ALMOST ADAM

I'm hallucinating, Ken thought.

The boy's little face had a protruding chin, a mouth with well-shaped lips that were distinctly pink in the light-brown face. The nose was flat, nostrils tiny but well rounded, and seeming to sniff and sort out scents at a fast and busy pace. The boy's cheeks were full, his eye sockets strong, and his low forehead frowning with sudden thoughts.

Ken stared at the boy, feeling as if he were tumbling down a funnel of time.

The child turned and scaled the rampart of rocks, agile and sure-footed. The heels of his feet cut quickly against the grayish yellow stone faces.

Then he vanished.

———

"Very rich, high concept . . .
A story liberally dosed with insight into archeology,
primitive and pop psychology,
academic in-fighting and African politics . . .
Popescu has come up with a credible and
likable creation."

Chicago Sun-Times

ALMOST ADAM

PETRU POPESCU

AVON BOOKS  NEW YORK

**VISIT OUR WEBSITE AT
http://AvonBooks.com**

AVON BOOKS
A division of
The Hearst Corporation
1350 Avenue of the Americas
New York, New York 10019

Copyright © 1996 by Popescu/Friedman, Inc.
Published by arrangement with the author
Library of Congress Catalog Card Number: 96-3490
ISBN: 0-380-72824-9

Published in hardcover by William Morrow and Company, Inc.; for information address Permissions Department, William Morrow and Company, Inc., 1350 Avenue of the Americas, New York, New York 10019.

First Avon Books Printing: February 1997

AVON TRADEMARK REG. U.S. PAT. OFF. AND IN OTHER COUNTRIES, MARCA
REGISTRADA, HECHO EN U.S.A.

Printed in the U.S.A.

RA   10 9 8 7 6 5 4 3 2 1

TO IRIS, ADAM, AND CHLOE

AUSTRALOPITHECINES: Bipedal early humans, with average brain sizes of 500 cubic centimeters. They inhabited Africa during the Pliocene era.

PLIOCENE: The geologic era from 5 million to 1.5 million years ago. During that time, early humans appeared in Africa.

FOSSIL (from the Latin for something "dug up from the ground"): The remains of an organism, preserved in rock. Generally only the hard parts of animals and humans—the teeth and bones—are preserved.

I do not think any spectacle can be more interesting than the first sight of man in his primitive wildness.

—CHARLES DARWIN
Letter to John Henslow

The crust of the earth with its imbedded remains must not be looked at as a well-filled museum, but as a poor collection made at hazard and at rare intervals.

—CHARLES DARWIN
The Origin of Species

If all men were dead, then monkeys make men. Men make angels.

—CHARLES DARWIN
Notebook on *The Transmutation of Species*

Contents

Prologue

M Y NAME IS I.V.H. I WRITE THIS USING ONLY MY INI-tials because I am limited by the oath I took as an officer in this war we have already lost.

Yet I am, with near certainty, the only civilized man who has ever visited this area. If I don't make it out of this hell, it is my duty to all of us to describe my discovery, however briefly. I sweat as I write these lines, and my brain feels like it's lighting up and crackling from a burst of neural fireworks.

We are not alone on this planet.

We are not its only thinking, bipedal, intellectually developed and morally capable—or incapable—higher primates.

We are not the earth's only humans. There are others, surviving here at an early evolutionary stage. I know this because I have seen them.

Amazing. Out of this world.

In view of my discovery, the history of humanity as we study it in high school becomes only half of itself. These other humans were here all along. They were here during the Ming dynasty and through the Renaissance, when Shakespeare wrote his plays and during the American Civil War, and later. In pockets of tropical forest, in Africa but perhaps on other continents too. Evolving more slowly than the rest of the planet, on a clock of their own, which might have untold consequences for the future.

Sorry—they *will* have untold consequences for the future.

For now I've found them. Even if I keep this a secret, in response to the secrecy-of-war acts, or out of scientific concern, if these creatures survive, they will be found again. So the genie is out of the bottle.

I've barely jotted down these lines, and all that's rational in me cries out against them: No, no, no, this cannot be true. I've been alone in this wilderness for too long. I've been too cut off and depleted and bombarded by strange new stimuli to make sense anymore. I've been living a dry delirium. I must have been seeing hallucinations, not living beings.

But with as much stubbornness, my mind is able to bring some reason to this situation. The survival of such an ancient breed is not only possible, it's perhaps logical. As for being discovered so late—well, the earth still has not been completely explored; in fact, it's only partially known. Most explorers reach their geographic destinations by traveling to them along the most direct routes possible. But around and alongside, there are vast tracts of nature that would take years to search step by step, yard by square yard. Any number of secrets could be hidden in those places, and that can be proved by what I've seen today.

We have only begun our study of the planet, by beginning to pierce the secrets of its habitats. Everywhere, species vastly different in age coexist and interact. Everywhere, many ancient species are still alive, and they share habitats with the new species that they gave birth to. In all the biological realms, ancestor breeds coexist with their descendant breeds.

That puts the question of our human ancestors in a totally different light.

In geological time, two million years is a blink of an eye. If the time clocks of the earth's habitats and species are so different, and their paces of transformation so astoundingly varied, we have to accept that the earth's time is a kind of continuum made of both past and present. Some beings belong to our immediate present while others are part of a lingering present that started long ago, but is still not over.

Even as I jot down these words, I feel that my pen carves the paper differently. It is so much lighter when noting theories, *words,* so much heavier and more lasting when it describes what I see, right here in front of me in this sun-bleached grassland. Since this morning, I've been observing two protohumans, a male and a female. They might be twelve years old and are barely larger than our sapiens children, but their organs are fully formed, and they are mating. Their behavior makes me wonder if they are mating for the first time.

I put away my pad and turn my binoculars on them. I focus the ring of this war tool meant to help kill soldiers, and I zoom in on the creation of primal life. They are so absorbed that I start moving closer to them until I distinctly hear their sounds.

I never thought that science might appear so pedestrian and shallow, and ultimately missing the point, compared to myth and poetry. I feel like invoking Hanuman, the monkey god of the Hindu myths of creation. Hanuman, if you were here with me, you'd be enchanted to see these two young graciles mating in the grass. These two "talk" just now, in extremely simple utterances. I keep listening until I distinguish differences between their anguished little grunts; some sound like exclamations of pain and others like warnings to each other to be careful. The female seems to complain, and that may well prove that she is a virgin. I gag at the thought—virginity, that distinctive mark of female humanness, observed here, in this place unchanged since the time of the Pliocene.

For all his small body, the male is endowed with large genitals, the mark of the jump from ape to hominid. But he too behaves uncertainly, as if inexperienced. Their brave passion is simply one of the humanest sights I've ever seen. Two mammals mate with awareness of each other, with urge, with need to quench their hormonal stirrings—but not with feeling for each other. Yet feeling for each other is exactly what exudes from this scene, and from these two bodies lush with young sweat.

I keep observing, barely breathing. She encourages him, and they finally fuse in a quiet, concentrated making of babies.

I came here as a soldier, an agent of aggression and death. I tremble watching this display of primal love, fiercely dedicated to producing offspring. We were like them only two million years ago, a blink of an eye in geological time. I wish we had remained like them. What did we know then that we later forgot, as our history marched through population explosions, conquests of new landmasses, wars, and inventions? And is what we gained worth what we forgot?

I look at that pair and cannot put into words the desperately loving way in which they are fused into each other. Do we, in our present state of evolution, match such depth of feeling, such desperation for our breed to make it into the future? Or is that already part of what we have forgotten?

Afraid to disturb them, I step back.

As soon as I lose sight of them, I'm faced again with the meaning of what I've just seen. With the incredible notion that as humans *we are not alone*. Not just in the far universe, but right here on earth.

I feel like I'm going crazy. The genie is out of the bottle. . . .

From a notebook written in spring 1954, after the guerrilla wars in Western Kenya

Part One

FOOTPRINTS

Western Kenya
End of May 1995
After the Rainy Season

T HE SMALL PLANE, A SINGLE-ENGINE BEECH LIGHTNING
38 P, was shaking like a bucking bronco, fighting to
keep a steady course. It was flying straight toward the southern spurs of the mountainous Mau escarpment.

The Mau, a clifflike fortification that rose ten thousand feet
high and ran almost north-south for over two hundred miles,
closed off Kenya's stretch of the Great Rift Valley, forming
what looked like a natural western wall. The Mau was an
astounding-looking formation. Its lower slopes were barren
and eroded, covered only by stubbly, hard savanna scrub.
Yet about halfway up, the Mau sprouted tree stands that got
thicker and thicker until they formed a vast forest that completely covered the mountain's crests. In the southern end of
the Mau, its forest descended all the way down, leaving occasional bald spurs and heels, until it reached the Dogilani
savanna, a plain of tall tasseled, sun-bleached grasses, dotted
every now and then by rare tree groves, and by a few water
holes that shone blindingly in the sunlight.

The shores of these water holes were bustling with thirsty
antelopes, duikers, and buffaloes. The grasses rippled with
lions and leopards stalking their drinking prey. The skies
were crisscrossed by predatory birds, eager to make off with
the felines' kills.

The savanna—vast and sprinkled with blood from the con-

3

stant fighting between animals of different species—looked as if it belonged to the current time. The barren and rocky spurs of the Mau were lifelessly suspended in an earlier time. Yet the most mysterious part, the lush forested crests that rose high above the savanna, was of another time altogether.

It was around noon and the air on the Dogilani plain had been heated by the sun throughout the morning and was expanding rapidly, laterally and upward, attacking the cold air that came down from the upper slopes of the Mau. The cold air fought back, stabbing its opponent with long daggers of frigid wind. These daggers caused the wind currents on both sides, blowing in conflicting directions, to become so strong that they shook the three-ton airplane as if it were a toy.

Hendrijks, the pilot, a Cape Dutchman in his sixties who had buzzed around these plateaus and mountains all his life, was desperately fighting the crosscurrents. His face, which was usually bright red from the genes of his ancestry plus all the alcohol he drank, had taken on a yellowish shade of fear. Behind him there were two other seats, side by side. Strapped into one of them, Kenyan geologist Ngili Ngiamena clutched the armrests with his graceful Masai hands, and kept urging Hendrijks to fly on ahead. The almost perfectly vertical wall of the Mau zoomed toward them, looking as if it would meet the plane any second, flatten its fuselage, and wrap it in a giant ball of fire and smoke.

In the other seat, the American paleoanthropologist Ken Lauder was leaning to the right, his body hanging out of the plane through the missing door of the starboard hatch. His seat belt cut painfully into his stomach. Ken was aiming the lens of a camera down at the lower slopes passing under the plane. His hands, arms, shoulders, and upper torso were all tightened together, trying to keep him from being dragged out of the plane by the slipstream that rushed past him like a giant frozen breath exhaled by the approaching mountain.

The wind was so powerful it peeled back his eyelids. Ken pulled himself into the cabin and yelled at the pilot to cut the speed so he could take his pictures. But if Hendrijks slowed down, he would lose the engine power he needed to break through the conflicting currents. As it was, every time the plane hit one, it felt as if it had run into an unseen brick wall and had pierced through it by some miracle of physics.

The jumble of eroded crests and ridges below kept causing the direction of the currents to change, and the hot gusts of air pushed the plane up, while the cold ones pulled it down. The plane's fuselage groaned and creaked, close to disintegration, and Ken yelled again at the pilot. Hendrijks had circled above one barren spur too fast, and Ken had missed his shot—could Hendrijks do it again, slower?

"Can't do it any slower!" shouted the pilot. "Got to have speed, to have power to fight the currents!"

Meanwhile, the wall of the Mau, its lower half gray from erosion, its upper half shiny green with scrub and trees, seemed to lunge out at the plane.

Hendrijks yelled that he was going to turn around, giving Ken a second chance to aim his camera. Ken took a deep breath and tested his safety belt with his hand. Correctly buckled, it had not snapped yet, and maybe it wouldn't snap at all.

Hendrijks banked. A pit of cold air opened underneath the plane, catching the right wing tip, momentarily pointing it straight at the ground. Ken almost flew out of the hatch, camera and all. His left foot, jammed under Hendrijks's seat, became an anchor that kept him from bailing out of the plane completely. The other anchor was his seat belt. Hendrijks fought to rebalance the plane, feeling his way in the windshear like a swimmer on the edge of an undertow from which he might never surface.

"Get it now, get it now, goddamn it!" he screamed.

The plane straightened its course. Underneath, the eroded incline was separated into five sections by dried-up mountain streams, making it look like a giant sphinx's paw.

On the paw's middle section, as if on a giant knuckle, was the particular spot that Ken was trying to photograph.

The slipstream made Ken's eyes water—he realized that by the time he was above his target, he'd have to photograph it blind. His camera lens was coming onto the target. He clicked, desperately trying to glimpse the thing he was aiming at, but he simply couldn't see through the eyepiece.

Still, he was sure he was getting it; how could he not? The thought filled his chest with such a sense of triumph that he opened his mouth to yell with joy, and . . .

He saw that middle section, as they zoomed above it, and beyond. The midday winds had kicked up the dust of the eroded surrounding slopes, obscuring it, one wave of dust after another. Wave, then respite and visibility, then another wave. When a wave blew, the paw was wrapped in a whipped-up maelstrom of dust.

Most likely, the only thing Ken had caught in his lens was a lot of dust. The only thing he would have on film was the general pawlike formation, and the dust churning up, covering it. The plane had cost him and Ngili a thousand dollars per week, and a case of scotch for Hendrijks, and now they were going to miss the week's last and most intriguing sighting.

He pulled himself inside again. "Go back," he shouted at Hendrijks. "Go back!"

"Didn't you get it?"

"I didn't!" He bashed his fist against the cabin wall. The thin shell of aluminum boomed, like a tin drum. "Go back over it slowly one more time!"

"Are you mad?" asked Ngili from the seat beside him. "He can't go any slower than this. He needs the speed to fight the wind!"

"Go faster then, but lower!"

"Faster?" yelled Hendrijks, turning to glance at Ken. There was not a trace of the usual red in his skin, as if his pigmentation had mutated abruptly and forever. "You want me to crash into that wall? I barely had room to turn back last time, didn't you see?"

"There's a way to do it!" Ken yelled back. "Go lower. Just remember where the wind changes!"

"How can I remember? It changes all the time!"

"Then we're not paying you your thousand bucks!"

The shaking and banking of the plane, the moaning slipstream through the open hatch, and the closeness of danger made Ken feel that they had already met the odds of their death, and survived them. They had been kept from catastrophe by an enormous act of willpower on his part. He dropped the camera onto his stomach, seized Hendrijks's fleshy shoulders, and shook him, getting the clear impression that he was shaking the whole plane.

"Do it! You're the best goddamned pilot in Kenya! Do it, or we're not paying a cent!"

The Dutchman shouted back that he didn't care, he was turning the plane back, out of this windy hell. Ken begged him. One more time, go lower. The last time.

He would not get another chance. This was Ken's last chance at getting a picture of what he had spotted from the plane a half hour before.

HE AND NGILI HAD GONE UP WITH HENDRIJKS EARLY THAT morning to complete an aerial stratigraphy of Dogilani and this southern end of the Mau. Its rock formations were easily five million years old. For this reason, the Mau seemed to sail above the Dogilani plain like a Pliocene battleship.

The Pliocene Era, which had lasted from five million years ago until 1.5 million years ago, was filled with important events. In the Pliocene, the earth's continents had reached their present positions. The Rift Valley was formed then, as two tectonic plates jostling under the earth's surface dug a north-south fault line between them that was almost as long as Africa. The climate on the two sides of the Rift had become sharply divergent. The west side had stayed rainy and had maintained its ancient forests, while the east had dried up, favoring grasslands where hoofed animals had multiplied to enormous herds. In the east, after the forests had shrunk, some of the forest apes had dared to tread into the open spaces, and had become the human race.

The southern Mau, with that stretch of lush savanna spreading up to its dried spurs and the ancient forests decorating its crests, looked like a wilderness left over from the time when man was becoming man.

Flying about and jotting down various rock formations, which Ken photographed and Ngili classified, they had passed less than a hundred feet above a round bald spur, so that Ngili could take a good look at its state of erosion. The time was 11:15 A.M., as noted by Ken, who was also diagramming the distance between various rock formations, using the flight time as an indicator.

Outlined on that spur were footprints which Ken recognized because they were set in a large circle, an intriguing pattern in this windswept wilderness. He asked the pilot to turn around and fly over the spur again. Hendrijks complied. Around they went, and came back lower, and Ken and Ngili both clearly saw that dark circle. When they flew down even lower, the circle broke into dots, like beads in a necklace. Lower still, practically a few feet above the ground, the dots became oval and elongated. Footprints. Made by someone who had walked on top of that spur, in a circle.

Ken and Ngili had looked at each other as only two scientists would if their field was prehistory. What if those were prehistoric footprints? What if they had been left by hominids, by early humans?

It wasn't really such a farfetched thought. Between the rainy seasons, the Mau's lower spurs were bone dry, constantly shaved by winds that unearthed the older layers of terrain beneath. And if something really was preserved on such surfaces, chances were that it was ancient, and petrified.

The footprints looked ancient anyway. They were low, and carved deeply into the sunlit ground. Ken could tell that, even at such a fleeting glance, because the dips in the prints were filled with shade, making them look like little pools of darkness, in contrast to the dusty glare of the surrounding surfaces.

Hendrijks had banked the plane a little more steeply and leaned into the cockpit window, to see for himself. He growled dismissively. "Nothing to get worked up about; those are footprints left by goat herdsmen."

"Why would they take their goats up on that barren spur?" asked Ken. "There's nothing to graze there. And where are the goats' hoofprints? I don't see any pointy little holes."

"This area's known to be totally uninhabited," added Ngili.

"Maybe the prints are older," argued Hendrijks. "Maybe there was grass down there a hundred years back."

"If they're that old, why couldn't they be older?" Ken countered.

Ngili nodded. "And that still doesn't explain the absence of the herds' prints."

Hendrijks had thrown up his hands, freeing the controls for an instant. What a storm of talk, he thought, about something he would've never given any attention to. He was crazy to waste his time out here with these lunatic scientists. But he wasn't exactly wasting his time. A thousand dollars was good payment for a week of aerial stratigraphy, and Hendrijks was getting on in years, and the trade was full of new bush pilots now, Africans.

He had finally agreed to fly back and find the spur, so Ken could take some pictures.

It had taken them over a half hour of zigzagging flight to find that spur again, among scores of identical spurs, because they had not dropped markings, the sunlight had changed, and the Mau's volcanic rocks, rich in iron, confused the plane's compass.

And by then the winds had started to stir up that noontime witch's cauldron.

KEN TRIED TO REPLACE THE WIDE LENS ON HIS MINOLTA with a longer one. The wide lens, detached, slipped through his fingers and slammed down onto the plane's bottom.

He didn't care. He ground in the long lens. He felt it finding its grooves, turning, coming to a tight fit. He turned toward Ngili and met his African friend's eyes, irises black like bullets of onyx. Ngili's skin, usually shiny as if freshly polished, was now flat and dull. He was turning pale the way Africans turned pale—they didn't lose color, they lost shine.

Ngili looked him straight in the face and said in a voice that sounded remarkably calm and together, "This plane's not going to make it."

"It did so far, didn't it? Just one more time."

"You're mad."

Ngili never said "crazy," he always said "mad," like the English. He spoke a flawless English with a tribal Masai singsong, even though he wasn't a tribal Masai. He was born and raised in Nairobi and had graduated from the University of Kenya. He had met Ken at the university and shared classes with him before Ngili specialized in geology and Ken in paleoanthropology.

They were good friends, and made a striking pair. Ngili was super thin, and all his limbs seemed fluted, including his tall, elegant Masai face. Ken was slim but muscular, looking younger than his twenty-eight years, with a sunbaked face pierced by vivacious light-brown eyes. He had a strong nose with well-sculpted nostrils, and a forehead swept by a rough tousle of sun-bleached brown hair. His lips were rather thin but his jaw was strong, with a short cleft in his chin completing an impression of liveliness and energy.

"I'm not mad. Hendrijks can do it, if he doesn't lose his head."

"Maybe he won't lose his head," Ngili said calmly. "But you're still mad."

All right, Ken thought to himself. Maybe I am mad. And I'll die mad today, in Africa.

The plane was slowing down.

Ken looked down and saw the spur coming under the plane. He realized that Hendrijks had gathered his courage and was coming onto the desired spot with all the skills of his long years of flying. As he tried to guess the wind, he was pulling down the flaps, slowing the plane as if coming in for a landing, except that he couldn't set it down even if he wanted to; there was nothing down there flat enough to land a plane on. So Hendrijks's plan was to abort, to max the power, and lift again right in the ugly face of the escarpment.

For an instant, Ken felt the deepest respect for the old drunk. His breed was almost extinct. And this might be his last stunt.

"You're the greatest," he shouted, slapping him on his fleshy shoulder.

"*Dankje,*" Hendrijks thanked him, in his native Cape Dutch, a language he almost never used. Ken thought, maybe using Dutch came from the nearness of death, for the three of them might die in the next few minutes.

Ken thought with bizarre clarity: For every human being alive on earth right now, there were probably a hundred-odd dead humans, stuck in the ground, deceased somewhere along the past five million years. Some had endured as fossils. Others—most of them—had long ago been recycled into minerals and into new organic growths. No one really knew why, when, or how.

No one really knew anything. Almost all evidence in paleontology and the combined related sciences was controversial. There was hardly any certainty or consensus. There was only . . . science.

And now for the sake of science, they might crash and die. He should have been frightened, but he had no time. They were almost over the spot, and he had to shoot it.

The plane was gliding like a bird coming to a roosting spot, weighted by its eggs.

The slipstream was less cruel this time. Ken's eyes were not as watery. He could see through the camera's eyepiece.

The wind was still gusting down below, blowing dust, covering and uncovering the spot for seconds at a time, almost at regular intervals.

His mind had to enter that sequence, making his camera click as one sheet of dust lifted, leaving the top of the spur clear, right before another sheet of dust covered it again. He saw a flurry of dust forming, looking bright yellow, as if oxidized by the sun. It passed, and what lay underneath became almost painfully clear, like the bottom of a sea drained of waters for the first time, showing its marine plants and deposits at their true scale and in their true light.

He clicked. The dust came, covered. Again the wind cleaned the spot, and he clicked again, a beautiful close shot.

He felt the seat belt snap, breaking under his weight, yet he didn't fall. Ngili threw both his arms about him, hooked one hand under Ken's right armpit and dug the fingers of his other hand into the belt of Ken's bush pants. Ken felt Ngili's nails, screeching against his belt, grabbing with it his shirt, his flesh. He felt that nothing else mattered, and clicked, clicked, in sequence with the wind and the dust spreading like a yellow curtain, then blowing off.

The plane made a tremendous jolt as it was hit simultaneously by two opposing air currents. Ngili cried out, and Hendrijks was thrown forward into the controls; desperately, he maxed the power lever. The downward tow of the wind and the weight of the plane seemed to guarantee that it would crash.

The machine roared upward, found itself inches, it seemed, from the wall of the Mau, and banked steeply. The movement sucked Ken even farther out of the plane. Ngili's hand cut into the flesh of Ken's arm, and blood spurted from under his fingernails as he clung to his friend's body. From the bottom of the plane, the lens Ken had dropped earlier found its way to the open hatch, clanked over its edge, and flew into the void. Ken watched it fall, amazed that he wasn't falling too, falling after the lens, headfirst.

He felt no fear, just a monster curiosity about what he thought were his last moments.

In slow free fall, the camera lens made it to the eroded big spur of rock, crashed into it, and fragmented on impact.

Ngili kept his hand under the belt fastening Ken's pants. Made of hard leather, it resisted that tremendous downward pull.

Hendrijks felt the shifting weight of the two men behind him. He straightened the plane so abruptly that Ken jolted up toward the door, and Ngili pulled him, hurling him inside. Ken hit the ceiling with the crown of his head. Hendrijks turned and grinned, and there was blood streaming from his nose, which had smashed against the controls. The plane was bucking so wildly that Ken thought it might have lost its tail.

"I'm g-going to t-turn," announced Hendrijks, stammering from the movement of the plane, "and t-try to make it somewhere down there. . . ." With a bloodied grin, he pointed toward the savanna stretching south of the Mau's slopes.

Ken and Ngili looked. They saw the acacia groves and tracts of tall grass alternating with rocky outcrops and monticules—low little hillocks of dirt. The savanna seemed so peaceful and welcoming, an earthscape made of wide, generous features. Far to the southwest, they could see a retreating storm's distant, unthreatening flashes of lightning. Everywhere against the vegetation's green and yellow stood the warm browns and grays of grazing animals.

"Do it," agreed Ken unnecessarily.

It seemed inconceivable that the plane could still have the strength to defeat all those currents as it descended. Ken and Ngili braced themselves. Ken voided his mind of all thoughts; all that was left in his brain was a giant hum of willpower, striving desperately for the engine, body, wings, struts and hubs and screws, to make it. It was like a final long heave in a birth-giving ordeal. From the womb of the winds, the plane emerged, and finally slipped free, into warm savanna air.

Still Ken and Ngili could not believe they had survived, but fought to push the plane along with their minds, while Hendrijks dragged lower and lower, with the last eroded slopes zooming back right under the fuselage. The plane cleared the last slope and swooped over the savanna, shaving the top of an acacia tree, making it even flatter than it already was.

Then the wheels touched down.

T AXIING THE SAVANNA, THE PLANE'S WHEELS RIPPED
across the red oat grass that covered the ground. The
grass looked level, but the ground underneath was broken by
holes and wrinkles that made the plane bounce like a toy,
shaking its passengers as fiercely as they had been up among
the winds. The wheels encountered a line of rocks, hopped
over them, hacked like machetes across clumps of whistling
thorns, and finally came to a halt.

Ken and Ngili jumped out through the doorless hatch as
soon as the plane came to a stop.

They crashed onto the grass, stunned to be alive. They
saw that there was a crack in the plane's rudder, and the end
of the right trim tab was missing. Hendrijks cut the engine,
jumped out too, and sprawled flat on the grass, grumbling
about the thousand dollars and two, *two* cases of whiskey.

Ken looked at Ngili, whose face was shiny again.

"You got 'em?" Ngili asked, pointing at Ken's camera.
"You got those bloody footprints?"

Ken nodded. "I got the spur all right, clear and free of
dust. The footprints, I don't know how clear they'll come
out; we'll only know when we get them developed."

"I hope our stunt up there wasn't for nothing," chuckled
Ngili.

They remained lying in the grass. Finally Hendrijks got

up, climbed back into the plane, and started looking for his pipe. He couldn't find it. Almost everything inside the fuselage had been jolted out of its normal location. Even the flight log had been hurled back and was scattered all over the rear of the plane. A box of crackers had bounced about until it popped open, spreading crackers everywhere. Hendrijks cursed that his plane was a mess. His bottle of bush whiskey had survived but was leaking onto the floor. Hendrijks hopped back out and walked around the plane, touching ailerons, flaps, wing struts, the propeller. He was making sure that the plane had not suffered more damage.

Finally, he called to the two young men. "I want to fix the rudder," he announced. "I'm not going to fly back with it in this state."

"How long will it take you to do it?" asked Ken, still lying on the grass. He knew that Hendrijks, like many old-timers, was a competent plane mechanic.

"A few hours at least. I've got wire, screws, brackets . . ." Hendrijks paused, looked thoughtfully at the sun. "But if I'm not done by sunset, we'll have to fly back tomorrow morning."

"I'd rather we spend the night here than do a hasty job." Ken and Ngili had spent many nights in the wild, on archaeological digs; sleeping under the savanna's stars did not scare them.

"In that case, help me filter the gasoline first. That takes some time."

The plane carried extra canisters of gasoline that had to be transferred into the nearly empty tanks, filtered through a shammy skin, to free the gasoline of impurities that might make the engine miss. Had one prolonged miss occurred while they were flying up next to the Mau's wall, they would be dead by now.

Ngili and Ken got up to help Hendrijks with the gasoline. They rolled a rock under the plane's tail, to make a natural ladder for Hendrijks to stand on so he could tinker with the rudder. Hendrijks gruffly ordered Ken to get the machete out of the plane and hack some branches of whistling thorns; if they were going to spend the night here, they would need to light a fire.

Minutes later, Ken hacked at the thorns, named for the sound of the wind passing through them. Ken noticed that these bushes were taller, and their fiber was tougher to cut than usual. Maybe they were as knotty and stubborn as in the Pliocene, or maybe he was just very tired. He glanced around. A bank of little trees was loaded with round ink-black berries that shone like human eyes. They even looked attentive in a human way—almost menacing.

"Hey, Ngili, there's some flora here like I've never seen before."

"I see some wildebeests like I've never seen before. They're incredibly fat and relaxed. Hey, there's a female who's giving birth," Ngili chuckled, passing the binoculars to Ken.

Ken looked, and located the wildebeests, about twenty or thirty of them. Brought close by the lens, they seemed to be grazing inches from his nose. As their name suggested, wildebeests easily got excited about anything: a gnat in the tail, a sharp stone in the hoof, or just hot savanna emptiness, into which they charged for no reason, as if they'd seen a ghost. They were always hyperactive. But here, they lazily moved their mouths from one plot of grass to the next, exceptionally placid.

The foaling female stood with her legs slightly apart, with a concentrated expression on her long face. From her rump emerged what looked like a big, shiny black gob with a high bristling end. The bristles were the calf's horns and forelegs and tiny hooves, and the gob its head and chest, shiny from a placental substance that had not yet broken. Inside that clammy cocoon, the calf's legs kicked already, though half the foal was still inside its mother.

Ken turned the binoculars laterally and saw that other females also had foals. A number of calves were staggering about vulnerably, as if they had been born over the last hour.

"This is pretty weird," he mumbled.

"What's weird?"

be
Ke
ve
job

to l

her
here

T
stirr
of th
they
Raci
grazi
Keny
their

tense gallops away from the plunges of lion
During that last minute of their convers
exited its mother. It fell in a heap in t
shiny head, connected to the mothe
of placenta. Then it tossed its h
placental strings, and tried to
abandoning her delivery po
the calf with her tongue
"So sweet," chuc
dise."

Ken laughed
adise after a
He slapp
wande
tin

anothe ...gratory cycle.

Those cycles determined all their other activities, including their well-regulated mating and birthing seasons.

"Maybe these wildebeests never ran with the migrating ones," joked Ngili. "Maybe they were always here."

"Maybe," said Ken. He looked at the tall, lush grasses. Maybe this savanna had never experienced the depletion of the Tanzanian savannas, in which case the wildebeests had no reason to migrate. And they could mate and give birth whenever they wished.

"There are plenty of duiker antelopes too," Ken muttered, scanning on through the binoculars.

"Anything weird about those?"

"Nope. Just fat and happy, and terribly relaxed. Like the wildebeests."

The duikers, brown-red antelopes with short horns and a wide black streak down their foreheads, were barely moving. There were no felines on the prowl just now, Ken figured. After dark, this sleepiness would quickly be replaced by and leopards.

...ation, the foal had

...e grass, but raised a

... by long silvery strings

...ead sideways, breaking the

...se, but fell back. The mother,

...tion, turned and started cleaning

...kled Ngili. "Oh, this is such a para-

...and said anything would have felt like a par-
...most having crashed in Hendrijks's flying box.
...d his arm around his friend's shoulders, and they
...ed back over spiny bush and hot savanna grass, chat-
...g and laughing.

"I won't be finished tonight," announced Hendrijks, slur-ring because he held two long screws in a corner of his mouth; his hands were busy with a steel bracket. He took the screws out of his mouth. "Ngili, get on the radio and tell Embakasi airport that we're changing our flight plan and ask for a weather report." His tone was usually gruff, but it was gruffer to Ngili than to Ken.

Ngili climbed into the plane and called Nairobi. He got a good weather report; there was a dust storm south of the Tanzanian border, and it was moving up, but it would prob-ably blow over before crossing into Kenya. Ngili asked the tower to phone a message to his family, telling them that he would be spending the night in the savanna. Their projected new return was by noon tomorrow.

They had left that morning with a picnic ice chest full of sandwiches, Cokes, cans of Kane, the Kenyan national soft drink, and a couple of beers for Hendrijks. The ice chest had survived, and Hendrijks broke out some Cokes.

Ken heaped the hacked branches next to the plane, ready to make a fire. Hendrijks put away his tools, Ngili sat on the grass with his stratigraphy notes, made crimson by the fiery sunset light, and Ken walked purposelessly just less than half a mile into the grassland, toward a monticule, a low mound that rose out of the barren ground.

Coming close, he saw that the mound was eroded.

When he circled around it, he found on its other side a skull, a hominid skull. Ken's first reaction was that this wasn't possible.

But it was. He was being watched by the brown eye sockets of a fossil skull.

THE SKULL SAT ON THE TIP OF THE MOUND, HARDLY BURIED at all. Its upper jaw barely bit into the gravel. That upper jaw had kept a lot of its teeth, which were clearly visible, firmly imbedded in its maxilla, or jawbone.

As Ken stepped toward it, he heard the rough savanna dirt disintegrating under his feet. The ground around the monticule was ancient and badly eroded. Under Ken's weight, its molecules broke and became dust.

The skull had been encapsulated in that ancient soil until the last fall or the spring before it. Fall and spring were rainy seasons. Some freshet, some stream issued from rainwater pooled up in a Mau crevice, must have gushed down here during the last rainy season and washed off the top of the mound, exposing an extremely brittle layer of soil underneath. Then the wind had started its work, peeling layer after layer, until it revealed the skull, returning it to the living world.

Ken saw a small brown bone next to the skull. He stepped close, hung his face above it, determined not to disturb it with anything except his hungry stare. It was a neck vertebra, sticking out of the monticule. Most of the skeleton was probably still there, buried below the skull.

Ken felt a powerful urge to call Ngili but resisted. If this was the skeleton of an ancient herdsman, the find would be interesting but not earthshaking. If, however, it was something older . . .

Again Ken felt the tension he had felt on the plane when he was photographing the footprints. His breath came in short, labored puffs, as he noticed that the skull's forehead sloped back unusually far. The skull was either ancient or it had belonged to some modern population with a uniquely narrow facial angle. But that was unlikely because there weren't any native tribes who had foreheads that slanted back that far. Ken squatted before the skull, and stared dead straight at it against the bleeding African sunset. On the crown of the skull, clearly visible from the front, he saw a sort of elevation. A cranial crest.

The only breed of ancient humans who had that crest was *Australopithecus robustus,* an ape-man once thought to be the famous evolutionary missing link. His species developed that crest in order to support the massive cheek and jaw muscles of a primitive human model. *Robustus,* a number of whose fossils had been found in Africa, had protruding, heavy jaws and needed very enlarged neck vertebrae to hold up a head that was heavy, not from its brain content—it held only five hundred cubic centimeters of brain—but from its solid, stocky skull bones.

Ken knew that there was a quick way to test whether the skull was ancient, and an even quicker way to test whether it belonged to an early human, or to some super monkey. Ken decided to carry out those preliminary tests by himself. No need to get Ngili excited as yet. He tentatively moved his hand out to touch the skull, fearing that it might crumble.

He took a deep breath, trying to control his emotions. *Come on, Lauder. Settle down. You need your nerves intact. We're talking science here, evolution of man.*

Then he exhaled harshly. He touched the skull. It didn't crumble but moved under his fingers, so easy to pull free, so ripe for collection, like a piece of fruit ready to fall off a branch.

He lifted it, feeling the ancient gravel come off between his fingers. He turned it upside down and stared at the horseshoe pattern of time-blackened teeth. Their pattern was round, humanlike. Gorillas' and baboons' teeth were set in a rectangular, boxlike pattern. The upper canines were flat, worn down by chewing; the person who once chewed with them had died in his early twenties, the maximum life span of an australopithecine.

Ken controlled his excitement and continued examining the fossil. The molars' tops showed cusps, elevations of their enamel surface. Squinting in the fading sunlight, Ken counted the cusps. There were five of them, set in an irregular Y pattern.

Good. That pattern had appeared in the common ancestor of apes and humans. Monkeys never developed more than four cusps on their molars. Judging by the cusps, this could have been a large ape. But had this been an ape, its upper canines should have been long and curved backward, shaped to interlock with equally long canines in the lower jaw.

These canines were clearly flat, humanlike.

Ken swallowed, passing his tongue over his dry lips.

Now for the empirical field test to determine how old the buried skeleton was.

He weighed the skull in his palm. For its size, it seemed heavy, indicating mineralization. Fossils, sucked into the ground millions of years back, went through the so-called petrification cycle, during which they were surrounded from all sides by minerals and were squeezed and compressed until, ever so slowly, the minerals made their way into the myriads of pores and air canals of the original bone tissue. Filling with minerals, the bones themselves became minerals. They became rock and stone.

Since stone was heavier than bone tissue, ancient bones had to be heavier than recent ones.

The one in Ken's hand felt considerably heavier than a recent one would have. Advanced degree of mineralization. But the test was not over yet. Ken carefully brought the skull close to his mouth, chose a spot on the crown, and licked it. He got the fine savanna dust in his mouth. He gathered it with his tongue and lips, spat it out, and licked the skull again. Cleaning it. Getting the tip of his tongue onto the actual bone. The bone tasted smooth, continuous. Unpetrified bones would taste porous because their myriads of air canals were still open, which made them act like tiny suction cups.

That porousness, though invisible to the eye, would not escape the human tongue. Recent bones made the human tongue stick to them. But it was different with this old one. The cleaner it became from Ken's scientific kiss, the smoother and leaner and more perfect it felt to the tongue tip—like a stone. A lean clean stone.

It *was* a stone. It was a fossil australopithecine.

That meant it could have lived anytime during the Pliocene. Anytime from five million years ago to one and a half million years ago, when the earth's last ape-men had fathered the next stage of human evolution.

WITH THE GREATEST CARE, KEN PLACED THE FOSSIL SKULL back in its little bed of gravel. He straightened his body and called Ngili. Not loud enough; he was tired and breathless, and too excited by what he had just found. But the second time, he yelled Ngili's name at the whole savanna.

Ngili dropped his notebook and hurried toward his friend.

Hendrijks, busy kindling the fire, barely looked up. He was happy not to have to fly with a cracked tail into the rising night winds, but instead to wait for the calm of the early morning. One stunt per day was enough; that was why he had stopped the repair work, which he could easily have finished. Hendrijks planned to die in his Nairobi bed, in the comfort of his savings, pinching some café-au-lait ass to remind him of *his* Africa, when whites were whites and blacks were blacks. Whoever heard of savant Americans (Ken was from Oakland, California) coming here to fraternize with Masai geologists? Whoever heard of Masai geologists in the first place, or of Masais with bank accounts and positions in the government?

That final thought referred to Ngili's family. The Ngiamenas were rich. They owned plantations of coffee and sisal, seized from Brits who had fled Kenya back in 1953. Ngili's father was a powerful man, the superintendent of the game parks and reserves, a job that made him automatically a member of the cabinet. He owed the position to his longtime friendship with Kenya's first black president, Jomo Kenyatta.

Hendrijks didn't understand any of this. Nor did he understand, when he finally looked up, why Ken was licking a brown, round thing that looked from here like a gross coconut, though there were no coconut palms around, just acacias, Kaffir booms, and baobabs. And why Ngili took that coconut from Ken's hands, and after some staring at it, licked it too.

KEN RUSHED BACK TO THE PLANE. HENDRIJKS WAS NOW seated by the fire, with the whiskey bottle in his lap. He no longer had questions about the scientists' strange behavior, his mind already floating into the fog of whiskey and post-colonial melancholy into which he escaped every evening.

Ken asked him if there were any brushes on the plane. Hendrijks replied that he had a shaving brush and a razor in a bag of toiletries he kept under the pilot's seat. Ken could borrow them if he wished. Ken said thanks, climbed into the cabin, found the bag of toiletries, jumped out again, and rushed with brush and razor to where Ngili, with the machete, was sectioning off the soil around the fossil into slices ever so thin—the soil coming off like sand, like ashes.

Ken dug with the razor and brushed the debris off the surfacing bones with the shaving brush. Ngili had freed more vertebrae, plus the collarbones. These were very hard to find intact; they were so small and delicate they easily got smashed when geologists' hammers pounded their way through the breccia that most often encased fossils. Breccia, a mix of gravel and limestone, was nature's own cement. After the collarbones, ribs appeared, frittered and broken, but nonetheless present.

Then the machete encountered a harder lower bed, and Ken said that this was as far as he wanted to go tonight. He didn't want to jeopardize the state of the fossil by digging it out by flashlight.

By now all the sky around them was ink blue. As a Masai

poet said, the night spat mouthfuls of stars into the bowl of the heavens.

Ngili spoke, shivering from excitement and from the growing evening cold. "If Hendrijks could spare a tarp, we could make a shelter over this mound, and a marker of crossed stones right next to it. Then we could return with a bona fide digging permit, and a digging crew. . . ."

Ken jumped. "And leave the find exposed? It could be destroyed by animals. . . . Or even taken away by some other guy passing through. . . ."

"What other guy? No one comes here, not even poachers." Ngili held up the dusty machete, its blade already becoming blunt. "Ken, we won't be able to wrench this whole thing out with improvised tools."

"Why not? Look at how much we've got out already."

"But we still need a digging permit!"

The regulations about digging for antiquities, recently toughened, required a bona fide permit, granted by a combined board of the university's paleontology department and the government's commission for antiquities. Getting the permit might take a couple of months, particularly with Ken and Ngili's mentor, Professor Randall Phillips, a paleoanatomist, leaving Nairobi in just a few days for a sabbatical at the University of California, Davis. They would not have time to write up a proposal, present it to Randall, and have him submit it to the board. Instead, they would have to get their permit from Cyril Anderson, the head of the department and co-curator of the university's fossils vault. Cyril might not grant them a permit at all because the field evidence had been gathered so primitively.

"You know what a stickler for procedure Cyril is," Ngili finished his reasoning. "If he knew how we worked here, with old dirty blades and practically in the dark, he'd report us to the board."

"And get the permit for himself," added Ken with uncharacteristic rancor. "I have another plan. Look around," he urged Ngili, sweeping his arm at an irregular horizon of mounds like the one they had dug up. "There might be bones in most of those humps. This might be a fossil bed as rich as Olduvai in Tanzania, or the Afar in Ethiopia. The degree of erosion is very uniform, so the fossils must all be pretty close to the surface, and second, this is a very isolated place. Ideal for a stable and self-contained australopithecine population. How big d'you think this plain is?''

"Let's see.''

Ngili pulled out a geological map and deployed it. Ken lit it with the flashlight, and Ngili calculated the distances by measuring them on the map between his dusty thumb and index finger. "Due south, it's over a hundred miles between where we are and the Tanzanian border. Due west, it must be about a hundred and twenty miles from here to the nearest villages by the lake. . . .''

Ken bent over the map, following Ngili's dusty fingers and the dancing dot of the flashlight. The lake, far to the west, was Lake Victoria. They could see on the map why there had been no human inroads here, why this plain had not attracted explorers, or settlers. Except for its wildlife, it had no natural riches. And it was enclosed on all sides. The forested Mau shut off one side, the brutally dry trench of the Rift Valley another, and the Tanzanian border to the far south, yet another. Although that border was just an imaginary line drawn on a map, the border region was made of flatlands that were forbiddingly hot and empty.

The only nearby area that was inhabited, the lakeshore, was settled by fishermen who preferred to stay by the lake and catch their fish.

As for the Rift Valley, which Ken and Ngili had seen from the plane, it looked like an ugly, badly healed scar. No roads crossed it in that area, but it was probably passable by safari trucks.

"There're at least five thousand square miles of unexplored terrain here,'' said Ngili, "and we're standing right in it.''

"Some habitat, huh?'' blurted Ken.

They fell silent, inebriated with the feel of the place. Ken enjoyed the sensation of being at man's zero hour. He tried to imagine that there was nothing left behind them, no humankind. To think that beyond the Rift's eastern wall, the Aberdares, there was no Nairobi, no giant urban sprawl congested by three million twisted lives. There was no civil war raging on the other side of Lake Victoria, in Rwanda. There were no famished files of refugees, trekking along muddy roads into unwelcoming neighbor countries. There was nothing but this place, and he and his friend.

Then he remembered the plane, the pilot, and their purpose here. He boosted himself back to his practical, energetic state. "Here's my plan. We take the fossil back now, with some soil samples, and give the bones and soil to Randall to take to the lab at Davis. He'll give them to Aaron Levinson." Aaron Levinson was the world's top expert in dating fossils with potassium-argon. "Levinson 'bakes' them in his machine, and certifies their antiquity. Randall presents the find to the international community. We'll get grants and support from scientists who can supersede Cyril Anderson."

Ken stared at those mounds of eroded dirt with such a glow in his eyes that Ngili felt the need to pat him on the arm. "That's a great plan. All it needs is for this to be truly old." He pointed at the fossil.

"Look at the shape of this skull!" Ken urged hotly. "It's a classic *Australopithecus robustus,* at least two million years old, maybe even three!"

Ngili agreed about the shape. It was textbook *Australopithecus robustus.* And there was so much of it here, already twenty times more bone than an australopithecine skullcap Ken had recently bought at a store in Nairobi known as Zhang Chen's Herb and Fossil Shop.

Zhang Chen was a Kenya-born Chinese who sold herbs and "dragon bones." These were old monkey or human bones, to be ground and swallowed as a remedy against impotence.

"With as many dragon bones as we have here," chuckled Ngili, "you and I could people this whole savanna."

Ken smiled. Several times in man's quest to find his forebears, dragon bones had led scientists to amazing discoveries.

In 1899, K. A. Haberer, a German naturalist journeying across China, had spotted in a country drugstore a whole range of human teeth, skullcaps, ribs, knees. These were guaranteed, the druggist swore, to repair impotence, gallstones, liver trouble, and even malaria. Haberer bought practically everything in the store. His purchase led to finding the site of one of the world's most famed human fossils, *Sinanthropus pekinensis,* Peking Man.

Zhang Chen sold herbs to Nairobi locals, and ground-up stuff such as ape bones and rhino horns to customers in Hong Kong and Singapore. The rhino horns, of course, came from rhinos that had been shot illegally in game parks. Zhang also sold fossilized mollusks and fishes, whose real value he was unaware of. Among his clientele were a number of students in natural sciences, plus some eccentrics eager for bargains.

Zhang had charged Ken pretty steeply, however, for that skullcap, while claiming that he had no idea where it had been found. Ken and Ngili had asked Randall Phillips to have the skullcap dated, but Randall had laughed. A skullcap lying in a cookie jar in a Chinese merchant's store had been weathered and contaminated far too much to still be testable. It didn't matter that it had a perfect australopithecine profile.

"Let's go with your plan," said Ngili, "although everyone will ask, why didn't we test our find in Nairobi? The university lab just got a brand-new potassium-argon machine. That cute blond palynologist Corinne Gramm is playing with it." Palynologist meant expert in fossil pollens.

"Yeah, but that cute blond palynologist is now Cyril Anderson's wife."

Ken thought about Corinne Gramm, who along with Ken and Ngili had taken Cyril's course in human evolution. Ken remembered her hands, working on the first samples he took to the lab as a student. They were agile, attractive hands, stained with lab acids. She was five three or four, gray-eyed, not strikingly beautiful, yet the cleanness of her features and the straightness of her manner made her attractive.

After getting her degree, Corinne had married Anderson, who was at least thirty years her senior. Their marriage had been the thing to gossip about in the scientific community. Paleontology was a super competitive science. Too few good remains came out of the ground, so rookies had a hell of a time getting projects funded and establishing their names. A rookie who pole-vaulted into a marriage with a scientific superstar instantly gained everyone's animosity.

As for Cyril Anderson, he had a reputation for taking over projects, pushing the finders, especially if they were young, into the background and associating the find with one of his own theories. Usually the dust wasn't quite off a newly discovered skull when Cyril, whether he had found it or not, was already on TV talking about its meaning.

"You're right. Too bad Cyril is Cyril," said Ngili.

THEY WALKED BACK TO THE PLANE, WHICH HENDRIJKS HAD moored with lines to the nearest and thickest whistling-thorn bushes.

The pilot was sitting like an Oriental sage, except that his meditation was nothing but brain-dead drunkenness. They were quite close when he keeled over, falling on one side, whiskey bottle sliding from his lap. Ngili leaped like a leopard to save the whiskey from pouring out into the savanna ground.

"Well done," cheered Ken. "For such a good deed, the old buzzard ought to give us a discount."

"Don't worry about the money," replied Ngili. "Um'tu will chip in."

Um'tu, "the man" in Swahili, was the name Ngili and his sister, Yinka, used for their father. And that was Ngili's standard reply about money: Don't worry, Um'tu would chip in if he or his friend came up short because the Ngiamenas were wealthy, and this was Ngili's last year of playing scientist. His father, Jakub Ngiamena, had already tagged Ngili for a government job, perhaps an ambassadorship.

Ken couldn't imagine Ngili ever giving up geology. But this was Africa, where duty to tribe and family prevailed over many personal choices. Ngili, who was Cambridge-educated, spoke English better than an Englishman, and was smart and urbane, might soon represent his country in international forums, sporting on national days a feathered tiara or a leopard skin hat. Perhaps. The future was hard to decipher. Meanwhile, both of them profited from their friendship in addition to enjoying it. Ken gained a level of introduction and help few foreigners had in Kenya. And Ngili had in Ken a peer he could talk to who would never judge him as being disloyal to his roots.

Neither of them had eaten anything since lunch, and the plane didn't carry any extra food. Ngili, whose stomach growled audibly, searched for the plastic garbage bag with the remains of their sandwiches, but didn't find any leftovers. All that was left were the crackers trampled on the floor. Accidentally leaning on a panel, Ngili caused it to lift; beneath it, in a storage bin, were several boxes of crackers, two leftover Cokes, and two cans of sliced Hawaiian pineapple. Hendrijks had prudently stashed them all out of sight.

"What a pack rat our great pilot is," snickered Ngili.

"Let him be, he did fine today."

"He didn't do fine when it came to sharing the food." Ngili's eyes brimmed with the contempt of a tribal son who would never think of hoarding food away from the others.

"So eat his crackers," said Ken. He had a slight headache but still wasn't really hungry.

"Nah," said Ngili. "My kind used to go for days without food. A little fasting won't kill me." He uncapped a Coke bottle and gurgled it. Ken didn't comment on the effects of caffeine and sugar on a food-deprived body.

There was a container of purified water, and Ken drank some of that. Then the two of them carried several blankets and an old tarp reeking of gasoline outside, to make beds. Ken threw a blanket over Hendrijks, who turned on his back and snored.

The fire was still crackling. Ken felt that his mind was crackling in tune with it. He started to divide the bedding. Ngili noticed, and asked him what the hell he was doing.

"A shrew might take a liking to that dug-up mound," said

Ken. "Or an owl might choose the skull for a perch. I wouldn't like that at all."

"You'll freeze, you idiot. Sleep here; when the fire goes out, we'll need all the available body heat."

"If it gets too cold, I'll come back here."

"As I often say, you're mad."

"I know. See you on the dig in the morning."

G ENTLY, KEN SPREAD THE TARP OVER THE EXPOSED fossil, then lay down by the dig, wrapped in a blanket, convinced that he would never go to sleep.

The fossil had taken his mind off the footprints, but now he remembered them, lying on that spur in an almost circular pattern. It was as if some hominids had walked there two million years ago, in a circle, for some reason known just to them.

Why in a circle?

If they were australopithecines, the question was even more puzzling.

The only other such trail of footprints had been discovered at Laetoli, in Tanzania. There, in 1976, Mary Leakey had astounded the world by discovering a double trail of hominid prints. Two early humans, one surely adult, the other perhaps a child, had walked on a thin sheet of volcanic ash that had forever preserved their footprints. They had walked, over three million years before modern man, on feet looking almost modern—only the toes were longer, with the big toe slightly separated and pointing out.

The two protohumans of Laetoli had walked in an almost straight line. They had been headed toward something, maybe food or a home base, or away from something, perhaps danger. Very likely the danger had been the volcanic

31

eruption whose spit of ash had captured their prints.

If the protohumans who made these prints on the spur were of the same breed, the shape and purpose of their movement appeared even more exciting and mysterious to Ken.

Why in a circle?

He didn't know. But the excitement of a find was always made up of two parts: the find itself, and the gradual deciphering of its meaning.

He almost couldn't believe that he, Ken Lauder of Oakland, California, who had first arrived in Africa with the Peace Corps, who had studied paleoanthropology at the University of Kenya while supporting himself as a bush tracker, a safari guide, a bartender at Nairobi's Naivasha Hotel, who had joined expeditions as a truck driver, and had earned his degree on merciless digs that had taken down other students with heatstroke and dysentery—in a word, the old he, whom he knew only too well, had made two discoveries in one day.

One, the fossil, of definite scientific value.

He didn't even want to think about the other one in too much detail. It ignited his mind. Another trail of hominid prints, a second Laetoli? No, no, impossible. A case of "Dubois syndrome," as Randall Phillips would say warningly to students too certain of the value of their discoveries. Even before Eugène Dubois, discoverer of Java Man, had landed in Java back in 1891, he had been adamant that he and no other would find the first "missing link." That was *faith*, Randall was fond of saying, not science.

Yet it seemed that in this field one needed faith almost as much as science.

Ken was quite sure that he shouldn't present his find to Cyril Anderson. And yet, he felt frustrated. Cyril was an institution, and not just through academic merit; in fact, academic merit was the smaller part of his aura. Cyril had worked with Louis Leakey, the father of modern paleoanthropology. While very young, Cyril had been an assistant to Raymond Dart, who first found *Australopithecus* and coined that species' name. Dart was also the first to propose that mankind's birthplace was Africa. His proposal kicked up a storm of scientific protest. No, no, no, the ancestor of our race could not have been from Africa! What Dart had found was some chimplike, gorillalike, baboonlike offshoot!

Over half a century had passed, and Africa had been accepted as mankind's birthplace. By association, Cyril had come to symbolize the soul of that pioneering generation. The glow of Leakey and Dart, reflected upon a successor, created superstardom. Superstardom translated into academic honors and lucrative book deals, and the co-curatorship of the university's fossils vault.

The vault was an amazing place. Located in the basement of the building that housed the paleontology department, down a corridor branching to the right from the one leading to the lab (Ken remembered again that Corinne was now running it), there was a shelterlike construction, with a steel door as solid as a New York bank's. It was a fort, holding in labeled aluminum boxes the most famous hominid bones in the world. They lay inside their little metal coffins, on couches of cloth and burlap, under the surveillance of closed-circuit TV cameras and of several thermometers and humidity gauges—several, so that the vault's inner atmospheric conditions could not fall victim to a single instrument's failure.

Ken reminisced about the fabulous place. Down there were stored the remains of early hominids, their succession like a series of technologic breakthroughs, though in this case the technology was man's reproductive system, and the assembly line was the harsh prehistoric savanna Ken intended to explore further. Down there were bones and skulls of *Homo habilis,* the toolmaker, and early *Homo sapiens,* the thinker. And a cohort of earlier models, the australopithecines, the ape-humans, whether smaller-boned specimens called graciles, or the sturdier versions known as robusts. They were still so close to the apes that they were once called the missing links.

Now, after so many ape-humans had been found, the chain's so-called missing links were longer than the other links, and between the sheer ape and the full-fledged human there was an intriguing middle stage, whose mystery fascinated Ken. If the fossil he had found really was two million years old, it could illuminate that mystery.

Ken remembered that Corinne had free access to what the rest of the world never got to see. Ninety-nine point nine percent of mankind would never get a chance to view their ultimate ancestors. But she, most likely, could visit the crown jewels of human evolution whenever she wished. Just as Leakey and Dart had imparted aura onto Cyril, Cyril was now imparting aura onto his wife.

There was no denying that Cyril was a character. He was a large, white-haired, stoop-shouldered, Kenya-born Englishman, who spoke with teatime affectation but in a voice of wonderful range, which made that affectation delightful instead of comical. Cyril sang his lectures. He wore checkered jackets and starched shirts and club ties, and when the temperate climate of Nairobi turned to rain, he walked the campus spreading a black, Victorian umbrella.

Cyril's office in the paleontology building—just like him—was vast, over the top, and crammed with mementos of his historic friendships. His desk looked like a lab bench, except that the instruments on it were not soiled by lab work, but were sparkling clean—one, a sieve for washing specimens, had obviously never been used, for it was made of gold. It was a gift from the Mitsubishi Corporation, cosponsors of a BBC documentary Anderson had narrated.

"Cyril is the perfect pop star for the *Man's Origins* show," Randall Phillips had once characterized him to Ken. "The right accent, the right associations, and a lot of sweep. He sweeps from the Cambrian to today in one sentence. He sweeps back to the Cambrian in his next sentence. We're a science short on fact and long on sweep. Now, Cyril's so long on sweep, he has no fact left at all. But he's got this image, the Philosopher of Man. That's what people fall for."

"You sound jealous," Ken had replied. He could say it because Randall had offered him his friendship, beyond age and academic achievement.

"I *am* jealous," agreed Randall. "I put my last thirty years into science, and Cyril put them into his own success. Who do you think had more fun?''

INITIALLY, KEN HAD FALLEN FOR CYRIL'S IMAGE. THE FIRST time he had glimpsed Cyril was back in 1985, in New York, when some of the world's most precious fossils, insured for half a million dollars each, had been brought to be exhibited at the American Museum of Natural History in a show called "Ancestors: Three Million Years of Humanity."

It was a cold spring day, with the sky pouring rain on a crowd that besieged the museum, spilling across Central Park West and blocking the traffic. Squashed in that crowd stood Ken, age seventeen. He had flown into New York the day before, alone, on an economy ticket bought with savings from summer jobs, to see the Ancestors show. Ken had started as an amateur paleontologist three years before on the beaches of Northern California, looking for the imprint of fossil plankton in limestone rocks.

And now he watched Louis Leakey and Cyril Anderson walk up the museum's stairs—the mayor of New York striding with them. Leakey smiled to the crowd, quickly but warmly, a famous man who had remained simple at heart. One step behind, Anderson grinned widely at the reporters' flashing cameras. His hair had not yet gone from gray to white. He had beautiful white hands which held high his black umbrella, and a copy of *The New York Times* with his face splattered across the front page. The headline read: PHILOSOPHER OF MAN ASKS: WILL MAN MAKE IT ANOTHER MILLION YEARS?

As Ken watched elatedly, the distinguished group disappeared inside for the unveiling of bones ancestral to all the people crushing each other out in the street.

That night, in a cheap, almost scary hotel on Fortieth Street, Ken had sat rereading the *Times* story on Anderson. Then he had watched Anderson on TV. Leakey and other scientists were restrained in their statements, but Anderson asked in a full voice the questions on most laypeople's minds: are humans today essentially the same as three million years ago? Where is humankind headed? Is it "spent"? Or is it still full of energy, and capable of change? His answers were not scientific. They were visionary and poetic. But everyone loved them, and so did Ken. Anderson made Ken dream of humanness, and of Africa.

Two days later, after two more pilgrimages to the exhibit, Ken took his economy seat on his return flight to Oakland. He nurtured in his head a plan that was a leap in his destiny, just as the trip to New York had been. To go to Africa.

There was little to share with his family about that plan. Ken lived with his mother, but did not know where his father was. His parents had met in San Francisco as flower children, and produced him between hits of pot. The pregnancy awakened them to reality. They moved to Oakland. The father took a job in a post office. One day when Ken was five, he left home to go to work and was never heard from again. The mother raised Ken by making and selling dresses of organic fiber. She spoke little. For days on end, she did not speak at all.

Thus, Ken grew up free. Who was to say that he couldn't go to Africa? The Peace Corps was as good a way as any other.

Ken arrived in Nairobi and found Anderson embroiled in academic intrigues. There was a man who had built the paleontology department, Randall Phillips. Randall was in line to become full curator of the fossils vault. Anderson wooed Kenya's government, arguing that he could be good P.R. for the young country if he were named co-curator. Randall could not oppose Anderson's co-curatorship if it was recommended by the prime minister's office; one didn't take the prime minister lightly.

After the co-curatorship was created, Anderson began to bar Phillips's path to the full curatorship. He continued wooing the government, offering his renown and connections to help bring in foreign loans. And by the way, Anderson seemed to ask, was Phillips the brightest banner that one could fly, not just over the vault but over the whole world-famed department of paleontology?

Just recently Randall had announced that he would take a sabbatical in the States, his first one away from Nairobi. This meant that Cyril could easily take over the department. The students loved Cyril's voice. And they had never liked Randall's. Randall was flat, impatient, and sarcastic. He was no priest of the past, leading his converts into a marvelous initiation.

The rest, as usual, was history.

ENOUGH, THOUGHT KEN. HERE HE WAS, IN THE MIDDLE OF the wilderness, playing back the department wars. You've been hanging around Randall Phillips too long, he scolded himself; give Caruso a break—Caruso was Randall's nickname for Anderson.

He found that hard, and knew why. Anderson had destroyed Ken's illusions about the world of science. As a full-time student, Ken had tried to join Cyril's tutorial list, but it was already so booked that he had to look around for another tutor. He chose Randall on academic merit, unaware of how risky that choice was. He found himself shunned from then on, at the library, in class, in the lab, in a manner that sharply stung a young enthusiast. Anderson was quite obvious about whom he considered to be "his" people. When Ken turned in his degree paper, Anderson reviewed it and gave Ken only one half page of typed notes. The meeting lasted five minutes.

Luckily, Ken had already figured out that what counted in this science was the fieldwork. He made his own connections, befriended Ngili, and went on independent digs, guerrilla style. When he got his degree, Anderson raised no obstacles; Ken was too unimportant. Anderson did not know that before he and Corinne were married she and Ken had had a brief romance just after Ken first met her at the lab.

When it was over, after two months of secretive meetings in Ken's apartment—direct as a scientist, Corinne was fiercely private as a woman—they agreed to act as if nothing had ever happened between them. When she married Anderson, Ken told himself that he did not care, that she was a good palynologist, and Cyril was lucky, as usual.

Ken had a degree now and wanted to stay on in Africa. To learn, and to become a true paleontologist. For that he needed experience so he plunged himself back into fieldwork. He went on exotic digs, such as Tilemsi in the Sahara, where the moonscapelike soil broke at the gentlest touch, exposing 300-million-year-old eggs of the crocodiles and turtles that once teemed in a landlocked sea. He went to Olduvai, eroded not just by time but also by the antlike toil of scores of scientists, who packed Olduvai more for its fame than for the richness of its fossil beds. He worked hard and suffered from heat and cold, dehydration and diarrhea, bug bites and crotch rot. He went to Lake Turkana. To Koobi Fora, to Kromdraai. To all the legendary digging sites.

He managed to get into those places, sometimes by taking jobs as a truck driver or a caterer. He would slip into the sites after dark or before dawn, sometimes bribing local guards. But he managed to be there, even though he knew that he would not come out with any significant fossils of his own because his time was too short, and the plum pieces had already been picked. But the main thing was to be there, with the giants. The giants of the past, the fossils; the giants of the present, their discoverers.

He lost his romanticism, and that felt good. Like the taste of truth on one's tongue, refreshingly sharp.

Still, his feelings toward Anderson were harsh, and not only because the other man had helped kill his illusions. Why, Ken wondered, did such a man have to be vacuous, egotistical, and petty? There was no reason; fate had endowed him with everything. Anderson could have been a god. Instead, he was a politician.

KEN DID NOT KNOW WHEN HE FELL ASLEEP, OR FOR HOW long. He became aware that he was waking up, and that something was stirring nearby.

Above the savanna, the moon was playing with thin, plume-shaped clouds. He sat up and glanced at the mound, and saw that the tarp had slipped off the fossil, blown by the breeze or shaken off by some settling of the soil. Uncovered, the skull faced Ken. The eye sockets, darker than the rest of the dark face, stared straight back at him.

He shivered because it was cold. He addressed the skull in his mind: Though I'm sure you felt the cold when you walked around on that spur, you don't have to worry about being cold now. That's one of death's privileges.

In a silence that seemed strangely expressive, the uncovered skull stared back, as if the ape-man it had once been could hear Ken's thoughts. It was sorry it could not answer and explain why it had once walked in that circle, with its relatives, on that barren paw. But australopithecines had not developed a spoken language.

The moon ducked out of a cloud. The fossil's eyes looked darker, as if filled with a real stare, while the increased light played on the top of its braincase, now shiny from having been cleaned. The magic of the night somehow made it hard to believe that though brainless and eyeless, the skull did not have some kind of awareness of the living world it had again joined.

Ken heard the wings of a bat ripping the air jaggedly. Then he heard tiny steps. He turned and saw a little troop of elephant-nosed shrews. Mouselike except for their trunk-shaped, flexible snouts, they traversed a small open space between one clump of bushes and another. The largest, probably the mother, led the pack, with her trunk-shaped nose to the ground. Ken peeled off his blanket, got up, following their movement with his eyes, and saw a golden jackal, standing dead still in a bush. He could see its yellow coat against the leaves, waiting for the shrews to get closer.

Not so fast, Ken thought, and groped inside the blanket for a flashlight he had taken from the plane. All he had to do was shine it, and the jackal would run. He found the flashlight, aimed it at the jackal, and pressed the button.

No light came.

He flicked the button again. No light. The battery was dead.

Great, just like Hendrijks, thought Ken, annoyed that he could not avert the little drama. Hendrijks never took care of his smaller gear; all he cared about was his plane.

The jackal lunged, grabbed the mother shrew, breaking its spine with a quick snapping sound. There was a squeak of death, and then the jackal galloped off with the prey in its mouth, while the little shrews scattered.

Ken stuck the useless flashlight in his pocket, draped the blanket around his shoulders, and paced around the mound of dirt, shivering. In the glow of the clouded moon, he saw dark shapes moving in the vast savanna. Hyenas and wild dogs barked, and he saw a string of round creatures, running maybe two hundred yards off. They looked like a sliding black necklace. Bushpigs, he guessed. They were not great to meet in a pack because they could chew a human to the bone in minutes. But they would not attack him, he reassured himself. There were wild beasts all over this place, but none of them were hungry enough tonight that they would stoop to eating a human being.

His mind tried to control his fear, but his body experienced it clearly. His penis contracted, and his testicles felt bean-sized as they were pulled in by his tightened scrotum, closer to the doubtful protection of his body. All of a sudden, he thought the idea of guarding these old bones while possibly risking his own seemed stupid. He looked off at the plane, which was the brightest thing in the savanna. It seemed to lie moored very far from him. He debated walking to it, but could not decide whether he was being wise, or just overly nervous from the darkness and the dead flashlight.

He felt as if the night were a time machine, and it had catapulted him back to prehistory. The bones he stood by belonged to a fellow human who was alive just days before. A fellow hunter, a comrade. Or a female, a spouse. Deprived of comrade or spouse, he felt the entire weight of fear.

Then his fear was combined with a curious fantasy. He felt a weight in the back of his legs, in his calves, as if they'd grown thicker, and shorter. What was it like to share the savanna with bushpigs and lions, and be only four feet tall, instead of six? To have no flashlight, just the light-processing powers of australopithecine eyes? And to have no natural defense from lions or other predators?

He shivered. *I'll lie down,* he told himself. *It's cold, and I'm shivering from the cold.* He came around the little mound, and stood agog, too frightened now even to be aware of his fright.

A lion was stepping toward the tarp that had slipped off the fossil. It was a young male, and it carried a good-sized black mane. It advanced with small steps, low-shouldered, looking almost hunchbacked. It kept its head bowed, sniffing the dirty odor of the tarp, and had the expression of lions when they are confused by something unexpected. It had a look of near humbleness, which meant nothing but a temporary stand-down of its aggressive instinct.

Ken stopped moving and gritted his teeth to prevent them from chattering. At the same time, he could not help a feeling of sheer visual pleasure, of admiration for the cat's smooth movements. The lion was stepping with the candid strength of novice predators. Was it encountering a human, or a human-made artifact, for the first time?

He watched the animal come to the edge of the tarp and stop, thrashing its tail. It brought its nose very low, then put forth a paw, and researched the strange object with a sweep of claws that screeched against the tarp's rainproof fabric. Then it raised its head and saw Ken.

He had only one way of handling this—by staring right back. Ken did so, thinking of how his primate eyes were so much less luminescent compared to the cat's, thinking that if he wasn't mauled, he'd probably have his sweat glands to thank; to a lion, a human stank badly and intimidatingly.

The lion lowered its face, back to its pose of feline modesty. Its eyes straight on Ken, it seemed to pour its body down into its haunches, as it sat on the ground.

Ken let out a cough. The round ears buried in the dark mane pricked up, and the animal dropped its jaw and growled. Then it took a loping leap, straight toward Ken. Ken raised the only object he had as a weapon, the flashlight.

No, he thought painfully. *This cannot end like this. This is too stupid.*

He wondered if he stood a tiny chance of survival by hitting full force at the feline's face. The lion was shrinking the distance between them. This will be over fast.

Out of pure nervousness, Ken's finger pushed the flashlight's on button. He expected nothing. But from the dying battery, a last surge of power kindled the bulb. A full, handsome beam of light flooded the loping lion's face.

Blinded, the lion leaped up, to halt his own movement. A screech rather than a roar came from his chest, and from the sloppy leap and that momentary blindness, he fell backward with a thud.

That instant was enough. Ken did not know when he had moved, but he found himself still facing the lion, but twenty yards away. The lion rose, turned, walked off, its nervousness apparent only in the way it thrashed its tail.

The flashlight flickered, then died again. But Ken breathed freely, feeling as if the whole night had been lifted off his neck and chest.

He stepped back to the dug-up mound. Without thought, he bent down to pick up the tarp and spread it again over the fossil.

Then he hurried toward the plane, without panic but without wasting an instant. On his way, he kept hearing stirrings of night life, many and varied. There was plenty of game here to hunt. Plenty to poach, too. If the night was so full of action now, imagine how it had been three million years ago.

T HE FIRST THING KEN HEARD WHEN HE WOKE WAS THE
rude, penetrating calls of a bush bird: *go-waar, go-
waar!* The sound helped him picture the bird before he even
opened his eyes. It was a gray turaco, popularly known as
the "go-away-bird," common in deserts and acacia scrub.

He heard strong, repeated calls from several birds, followed by a dry, brief crack: a gunshot. He bolted up, rubbed
his eyes roughly, and glanced at the plane, which looked
curiously lopsided. He saw Hendrijks standing with a hunting
rifle in his hands. The top of the fuselage seemed to take off,
fluttering and flapping. The go-away birds had been perching
on it, and the shot had propelled them into flight. Hendrijks,
rifle in hand, ran around the plane, stood in the clear, and
fired the rifle again, several times. Rushing in from the savanna, Ngili called out at Hendrijks to stop shooting. Ngili
was brandishing the machete—Ken noticed that the machete's blade was already yellow from fresh digging, and its
tip was twisted. He wondered how early Ngili had gotten up.
Hendrijks turned, tripped, and inadvertently loosed a bullet
that meowed right by Ngili, who ducked, then charged forth
with the machete, his face rigid with anger.

Ken darted toward the two. His thoughts were still fuzzy,
but his body bubbled with tension; the day was starting
badly, really badly. He arrived at the point of precollision of

43

two furious males and managed to stand between them, asking, in a voice still groggy from sleep, what the hell had happened.

"Look at my plane!" was all that Hendrijks could articulate.

Just then, Hendrijks spotted a pair of go-away birds circling back. He tried to point his rifle, but Ngili almost collared him. The insufferable birds alighted on the plane again and resumed their obnoxious "go-away! go-away!"

Ken stared at the plane. An undercarriage leg, the one on the port side, had shrunk to half the length of the other leg. The plane leaned on the side of the shorter leg, its wing tip close to the ground.

Ken asked when it had happened. Hendrijks barked that sometime last night, while they were asleep, the springs inside the leg, which probably had been damaged when they landed, had collapsed. Hendrijks's explosion at the birds was from the frustration of discovering the damage. Now he spotted the machete in Ngili's hand, and found cause for more grief in the way it looked. Ngili explained that he had used it to dig. Hendrijks shouted it was *his* machete, and he should not have done that. Ngili reminded him that last night Hendrijks had allowed them to use the machete, the shaving brush, and even his razor. Hendrijks jumped at the mention of the razor, ready to fight again.

Ken pulled Ngili away from the pilot. Then he grabbed Hendrijks by the shoulders, and stared into his pink face. "Can you take off on that leg?" Hendrijks glanced at the lowered wing, and gritted his teeth, but nodded. "Then why don't you pull yourself together, and finish fixing the rudder?" Hendrijks unexpectedly pushed back Ken's arms with a thrust beyond his real strength.

"I'm putting one last bracket around the rudder," he yelled, "and after that I'm leaving. You two have an hour. If you're not in the plane in one hour, I'm taking off without you!"

He climbed into the cockpit, leaving Ken and Ngili facing each other.

Ken took Ngili's arm. "Don't worry. He's letting off steam. He's just hungover and upset."

Ngili was breathing deeply. "Letting off steam with a loaded rifle? I'd rather have a fistfight." Then he turned and headed into the savanna, calling over his shoulder, "Come on, I found something else!" He seemed very spirited, even though his face was gaunt and his stomach growled more loudly than it had last night.

"Look at this branch of whistling thorns," said Ngili, setting down a clump of the thorns harvested with the machete the night before. One thorny branch had a gob of dried-up mud, the size of an apple, impaled on its tip.

That apple of mud was an ants' nest. Ngili picked up the thorns, and led Ken a few steps away, to an irregular machete-cut pit in the ground, where Ngili had freed a slab of ancient limestone and laid it on the ground. He placed the whistling thorns side by side with the sample of rock.

The same pattern of whistling thorns was impressed clearly upon the inside of the rock. The same knotty, twisted profiles of branches, the same studding of thorns, and even an identical ants' nest, apple-sized, impaled on a branch tip, were imprinted on the rock. They were petrified, fossilized.

The live whistling thorns looked the same as their ancestors.

"How about this, Professor Lauder?" asked Ngili, his voice gushing.

"Fabulous. You made me a professor already?"

"*They* should make you one, though of course they won't."

Ngili energetically prowled back and forth past the fossil plants. He was handsome, unshaven, red-eyed from his Masai genes and from his lack of sleep. "This is the best proof for your theory, Ken. This habitat hasn't changed for at least three million years." He dropped on his knees, caressing with dusty fingertips the shape of the ancient flowers, careful not to weigh down their delicately preserved shapes. "Had the levels of temperature, or the amounts of rainfall varied considerably since the Pliocene, these plants would have disappeared, or gone through so many adaptations they would've looked like a fern next to a cactus. But look, they're absolutely identical, back then and today.''

Ken cleared his voice. ''You really think this is so conclusive?''

''This is just one sample. God knows how many other shrubs and grasses out here look the same live and embedded in the rock. But what kept the weather conditions stable?''

''That!'' blurted Ken, pointing up. Ngili looked up to the crests of the Mau. They were wrapped in thick, milky mist. ''The Mau is a weather stabilizer. It maintains the humidity. There are scorching rainless days here, no doubt, but that mist comes down in rainfall on the crests, and the cool humid steam makes it to the plain. It's not obvious, but this place is among the wettest savannas in Africa.''

''In that case''—Ngili opened his fluted Masai arms at the surrounding savanna—''Ken, this is it, this is live Pliocene. And you guessed it was here.''

''Thank you.'' Ken felt emotional, shy, and blessed beyond belief. Ngili lowered his arms, and Ken grabbed one of the dusty Masai palms, and shook it.

''You're a good friend, Ngili.''

''Thanks. I hope I'll be a good geologist.''

''If your father lets you.''

''He might start bending after this kind of find. Ken!'' Ngili shouted. ''We could get a dig permit, maybe some funding, on this alone. The unchanged continuity of the habitat.''

''But we also got a fossil,'' Ken reminded him.

''Right, and if this creature's pelvis and feet show a reasonable degree of bipedalism''—which meant that the ancient ape-human had walked erect—''then we've got it made, we've got the ancient humans in their exact ancient habitat!'' Brusquely, he bent down to examine a print of a lion's paw. He glanced away at the tarp lying ruffled on the ground, then started laughing. ''Is this what chased you back to the plane last night?''

Ken nodded and described the encounter with the lion.

"Idiot," said Ngili. "You could've died before completing your great find." Which reminded them that they still had some digging to do. They grabbed their improvised tools, Ngili the machete, Ken the razor.

"Remember, the pelvis tells all," joked Ken. "And we're in the era of pelvis."

The way a fossil's thighbones are joined into the pelvic joints indicates whether the creature walked erect regularly, and the broadness of the pelvis indicates whether the specimen was male or female. The "era of pelvis" was only half a joke, because it referred to a radical change in scientific belief about what had brought about bipedalism.

Scientists had traditionally thought that humans did not walk erect before their brains swelled from the average five hundred cubic centimeters of *Australopithecus* to the average seven hundred fifty cubic centimeters of *Homo habilis,* the toolmaker. Walking erect was thought to be the direct consequence of the brain getting bigger. But in the mid-seventies, more complete skeletons of australopithecines were discovered, including the famous hominid, Lucy, whose pelvis proved that she was already bipedal 3.2 million years ago, and with only four hundred cubic centimeters of brain-power.

Those discoveries stood evolutionary theory on its head, so to speak. If walking erect was possible with an ape-sized brain, that meant that something else had made early humans hip to the benefits of walking on two feet and never dropping back on all fours again. But no one knew what that was. The clues were being provided, bit by bit, by petrified remains like the one Ken and Ngili were freeing out of the ground.

Now Ken's stomach was growling too, and his headache was back. Yet he went to work, chipping away with Hendrijks's razor.

He wondered whether this find presaged more years of lonely work for him or, on the contrary, a better chance of making regular money, getting married, having children. Hard to tell, since in his case, the future's crystal ball was a buried ape-man's pelvis.

That pelvis contained incredibly fascinating information, if only one could decipher it. During the ape-man stage, the anatomy of early humans had undergone drastic changes. No one knew exactly how or why they happened, but as hominids rose on two legs, the females began to carry their genitals hidden between their legs, instead of hanging them on their behinds, grossly inflated by estrus and entirely obvious. The males started carrying their penes frontally, totally exposed, and larger and more visible than in any other mammal. During the ape-man stage, the penis bone mysteriously disappeared, and the penis increased almost four times in size, becoming solely dependent for its erections on rich irrigations of blood. The ape-man had blood coursing through him much faster than did any apes, and there was more of it. The females had more too, and they started leaking it out once monthly. Sex, still one of the most mysterious functions of life, had changed fundamentally along the passage from full ape to modern human.

Ken worked at the mystery in front of him with the razor, feeling the thin blade throb as the soil got harder and harder. Suddenly the razor jolted in his hand and the blade broke.

Ken stared at the piece of steel sticking out of the handle. He packed the broken razor back in its case and put it in his pocket, then looked around for another tool to dig with. He unbuckled his belt, took off the round brass buckle, and used it.

"Breccia," said Ngili, referring to the limestone-and-gravel concrete of the ages. "Now I'm hitting breccia, all over. From the waist down, this guy's encased in it."

He wiped his forehead with his sleeve. Ken made a joke that the Mafia of the Pliocene Era had sealed its fossils in cement.

"We're not going to be able to free this thing in one morning. It might take the whole day, and some of tomorrow."

"We gotta go talk to Hendrijks."

"He's here to talk to us," said Ngili, and pointed.

Hendrijks was zigzagging between bushes, his rifle on his shoulder. As he approached, Ken noticed a dozen antelopes, black-fronted duikers, pulling their mouths out of tall grass as Hendrijks walked by.

He heard Hendrijks's boots thudding closer. Hendrijks was wearing his bush hat. Under its brim, his face looked grayish and granulated, like weathered rock.

"You look so serious. What's up?" Ken asked, to take the initiative.

"I just listened to another weather report," said Hendrijks. "That dust storm is moving in from Tanzania. It will hit here around four in the afternoon."

"Maybe we'll be ready by then."

"I want to be gone long before. I can't afford to be blown off course with the plane in the condition it's in."

"You said you had only one more bracket to put around the rudder."

"I did that."

"Then the plane's in fine condition, and so are you," said Ken.

"Maybe you're just hungry," Ngili added in an acid tone.

Hendrijks stared at Ngili with such anger that Ken wondered what the hell was the matter with the old guy; he'd never seen him like that before.

"Let's make a new deal," Ken said amicably. "We might need to stay another day here. Let's talk price for another day."

"I don't stay here, not for anything," said Hendrijks. "And I don't want those bones in my plane. You leave markers, we go. Someone else brings you back next week."

Hendrijks glanced around. With the morning sun up, the savanna looked glorious, struck with white and red flowers, and undulating with animals' backs. Yet the pilot scanned it with a narrowed, opaque look, as if it were some ghostly graveyard. He cleared his throat, adding a little more softly that he'd barely made out the report about that dust storm. The plane's radio seemed close to dying. He did not want to risk other mishaps, and this stop felt like bad luck. Real bad luck. Ngili told him not to be superstitious.

"You say that? *You?*" asked Hendrijks with audible subtext. Ngili glared at him, threw the machete on the ground, and said that if Kenya had public campaigns against kamba witch doctors, Hendrijks could also afford to act reasonably.

The granulated face under the bush hat seemed alive with a second life, that of its skin; the pimples and wrinkles on it appeared to throb with contained anger.

"We have no food," snapped Hendrijks.

"You've got a *bunduki* right there on your shoulder," said Ngili, using the Swahili for rifle. "I've seen fifty wild hares in these bushes. You can catch them with your bare hands. We did it when we were children."

Ken had seen that done, by tribal children and also by adults. Hares raced away straight into the bushes, but almost invariably veered at a right angle to the right or the left, and then glued themselves to the ground, waiting for the peril to pass. If their pursuers dived to that spot, even if they couldn't see the rabbit, half the time they would land on top of it.

"You caught hares, and then ate them raw?" asked Hendrijks.

"I'm going to let that pass," announced Ngili.

"I'm not going to let your airs pass!"

"I have no airs," said Ngili coolly. "You're a mess this morning. When you drink too much, you're a mess."

Hendrijks turned almost lilac. He uttered a sound Ken never thought him capable of making, a kind of hiss.

"Don't you dare call me a mess," he said. "Don't you dare call me anything. You hear, boy?"

"*Toto*'s more like it," said Ngili. "Why waste your time with boy? Call me *toto*, or *mpishi*." These words meant "house servant" and "cook," in the minimal Swahili of the former white masters. Ngili's voice had gotten strange too; it was a snarl through gnashed teeth. "Or kaffir, huh? Aren't you from where they used to call them kaffirs?"

"Guys, guys!" Ken called out.

He could not believe it. He saw Hendrijks's right hand grab the strap of the rifle. Hendrijks stepped closer to Ngili, who did not budge an inch, and told the young geologist that he was born rich and knew nothing from nothing. Hendrijks had flown about Africa twice as long as Ngili had lived, had worked in this land, had suffered. Ngili told him that Hendrijks's kind had never suffered in Africa one day. Hendrijks yelled that during the guerrilla war preceding independence, whites had had to lock their bedrooms so they would not be killed in their sleep by black servants they'd done everything for, saved the black men from charges of theft, saved the black girls from being sold at the market for a box of soap each! He seemed belatedly to realize what he had been saying. "Your father would know what I'm talking about. . . ." he trailed confusedly.

Ngili's eyes had narrowed till they looked like the blade of the machete.

"Enough." Ken marched over, put himself between the two. He told Hendrijks to get the hell back inside that plane, get a drink of water, come back cooled off, and apologize to Ngili. But Hendrijks looked as puffed up as a bullfrog in heat. "I'm leaving," he threatened, and turned and shoved off.

Ken looked at Ngili. He felt like touching Ngili's arm, in the way he had learned from Africans, who rarely consider physical expressions of warmth inappropriate, even between men. But at this moment, he didn't want Ngili to think he was babying him. Instead, he muttered something about the jerks of Hendrijks's generation.

"We can let him go," said Ngili, tense but cool. "As long as we manage to get inside the plane before he takes off, radio Nairobi, and get another pilot to pick us up. I don't want Um'tu to get worried."

His face looked carved, from hunger, from contained anger. Usually Ngili looked almost too pretty. Now he looked less perfect, but real in a harsh, basic way.

"That bastard's bluffing," Ken muttered. He took the machete. "Come on, let's work."

The machete began to cut a circular trench around a big boulder of breccia in which the lower part of the fossil was encased. They had to dig deep enough to reach under the fossil without damaging it, and then pull out that whole big piece, with the fossil intact inside it.

The machete opened the way, the buckle followed. The progress was inch by inch, excruciating. Ken pondered the wisdom of trying. But as Ngili pointed out, without that pelvis they didn't really know what they had found.

Ken figured that the job would take at least until sundown. When they heard the airplane, it sounded like a dream.

When they looked, Hendrijks had turned the machine toward the Mau, to gain advantage from a light mountainbound wind, and was revving up the engine. Son of a bitch. Bastard. Stinking old shit, cursed Ken, getting out of the trench, and switching his energy to running, running as fast as he could to catch up with the departing plane.

Ngili jumped up too and raced behind Ken. The propeller was already raising a little cyclone of dusty air, which hit them in their faces, blowing open their sweat-soaked shirts and whipping back Ken's bleached and dirty hair.

Ken made it to the plane, avoiding the port side, whose wing slashed down at a menacing angle. He raced under the right wing, and stopped far ahead of the propeller. Hendrijks was taxiing slowly, as if reconnoitering, and his side window was open. Ken hand-signaled, arms raised and crossed repeatedly above his head: "Stop! Stop!"

The propeller slowed, became visible. Hendrijks had cut the power to half. He put his head out and yelled that he would take Ken. Not Ngili.

"Forget it," Ken yelled back. "I'm not going either."

Hendrijks yelled at Ken to scramble in; Ngili could wait for another plane, which Ken would send from Nairobi.

Ken mouthed "Fuck you" against the noise of the propeller.

Ngili caught up with him and grabbed Ken's elbow and urged him to leave with Hendrijks. Once in Nairobi, all Ngili had to do was call his father from the airport. Ken shook his head and grunted against the propeller's sound that Hendrijks was bluffing. He stepped out of the plane's way.

Hendrijks revved up again. The aluminum toy bounced away, shaving the bushes with its lowered wing tip. It raced off at full takeoff speed, with the wind in its tail and its wing tip snagging bush and a small tree.

Then it slowed down, turned, and taxied back.

The portside wing tip looked shredded; the navigation light hung from it, its bulb broken, like a car's shattered headlight after an accident. Ken's eyes scanned the terrain—with the port wing at such an angle, there was no place in sight where the plane could take off without snagging branches or hitting rocks.

The plane stopped. Hendrijks came out. He walked almost briskly toward Ken and Ngili, explaining loudly, "The undercarriage is shot. We can't take off without clearing a takeoff strip first." Ken noticed the *we*. Hendrijks stopped right by them: "After you two get some rest, we clear a strip together, okay? And if it must be tomorrow, it is tomorrow. Okay?"

For an instant, Ngili looked ready to total him. Ken's eyes begged his friend not to do it. Then he reminded the pilot that they had to finish unearthing that fossil.

Hendrijks grinned. "Of course. D'you want some water? There's still some." He led the way toward the plane.

Ngili mouthed silently at Ken, "Radio." Ken nodded. One by one, they climbed in. Ngili took a tin cup from Hendrijks's hand, and Hendrijks poured him water, while Ken reached for the earphones, hooked them on, and turned on the radio. He started to call out the plane's identification tag, then stopped. He was not talking into the usual crackle of airwaves, but into a blank silence. He pressed the buttons, then listened, holding his breath. But the radio was dead.

Hendrijks took the set, put on the earphones, played with the buttons. Then he took off the lifeless set and laid it down by the pilot's seat.

"Give me that rifle," said Ken.

Hendrijks had recovered his common sense; he knew when to resist and when not to. He handed Ken the extra light, insignificant-looking weapon. Ken took it, told Hendrijks to lash down the plane again and Ngili to pull the tarp over the dig and rest. Ken was going to get them all some dinner.

K EN WALKED INTO THE HIGH GRASS, LOOKING FOR ACA-
cia groves. Acacias, the typical, flat-topped, thorny savanna trees, provided only light shade because their leaves
were thin like pins and clustered horizontally, like green trays
held up to the sun. Still, their shelter was better than the
harsh direct sunlight. Most antelopes would be at rest at this
hour in the shade, chewing on the morning's grass intake.

The morning would have been a much better time for
hunting, but he had no choice about that now.

Big acacias rose by a long line of rocky outcrops, an almost uninterrupted rocky palisade that divided the grassland,
pulling the eye away until it joined the last spurs of the Mau.
Ken headed for the palisade, expecting to find duikers, which
had small hooves, equally able to trot the savanna and to
straggle into the rocks. Chasing the duikers toward the rocks
was good strategy. Out in the tall grasses, if he missed his
shots, they would scatter in all directions. By the palisade,
they would show against the rocks like big bouncing targets.

He could tell from his unsure steps how tired he was, and
also how depleted by hunger.

He arrived at the tree line and found that the acacias'
trunks were charcoal black. They had survived a bush fire.
They gave little shade, yet the duikers were there, sprawled,
looking like rufous pillows with antelope heads. The black

stripes down their foreheads moved gently up and down as they chewed, and their little black forelegs and hooves at rest looked delicate, too unsturdy to carry them. Ken decided to get as close to them as possible. He did not want to waste bullets or to prolong an animal's death with a bad shot. They looked at him innocently, and started to get up, but without any fear. All animals around here seemed either unused to man, he reflected, or unafraid of him.

Slowed down by the noontime heat, he wondered if he would have the stamina to carry a dead duiker. He raised the rifle and played with the sights against an array of dark foreheads, delaying his shot and allowing more of the animals to rise and flow toward the rocks. He saw that there was a series of walkways between the rocks, all overgrown with red oat grass and horsetails. Beyond them, the rocks built upward into an irregular second story. This could be an ideal land for poaching, full of excellent natural ambush sites.

He tripped, and his left ankle twisted outward. He let out a sound of pain, and the duikers, now fully alerted, flowed faster into the rocks, while Ken chased them from behind, limping and grimacing, but still sure of his first shot. Then he shouldered the rifle, froze his body, fired, and missed. The last duikers disappeared, the little brooms of their tails whipping in alert.

Now he was alone, without targets.

Ken chuckled, feeling relaxed and stupid. He got down on his knees, massaged his swelling ankle, then limped into the rocks, convinced that he could catch up with the little herd. He looked down for hoofprints, saw them stretching far ahead. He stopped, wondering whether to continue. The farther he went, the farther he'd have to carry a kill back to the plane, limping on that injured ankle.

He walked back, unalert and hungry and finally irritated, until he found himself back by the acacias. He looked down for animals' prints to evaluate other hunting possibilities and noticed that some of them had stepped over an elongated footprint, with a deep heel mark. He stopped, too amazed and tired to feel truly shocked.

The print's toes were longish, well formed. The big toe leaned outward. He put his boot next to it, and saw that the footprint was half the size of his own. In size, it looked like a child's. In all other features, it looked like an early hominid's.

He stepped back so as not to disturb it, and stepped on another footprint. He jumped sideways to avoid trampling a brief trail of them, all crisscrossed by antelope prints.

His heart caught up with his brain and started to pound. He started counting . . . one, two, three, four. . . . There were seven prints in all, some almost erased by the animals.

He sank to the ground and carefully put a palm over one of the prints. The dirt broke under his fingers and the toe marks lost their shape. The prints were recent.

They were hours old, maybe a couple of days at most. They could not be any older, not with that constant traffic of antelopes' feet.

These prints were recent.

Then he heard hooves, thudding like drums. Bleating thinly, the duikers were stampeding back. He looked up from where he was and saw a large buck—thirty to forty inches at the shoulder—that seemed to be racing right at him. A thick streak of blood ran down its forehead. Ken raised the rifle but did not need to aim. The target was coming right at him. He pulled the trigger, saw the brief flame at the end of the barrel. On the buck's chest, a tiny gash popped open. The buck skidded and fell, dragged itself over the hominid footprints, and lay still.

Birds Ken had not even noticed flapped and cawed into flight. A pair of gray turacos flitted upward, screaming back that rude go-away call. Very close, a crested hare bounced up and away into the grass.

He felt as if he were waking up. The duiker was dying at his feet, black blood spurting from its chest wound, while the blood from the wound on its forehead had almost dried up.

Ken reloaded the rifle and stood over the animal, his eyes going from the wound in the chest, which he knew he had inflicted, to the one in the forehead, which he knew he had not. It was as if he saw, with three simultaneous glances, three different images. One was the footprints he had just stepped on. Another was the wound on the buck's forehead. And out of those two, yet at the same time, he pulled a third image, of someone else, someone naked, brown-skinned, and with a low forehead, walking at the other end of the path the duikers had taken.

A creature was hiding in those rocks. The creature who left hominid footprints. It must have been surprised by the duikers, and had struck the buck that led the stampede.

Otherwise, why would they have stampeded back, those stupid antelopes, after Ken chased them off, and even fired at them?

There was someone ahead, in those rocks.

As the buck raced unawares into those rocks, that someone had hurled something at it, hard enough to injure it, though not hard enough to kill it.

Ken had finished the kill.

Ken checked the rifle, even though he had reloaded it literally seconds before.

He was shaking.

He finally shouldered the rifle, bent to pick up the buck, and laid it over his shoulder, its bloodied horns hanging in front. He headed down the path the duikers had taken.

It was overgrown with oat grass and other weeds, thrashed twice by the animals' panicked rush.

Once on the path, Ken slowed down, feeling the weight of the buck on his shoulder. He looked up. He was inside a narrow, twisting passage walled in on both sides by jumbles of rocks.

He saw no one.

Ken stepped forward slowly. Step step step.

He passed several bizarre rock formations, sculpted by the tireless fantasy of the heat and the wind. Then the path widened. A kind of clearing opened ahead, a natural corral fenced in by low rocky piles. When Ken stepped inside it, he felt that he looked dangerously different from the rest of the habitat.

There was a lot of gravel here, and more trampled weeds that would not preserve footprints, but . . .

In the middle of the clearing, on grass that had been torn and flattened, lay a black stone about half the size of Ken's hand, as obvious as if someone had purposely laid it down there. It was the only black object in the whole scene; the surrounding rocks were limestone, ranging from gray to yellow, and the weeds were a dusty green.

Ken picked up the stone. His fingers shrank from a clammy sensation. He turned the stone and raised it to his eyes. It was flat and chipped, as if it had been hit against some other stone. One end was wet with a blackish fluid. Ken dropped the stone and raised his fingers to his lips.

Blood. The buck's blood.

After an instant, he bent down and put the buck onto the flattened grass. He straightened, grabbed the rifle, held it at the ready, his finger on the trigger.

He felt as if he were having an extra awareness of himself, through someone else's eyes. The other hunter's. Ken had taken away his or her prey. Ken had finished with his bullet the hunt that the other had started.

He did not feel deluded, or hallucinatory. He was awake, reasonable, logical. He simply imagined himself being watched by the other hunter, and was afraid of the other hunter's reaction. From between the cracked ledges, from within the bushes, he was being watched.

He waited.

But after an instant, he realized he was alone. The other hunter had left, alerted to the intruder by his gunshot. As for the throwing of the stone, Ken wondered if it might have been a defensive act, rather than an attempt to hunt and kill.

Still, there was the stone, the buck's injury, and the footprints.

Someone was hiding somewhere in those rocks.

He looked at the stone again, following an irresistible need to do everything twice, even to think everything twice. He stared at the blood, which was coagulating, looking more and more like a brown smudge of dirt on the jagged end of that stone. There was no way to keep it from drying up. There was no way to carry it back protected, unless he abandoned his catch, along with the rifle.

He searched his pockets. He found a handful of Kenyan change in one, and his cigarette lighter in the other. He always carried a cigarette lighter in the bush, to kindle campfires. He moved the cigarette lighter into the pocket with the change, and dropped the stone, by itself, into his other pocket.

Then he picked up the antelope and the rifle, and went back along the twisting path between the rocks.

He hiked back into the plain, the head of the duiker dangling over his right shoulder, its blood staining his shirt. The blood helped convince him that he had not hallucinated or lived an instant of insanity.

IN THE LITTLE SPACE ENCLOSED BETWEEN ROCKS, A FEW instants passed, or perhaps a few minutes.

The duration of time had suddenly changed. The hunter who used the stones had a good sense of the passage of time, but his was global time. For him, it had not yet been broken into artificial little spans, like hours or minutes.

The hunter with stones came out of hiding and stalked the alien visitor along that twisting passageway. And when he did this, he stepped ever so carefully, his heartbeat filling his entire body, which stood under four feet tall and weighed less than a fifth of the visitor's.

"*Haaah,*" he gasped, a flat sound that came from a larynx resting high in the throat, close to his long mouth with its low-hanging palate. The meaning of that last gasp was unmistakable. It was pure fear.

Yet it was different from the hunter's usual fear.

Had he thought in words, he might have described this fear as dreamlike.

The things he had seen since the previous evening were

so enormously unusual that they compared only with those disjointed, scary, strange combinations of reality he conjured up in his mind while he was asleep and dreaming. Or maybe with the shocking way his habitat looked when flashes of lightning lit up the heavens and earth.

He put his long feet with their outward splayed big toes directly on the oval marks left by the intruder's boots, and felt the physical sensations rise from the palms of his feet and from his toes, racing along his nerves and synapsing inside his brain, in a cognitive storm. The boots had flattened the dirt and gravel into straight leveled surfaces totally unknown to the hunter's senses.

He'd never had these sensations before, and they were so intriguing that the hunter stopped, bent down, and put a long narrow palm with long fingers over one boot print, to see what such perfection felt like.

He had never encountered a perfectly flat surface, or a straight line.

He bounced up to his feet and hurried on. His field of vision, made by the overlapping angles of his close-set frontal eyes, offered an acutely, almost painfully clear view of anything as far as two hundred yards away. His eyes were almost weapons. They took reality apart, with a precision that was developed in an earlier habitat, far darker and more confusing.

Arriving at the point where the rocky passage opened into the savanna, the hunter dared himself out into the open. He stood just at the edge of the tall swaying grasses, staring above them, not still but letting his face bob about. At a distance, he didn't look much different from a lurking savanna animal.

He stared at the visitor, hardly able to believe how much the strange tall creature resembled himself. Like the hunter, the visitor used a peculiar motion to cut through the open spaces. Only his lower limbs were on the ground. But they carried his whole body.

At about two hundred yards away, the hunter's vision underwent an unexpected change. It was still clear, but it became flat, as if whatever was beyond that invisible landmark didn't need to be known as well.

But today the hunter was forced to stare far into that shallow beyond, because *out there* lay an amazing thing, associated with all those strange visitors. The day before, he had seen two of them up close—one of them strangely light-skinned, the other dark like the flesh of a tree after a bush fire.

The third visitor had stayed close to that distant thing, which was big and tuber-shaped, like an oversized edible root. The tuber shone as if a film of savanna dew clung to it, wrapping it completely, strangely unwilling to dry out under the fierce sunshine.

The three creatures had a strange way of vanishing inside that tuber, and of reappearing out of it.

Just now, tassels of grass moved in front of the hunter's round, deep-set nostrils—fragments from his immediate system of reference—while far ahead, the other hunter, buck on his shoulders, moved against a sky that darkened suddenly. A smoky, dirty tower of dust sprouted on the horizon, and moved closer.

The hunter with stones wondered if the dust storm would make the tuber disappear, or the three creatures that had come in it. He stood and wondered about this until the dust tower was almost upon the plane. The tuber did not disappear.

The hunter turned, and as the dust started raining down, he looked for shelter among the rocks.

REMEMBERING THE DUST STORM MENTIONED BY HENDRIJKS, Ken started running toward the Beech Lightning as fast as he could, encumbered by the prey and stabbed by pains in his sprained ankle.

Instants after he reached the plane and threw the dead buck on the ground, the dust bore down on the grasses and trees.

Through the storm, Ken and Ngili lay on the ground under a tarp, blindly holding on to the ropes that moored one of the Beech Lightning's front wheels, while Hendrijks did the same with the other wheel, all three adding weight to the plane. Their lungs heaved in the scant air inside the tarp, which was hot but free of dust. The wind pulled and rattled the fuselage, and made the tail and the aft wheel yaw back and forth on the ground.

The storm came in big ripples of sand, and in its moments of relative calm Ken talked feverishly to Ngili. "What do you think? What do you think?" he asked him over and over.

"I think that buck might have raced ahead of the herd in panic and bumped its forehead into some rocky outcrop. Unless . . ."

Ngili paused. Ken heard the dust, the savanna gravel being churned onto the tarp; the finest rain could never match that sound, that infinitesimal pitter-patter.

"Unless you yourself hit it with your first shot," Ngili completed his thought.

Ken tried hard to remember, to be absolutely certain that the hunger and fatigue he was experiencing as he came upon the duikers had not confused his memories.

He replied with certainty, heaving in the hot rarefied air of that little cocoon. "I fired that first shot as the duikers were running away from me. That bullet couldn't have gone past the buck's butt and around its front and hit it in the forehead. It was just a lost shot. Someone else stood back there, at the end of the path. Someone who threw this stone at the buck."

He pulled the black stone out of his pocket. "The buck turned, and the herd ran back, and I shot the buck in the chest."

Ngili flicked on a flashlight, whose battery was still alive. He took the stone, examining it from every possible angle. It was completely dry by now, and clean from being turned over between feverish fingers.

"There're no black rocks over there? No basaltic deposits of any sort?" asked Ngili.

"No, I swear. At least I didn't see any."

"You don't have to swear."

"I'm sure this is what hit the buck." Ken took back the stone. It felt as real as before, and as mysterious. "So, what's your theory?"

"I don't have one. I don't doubt your word, but I don't have any explanation." Ngili paused and reflected, with the sand of the ages raining on their shoulders and heads. "Did they look hominid, those prints?"

"Totally. Good ball of the foot, well developed, good heel. The big toe is splayed. The other toes are long, and lightly curved downward. Probably better for climbing a tree than your toes or mine."

"Are you sure you saw all that?"

"God. Am I sure? After today, I'm not sure of anything."

"Maybe there were tribes here once."

"Once? What about now?"

"Tell me again, how long were those prints?"

With the ability of a trained field researcher, Ken pictured a ruler next to the footprints. "Some six inches each."

Ngili did not comment. There was nothing to say. That size of foot could only be a child's, or a chimp's. But chimps did not really have feet; like all apes, they had four hands, two on top, two on the bottom.

There was no way that they would find the footprints the next morning, not after hours of the wind churning dust onto the plain and that rocky palisade.

But they could take a compass out there, to make a positional record.

Ken thought of the other footprints, the ones lying on the Mau spur. They too would disappear under several inches of dust.

BEFORE MIDNIGHT, THE STORM WAS OVER. THE SAvanna looked snowed under. The three men shook the dust off the hacked stems of whistling thorns, to make another fire. Ken and Ngili dusted off the duiker. They skinned it with a knife lent by Hendrijks. There was a bullet wound in its chest, but no second bullet hole anywhere on its head or front parts.

They roasted the duiker. Hendrijks shared the leftover whiskey, and kept asking one question: How early would Ken and Ngili start clearing that takeoff strip the next morning? As soon as they put the fossil and other samples in the plane was the scientists' answer.

The radio remained dead.

They slept in their sheets of tarp, burping in their sleep from the unevenly cooked antelope meat, sneezing from fine dust that kept settling upon the plain and entering the cracks over their covers.

When they got up, it was dawn. Hendrijks, already awake, sat by the lopsided plane like a gray-faced gorilla in a temple of ashes.

Ken and Ngili finished unearthing the block of breccia sealing the fossil's lower parts. They left it by the dug-up mound and made a positional record, using the camera, a compass, and a roll of measuring tape they had found in the plane's tool kit. Ken took photographs of the mound, and of the surrounding rock formations, keeping them to a minimum. He wished he had more film, but after the feast of clicking he had done while hanging from the plane, he was halfway through his last roll.

The plane's radio was still not working.

Ken and Ngili went toward the acacias, to make another positional record.

"We've been missing now over thirty-six hours," mumbled Ngili. "Um'tu must be terribly worried."

"You have such a bond with your father. You mention your mother and Yinka and Gwee half as often." Yinka was Ngili's younger sister, and Gwee was the baby brother.

"That's normal. Being the male firstborn, I'm very important to Um'tu. Doesn't your father feel the same way about you?"

Ken laughed: "Don't you remember that my father left when I was five, and we never heard from him again? That's how important I was to *my* father."

Ngili could not comprehend such a story. "Your father's out here," he said, pointing with his chin at the dust-coated outback.

Ken felt a brusque throb. It entered at the top of his spine and vibrated coldly down his back, leaving him shaking with fear. Ngili read something mind-chilling in his friend's expression, for he added quickly, "I mean to say, without such a pitiful childhood, you would not have been you, and you probably would've never come to Africa."

Ken still felt the shaking. His heart was gripped by a claw.

The bush was stirring, rodents were scurrying, breaking the seal of dust off their lairs' doors. Birds flapped about, some still shaking the dust from their plumage.

They repeated the process by the acacias, whose branches looked golden. Ken found the path between rocks where he had tracked the duikers the day before. He led Ngili, both stepping on a layer of dust as fine as flour.

Ken was surprised to realize how little he remembered of the path; he had been in such a state that he had hardly paid attention to the rock formations. At one point, the path diverged into two new ones. Ken did not remember this fork in the road, but he conquered his hesitation and turned left.

They couldn't find the little clearing, or the trampled weeds. After several hundred yards between boulders of limestone, the new path opened into a wide, irregular plateau between more boulders and scarred ledges, beyond which the rock formations tapered away into another tract of savanna. Ken was sure he had not been here—yet at the same time he again had the uneasy feeling he'd had the day before, that he was being watched by unseen eyes.

Suddenly, Ngili gave out a short, high "Ha!" that sounded as if he had tripped and injured himself. Ken spun around, and found him behind a line of bushes and under a rock overhang, both concealing him almost completely.

On the ground inside that narrow niche lay several big stone pebbles that had escaped the dust's invasion. The pebbles were black, basaltic. And there were several footprints on the ground, small prints, half the size of Ngili's foot.

Ngili was lifting one of the stones toward the hesitant sunrays. It was round, an almost perfect spheroid. But one end was chipped, flaked off into a hunting device.

Ken took the stone from Ngili's hand. He pulled out the other one, comparing them. "This creature hunts on a regular basis," he said.

The stones were different in weight and shape, yet they were enormously similar, like two animals of the same species. The flakings, present in both, made them so.

Ngili looked at Ken while blinking rapidly. Ken almost felt his friend's brain crackling from mind enlargements coming in rapid sequence. "It can't be a chimp. Chimps don't hunt with stones."

They squatted down on the ground, sharing now that feeling of being watched. Of being listened to as well.

"Got any shots left in that camera?" whispered Ngili.

Ken nodded.

They had no equipment with them to make casts. But they had a camera. Ken aimed it at the footprints, feeling as if he were peering through the eyepiece not into that dusty spring morning but into the Pliocene.

"Don't use all the shots," warned Ngili.

They were thinking with one mind; Ken planned to keep a few shots. Just in case.

Ken let the camera hang down on his chest and picked up the stone again. The surrounding boulders and ledges were all made of yellow limestone, sedimentary rock rich in calcium carbonate. The little stone projectiles were all basaltic, pieces of volcanic rock, much harder and older. They had been brought over some distance, from a bed of basaltic rock.

That made them "manuports," stones made into tools by the simple fact that a hominid had carried them outside their natural location, to use them here. That alone was extremely significant. The flaking was also significant, but it was harder to establish whether the flaking was man-made or had occurred naturally.

"Wait," said Ngili, "if we talk manuports, we're already talking hominids."

"What else is there?"

"A tribal straggler maybe. A derelict of some kind."

"Out here? Didn't you say yourself that this region was totally uninhabited?"

Ken found it amazing that they would have a scientific debate possibly in earshot of whatever had crouched low in the bushes the day before, and had almost killed that duiker.

"I did say that," acknowledged Ngili, "but there was a time when tribes used to maroon their killers or rapists, their undesirables, precisely in locations like this."

"Really? When was that?"

"Not that far back. Thirty, forty years ago."

"But look at the prints!" Ken pulled Ngili back to the area under the overhang. "Look at their shape and size."

"It cannot be," said Ngili. "Most likely, it's a lost tribal child, maybe with some anatomic features that look atavistic, but . . ." Struggling with notions that would not fit together, he muttered to himself, "But they cannot be truly atavistic . . . because protohuman atavisms would not survive that long.''

Ken pressed his hands to his temples; he could not think straight. He urged his friend to follow him back to the plane, where they had to finish packing up that fossil.

He slipped three more stones into his pocket and led Ngili out of the rocks. The day before, he had taken that creature's prey; today, he was making away with its weapons or tools. Whatever this creature was, he was presenting himself to it as a thief.

Hendrijks was walking toward the fossil site with his rifle shouldered. He looked entirely out of place in that landscape.

Hendrijks bitched that the scientists were not ready. He told them that a small plane had just passed him southbound, flying low, and he had waved his arms and fired his rifle in the air, but got no rocking of the wing tips, no signal from the pilot that he had noticed him or the parked Beech Lightning. Ken glanced at Ngili, who shrugged—neither of them had heard the rifle shots, or the buzzing of an engine. But that was not too incredible, given how absorbed they had been.

Ngili told Hendrijks to put down the blooming rifle and lend a hand with the boulder of breccia. The three of them staggered with it toward the plane, panting and cursing and stopping several times.

Finally, they laid it down in the fuselage and secured it from knocking about by pushing the ice chest and a cardboard box against it. Ken waited for Hendrijks to turn and face him, then sharply asked Hendrijks whether he had ever been in the Dogilani savanna before.

Something moved in the pilot's face. "I flew over these parts back in '52 and '53," he grumbled, looking straight back at Ken, as if Ken's stare had mesmerized him into speaking the truth.

"Did you land here?"

"No." Hendrijks gave Ngili a careful look. "I was carrying British soldiers from Uganda to Nairobi, to help put down the Kenyan independence uprising."

"Back then, did you see those footprints we photographed yesterday?"

Hendrijks shifted in place, bumping the cabin wall with his fleshy mass. Knocked off the top of the fuselage, a thin sheet of dust rained past one of the windows. "I saw some prints around there," he admitted. "I was flying low, and I saw some dark marks that looked like prints."

"Where? On the same spur?"

"How could I tell? I didn't think they were worth much attention." He sounded sincere.

"Did you see the . . ." Ken swallowed dryly. "Did you see anyone? Any people that might've left those prints?"

"I saw no people, just the prints."

"So what's spooking you about this place?"

"Nothing," snapped Hendrijks. "Go get your other bones and my rifle. I'm going to test the engine."

The two friends jumped down and hurried back to the fossil site.

By now, Ken was thinking coherently. They would have to fly back to Nairobi, hand the bones and soil samples to Randall, and return here as soon as possible with film and maybe a video camera too, and plaster casts to lift foot imprints, and digging gear and food. A regular expedition, officially sanctioned or not. He did not want to speculate any more about who or what exactly lived out here, except that the creature was a hunter, and it had used manuports before.

Hiking back to the plane with the skull, the fossil plants, and the rifle, they saw a large yellowish hump moving across the plain, coming toward them rapidly. It was a vehicle. A British-made Safari Cub, the type of van used to drive tourists around game parks, with a pop-up roof for taking pictures of wildlife. Except that this one had lost its pop-up roof and its doors. Its surface was covered in golden dust that flew back in a gracefully elongating plume each time it hurtled over a wrinkle of the ground.

Ngili stared in surprise. "Maybe they're park rangers sent by my father."

"Whoever they are," chuckled Ken, "they're right in time to help us clear that takeoff strip."

A silhouette emerged through the Safari Cub's open roof. The exhaust backfired loudly and repeatedly. Suddenly Ken realized that the exhaust wasn't producing the noise. It was a gunman firing a shotgun at the plane. Hendrijks, outlined against the plane, ducked to the ground, while the Cub's driver floored the gas.

"They're gonna ram the plane!" yelled Ken, as the Cub's course became unmistakably clear.

He grabbed the rifle. The Cub roared toward the Beech Lightning, then met that string of low rocks the Lightning had run over while landing, which was now concealed by the dust. The Cub jumped over it, coming clear on the other side with a scream of dying shock absorbers.

The engine stalled. Ken and Ngili heard the ignition as the driver tried to revive it.

The engine sputtered alive and moaned as the driver floored the gas again.

The Cub started forward like a charging rhino.

Ken was now just a few hundred yards away, with Ngili yelling savagely behind him to shoot the Cub's tires. Ken dropped in the grass like an anchor, his face against the sights. He found the turning front wheel with his scope and pulled the trigger. The man with the shotgun turned. He fired at Ken and Ngili, his bullets slashing dust-laden twigs. Then the Cub flipped onto its side, as if knocked over by a god's invisible hand.

The driver scrambled out and ran away into the savanna.

Ken and Ngili raced over. The gunman had been thrown out of the cab. Arms and legs spread, he lay lifeless. Blood was oozing from his fractured temple, reaching the ground and being sucked in by the dust, as if by blotting paper.

The man was a middle-aged, short, malnourished African. His reddish palms, crooked fingers ending in overgrown fingernails, opened to the sky in an indecipherable plea. His eyes were open, but already glassy; they looked bloodshot, almost as if from inner bleeding. He wore a nondescript sweater, fatigue pants in camouflage colors, and sandals with car-tire soles on his bare feet.

Hendrijks was hurrying over, shouting something in which Ken distinguished the word "poachers."

Ken glanced inside the Cub. The van was only a few years old, but rough driving and the harsh sun had corroded it on all sides, cracking the paint, breaking and parching the upholstery, cooking the seats. It reeked of some unidentifiable filth, but otherwise was absolutely bare, showing not even a cheap good-luck amulet hanging from the rearview mirror. Its glove compartment had burst open, exposing nothing but a featureless boxlike interior.

It had no license plates. Its exposed underside, a darkly dirty jumble of transmission and fuel lines, smelled of hot oil and smoky brakes.

Ken took a deep breath. There was a jangle of thoughts in his head, too many and too fast.

He fought his repulsion, squatted, and ran his hands over the gunman's body, turning it over, feeling for a wallet or any personal belongings. The body was warm, smelly from sweat and from no washing, and so thin that it felt light as a dummy—the strange assailant was skin and bone. As Ken searched the body, all his thoughts became one: What's going on? What's going on?

Meanwhile, the fleeing driver looked like a dot on the yellow plain, moving away, away.

"Nothing, he doesn't carry no papers, nothing?" asked Hendrijks. Ken rose, shaking his head. He wiped his hands on his pants. Hendrijks gave the cadaver a kick.

"Stop it." Ken growled.

"I stopped," said the Dutchman. "We go now. Don't look more, it helps nothing. We take off now."

He picked up his rifle and headed off, back to the plane.

Left by the body, Ken and Ngili looked at each other, out of words, out of explanations.

"D'you think they were poachers?" asked Ken finally.

Ngili shook his head. "Poachers don't charge at an airplane if they see it parked in the savanna. They wait for the scene to clear, so they can go on about their business. Does this guy smell of poaching?" he asked rhetorically. He bent down, turned the body on one side, and searched it again, touching it lightly but thoroughly. "He smells of crime, that's for sure. You missed this."

From under the gunman's sweater, Ngili pulled a small Walther PPK pistol. He opened the magazine and showed Ken six live bullets, then clicked it shut again, and put the weapon in his friend's hand. "Take it, it could be useful evidence. It's good protection anyway, and you're more vulnerable than I am."

"How's that?" Ken asked hoarsely, his voice coming out over what felt like a roll of sandpaper in his throat.

"Because suppose this isn't over." Ngili paused to look at the body lying at his feet. "You have no family protection, you're a foreigner, and you're so bloody conspicuous, 'cause you're white. So whatever this means, you're more at risk than I am."

Ken took the Walther and slipped it into his pocket. It clanked against one of those prehistoric stones, one weapon meeting another. Then Ken picked up the shotgun, held it by the barrel, and whacked it hard against a boulder. The stock came off, the barrel twisted, trigger and trigger guard clanked loose upon the stone.

"Let's gather the fossil plants faster," said Ngili. "The Cub's driver might make it to some sort of base camp. If he sends more gunmen this way, we'll be sitting ducks."

"Should we call the police when we get to Nairobi?" asked Ken.

Ngili reflected, then spoke. "I wouldn't do it. It's the best way to make our return here more complicated. I'd rather tell everything to my father."

"What can your father do?"

"Send some trusted scouts here, to search the area. If they find it safe, we can return and deal with that other riddle."

Ken thought of that other riddle. The mysterious creature. They would be leaving it so close to those gunmen's unexplained menace.

He looked away, toward that rocky palisade.

Ngili followed his friend's gaze. "Come on," he said softly. "That thing out there knows the savanna better than anyone, and can hide better than anyone. Come on now, help me."

He started cleaning the fossil whistling thorns. As he helped Ngili, Ken kept repeating. "What the hell is going on?"

Ngili shrugged, obviously worried.

Despite what had just happened, both of them carried the petrified plants to the plane with the utmost care.

In the plane, Ken combed his fingers through his hair, straightened his clothes, and realized that he was missing his cigarette lighter. He thought about jumping back out to try to find it, but he could have dropped it in a dozen places, including while running and firing back at the Safari Cub. He was uncomfortable about leaving a flammable object behind him, but in a month the bush would be cracking from dryness, and the sun would cause more spontaneous fires than any man-made object could.

Hendrijks told them to put the boulder of breccia on the starboard side, and to sit next to it. That added weight would cause the right wing to descend, while the drooping left wing would rise a couple of feet. They did as they were told, and indeed the wing lifted just enough to stop scraping the ground. That was it, said Hendrijks. He was going to chance it that way.

He rolled the Beech Lightning back toward the hulk of the Safari Cub, then turned, revved hard toward those low rocks, and cleverly bumped into them, kicking the plane up into flight.

The wings instantly balanced, and the Beech Lightning soared off, making everything below seem unreal. Ken, arms spread protectively over the fossil, twisted his neck and glued his face to the window, scanning the bush for a poachers' camp. He saw only the vast yellow expanse, specked with animals but otherwise majestically empty.

Hendrijks took a course way south, to make absolutely

sure that none of those violent winds would hit them again. In a while, he punched the radio button and swore, "*Got Verdomma*, God damn, what do you know?" The plane's radio was crackling back to life. He made contact with Embakasi airport and announced their arrival.

After that, Ngili took the radio to call his father.

Ken listened as Ngili talked on the radio, heard him and did not hear him. He heard himself instead, the memory of himself, his boots crushing the savanna scree, his footfalls pounding that dust, following the steps of the other hunter. Could it be? Had he always expected such an encounter? Was he now fated to live it?

"Dubois syndrome!" he commented to himself, and even heard Randall Phillips chuckling.

No, it couldn't be. Though high-strung and exhausted, he was a sane young man, a researcher, patient and skeptical most of the time, a scientist. He had to come back here, that was all. He would come back, as a scientist.

He relaxed in his seat and closed his eyes. But as soon as he did so, that tireless thought returned, circling like a savanna vulture: What's going on? What's going on?

THE HUNTER WITH STONES HAD WATCHED THE SAFARI CUB from a few hundred feet away, seeing it in that distant perspective where, for him, the relative size and position of things became flat and crowded. Because of this perspective, the gunfight, the overturning of the van, the hurried frenzy of the aliens had seemed to him to have a playful feel of unreality. But still he had been so captivated by it that his long hands balled up into fists. One of his fists closed around a hunting stone, squeezing it more tightly and more precisely than any ape could have.

The van had stopped moving moments after it had appeared, as if some large savanna beast, a charging water buffalo or rhino, had been struck by a fatal snakebite. But the hunter had never seen a snake make such a beast go motionless so instantly.

That charging thing remained still, and the visitors hurried back to their tuber, whose shine was dulled from the dust storm. That told the hunter that what he saw was not a dream because he knew that the dust storm had happened. The tuber made noise as it began to move. It was alive. It turned around, and the hunter saw its wings again, stretched out, buglike. It really did behave like a big bug, stirring and buzzing again, as if it were reanimating after a cold night or a rainfall.

It took off on its wings, soaring high, higher than the hunter had ever seen another bug do, even if carried upward by a strong gust of wind. He expected a bird, a vulture or a marabou stork, to sweep down and peck the shiny tuber/bug out of the sky. But the birds did not claim this easy prey, not one of them, even though the tuber/bug was big and noisy and stayed up in the sky quite a while.

Finally, it left the savanna, unharmed. It vanished beyond the horizon. The sky left behind was again silent and empty.

It was all over, as if he had just awakened to his familiar world. Maybe this was only a dream.

But no, it was not. Walking back to his sleeping lair in the rocks, the hunter stepped on the cigarette lighter, which lay just inches from the path both hunter and intruder had walked on back and forth. The lighter was almost hidden under a big palmated leaf loaded with dust. A thin sprinkle of dust had filtered onto the lighter, yet when the hunter's long-toed foot padded down on it, his naked skin ignored the dust and reexperienced another world.

The hunter bent down to pick up the lighter. As he lifted it, its coat of settled dust broke, and his elongated fingers analyzed it. *Totally smooth, untextured and ungrainy,* but also *finite* in a *straight square-cut way* (everything else in the savanna ended in rough, irregular edges, or in vague, amorphous dilutions). He forced his brain to make room for these new notions. Terribly curious, the hunter turned the cigarette lighter in his elongated fingers, realizing without words that the creature who had stolen his hunting stones had left this strange little stone in its place.

His mind recalled the face of the alien visitor, which the hunter had watched the day before from just a few yards away. That face was different from his own. And yet, in certain features, especially in the setting of its eyes and the quality of its stare, it was disturbingly alike. Also disturbingly alike was the way the alien walked.

With that object in his hand, the little hunter faced the tall visitor in his mind, so close that there seemed to be a silent exchange between the two. It was a strange yearning that took shape, an expectation that there could be other encounters. This expectation settled itself into the brain of the brown-skinned hominid boy.

Part Two

LIVE PLIOCENE

F ROM THE SKY, NAIROBI'S VERTICAL DOWNTOWN AND
its low, sprawling suburbs looked like any American
city. Jomo Kenyatta Airport, which many called by its old
name, Embakasi, looked like a strange squid made out of
concrete, with its terminals reaching out like tentacles from
its spherical body.

Around the airport, the desertlike scrub was slashed by
roads. When Ken first came to Africa, those roads were still
crossed by antelopes, and the ten-mile distance to the capital
was nothing more than a pleasant stretch of fields dotted with
acacia trees. But now the herds had disappeared and the
roads were choking with vehicles. The fields were vanishing
under shantytowns. Most of the acacias had been cut down
by squatters and used for cooking fires.

Hendrijks brought the plane down over squatter homes
made up of cardboard huts, tents sewn up from plastic bags,
and tribal lean-tos of branches covered with rags. Many of
these homes didn't have roofs because the rainy season was
over, and it was easier to open the roofs for light and ven-
tilation than to cut windows through the fragile walls. Inside,
mothers suckled their babies or cooked, while older children
looked up and waved at the passing plane.

As they approached the landing strip, Hendrijks told Ken
and Ngili to move to the plane's starboard side, then he

touched down with a squeak. The right wing tip scratched the ground and sent up a cloud of sparks, but righted itself to just a few fingers above the tarmac. Hendrijks braked, all the seams of his plane creaking and moaning, then crept toward the light-aircraft terminal.

On the tarmac, alone in the path of the airplane, stood an African man, tall and ample, in a bright red *kikoi,* the one-piece Masai tribal robe. He anxiously watched the lopsided plane. As it taxied in, he relaxed and waved with a vast pink palm.

"Um'tu!" smiled Ngili, jumping up.

Hendrijks yelled at him to sit down, rolled forward a few more yards, and parked by a chain-link fence separating the terminal from the scrub. Beyond the fence, the scrub was cut by a long strip of tar—a jet runway that was still unfinished.

Hendrijks wiped his forehead and growled toward Ngili. "I see that your father's here. I want him to write me two checks. One for the week, one for the damage to my plane."

"He'll pay you the thousand now," answered Ngili, "but how can you estimate the damage without a mechanical inspection?"

"Then I'll drop an invoice at his office. I want to be reimbursed for the repairs to the last shilling!" Ken saw the anger in Hendrijks's alcohol-pickled face, and felt like grinning. Ngili's father knew about planes; he would pay for the cost of the repairs, but not more.

The hatch opened and Ngili and Ken jumped out. The dry Nairobi air was spiced with smoke. There was the sound of loud cracks, like those of African cattle whips, and of high angry voices, which Ken ignored at first. There was often some commotion going on in an African airport.

Jakub Ngiamena, MP and superintendent of game parks, ran forward to hug his firstborn. In his flowing kikoi, he looked like one of the tribal kings who had given shelter to a trek-weary David Livingstone. He wore the garb to honor his heritage, but also because he weighed four hundred pounds. Inside his embrace, Ngili looked like a thin, wiry stem.

By the terminal's glass door, which for an instant seemed strange to his savanna-adjusted eyes, Ken saw Ngili's younger sister, Yinka, who worked as a reporter with the *Nairobi Daily Herald*. She was also tall and thin and wore a kikoi—hers was deep blue. A glint of gold highlighted her forehead.

Ken raised his hand and waved, but Yinka did not wave back; she just focused her eyes on Ken. Like all the Ngiamenas, she had fantastic jet-black eyes.

Jakub Ngiamena let go of his son and hugged Ken. "How are you, my son's best friend?" he inquired poetically. "Hurry up, let's go!" he urged in the same breath, glancing worriedly somewhere beyond the plane.

Ken followed Ngiamena's glance and looked through the chain-link fence at the unfinished runway. Next to it was a squatters' camp. For a few seconds, he could clearly see the strip of black tar shimmering in the heat and the small and puckered huts and tents. Then, things happened fast. A herd of bulldozers hurtled at the squatters' camp, ramming their blades at the shacks and tents, making them fall the instant they were touched. Men, women, and children fled out of the camp and across the unfinished runway toward the airport. In seconds, the wire mesh of the fence turned solid with brown hands and feet climbing it.

Behind them, the bulldozers attacked the next row of shacks and tents, chasing another wave of squatters toward the airport. Running and bending and running before the bulldozers, they looked like worshippers caught in an earthquake. The women stooped to pick up children; the men grabbed mattresses and cooking utensils and lunged to catch chickens and untie goats. A bulldozer reached several goats still tied to a post and crushed them while they were still kicking and bleating.

The bullwhip cracks were gunshots. A police helicopter hovered above, and a voice thundered out of it, in English and then in Swahili, warning the squatters to stay away from the airport. Police and army vans raced across the tarmac to link up with the bulldozers. The combined noise became deafeningly loud.

"What's happening?" Ngili yelled a question at his father.

"Rwandan refugees!" the big man yelled back. "They're infiltrating our squatter camps, so the army's evicting them. Hurry up. You bring anything back with you?"

"Some bones that are very valuable! They're still on the plane!"

"Then get them out quick, or forget them!"

They were shouting as if in a gale. Ken raced to the plane and dived inside with Ngili right behind him. Ngiamena glanced at the chain-link fence, as it rippled under the fugitives' weight. A few more seconds and it would break.

Ken and Ngili stumbled out of the plane carrying the boulder of breccia. Yinka walked over, and despite the commotion she was moving quite slowly. The glow on her forehead came from a golden tribal chain hanging just above her eyebrows.

"There are more bones on the plane. Yinka, can you help us?" panted Ngili.

She looked at him like a princess asked to do menial work. Her face was very Masai—narrow, with a small straight nose, sculpted nostrils, and a delicate dip in her upper lip. She raised a long hand with naturally pink fingernails and pushed the gold chain up from her eyebrows.

"Move, Yinka!" ordered Ngiamena, his voice injecting some urgency into her elegant movements.

Finally the fence broke under the weight of several hundred men, women and children. Ken saw a woman perched on the collapsing wire, trying to hand an infant to a man who had jumped onto the tarmac. The man tripped and disappeared, and she dropped the child into a mass of bodies falling with screams onto the tarmac.

Ngili pulled at the boulder of breccia, dragging Ken with it toward the terminal. Yinka and Jakub Ngiamena scooped the last bundles of bones out of the plane while Hendrijks was yelling about his money. The noise was so loud that Jakub lip-read his words rather than heard them. The refugees who had collapsed with the fence charged forth again, coming so close that Hendrijks forgot the money and rushed to protect his plane. Ngiamena hurried after Ngili, Yinka, and Ken. Ahead, the terminal's glass doors whooshed open with a sci-fi sound.

Hendrijks clambered to his plane, grabbed his rifle, and stood frozen with it at the ready, until the army and the police pushed the refugees back to the area where the bulldozers were grinding and flattening their last homes. Only then could Hendrijks breathe in relief. He'd seen his share of African stampedes, both animal and human, and this one had been close.

He'd heard Ngiamena say those people were Rwandans, but to Hendrijks they looked just like homeless Kenyans, with their dirty kikois and torn T-shirts and jeans, their feet bare or in sandals with soles made of tires. They were all just blacks, whom the British had idiotically freed back in the sixties. *This land hasn't had a decent rule since. What the hell was in the minds of the British back then? And after the bloodiest uprisings, when a white man couldn't walk to an outhouse to crap without risking a guerrilla's bullet.*

Inside the terminal, Ngiamena flagged down two porters, both barefoot but wearing union caps, who stared at the lump of earth Ken and Ngili were carrying, then rushed to help them. Ken and Ngili showed them how to carry it safely.

"Thanks, Yinka," Ken said, rubbing his scratched hands. She was holding several bones that had lost their wrap completely—petrified pieces of prehistory rubbing against her smart kikoi. "Ngili and I found an incredible fossil."

She gave him a cool smile. "I'm happy for you, settler."

Being called "settler" in Kenya was like being called "white boy" in America. Ken ignored her taunt; it wasn't her first. Yinka was only lightly adorned today. Ken had seen her balance a whole jewelry shop on her forehead, tripping as she walked because she could barely see from under their jingling mass.

They hurried across the terminal and stepped outside the main entrance. Here, things seemed peaceful. A large sign boasted a million tourists per year—everyone knew that the real figure was drastically lower. Gridlocked cars were assailed by street kids with dripping washrags. Grown men hawked green bananas and bags of coffee. Women waved flyers advertising safari tours, hotels, curio shops.

Ngiamena led the way to a parked car that appeared to be snowed under because four street kids were foaming it zealously. Ngiamena yelled at them to rinse it, and they did, splashing soapy water from tin buckets. The car was a Mercedes 600, a little chipped, its doors scratched, one hubcap missing, but still a Mercedes 600 in Africa.

Ken had left his Land Rover parked at the Ngiamenas' mansion, in the exclusive suburb of Karen. He asked Ngili's father if they could stop at a photo studio on the way; he was anxious to have the photos of the footprints developed. Ngiamena agreed, threw a volley of coins at the kids, then paid the porters. With great precaution, Ngili and Ken loaded the bones into the luxury car.

"Um'tu, Yinka, we found the most exciting fossil, in a unique habitat," Ngili kept repeating, but they didn't seem to share his enthusiasm. "What's the matter with you?"

"It's been very stressful here," said Jakub. "The army's flying the Rwandans back home. But to return them, we have to find them first, so the police are raiding the shantytowns. It's too bad, but the Rwandans are really stretching our social services. . . ." Next to him, Yinka raised her crescent-shaped eyebrows at the mention of social services.

Ngili gaped at his father. "What Rwandans, Um'tu? Those poor bastards didn't look like Rwandans."

"Well, the police say they are. This is called Operation Clean Sweep. Sit in front with me, Yinka. Boys, can you hold that big lump of dirt on your knees?"

"It's too heavy, Um'tu. I'll put my shirt under it."

Ngili peeled off his shirt and stretched it over the backseat, and the two friends sat propping up the breccia between them, while Yinka climbed in front, next to her father.

Just as Ngiamena was starting his car there was the deep growly noise of airplane engines hovering extremely low. It filled the car, becoming insufferable. In the street, the army of hawkers leaned their heads back and watched a transport plane with the insignia of the Kenyan military on its wings as it seemed ready to drop onto the traffic.

Then the plane headed toward the city. Taking advantage of the other drivers' distraction, Ngiamena boosted his car up a ramp, onto a six-lane freeway. It had been completed less than a year before, and had already lost half the width of its paved surface. Ken looked out the window and saw the plane drag itself toward Ngong Hills, where the city's most exclusive suburbs nested between golf courses and horseriding tracks.

"Why is it flying so low?" he asked nervously. It looked as if the plane was doomed to crash into the hills' bluish crest.

"Because it's crammed with two hundred refugees in a body designed for a hundred," explained Yinka from the front seat. "And also to give a message. Think about it. What's out there?" she asked, pointing at Ngong Hills.

"Your house?" tried Ken.

"Cold, settler."

"The foreign embassies?" he tried again.

"Getting hot."

"The U.S. ambassador's residence?" Ken breathed as the plane barely cleared the hills.

"Very hot. Burning. Those planes will crawl over the U.S. ambassador's residence again and again, till he and all the other diplomats get the message: We've got Rwandans, help us." Yinka paused, looked at her father. "Now, there are those who say that Operation Clean Sweep is not about Rwandans at all, but about our own homeless being cleaned out of the capital."

"Christ, what a way to solve a social problem," muttered Ken.

"Isn't it a clever one, settler? Clean Nairobi, and start a new drive for foreign aid." Yinka spoke an even more agile, flawless English than Ngili. She put a long forearm on the back of her seat and looked straight at Ken. "I bet one of our generals thought up this ploy; it's too clever for a civilian's mind."

"Where'd you come up with this, Yinka?" asked Ngiamena. "There's no perverse scheme to scare the foreign diplomats." He grinned tensely at the backseat. "This is because we're African, Ken. We're prone to the most excessive flights of imagination."

"What do you think, Ken? Are our Rwandan refugees imaginary or real?" asked Yinka. Her irises looked deeply black, but when a sunray hit them they took on an underhue of lustrous brown that was far warmer and softer.

Ken became alert. Yinka was trying to lure him into a political debate, and he was determined not to let her, even though he kept remembering those men and women clutching on to their children and belongings. Clutching them as frantically as he and Ngili had clutched their fossil. Ken silenced an inner voice that kept asking him what he could have done about the scene at the airport. The humbling truth was that he could have done nothing. He was one powerless foreigner facing a land in pain. President Donald Angus Noi was turning Kenya into a naked dictatorship, with some vestige of freedom vanishing every day. This was not the country Ken had once known.

"By the way," said Yinka, turning toward Ken and her brother, "my paper just folded. I'm unemployed."

"What?" Ngili sat up sharply. His handsome torso was glossy from sweat dried off by the car's air conditioning.

"Are you joking, Yinka?" asked Ken.

"Not at all. There's no more *Nairobi Daily Herald*."

Ken heard the bitterness in her voice. Yinka had studied journalism in England and returned home full of idealism about how a free press could tackle her country's social wrongs. Of course, the fact that she had a plum job at the capital's best paper helped her idealism. And thanks to her father's influence, she could afford to write acidic pieces about the country's woes without being fined as a rumormonger.

But now the *Nairobi Daily Herald* had folded, following

a string of closures of the country's most imaginative and liberal newspapers and magazines.

Ken glanced at Jakub Ngiamena. He was driving aggressively, and the cars zooming by in the opposite direction seemed to be aiming for the Mercedes's side mirrors with theirs, but that was routine on Nairobi's roads. Jakub didn't usually drive like this, but today he dared the oncoming traffic, making it shy away to the outer lanes, while he barely turned the wheel of his German juggernaut.

Something was going on.

Ken's immediate thoughts were selfish. Would the political situation affect the activities of foreign scientists, especially his own? And was the Ngiamenas' influence perhaps on the wane? The older man was answering his children in a particular way today—he was giving them the government line.

Ken had benefited greatly from being virtually adopted by the Ngiamenas. When he needed an extension of his visa, for instance, a hassle for any other foreign scientist, all he'd had to do was hand his passport to Ngili, who gave it to his father. The next day, without waiting or bribes, the new visa was stamped in his passport. And there were other benefits, less practical but emotionally more satisfying. Like the surprise birthday party the Ngiamenas had given him when he turned twenty-seven. Or their interest in his views about Africa, which he still had to express with care because Africans were as touchy about outsiders' opinions as they were curious about them. The Ngiamenas were always warm and welcoming to Ken when he came back from a dig—they would prepare a lavish dinner and sit Ken at the table opposite Jakub, the tribal king. Of course, there were some problems in this relationship, such as their exaggerated awareness that he was American, and their attempts to win him over during a political quarrel. Still, Ken could not imagine his Africa without the Ngiamenas, which made it all the more difficult to watch them fight.

Jakub spoke harshly. "Enough of your nonsense, Yinka. The government did not close your paper."

She curled her lips disdainfully, their inside brightly pink like a ripe fruit. "I know, it was a coincidence. We published a special report about Nairobi. The street crime, the decay of what we once called the city of flowers, the appearance of jackals in our slums—an interesting ecological side effect of a dictatorship. The next day, it just happened that the president called his economic advisers and made the price of printing paper prohibitively high."

"Yin-*kah*!" A vein throbbed in the side of Jakub's neck.

"Yes, Um'tu?" she asked, mocking a good daughter's tone.

"We are not a dictatorship. Heavy-handed yes, confused yes, mistaken all too often. But we are free. We spilled blood for our freedom, and what we do with it now is our business!"

Jakub's voice had filled the car. Yinka's eyes closed for a second, then reopened at half-mast, as if filtering out a silent response to her father's explosion. Jakub continued, just a few decibels lower. "We gave you children freedom, money, opportunities. Nice expensive toys, that we as children did not have to play with. But now we have serious problems, so it's time that you put aside your toys."

Ngili leaned forward. "Um'tu, stop it!" he pleaded.

Yinka's eyes had ignited—it was said that Masais blushed with the whites of their eyes. Ken waited for an outburst of injured pride, but she answered surprisingly softly. "It's all right, Ngili. I'll take my place in African society, like a woman should. Thanks, Um'tu. You can take back my toy."

"But Yinka, I'm not the one who . . ." Exasperated, Jakub shook his head. Suddenly, his arms froze on the steering wheel.

A *matatu*, Nairobi's crossbreed of taxi and pickup truck, was rushing head-on toward the Mercedes. As the distance between the vehicles shrank, a load of African men on its platform stood up and started to cheer. Ngili rose in the backseat, and Yinka gaped as the matatu got closer and closer. Ken saw Ngiamena's arms turn the wheel, to steer the Mercedes to the freeway's shoulder. But the other driver lost his nerve and flew to the side, his passengers falling all over each other, but still cheering.

Steering back to the middle lane, Jakub breathed heavily. "Most of the men in that truck have wives and children. . . . Did you see how they played with their lives?" Sweat rolled down his temple, following the minute arabesques of his graying curly hairs. He mopped it with a thick thumb. "Africa, huh?" he commented to Ken. "I think I'll rest my case. So . . . what did you dig up that's so exciting, Ngili?" He still did not sound enthusiastic, but maybe he was tired.

"A robust *Australopithecus*. If its feet are intact in here"—Ngili tapped at the breccia—"we'll get some new clues about bipedalism that will put me and Ken on the map. You said you'd stop at that photo shop, Um'tu."

"I didn't forget, son. Here we go." Jakub turned the wheel and took a cracked ramp into the smoky, bustling downtown.

Minutes later, the Mercedes inched along in tight downtown traffic, surrounded by chugging matatus and dented cars and trucks of every conceivable vintage. The traffic was so slow that Ken offered to get off and run to the photo shop; he'd catch up with the Mercedes halfway down the next block. Ngili wanted to come too, but his father stopped him. They had some family matters to discuss.

Ken assumed that Jakub meant preparations for the impending marriage of Gwee, Ngili's younger brother. Two days before flying to Dogilani, Ken and Ngili had used Ken's Land Rover to deliver a ten-gallon canister of raw honey to the bride's house. Honey signaled Gwee's intent to marry the girl. Known in Masai custom as *esiret e nkoshoke,* "the gift of the stomach," it was to be eaten by the bride's clanswomen if the young man's declaration was accepted. Acceptance was conveyed by not pushing the canister back out of the bride's front door. Ken and Ngili had waited by the front door for one hour, but nothing was ejected. They returned to the Ngiamena mansion and told Gwee he could drive back there in person with a much larger load of honey, to be brewed into *tembo,* native beer, for the bride's menfolk.

For Gwee's wedding, the Ngiamenas had decided to go

heavily tribal. The girls in the family had been busy rehearsing Masai dances, and a rented hall at the Naivasha Hotel was being decorated with shields and spears. The two families exchanged arguments about how to appear most authentic, because both of them now belonged to the city elite, and had not hunted or walked cattle in the savanna since before independence.

Ken dashed across the chugging traffic toward a two-story mall. He climbed to the second floor, rushed under a fibrillating neon sign, and entered Theo's Safari Aids & One Hour Photo Shop.

"I CAN'T HAVE YOUR PICTURES DEVELOPED BEFORE seven," explained Theo, a heavyset, talkative man with a Greek face. "I'm finishing a big job for some East Indians who are leaving the country. They took a million farewell shots of their house and swimming pool." He labeled Ken's film rolls and dropped them in a bin marked TO DO.

"All right." Ken checked his watch. It was almost five in the evening. "As long as I get them tonight . . ."

Gaunt, tanned, dirty, Ken had such a glimmer in his eyes that Theo felt thrilled too, even before dipping Ken's film into the developing tank. Theo had been processing Ken's photos for years; he sold safari gear to scientists, and felt that he belonged to the milieu.

"Is this it? The big one?" he asked, meaning the kind of discovery that would make Ken a star in the world of paleontology.

"Maybe." The thought of how valuable the find might be coursed through Ken's veins like a shot of eighty proof alcohol. "Theo, I have a favor to ask. You're going to be the first to see what's in those shots. Don't tell anybody about it, okay?"

"Don't worry. I'm a professional. Besides"—Theo's face darkened beyond its Greek pigmentation—"I don't like what's happening around here, so me and my brother are leaving soon too."

"You're kidding. Where are you going?"

"South, I guess, maybe try for Jo'burg. Mr. Mandela seems to have things under control. Or maybe Texas—we have a cousin in Texas."

"That's south all right. They'll love your other stuff, over there."

The other stuff filled the rest of the store. Pistols and hunting rifles, their metal combining in a cool wall-to-wall shine. Watching and listening devices: binoculars, infrared night-viewers, extra-minuscule mikes. The mikes were battery-powered and guaranteed to pick up the savanna's most intimate sounds. You wanted the night cough of a leopard? The sloshing and crunching of a hyena's jaws? You could buy them right here, with those state-of-the-art gadgets.

"Need any of those babies?" asked Theo. "I'm slashing their prices every day."

Ken glanced at his watch again; the Mercedes should still be inching down the same block. He stepped toward the safari aids. He yearned to make enough money to buy most of them. Theo tried to push an Iridium cellular phone with a miniature antenna. It weighed only twelve ounces, complete with its lithium ion battery. It could call from any location on earth to any other location that had telephones by bouncing its impulses off seventy-seven satellites in low orbits. That was why it was called Iridium, the seventy-seventh element in the chemical table.

"No, thanks. I don't need anything that sophisticated."

"It's only a grand, Ken." Theo's face suffered, mentioning the price. "You can call your mother in Oakland direct from the jungle. When's the last time you talked to your mother?"

"I visited her last Christmas."

"Is she doing all right?"

"Sure. She's fine."

In Ken's memory, a tall skinny woman in organic-fiber clothes hugged him stiffly as he deplaned in Oakland. Her upper lip was streaked by tiny broken capillaries from years of chain-smoking. The smell of cigarettes was the smell of

Ken's childhood. His mother still smoked, but ate macrobiotic, and was writing a New Age cookbook. After several years of being in touch only by postcards, Ken had flown home to see her, and she had thrown a party to show him off, in the same clapboard house where he had grown up. The music was New Age mixed with the Grateful Dead. Some of his mother's friends had known Ken's father, the pothead postman.

He had spent five days in the clapboard house in Oakland, waiting for his mother to ask him something, anything, about how he lived, about what he had become. Instead, she asked him to send her African organic fibers and food recipes.

"Ken, I'm going to miss you, you devil," Theo said spontaneously. They faced each other awkwardly, two men who hadn't noticed how close they had become.

Behind them, a newspaper boy threw the afternoon edition of the *East African Standard* into the store. Theo picked it up, glanced at the front page, frowned. The headline read: RICHARD LEAKEY JOINS KENYAN OPPOSITION IN LONDON. FAMOUS SCIENTIST'S BETRAYAL ANGERS AFRICANS.

Below was a shot of the Leakey estate outside Nairobi and an enraged crowd tearing down its gate.

"This was bound to happen," said Theo, with a true confrere's concern. "Now, what kind of government backlash are we to expect against other scientists? Not you, Ken, you're running with the right crowd."

"Don't be so sure," mumbled Ken, remembering Jakub's unusual behavior in the car. His eyes spotted a dense little announcement that he had missed the first time. It was boxed to the left of the Leakey story, under the title FROM THE OFFICE OF THE PRESIDENT OF THE REPUBLIC.

Ken read the lines so fast that the words made no sense. Then he read them again. "It is with deep regret," the office of the president stated, that "due to abuses of the country's hospitality by certain foreign researchers, all research in progress by foreign-born scientists is to be immediately halted. The appropriateness of each project's continuation will be reviewed by a government commission, whose scope and powers are to be decided by the parliament.''

Ken pulled at the collar of his work shirt, causing the top button's thread to break. The button rolled on the floor, but neither man paid it any attention.

"Shit," said Theo sympathetically. "Now maybe we'll meet on a plane out of here.''

A massive headache rammed at Ken's temples. He fought it with a desperate hope that the announcement did not mean what it said. It was not clear what the government meant by "immediately." In Africa, that was a variable term. "I gotta go," he exhaled, letting the paper drop.

"You okay?"

"As okay as one can expect. I'll see you at seven.''

KEN RUSHED OUT OF THE SHOP IN A STATE OF CONTROLLED panic and was surprised by how normal the street looked. He walked through the colorful crowds, sweating coldly and quietly. He might never get his chance to return to Dogilani.

Richard Leakey had once been Kenya's conservation boss, appointed by the government in an effort to regain its credibility and resecure foreign loans. But the outspoken Leakey had never clicked with the regime, and was now denouncing it openly. Ken feared that Leakey's entrance into politics would push the regime to become even more authoritarian and paranoid. He heard another of the army planes cruise above the city and wondered what might come after this Operation Clean Sweep. A full state of emergency? Curfews? The expulsion of foreigners, including scientists? Things like that were happening in many parts of Africa—why couldn't they happen here?

He felt somewhat encouraged by the street's movement and variety. Ignorant of the crisis, the African soul was determined to live, and live joyfully. Kids danced and played rap music on tin cans. On balconies, girls in bikinis chatted and rubbed Coppertone on their black skins. Businessmen in three-piece suits stopped to buy spells for a few shillings from roving kamba doctors. Women had their toenails done on the sidewalk. Craftsmen carved wood and hammered brass. *Pipits,* street urchins called so after a fast-running bush bird, dashed about offering their services. Even the smells had an exciting pungency, of smoke from burning garbage, sweet rottenness from withering fruit, and sweat from hot bodies.

There had to be a way out of this fix. The new decree might never be enforced. Many scientists were sponsored by foreign corporations that could apply significant political pressure.

One block down, Ken saw Yinka leaning out of the Mercedes window to buy a copy of the *East African Standard.*

He hurried across the traffic, opened the door, jumped in. "Did you see what's on the front page?" he asked. Ngili was staring down at the slab of breccia. "It's terrible, I'm practically banned from returning to Dogilani."

Ngili did not look up. Yinka had spread the paper on her knees but was not reading it. Jakub Ngiamena towered silently behind the wheel.

"What's happening?" Ken asked.

Yinka furiously pushed her gold chain up from her eyebrows, then told him that her father had just ordered Ngili to cancel all plans for further expeditions. In view of the political situation, Ngili was to report to the Foreign Office the following Monday, for a crash training before joining the country's diplomatic service.

ABOVE THE SAVANNA, THE SUN HAD STARTED ITS downward cruise toward the hazy horizon. The hominid boy sat on a tall *kopje,* a pile of savanna rocks that had been dragged to that spot millions of years before by the drifting movement of a glacier or by the impetuous push of lava streaming down from an erupting volcano.

To a geologist's eye, the yellowish brown and the deep irregular cracks of those rocks would suggest a glacier's drift rather than a volcano's eruption. Had they been spat out of the earth's fiery throat, they would have been dark gray or black, and harder to scar by the cycles of daytime heat and nighttime chill. The pile's top boulder sat on the pointed fulcrums of two smaller stones, looking as if it might roll off them at any time. That too indicated the giant power of the glacier, which had lifted those rocks like pebbles, dragging them blindly, then randomly heaping them on top of one another. When the glacier started to melt as the temperature warmed, the rocks remained where the ice had clustered them, marvels of balance that would one day look dangerously unstable to human eyes.

But right now, the hominid boy sat on his throne of rock, utterly unconcerned with how precarious it looked. And the rock was as unaffected by the boy's presence as it had been by birds nesting, baboons chasing each other, and downpours of rain that had eroded its cracks.

The boy sat quietly, seemingly without thought, but he was dealing with a complex issue. He had watched the visitors and their tuber/bug for almost three days until they had disappeared, like fantastic creatures in a dream. The boy did not think ''dream'' as a word, for he had no words for anything, although he did use sounds. When his mind evoked something, it was really an *awareness* of something familiar, something known well enough to be part of his mental storage.

(Dream) was something that (happened) during his (sleep).

But this last dream had happened very differently. He did not remember falling asleep, the familiar sensations of waking up, and stretching, and smelling the morning air. He didn't know when he had entered this peculiar dream, nor when he had exited it.

Unlike any of his other dreams, this one had left behind changes to his world, pieces of another world. Like the shiny little stone left on the ground for him by that light-skinned visitor.

He held his breath, aiming his full-lipped, pouting mouth at the place he had watched for three days, his narrowly set eyes scanning it with anxious beams. He was seized by a tremor of decision. His long, wispy hairs, straight and dirty, almost stood up on his head. His ears, well set off from his head, vibrated as they collected the surrounding sounds. His nose, small and practically without a bridge, searched the air, his nostrils rounded into two palpitating little holes.

He decided to investigate the wide grooves the tuber/bug had left as it rolled away on its strange round feet, toward its takeoff.

The boy was almost four feet tall, with a flat stomach and arms and legs undulating with muscles. His torso was free of hair, but a fine coat of downy growth started on his lower back, stopping at his buttocks, whose lean skin was dirtied from sitting on dusty rocks. Short fine hairs sprouted timidly around his groin. A curved little penis hung at his crotch, delicate in contrast to his well-muscled body.

His knees were round, oversized. All his flesh had concentrated in his muscled masses—otherwise he carried not an ounce of fat. Down his lean back, his vertebrae showed like a vertical string of beads, and his shoulder blades moved in relief under his coffee skin, like little spatulate wings. His big toes, which pointed outward, were agitated by long nervous throbs. They clutched down at the rock, and then all ten toes twitched minutely, like a perched bird's claws before it lifted off into flight. In anticipation of his daring move, his scrotal sack tightened around his little testicles, and the hairs on the sack pricked up, scratching at his thighs.

To encourage himself, he opened his mouth and let out not a gasp of fear but a low and harsh "rrrr" sound, like a threat. Then he slid down from the rock and started ahead, clutching an almost spherical stone in his right hand. The skin of his hands was light brown and crisscrossed with the scars of so many gashes and scratches that his little hands looked tattooed. Larger scratches on his chest, belly, back, and thighs completed that tattoolike pattern.

On his belly, a short but deep and frightful scar marked the spot where a warthog had gored him before the last rainy season. Healed now, it was lighter in color than the skin surrounding it. Just above it, his navel, small and round and dark, looked like a pretty little bug asleep on the body of a host animal.

He gave the savanna one last inspecting look.

Almost everywhere, close or far, the horns of duikers, topis, wildebeests, sables, and impalas rose above the grass like periscopes. There were flat, dry whacks of duelling bucks' horns, and the herbivores bellowed and brayed so continuously that they sounded like one voice with an astounding skill at changing its pitch.

To the boy's left, in medium-tall grass, a company of vultures was hopping on the ground, flapping about and cackling. The boy knew that meant they were waiting their turn to pick at a kill. He could not see it, but he knew the kill had been brought down by lions. If lions brought down anything, the other meat-eaters had to wait until the lions were full and happy. That was true only for lions. No other carnivores got that mark of respect. Just now, the lions were busy eating, and the birds of prey were busy waiting for them to finish and take a nap. That gave the boy time to explore the mystery left behind by those fantastic creatures.

He gripped his stone tighter, lowered his face, and started walking, swishing fast through the grass. The spot where the tuber/bug had landed was out of his territory. It lay several lion's dashes away from the rocky palisade and from the acacia grove—spaces where he felt safe because the tall rocks and knotty branches provided excellent lookouts against flesh-eating predators. The boy remembered these things with his body as much as with his mind. His legs and arms, his fingers and toes remembered how easily they had climbed a specific stand of trees or ladder of stone. His senses computed his chances of survival in a particular tract of terrain with more accuracy than would the mind of a sapiens two million years into the future.

This space between his home grounds and the tuber/bug's landing site was dangerous because it contained no trees or tall rocks. His only concealment from large carnivores was swaying, swinging grasses.

Yet even against such (dangers), he had to enter that (area), to examine what was left of the (dream), and to draw some (conclusions) about it.

The boy was now a whole feline's dash into the grassland, under the afternoon sun, feeling his pores open and sweat both from the heat and from fear. He stopped by a tall and narrow anthill; rising some twenty feet in the air, it looked like a limbless tree, strange and wasted, as if struck by lightning. The ants quickly found his feet, but he hardly felt their bites. He was rather fond of ants. He had once slipped inside such an anthill to escape the charge of a warthog, but the stinging little beasts had chased him out. The warthog had promptly gored his belly with one curled-up tusk, then run off, its tail like a flapping little white flag streaked with black, unfittingly cute for the animal with such hideous warts, horns, and tusks.

Writhing on the ground and bleeding, the boy had imagined his death as clearly as his brain of five hundred cubic centimeters could conceive such a dreadful notion. But he had lived, thanks to the ants. He had used his fingers to squeeze the lips of his bleeding wound together while the ants swarmed over his belly and kept stinging him. He barely felt their stings though, because the pain they inflicted was obscured by the agony of the slash. The ants pinched at the lips of the wound, and the boy brushed them off with his other hand, breaking off their bodies but leaving their jaws sewn into his skin. Finally, a good stretch of the wound had been sutured shut by the jaws of the ants. He crawled to a water hole, and applied a bandage of fresh mud on the rest of his cut. The cut healed. The barbaric surgery of those insects had saved the boy from an injury that should have festered and killed him.

The boy had reacted to his own survival like any child. He quickly forgot the mortal danger and started to play. He became fascinated with ants and other bugs, watched their movements, noted the diversity of their colors and shapes, and chased them the way lion cubs chased rodents. He caught many bugs, and put them in his mouth, and learned that some were good to eat.

He slapped the ants off his legs, threw a few crushed ones into his mouth, and hurried on to the tracks left by the tuber/bug. As the boy stepped, he was using his long agile toes to grip the ground lightly each time they landed on it. His toes pinched at the space where he was stepping, as if they were alert antennas checking for unseen hazards. The muscles on the back of his calves bulged, giving him a good bounce upward.

There was some anxiety in his bounce. As one foot lifted and another prepared to land, the memory of the boy's species brought back a time of great panic and choice, when his ancestors had urged themselves to stay upright. They had to figure out how to keep supporting themselves on a spine that had not been designed to carry so much weight. Their very survival had depended on lifting their faces up, up, up, to the highest point of their bodies.

That way, their round brown eyes could sweep the horizon, looking out for predators. Now that memory lived wordlessly in the foundation of the boy's mind.

He stepped inside the groove left by one of the plane's wheels, and breathed heavily. He looked at the tracks. The child was here now, and his dream had ended, yet it hadn't. His dream had left stuff behind it.

He sat down on the dirt, thinking wordlessly.

(Dreams) left no (evidence).

Dreams left nothing behind them, except the dreamer himself.

That was himself, and he was here.

But so were the traces left by the dream.

He dropped his hunting stone, put both palms forward, and felt the inside of a wheel's track. It felt smooth and round like few shapes he had touched before. Under his touch, the dust broke and rolled away, stroking his skin with the fine particles of dirt moving under his palms.

He heard a light sizzling sound, and jumped up, his right fist instantly clenched around the black stone.

It was only a snake, a small green mamba, hissing as it retreated from a secretary bird. Unimpressed by the hiss, the bird kept stepping on its stilt-shaped legs, making the snake roll backward into the wheel track. Then the bird jumped straight at the mamba's head, crushing it with a foot that struck like a sledgehammer. The mamba writhed, then became still. The secretary bird picked at the crushed head, and cawed.

Somehow, this triumph of one beast over another inspired the little hominid with a sense of his own power. The tightness in his muscles decreased. His shutoff valves and lids gave way. Like an animal scenting his territory, he pointed his little penis and urinated on one of the tracks, as if putting that dream under his control.

He was less frightened now, and was almost ready to play.

He hurried with that agile, spirited bounce in his steps toward a raucous chorus of cawing birds that was coming from behind a large mass, larger than a rhino, that was lying motionless, surrounded by tufts of grass. Its color was still blurred by dust clinging on after the dust storm.

He stopped just a few steps from the overturned Safari Cub, gripping his stone tighter. The big beast could easily stagger to its feet and attack, though the birds that were cawing so close to it were a good sign that the big beast had lost its power and was probably dead. He raised his fist, ready to release the stone, and walked around the overturned Safari Cub so softly that his feet lifted and fell without sound.

He stood still by the roof of the vehicle, trying to detect a breath coming out of it, or a gurgle of digesting bowels. At the same time, he was looking for a head or a tail, a front or a rear. But this thing wasn't like the other large creatures he knew in the savanna. It smelled smoky and hot, but in a repellent way that was different from the smoldering fields after a bush fire. Also, this big animal didn't have any ticks or bugs or other little parasite creatures clinging to it.

The boy inched around the shell of the overturned vehicle. The roof's pop-up top was missing, so he peered into an empty space. He became unafraid, and touched the roof with one palm, while the other prudently gripped his stone. The roof of the van was flat, dull, lifeless. He did not like it.

He circled around to the vehicle's other side, its fuel and transmission lines still exuding heat. He wrinkled his nose. He had once smelled a sulfurous fumarole, and vaguely remembered that suffocating sour smell coming from the bowels of the earth.

He noted that this thing was not disappearing. Unlike the tuber/bug, it was staying here, a fixed part of the scenery.

He heard the tearing, cutting, and swallowing sounds made by the birds. Stepping around the animals, he avoided a strange lower horn poking out (the van's bent front bumper), and saw the birds and what they were eating.

A griffon vulture, its talons anchored in the chest of the dead gunman, was picking an eye out of his head. Two black kites and several hawks hopped around the face, trying to slice off a morsel, but each time they got close, the much larger griffon lashed out with its beak or flapped its enormous gray wings to protect its hold on the prey; finally, it flitted off the chest and perched on the bloodied face itself, to eat from the soft neck and throat. Cawing and cackling, the other birds attacked the dead hands and feet, or groped about in frustration, looking for entries through the torn clothes to more naked flesh.

The creature they were eating looked like the other dream creatures, except that it was dead. But again, this dreamed-up fantasy had made itself a part of the boy's world. The feeding birds were proof of that.

Fascinated, he watched how quickly the birds were changing the dead gunman's appearance. Both eyes were missing now and bright red pits of bare flesh stared hideously from inside the face. The pointed tip of the chin protruded strangely, all pecked up and morseled, while the nose, half torn off, was still much larger than the boy's. The gunman's forehead was also bright red from temple to temple; its skin had been completely peeled off by beaks. He still had the look of the other visitors, the ones who arrived by tuber/bug, but in a bloodied, horrid way.

The boy's hair flared up around his face. The ''rrrrr'' sound coming out of his throat became a long, doglike howl, and for an instant he looked ready to jump at the corpse and maul it worse than the vultures had, with a fearful rage. He had seen death, many times. But not this death. The boy's yell made the birds caw into flight, their wing joints snapping from the hurried pull of their chest muscles. The boy tripped, fell backward, jumped up again, and realized he had lost his stone.

He looked for it on the ground, and could not find it.

A clinking sound made him bolt. A piece of glass fell out of the Cub's smashed windshield into a pool of broken glass by the van's front.

He could not find his stone, though he circled around the van and the corpse several times. Finally, he looked over the tall grass toward the acacia grove, trying to decide whether to go back slowly or to run. He had other hunting stones in the grove, in several little clutches positioned by bushes and trees. The grove's branches were easy to climb, and the rocks rose right behind the trees.

Running was dangerous because it attracted carnivores, but it was faster, so he settled on running. At that hour, most of the big predators were napping, lazy and full. He could smell the unfinished kills heated by the sun, and he could hear the thick buzzing of bush flies feasting on the antelope bowels that lay all over the grass.

He took off toward the acacias and was halfway there when he saw the hump of a solitary lion ahead of him. He slowed down to assess which direction it was moving in. The lion raised its head higher than the boy's—it was a very large, young male, five feet at the shoulder, with a sparse, ungrown mane. He could lunge and catch the boy in a few quick bounces.

The lion saw the boy.

The boy's fist-sized mind noted that he should have taken along more than one stone. He could see the acacias rustling their spiny leaves right behind the lion. This was the boy's territory, where there were trees he had climbed countless times.

But the lion was moving in an arc, right between him and the trees.

His encounter with the plane's tracks and the van had made the boy sweat so much that now he was very thirsty and his tongue was clicking dryly against his teeth. The lion was picking up his scent, just as the boy was starting to smell the lion's stench of short hairs that had been muddied in water holes and dragged over ripped-up herbivore flesh. It was mixed with a rank smell from his musk glands, which were secreting more richly than usual; this was a young lion, hot-blooded and inexperienced and looking to mount. But there was one ray of hope—the lion moved casually, as if he had already eaten.

The boy could stand still, or go straight at the lion, behaving like an animal many times his size and strength.

The decision was the lion's. It crouched, then loped at the boy, mowed the tall grass aside with its chest, trampling it with his hind legs and lashing it with its tufted tail, as it charged, enormous, lethal, but unhungry and playful. Ready to kill, not for food but to have fun.

The hominid boy stood looking at the long yellow jumps coming closer. Nothing could stop them.

He suddenly became nothing but a blob of live fear. He raced back, across tall grass, letting out a loud piercing sound.

The bulky heads of several water buffaloes lifted above the grass. One of them was quite close, its eyes placidly at half-mast, its nostrils picked at by a starling. The boy noticed that those nostrils were gigantic, big enough for the bird perched on its nose to reach its whole head inside them, gulping up flies and other little pests. Racing toward them, the boy's mind formed a wordless hope that the lion would stop its loping the closer it got to the buffaloes. He let out that piercing yell again, a nearly human sound of despair that made the buffaloes erupt forcefully above the grass, their paddle-shaped ears swatting back and forth. Cattle egrets, white and small, flapped into flight above them. The closest buffalo, a big bull, bellowed deeply, then put his head down and thundered forth to charge at the brown-skinned boy.

The boy was not afraid of the bull's open mouth. It ate grass and leaves. Its hooves were the thing to look out for, so he leaped sideways, out of their path.

Confused, the bull slowed down. The boy raced around its massive flank, and was lashed hard in the chest by the bull's thick black tail. He gripped the tail, and might have sunk his teeth into it had the bull needed any added prompting. But the bull broke into a godlike gallop, yanking the boy off his feet and dragging him behind the bull's dark rump.

Now the bull found the lion loping right at it. Still galloping, it lowered its massive horns. To arrest his run, the lion swerved away in midair and fell on his belly in the grass like a swimmer in a clumsy dive. When the lion got up, the bull had charged past him. The boy let go of the bull's tail, tumbled to the ground, pulled himself up, and raced off toward the lifesaving acacias.

The acacias were easy to climb. Most of their foliage was at the top of their upper branches, like flat umbrellas. Their leafless lower branches were easy to check for leopards. When a leopard climbed an acacia, it usually did so with an antelope dangling in its jaws; the prey's flopping limbs and the leopard's spotted coat were easy to spot against an acacia's gray bark.

There were over a dozen acacias in that little grove, set in an irregular boxlike pattern. The boy didn't know numbers, but he knew the difference between many and few, and between rich and complex as opposed to rare and insignificant. The running distances between the trees were of diverse lengths, and were interrupted by bushes that offered additional cover. All these elements gave him a lot of ways to escape if a predator came into the grove.

In fact, this grove was his favorite hunting ground. Here, he brought down duikers, which kept stupidly returning to ruminate right under the acacias, where the boy had successfully stoned his first one before the last rainy season.

Also in the wider perimeter of his home base were the rocks, where he rested and slept. At the rocks' highest points he could see in all directions. The boy shot his eyes upward, chose an empty acacia, and hugged its trunk. His hands and feet gripped at the bark. His elbow hinges bent and pulled, his ball-and-socket hip joints pushed. Like a natural machine, he craned himself up.

Below him, the lion and the buffalo chose to avoid a serious confrontation. The lion crouched down and waited, its tufted tail whipping up little puffs of dust. The buffalo stared darkly at the lion, then orbited slowly back toward his herd.

When the lion finally looked for the boy, he saw a dash of brown flesh diving out of an acacia so quickly that the feline's eyes continued to stare at the empty tree. The boy hopped to the ground, thudded toward another acacia, bent toward its base. He grabbed something, then scurried up the trunk like an insect that had no use for gravity.

The lion trotted toward the tree. The boy was eight feet from the ground now, throwing a leg over a branch.

He had stored several black stones at the foot of that tree, like a tiny ammunition pile. Now he was gripping two of them.

The lion leaped. He soared, almost touching the branch with his gaping jaws. The boy's brown arm folded like a crane joint. Then he threw one stone across barely a foot of distance at the lion's upper fangs. He missed by inches—the lion took a blinding whack under one eye, yowled in pain, and crashed back to the ground.

Just then, another lion let out a rusty, hollow wail. Still stunned, the young lion rose, hesitated, then hunched away, head low, tail slapping the grass. The boy saw him join the other, clearly older lion, and both of them slunk away from the trees. A good distance farther, they fell to rest in tall grass.

For now, the boy was out of danger. He lifted his protruding mouth and yapped out a high-pitched laugh. It was a laugh of hominid triumph, cutting across his fear, building an upsurge of confidence that was out of all proportion to his small flat teeth and round unaggressive nails. Now that his danger mode was over, his play mode returned. He dropped from branch to branch, back to the ground. Running, he crossed the brief space between the trees and the rocky palisade.

I N DOWNTOWN NAIROBI, LESS THAN HALF AN HOUR HAD passed, and the Mercedes was still chugging back to the freeway toward Karen.

No one was talking inside the car. Jakub's decision was not a surprise. It had always been assumed that Jakub's first-born would sooner or later be asked to play his role in public life. But now that the decision was here, Ngili was having trouble believing it.

He's not going to take it, Ken thought. Ngili's not going to take it, firstborn or not.

Yinka looked at Ken. She felt bad for Ngili and was angry with her father, but she was more curious about Ken's reaction than about Ngili's. Yinka could predict white people's reactions fairly accurately, and took great pride in that skill. However, she was less sure about Ken, who missed some standard white motivations, and possessed some others, all his own.

Kenya had gained its independence from the British in 1963, after a devastating guerrilla war that had lasted ten years. Both Yinka and Ngili were born after independence. When she was six and Ngili was eight, they were sent to live with their grandparents in a village because it was fashionable among the new black elite to send one's children back to one's roots. They were teenagers before they ever saw a white person. By the time they returned to Nairobi for high school and college, Kenya had become one of Africa's most promising new nations, with the power firmly in the hands of Jomo ("Burning Spear") Kenyatta and a few of his friends. One of his friends was Jakub Ngiamena, also known in the independence movement as Simba, "lion" in Swahili.

Simba Ngiamena put his children in the best schools in Nairobi, where they were faced with what was left of the white community. Yinka became friends with little white girls, most of them of English descent. She met their white parents, all of whom had been important in the British Protectorate of Kenya but were no longer so in this free black republic. Now they were "clingers."

Most white clingers had simple motivations; they stayed in Kenya to make money. Others were the scientists who studied Africa, and then there were the old white hunters who would not fit in anywhere else. For most whites, money meant status, safety, and confidence. In post-colonial Nairobi, every white person's confidence was quite simply buttressed by a business, a bank account, a piece of land. To maintain those assets, the whites made predictable alliances with the blacks in power. If a white person's alliances foundered, he had to leave the country. It was that simple.

It was almost impossible to watch the whites play by such a crude set of rules and not think that they were crude themselves, and soulless and lacking all inner complication. Yinka found the whites shockingly uncomplicated, yet surprisingly conceited, given their precarious position. A white man who was complicated and not conceited was a contradiction in terms. An impossibility.

Ken was such an impossibility, the only one of his kind that she had met.

Ken acted confident though he had no bank account. Ken acted confident without any visible support and entitlement, unless, reasoned Yinka, he got all his confidence by being friends with her brother.

She also thought he wasn't bad-looking for a white man. Yinka had had several white lovers while studying journalism in England. She found it easier to copulate with white men than to look at them. Naked in bed, they reminded her of African mole shrews, discolored and tiny-eyed. Occasionally, a tanned one reminded her of a normal, dark anatomy. Ken was one of the few acceptable-looking whites she had met. He tanned well, and was often unshaven. He smelled racy when he returned from a dig after not showering for days, but so did Ngili. They were not dirty per se because the savanna was not dirty; it was a place of natural odors and excretions, dried off by the wind and burned away by the sun.

She was surprised by how lasting Ken's relationship with her brother had turned out to be. But Ken had a lot to gain from that relationship. Yinka predicted that Ken would not challenge her father's decision about Ngili's future. He could still benefit from the Ngiamenas' goodwill, even if Ngili was forced to give up geology.

Ken looked as if he had been awakened to a rude reality. That amused Yinka. *Mzoori*, great, she thought. Let's see the settler come back from his prehistoric fantasy and deal with the real Africa.

Ken looked at Jakub's massive back, cleared his throat, and spoke in an uneven and rocky voice. "I'm sorry, sir, but . . . keeping Ngili in Nairobi means denying all his years of study. Especially now, when we've found something that can make us known and respected in the field . . ."

"I'm sorry, Mr. Lauder, but you don't understand the situation." Jakub had not called him Mr. Lauder in years.

"I'm afraid, sir, that you don't understand Ngili."

"Ngili is my son, Mr. Lauder. We have a different sense of family here. The fact that you two are friends gives you no right to confuse his priorities."

"I think Ngili's quite clear about his priorities. What's of more value to this nation—another diplomat or a world-class scientist?"

"Mr. Lauder, enough. We've been very hospitable to you, and we'll continue to be so, if you recognize that this is none of your business."

The dismissal could not have been more clear. Yinka was amazed that the settler had spoken out, and in such uncompromising terms.

Ken looked crestfallen, no doubt because of the threat to his great scientific opportunity. Then he locked his jaw so hard that Yinka expected him to open the car door and step out of the car and out of the Ngiamenas' lives. But he remained seated next to her brother. She wondered whether that signaled weakness, and then she remembered that Ken's Land Rover was parked at their house.

Ken said in a low voice, "You're right, it's none of my business. Only Ngili can decide about his own future."

Yinka studied her brother. Ngili ground his teeth, but said nothing. Several minutes passed. Yinka saw from the throb of her father's hands on the wheel that he was tensing up. Jakub fought his way back onto the freeway almost recklessly.

Ngili sat draped in silence, his face sculpted like that of a tribal deity, and still said nothing. The other three people in the car had the same thought at once, in almost identical words: What was the firstborn going to do, obey his father or defy him?

WAITING FOR THE CAR TO MAKE IT TO KAREN, KEN TRIED to form rational, practical thoughts. Without Ngili, things would be tough. Ngili had provided introductions, scientific comradeship, limitless knowledge of Swahili, and money when their resources ran out. It would be tough to work alone again. Ken pressed his knee onto the jagged breccia. He felt an immediate connection with that morning's mystery. The footprints, and then the dead gunman lying by the overturned Safari Cub.

The dead man's Walther pistol was tucked in his belt. Instead of giving him a feeling of protection, the weapon made him intensely aware of his vulnerability.

Ken and Ngili had first met six years before, while tending bar at that hotel, the Naivasha, whose grand ballroom was now rented by the Ngiamenas for Gwee's wedding. Ken had taken the job to finance a generator and a water purifier for his future digs (a previous bartending job had paid for his used Land Rover). One evening, the hotel manager asked him to give a crash course in mixing drinks to a freshly hired young Kenyan. The new employee acted as if he had never washed a glass in his life, but he still got the job because his name was Ngili Ngiamena.

Ngili had left home after his father forbade him to study geology. He needed a place to stay, and a coach in bartending. Ken let him room with him in his cheap apartment on Tom Mboia Road and taught him how to mix drinks and wash glasses, empty ashtrays and rearrange chairs, clean the bar's toilets and bow when tipped. More important, he told Ngili that he was also humbling himself for science.

That bonded them. They talked science, and shined the bar's antique, badly chipped ivory rail. In the thirties, white hunters drinking at that rail often nicked on it what they owed and paid their bill in antelope horns or lion skins. Or so said a legend, repeated ad nauseam to safari groups. Ken and Ngili were unimpressed with that kind of legend. They dreamed of finding the next Lucy.

There were compensations for the humbling work. They played tennis on the Naivasha's courts, free because the tennis coach was a cousin of Ngili's. They played doubles with English and Dutch and German and American girls (''pink memsahib pussy,'' Ngili called them), who went wild for the Masai prince and his Africa-wise white friend. Often, after a double, they picked up the girls, piled them into Ken's Land Rover, and rushed to Ken's apartment, where fossils wrapped in burlap and calipers and other anthropological paraphernalia gave the girls an extra thrill. Ken downed the shades, Ngili poured glasses of Mount Kenya liqueur, the girls took off their tennis outfits, and seconds later all four were airborne. The next morning Ken and Ngili sprinted over the university's lawns so they wouldn't be late for Randall Phillips's classes in human evolution.

After four months, Ngili's father relented and agreed that

he could study geology—for now. That temporary "now" contained a promise of African permanence. In any case, Ngili returned to the family's warm cocoon, bringing Ken with him.

Then Ken and Ngili went on their first digs and got hit over the head with the notion that out there, between nameless hills, with wildebeests bobbing in swaying grasses like dark swimmers in high waves, *there,* in the countless ravines of the Rift Valley, man's genes had been mixed as if in a test tube, by the hands of a science-minded God. And this bonded them again, and changed them. As Ngili said one night, by a dig's campfire, "Good-bye to tennis and to pink memsahib pussy; it's science from now on."

At that very moment, as if to mark Ngili's words, they heard a prophetic rumbling of lions. It reminded whoever cared that lions had not changed their physiology or behavior for millions of years. They had witnessed the dawn of man. That, too, was part of science.

But now, for Ngili, science had to end.

"Here we are," said Jakub Ngiamena.

They had entered Karen. As if a distorting lens had fallen off a viewer, the roadway seemed to straighten itself. Sidewalks appeared, along which acacias of the garden type incised the air with their needle-shaped leaves. Wood and wrought-iron fences protected handsome mansions. Shiny Jaguars, BMWs, and Toyotas appeared in driveways. No policemen were visible, but its very ambience gave this neighborhood a feeling of safety. White residents in shorts and flowery shirts watered the grass, or taught children how to swim in tiled pools. None of them were taking nostalgic pictures indicating their pending departure.

A black postman in a pith helmet walked leisurely by, pushing letters into mailboxes. Apart from the postman, there were no Africans on this street. A basketball sprang out of a yard, and Ngiamena braked while a ruddy white boy rushed into the street to pick it up.

Ngiamena rolled the car through a stately gate and up an alley of flowering Cape chestnut trees. Half hidden in the trees, a columned manse showed, with a row of coffee bushes by the steps. The previous owners were coffee producers who had left Africa long ago. Ken knew how much Yinka had fought Jakub to erase the evidence of the former order, but as if to teach his children a lesson, Jakub had refused. Our power rose on an older power, he had told them.

A multicar garage showed at the right. Parked in front, dusty, lopsided from a chassis bent during a drive in the savanna, was Ken's old Land Rover.

Ngiamena got out of the car. Patrick, the family's aging butler, stepped out of the house with a welcoming tray of papaya drinks. He was mahogany-black and had tribal tattoos on his cheeks. He too had been inherited from the old order and often joked about how much better the Ngiamenas were to him, letting him wear a kikoi and go barefoot, instead of insisting on the old order's jacket and black shoes.

Patrick rolled his eyes, seeing Ngiamena and Yinka and Ngili and his friend all get out of the car with such tense expressions. But he said nothing and rushed back inside to bring a T-shirt for Ngili, while Ngili and Ken started to transfer bundles of tarp from the Mercedes to the dusty Land Rover.

"We're going to eat something, and then take these over to Randall Phillips," mumbled Ngili, looking down, as if talking to himself. "And I'm not going to report to the Foreign Office on Monday." He said it low, as if to himself, but everyone heard him. Climbing the front steps, Jakub turned and watched his son move with the bones from one vehicle to the other. "I'm not going to give up science," Ngili stated, quite loud now but still not looking at his father.

Jakub spoke from the steps; his height added to his stature. "I made a decision, Ngili. As of Monday, you will attend a special course at the Foreign Office School of Diplomacy. In a few months, you will join Kenya's New York mission to the United Nations, as a press attaché." In the driveway, with a papaya drink in her hand, Yinka giggled at the word "press."

Ngiamena ignored her, and walked down into Ngili's path.

"This is one of those times when a country needs her best young men out in front. The government feels . . ."

Ngili sidestepped him, and almost threw a bundle in the Land Rover, making Ken grit his teeth. He came back, now staring straight at his father, his eyes fiery. "The government got us into this mess! They emptied the treasury to fill their pockets. They decreed AIDS to be a ploy against our national image. Our economy is collapsing, our administration is moribund, the poaching's getting worse than in the days of the sultan of Zanzibar . . ."

"I'm so very sorry," said a quiet, rich voice. "I think I came at the time of a family difference . . . "

All turned. Cyril Anderson was stepping toward the house. He carried a manila envelope. He saluted each of the Ngiamenas, with an extra smile for the father.

Ken noticed that Cyril was not wearing his usual tweeds and club tie, but a light khaki jacket, gabardine pants, and sandals. Almost a safari outfit. That was quite unusual. What was Cyril up to?

"Maybe you will help us resolve this," said Jakub. He shook hands with Anderson, his pink African palm against Anderson's big blue-veined hand. "Patrick, will you set up for coffee on the terrace?"

"Yes, *mkubwa*," said Patrick, using a term for master from the old order.

Anderson also lived in Karen. Seeing no vehicle at the end of the driveway, Ken concluded that he had walked over. When had he become so friendly with Jakub? Ken tensed up as Jakub explained openly why he and his son were fighting. Ngili had to respond to the call of duty; the exciting stuff he and Ken had found could wait for now, as it had for thousands of years.

Anderson narrowed his eyes at the wrapped objects being transferred from one car to the other. Then he smiled at Ngili. "You and I might have the same dilemma."

"How's that?" asked Ngili, hostile.

"I got a government offer to become state minister for culture and antiquities. A newly created position." Anderson held up the manila envelope: "This is an overview of my office and duties. I'm wondering how to respond."

"It's an honor," said Ngiamena, "and you'd be right for the job."

This had to be the direct consequence of Leakey's defection, thought Ken. As for the change in Cyril's clothing, why, Cyril was already trying to look more like Leakey. Ken had to fight to suppress a grin, but it froze on his lips as he realized that . . .

The state commission decreed to review foreign scientists' work would no doubt be chaired by the new minister for culture and antiquities. And that was going to be Cyril Anderson.

"I'd do it for science," said Anderson, smiling at his little audience. "We are a country too important for man's understanding of himself. We need political stability, and I'd be glad to help. But . . . this offer does not have a budget attached and no clear provision that I'd be allowed to choose my staff."

Negotiation? wondered Ken. Probably.

"Let's chat about that," said Jakub. "I don't know what your requirements are, but I'd be glad to hear them and convey them, if they're reasonable."

How nicely everything was falling into place!

Ken reminded himself that he needed to call Randall. He caught Ngili's eyes, motioned at the Mercedes, and they both bent down inside the car, anchoring their arms around the breccia. They pulled it out and shuffled with it to the Land Rover.

"What are you going to do?" he whispered at his friend, as they lifted the breccia onto the Land Rover's sun-scorched backseat.

"I don't know," muttered Ngili. "Did you read that thing in the paper?"

"Yeah, I read it at Theo's."

"What are you going to do?"

"I've no idea. But we have to help each other."

"I don't think you can help me this time," said Ngili.

"It's funny—according to that government statement, *I* could go back to Dogilani, but not you."

"Maybe we should switch identities."

Ngili uttered a dry laugh, and walked back toward Anderson and Ngiamena.

Anderson smiled. "There are ways to combine duty with pleasure," he said. "I might take a fossil exhibit to New York, for the country's image. Would you like to be the exhibit's director, Ngili?"

Ngili stared back blankly, then shrugged. Patrick leaned out of a window and called that coffee was served on the terrace.

"Uh, are you going to have coffee with us, Ken?" asked Ngiamena. "Or maybe you want to take a shower first . . . ?" He looked with exaggerated concern at Ken's crumpled shirt.

Ken was surprised by Ngiamena's obviousness. "If you don't mind, I have a couple of phone calls to make," he answered awkwardly.

"By all means, use the set in the den." Ngiamena turned toward Yinka. "What are you going to do?" he asked, making it clear that she was not included in the coffee party.

"I have no phone calls to make, so I'm going to try on my wedding kikoi," she said calmly, and strode off. Despite feeling glum, Ken pictured a lioness heading for a solo hunt, from which she'd bring back nothing to the surly old male.

Ngiamena put his big hand on Ngili's back and pushed him toward the terrace. Behind them, Anderson walked past Ken. The roar of another army plane grew over Karen, so labored that Ken muttered, "The way those idiots are flying, they'll crash and kill two hundred people."

"And give them a merciful end," said Anderson. Ken stared at him. Anderson met the stare with a clear smile. "Did you bring back something interesting? What's inside that lump of breccia?"

"An ape," lied Ken angrily.

"If it's more than that, let me know." Anderson smiled again, and walked off toward the terrace.

* * *

"YOU DUG OUT A FOSSIL WITH *WHAT*?" ASKED RANDALL
Phillips at the other end of the telephone line. He broke into
a heady little laugh as Ken described again the tools they
had used, the machete, the razor, the belt buckle. "Amazing,
absolutely amazing! Wish I could tell this story to the guys
at the Berkeley Institute of Human Origins . . ."

"Please don't. They'll hem and haw that the fossil wasn't
collected properly."

Ensconced in the Ngiamenas' den, Ken was using an old
phone set of Bakelite, a colonial relic well shined by Patrick.
Through the nearest window he could see out to the terrace.
There Jakub, Anderson, and Ngili were sipping *kahawa*, the
strong Kenyan coffee, from cups with minuscule coffee
beans of china beaded around their rims to give to the guests'
lips a pleasantly granulated feel.

Anderson was talking. Leaning toward Ngili and rounding
the air with his handsome white hands. He looked confident
of his powers of persuasion.

Three miles away, in a declining neighborhood, Randall
Phillips snorted with excitement. "Can you bring that thing
over?" he asked. "Not right now, in a couple of hours. Marcia and I just had a fight. She's upset about leaving Kenya,
though she's the one who pushed for it, so she went ballistic
because I forgot to buy an extra suitcase."

"I'll buy you a suitcase on the way," said Ken. "You'll
need it to pack the samples of bones and soil."

"Fine. Shit, are they really making Caruso minister of
antiquities? Maybe I shouldn't leave, maybe he'll give up
the fossils vault's curatorship. . . . Nah, that man never gave
up anything," Randall mused bitterly. "It's okay; I'll live
in California, where my kids will learn disrespect for their
parents, and Marcia will get a face-lift. So, is that everything?"

"No," answered Ken. He described the circular pattern of
footprints on the spur. Then the footprints they saw after the
dust storm.

Randall listened attentively. He was so quiet that it made Ken nervous.

Then he spoke. "Wow," he said, honest and unscientific.

Ken pictured his old teacher. Randall Phillips was short, and muscular like a marine, but with a podgy midriff, a receding hairline, and thick glasses. A bulging, balding, myopic marine. He had two academic specialties, paleoanatomy and human evolution. He was really tough to impress, and Ken had just impressed him twice.

"Give me some more facts," said Randall.

"I don't have any more facts. All I have is evidence that someone with protohuman feet is hunting with protohuman implements in a protohuman habitat. My evidence consists of photographs and stones. The photographs are being developed, the stones are in my pocket."

He slipped his hand down the side of his body, found the stones, and stroked their silent, inanimate shapes.

"Wow," said Randall again. "What the hell's that thing out there?"

Ken took a deep breath. "I don't know what it is, but I have an idea of what it's not. I've turned this enigma on all sides, and I reviewed the reasonable explanations, which are three: a wild child, a tribal straggler, or an unknown variety of ape." He took another deep breath, and continued fast. "Now, Randall, none of these explanations seems right to me. The ape hypothesis is the least likely, because apes have hands instead of feet, and even if they hunt, which only chimps do regularly, they don't use hunting tools." He stopped, caught his breath, and waited nervously for Randall's answer.

"All right," said Randall patiently. "So that leaves the straggler and wild child theories."

"Right. Let's presume that a straggler, which is a pretty rare case in itself, also happens to have the most incredible atavistic feet. Now, don't you think that a straggler, whether a tribesman or a fellow scientist, would've tried to signal his presence in order to be rescued? I mean, we were there, right smack in the middle of an open field, for three days! There's no way that anyone could've missed us, or the plane! As for a wild child, how could one survive out there?'' Ken laughed tensely and dryly. ''I slept just a few hours by the digging site, and I woke up practically nose to nose with a lion. The chances of a child surviving in that place alone are one in a million! Don't you think? What do you think, Randall?''

''I think you're right,'' agreed Randall. ''None of those hypotheses seems entirely convincing.''

Ken breathed deeply. He felt a strange relief.

''So what are we dealing with?'' asked Randall.

''I don't know. I just have a strong feeling that whatever it is, it did not get lost out there by accident. It belongs to the habitat.''

''All right . . .'' Randall's voice grew heavier, as if his scientific mind were plunging into the lower depths of the puzzle. ''So you brought back from Dogilani a fossil, and some evidence of a living thing. A fossil is a fossil is a fossil. It's solid, real, datable. This other thing is what exactly? Another Big Foot?''

''Randall!'' Ken felt insulted.

''Let me reformulate. A child can get lost in the savanna, and so can an adult. But if this creature was born in the savanna, then you're not talking one creature only, you're talking a family. You're talking population.'' There was a pause. ''Or do you want me to believe that some fossil came back to life and started walking around? Ken?''

Ken opened his mouth to answer but did not utter a sound.

His mind seemed to expand in all directions. Inside that vastness rushing into his head, he found himself in the savanna, facing the crouching brown creature.

The hominid that hunted with black stones. The hominid he had never seen, except for its footprints. The hominid looked up, straight at Ken.

Ken shrank back in fright. He uttered a throttled sound, breathed deeply, and the hominid disappeared.

All right, Ken thought, this is just fatigue. Fatigue, hunger, depletion. Of the body, of the brain.

He regained control. ''I've nothing else to say, Randall.

I'll pick up those pictures in an hour, and we'll look at them together."

"Very well, I can't wait to see them. By the way, do you remember Raj Haksar? Used to chair the department of cultural anthropology?"

Ken nodded. "Sure. Tribal Customs. Rites of passage and manhood. He must be professor emeritus by now." He remembered Haksar as a wrinkled East Indian, small and frail and excessively polite with his students.

"Yeah, he retired a few years ago. But he'd be good to speak to, just in case those footprints were left by a boy on a tribal 'walk.' ''

Ken jumped. "What 'walk'? What are you talking about? There are no tribes living at Dogilani!"

Ken had already thought of this possibility and discarded it.

A walk was a solitary savanna or jungle trek, which young tribal males had to take to prove their manhood. They had to go into the bush totally unaccompanied and unaided, surviving on their own resources. Sometimes they were allowed to take spears or bows and arrows with them, but most often not. The walk could last several weeks, and the walkers' ages varied with the tribes. In a few tribes, the boys taking the rite walked as early as age nine.

"I know. I'm just playing devil's advocate," answered Randall, "and I haven't even seen your pictures yet. But if your footprints were not made by a tribal boy on a walk, or by an ape, or a straggler, then, to quote Sherlock Holmes, what is left, no matter how improbable, must be the truth. And what is left is a protohuman. Are you prepared to claim that there are live protohumans at Dogilani?"

A vicious headache ground at Ken's temples. He searched his mind for the brown creature, but instead found the notion of the brown creature, the notion of a live protohuman. He felt utterly intimidated by its enormity, and embarrassed for having acted so certain and excited in front of his old teacher.

"D'you have a phone number on Haksar?" he muttered.

"He must be in the directory, unless he died. All right,

hotshot,'' Randall concluded quizzically. ''Bring your mystery over. By the way, see that Caruso doesn't get wind of your find before you even know what it is. He'll knock you aside—now he has the perfect excuse—then figure an explanation, and have it all over the news.''

''I know. Ease up, Randall. I'm not irresponsible.''

''I never said you were,'' chuckled Randall. ''See you.''

They hung up.

Ken stood staring distractedly at a Victorian advertising sheet framed above the phone.

COMMERCIAL HOTEL NAIROBI.
CHARGES REASONABLE. PORTERS IN UNIFORM
AWAIT ALL TRAINS.
CAPE COLONISTS WILL FIND
AN OLD FRIEND IN THE PROPRIETOR.

The house was unusually deserted and silent. Ngili's mother, Itina, and Gwee and Wambui, the nanny who had raised all the little Ngiamenas, were out on wedding-related errands. Ken glanced out the window, at the terrace. Jakub was the one talking now, and Ngili was listening. Jakub was pressing his fleshy palms on the wooden table. Ken prayed that the old man was showing some flexibility. Then a stubborn thought filled his mind: *It could not have been a walk.*

A WALK WAS A TRIBAL RITE THAT HAD CAUSED MUCH INK to flow. It had also caused the death of a few romantic anthropologists who had tried to pursue the walking boys in the wild, ignoring the risks of snakebite, dysentery, and dehydration.

It was a heroically gruesome test of endurance. The boys had to survive on game and on foraging, forgoing all other sources of food. If they cheated, they would be banished from the tribe. In a few cases, tribal walkers who accepted food from missionaries or explorers had been killed by parents who would not tolerate the breaking of a tribal vow.

The course on tribal customs was part of Ken's freshman year curriculum. Ken remembered that Haksar had started it by showing his freshmen a series of stills of tribal boys' feet, taken after the successful completion of walks. The boys' feet were dusty, muddy, caked with blood. Some showed unhealed injuries and fractures that made the students wince. Instead of deploring the barbaric rite, Haksar had become lyrical about the walkers' strength and endurance. "African boys are the bravest in the world, ladies and gentlemen, as they plunge into the life-and-death test of the walk. But they are not even aware of their bravery, just as their feet, the most robust in any human population, step readily over rugged terrain, hot sand, cutting thorns, and deadly spiders and reptiles. African feet, ladies and gentlemen, have the unconscious bravery of man's march toward his future. . . ."

He had paused and stared down at the feet of his African students showing under the auditorium's desks. There had been a long shuffling noise, as the students had scrambled to push their toes back into the sandals and slippers they had innocently kicked off during the course. Many had never worn shoes before enrolling at the university. Haksar had smiled and continued, explaining how those boys made the wild yield its natural foods with their bare hands. They drank water squeezed out of leaves and tubers, and waited hours by wild beehives for a chance to dip out a mouthful of wild honey. Vanquishing their repulsion, they dug out carcasses buried by hyenas, and broke bones that the hyenas' mighty jaws had left unbroken, just to lap a few grams of rotting bone marrow. They collected larvae and pupae of bugs, crushed and ate them. When the heat became insufferable, they peed on the ground, kneaded the dirt into mud, spread the mud in the shade of a tree and lay on top of it, to provide their bodies with some cool humidity. They ate eggs of all kinds, even crocodile eggs if they could safely get to a clutch of thirty to forty soft-shelled balls with shades of embryos inside them, left hatching in the sun by a careless crocodile mother.

In short, a walker became a living encyclopedia of natural survival. If he made it, he would pass his knowledge on to his own sons, then let them test it again, alone, in the wild.

At the end of his lecture, Haksar had received spontaneous applause, yet, crossing a hallway toward his next class, Ken had heard two African freshmen comment that Haksar was fun for an old "curry breath"—an insult held over from the British. The young Africans wore polo shirts, pressed khaki slacks, loafers without socks. One of them caught Ken's surprised stare. "What's wrong, mate?" he asked cheerfully.

Ken found a fast comeback. "Everything's fine. Just the way it's always been."

He walked off, wondering if Haksar knew that his students called him a curry breath, or a tandoori. Of course Haksar had to know. He had lived all his life in Kenya, dealt all his life with its racial and tribal complications. During the colonial period, the whites were on top, the blacks at the bottom, and while hating each other they both hated the middle, the East Indians. Tribally, the situation was no better. After independence, seventy tribes in Kenya and over two hundred in East Africa reverted to their old rivalries, turning the area into a simmering cauldron of jealousy and distrust.

But there were no tribes at Dogilani to send their boys on ritual treks.

Or maybe . . . There were no *known* tribes.

But the hypothesis of an unknown tribe made no sense either. The African scrubland was not Amazonia. Where would an uncontacted tribe hide?

Ken's headache was getting worse. He massaged his temples, then lifted his hands in front of his eyes and stared at them. He imagined them throwing stones. He imagined a brown hominid paw throwing stones. Throwing with aim, with good hand-and-eye coordination, which no ape possessed, even though apes threw dirt and sticks during their displays of anger. Throwing with aim meant regular hunting, which meant humanness.

Another roar of a transport plane. It made the windows throb. It made a door shake at the other end of the den. The door started to swing open. Ken heard a radio. Digo drums, quickly drowned out by the plane's noise.

The door slid open completely, revealing a bedroom, and a young woman in profile, facing a mirror. It was Yinka, and she was nude except for a pair of white cotton underpants. The plane's noise made her grimace, but she continued facing the mirror, raising a handful of strings of colored beads. She slipped one around her neck, doubled up another and fitted it on her left wrist.

She had small breasts. Masai breasts, whose girlishness would last till they filled with the milk of motherhood. They were cute, but unarousing. What made Ken swallow dryly were her thighs: long, lean, shinily fawn. As if lit from inside. Yinka was about five six, but her thighs looked long and slow and undisturbable. Like a giraffe's limbs, slow even when the creature was at a full gallop.

She lifted a foot, brought it behind her other knee, and stood naturally in the one-leg perching pose of Masai cattle guards supervising a herd. They could hold this for hours. Like a true African, Yinka was trying on her beads one-legged, and without covering her breasts.

The plane's roar subsided. Ken heard the Digo drums, five of them, each tuned to a different note. Their intense and well-timed beat reminded Ken of the Mombasa Lions, a popular group. He told himself he had to tiptoe out before Yinka saw him, but he couldn't make himself move. He stood and watched her innocent nudity.

Yinka turned. She saw him.

He remained still, cheeks ablaze. She studied him impenetrably, as she had done at the airport. Then she moved those imperturbable legs and faced him full front. Her thighs were perfect, with a light hazing of pubic hair shading her flesh where it was cut by her underpants. She spoke dryly: "What are you doing, settler? Taking a good old colonial peek at a naked black girl?"

She stepped out of sight but didn't shut the door. He heard quick sounds of a garment being pulled on. She reappeared in a white kikoi hemmed with silhouettes of archers chasing antelopes. She advanced toward him, her voice calm: "What's the matter, Ken? Spent too much time watching the baboons mounting each other on hot rocks?"

He broke into a hollow laugh. "I might apologize if you cut out those sarcastic remarks, starting with that stupid 'settler.'"

She looked at him coolly. "I was only half joking. Didn't you apply for residency in this country?"

"I *what* . . . ?" He gaped at her kikoi. It draped her breasts tightly and narrowly.

"You applied for residency in this country. I know it from a source in the Ministry of the Interior. I thought you did it to help with your dig permits and things . . ."

"I never applied for anything like that."

"You're on some government list . . ."

"Maybe I'm on a list to be thrown out of the country; that wouldn't surprise me these days!"

"Want to meet some American students in journalism?" she asked without transition. Ken wondered if she hadn't invented the government list to justify her teasing of him. "They're here on a cultural exchange, one man, two women. All black, of course."

"I'm sure they can amuse themselves without me."

"The guy does. He has more dates than he can handle. But the girls don't, because our boys want white girls. So they're desperate. What do you say, set . . . Sorry. Between our black boys' prejudice and your black girls' horniness, this is your chance."

"No, thanks. I prefer watching the baboons; they have interesting reproductive strategies."

He marched out of the den, emerged on the front steps, stopped and inhaled the warm evening air.

He was surprised to hear her footsteps behind him. She walked out and stood next to him. They faced the bleeding sunset sky.

"There are two things you shouldn't do these days," she said. "First, do not take any fossil stuff out of the country. Aside from the existing laws, an additional law against the pilfering of our national wealth will be passed, aimed specifically at scientific finds by foreigners. And second, do not antagonize my father.''

''I'd already figured the second, and I was fearing the first. Thanks anyway. When do you think that new law will become effective?''

''Probably later this week.''

Randall was leaving tomorrow. He could still take a few bits of fossil with him, packed in an innocuous little container, like a tobacco pouch or a tin of candies.

Yinka stared at Ken with that brown lustrous stare, whose depth he usually tried to avoid. ''You want to get back to that savanna of yours? Convince Ngili to go to the School of Diplomacy, and then you can ask Um'tu to help you. He'll find a way.''

He choked, partly because her lustrous stare made the suggestion seem simple, and almost innocent. ''How could I do that to Ngili? He's my *friend*. It's out of the question.''

''Your choice. What's so hot about that skeleton you brought back?''

''It's sexy,'' he blurted. ''Did you know that two million years ago protohumans invented orgasm? The males had more blood in them than the apes, so their erections were far more tumescent and satisfying.'' She narrowed her eyes. He was trying to shock her, but he couldn't tell if he was succeeding. ''As for their females, they developed that bottle-neck-shaped uterus, which contracted and dipped into the pool of sperm after it was deposited in their vaginas! That was how female orgasm started, and it was developed so that females could make babies with a mate of their choice. If they liked him, they came; if they didn't like him, they stayed dry, and no children resulted. That was the first time females had any choice in how they reproduced.''

''That really happened?'' she asked.

''You bet it happened. It was big progress in reproductive strategy. That's why even today women take longer to reach their orgasms than men. It's not democratic, but it's good for the future of the race.''

She smiled. They saw Ngili arriving from the terrace. "Hey, Ngili," she called to him, "did you ever hear Ken's theories on protohuman orgasm?"

Ngili walked up to Yinka and put his arm around her. "Ken's theories, like all theories, are hard to prove. But he's right that there are some indications that australopithecines initiated monogamy, and that improved their caring for their offspring, and considerably increased their population."

"Fascinating," said Yinka. "Is all that out of Ken's head?"

"Most of it," Ngili smiled rather tensely. "I only sample rocks."

"White boy, very smart fellow," Yinka said, in imitation of an African simpleton. Uncharacteristically serious, she gave Ken her lustrous eyes. "Ken?"

"What?"

"When did love come about?"

He pondered. When did attachments comparable with modern ones start to form? It was less a question of date than of stage of development. Somewhere inside that maze of positive biofeedback that made australopithecines and habilines the human race's great experimenters, sexual life improved in quality to such an extent that males started to be monogamous.

"Simplifying it, we fell in love while mating face-to-face, rather than face-to-back," he explained. "Face-to-face made it more pleasurable to have one mate than to frolic with a whole horde. Face-to-face bonded our primal human pairs, benefiting the children, for whom the monogamous parents began to forage and hunt with enormously improved success. . . ."

He trailed off. Ngili had just turned and started back toward the house.

"Fascinating," Yinka repeated. "You sure you don't want to meet those journalist girls?"

"No, thanks."

He hesitated. Then he asked Yinka to follow him to the Land Rover. He unwrapped the fragment of stone encrusted with fossil whistling thorns and showed it to her. Her eyes widened, and she breathed deeply and slowly, as she looked at the shape of the thorns, so perfectly petrified. Ken re-wrapped the fossil thorns. "I'm going to give you these. I want you to have them."

A delicate smile parted her lips. Their insides shone, crimson and carnal: "You're finally bringing me flowers, Ken?"

He laughed. "Yes, in my own way. These last a long time, and ask for very little caring."

"They're probably very valuable. Why are you giving them to me?"

"I'm buying your silence about this whole thing," he grinned. Then he became serious. "I don't know. In case Ngili does become a diplomat, and I return to Dogilani by myself, and . . . something unexpected happens to me. You'll have the proof of what we set out to investigate. A live Pliocene habitat."

She shook her head with conviction. "Nothing's going to happen to you. After he cools off, Um'tu will send an army of park rangers to Dogilani, to make sure it's safe."

"Terrific," he muttered. "Great for the wildlife, great for the habitat."

"What the hell's so special about that scrubland?" she asked with annoyance. "Why is Ngili acting like not going back there is some kind of death sentence?"

"It's a fascinating place, Yinka. I found a fabulous fossil one hour after landing there." He pointed to the bundle of petrified flowers. "And then the next morning, Ngili found these. But even more important, I think the combination of the isolation of that area and some unique weather patterns there have created an ecology that has stayed the same for more than two million years. There might be some live species there, undisturbed and unchanged since before Adam."

She glanced at the petrified flowers, then uttered a little laugh. "That's impossible. No such place exists on earth."

"Maybe. But I still have to go back and check it out."

She reflected, then spoke with that underlying anger that indicated emotion in her. "You mean, that place and its species stayed undiscovered through the last twenty years of satellite photography? You're aware, aren't you, that your intelligence agencies spy on Africa with relish? When Idi Amin ruled in Uganda, the CIA photographed every inch of Kenyan territory, under the pretext of our next-door neighbor's PLO connections . . .''

"That's a very nice patriotic speech, Yinka. As for every inch, let me tell you something. In satellite photography, the smallest resolutions available are of a few meters in actual earth size; in other words, they're not small enough to record human beings. From a hundred and fifty miles up in the sky, a human being is not even as large as half a pixel, half of a black or white dot making up the smallest contrast unit that creates a visual image. You simply cannot see humans, or animals, or even herds from a satellite, except perhaps as meaningless blurs.''

She raised her long Masai neck. "But there might be finer resolutions that are classified, don't you think? Your CIA is not going to go public with its best technology.''

"I think that's journalism, Yinka. Anyway, I've got to go back there.''

Great, go back there alone, you fool, she thought, tired of everyone's unrelenting egos—her father's, her brother's, this white American's. "Are you coming to Gwee's wedding?'' she asked with the same lack of transition. She started to laugh. "We're going to dance the up-and-down. Can you imagine the prime minister dancing the up-and-down, or Cyril Anderson?''

He laughed too, picturing Cyril dancing the up-and-down. He'd have to do it, especially if he joined the cabinet.

The up-and-down was a dance of sexual prowess performed by young Masai warriors in front of their future brides. The young men hopped in place with tall vertical leaps. The brides, their faces hidden under piles of chains, bangles, and hoops, peered under their adornments, giggling crazily, to catch glimpses of the warriors' manhoods, occasionally revealed as their kikois flew up and down.

"I'll be there," he promised. "We'll dance the up-and-down together."

She suddenly squeezed his hand. Her fingers were cool, but they sent his blood into his face. She stared at him blankly, while giving him that secret signal of interest, then she relaxed her hand in his. Ken held his breath and stroked her fingers, enjoying the feel of a feminine hand, practically forgotten.

Then she freed her hand.

Ngiamena and Anderson were walking over from the terrace. Anderson was finishing a sentence. "That's the best thing to dazzle them with, in New York and Washington." Ken guessed that he meant the fossil vault; he was preparing to take it on the road again. "After they're dazzled, I'll talk of the country and ask them straight out who's going to chip in, and how much."

"It's a good plan. I hope it works," said Ngiamena.

"It will," said Anderson, calm, Olympian. They walked in ahead of Ken and Yinka.

THE OPEN-AIR MARKET AT MUINDI MBINGU ROAD WAS LIKE a bazaar in *A Thousand and One Nights*. It sold food and spices, goats and guard dogs, pet parrots and monkeys, bamboo garden chairs, brass pots and pans, Persian rugs of doubtful value, and wedding rings of unmarked gold and silver. Ironically, the fresh-meat section was right next to a row of shacks with narrow doors covered by flapping shower curtains. Inside was a community of prostitutes, with their names advertised outside on little wooden shingles. The prostitutes were friendly and cheerful. Minimally dressed, they walked around the market to buy a cup of kahawa or shop for groceries, and usually returned to their shacks with a customer. One called herself Madonna. Another was known as No Knob Annie, because of the extra business she did by showing city folk that she had no "knob," no clitoris. Her clitoris and part of her labia had been shorn off at puberty, in some village that still practiced female circumcision, which was deemed to make women faithful in marriage. The tradition continued in rural areas, even though it had been banned by law. Annie had not become a dutiful African wife, but she had turned her loss into a little tourist attraction.

Energized by showers and a quick dinner of steak, *githeri*—a corn and beans dish—and *matoke*—a kind of Ugandan banana quiche—Ken and Ngili walked around looking for a suitcase for Randall. Ken asked Ngili what had been said over coffee on the Ngiamenas' terrace. Ngili described how his father, in an attempt to find a compromise, had pressed Ngili to accept Cyril's offer of custodianship of an itinerant fossil show. That would be a great opportunity for Ngili to meet the world's top paleontologists, and it could easily be combined with a diplomat's duties.

"But that's not the same as going back to complete our find, Ngili. That's *our find* out there, and it might be extraordinary! I know we have only a few pieces of the puzzle, but we can find the others," Ken pleaded, against the raucous din of Muindi Mbingu Road. "If you think it can help, let me talk to your father. . . ."

"No," said Ngili grimly. "It's not your place to intervene."

"Oh, for Christ's sake. Is this the time for African formality? This is important for the world."

"You don't know if it's that important. And I don't want to hurt my father."

"In what way would you hurt him?" From Ngili's tightened features, Ken guessed that he would not get a straight answer. He wondered if Jakub feared losing his status with the country's fickle, unpredictable president. That would explain his show of patriotic dutifulness, but . . . Jakub was doing it at his son's expense.

Ken thought there was already a note of self-betrayal in Ngili's voice. Frustrated, but above all insecure about continuing that big undertaking alone, he snapped, "You don't want to hurt your father? He has no problem hurting you."

Ngili snapped back, "What do you know? What the hell do you *really know* about African fathers and sons?"

He marched off dramatically, then stopped by a pile of travel articles. He asked haughtily in Swahili to be shown some suitcases, chose one, then bargained hard. Ken pulled out a roll of bills to pay half the price. Ngili pushed Ken's hand away, counted the whole price out of his own wallet, then grabbed the suitcase.

"Listen," he said tensely, leading the way out of the market, "my sister likes you. Did you encourage her?"

"What?" Ken started laughing. The notion of encouraging Yinka was comical; she would do what she wanted to do without any prodding. He was tempted to say yes, but he realized that in his present state Ngili could not take any jokes.

"I never made a pass at her, if that's what you mean," he said stiffly.

"That's probably why she likes you."

"She doesn't, Ngili, not the way you think," he said appeasingly, and remembered the soft but strong feel of her fingers against his palm, which was hardened by years of using rock hammers.

"I saw it. Even in the car, the way she kept turning to you and giving you those looks. Do not encourage her from now on. All right?"

"She was venting in the car, about the political situation. Yinka's a big girl, she can take care of herself."

"She's an African girl, and you're a white American," ruled Ngili severely. "Out here, we take care of our sisters. You and I are different, we're men and we share something—we share the past. But you and she share nothing. You understand?"

He made it to the parked Land Rover ahead of Ken, and stamped his feet impatiently.

Ken had stopped by a square enclosure of empty cardboard boxes printed with brand names of computers and TV sets: IBM, Apple, Sony. GOD'S GARDEN OF PEACE—PLEASE HELP read a sign hand-painted over the brand names. Inside that enclosure, emaciated, covered in pustules, an AIDS-stricken family was dying quietly. There were holes in the ramparts of cardboard. Passersby pushed offerings of a few shillings into the holes. The coins clinked on the other side into tin cans affixed to the walls.

Ken had not stopped for effect. He still held his rejected share of the price of Randall's suitcase. He saw the garden of peace and death, and felt as if a mute call was passing between the money in his hand and those collection holes, dark and sad, like eyeless sockets. He rolled the bills into one wad, pushed it into one of the holes. A whoop of excitement rose behind the wall, and an unseen victim snatched the unusually large gift.

"Ahsante, ahsante sana," said a man's hoarse voice from inside. "Thank you very much." A woman laughed in the garden of peace, a young laugh.

By the Land Rover, Ngili called for Ken to hurry up. I'm coming, you big baby, Ken thought angrily. He climbed into the car, determined to drive to Randall's in silence, but as he plunged the key into the ignition, he couldn't help himself.

"Just what the hell did you mean, putting me on notice like that?" he raged back at Ngili. "As your friend, do you think I would ever insult your sister? And how exactly are you taking care of her, by treating her like your property? By denying her the freedom to like me, or anyone else?"

"Spare me that song, freedom," scoffed Ngili, with a mean twist to his features. "It's a great American hit, but it doesn't play so well here. I've been wanting to tell you this for a while, Ken. You're naive, and presumptuous."

"And you are spoiled, and don't know your own powers."

Ngili did not answer. Ken drove out of the market. Stopping at a cracked traffic light, he glanced at his watch. Theo had developed the pictures by now. He decided to head for the photo shop. He stared west, above the street's confusion.

Dogilani lay straight toward the twilight's lingering gleam. The past. The past was better, cleaner. The past had room in it for everyone.

I N THE SAVANNA, THE HOMINID BOY WALKED UP A PATH
that ran between rocks and squatted by a clutch of black
stones he had hidden in a clump of oat grass. He grabbed
one more stone and stuck it inside his left armpit, then let
his arm hang over it, as if he were hiding it in a pocket.

This was his territory, where he had stored stones in places
that were well engraved on his mind. They were there, waiting for him whenever he needed them. No predator would
disturb them nor would any predator connect them with the
boy; the only time that connection was made was while the
predator was getting a number of stones thrown at it, one
after another. This would have an intimidating effect on any
beast, and by the time it wore off, the thrower was already
up in a tree, or climbing a rock.

The boy's stones were a deep black, completely unlike the
surrounding yellowish rock outcrops. When he had first settled in this area, he had found many of these stones, lying
in the open or hidden in the grass. Over the following months
of making himself at home, he had gathered them and then
placed them along his pathways and by his ambush sites.
Now he handled them daily, throwing them at his prey and
gathering them after the prey was down, dropping them back
onto their little piles, and picking them up again. At night,
he grabbed one in his hand before he went to sleep, and when

he woke up, his fingers were still clutched around it.

He stepped into the clearing between the rocks where the dream creatures had examined his footprints. They had moved about, crouched to look at his footprints, then picked up his stones and examined them, not by leaning down to sniff at them but by lifting them and holding them in front of their eyes. *They had not sniffed at anything.* They had just touched, picked up, and looked.

He stopped, and remembered what the creatures looked like.

Their (faces). The (expression) on their faces.

He had no name for it, but he knew that they had been amazed by what they were seeing. This was not an alien emotion to him; however, he had been deeply struck by how much of it the creatures had displayed. They had kept blinking in utter puzzlement, while their lips made sounds like the beaks of turaco birds.

His world was full of novelty, but he had never before been as utterly dumbfounded as he had been by the alien creatures' visit and what they had left behind. He squatted by the creatures' footprints, which were oval and without toe marks. He might not even have recognized them as footprints except that he'd seen the creatures walking among the rocks.

He clutched his stones harder. He was tense and fearful, almost expecting a punishment, as he shuffled his bare feet over the alien footprints.

Nothing happened.

He erased them completely, then destroyed his own footprints by rounding the ball of his right foot over them, breaking their contours. Then he reached inside another clutch of stones and brought out the cigarette lighter. He had stored it there earlier. He was fascinated by it, even though after he'd tried throwing it, he'd decided that it had very poor hunting value.

He had dropped it on a sunlit stone ledge. Not much later, he picked it up again, burned his fingers, dropped it by a bush and circled around it, angry that the alien visitor had played a trick on him. He had torn a leaf and used it to pick the treasure up again, feeling its warmth through the leafy tissue.

Now, holding the strange stone, he could not tell how much of this had been a dream, and when exactly it had started and ended. The day before, when the duikers had unexpectedly charged into the rocks, he had barely had time to grab one hunting stone before the big buck in front galloped right toward him. The boy had hit the buck and stopped the charge. The buck had turned around, leading the herd back out of the rocks. The hunting stone had fallen on a clump of weed trampled by the herd.

A brief time had passed until the creature had appeared with the buck on its shoulders. The creature's head looked top-heavy, while its face reminded the boy of a lion's because of its brown eyes, pink muzzle, and short brown mane. Lion-face.

The creature had come into the space between the rocks, barely an arm's reach from a green bush of tanglehead thorns loaded with ripe berries. The creature had stopped by the bush, looking toweringly tall, taller than any creature the boy had seen, other than an elephant or giraffe.

The creature had dropped the dead buck, picked up the hunting stone, looked at it, and noticed the fresh blood on it. All this time, the boy had crouched behind the tanglehead bush. The creature had looked closely at the bush, but had not noticed two berries that were alive with a tremor—the boy's eyes.

The boy remembered that the creature carried other things, but he hadn't paid much attention to them because he had been so fascinated with lion-face and how he looked and moved. Lion-face had not sniffed at anything. He had held himself up on his hind legs at all times, even when the duiker's body was on his shoulders, and walked erect, sometimes fast, sometimes slow, the same way the boy did.

The creature walked, and stood, and carried things just like the boy did.

The boy had no difficulty remembering the unknown man with the duiker on his shoulders. He had been too deeply struck by that unusually alien yet bafflingly familiar stance. To remember the man he had only to give in to the urge of remembering. He had tried to keep down that urge, to suppress what it meant, because . . . *the boy had never met someone else that walked like him, or stood erect like him, or did anything else like him. There had never been someone else like him. Or had there?*

He gave himself a task. He would remember something utterly familiar, something that evoked his life exactly as it had been before the creatures came. He decided to focus on the place where he slept.

He "thought" of the little trove of personal belongings he'd had for some time. He saw his trove on the screen of his memory. A baby warthog's tooth, long, sharp, with a spiked tip. He liked to play with it, to scratch his skin with it, and to draw meaningless patterns with it on the dust gathered in the kopje's crevices. He also kept several stones by him as faithful guardians when he slept.

He had a gray vulture's feather, long, streaked with black and ending in black ruffles. It was one of the lightest objects he had ever handled. And he had a bone that was white and dry and utterly clean of tissue. He did not remember how he had come across that bone. Now he added the strange shiny stone to his treasures.

He began scaling the rocks, feeling the sun on the top of his head, his chest pulling in lungfuls of dry warm air. He stepped slowly, carrying his throwing stones almost loosely. Most of the time, he was higher than all the other beings of the savanna, except the birds. From high up in a tree, or from atop his rocky ramparts, he could tell where the wild's raiders and killers were and whether they were approaching, and what kind of mood they were in. Being higher, like standing upright, were his basic survival principles. Survival was so well imprinted in his brain and coordinated with his actions that he was almost never caught short.

The big killers would love to catch and disembowel such a soft being, paying no attention to his dying cries. His skin was thin and his flesh easy to get to. He didn't have a tough hide covering his body's lean and nutritious muscles and tissues. His bones were light, gracile, delicious to chew on. As for personal weapons, he had no claws, and his teeth were insignificant.

His best weapon was his mind. At the evolutionary stage of five hundred cubic centimeters, it had already evolved the incredible function of strategy and planning.

THE CLOSER HE GOT TO THE PALISADE'S TOP THE MORE aware he became of the change in the light, as the sun descended. From this height, subtle changes in the colors, in the temperature, even in the taste of the air, became obvious long before they were felt by the creatures roaming lower down. A scent of humidity seeped down from the crest of the Mau, where a mist that was invisible earlier was turning into a crown of clouds.

The clouds were holding on to a rainfall that might make it to the ground if the night got cold enough.

It was still full daylight, but the boy could smell the night coming on.

In the grasslands, the terrain had started changing. The shadows stretched, the dents in the ground deepened. The foliage and flowers acquired a sharpness of tone they had lacked under the flat shine of the sun. Soon the sun would die as it did every evening, letting the savanna slip into the anxious limbo of dusk. Dusk sounded the waking call for nocturnal animals, and the invitation for diurnals to return to their holes, burrows, and nests. Some would survive the night, others would not.

Close to the top of the rocks, the boy hung his head back, and gave the sky a good thorough scan. The air seemed to be made of liquid gold, a golden lake swallowing the sun's fiery ball. The griffon vulture he had seen before wheeled slowly above him, letting itself drift on high currents, turning, letting itself drift off again. Lower down, two black kites flew in wide orbits, turning their heads to stare fixedly at the ground from one eye, then from the other.

As usual, the birds of prey were on constant watch for the movements of land predators. When they spotted a chase, the birds would dive, the wind whistling shrilly through their plumage, sometimes anticipating the place of the kill with amazing accuracy. By the time lions or hyenas brought a wildebeest down in the scrub, in a brief final combat that uprooted bushes and made the dust fly, the birds would be already on the ground, ready to join the feeding. By watching the sky and the brush, the boy could read signs that other creatures didn't notice.

He sauntered up onto a flat ridge lying beneath the top boulder and heard grunts and squeals. His heart started drumming inside his chest, while his inner organs tightened almost as dramatically as they had done before reaching the plane's tracks.

A troop of baboons was occupying his ridge.

He trembled, feeling in his bones a day that had already had its share of danger. He had been mauled by baboons before—one deep scar on his back was from a large male that had caught him in open scrubland several rainy seasons back, and had nearly killed him. Since then, the boy had learned to avoid them. It did not do much good to stone them because baboons always moved in hordes more numerous than his stones.

He was shocked to see them. Baboons usually hunted small game, but the only thing they'd find on these rocks were a few lizards. But this troop's dominant male was tearing up a piece of meat with his doglike muzzle. Three subordinate males sat by on their rears, watching their leader with such attention that their muzzles moved in tune with his as he bit down repeatedly.

The big baboon was trying to crack the skull of a duiker and get to the brains. Immediately, the boy's nostrils were hit by a pleasant stench of decomposition. The duiker was a kill he'd made before the creatures' visit. The baboons had smelled it and followed its odor to a crack in the rocks where the boy had been keeping his larder.

The boy did not react immediately; the invasion of his

habitat was too unexpected. He stood totally visible and unprotected, watching the monkeys stuff little pieces of meat
in their mouths, menacingly hissing at each other and slapping off a thick cloud of flies. The troop was made up of
adult males and females, and of weaned youngsters, and infants, all restless because the older adults were determined
to keep the carcass to themselves. The females and the
youngsters made this marauding troop even more aggressive.
With their fearsome canines bared to their gums, the big
males would charge any intruder except a leopard or lion. If
they saw the boy, they would kill him even before the females could load the children protectively in their arms and
on their backs.

But, luckily, for the moment they were busy, some eating,
some watching those who ate.

The only weapon the boy had against a troop of baboons
was to flee.

He felt the rock behind him with his foot, and found it
flat and continuous. He stepped backward, eyes darting to
see if any monkey had spotted him. He finally turned, ready
to race down the rocks.

He stopped. His retreat had been cut off by two large
males hurrying up from a lower ledge, coming straight at
him. The leading one clambered strangely on three legs, one
hand clutching something glaringly white. His eyes, shaped
like shiny black seeds, seemed to light up on seeing the boy.
Farther down, more baboons scrambled about the rocks, their
tails held up in a curl, the tips hanging away from their bodies, as if they were always trying to excrete.

Terrified, the boy opened his mouth and his larynx started,
at its lowest point, that boiling, bubbling "rrr" sound. He
knew he would die. In a few instants, they would be eating
him along with the rotting duiker. In a few hours, the birds
would pick his bones, and ultimately he would be scattered
all over the savanna, some part of him dropped off by a bird,
another dragged off by a rodent, others left to dry where he
had been eaten, until the next rains would wash him into the
nameless organic litter of a past season.

He groped desperately for a way to survive. The first male bared his teeth, one hand still holding a white arm bone. The baboons had found and raided his sleeping place.

That produced a spark inside him. He grabbed the monkey by its middle just as it hopped to the same level with him. He whirled the snarling animal so hard that it dropped the bone; then the boy flung the baboon from his hands, whacking its skull against a rock. Blood gushed and brains foamed out of the split skull. Before the baboon could live its last spasms, the boy had already picked it up again, and flung it at the others like a club. The monkey's body mowed down its kin. The boy's growling "rrr" rose to a pitched howl. He clutched the dead monkey again, and rammed the dominant male, while the male's jaws snapped and his fangs gored the furry hulk and finally cut into the boy's right arm.

But the boy did not stop his blows, or his howling. As he rammed and hit, the hulk in his clenched hands became more and more shapeless and bloodied, and the male baboons kept dropping before him. All this while, the females squealed, calling the males into retreat. A baboon finally jumped on the boy's back, but he threw himself backward against the rocks' top boulder, first feeling teeth and claws enter his back, then feeling the baboon's body being crushed and finally hanging limp. He threw off the dead body, turned and sank his short teeth into the neck convulsed by death.

The glint of his teeth on the dying neck pushed the other baboons away, screaming and spitting.

He stood between the monkeys he had killed, on the clearing rocks, alive.

HE HAD NEVER KILLED ANYTHING AS BIG AS THE BABOONS, and never more than one at a time. In fact, he had always turned and slunk away from a horde of hostile baboons, letting them enjoy their power. But never before had his lair been invaded. His throat was raw.

He did not know the angry being that had come out of him, and killed, but it felt reassuring, frighteningly reassuring that he could summon him up, and ask for his help again.

He looked around, for once knowing without doubt that he was out of the dream. He spotted the white arm bone stolen from his lair. He picked it up but let it drop again, as if the tie between himself and that familiar object had been broken. He looked for the odd shiny stone which he had brought with him out of the dream, but could not find it. This time, it was gone for good.

He looked for his hunting stones, but could not find them either. They had been lost in the fight's blinding storm of blows, jumps, and charges.

The rocks were littered with the bodies of the dead monkeys, smeared with blood that had spurted wildly out of one baboon's cracked skull, and fouled by excrement some of the juveniles had loosed while watching the boy's unleashed fury.

He walked to a lower layer of rocks and bent so he could enter the crack where he had been sleeping. As he did, he stepped on a fresh plot of excrement. He adjusted his eyes to see the narrow space. Not only was his personal trove gone, but his bed of dried leaves had been kicked and trampled. His nest was a reeking hole of monkey hairs, feces, and wet stains from urine and drool.

He crawled out backward and cleaned his feet by wiping them repeatedly on a flat piece of rock. Then he climbed back to the site of the battle, where birds were already circling above the dead monkeys. A dry rush of anger made him kick the bodies until they tumbled off the rocks' edge. Instants later, two columns of descending birds pointed to the spot where they had settled among the lower bushes.

He lay down, beginning to feel pain in his fresh wounds.

The sun was setting.

The moon rose.

He was lying flat on the top ledge, by the big boulder, sleepless.

Thin plumes of cloud tore from the crest of the Mau and sailed slowly east, like wild cotton fluff breaking and spinning off. To the hominid boy's eyes, they looked like hunched silhouettes, exiting that forested crest and beginning to walk, scared and undecided, across the sky's dark savanna.

The boy closed his eyes and the light-skinned creature came back into his memory in such vivid detail that the boy started shaking again, fearing and yet wishing that he could open his eyes and find the creature next to him, lit by the moon, lowering his strange face over the boy's own.

The boy breathed deeply. In his mind, he stared at the imagined creature, and the creature stared back. For a good spell of time, they sized each other up.

Then the boy opened his eyes.

He was alone, but his mind was not. His mind raised a yearning about that stranger. And that yearning reached toward the moon above, and then toward the savanna's distant edges.

A beam of memory went out of the narrow braincase of the hominid boy, across the world he knew, searching for that unknown man.

"A MAZING. THE FOSSIL'S SO COMPLETE, IT'S AMAZ-
ing." Randall Phillips held a power drill, guiding it
through the outer layers of the breccia in a zigzag pattern.
He stopped, pulled off his eye goggles, and inhaled the air
heated by the drill's fight with the two-million-year-old na-
ture-made concrete.

They worked on a plain kitchen table that was old and
chipped and limping on one leg. Marcia Phillips, a large,
morose woman with an almost faded American accent, had
washed the table with soap and water before Ken and Ngili
had gotten there, as a minimal precaution against contami-
nation. Randall had moved the table into the Phillips's empty
garage, where the floor was marked with black drippings of
crankcase oil and smudges from tires. The Phillipses had
already sold their cars and would buy new ones in California.

"This is the most complete australopithecine skeleton ever
found, which is enough to put you two on the map. How
much of Lucy's skeleton was dug up, forty percent?" Ken's
heart beat fast. Randall was comparing their find with that
world-renowned discovery. "This one's seventy percent intact, easy."

In 1974 at Hadar in Ethiopia, Don Johanson of Berkeley
had found an ape-woman whose anatomy proved that she
had walked erect over three million years before the current

146

era. But Lucy's feet had not been found; the proof that she had walked erect rested on the structure of a hip joint. The only complete piece of Lucy's head was her lower jaw.

The feet of Ken's fossil were still encased in breccia. But Randall was already convinced that she (the broad pelvis suggested a woman) had stood erect. "Look at this knee joint!" he said. "Her leg bones locked into each other at the knee like tent poles!"

Ken turned toward Ngili and they tensely exchanged a glowing look.

The knee joint was practically a classroom demonstration of how a human's legs, unlike a gorilla's or a chimp's, stood vertically like pillars supporting the rest of the body, and how they helped keep the body in balance. A human's strongly developed buttock muscle, the gluteus maximus, helped keep the spine straight, and propelled the body forward in its wide human strides. Together, the pelvis and knee showed that this female was fully adapted to verticality. Gorillas and chimps, although they walked occasionally, had no buttocks to speak of to help them balance their spines and upper bodies, and their knees did not lock. When they stood up, they did so with bent knees. When they walked on two legs, their torsos hung forward in an uncomfortable crouching stance, a position that was tiring and soon abandoned.

Ken stroked the leg bones with his glance, seeing in his mind the live female. Standing. Stepping. Clumsy and yet graceful. He looked at her teeth, flattened from eating seeds, grass, and tubers. The lips over them would have been fleshy and fresh, breathing out a scent of vegetal diet.

"You with us, Ken?" asked Randall sarcastically. "You look like this damsel's getting you wet in the pants. Hammer!" he blurted an order.

Ken stepped forward with a rock hammer. He inserted its pointed end at regular intervals along the drill's trail, then turned the hammer upward and sideways, tearing off large shards of breccia plaque.

"Chisel! Needle!" Randall kept ordering, like a surgeon asking for scalpels and clamps.

Ken and Ngili hurried with the tools, removing debris that had stubbornly fused to the bone. The bone and the debris were often so similar in color that only Randall's experienced eye could identify where the debris stopped and the fossil started. Ken did some minute cleaning by removing atoms of dirt with a mounted needle, while Ngili dipped the cleaned bone pieces into a bucket that contained a weak solution of soda.

The process was slow, and incredibly straining. The cleaning had to be done with pinpoint accuracy, like laser surgery.

Only a tiny piece of the lower jaw was missing from the skull. Shoulders, arms, hands, rib cage, and spine were all there, at least 70 percent complete. The left ribs were crushed in, as if the body had been struck with a giant mallet. The right hip joint and thighbone were intact, but the right lower leg bones, the tibia and fibula, were broken in many small pieces. The left thighbone was broken in three segments. Below the knee, the left leg looked as if it had been crushed by the same deadly pressure first noticed in the ribs. Still, most of those bones could be easily reassembled. Which meant that the ancient lady was still intact.

"She looks like she's been trampled to death by a proto-rhinoceros or a deinotherium," said Ken.

"It's more likely that it happened after her death," said Ngili. "The terrain weighing on top of her settled and crushed some of her left side."

"I suppose you're right," Ken told Ngili.

"I think we'll have trouble with the feet," said Randall. "The tibias are frittering above the ankles."

Ken felt that his heart had been pounding nonstop since they had started working. "Let's hurry and find out the state of the feet," he urged. He could not imagine their luck running out, but that might happen, and the definite proof of bipedalism was still in the feet.

"Hold on," answered Randall. "Now, this pelvic girdle's definitely so broad, I'd say this ancient Frau already had children. She's beautiful, so generous and basic. You lucky punks. Ken, d'you think your photo man finished developing your pictures?''

He'd already asked that several times.

Ken shrugged in frustration. On the way over, he and Ngili had stopped at the photo shop only to find that Theo had not finished the job. "Sorry, Ken, those East Indians came back to have some farewell shots enlarged. Give me the number you'll be at. I'll call you when yours are ready.''

Ken had given him Randall's number. Now it was past nine, and Theo had not called yet. Ken had tried his number, twice. Both times it was busy.

"I'll call him again in a few minutes.''

"Hammer,'' Randall ordered again.

THE PHILLIPS HOUSE WAS UP FOR SALE BUT HAD FETCHED no offers. It stood in an area that was once prized but was now entirely invaded by low-income tandooris, the kind that prayed at the Hindu temple and left their shoes outside their doors. The African upwardly mobiles would not settle among this minority, even though they had lived in the land for over three hundred years. For over a year, the tandooris had been repeatedly hit with new regulations against their businesses. So they were leaving, in a firm constant flow.

Randall had dug up all the paleo gear he had not shipped off to Davis, California, but his brushes were packed. With the drilling over except for the feet, he ran next door to borrow a few brushes from a neighbor who painted restaurant signs—tandoori, of course, both he and the restaurants. In his absence, Randall's wife, Marcia, helped the two ex-students wash the table again. "It's a shame, what's happening to the East Indians,'' she said. "They built this country. Even more than the English.''

Ngili chuckled coldly. "Thanks, Marcia. You left us blacks out altogether. Like in the time of the color bar.''

"Take a look at your own prejudice,'' Marcia retorted with unexpected hostility. "Ride a local train and see how many stations haven't even replaced their old rest-room signs for 'Europeans' and 'coloreds.' If that's the message your government gives to your own people, why should I be so politically correct?''

Her face was flushed. Ken smelled a pickled odor on her body from long-term imbibation with whiskey. Marcia was a drinker; everyone who knew the Phillipses knew that. Their marriage was lasting out of inertia. Ngili clenched his teeth and stepped up to a yellowed sofa loaded with discarded objects, including an old radio. He turned on the radio. A familiar hoarse voice came out, making Ngili freeze in surprise.

"We are like a pride of lions," said Jakub Ngiamena's voice. "In these days when the world heaps judgment on our nation, we must remember that we are not like other nations. Our old lions are still the pride's guarantee of leadership and prosperity. I advise our youth to follow our government, and our president. . . .''

Another voice interjected, young and jarringly contemporary. "You are listening to Jakub Ngiamena, superintendent of the game reserves and a member of the cabinet. Mr. Ngiamena, your style is particularly indebted to Masai poetry. . . .''

Randall reentered the garage just then, carrying a clump of brushes. "Hey, hey," he quipped, "your old man's not given to such endorsements. What's going on, Ngili?''

"Nothing's going on! As a member of the government, my father's supporting the government—what's so unusual about that?'' Ngili lunged at the radio and in turning it off slammed it against the threadbare back of the old sofa.

"So what's happening next?'' asked Randall. "It smells like martial law to me, maybe even a dissolving of the parliament.''

"What d'you care? You're leaving tomorrow.''

Ngili's English had lost its Cambridge perfection. His voice was dull, its vowels reduced to a basic aah, like a true African's. Tamarrah.

Randall put his hand on Ngili's shoulder. "I care about my students. And I'm sorry for your father to be mixed up in this; he's a decent guy." He grabbed his eye goggles. "All right. Ken, Ngili, ready? Let's take off her socks."

The thin smoke from the drill tip started tickling their nostrils again. A dark rain of breccia chips fell on the garage floor.

With every push of the drill and chip of the hammer, what remained of the initial slab grew smaller. Ken wondered if the feeling he had resembled a sculptor's elation as his chisel freed from amorphous marble the finite form of a statue. No. It was more like a sexual fulfillment. What he had lusted to see, he was finally seeing. Sick, Yinka would say. He pictured her in the room, witnessing his obsession, and grinned. That's right, Yinka. A woman like the one in the breccia was worth pursuing.

Suddenly, the last breccia around the right foot disintegrated in a cloud of grayish dust. When the dust scattered, they saw the foot bones. Or what was left of them.

They had been completely broken, mashed into bits by the pressure of the protowoman's anonymous grave. Even though he was sullen, Ngili looked up at Ken with genuine sympathy.

Ken rushed to hold Randall's hand back. "Stop that drill—it's blasting the foot into dust!"

"It's already dust!" Randall almost yelled, as disappointed as his ex-student. "You think you can do better with the hammer? Go on!" He turned off the drill, stepped back, and crossed his arms.

Shaking, feeling as if the whole significance of the find was disappearing before his eyes, Ken bent down with rock hammer and needle over what was left of the breccia: one narrow slab, encasing the other foot. Hands loaded with his tools, he shook his head to help clear his mind and focus his eyes, then scraped at the breccia, barely breathing.

Under a hard outer layer, the breccia became so frail that it started pulverizing as soon as he touched it.

He pried deeper, his heart pounding slowly, feeling an ugly premonition. He opened the crackling cocoon, and it collapsed in upon itself.

In the silence of the garage, there was a clucking sound, made by Randall's tongue against his upper teeth.

Then Randall moved in with mature energy, like a surgeon restoring confidence to a patient after an amputation. "All right, all right. What have we here? The Pliocene Aphrodite without feet? No big deal, she's still Aphrodite. Most of those wonderful statues were unearthed without a nose, and often without a head. Ken, Ngili. Yours is still one of the most intact australopithecines yet discovered. Look at this, for instance." He lifted the hip joint, cleaned up earlier, touched lightly several uneven crests inside the joint. "This is the ligamentum teres that keeps the hip together. Fossilized. Petrified. Human parts that are not bones hardly ever make it to petrification. We can base some incredible computer projections on this ligament alone. We can reconstruct the functioning of this with such precision"—he moved the joined pelvis and hip bone—"that we'll be able to determine the mass of her ligaments and muscles, the length of her stride, even her age, as precisely as by analyzing her teeth!"

He stopped talking and tried to assess the mood of his students. "Don't be so downcast. On what you have here, we can start explaining a lot of evolutionary mysteries. We can start glimpsing why man got up and stayed up, which is the biggest evolutionary why."

"We can't really," said Ken. "Not without the feet."

"So why didn't you bring the feet too, you sloppy cowboys?" Randall tried a lame joke. "Come on, you'll go back there and dig some more, and you'll find some intact feet. Meanwhile, I'll still take this to California and date it. Come on, it's too late for me to probe into the forming of humanness, but not for you two," Randall concluded, with the latent bitterness that Ken had detected on the phone.

"Are you going to take the ligament part to California?" asked Ken.

"Absolutely. I'll tie it around my neck if I have to, to pass it through customs." He slapped Ken's shoulder. "Hey, I'm disappointed too, and you know what a foot fetishist I am."

Ken turned to Ngili. "You should go call your father."

Ngili stared back blankly. Ken urged, softly but clearly. "Go call him, Ngili. No matter what you and I decide, resolve it with your father, and you'll see how much better you'll feel."

Ngili hesitated, then spun around and hurried out of the garage, toward the house.

"Now, while he's not here, let's decide how much of this wench I take with me, and how much I leave to the Kenyan government," said Randall. Ken had a shocked look on his face. "Don't stare like that. Fossils are Kenyan property, and you know Ngili would do anything to get back into his father's good graces. That's as good as losing the find to the current political crisis."

Ken felt a jab in his chest. Randall had voiced his own fear. It was ugly, and he fought it. "You're acting paranoid, Randall. Ngili's a scientist."

"We're all scientists till it comes to the crunch. It was nice of you to tell him to call his old man, but it wasn't selfless. If they make peace, you'll go back to Dogilani very comfortably." Ken felt himself blush; Randall was right. Ken did care about Ngili, yet his advice was not selfless, at least not entirely. "By the way, you should appoint me scientific coordinator of the project. That way, if something happens to you, I can raise some international ruckus to protect you and the fossil."

Ken pondered. Randall was right. But he was promoting himself so unambiguously. And yet, how could Ken protest?

"Fine," he said, fighting an awareness of his political skills which was novel, and not that pleasant.

"Thank you," said Randall. "You made the right decision. Ngili should ask his father to store the rest of the fossil and to see that I get no trouble at the airport tomorrow, when I'll walk through customs with my grumpy wife and squabbling kids, and a Pliocene skull and pelvis." Ken was pacing uneasily. "What's the matter?"

"You've become cynical, Randall. I don't like that."

"I don't either, if that makes you feel better. In time, it happens to everyone. Now, Ken . . ."

"What?"

"Those footprints you saw at Dogilani . . . Your pilot, Hendrijks, did he say that he had seen that kind of footprint there before?"

"He did. But who knows, he's a lying old drunk."

"I'd get hold of him if I were you and try to find out what he saw." Randall paused, seeming unusually preoccupied. Then he pointed to the bones. "Ken, what if this is just a subfossil?"

"A *what*?"

"A partially mineralized skeleton, but one that's really quite recent. Under ten thousand years old." Ten thousand years was the threshold that separated fossils from subfossils.

"Randall! Who's got the Dubois syndrome now?"

Randall paced agitatedly. Now they were both pacing. "Ken, this skeleton's so whole, it's almost bizarre. Even without the feet, it's seventy, perhaps seventy-five percent intact. I don't know how the hell it went through burial and petrification and uplift and fracturing and erosion and still remained so undamaged."

Randall was describing the cycles of a fossil's movement through the earth's strata. Those cycles had buried it deep, then jolted it upward, then sunk it again, then disturbed it again, rupturing its bed through earthquakes or spells of volcanic activity. Time had submitted that perishable material, a human skeleton, to the most incredible wear and tear. Not for just a few years, but for millions of years. Even with minerals invading the bones' pores and turning them gradually into stones, it was amazing that the woman's remains had not lost their shape and appearance, becoming completely unidentifiable shards of rock.

Ken grinned, enjoying the find's uniqueness again. "Geologically, it's possible, Randall. All those cycles were minimal at Dogilani. As the habitat remained unchanged, so did its stratigraphy. You should come out there, Randall. It's like the beginning of the world. Live Pliocene . . ."

"How big would you say that plain is?"

"Some five thousand square miles."

"A band of African bushmen needs only four hundred square miles for a stable home range," Randall reflected aloud. "And they roam more than any other nomadic tribe in Africa. On the other hand, a horde of baboons needs under twenty square miles, and a gorilla family under ten. That means . . ."

Randall seemed to be talking only to himself, as he almost whispered. "That means that there's more than enough space there to sustain an ancient population. A population bred by mommies like this one. Two curves of high improbability— the survival of such a population and your finding it—may have intersected three days ago, when you landed in that spot. We'll get a strong clue if that's so when I get to Davis and measure the age of this fossil."

Ken felt the need to glance around. Dusty spaces, a broken tool closet. The discarded sofa, the old radio. A coiled-up garden hose, a lawn mower. He glanced up. Minuscule bugs had found their way inside the two naked lightbulbs hanging under the ceiling. Fried by the electric blaze, they lay now on the glass bubbles' bottoms, as black organic sediment heated and reheated by the incandescent wires.

Reality was holding, even though Randall's words were as amazing as the turnaround in his thoughts, from skepticism to wild speculation.

"Ken. Go get those pictures."

"Right. I'll call Theo again. He's got to be done with them by now."

Ken hurried out of the garage. He crossed a narrow backyard, entered the kitchen, saw Ngili sitting on a bare counter, talking into the kitchen phone set. To his father, no doubt. Ngili looked fairly relaxed, and waved briefly at Ken.

Ken felt that headache again. He entered a cluttered master bedroom and stopped; snoring lightly, Marcia lay on the bed in her clothes, next to an open and partially filled suitcase. The phone was on the night table, and there was a half-filled glass of whiskey by it.

Ken tiptoed over, picked up the phone, dialed Theo's number.

Still busy.

A dry heat ignited his cheeks. Had something happened at Theo's shop? A fire, a break-in, a raid by the brutal and corrupt Nairobi police?

He decided to drive over to Theo's.

R ANDALL'S WORDS ABOUT THE SIZE OF DOGILANI AND the possibility that it could sustain an ancient breed had made Ken surreally excited. He drove his Land Rover sweating, one instant thinking he was insane, the next believing that he was on the edge of an unparalleled revelation about mankind.

If there was a hominid breed out there, that meant that there was more than one human species alive on earth.

There was more than one human species alive on earth. . . .

He gasped. Whether that species was left over from an earlier stage, or whether it was an offshoot into a divergent new stage, it meant that mankind *was still evolving*.

Ken slammed on the brakes, almost hitting the car ahead. Now was not the time for an accident. He rolled past the last East Indian block, with groups of boys in white shirts and dark slacks lolling on the sidewalks, stopping to chat with girls who peered out of latticed windows, protected by the looming shadows of their mothers.

When he reached the African side, the scene changed drastically. Despite the late hour, nearly naked kids still chased each other on the sidewalks, and the bars and restaurants were open and blaring music. Traffic was chaotic, with teenagers cruising by, yelling at each other from dented cars while they openly swilled beers. A drive-in movie screen projected its giant faces into the sky, above the low roofs.

Suddenly all the power in the street went out. The street-lights, the apartment windows and doorways vanished as if a main switch had been flicked off. Only the crawling head-lights of cars remained, under a tatter of moon.

A pickup truck hit Ken's back bumper, but he decided to ignore it. He sped off, praying that the power cut had nothing to do with the political situation. Suddenly, ahead of him, the sky seemed to be cracked in half by a giant reflector's beam springing upward, drowning the moon's yellow glow.

The beam completely mesmerized the cruising teenagers. Repeated thuds were heard, from cars crashing into each other. Ahead of Ken, the traffic froze. Theo's shop was only two blocks away. Ken decided to park his car and continue on foot.

Forcing his front wheels onto the sidewalk, he pulled tightly between two trees and locked the steering wheel, hoping that the tightness of the spot would lessen the risk of the Land Rover being stolen. He jumped out, then jumped back in. He punched open the glove compartment, took out the Walther pistol, and slipped it into his belt. He jumped out again.

Immediately he saw another driver, an African, pull his car, a mangled Toyota, onto the sidewalk just a few feet down and step out. Ken gave him a grin of comradeship in distress. The man, tall, in a plain shirt of military cut, stared back and pointed his finger, as if to say that he had wanted Ken's parking spot. Then he vanished among the stalled traffic.

Ken hurried ahead on the sidewalk. He trampled over the white sudsy foam spilled by a family's washing, avoided clothes hung to dry on a tree, and received in his face a glare of light so enormous that he felt he was being X-rayed from top to toe, along with the whole street.

It was that same giant spotlight, beaming from somewhere close. Its angle had been tilted to sweep horizontally. Ken was now right behind the mall containing Theo's shop. The back stairway leading to it started at the edge of a narrow parking lot. Several pipits were digging inside a garbage bin. Ken paced swiftly to the stairs and sprinted up. He made it to the second-floor concourse, stopped to breathe, and was X-rayed again by that giant bluish light.

Blinking, he peered down. In front of the mall, an army truck idled with that giant reflector light mounted on its flat-bed. Three soldiers hung from the reflector's handles, using their weight to alter its angle. Next to the truck was a tank, whose commander stood halfway out of the hatch, giving orders to the soldiers manning the reflector. The reflector slowly swept the apartment fronts, courtyards, and shops. Other armed soldiers laughed and prowled the street. The faces of African men and women began to emerge out of the darkness of windows and doorways. In Swahili, the tank's commander told them that they had nothing to fear.

As more faces inched out of the darkness, the bluish glow of the reflector gave their skins a strange, almost aquamarine color. The reflector stopped on the glass front of a bar. Several young women in miniskirts and high heels stepped out of the bar. One waved timidly at the soldiers.

"You like what you see?" asked a voice right next to Ken.

He jumped. It was Theo. The big light crawled over the two of them just then, turning Theo's face the same aquamarine hue. The photo shop's doorway was two steps away, open wide. Theo's brother was inside, sorting out papers by the light of a candle. Ken started mumbling that he had been calling all evening.

"We've been on the phone with a stockbroker, asking advice about our portfolio," Theo explained. "We own some stock that we need to sell pronto; we've decided to leave in forty-eight hours."

"Why so fast? What happened?"

"Didn't you hear? The president decreed martial law. He said that everyone should pull up their socks, but me and my brother have been pulling at our socks till we tore holes in 'em, so we're leaving. I don't think anyone's too glad to pull up their socks again, that's why the army's in the streets.''

"Pulling up one's socks" was a colonial expression the president was very fond of. He often promised to be the first to pull up his socks. The trouble was that it had come to mean "tightening one's belt," in an area where people's belts were already very tight.

"I didn't know any of that. Did you finish my pictures?"

"Sure, let me bring them to you out here. When the power cut hit us, we were just carrying some boxes that spilled all over the place."

Theo hurried into the shop, toward the dancing flame of the candle. Ken stared out at the street. People kept emerging from their houses, cautious but also eager for a party. The tank commander chatted with the crowd, while the soldiers kept brandishing the beam at the bar. Ken knew the place by sight and suspected it to be a front for a whorehouse, because its waitresses were unusually good-looking and clumsy.

"Here," said Theo. He pushed an envelope into Ken's hand. "You want to come in? You shouldn't be out in the street at this time."

"No, I gotta get back. . . ."

The beam moved off the bar, back onto the mall's concourse. Ken felt it on the back of his neck. Like a giant nonwarmth, it flooded the concourse and the back stairs. Ken looked up at the top of the stairs, where a man was raising a big automatic with both hands, pointing it at Ken.

Ken gasped, recognizing the African who had parked close to him in the street. The big light hit the gunman, making him blink.

Ken yelled and ducked, feeling Theo plunge at the concourse in sync with him, and tore the Walther out of his belt. He saw the bullets coming from the other man's gun. He aimed his own shots at the gunman's joined hands. The light crawled away just as the man let out a loud shout of pain.

In the street, some of the soldiers fired their rifles in the air. Theo scrambled toward the shop on all fours and in a flash was back out with an assault rifle that looked mountainous against his short stature. He pointed it, yelling at Ken to move, but never fired it. He stopped at the top of the stairs and looked out at the parking lot.

Ken didn't remember letting go of the envelope, but his pictures had landed all over the concourse. One was still wheeling slowly up in the air. He grabbed it with his badly shaking hand and bent to pick up the others. Then he ran to Theo, at the top of the stairs.

"You didn't get him," Theo grunted. "Give me that." His strong left hand whipped the Walther away from Ken. "This isn't a gun, it's a popcorn shooter! Who's after you? What the fuck's going on?"

Only two seconds seemed to pass, but it could have been ten, or even a hundred. The power came back on, and Ken could clearly see the parking lot, which was now totally empty.

At the top of the stairs, next to Theo, Ken was still trembling. He could think of only one thing to say to Theo. "That gunman . . . was after me . . . I saw him earlier, in the street."

"Where?"

"Where I parked my jeep . . ."

"You're so goddamn lucky," said Theo. "You were standing against that rail like a target at a shooting range. That beam blinded him; otherwise you would've been dead."

Two more seconds passed, or ten, or a hundred. They were back in the shop now. Someone inside Ken moved Ken's hands; someone inside him talked out of his lips. He paid for the photos and started to say good-bye to Theo and his brother.

"You crazy?" exploded Theo. "They're probably waiting for you by your jeep. Ken, what's going on? Are you mixed up in ivory, or other poached stuff?"

"No, I never got mixed up in anything! Not in anything, except . . ." He wanted to say "science," but the word felt enormously irrelevant. "I'll take a matatu," he said, and realized instantly that he'd never find a taxi in that madness. "Or I'll walk."

"Armed with that toy?"

Suddenly, both brothers grabbed Ken's hand and slapped into his palm a Rhino .38. Solid, South African. "You want to see your mom soon?" asked Theo. Ken shook his head and laughed crazily, no, not his mom; there was other stuff he'd sooner see than his mom.

"You'll find your Land Rover tomorrow, where you left it," said the brother. "Without battery or tires, but you'll find it. Come with us, we'll give you a lift."

TWO SECONDS, TEN, A HUNDRED, A THOUSAND. KEN WAS IN the car, behind the Greek brothers. Theo drove. The city was in an uproar. Tanks and military trucks were stopped at most intersections, and some trucks were handing out beer. Men and women drank the beer. Confused dances started, broke off. Portraits of the president were held up above the crowds.

"That jerk should feed his people instead of getting them drunk," said Theo's brother.

Ken thought of Ngili, of Yinka. He hoped Yinka wasn't watching the madness of the starved city. The pictures were on his lap.

"These came out blurred, all of them," Theo said, pointing at the circular pattern of footprints on the bald spur. "Your film wasn't fast enough for the speed of the plane. But you can tell they're man-made because they're so regular. Now *these,* they're great." He whistled, pointing at the savanna creature's prints. "What kind of animal made them, a colobus monkey?"

Ken smiled but had no energy to respond. A colobus monkey's feet didn't look like that. Several of the shots also showed the much larger print of Ken's boot, which he had stamped in the sand to compare the sizes. The hominid footprints were less than half the size of his own footprints. They looked like a child's feet. A naked child, in the savanna.

The Rhino .38 lay on Ken's lap, next to the pictures. Ken's hand made a fist, and hugged the gun's grips. Theo glimpsed the movement in the rearview mirror. "Easy, don't blow *us* apart."

"Do you have any more clips for this gun?"

"Don't you remember? I slipped two in your pocket back at the shop. Where the hell are you?"

"Right here."

And tomorrow, I'll get back there somehow. If I survive the night.

He had ten thousand shillings in the bank. Enough to entice Hendrijks, or some other old buzzard, to fly him back there. *If he says no, I'll put this to his head.*

He wasn't trembling anymore.

Theo's car, a tough little Mini Morris, hurtled into Randall's street. The East Indian section was markedly quiet. A car parked ahead flashed its powerful headlights. It was Jakub's Mercedes 600. Ngili, Jakub, and Randall were standing on the sidewalk, watching the car's approach. Theo defiantly stopped his Mini Morris headlights to headlights with the Mercedes. Ken stepped out.

"What's wrong?" Ngili asked, rushing to Ken.

Ken knew he could not hide what had happened. "Someone shot at me in front of Theo's store." He paused, examined the other men's expressions. "Maybe it was a mistake. Maybe he thought I was someone else."

Jakub Ngiamena gaped. Randall quickly glanced back at the house where his wife and children slept.

Jakub Ngiamena moved his majestically fat body, looking puzzled and concerned. "Ken, you want to stay at our place tonight?"

"Uh . . . no, I'd rather go back to my apartment."

"We'll drive Ken home," Theo called out from his little car.

Ken asked Theo to wait just five minutes. He held up the envelope of pictures for Randall, who took it and walked with it into the house, followed by everyone except Theo and his brother.

Inside, Randall spread out the pictures, and everyone studied them in silence. Then Ngili looked at Ken, who said, "I think it's best that you keep the bones for now."

"That's what we were planning," said Jakub. "I'm going

to put them in our own safe, until martial law is lifted.''

"Don't go home," said Ngili. His eyes did not leave Ken's face.

"If I don't go home, how will I know if this attack was a mistake or not?"

"Come with us," Jakub repeated. "Yinka was out too when all this started and hasn't come back yet."

"Thank you, I'm going home."

"Call Kwezi," said Jakub. Kwezi was the doorman at Ken's building. Jakub remembered his name from the days when Ngili was rooming with Ken. "Make sure no one suspicious is waiting around."

"All right." Turning to Randall, Ken motioned toward the pictures. "What do you think?"

Randall pursed his lips. Then he answered, choosing his words. "What do I think? I think they're very, very intriguing. I should take a couple of them with me, since I'm taking the samples of bones and soil. I'd like one with your boot in it too, for size comparison."

Ken slowly chose two shots, handed them to Randall. Ngili read in the slowness of Ken's movements a momentous decision. He stepped around the table and stood next to his friend, "Ken, what are you going to do?"

"I'm going to go back there somehow. Soon, maybe even tomorrow." Jakub frowned and started to say something. Ken raised his hand in a pleading gesture, and Jakub stopped speaking. "I have to, whether you, Ngili, can come with me or not. We discovered something incredible, in a place that looked inaccessible, and yet we were attacked there. And I've been attacked again, just now, although I've never been in trouble in this country before." Jakub watched him closely, his frown deepening. "It's hard to believe that there's no connection between these two attacks. On the other hand, why did the first one happen out there, next to our find? I don't know the answers to any of these questions, and I don't know how to look for these answers. But whatever they are, someone's got to go back out there, both to complete our find and to protect it."

He paused. Then he reached for the spread of pictures, selected several, and put them in his breast pocket. He stacked up the others with the negatives on top and handed them to Jakub.

Jakub accepted the pictures. "There might be a very simple explanation for the first attack. Some fugitives from justice crossed the border from Tanzania, in a stolen safari vehicle, and got lost. They mistook your plane for a ranger's plane, and decided not to take chances."

"I sure hope that's true," said Ken. "At any rate, given what these pictures seem to show, I think it's clear why we should keep the secret right now, until we know exactly what we're dealing with."

"You can be assured of my silence," smiled Ngiamena. "I have other concerns just now. But Ken, I still think that you should sleep on this first."

"I'll try to," Ken laughed humorlessly.

"Ken, don't go back there without telling me," said Ngili strongly.

"I won't."

"Good night, my son's friend. Good night, Professor Phillips," said Jakub. He exited followed by Ngili, like a king with a one-man suite.

Randall stared at Ken as if he were seeing him for the first time. "Are you really determined to go back there?" Ken nodded tensely, stabbing the air with his chin.

"Dammit, I used to have a gun someplace," said Randall. "Do you think I should try to find it?"

THEO AND HIS BROTHER DROVE KEN BACK TO HIS APARTment on Tom Mboia Road. The wide street looked deserted; its population had spilled out, toward downtown. Theo drove slowly, while his brother examined the parked cars, the assault gun on his lap, his finger in the trigger guard. They saw no one sitting in the parked cars, no suspicious shadows in the street. Theo pulled up in front of Ken's apartment building. The entrance was well lit. The brothers stepped out with Ken, but he stopped them from coming into the lobby.

He made sure the Rhino's safety catch was on but could be flicked off with a push of the thumb. He stuck it inside his right pants pocket and walked in.

Kwezi the doorman was watching TV on a small old black-and-white set. The TV broadcast downtown scenes, intercut with newsreels prominently featuring the president. A few street kids that Kwezi let sleep on the lobby floor most nights were sprawled around his desk.

"Welcome back, Mr. Ken," said Kwezi, then held up a white envelope. "A gentleman just dropped this off for you."

He took the envelope. The paper felt expensive. "Who was it?"

"A Mr. Anderson."

Ken was too stunned to react. He cleared his throat and asked Kwezi if anyone else had been looking for him, anyone in the slightest way suspicious. Kwezi shook his head. "But there's someone waiting for you now, Mr. Ken." He gestured toward a plain wooden bench, almost hidden behind a row of potted palms.

Ken's hand slipped to his right pocket, while he tried to make out the guest through the palms. A fluid body draped the bench, contrasting with its square, uninviting angles.

"Hi, settler," said Yinka from behind the palms.

KEN LOOKED BACK ACROSS THE ENTRANCE AND GES-tured to Theo to wait. Then he hurried inside the en-closure of palms.

Yinka remained seated. But her expression changed when Ken bent down toward her and spoke, his eyes shining al-most feverishly. "I've just been dropped off by a friend who could drive you back to Ngong Hills, so I'd like you to leave now. Someone tried to shoot me about an hour ago, and I don't know how safe you would be here with me." It oc-curred to him that she might have come here because of the street madness, and added, "It's not too crazy outside. I'll ask Theo . . ."

"I have a car," she cut him off. "If it's not safe here, why are you back? And who tried to shoot you?"

Ken shrugged silently.

"You look well equipped to repulse further attacks." She grinned and got up.

Ken glanced down at his pants. A gross erection bulged out his right pocket, where he had stuck the Rhino gun. He self-consciously pulled the bottom of his jacket over the bulging pocket. "What do you want, Yinka?"

"What's Anderson writing to you?"

"Did you see him come in?"

"I saw *them*. I peeked through the plants. If you ask me

upstairs, I'll tell you who else was with him."

"I don't want to ask you upstairs. Go home—your dad's worried about you."

"Let him be worried. I've figured out how you can get back to Dogilani."

"How nice of you. Actually, I have my own way to get back."

Like a young giraffe, she stretched herself up from her semi-reclining position and threw her long legs toward the entrance. He hesitated, then blocked her way, apologizing. All right, she could come upstairs. He turned and signaled Theo that he was okay and they could go home.

Dogilani, he thought. Whatever help Yinka was offering, he had to consider it.

"What's the bwana professor writing to you?" she asked.

He tore open the envelope.

A handwritten note, on Anderson's stationery, invited Ken to a meeting in his tutorial rooms, to share the results of his trip to Dogilani. (How the hell did he know where they had been? Ken wondered angrily.) Anderson expected to be fully apprised of the nature of the project, offering in exchange his support for Ken's further expeditions. The political situation, he stressed, required his kind of clout to keep any independent research going. "Ken, now is not the time for scientific charades," the note concluded, friendly yet ominous. It was signed "C.H.A.," for Cyril Hewett Anderson.

He handed Yinka the note, while he pondered. Anderson knew. He knew, but he didn't really know. Yinka scanned the lines, made a disinterested face, handed it back.

"Who came here with him?" he asked.

"That old emeritus, Raj Haksar. And they were at our house together yesterday."

"What the hell were they doing there?"

"Yesterday afternoon, after you and Ngili had been out of radio contact for twenty-four hours, Um'tu got nervous and called Anderson. I was in Um'tu's office and I heard him say that you had flown out to do some stratigraphy. He asked Cyril whether he had any idea where you might've gotten lost. Cyril asked if there were any notes of your earlier surveys lying around. Um'tu told him to hold, and went into Ngili's study to look. I picked up the phone in the office and listened in because I wanted to know where Ngili was. Um'tu found some stratigraphic notes in the study and read them to Cyril, and Cyril said that from the rock composition, you were near the Mau's southernmost spur. Probably at Dogilani. Then he asked Um'tu if he could come by.''

''And he did?''

''He came about half an hour later, with Haksar. Um'tu asked me to make tea, so I played nice African daughter''— Yinka scornfully curled down her lower lip—''and brought the tea in, and heard most of what they were saying. Anderson didn't seem to have much to do with Dogilani, but Haksar was talking about some natives living in the area. He was afraid you might be disturbing their habitat.''

Ken's adrenaline kicked back in. ''What kind of natives?''

''I didn't hear the tribal specifics, I was moving around, but I think he said that they were nomadic. Then Haksar asked Um'tu not to tell either you or Ngili about the conversation.''

''Didn't your father think that odd?''

''He did and said so. Haksar said something about planning to go there, and how competitive your field was. Um'tu promised, he didn't care, all he wanted was to know where Ngili was, so he could send out a game park plane to find you.''

''Did he send that plane?''

Ken suddenly remembered Hendrijks mentioning a plane passing overhead while he and Ngili were photographing the footprints.

''Mhm, he sent it early this morning, but by the time it spotted the Beech Lightning on the ground, it was almost out of fuel and could not make radio contact with the Lightning, so it flew back. A few hours later, I guess you got your own radio fixed, because Embakasi airport called to tell us that you had just asked permission for landing.''

She took a breath. Ken was tense and silent.

So Haksar knew something about Dogilani's odd inhabitants. But how much did he know?

He reasoned quickly: Perhaps not much at all; Haksar wasn't a field researcher. Rather than visiting Dogilani himself, he had more likely come across some old field report, or just rumors. Still, Anderson had become interested; otherwise he wouldn't have written Ken such a note, which he now felt had been penned with Haksar peering over Anderson's shoulder. Anderson and Haksar did not go together. But Dogilani had brought them together.

Had a layman been to Dogilani and sighted some protohumans? Had the word somehow gotten out? Hendrijks's face flashed through Ken's mind. He remembered what Randall had said: If I were you, I'd get hold of that pilot. . . .

Very well, Menheer Hendrijks, he thought, using one of the few Dutch words he knew. I'll find out what you know. I'll do even better—I'll take you back there with me to stop you from talking.

"Come upstairs," he said, and took Yinka's arm.

He led her into the elevator. Its light was long defunct, its wooden walls cracked, its linoleum-covered floor smelly. He leaned closer to the scent of the young woman. She did not pull back.

"I have a very simple plan," she said above the creaking elevator cables, "about how you could go back there this week."

"This week?"

She nodded.

"What's the catch?"

"None. You convince Ngili to stay here now and do his bit for the country, by telling him he can get back on the project later with full co-authorship. Meanwhile, this crisis will hopefully pass. For that kind of arrangement, I'll make Um'tu send you to Dogilani on a game park permit, with game park funding."

"That sounds terribly generous."

"It's not. My father fears that his power's on the wane.

He wants to recapture it by making a show of commitment, and feels that Ngili can help him."

That explained the old man's strained behavior, his radio address. . . .

"There is a catch though," Ken observed. "I'd be in the savanna alone." *Alone like that child.*

She sized him up, her fantastic eyes made more fantastic by the passing of the floors, some deep in darkness, others lit lugubriously by rusty brass sconces: "Isn't that what you really want?"

"Yeah, that's what I want. What do you want?"

"I'm sick of small-time journalism," she replied unhesitantly, "and I feel that I've paid my dues to the people. You find anything sensational out there, I want to be the first on the scene. And I want . . ."

The elevator stopped. Ken's floor was totally unlit. Her eyes became pits of night again. "I want to understand you."

"Why?"

"My business. All right, settler? We have a deal?" They stood face-to-face, hearing the elevator cables creak above them. "You could be back at Dogilani next week."

Jesus, he thought. Next week.

"Okay. You've got a deal. Ngili must be home by now, let's call him."

He led her to his apartment door. He felt a little dizzy and had trouble fitting the key into the lock. While he opened the door, she commented that she still didn't know what exactly got everyone so worked up about the study of early humans. Then she entered the narrow living room and suppressed a little cry, seeing the two naked creatures standing inside, the ape-man and the ape-woman.

They were life-size plaster casts of an australopithecine male-female pair, standing just under five feet tall, their light-brown skin overgrown with short black hair. Their mouths had thin, far-protruding lips; their noses were flat, without bridges. Their foreheads sloped back into their low skull tops. They had glass eyes with stark brown irises and opalescent whites, deeply buried under overhung eyebrows.

They were so realistic that Yinka fought a feeling that something was alive inside them. Captured and kept prisoner in there by the ever unpredictable Ken Lauder.

"So this is your family?" she joked.

He muttered that they were teaching props he had bought when the university refurbished its paleoanatomy lab. He shoved a pile of scientific magazines off a couch to make room for her to sit down, then picked up the phone.

FIRST, KEN TALKED TO NGILI, WHO SOUNDED TIRED, BUT calm and levelheaded. He agreed to the plan, on condition that he could fly to Dogilani every week to check on the state of the search, to bring Ken his supplies, and to pick up his field reports. He could schedule the supply flights on the weekends and was sure that his father would accept that arrangement. Then Yinka talked to Ngili and said at one point, "Fine, come pick me up if it makes you feel better." And then, "Cut it out, I'm not twelve anymore." Ken guessed that Ngili was taking her to task about coming to Ken's place alone.

Ken felt that Ngili was being the older brother for the sake of form. Ngili was back to being himself—they were all back to their normal selves, now that Ngili had appeased the tension with his father.

Fatherhood, thought Ken. One of the mysteries of humanness.

Peace, sweet, exhausted peace, invaded his limbs. He was going back to Dogilani, and that was all that mattered. When Yinka hung up, he asked her if she wanted a drink, and she shook her head. He felt he needed one, so he hunted through his closets, located two fingers of Johnnie Walker at the bottom of a dusty bottle, and poured them into a glass.

He took a swig, and watched Yinka, who stood in the living room facing the protohuman creatures.

The man was the furrier one. Rich hair paraded up and down his chest and belly, exploding at the crotch into a wide frontal forest. Out of that forest, the penis at rest hung down like a thick brown finger. The woman's genital area was equally well marked; a hazing of hair started under her navel and dripped down till it was sucked into a busy pubic triangle, coarse and tufting outward. Overall, she was much less hairy, which revealed that she had no pouches of fat; even her buttocks and thighs stored their extra fat inside girdings of muscles. She had almost no facial hair, just a haze of down on her upper lip, which Yinka thought had a sort of animal sexiness.

Altogether, the female looked less apelike. She was closer, over hundreds of thousands of years, to the women who would one day wear lipstick and use deodorants. The man stepped ahead of the woman, his expression one of quest. The woman's expression was expectation. She seemed more anxious, yet also confident that whatever the man would find, he, or they, would handle it.

Yinka burst into a nervous little chuckle. "This couple looks like they're out to conquer the world."

"They were. And who's to say that they didn't know it?" he asked, taking another swig.

"But their pose is so traditional. Look, she even walks behind the male."

He shrugged. "These casts are about forty years old. But the reality is, their respective habitat was not London or New York. It was the savanna two million years ago, so the male was supposed to be the protector, the path opener."

"Yeah, yeah, the protector, the opener, the leader. All that crap."

He frowned, then explained like a professor in a classroom. "Australopithecine women were not stupid, Yinka. They had a job to do, which was to make children for the species, and they were not going to jump into a sabertooth's gaping jaws just to make a point. That was the man's job, and he knew that he was expendable that way. If he opened the path into a sabertooth's jaws, tough shit for him. That was a deal that greatly advantaged the woman, wouldn't you say?"

"Well, sure, when you present it like that. Why would the man accept it?"

"Because he was devoted to passing on his genes, mixed with hers of course, even if that implied dying for his genes. She didn't refuse to bear children either, even though she could die in childbirth, and often did."

Yinka was silent.

Then she commented sarcastically that the artist had gone ape over his casts' genitals. Ken replied that the australopithecines had been in a state of sexual experimentation. The position of their genitals had shifted, the male's becoming more exposed than in any other mammal, while the female's were now practically hidden, compared to the purple, estrus-inflated genitals of a female ape. It was normal for nature to go overboard in advertising their new locations. It had done the same with the milk glands, by placing them in cup-shaped tits. Meanwhile, the hidden female sex had acquired mystery, a quality unknown or unimportant in other animals but essential in humans for the creation of monogamous relationships.

"Sounds like sex made us human," she smiled.

He sized her up, as if deciding to let her into a secret. "You want to know my theory?" She turned toward him, all attention. "Five major transitions made us human. One: eyes in front, instead of on the sides of the face, giving us three-dimensional vision so we no longer had to rely on a sniffing wet nose for orientation. Two: stepping on flat open ground, imposed by the shrinking of the forests, and then standing up to detect the movements of predators we could not outrun or outbite with our modest flat teeth. It was essential that we keep our distance from them, which we couldn't do without standing up. Three: using our hands to help our poor teeth in catching our food and tearing it up. Four: loss of our body hair, so we could develop sweat glands and survive the lethal savanna sun. As a result, we acquired our naked skins. And finally . . . there was pleasure, which was much enhanced by our naked skins," he concluded, and enjoyed the look of astonishment on her face.

"Pleasure?" she repeated.

"Pleasure. More than any other animal, we have cells equipped to experience pleasure in our bodies, and connections for processing pleasure in our brains. I'm not forgetting that the enlargement of our brains allowed us to think abstractly, but I think that humanness is, above all, *appreciation*. That's how we separated from the rest of nature. That's how we finally became aware of ourselves."

She took a quick circular look at his messy apartment. "For someone so aware of pleasure," she murmured, "you don't seem to appreciate that lifestyle very much. Am I going to see you again before you go back to Dogilani?"

"Probably not."

He was turning the nearly empty glass in his fingers. She took it from him, swallowed the last drops, then let the glass fall. In one uninterrupted motion, she wrapped her long arms around his neck, pulled his face close, and gave him a kiss with her lips and tongue—it was intimate but a little cool and distant, as if she were testing him. All her body, flexuous and strong, adhered to his. He felt her flat taut stomach, her hard round knees, and her breasts, which seemed strong and fleshy and larger than they had looked earlier that day.

She pushed him away. They stood face-to-face, looking at each other. The phone rang, once only.

He whispered, "That's Kwezi from downstairs. Ngili's probably here."

"Good luck, settler."

"So long."

He closed the door after her. He sat at a cluttered desk and touched his lips with his open palm, as if to convince himself that she had indeed kissed him.

He got up again and made sure the door was locked. He took out the Rhino .38 and set it on a desk, safety catch off.

He took a pen and a pad and started making notes about the gear he needed. He pulled out old checklists of dehydrated foods, camp appliances and equipment, and a giant map of Western Kenya. He had started jotting down a reminder note about halazone tablets to purify wilderness water, when his head slid forward, and his whole upper body settled on the desk.

Ken slept.

Six hours later, the African sun unleashed the blue heat of a new day, but the rays making their way through the blinds of Ken's apartment did not disturb him. With his head on his desk, he slept.

IN THE SAVANNA, THE SUN SOARED WITH THE USUAL DRAmatic speed of African dawns. The hominid boy was already awake and tossing in his niche of stone.

He heard the thud of bare feet approaching between the border of the tall grasses, whose tasseled heads swayed in the morning breeze, and the rampart of rocks.

Several pairs of those feet trod the path along the base of the rocks, their massive naked *calcanea* (heels) crushing the sand. Their great toes, long and set at a wide angle, made their gait heavy. They flattened the sand noisily, while their concave chests let out a harsh, almost painful panting.

The stepping and panting made the air vibrate, and the sound waves pierced the air in all directions, reaching the hominid boy's long-lobed ears. In sub-fragments of seconds, the boy's brain processed the heavy-treading sounds. He rose, shaking fearfully, grabbed two hunting stones, then inched his face over the edge of the rock, to look down.

In the bluish haze of the still unlit path, he saw hairy humps of necks and shoulders looking deeply dark, almost ink-black. The boy set his clutched fists on the rocky ledge, while he gritted his teeth so as not to utter even a hint of sound. He glued himself onto the rock face, and his mind felt like a box of smoke.

Then his memory returned. He remembered. He remembered the big creatures passing below, and what their presence meant.

It was almost at that moment that he glimpsed the cigarette lighter. The odd shiny stone, a gift left for him by the alien who traveled in a tuber/bug. Thrown out of his sleeping niche by the baboons, it had fallen in a crack of the rock.

It had reappeared almost magically. The boy's lips opened in a grin of wonderment.

He scooped it out of the crack with a long slim finger, then plunged back into his niche and reappeared with the white arm bone, which he had found earlier. He stuck the lighter under his arm, put the arm bone in his teeth, and listened.

The footfalls had stopped. They restarted in several directions at once, as the heavy-treading patrol split up to search the rocks.

His little mind instantly saw his chance to move. These unseen raiders would hear each other's footsteps now. And guessing direction was not their strength.

He threw one hunting stone at the path, away from the rising sun. He heard its clatter, followed by a scramble of heavy bodies. He raced to the edge of the rock and took a wide, unseeing leap over the path. Landing in grass, he thrashed hard and noisily in the midst of it. Then he slipped back to the path, crouched, and watched.

The big shadows crossed the path back and forth, in confusion. Then they left it, and started to search the grass.

He rose. Glancing over his shoulder, he silently hurried around a corner of the rocky palisade, then followed its ramparts as they straightened and marched northward, like a petrified army, until they ended in a buildup of ledges and terraces that blended into the Mau foothills.

The sun continued its ascent, setting in motion another day. In the distant city, hours passed. In the bush, biotic potentials were realized, and species marked another step toward their survival or extinction.

SEVEN HOURS LATER, THE COMPUTER HUMMED IN KEN'S apartment, flashing up research mailed in on the Internet. An outdated StyleWriter slowly printed an article published in the *Quarterly Review of Biology*. Ken did sit-ups by the printer, an eye out for the path of the perforated paper.

The phone rang. He got up, grimacing from the fatigue in his back and shoulders, and picked up the receiver.

"Cup of coffee for an unemployed reporter?" quipped Yinka.

Surprised, he started to chuckle. "Where are you?"

"Right around the corner."

"I think I'm out of coffee, but maybe I've got some tea. . . ."

"Great. I'll be there."

"Wait." He had planned to spend the day hunting expedition supplies. "Maybe this is not a good time, my place is a mess. . . ."

"You have two minutes."

"What are you doing in this part of town?"

"I went to a lunch at what's left of the foreign press club. Don't worry about the mess, I have a messy brother, you know."

"All right." After all, she had helped him set up the expedition. "Can you make it five minutes?"

"Two. I can see your building." She hung up.

He shook his head. The StyleWriter had finished printing. He tore off the last page, picked up the little stack of papers, and paced around with it looking for his robe. He found it draped over a chair in the living room. He flung the papers on the couch, grabbed the robe, rushed into the bathroom, praying that water was running. It was. He stormed into a cold shower, scraped his skin with his nails as he soaped himself, rinsed, dried off, boxed his way into his robe just as the doorman rang to announce Yinka.

He told the doorman to let her come up, rushed back into the bathroom, knocked the toothbrush out of its glass, crushed the last drops from a tube of toothpaste, brushed hard, making his gums bleed, and rushed back into the living room.

There was a knock on the door, quick and light, a woman's knock.

He opened the door. Yinka stepped in, in a plain cotton dress, white with narrow lapels, and white high-heeled shoes that made her look taller. He felt as if he were seeing her for the first time. "You look so formal."

He passed his palm over his chin. He had forgotten to shave.

"Yep. I thought I'd dress up; it was a funeral of sorts."

He heard in her voice the same inflection as during the ride in her father's car. Controlled anger. She glanced at the apartment, at the plaster casts, more obviously fake now, in the daylight.

"You okay, Yinka?"

"Medium enraged. Where's the tea?"

"Sit right here. I'll make it."

He hurried into the narrow kitchen unit, rattled a cupboard open to pull out the cups. *I better steady my hands; what will she think?* He became angry. When had he started to care so much about what Yinka Ngiamena might think? *I guess I'm really tired.* He knocked the cupboard shut with his elbow.

"I got Um'tu to commit to two survival caches for you," she called from the living room. "From his game reserve inventory. You'll need them, assuming you hang around there alone for a while."

He almost dropped a cup he was dusting off with the edge of his robe. "How did you make him agree to that?" The survival caches, little camps in themselves, were the most prized safari matériel in existence. Stolen ones cost a thousand dollars on the black market.

"Because his darling daughter might hop out there later, to write a story."

Ken jumped. She'd noiselessly stepped into the kitchen and was standing in half-profile against a window framing a slice of smoky Nairobi. She did not look at him. "Um'tu'll have the caches parachuted into the bush, but of course you can tell the pilot *where* to drop them, and if you break into one, you won't have to pay for it." Still without looking at him, she exited on those threateningly silent high heels.

He stuffed tea leaves into a greened-up strainer, while the kettle started exhaling little clouds out of a spout showing the brass under the peeled-off enamel. He poured hot water into two cups, dropped the strainer into one, balanced the whole on a faded tray, and stepped in from the kitchen.

She was standing by the couch, scanning the pages from the *Quarterly Review of Biology*.

"What's this?" she asked, holding them up.

The title was written in a plain, undecorative font: "Mysterious Female Sexuality: A Weapon in the Reproductive War."

"It's research." He lifted the tea strainer from her cup, sank it into his own, presented her with her tea. She flung the pages onto the couch, strode to a window with a bigger slice of Nairobi in it. "The light's harsh. D'you mind?" She canceled the view with a drop of the aluminum blinds, then sat on the couch and picked up her steaming cup. "You happy, settler?"

"Sure. How much blood do I have to spill, to repay myself?"

"You have to write Um'tu a report about the fauna. No strain for someone with your IQ."

He sipped his tea, found it hot and tasteless. He looked at her legs, swallowed, looked at her directly. She put her cup down. "I'm upset, settler."

"Because of the political situation?"

"Because of everything. My paper closed down, Gwee is getting married—he was the baby brother I could push around, but now I'm losing him—and you're going off to fame and adventure. . . ."

"Am I that important?"

"Your expedition's the only thing I can contribute something to at this time. So. Tell me about mysterious female sexuality."

"As a topic for tea?"

"Seriously. Maybe I can become a science writer."

Her fixed attentive gaze, like a student's, put him at ease, but the sight of her knees made him want her to leave as soon as possible. He explained, in a tone that he wanted detached and casual, that female sexuality had grown more and more enigmatic with the advance in human evolution. Ovulation in chimps, cows, bitches, lionesses, was obvious; they all gave out scents and signaled their readiness with a randiness impossible to miss. Not human females. A slight rise in their body temperature was the only indication of ovulation, a very unreliable one and easy to miss. And yet, that change from overt advertising to almost total secrecy had to deal with maximizing reproductive odds. No species initiated such changes unless they benefited the species' reproduction.

He noticed that she was following him with a darker and darker gaze, and an increasingly more rigid posture. "You praised monogamy last time," she interrupted. "It doesn't look like this mystery encourages monogamy."

"It does in a way, because it drives the males crazy trying to keep the females to themselves. Meanwhile, it allows women the option of infidelity that can go undetected. The official mate often provides an excellent nest, but not always the best genes." He got up and put away his cup, freeing himself of an awkward rattling object. As he turned back toward her, her gaze was even darker, and her posture was full of compressed tension. "There are studies showing that women climax more often when they have affairs," he added in an uncertain voice, "which may seem obvious, but in illicit affairs the males also produce more sperm, thus 'flooding out' the competition of a husband or of another lover. . . ."

She put down her cup and rose too. "We're such secretive selfish bitches, according to you."

"Selfish is too hard a word. I think that life in the savanna was so full of dangers that females had to be opportunists. If they lost a mate to a feline, they had to acquire another mate—but how to convince him to raise her earlier offspring? So maybe affairs were a way to create secondary bonds, to be called into play when the primary ones ceased, especially if they ceased tragically. Maybe keeping a male in a state of jealous insecurity was a way to make him stay in the . . . relationship. God, I hate that word." He laughed dryly.

"Are you going to miss Gwee's wedding?"

Gwee's wedding. Hmm. He'd forgotten about that. He almost blushed.

"Of course you will. You're such a selfish male."

She took his hand, kneaded it in her strong narrow fingers, then pulled his arm over her tall shoulder, and kissed him on the mouth, urgently, almost clumsily. "The truth is, you don't know a bloody thing about women," she whispered, "so why am I so nervous that you'll see everything about me, with that scientific mind of yours?"

She kissed him again, then pulled back, lips shining wet, her sloppiness making her imperfect, a different woman. "D'you have a bed, ape-man?" she asked, and he realized that she had really come to make love. Not to drink tea and fume about the political situation.

He pointed with his chin to the bedroom door. She turned and headed for it, starting to unbutton her dress. He followed her, stepping into the bedroom as she undid a zipper on her side, making the dress lose its shape. She slid her shoulders out of it, let it drop to the floor, unclasped a minimal bra and threw it away at random, kicked off her shoes, then bent to take off her underpants. Instantly naked, she stepped up to him, tall and leggy.

"Take this rag off," she whispered, pulling at his robe.

He let the robe drop to the floor and found himself naked and aroused, in the semi-darkness that smoothed the visual shock of nakedness but concealed nothing. He pulled a deep breath and guided her to the bed. A black-and-white picture of him and Ngili on their first dig grinned from a dresser.

Her breasts were rounded and lovely, and there was not a crease on her belly. She had a small pubic patch, attractively discreet. She lay on her back. He lay next to her, took her in his arms, and she whispered with shock that he was burning up.

"That's the difference between males and females in the reproductive war," he muttered with chattering teeth.

"We're obvious. You're cool, mysterious, and calculating."

"Shut up."

She pulled him over her. But somehow, he just could not instantly put it in, not into this dark nymph, even though she rubbed her legs and distanced her thighs. "Did you come to make love to me, or to my theories?"

"To your courage. Your sexiest part."

There was no foreplay. She was open, and they connected without any awkwardness. He made room for himself inside her, while she kissed him repeatedly with an anxious tremor, as if fearing pain. He breathed in her ear, asking if he was hurting her. She shook her head impatiently, holding on to some inner concentration, and started moving under him, slowly, then fast. He held back his climax, surprised by how much he wanted her to enjoy this.

He found a way to delay his urge, remained almost still, just listened to her breathing and felt that long wonderful body. With hungry fantasy from having been celibate for so long, he pictured her belly, her navel, her breathtaking thighs, her pubic hairs mingled with his own, her skin above all. All in motion against his larger, slower body. Then she stopped moving, her vagina absorbing him to the root of his penis, and they fused for a long, hot, and mindless time. He probed at the very depth of her vagina, till finally he could no longer fight it. He gritted his teeth not to moan. She hugged him hard, and he felt her body vibrate downward, from maximum tension to relaxation.

He let go of her, lay on his back, glanced at the naked woman. She lay on her side, eyes open and directed at him. Then she put a long hand on his cheek and moved it hard against his rough stubble. She whispered, "So. Is this the way they did it back then?"

He felt like telling her, Yes, but with considerably less interference from possessive brothers, and political and cultural barriers. But he remained silent. *This probably won't happen again—don't spoil it, Lauder.* Whether she guessed what he was thinking or not, she seemed aware of the moment's melancholy magic, for she pushed herself over him, as if forbidding him to think. She stared at him with curiosity, then whispered a question: "How can you live without women?" He heard in it the African mind, ever unwilling to accept celibacy, monkhood, waste of the body that was designed first and foremost to be fertile.

He grinned. "Right now, I'm asking myself the same question."

Maybe she heard in his answer something unspoken, because she crushed herself onto the whole length of his body, hurting him with a hard and restless mons, and they kissed without talking, faces wet from each other, open eyes no longer shy, until they fitted into each other again, naturally, a hard penis, a ready opening. He thought of only one thing, that this *was* the last time, and that stirred a violent urge, a silent despair to enter and possess her as completely as possible. He rolled on top of her. She started fighting him, not able to shake him off, he was too heavy, but grinding him with her vagina and labia, as if punishing him for having a passing power over her. She bit his shoulder, and he felt spasms in her breasts and belly. He became madly aroused and mated abruptly, hitting, plunging, pounding, while she bit her lower lip and hugged him ferociously but made no sound at all, until sweat erupted on her forehead.

Finally, they disengaged. He squeezed her to him, feeling ridiculously moved, almost in love, and praying that it didn't show. After an instant, she shook briefly and laughed. "Hey, ape-man, I came just now. After you, like you said."

"You're making it up."

"No, I'm not, I did come. Only a bit, but I did. You're a good lover," she added objectively.

He was angry at her detached tone. "Thanks. Don't be kind."

With a quick kiss, she rose and stepped toward the bathroom. He heard her turn on the shower taps.

Waiting for her, he lived a feeling of déjà vu from his college days, when, after managing to take to bed some truly good-looking woman, he saw his familiar surroundings through the aura of that naked goddess's presence. It was as if his lover had already departed, though she was still there. This shower, she had used. That bed, she had lain in, with him. He had never been able to hold on to those special ones, the ones he really liked, despite his potency, which he knew to be at least standard, or his desire to see them again. They all broke it off for some reason or other, sensing a lack of availability in him. Now he wasn't as young, but his restlessness was still in him. The woman who had just opened to him the depth of her femalehood was in fact the one sending him off to his next wilderness stint. He couldn't blame her for not saying more, after she had twice fused with him, skin to skin, mouth to mouth, fertile organs to fertile organs, but with no certainty that she would ever know him better.

He showered after her, stepped back into the bedroom, and found her back in her cool white outfit, putting on her shoes. She asked him to make more tea. But when he brought the tea, she just touched her lips to her cup, kissed him, and was gone.

To keep from thinking, Ken straightened out the room, and found a note. It read:

> Settler,
>
> I just behaved like a female opportunist, but as far as you and I are concerned, that's the only way to escape this world cut up into black and white, Kenyan and American, male and female, present and past. Please, don't get killed out there. Come back, and _maybe_ you'll show me what else they did to each other back then. Y.

He guessed that she had started the note while he was in the bathroom, and then asked him to make more tea so she could finish it. A surprise, from someone never at a loss for words.

Had she written it so he could have something from her?

Ordinarily, he would've grinned to himself, proud of such proof of a woman's caring. Now, he did not feel like grinning. He threw on pants and a T-shirt, and went out to look for expedition supplies.

Part Three

HUMANHUNT

NOT FAR FROM HIS OLD LAIR, THE BOY FELT ALMOST
safe. He stopped, knelt by a cluster of giant oil grass,
and industriously tore up a good number of blades; then,
choosing the wider ones, he wove a little pouch with a sash
that would hold his possessions—the arm bone, the cigarette
lighter, and his remaining hunting stone.

He strapped the pouch on his shoulder and walked on,
staying between the border of the tall grasses and the ramparts of rocks.

He walked with a purposeful, even stride, though he didn't
really know where he was going. He kept leaning back his
head, searching the sky for the tuber/bug, but there was no
trace of it; this surprised him, because it was still dawn, and
bugs always flew busily at dawn and dusk.

Sometime later, he caught a mole shrew and ate it, but
lost his stone during the hunt. Luckily it didn't take him long
to find a new stone, which he knocked hard against the rocky
rampart, breaking off sharp flakes and leaving an irregularly
round core. He now carried this core of stone in his mouth,
activating his salivary glands and making him less thirsty.

He stuck the flakes, good for cutting, in his grass pouch.

The boy walked on north, with no discomfort other than
an occasional burp. Later, the day ended, and he perched on
a ledge, pondering the return of the big creatures, when sud-

denly he heard the tuber/bug flying over his head. He glimpsed it quickly and lost sight of it as it plunged into a cloud. It did not occur to him that this might not be the same tuber/bug. He just grinned widely. He'd known all along that it would return.

AT THE FOOT OF THE MAU, THE TERRAIN BECAME ROCKIER. Sharp streams of mountain water trickled down more often. The mists wrapping the crests condensed into brief cool showers, falling down quickly and drenching the foothills.

Walking on, the boy came to a wide field of broken black rocks—giant plates of dried lava that had been split up into flat ledge faces arrested at strange angles. They formed a maze of ancient black rubble, labyrinthine and infinite. This collection of clefts, chimneys, tunnels, and quarries created a magical and cheerful architecture, providing a myriad of complex hiding places.

Forgetting everything else, the boy dropped his pouch. Giving out a big whoop of play, he leaped from boulder crest to boulder crest, agile and steady on his hardened feet, enjoying a rush from his challenged muscles. He looked a bit like a hairless chimp at play.

Suddenly, above him, a thunderstorm began drumming hard, and a lashing rain started.

The boulders were becoming slippery, which increased the challenge of the boy's game.

Ignoring the dangers, he leaped about on the crests, uttering howls, a primal hominid inventing a dance with no name.

Scratches bled his feet. He did not feel them. He danced on, youth gorging itself on the illusion of immortality reinforced with every leap.

Lightning struck just a few yards down, the grounded electricity flaming around the stone, smoking it up. The deafening discharge caught the boy as he was leaping up in the air. Startled by the noise, he fell, tumbled from a high slate of lava to a lower one, and lay still.

As the rain eased, he came to his senses. He rose with

pain, but without serious impairment, and remembered his pouch.

He climbed down from the labyrinth and found the pouch by sheer luck. Just then, a buried memory surfaced in his brain, vivid and detailed. He stood with raindrops drying on his skin, watching the memory as if it were a live scene.

He saw hominids, males and females, running from the savanna toward the rocky maze, looking for hiding places.

They did not make it to those hiding places.

He walked among the rocks until a vast, quarrylike dip in the rocks opened before him. He entered, stood there a moment looking, then turned abruptly and walked out. Then he returned. He faced a field of bones, fleshless, cleaned by wild animals and by time, and washed again by the rain.

He stood silently, suffering the memory until it subsided.

He thought again about the creature he had seen digging up those bones from the savanna gravel. The alien and his mate had dug them up with a care that told him something that even they did not know about themselves.

He remembered the lion-faced alien's hands, freeing the bones. Slowly, patiently, kindly.

The boy lay down in a narrow chimney of lava, his own thoughts having exhausted him.

HE AWOKE TO THE WET NEW DAWN OF A RAINSTORM.

He walked out of his shelter. A replenished little stream gushed down past him to a water hole marked by reeds growing irregularly into the water. Blurred by mist, water buffaloes stood stoically on the shore. A wildebeest, stung perhaps by a bug seeking a dry refuge on its body, bounced up, all four legs kicking at the air, then plowed headfirst into its own herd, trying to start a stampede but causing only a ripple.

The boy heard the tuber/bug again. The plane swooped low, like a giant bee threatening to land. The wildebeests' stampede instantly restarted, plunging them wildly at the wa-

ter buffaloes, who mooed with annoyance and broke into a
halfhearted run.

THE AFRICAN PILOT TURNED TOWARD NGILI, WHO WAS
seated next to him in the old Helio Courier that belonged to
the game park department. Clouds were forming ahead,
building up from wispy plumes into grayish cotton bales. The
pilot wanted to know whether he should still bail out a cache
of instruments and supplies, which Ken wanted dropped by
the southernmost spur of the Mau.

It had been exactly one week since Ken struck his deal
with the Ngiamenas.

Ngili took the radio and talked to Ken, who was organizing his camp twenty miles to the south of that spur and
about a half mile from where they had landed with Hendrijks
and found the fossil. Ken had arrived the previous morning,
after a hard four-day ride from Nairobi in a truck driven by
a game park scout. Behind the truck, another game park
scout drove Ken's Land Rover, freshly reinforced with new
bull bars at the front.

He had managed to find the collapsed and hollowed fossil-
yielding mound without Hendrijks's help. For the last seven
days, no one had seen or heard from Hendrijks. His phone
rang, but no one answered it. His downtown office was
locked up, its glass door shut off from the inside with a pull-
down shade that looked flea-bitten. Even more strangely,
Hendrijks had not called or shown up to claim his check.

"Drop the cache now," instructed Ken, "before the
clouds build up. Over."

"It's a distance from where you wanted it, several miles
from the spur. Over."

"That was an arbitrary site," said Ken. "Drop the cache,
and get the position. The parachute's bright orange. I should
be able to spot it later. Over."

"Very well. See you back there in a few minutes," said
Ngili. "Over and out."

* * *

UNDER THE PLANE, THE HOMINID BOY DID NOT THINK OF hiding. He was scared but so fascinated that he stood still as the plane soared above him. A break appeared in the body of the tuber/bug, and a strange object like an ejected egg fell out and sailed down, carried by an orange flowerlike shape. The tuber/bug soared away, while its egg clattered onto the rocks. The wet parachute heaped over itself and caught the top of a tall slate of lava. Its orange fabric looked so strikingly different from the surrounding native colors that the boy wondered if he was dreaming again.

He heard a grating noise. The load carried by the parachute was a large metal cylinder. Having fallen on an inclined rock surface, it was now slipping down, scratching the rock, stretching the lines attaching it to the rain-drenched parachute.

The boy rushed to see the case, whose slide down the rock fascinated him. Pulling at the snagged parachute, the lines rubbed against the slate's jagged sides. They began to sever. One snapped. The increased weight of the case pulled on the remaining three lines, each one snapping in turn, one after the other. The case fell, and disappeared down a lava chimney.

The parachute remained, like a huge orange flower, weighted by rain.

The plane buzzed away from the spurs toward the southwest, where it would drop another survival cache.

"PROFESSAH LAUDAH? I AM SAH-GEANT JONAS MODIBO, Professah," said the little African man with a tribal tattoo of inky dots set in an irregular square on his left cheek. "I come to ah-sist wid your camp. Da situation is dat as far as I see dey is no poaching situation in da area, but I come to ah-sist." He was five feet tall, had a thick tribal accent (it did not sound Kikuyu—was it Kipsigi? Luo? Ken wondered fleetingly), and wore an old British army greatcoat, the bottom part cut off to adjust to his short stature.

Standing in the savanna half a mile from the fossil-yielding monticule, Ken could not believe what he was seeing. The man looked to be in his fifties. He carried a British Enfield carbine of World War II vintage, slung onto his shoulder not by a leather strap but by a cord of what appeared to be knitted animal hair.

Ken had pitched his camp in the barest spot he could find, just wild grass and bushes, so he would be disturbing as little as possible the habitat he planned to observe. The site gave him a clear view in all directions, including the rocky palisades and the scattered groves of acacias. However, it also had the disadvantage of being in the harsh hot sunlight, which flooded the place, giving it the surreal, overexposed look of a nightmare.

Sweating under an old bush hat, Ken listened to Modibo, who had appeared from nowhere, walking over the savanna in old ankle-high boots, sockless it seemed. Modibo claimed that the game park department had relayed a request to a border post Ken had never heard of to deploy an NCO with bush-tracking skills to Professah Laudah's campsite. Because, as Modibo put it, ten days before, the professah had had "visitors."

"How exactly did the game park department get in touch with you?"

"Not game park. Ar-mee. I am ar-mee, border patrol. By radio telephone from Nairobi over to my post."

"And how did you get here?" The closest border post had to be almost a hundred miles away.

"Ar-mee truck from border wid Tanzania to about thirty mile from here. Den tree day walk over."

"You walked that distance alone?"

"Yess. Survey predators, for your protek-shion, Professah." Jonas Modibo broke into an almost happy smile, and reached a clawlike dark hand inside the faded greatcoat: "Dis ez my ah-creditation."

Though he looked as if he might be naked under his coat,

he brought out a wallet-sized army ID booklet, crumpled and dirty, but inside was a picture, stamps, and a valid date.

Behind Ken, Jakub Ngiamena's park scouts gaped at the odd little man. In their khaki tunics and shorts and dark blue berets, they looked *très chic* by comparison, even after two days of dusty driving through the Nyiri Desert and one night of camping out. They listened as Modibo said, "My order come from army, who got it from Superintendent Ngiamena office." He pronounced it Nyamena, with a strong nasal exhalation, making Ken wonder whether that was the initial pronunciation before the Ngiamenas moved into towns and joined the detribalized elite.

A feeling of incredulousness swept over Ken that was so strong it made everything else hard to believe.

"You making this up, Sergeant?"

"I am not, Professah."

Ken glanced at the team of park scouts. The team leader, a good-looking young warden, shrugged in complete ignorance of this additional arrangement. He and the other scout had "swept" the bushes and rock ranges the day before, by truck and on foot. They agreed with Modibo that there were no poachers here, at least none that could be easily sighted.

"Did you see any lions?" asked Ken, just to say something.

"Yes, two male. One ol', one young. Dey ben goin afta a pra-ahd of some"—Modibo narrowed his eyes, counting in his mind—"maybe five lioness wid cubs."

Ken nodded. He knew of that practice. Lazy male lions tried to join prides by killing the lionesses' cubs. If they managed to kill most of the cubs, the lionesses would soon fall into heat again. They would start rolling in the dirt and whipping their tails and growling for the males to come over and make new babies with them. The pressure to be fertile was carved into their genetic code deeper than the rage of pained motherhood. So the males took over the pride, and took advantage of the lionesses' hunting services.

"Did you see anything like this?" Ken was holding a clipboard with his checklists of equipment and maps, and a notepad. He made a quick sketch of the hominid footprint and showed it to Sergeant Modibo.

The tattered black man took a quick look. "No. Why? Your visitors has funny feet?" He indicated with his chin the ten-day-old wreck of the Safari Cub, which had become amazingly integrated to the bush, due to dust, spots of pollen, bugs crushed against its sides, and birds perching on it.

"No, I'm referring to the footprints of a kind of . . . primate creature."

The old soldier ignored this. "Dis camp not good here," he said authoritatively. "Bad situation, right in da path of herd stampedes. Dere's one dat come right now." He threw himself at the ground, buried his ear in the dirt. "Right now. Move camp *dere*." He rose and flagged his hand at a barren, steep hillside with a flat top.

Ken whipped his binoculars out of their case, scanned the horizon three hundred and sixty degrees. He saw rain clouds obscuring the Mau, but no dust stirred up by racing herbivores. Of course, if it was raining, the dust might be wet close to the Mau. He threw himself at the ground at once with one of the scouts, and they rose glancing at each other and shrugging; they didn't hear any distant drumming of hooves.

Modibo stared at him as if reading his mind. "Just wait, dey come. And you don want your papers wrinkled, Professah."

"I'm not a professor," blurted Ken. "And we're not moving this camp."

Ten minutes later, Ngili called. Out the plane's window, he had seen a pack of running wildebeests and buffaloes; they were widening their ripples away from the wet black rocks, into longer ripples that kicked off a panic in the other herds. Ngili told Ken that in an hour they might be visited by a charging stampede.

Forty minutes later, a black river of buffaloes poured past the hill, followed by prancing and leaping wildebeests. When their charge was over, Modibo, who was sitting on the dry grass munching on a coarse *posho* biscuit he had taken out of his tattered greatcoat, got up and left without a word. Ken saw him stop by the Safari Cub. He examined it, crawled inside, and reappeared holding a shiny wrench.

He came back and told Ken his theory that the gunmen were escaped criminals from Tanzania. They crossed the desert sometimes, in stolen vehicles, aiming for the relative haven of Uganda.

"Your friend's plane is coming," he warned Ken, who strained his ear but didn't hear an engine. Minutes later, a dark triangle that had looked like a hovering vulture grew into something rigid and man-made. It bounced as it landed on a strip cleared by the scouts and the buffaloes' hooves.

The sonofabitch must be psychic, thought Ken. Maybe he had spotted the plane, but there was no way a normal ear could have heard those distant hooves of the stampede. And how the hell had he detected that wrench in the Cub? He and Ngili had scoured the Cub and found it empty as a shell.

DRIVEN UPHILL BY ONE OF THE SCOUTS, KEN'S LAND ROVER stalled. It was restarted and made it to the top, coughing like an old man after a strenuous walk. Modibo shot up from the grass, brandishing the wrench and declaring that he had been a mechanic in the army and should be allowed to look at the engine. Before Ken could object, he had already popped up the sun-heated hood and was looking inside. Ken rushed over and slammed down the hood, almost catching Modibo's fingers. He would attend to his jeep himself, later. Angry that he had lost control and shown it, he marched back to the tent, where a scout beckoned at him that he had a radio call from Nairobi.

Sweating from the walk uphill, Ngili surfaced on the hilltop and found Ken grinning into his radio. A woman's voice spoke, clear and melodious. "This is easier to say over the radio. You are an unusually free man, Ken—I mean, for someone without power or money. I hope you find some pleasure in being out there."

"Plenty!" yelled Ngili, hurrying toward the radio and his

sister's voice. "He's having a big rush tonight, by going alone on a predator check, over!"

"Were you listening in?" asked Yinka. "And what's a predator check?"

"I'm not going on any kind of check. Certainly not tonight," Ken cut in.

He was indeed planning a night survey of the lion prides and hyena packs, but not in the first few nights, when, after two days of low-flying airplane activity, the savanna would be stirred up into stampedes. The unavoidable ripples of stampedes had just started, and they would continue to the edge of the desert, then ripple back in counter-stampedes, until the scared animals would settle again into their grazing territories. There, attacks by carnivores would make them spook and stampede again, but for considerably shorter distances.

He said a hurried good-bye to Yinka, switched the radio off, and turned to Ngili. "You're so unnecessarily rude, it's not to be believed. And what the hell's the story on this busybody sergeant?" Modibo, crab-legged and pulling up his greatcoat, was urinating on a bush, revealing that indeed he wore nothing under the big top except shorts. "Would you call your father and ask him to get this guy out of here?"

"I'm certainly not going to call him for *that*. I didn't know about this guy, but he's good extra protection for you!"

"I don't need that extra protection. I thought this was going to be a one-man search!"

"Isn't it? Aren't you the only damn scientist present in four hundred square miles?"

The area had been defined by Ken himself, as a twenty-by-twenty-mile square of savanna, bordered by the rocky palisades on its north-south edge, with a survival cache in its northeast and southwest corners. He was planning to search it on foot, carrying his light tent and a two-gallon plastic container of water, combing back-and-forth stretches five miles wide. To cover as much territory as possible, he would move his base camp to the first cache, and then to the second, and go on as many secondary searches as he had the stamina for.

It was an extremely ambitious plan. He would probably conk out way sooner than he expected. On the other hand, he might find what he was looking for.

Ngili cooled off. "I'm sorry. The old bugger won't be in your way. He's just going to eat your food for a few days and take off. I'm mad because you're going to see what you're going to see without me."

"Maybe I won't see anything."

"You will too, all by yourself."

"Well, you've got to come to terms with that. You're flying in every week anyway. It's the best we could do, and you agreed to it."

"I know!" replied Ngili, with high passion bubbling in his voice. "Yinka was right. You're free, and I'm not as free as you. I'm not a lucky free Yankee orphan, okay?" In one of his mood switches, he touched Ken's arm, passion still high, but now warm and sincere. "I'm sorry, okay?"

"Okay." Ken rose and started walking away. "I'm going to ask this weird old bird how long he's planning to stick around."

But he did not, because Modibo was nowhere to be seen.

Ken asked the two scouts where Modibo had gone. They were busy checking the truck they would be driving back to Nairobi. Modibo had just advised them to leave sooner than they had planned because "dere was anodda big stampede coming, da biggest," and it would rut the ground at the base of the hill, making it undrivable. The scouts were impressed with such bush lore, and had asked Modibo how long he had been familiar with Dogilani. He had told them he'd been "in dis spot since da eah-ly fifties, one way oh anodda. As a Mau Mau guerrilla, den in private safari bizness, den in da ah-mee."

But now he was not anywhere on the hilltop, nor visible anywhere else. There was no proof of his presence, except for a few crumbs from his posho biscuit, and the bush he had sprinkled with his urine before leaving, like a beast marking his territory.

FINALLY, MODIBO REAPPEARED WHEN THE SCOUTS AND Ngili and Ken and the Kenyan pilot were sharing a tense dinner. Now the pilot also wanted to leave early, and that frustrated Ngili. As for Ken, he was tense because he was only halfway set up and had counted on more help before they left him alone.

Modibo sat down, grabbed a park scout's lunch ration, and ate it in complete silence, interrupting himself only to announce that those lionesses with cubs had just appeared in the direct vicinity of the camp. They had settled nearby in a grove of acacias.

"Very interesting," said Ken. "You come with me after sundown, to film them with my infrared camera?"

"No. I protect camp, dose my orders. I don film lions. Dose not my orders."

"Fine, Sergeant. We'll go through our respective duties after we eat."

"Sure, Professah." Modibo spat a piece of cold chicken. Ken rose and picked it up and threw it in a dump bag of plastic. "Rule number one," he said, "no one's sloppy around my camp."

"Sorry, you right," said Modibo with mock effusiveness. "About da lions, I come wid you if you want."

"No need to. Stick to your orders. By the way, where are your buffaloes? I don't hear or see any stampede."

"Dey come."

"Before you walked off, you made it sound like they were going to trample us in the next five minutes. You made everyone nervous and anxious to leave, and now I don't see any buffaloes," said Ken, talking more for the scouts and the pilot than for himself.

"Sorry. Dey come later." Modibo spat another speck of chicken, then picked it up with his fingers and made a show of pushing it into the dump bag.

"I'm going to warm up the engine," announced the Kenyan pilot, rising. He did not look at Modibo, but Ken knew that the pilot was focused on Modibo's impending stampede, which would destroy the air strip and strand him here with someone like Modibo, the least reassuring bush tracker Ken had ever met.

Ngili got up too. He averted his eyes. "Ken, I'll help you get some wood for the fire tonight."

By the time they came back with the wood, feeling closer to each other after a half hour of silent hacking under the sun's melted steel, Modibo had disappeared again.

And there were no buffaloes in sight, nor wildebeests.

Finally, they all said good-bye to one another. Ken shook hands with the scouts and the pilot. The scouts parted from Ngili and the pilot. Ken and Ngili hugged each other. *"Kwaheri na kuona,"* said Ngili to Ken. "Good-bye till we meet again."

In all his bush treks, Ken had never experienced two departures at once. The truck hurtled down from the hill and the plane bounced to its takeoff at the same time.

In minutes, the truck was a moving dot, and the plane a cross shining hard at the zenith of the still incandescent sky, as the pilot turned from his ascent and passed right above Ken toward Nairobi. The Helio's wings collected so much sun glare that they looked like laser beams.

It was impossible for Ken not to watch the decreasing truck and plane without some anxiety. Humanity was leaving one of its own behind, and that human happened to be him.

Ngili had told Ken to keep his radio on reception for a while, just in case he spotted the sergeant from the plane, although he believed the man was nearby and would reappear as unexpectedly as he had the other times.

Ngili had helped Ken chop dried whistling thorns into a little pile ready to be kindled into the camp's first fire; all Ken had to do was light it up. But Ken still had to secure his surroundings. He started that by walking back and forth over the flat hilltop, not gently as he usually would in a natural environment, but plodding heavily with his boots to scare away rodents and other small mammals, thus lessening the chances that a big snake, including the fatally poisonous black mamba, would show up later. Other death-inflicting creatures would hopefully be kept at bay by the fire.

As the sun went down, and the moon started to rise, Ken's radio crackled. Nigili had not spotted the sergeant or anyone else as he headed south. Now he was getting close to Nairobi and wanted to wish Ken good night.

Ken lay down in his tent, a few feet from the Land Rover. He thought he had fallen asleep, then found himself awake and rising, crawling outside, stepping into the Land Rover, and driving it off and parking it twenty yards away. Now, no one could sneak up on him by using the Land Rover for cover. Somewhat reassured by that thought, he returned to his sleeping bag and felt around for the Rhino .38. He loaded it and set it next to him, safety catch on. He knew it did not augur well that he was starting his solo search with such strained nerves.

HE BOLTED UP AGAIN, NOT KNOWING WHEN HE HAD NODDED off. He had fallen asleep by the tent, in the open.

Rawooo, went a male lion nearby, like a deep prehistoric warning.

And several females seemed to bark in response. They sounded angry and pained, as if wounded in their entrails.

What the hell is that idiot doing? Ken wondered. He was convinced that Modibo was stalking the lions, orders or no orders. He strained to hear the flat brief bang of the Enfield. A moonlighter like Modibo would not hesitate to kill lions to sell their skins to poachers.

He sat up, fighting an uncontrollable tightness in his chest that came from the close sounds of lions. He had been near them hundreds of times, but their power never failed to frighten him. He wasn't embarrassed about it; being afraid was almost genetic.

"Da lions caught someting," said Modibo.

Ken flinched so hard from the shock that he almost toppled

backward from his sitting position. Modibo was on his knees, less than a yard from Ken, his rifle lying on the grass next to him. He had raised his hands, with fingers spread and crooked, to mimic the lions' clawing action.

The lions caught something.

"What did they catch?" breathed Ken.

The sergeant stared, as if deciding whether to speak or not. "Can't say. Prey don cry, don make sound. Maybe dey picked someting dead already."

A thought stabbed Ken's mind. Maybe it was that child. *Maybe it was dead already.*

Steady, he urged himself. Don't go crazy.

But he could not stop his mind from rambling. *Was it the child? Was it dead already because Modibo killed it with one short, low, dry bang of his rifle?*

Modibo dropped his hands into his lap. As he did so, Ken realized that the other man was creeping forward to grab the Rhino .38, which was almost within his reach.

Ken also was in reach of a weapon. The sergeant's Enfield.

He calculated that his own arms were longer than Modibo's, and that this was a peculiar kind of Wild West gunfight; instead of just drawing, both gunfighters had to lunge out first and grab the other's weapon.

"What happened to that stampede?" Ken rasped. "Still not here?"

Modibo squinted in the dark, as if confused by the question.

Ken's hand shot forward, grabbed the Enfield's barrel. Though sweeping Ken's face with his little eyes, the sergeant was unprepared. When he brought down his claw, he struck grass. The rifle was already in Ken's hand.

"Come down with me, to see what the lions got," said Ken. He pulled the rifle entirely to his side, then threw himself back onto his sack of equipment. He felt the hard shapes of his Starlight nightviewers, of an extra field radio and a shovel—they cut into his spine and kidney area, but he did not care. He rose, holding the sack, the Rhino .38, and the rifle.

"You need so much protek-shion?" asked Modibo, looking up from his kneeling position like a goblin come alive. He scared Ken more than the fighting lions. "Where you going, professah? You leave me here without ah-ms?"

"The lions won't climb the hill to attack you, you should know that," muttered Ken. He felt embarrassed, yet relieved to be listening to his cowardice. The more he looked at that unkempt face, at its scraggly beard and mustache and inky tattooed dots, the more he felt that he wasn't even beginning to suspect the truth about the little man.

From down on his knees, Modibo laughed with a loudness that did not suit his tight little manner. It was big and dramatic: "Crazy *mzungu*," he said, using East Africa's derogatory word for white man.

"Right," said Ken. "Very crazy. You'll tell me more about that when I come back." He backtracked from the little man, leaving him on the top of the hill, alone, unmoving.

First let's see what the story is on those lions, he thought.

He heard the hill's gravel squeak under his boots and realized that he had not taken them off before going to sleep. Lucky mistake. Lucky everything, so far. He finally turned, threw the heavy sack of equipment on his shoulder, and started running full force into the night.

Ahead of him, a lioness burst out in a cry of pain or indignation, followed by the combined roar of two lions—that lioness or another one, and a male. They sounded as if they were fighting mouth to mouth, fang to fang.

Running, Ken rummaged among the equipment and pulled out his Starlight nightviewers. He stopped to put them on, then rushed again toward the roars of the lions. His nightviewers made the bush look phosphorescent green. Luminous points of green fire indicated the animals' eyes, or fangs glinting inside their open jaws. The horizon seemed lit by a green-amber breath from the cosmos beyond. The stars looked like eyes too, myriads of them, their fixedness giving them a quietly hellish look. They were dead and unmoving. Like the eyes of departed ancestors in African stories, they were still focused at the strange planet they had left behind them.

Whether it was fatigue, or the eeriness of the nightviewers' rendition of reality, Ken shivered. The acacias were coming closer, seeming to move with up and down jolts as Ken's steps carried him forward, altering the nightviewers' angle of vision. He suddenly heard a massive roar of lions. He was pierced by fright.

He saw a tangle of lions next to an acacia tree. They were tearing at something. He saw a dark body in their midst.

He rushed forward, shouting, "Ho! Ho!," an unplanned primal shout. He dropped the sack, found himself brandishing the African's rifle. Its stock was light, as if it were made of bamboo, and the barrel too heavy to aim. He dropped it, grabbed the reassuringly heavy Rhino.

The body inside the lions' tangle rose, then fell, then rose again, pulled up and knocked down by the lions. Ken was convinced that the body was that of the hominid. He felt the horror any human faced when another human was being ripped up by claws and fangs.

"HO!!!" Ken shouted dementedly, rushing forward. He could not fire at that tangle; there was no way he wouldn't hit the prey. He dropped the Rhino and the Enfield and charged forward with bare hands, then plunged to the ground to scoop up stones and throw them at the lions. He scraped hard, finding only pebbles and frittering sand. One of his thumb nails cracked, splitting painfully. He winced from the pain, but forgot it the next second. He arched his arm to throw a pebble, but stopped his move in midair. Two lionesses were jumping straight up at the lower branches of another acacia. They jumped and growled, as if teased by some presence in the tree.

He aimed his nightviewers at the strange scene, a dance of powerful hungry bodies. Then he looked up. The tree was richly foliated. He could not tell what they were jumping at. He scanned the leaves, saw a rounded shape in the fork of a high branch, and could not tell whether it was a crouched monkey, an outgrowth of bark, or an oversized nest.

In the first group of felines, the lions were silent now, pulling at a mangled body that was clearly dead. There was nothing he could do. A male lion slouched out of the fight with some shredded piece dangling in his mouth. Ken's breath stopped. He scanned in horror, assuming that this was a human's limb . . .

It was a dead cub hanging from the big male's jaws, and on the ground lay a dead lioness. Two other males were eating her. The other females began herding the surviving cubs away with strong pushes from their noses, and an occasional rough swat of paws.

The lions' prey was not a hominid.

The wayward young females stopped jumping at the other tree and joined the departing pride. Their tails hit puffs of dust perfectly visible in the amber light of the nightviewers. Ken wondered what other animal, now safely ensconced in the branches, had provoked them so. The males were left to devour what they had killed. They would surely pester that pride again, but not tomorrow. For the next couple of nights, they would lazily roll under the trees before they got hungry enough to attack their own kind again.

Ken stood watching the chewing males, watching the lionesses' hips sashay away in the moonlight. The show of the unending primacy of instinct was momentarily over.

He retraced his steps and found the weapons he had dropped. Bending to pick them up, he glanced randomly toward the hilltop, and was blinded by a beam of light, so unexpected and harsh that he uttered a muffled cry. Increasing the available light 70,000 times, his nightviewers had hit not a feeble moon ray or a glint of fangs from the savanna's fauna, but a source of live electricity. He fell to his knees, closed his eyes hard, then took off his nightviewers, letting them hang by their strap against his chest. Carefully, he blinked, easing his shocked eyesight into the savanna's darkness, lush and real.

Up on the hilltop, the flashlight was dancing around the square shape of the Land Rover. Ken's adjusting eyes told him that the vehicle's hood was up. Then the flashlight blinked off, and he heard a mechanical noise, like metal hitting metal.

Picking up the Rhino, the sack, and the rifle, he started back, his boots torturing the gravel. Coming level with the hilltop, he saw the jeep. Its hood was down now. He wondered whether he had just imagined it being up. Then the flashlight came on again. Modibo was seated at the jeep's wheel, the wrench flashing up in his hand, then hammering down with that noise of metal on metal.

Dead still, Ken stared as his brain processed the visual. Suddenly it came to him: Modibo had been driving that Safari Cub the week before; he had to be the one. And he had escaped into the wilderness.

He took a quick look at the dark hilltop, spotted a bush and silently dropped the Enfield behind it—just in case Modibo tried to wrestle the rifle from him. He stuck the Rhino in his belt and tried to step noiselessly up to the car. He reached the car door, shot his arm forward, and tore the door open.

The steering column looked disemboweled, with strips of plastic hanging out one slashed-open side, and the connecting bolts shone inside like bones exposed by a severe fracture. Modibo was battering the steering rod, trying to loosen the bolts that connected the steering rod to the device that moved the car's wheels.

Modibo turned and hit Ken over the head with the wrench so hard and fast that Ken fell forward over him. Ken smelled the insufferable odor of old unwashed male, a redolence of bad teeth and coarse food, a whiff of rancid butter that perhaps the sergeant had oiled into his hair. They kept him from fainting. He felt blood roll down his forehead, warm and sticky, and tasted it on the corner of his mouth, and saw it before his eyes. He now saw everything through a film of red.

Ken ducked another blow from the wrench. A third missed him. Ken grabbed the wrench. He flung it away, grabbed the sergeant by his sweaty neck, pulled him out of the Land Rover, then put all his strength into one punch. He hit the sergeant full in the chin, sending him crashing back into the jeep. His hands locked on Modibo's clammy neck again, and he shook him, hissing through a taste of blood, "Why?" And then, "Who? Who sent you?"

Modibo hung limply. Ken let him go and Modibo crashed forward, one knee hitting Ken's stomach, knocking him down. Whirling around, he stepped on Ken, groping to find the wrench in the dark. Ken's heart was in his throat. If he didn't catch the man, he was dead. He lunged and gripped a foot in a battered army boot. Modibo left the boot, dusty, smelly, in Ken's hand. He laughed like a gnome, and rushed down the incline, while Ken picked up his Rhino and threw himself behind the car's wheel. He swabbed the blood from his face with the back of his hand and cracked a bloodied grin. No way. No way would he let Modibo escape. Modibo had escaped on the morning of the Safari Cub's charge, and someone else had tried to kill Ken that same evening, in front of Theo's shop.

He stabbed the key into the ignition. The engine fired. He turned the wheel, hearing a grinding noise in the steering column, but the wheel responded. Modibo had not managed to destroy the steering rod. He punched the high beams on and roared down. Ahead, he could see the military greatcoat sweep the ground. The trail of gravel looked jagged and pitted. The Land Rover skidded, kicking a cloud of pebbles and gravel, and Ken braked hard.

The brakes sank to the car floor and failed to come up again. He pumped them. They remained stuck to the floor, lifeless.

Ken did the only thing he could—he hugged the wheel.

Modibo must have slashed open the high-pressure hoses transferring oil from the master cylinder to the disc brakes. He must have used a sturdy knife which he kept hidden in his inexhaustible military coat. He had done a very professional job; all it had taken was one hard slam on the brakes, and they exploded. Ken pictured the Land Rover's bottom, trailing tears of dark brake oil over the aeons-old scree of the hillside.

All that fought in his mind with the curves of the incline, with the treacherousness of the gravel, with the gaping drops of empty space he was passing at a dizzying speed, and into which his screeching wheels were now kicking pebbles. He yelled a high yell, to exorcise the unwanted thoughts. To concentrate, he looked away from the military coat running ahead. He hugged the wheel, hugged the road, hugged his life.

The Land Rover banged and rattled like an empty pail. It skidded frighteningly. Ken twisted the wheel hard into the skid to keep from tumbling over and downward. The jeep righted itself and roared down again as if chased by the furies. All Ken could do was drive, hugging the curves and trying to predict them, and praying.

The incline that had taken ten minutes to drive up took under two to drive down, but even that seemed an infinity. To slow down, Ken downshifted—without any results. At the bottom of the hill, the jeep was clocking a hundred an hour. It hit a boulder and leaped, cracking Ken's forehead into the rearview mirror. He didn't feel the blow because he was staring outside at Modibo, who was at the foot of the hill, standing almost at attention, coat open over his chest, white teeth flashing.

Ken could have shot him, had his hands not been fused to the wheel. He passed him close, taking him in, his brain fighting for any detail he could use to track him later. He had a sense of being in an unplayed game, of a race that was only starting. He had survived. He had not tumbled in his jeep to a fiery death—so why was Modibo laughing?

The jeep roared into the savanna, its headlights shining on a vast vista of horns. That was why Modibo was laughing. The water buffaloes were not stampeding, but *they were here,* trotting peacefully in the cool of the night. Their horns filled the flatland, a dozen yards from the hill.

Ken had no time to debate whether to stay with his runaway jeep or to jump off. He watched as his brand-new bull bars crashed into one of the huge buffaloes, whose widespread horns seemed to drag its head down. The bull was catapulted into the air and came down again like a jumping whale over the dark waves of other buffaloes. The herd shook from the commotion, like land from an earthquake. The jeep, still standing up, was thrust into the mass of buffaloes, like a bullet hitting with full impact.

CRUNNKK!! From the left side, a pair of horns bashed in the dented bodywork, above the left rear wheel. The side window shattered. From the right side, a female protecting her calf thrust her nimbler, less down-spread horns at the right tire. On reflex, Ken swung the wheel and rotated the jeep's front, causing the right end of the bull bars to gore the female at the neck. Ken cried out loud and hard. A week before, he had been attacked twice and had managed to trick death, but he wouldn't be so lucky this time, and that was why Modibo was laughing. He was doomed whether he left the jeep or not. He'd be found in bloodied pieces strung over the bush, man and car fused together with help from an evil-smelling engine fire. The horns would rock the jeep until they knocked it over, and fire was almost a given. And . . .

And *they* had the evidence of his find.

He realized it with a shiver so severe that the hairs all over his body hardened and felt like wires.

They, whoever they were, knew he had discovered that fossil. They also knew where he lived, or could easily find out. He had recorded his find on two floppy discs, which now contained detailed descriptions of the fossil and the footprints. He had stored these discs in his apartment, in a locked drawer whose key he carried on his key chain. But once his pursuers broke into his apartment, they'd need only a few minutes to break into that drawer too. He'd put the negatives of the film of the footprints in a bank box, but even that did not feel terribly safe now. Even his digging gear was evidence of his discovery, and it was all back at the camp, much of it in that sack of equipment he had so idiotically dropped on the hilltop.

He would never see that hilltop again; they'd gotten rid of him, and they had all his evidence.

They . . .

Who exactly were *they*?

And were they after him because of the fossil or because of the hominid footprints?

The horror of those thoughts brought him to his senses. However slim his chance of survival, the game had to be played out.

THE LAND ROVER WAS BEING ROLLED AND CONFUSEDLY bumped by horns every few seconds. Then the jeep moved into a different segment of the herd, where the buffaloes were smaller but seemed to attack more viciously, boring holes in the jeep's shell with their lowered horns. They were mostly females protecting calves. *Whack, dang, boom*—the hits came from all directions, as half a dozen mothers quickly figured out Ken's weakness and began ringing him in a circle of horns, crunching him simultaneously from the front, the sides, and the back. The jeep shook like a carcass that a dog had dug up from the trash and would not let go of. All the side windows had cracked and fallen off in shards, and a dented back door had popped out of joint, causing the dying overhead light in the jeep's ceiling to revive and flicker, which gave Ken trouble seeing ahead. Both headlights were gone now. All he could think was: Get away from those enraged mothers.

He still had some gasoline. The transmission and steering still worked. Even the dashboard radio worked, but Ken could not take the time to send distress signals. And besides, Modibo was probably rummaging through Ken's camp and would be the first to receive his distress message. In no time, he would radio his friends, who would rush in and kill Ken if he wasn't dead already.

He grinned with chattering teeth. The stampede was his best cover. If he survived. He gassed the jeep, pulled at the sluggish wheel—either some of the steering bolts had given way, or the wheels were mired in a collapsed buffalo. He pulled at it while gassing frantically, and . . .

Slowly the Land Rover emerged from the mothers' herd, back into the main one.

He was racing along with them now. Lateral jabs of horns were still aimed at him, but somehow the herd was letting him stampede with them, almost accepting him. His only chance was to ride the stampede and at the same time prolong it, powering the herd from inside by being the herd's nuisance. If this worked he would end up far away from his camp and from the gunmen.

And in the end, if all his gasoline was depleted and he was knocked over, the only way he'd survive would be for that to happen during daylight. He had to become the stampede. He had to be its soul, till the morning.

The torn-open back door rattled loosely, turning the bulb above him on, off, on. He could see ahead only when that crazy flickering above him was off, so he punched upward at the blinking bulb. A vicious burn singed his fist, and shards of glass from the bulb lacerated his skin, but he had done it. He had killed that killer light. Now he and the stampede, as one, rolled away under the moon.

T HERE PASSED A TIME THAT SEEMED TIMELESS, AND AT long last, on Ken's right, a streak of red cracked the horizon, like a gash in the skin of a pulpy ripe fruit. Ahead, the mists were thicker. Clouds churned over the savanna's northwestern edge. The Mau seemed very far away and was almost completely blocked off by the mist.

The Land Rover slowed down. Horns from behind attacked it instantly. He prayed the herd would abandon him next to a tree stand, the best momentary cover against discovery from above. He considered jumping from the jeep, but the dark humps around him were still dense and furious. The trees were coming. He tried to identify their species, so as to guess other features of the habitat. An unseen natural obstacle sprung the jeep upward. A wide blinding light invaded him as he flew up in the air, jeep and all, and his head collided hard with the jeep's ceiling.

The jeep crashed onto its side, and several pairs of horns instantly stabbed into it, powered by the herd's run. They became stuck in the vehicle's roof.

The horns dragged the jeep away, its weight slowing them down. Finally, like a stone jammed in the middle of a stream, the jeep stopped. Inside, the limp human looked dead while the buffaloes poured on past, and then they were gone.

An unmeasured time passed. The limp human coughed,

opened his eyes, and struggled with the car door. He opened
it and attempted to climb outside, but his knees folded under
him. He fell out of the Land Rover and crawled a few feet;
then his powers gave out again. He lay still, unconscious.

HE HEARD A TWITTERING OF BIRDS. A LOUD *VRRRRRR*
sound throbbed the air above his face. He thought: hum-
mingbirds. He blinked, opened his eyes, cracking a crust of
blood.

He was lying in a bush with small leaves and frail pale-
blue flowers. Above him, the crown of a big tree looked
soothingly dark. He tried to stagger up, felt a searing pain in
one ankle, and fell back by the bush. For now, he could not
stand on that ankle. That woke him from the lingering stupor
of his vehicle's crash.

THE LEOPARD HAD JUST HAD CUBS. HER BELLY STILL HUNG
down under her otherwise sleek body, distended and hollowed by pregnancy. She was furiously hungry; for the last
week she had eaten nothing but an insignificant bushbuck
and her own afterbirth. Hunger forced her out in daytime.
She walked into the clearing, between two large trees, where
fruit often fell to the ground, damaged by parasites, only to
be eaten by gazelles who would digest the fleshy part and
dump the seed pods out in their feces. So there might be
gazelles among those trees. The leopard tiptoed, but she was
too hungry to be quiet. She salivated, while curling the air
in her mouth with an audible *grrrrr*.

Slowly Ken began crawling toward the overturned Land
Rover, to try to find his gun. He had heard the leopard even
before seeing it; no other bush animal made that throaty rattling sound. When she stepped into view, one glance at her
belly, with its enlarged pink teats showing in the unkempt
fur, told Ken that she was a brand-new mother, which made
her doubly dangerous. Giving thanks that nothing else in him
was twisted or broken, he moved himself by digging his nails

into the ground and pulling. He was feeble, but alert. He had a chance with his Rhino pistol, if he could find it.

The leopard crouched down in surprise, tail beating at her fertile flanks, then got up and sniffed the air ahead. A sunbird buzzed by her nose, and she pawed at it, hating, like all felines, distractions before a kill. Her stomach was secreting gastric compounds that rose into her throat. She *grrr*-ed louder, drooling a clump of hungry foam.

Ken was at the front end of the jeep. The side ends of the bull bars, he noticed, had been torn off like matchsticks. Horn stabs all over the front looked like bullet holes and the bumper was entirely gone. The headlights were blind scooped-out metal sockets.

By mistake, he pushed at the ground with his feet. The maddening pain in his ankle shot into his brain. He sweated coldly. The sweat mixed with the blood on his face, producing a horrible appearance—not animal, not human. He grabbed the bull bars to pull himself up, but felt faint. He could not stand up at all. He could not open the dented doors.

Now the leopard was just a few feet away. He guessed that she was better than a hundred and sixty pounds. He feverishly grabbed at the belt around his middle; he still carried a large knife, bayonet-shaped, which he used for cutting wood to make fires.

He pulled it out of its leather sheath and tried to figure out the best position for using it. Lying on the ground, he would never defeat the leopard, unless by some luck he could get to her heart. Sitting with his back against what was left of the bull bars was a better option. He managed to push himself up, turned, and fell against the jeep. He folded his legs and sat, with the knife pointed forward.

She was crouching two yards away, preparing for her bring-down-the-prey leap.

He thought he had strong enough nerves to wait for the leap, but the fixed concentration in her glittering yellow eyes overpowered his self-control. She went down so close to the ground that she almost disappeared. He saw only her face, and her pale tongue waved out hungrily, smacking her black nose and wetting her spiny whiskers. The smacking panicked him. He opened his mouth.

"HQOOOOOO!!" he yelled, a loud and unending human voice. He yelled so hard that when he grew breathless he still snarled with his short flat teeth and closed his eyes and willed away the leopard.

She drew back, momentarily intimidated. He stuck the knife in his teeth, grabbed the bull bars, and pulled himself up again. He stepped on his excruciatingly painful ankle, and it held him. He then scrambled onto the side of the jeep facing up and found that the door had fallen in. He lowered himself inside, but did not see the pistol. He felt, groped, scoured the various niches of the car's inner space. His fingers found something, grabbed it, pulled, burning with hope fired up from his capillaries into his brain.

It was his set of nightviewers.

He dropped it back into the jeep, scoured with his fingers again. No weapon. It had probably been flung out by the power of the crash.

He felt he had exhausted all his powers of yelling. And the big cat was sitting on her spotted tail, a few yards from the jeep.

Unaware, he was leaning on the mangled rear door. With a jangle of bent metal, it ejected him outward. He tumbled and rolled, and the cat was instantly on him, as if on cue, lured by his sudden movement. A paw crushed the front of his field shirt, which was studded with copper buttons. Her whiskered nose lunged at his face, and he burst into the most godawful howl he had ever uttered, spitting his dying breath at the cat.

She shook her head, as if deafened by his shout, and stepped off his chest. She retreated backward, her tail swishing. He sat up, shaking so hard that his head bobbed about, making the cat throb and blur.

The closeness of death was making him rave. Even though there was no open sky above for him to pray to, he threw back his head in that typically human gesture of desperate supplication.

He saw a face above him, and it wasn't a child's. An adult—brown skin, low forehead, long lips, long arms—hung down from the acacia tree, almost right above him. It had the brawny arms of a strong, habitual arm-swinger, and its mouth was open. It seemed ready to join Ken in howling away at the leopard.

Two other creatures, a little higher up in the branches, were reaching down to pull at their curious mate, to stop him or her from letting on that they were there. Ken barely glimpsed the two other faces because they were hidden by leaves. Ken's mouth was gaping to issue another howl, but it never made a sound. The creature closer to him opened its lips, pursing them out into a funnellike shape, and emitted a howl that was high and screechy, but above all so penetrating that the leopard bounced back, lashing her hips with her tail in near-defeat. The creature let out another scream, an even louder kind of *eee-eee-eee-eehh* sound. It seemed to freeze all the surrounding animal movement. Even the sunbirds, bubbling across sunrays one instant before, seemed to disappear.

Then it waited, outlined clearly against the green of the leaves. Ken saw the curve of its chimplike braincase, and reckoned that it might, just might, carry five hundred cubic centimeters of brain. It was topped by a low but distinct jagged indentation, a sagittal crest to secure its massive jaw muscles.

It looked like a hominid.

Ken grinned with parched lips: Perfect dying dream, Lauder. At the right time, and in the right spot.

The other creatures began pulling up the lower one. They would not let it endanger itself more by participating in a fight that didn't concern them. It was a beautiful gesture meant to stop their idealistic kinsman who was feeling sympathy for the cornered alien below.

Ken became unsure whether or not he was dreaming this moment. The vision lasted only a few more seconds before the other two arm-swingers hoisted up the third one, revealing a humanlike buttock, no tail, no ischial callosities, no chimp excrescences.

Then all three vanished upward, into stirred leaves, letting Ken exult, about to faint and no longer caring. *You saw them, Lauder. Fate gave you that gift, so you can die now.*

Even if they were only a vision, he felt they had helped save his life. The leopard had turned away. Throat rattling menacingly, she rolled her shoulders and hips out of the clearing, toward more orthodox game.

He crawled into the jeep, pulled the mangled door shut, and enjoyed a brief sense of better odds.

FOR THE NEXT FEW MINUTES—OR WAS IT HOURS?—KEN searched the jeep but couldn't find his pistol. His mind would not accept the notion that he was without a weapon. A moment of lucidity came and he realized that the reason he was acting maniacally and illogically was because water depletion was already taking hold. Then the lucidity passed, and he was again searching for the weapon.

He crawled out again, pressing his forehead against the scrub to fight a vicious headache and to gain control of his racing thoughts. Perhaps the Rhino was lying in the nearby scrub, ejected by the impact of the crash but loaded and ready for use. His injured ankle stopped him from looking for it.

He had found his keys lying on the bottom of the jeep, and was now working the little ring that held the keys together, separating the ignition key from the keys to his Nairobi apartment, to his safe at the bank and to the drawer of his desk. He put the ignition key in a zippered breast pocket, and the other keys in his back pants pocket, next to his wallet and the foreigner's permit to seek work in the Republic of Kenya.

The limited search had exhausted him. He sat on the grass, his ankle swollen like a football. Jabs of pain shot up into his knee and thigh, with such sharp intensity that he had to clench his teeth not to moan. He had not eaten or drunk fluids for over sixteen hours. All he could do to improve his condition was rest.

Then he found the knife, in the grass, inches from where he was sitting. He could not remember when it had slipped out of his fingers.

With the knife clutched in his hand, he lay down on one side, reviewing his fantasy of the protohumans. It *was* fantasy, no doubt about it. Even that screeching yell. He decided that this was the best dying vision a man could have, and he closed his eyes.

HE FELT HE HAD SLEPT, BUT IT SEEMED AS IF ONLY MINUTES had passed. It was dusk again, and he was still lying by the jeep.

He had not eaten or drunk fluids for almost twenty-four hours.

The dusk was cool, and he felt rational again. He started mentally drawing up a list of his present handicaps. His ankle was swollen and he could not guess what its true state was. He did not know whether his jeep was drivable after tumbling onto one side, but it had to be righted first, and he was in no condition to try that by himself. The jeep had a battery-operated winch and cable mounted behind the bull bars, on a steel bracket. If he could secure the cable over a thicker acacia branch and turn on the winch, he could pull the jeep back to its upright position. He could not remember whether he had an extra canister of gasoline in the storage bin behind the backseat. And there was no way to patch the brakes.

More important, he had no food or water, and no compass—the compass had been left at the camp with the rest of his gear.

He could not help reminding himself how ample and sophisticated his camp supplies were. But now all of them were lost. They included his tent, his sleeping bag, his medical kit, his flashlights, all with spare batteries, his watch (last night, he had unstrapped it and pushed it into a hemmed pocket of his sleeping bag), his sunglasses, binoculars, camera with spare lenses and film rolls, maps, frying pan and cooking pots, notebooks and pens and pencils, signal flares, and a healthy stack of wet towelettes fit for all kinds of cleaning needs, sealed in a plastic bag. He also had water purification tablets and food—everything from dried soups and meat bars to cereal mixture and salt tablets.

He had brought along modern man's complete culture, and lost it in minutes.

Of all those losses, his watch was one of the most glaring. Literally so, for it was a digital Seiko that glittered reassuringly in the dark. In the bush, time was of little significance, and yet he was almost mystically wedded to its passing. Often, as night fell over majestic wilderness, he read the time to see exactly when the sun had exited, giving the signal to the night hunters.

No more time now. All gone, with man's other inventions.

He did not know how far he was from the camp. During his long drive, he had glanced repeatedly at the odometer, but now he couldn't remember the readings. Besides, the mileage was meaningless without knowing which direction he had been moving in, and the jeep did not have a dashboard compass. In daytime, he could orient himself by the sun and the crest of the Mau, provided that his ankle got better first so he could walk out of the trees.

Ken knew he could exist without any food at all for five to seven days, even sweating and evaporating at a high mineral-depleting rate. But if he didn't find water, his rationality would give out totally in seventy-two hours maximum, not to mention that he would lose all his strength. He would experience visual and auditory hallucinations, or the most bizarre of thoughts, including suicidal ones.

His first priority was water and the second was to reach one of the survival caches.

For that, he needed physical strength. He wondered how debilitated he might feel the next morning, assuming that tonight he would not have to repulse another leopard or some other ferocious animal attack, which could be fatal.

Then he remembered Sergeant Modibo and his gnarled,

gnomish laugh. Sergeant Modibo had not managed to kill him, nor had he failed either. On his list of dangers, Ken had to add the likelihood that Modibo and his friends might hunt him out. He remembered the Safari Cub. If they were organized at all, they had to have other vehicles.

He scolded himself for panicking. Modibo probably thought he was dead. And all these creatures drank water, so there had to be a water hole nearby. He didn't have any halazone purifying tablets, but he had drunk brown waterhole fluid before, suffered through the inescapable ensuing diarrhea, and survived. He'd reach that water hole somehow, crawling if he had to.

Stupid, he muttered, alone in the thickening dark. So stupid.

HE EXPECTED TO SLEEP, BUT COULD NOT. TRYING TO THINK positively, he kept reminding himself of the survival caches, which were approved by the largesse of Jakub Ngiamena, who expected a weekly report from Ken about the fauna, the flora, and the state of the terrain in the researched area.

Jakub Ngiamena . . .

"My order come from army," Modibo had said. "From army, who got it from Superintendent Ngiamena office."

Sergeant Modibo . . . Superintendent Ngiamena . . .

He threw himself upward and cried out, landing on his painful foot, and fell. But his physical fall was nothing compared to the crash of his mood, as he realized that if Ngiamena's office had contacted that border post, then it was possible that Ngiamena was the one who had ordered Modibo to . . . to . . . to kill him!

There was an explosion in Ken's head as he put the evil-smelling sergeant next to the majestic and paternal Masai king.

He was slipping his cables. Plain slipping his cables.

But was he really?

He reasoned feverishly: Why would Ngiamena *not* want to kill him? Ken was a foreigner, an American, a paleface, a bad influence, and an unwanted distraction to his daughter. Above all, Ken had discovered a unique treasure in a poor land during a time of rabid nationalism! He sweated coldly. Yinka had told him that the old man had problems. The Ngiamenas stood to lose their status, money, and place in the land's elite and history, but they could retain all that through some great act of faith toward their country during this crisis. And there was no better way to do this than to rescue this incredible find from the hands of this outsider, this intruder—or "agent," as they would no doubt describe him.

He was going mad from dehydration, food depletion, and the shock of his unexpected and frightening plight. Anyone in his situation would start seeing ghosts and plots everywhere. Ngiamena, a killer? He had fought the British, yes, but that was forty years back. But wait a second . . .

Ken shivered. He knew that lions, the symbol of noblesse on so many coats of arms, the pillared, pedestaled pride of so many monuments, were nothing but vicious and lazy killers who ate their own young, stole the lionesses' kills, and never shared food before their own bellies were full. They were foul-smelling, passive, childlike, and utterly murderous. He sniffed, trying to make out whether Simba Ngiamena smelled like a real lion. But just then Ngiamena turned into his own daughter. "We have a deal, settler?"

Yinka. Yinka smelled like a flower and was as cool as one. Or cool as water. In his dry, painful delirium, Ken realized how much he needed water. Yinka, water. Did her name mean spring or something like that in a tribal dialect? Yinka = water?

Yinka became Ngili. Ngili said, somber, vengeful: "You'll be the first scientist to see this. The only one in four hundred square miles."

That was true. A glitch of rationality lit his brain; if Modibo had been taken in by his trick, then he was alive and alone, the only human in four hundred square miles.

So water-depleted, he should've stopped sweating long before. Yet he still sweated against the coolness of the night,

praying for the craziness to stop. But it didn't stop. If Ngiamena had ordered his elimination, which made perfect sense,
where did that place Ngili?

Ngili!

No, he said to the night. No way. Jesus. Ngili was his best
friend. Ngili had saved his life only ten days before, as they
flew above that spur and Ken almost fell out of Hendrijks's
plane. No, no, Ngili was his friend. Still his friend. Despite
his ridiculous reaction to Yinka's interest in him, if she really
harbored such an interest . . .

Yinka . . .

He felt her kiss on his lips, in his mouth, and then realized
that he was tasting his thirst-parched palate. It felt dry as a
desert. He tore a button from his shirt and stuck it in his
mouth. He bit on the copper, letting his mouth react to its
presence. Its taste was bitter, oxidized. But his palate and
cheeks responded by secreting tiny drops of saliva.

Yinka had been the one who had talked him into the
deal. . . . Yinka was in it too. . . . All of them were in it. . . .

But why *him*? He was innocent. Why was he being punished?

Precisely because he was innocent, he decided. As a reminder of the Africans' own innocence, destroyed over cen-
turies of raiding and killing and pitiless foreign rule. Africa
had a history of cruelty.

He sat down in the darkness, shaking. He was sad, but he
recognized that his friends-turned-foes were owed some
amount of revenge. Their hate had been sown in them since
pharaonic and Roman times, when the first African slaves
were sold in Thebes, Byzantium, and Rome. Then the Arabs,
Turks, English, Dutch, French, German, Portuguese, Americans, all had raided them, burned them, lashed them, and
garrotted them, pushing them into ships where the chained
captives, not even free to jump overboard and drown, took
their own lives by holding their breaths till their hearts
stopped—a feat that Western medicine could not explain. So
the Africans hated as a matter of course, as a way of life and
an adjustment to history, and now they were using Ken Lau-

der to make them feel less hate. But they had a right to their hate, which would not be assuaged by the game of democracy and the revenues from game parks.

Ken began to shake so hard he drew his hands under his chest and curled his knees up to his face, vainly trying to control his body. It had been his mistake to take them for granted, to eat at their table and enjoy their help, to feel the privilege of friendship when it was nothing but a truce, to walk around beaming with the stupid Anglo-Saxon wishful thinking that the past was past. Well, it wasn't. And if he attempted to take away the bones of their ancestors, he insulted the memory of everything they had lost, and he deserved to be punished. He deserved to die ignorant of his sentence!

His blood was boiling. His brain was cooking.

He lay down. Above him, in the acacia, glittered a pair of eyes. Frontally placed, and widely spaced, as if in a human. They remained stable for maybe a few seconds, focusing on Ken. Then he heard a stirring of leaves and they disappeared.

I'm hallucinating, he decided.

The hallucination had changed his course of thought. He felt a little more rational again.

First priority, he thought, is not water. First priority is . . . *walking*!

He rose and hopscotched on his good ankle to the exposed roots of the acacia tree. It took a long time—a few inches a minute. A parasitical vine coiled around one of the roots. He forced his swollen ankle between the vine and the root, as if in a noose. Swearing and sweating, he fell to the ground. His injured foot was well moored inside that noose. He pulled, slowly.

The pain made him rain sweat on the ground around him.

He pulled again, and heard a crack in his ankle, as if a dislodged bone was being straightened. He bit his lower lip until it bled, and pulled again. The pain was mixed with a strange relief. He freed his foot, lapped the blood on his lower lip, and found that it tasted very soothing. He put his foot down, then staggered up. He could stand now with considerably less pain.

He could even take steps, painful but not excruciatingly so. He had straightened that dislocated bone. The swelling would go down. In the battle to maintain rationality, he had won the first fight. All he had to do was maintain it.

Maybe there wasn't a conspiracy . . .

He listened to the bush. Even now, every sound, every cricket buzz, every distant howl or roar, seemed inordinately beautiful. Next to a tree trunk, an enormous African firefly cut through the air, its abdomen blinking on and off like a plane's position signal, then sat on the trunk and kept blinking, calling for a mate. Its light, bright and yellow, made the insect seem big as a sparrow. A second one appeared and beelined to the first, its light blinking in tune, but emitting a different glare, less intense and greenish.

Ken realized that in the morning he would be thirty-six hours without food and drink. Still, he had survived. And maybe he had seen his dream creatures.

THE UNSEEN CHECKPOINT OF THIRTY-SIX HOURS OF DEHYdration came, and passed. Forty hours was approaching.

Ken had woken up with a precision of thought that almost scared him. There was water right at hand, he realized, in the Land Rover's radiator. He dragged himself inside the vehicle and used his knife to cut the leather upholstery off the seats. Once he had enough, he made a crudely round gourd with a narrow opening. He crawled with it to the jeep's front, unscrewed the radiator's drainage hole, knowing he could do it once only, and that he had to be prepared to catch every single drop of rusty radiator water. It gurgled down, perhaps twelve ounces, barely a beer can's worth. He closed his eyes and drank half of it—his throat so parched and his tongue so swollen that he almost didn't taste it.

Slowly, he became alert and felt some strength.

He limped out of the tree area and was shocked. He had expected the Mau to rise close in front of him, to what he felt was his west. Instead, the Mau was far away, looking low and discolored under a sky full of clouds. It seemed to rise almost to the north, better than a day's drive away from where he stood now. The stampede had carried Ken way down, close to the desert by the Tanzanian border.

Still, he felt better and clearer in his head. Just because he could move normally, the situation no longer seemed desperate. He limped back and found the extra gasoline in the jeep. Taking little breaks to rest, he poured the gasoline into the tank, then he passed the winch cable over the big tree root and turned on the winch.

The cable pulled and moaned, and the root creaked, but held fast.

Soon, the jeep was almost up, then it was up completely, drivable, even without brakes. He would drive it very slowly. To cool off the engine, he would simply turn it off.

He reversed the winch, to wind it back in its box. He checked the engine by turning it on and off again. He listened to the clearing, and found the tree above him excessively still.

He stared at random between two acacia trunks and saw a vehicle moving in the savanna, slowly. It was another Safari Cub.

Don't do this to me, he begged his tired, unreliable senses.

But the Cub did not vanish, no matter how hard he stared. He could hear its engine. A branch above him stirred loudly, forcing him to look up. Again, he resigned himself to see what looked real and perhaps *was* real. A brown silhouette was advancing toward the tip of a branch, until the creature stopped, making the branch sway under its weight. It leaned out toward the savanna, like a lookout.

A brown, hairy arm reached out from the creature's body. Its long palm went up to shade its eyes, in a gesture that was so human that Ken found himself giggling soundlessly—the giggle sent a cramp into his empty stomach. The creature's gesture was so human-before-humanness that for a moment Ken lost his focus on the Safari Cub out on the savanna.

Then he saw another creature. Perhaps it was the one who

had screamed the morning before and chased away the leopard. Or maybe it was another one. It was sitting in the fork of two big branches, looking down at Ken, then alternately out at the approaching vehicle, its eyes dilated with fear.

The Cub was driving slowly, then it stopped. Ken peered, with his hand shading his eyes against the savanna's glare. He counted four men stepping out of the vehicle. Three Africans, one white. They squatted down, and Ken figured that they were looking for the Land Rover's tracks under the buffaloes' prints. The buffaloes had battered his jeep tracks so badly that even Modibo would have a hell of a time reading them. And Modibo was there, he could see him. He was too far away for Ken to make out his features, but he recognized his crab-legged movements and that open greatcoat.

Ken heard a sound from above—a moan of low, quiet fear. He thought, If this is real, then I'm hearing the first sound from the Stone Age.

But he was too exhausted for emotion. Okay, he said silently to the mysterious hominids, you're scared of those bandits. I'll find a way to throw them off. I'll protect you.

He stuck the knife in his belt, grabbed his gourd of radiator fluid, and climbed into the jeep. He found his nightviewers, probably thrown out from under a seat as the jeep straightened up. He sat behind the wheel and revved up the engine.

The four men did not hear the Land Rover as it accelerated, nor could they see it because of the trees. When it raged out of the grove, it moved so fast that their eyes didn't locate it until it was already out in the clear and hurtling away.

They cursed, throwing themselves back into the Cub, and charged after the Land Rover, which moved as if possessed. It shot far ahead of them, then bounced up, perhaps from hitting a rock, then seemed to leap, and disappeared in a gully. Then suddenly, there was an outburst of smoke. A tall column of flying debris built up, then collapsed back on itself.

In the Cub, the three Africans cheered. "Great brake job," one of them said. He wore a faded uniform jacket, patched by hand, and a yellow knit cap. The other two also wore faded uniforms or fatigues, unmatched and ill-fitting.

The white man was unimpressed. "Great brake job, three days later. Let's get there and be sure he's dead."

In minutes, they found the little gully, which was almost completely filled by the smoking Land Rover. Nothing could be seen inside because of the heavy smoke.

Modibo stood sniffing as the fire singed his face. Then he turned slowly and told Hendrijks—softly, so that the others could not hear—that he did not smell a roasted body inside the jeep. "Maybe, da mzungu jump off. But no problem, dere's jus one water hole out here, and he won find it. So he die."

"What the fuck d'you mean he jumped, what the hell are you fucking talking about?" foamed Hendrijks. He stared hard at the fire and the smoke which was being blown away by a sluggish breeze. It was easier to see the Land Rover now, but it didn't look like there was a body inside it, though someone could be lying slumped and lifeless between the front seat and the dashboard.

Hendrijks was so frustrated that he took off his hat and slapped it against his knees, causing dust to blow straight into his face, making him choke. Through the dust, he thought he saw a grin on Modibo's face.

"Go find him," he yelled. "Now!"

"No," said Modibo quietly. "We go back. We're out o' water." He pronounced it waddah.

"What if he doesn't die?"

His voice wafted off with the wind and the smoke.

"He die," Modibo reassured him.

"Or I'll come back and get him myself," grunted Hendrijks.

Modibo stepped back toward the Cub, joined by the other men.

Hendrijks looked beyond the gully and the column of smoke. A range of rocky outcrops started some seventy yards off, blurred by the smoke wafting onto bare stone. I stretched to the misted Mau. He could not search it alone. He turned back and followed the Africans.

* * *

PEERING THROUGH THE NARROW INDENTATION IN THE TOP of a kopje, Ken had heard Hendrijks clearly: "What if he doesn't die?" And then: "I'll come back and get him myself."

He was shivering so hard that the nightviewers, hanging down his chest, were banging a rhythm against the rock. He pressed his chest down, to kill the sound of fear. He watched his pursuers step into the Cub and disappear.

What was Hendrijks doing here? How had Hendrijks joined forces with Modibo? And why did they want to kill Ken Lauder? He was searching for hominids, which could be of no value to Modibo or Hendrijks.

With another shiver, he remembered that Jakub Ngiamena himself had interviewed Hendrijks before advising Ken and Ngili to hire Hendrijks to fly them to Dogilani. Buy him his whiskey and leave him alone, he'll do a decent job. And they had dug out the fossil in his presence, and mentioned its value, and how it could change their lives.

Could it be the fossil? That seemed just too sophisticated for Hendrijks, or Modibo. Hendrijks was just a "winged pig," as Ngili once called him, an aging bush errand boy who flew for small wages, came back and blew his money in native discos, and snored his drinks off on a semen-stiffened mattress till his next job. As for Modibo . . .

But here he realized that by belittling Hendrijks or Modibo, he was simply trying to reassure himself. He really knew nothing about either one of them. And that still did not answer the main question: Why?

What was happening out here, that they so savagely meant to keep him away?

He decided to wait out the day in the shade and move again by night. Most kopje ranges abutted at the Mau, and that was where water was most likely to be found. He would follow the range. He looked back at the grove where he had spent almost two days. The trees looked magically beautiful, like dream trees.

After the sun went down, he drank the last drops from his makeshift flask, and kept licking its wet interior until he felt he could no longer move his tongue. Then he rolled on his back. The clouds were breaking. Frightened stars blinked in the skies.

The few drops of water and the night revived him. He felt more strength than over the last few days, though he still had not eaten. The mists lifted, and he could see the Mau where he expected it to be. Somehow he thought he could reach its foothills and the survival cache he believed was waiting there.

He started walking, wearing his nightviewers, which would help him see any attackers in the dark. He was frail but light on his feet. Far into the night, with the moon forming his shadow on the ground, he reached a jumble of blackish rock faces that rose before him, looking strange enough to be another hallucination.

He advanced toward them and touched them.

A flapping sound was coming from the top of an inclined rock slate. He managed to stand on a lower stone, getting close enough to the sound to figure out what it was.

It was the parachute, which he reached for with his fingers.

The parachute's lines to the cache's metal case had been cut. There was no reserve of water, food, or equipment attached to it.

In the dark, Ken's fingers probed the severed lines. The nylon ends felt so cleanly sectioned that all his thoughts came together in four words: *They* had been here. They had cut the lines and stolen the cache, thus topping the sabotage of his car, the chase through the bush, the search for his tracks and hiding place, and the promise to come back and finish him off.

They had dealt him the coup de grâce. And they might even be watching him from somewhere close by, enjoying his death throes, making sure that he didn't survive. There was no escape.

He waited. For several hours, death did not come. Death was late.

He wondered how much time there was left till the morning. Without his wristwatch, he had been without any mechanical sense of time for three or four days.

Finally, he attempted to get up, and succeeded. The moon, almost full, lit robustly the jumbled lava rocks. He staggered toward some trees rustling a small distance away. Under one of them was a wide pool of what looked like dark fruit. He fell into it and realized they were mungongo nuts. They were edible, a high source of protein, and a staple in some tribes' diets, including bushmen.

He had nothing to crack the nuts with so he put one in his teeth, lacerated his gums and bled his lips, but managed to bite the hard shell open. He was so eager, that the nut found its own way down his throat. He swallowed it whole, and choked and coughed himself back to breathing.

He managed to chew the second nut, ordering himself to do it slowly, and was helped by a strange emotional reaction: The nuts could prolong his life by a few hours, and that made him aware of how much he wanted to stay alive. His eyes misted up.

He chewed, swallowed, licked his lips, and attacked another nut. He was sweating hard, then had to get up and open his pants so he wouldn't wet himself. It seemed that all his bodily functions, alerted to the possibility of more life, were reasserting themselves.

He fell back down under the tree, ate more, and kept swallowing the blood from his lacerated lips, like a salty-sweet spice.

When he looked above, he saw more nuts in the tree. Clearly there were no tribes here or else they would've picked all the mungongos. For now, the tree was all his. He could count on at least one more meal.

He lay down by the rocks and fell asleep, wondering vaguely whether the trees and rocks had any consciousness of him, who had arrived from nowhere carrying with him, like a mobile pocket of time, the era he belonged to. He was up before the sun, tortured by a latent hunger, but feeling stronger and clear in his head. He crawled back under the tree, picked more mungongo nuts, and was overcome by how monotonously delicious they were. He then limped away to inspect his surroundings. The mist had thickened, curdling around rocks and trees.

He stopped frozen in place when he heard footfalls.

Hendrijks, he thought.

Through the night, Hendrijks ("I'll get him myself") had become even more menacing than Modibo.

The footfalls were close. He felt his torn clothes for the knife, found it, gripped it.

The footfalls faded in the gray mist.

He moved again. He had just found some food. If he wanted to survive he had to keep moving on. He stepped into the mist, his eyes straining to read the looming shadows, and gripped the knife. The mist started to lighten, and less than a quarter of a mile from the jumbled rocks, he found a shallow dip dotted with acacias. This led him to a muddy stream of water that had lost its flowing strength and was disappearing underground in a wide messy puddle.

He forgot the other dangers, dropped his knife and buried his face in the water, ignoring the vegetal spines, specks of dirt, and dead insects floating in it. He drank, feeling that he was ingesting not just with his throat and stomach but also with his lungs, heart, kidneys, and all of his body. He pictured the blessed fluid, dirty and rough-tasting (but it was *fluid*!), descending into his body, nourishing it, regenerating it. He stopped to feel the cool caress of the water on his cheeks. He drank again. He breathed, and drank on, blinded and deafened by the drinking.

Then the footsteps surfaced like a submarine reverberating deep in the water.

He bolted upward, dripping. The footsteps were coming closer.

He had the time to grip the knife and turn slightly on one side, to look up. Who or what was coming loomed enormously, as it ripped through the mist, almost running. He ordered his arm to flex back so that he would have the best thrust of the knife. A dark silhouette seemed to dive at him

Then it fell at the water, partially hidden by a wild agave bush, its red-and-blue flowers looking pale gray in the mist.

Ken heard a slurp of drinking, long and uninterrupted. His pursuer seemed almost as thirsty as he was. *Maybe as energy-depleted as he was.*

He crawled along the edge of the puddle, knife in hand, to see who it was. He got up on one knee and hung forward to peer above the bush. He saw someone's naked back as it rose to full stature. It was a shockingly tiny boy, his hair long and dusty and looking shingled-up with acacia spines and loose foliage. The boy drank, breathing loudly without taking his lips out of the water. Then he lifted his face and darted his eyes around. Then he drank again, again keeping his mouth in the water a long time, and snorting his breath in and out as he drank.

From the side, his lips were long, pursed down into a comically greedy shape. His nose was flat, with hardly any bridge, but with wide nostrils, which the boy flared vigorously. To Ken he immediately seemed both alert and expert at discerning unusual smells.

But the thing that made Ken stand frozen was not the boy's profile but instead, the way he was drinking.

Modern humans could not drink and breathe at the same time. Their larynxes were positioned too low for that. Apes did, and so did newborn babies, whose larynxes had not descended yet. The same was assumed of australopithecines.

What breathed and drank at once could be a baby, or an ape. But this was not a baby. It was too big. Nor was it an ape, because it had run fully erect to the puddle. This was a hominid boy, who drank like an *Australopithecus*.

WITHOUT THINKING, KEN COMMITTED THE CARDINAL sin of anthropology. He sprang onto his specimen and yelled out, *"Hujambo. Habari?* Hello. What's new?"

The boy dove into the spiny leaves of the agave bush, ignoring their jabs at his naked skin—the spiny leaves were not the kindest to a naked skin. Between two clusters of agave leaves, his little brown eye was sizing up Ken, who took a step forward and was hit so hard in the right shoulder that he reeled. A round stone rolled down the front of his filthy shirt. The boy bolted out of the agave bush, running in silhouette past Ken. His tiny fists were clenched fiercely next to his small, light-brown chest; open lips made a whistling sound, and nostrils flared in alarm. Ken could tell even from that one glimpse of the boy that the line uniting his forehead and lips slanted at almost forty-five degrees.

I'm hallucinating, Ken thought.

He shot his right hand at his mouth, bit his wrist as hard as he could. The pain made him shake.

A pair of naked buttocks, shining as if oiled even through the thinning mist, raced into the acacia trees, then vanished. Ken raced in pursuit. The boy had dived where the trees were thickest. Ken had to stop himself by hugging a low branch, his heart thundering. He wasn't recovered enough to be running yet.

He stepped out of the acacias and picked off the spines clinging to his shirt and sticking into his forearms. He rubbed his right pectoral, which was sore.

On the ground, he saw a blackish stone. He picked it up and felt its warmth, as if it had been held tightly in an anxious grip.

Here I am, stealing his weapons again, Ken thought crazily.

Or his tools.

Tools? If he's using tools, he's not an australopithecine anymore, he is *Homo habilis*, a handy human.

He sat on the ground, trying to recall, as fast and as richly as possible, everything he had experienced while seeing the boy. How long had it all lasted? Two, three minutes? Five? How long *really* had the boy been drinking from the puddle?

He jumped up, marched back to the acacias, no longer caring whether he made noise. The sound of his boots announced his arrival all too clearly. He was too driven to slow down or to take precautions. They, the killers, were probably not here. If they were, the hominid would not have come into the open as he had and drunk so greedily, like a child rendered thirsty by too many hours of sleep.

The ground around the acacias was dry and gravelly. He found some dips in it, but they were impossible to identify as footprints. He remembered that he had dropped his night-viewers and knife, and might not find them. He lost that unimportant thought as he had lost others before it.

Past the trees, there was that range of rocky outcrops that had been cracked and carved by heat and wind. The boy could be anywhere—hiding nearby or already on the run.

He stepped into an irregularly rectangular area closed off with a rocky rampart. Inside the rectangle, Ken dropped on his knees. He was surrounded by black stones like the one the boy had thrown at him. He caught his breath and counted them. Nine stones, small but heavy, basaltic. This must be a storing place, a little hunting pile. They had been chipped out of bigger rocks, and shaped into these hurling projectiles millions of years ago, or perhaps just months ago. The child and the stones belonged to the same time, and that time was way in the past . . . but it was also now!

Ken felt the need to do something, to utter some word, or perform some undefined gesture, just to release some tension. He needed to express how enormous and momentous this was. It was as if he had stepped through an unseen gate, into an age that was then and also now, and therefore timeless.

He did not know what to do. The thought of gunmen lurking not very far away—though he felt that their danger had diminished—helped settle him down. He slid his back down the rocky rampart and sat on the ground.

The sun was burning a hole in the mist. It appeared as a full fiery sphere, opening the skies. Now he could easily be spotted from a plane, but even that had lost its significance.

He was also now convinced that the day before he had seen protohumans in those trees above his fight with the leopard. They were protohumans, not chimps or colobus monkeys.

And if that boy was here, his kin must be here as well. The adults.

He could not act crazy just now. He still represented the modern era, and science, so he had to be cool. He looked up, and saw the boy again.

The first thing he noticed this time was the multitude of scars on his body.

THE BOY HAD REAPPEARED WHILE KEN WAS EXAMINING HIS hunting stones. He stood in the open space, looking at the modern man, wrinkling his tiny brow. Scars covered his arms, shoulders, and thighs, all looking completely healed. They were all rather light, as if they came from scratches by thorns, except for a large one that slashed his belly. That one too looked healed. Ken figured it had probably been stretched as his little body had grown, but he realized that it wasn't likely that he would ever learn what had injured the child, or how it had happened.

What he did know already was that this child had been alone for a while—and had survived.

Ken started to open his mouth; then he was silent. Speaking had become both meaningless and unnecessary.

He stared at the boy, feeling as if he were tumbling down a funnel of time.

The boy's little face had a protruding chin, a mouth with well-shaped lips that were distinctly pink in the light-brown face. Fine downy hair put a hazy spot on his upper lip, and the hair showed some discolored streaks, looking sun-bleached rather than dusty. Ken was somehow reassured that hair from a few million years back could be bleached under the savanna sun, just as his own was.

The boy was truly light-skinned—an early savanna biped that hadn't had a chance yet, genetically speaking, to build up enough melanin to counter the lethal tropical sun.

Ken felt his eyes being pulled in by every detail of this amazing appearance. The nose was flat, nostrils tiny but well rounded, and seeming to sniff and sort out scents at a fast and busy pace. The little chest swelled and shrank; the child panted, both from running and from tension. The boy's cheeks were full, his eye sockets strong, and his low forehead frowning from sudden thoughts. His little fist squeezed another black stone, with a precision grip Ken recognized instantly. The kid's thumb was pressed tightly against the visible end of the stone, its joints flexed, showing that it bent easily. The other fingers wrapped around the stone in a comfortably curved grasp, well out of the ape stage.

The back of his little hand was slightly hairy. He had hairs on his legs and arms, but few on his body. By contrast, the hair on his head was rich, and rose in those straight and dirty bleached strands. The feet, which Ken scanned quickly, were well formed and long-toed.

His curved little penis, dusty from his having crawled on his stomach, hung out of a little fold of fat, the only fat formation visible on the child's wiry body.

By now the sun was shining fully on this unbelievable scene. The boy was barely ten feet from Ken. And the distance in time between them seemed no longer to exist.

Ken searched his pockets, and came up with his apartment keys, which he held up and dangled.

The boy shuffled a couple of steps backward. His little arm throbbed, the stone lifted level with his little shoulder. He pursed out his lips, in a cute pose of childish fierceness. Ken dangled the keys, producing a tiny bell-like clinking, then let them drop on the ground.

The child turned and scaled the rampart of rocks, his shiny buttocks shaking from his agile and surefooted climb. The heels of his feet, lighter in pigmentation, cut quickly against the grayish-yellow stone faces.

He vanished. Ken jumped to the rocks and saw the child leap to the ground on the other side, landing on all fours. He bolted up and headed erect for the jumble of black lava rocks. He walked without any visible strain, and without any sidling secondary movements, but every now and then he bent as if to gain cover behind the richly tufting oat grass. For easily more than a minute, Ken could see his brown body. Then the boy turned, looked back, and seemed sucked in by the jumble of rocks.

Ken pondered following the boy, hoping for another encounter. What was this, actually? What was he doing now, exactly? he wondered, remembering that he had no implements, no instruments, no recording devices, not even a pen and pad, that he had left science behind.

He is more at home and prepared at the age of eight than I am at twenty-eight, Ken reflected, feeling that his lack of preparation was due to something other than the loss of his camp and the chase he had thwarted.

He guessed the child's age at eight, due to his size. Yet the boy's sureness of action, and the way he seemed so much in his element, and alone to boot, made Ken wonder if he wasn't much older. Most likely, neither age applied. But if the boy was of a different breed, his kind had its own age clocks, its own durations of childhood, pre-adulthood, and maturity.

Ken opened his shirt; he had a good-sized bruise on his

chest. He rubbed, then paced forward and picked up his keys.

The boy had not reacted to them. *Gotta impress 'im with some better gadgets, Lauder.*

Then he saw the boy, streaking out of the rocks. He was hurrying in that forward-hanging stance of his, but still unarguably bipedal, looking purposeful and concentrated. Ken smiled. All little boys everywhere were terribly busy, and this one was no different.

But he was not returning to the rampart. He glanced at Ken once, briefly, and then started cutting a path through the tall grasses, quickly disappearing. Ken climbed over the rocks and rushed into the grasses. They were beginning to straighten up again, hiding the child's passage. He panicked that he might lose track. *Shit, he was not being scientific at all, or even careful.* He threw his head back and scanned the sky and then the horizon for any sign of Hendrijks or other visitors. But there seemed to be no humanity, other than he and the boy.

The tasseled heads of the tall grass were closing up, drowning the boy's passage. He had to move quickly.

THE WATER HOLE WAS SMALL, NOT MUCH BIGGER THAN A tennis court, and so overgrown with grasses and reeds that Ken walked right into it. He parted a clump of reeds at the end of a closing footpath and suddenly dipped into green water to his knees. The water hole was tiny but deep. The unusual amount of rain in the area had kept it well supplied. Turaco birds, warblers, and chats fluttered upward, and the humid breeze of the water fanned Ken's hot face.

A white square-lipped rhinoceros rolled in the water hole's midst, as if this were its personal tub. The two-ton beast was known to be solitary and shy. Hearing Ken's splashing sounds, it waved its little ears and started climbing out on the other side, which was far less shrubby. Sighing obesely, the rhino trotted past three resting buffaloes and a bearded black buck that dropped its nose back into the water.

There were flowering bushes on the other side of the hole,

plundered en force by sunbirds hungry for pollen. Ken had seen sunbirds mostly in forests, but the ones here had successfully adapted to the grassland. There seemed to be more of them than starlings and warblers. The opposite shore had a kind of wet muddy beach where the hominid boy now lay. When the rhino lumbered out, the boy just rolled to one side, like an unconcerned zoo hand all too familiar with a heavy animal's antics.

Ken breathed, forgetting that he was in water to his knees. Now that he could see the boy, the dream was starting again.

If he doesn't put me through some crazy hide-and-seek, I may keep up with him, he thought. *If he does, then forget it, my stamina's nowhere close to his.*

He sensed that the boy had observed him before. His reactions were too unshocked and he seemed too comfortable having Ken there. But when had this happened? Most likely it had been during Ken's earlier stop in the savanna, with Ngili and Hendrijks. Yet that had occurred some twenty miles to the south—strange that the boy (if he was the same specimen) would change locations and reappear right in Ken's path. Maybe this wasn't the same hominid. . . .

The boy's hand-shaped feet had left fresh footprints in the mud of the water hole. Ken conjured up his memory of the photographs, then studied the footprints before him. They seemed identical.

Several stones lay in front of the boy on the shiny wet mud. Ken saw him pick up one, then put it back. He picked up another, dropped it down too, settled for a third, with the silent concentration of a human choosing from a pile of hard-to-distinguish cuff links that were small and similar, yet with a subtle difference that mattered to the owner. The boy chose his weapon and got up, headed for a particular destination. Then he gave Ken a look and seemed to abandon his earlier plan. He paced, studied the ground, dropped the stone, got down on all fours, and seemed to check the soil as intently as a physicist examining a nuclear core ready for fission.

A quote from Darwin ran through Ken's mind. "All creatures feel Wonder, and many exhibit Curiosity." Well, this one went from Curiosity to Wonder to Curiosity. He almost smiled at the ground, then frowned, lifted his eyebrows, knitted them again, and smiled again. Ken was becoming enraptured with the boy's intellectual exertion. Since the first time he had seen him, *thought* seemed to have been imprinted on the little hominid's face in all its variations: curiosity, choice, doubt, certainty, boldness, and gambling expectation. Maybe he did have more than five hundred cubic centimeters of brain.

And now the boy seemed to be studying the ground just for the sake of studying it. He might be the type who thought for long spells and emerged with sudden and unusual revelations. The boy suddenly stared up at Ken, his stare feeling like a shortcircuiting of time.

Ken grinned back. "Stop raving, Lauder," he muttered softly, getting out of the bilgey water and dripping as he stepped around the reeds to where the boy was, "he's not here for you to force theories on him. He's here to be here, and you might as well forget all else, and be here too. . . ."

It was hard. Ken had prided himself on being more practical than other researchers, less speculative and curly-minded than other paleontologists. He frowned when someone called him "cowboy Lauder," but deep inside he was flattered by what they meant. He was a finder more than he was a thinker, and that was good. He would have something to think about later, when he couldn't find things anymore, and he would write about prehistory from his experiences rather than rehashing other people's beliefs. Ken had certainly fantasized about a moment like this, when a unique search and observation would spark new and original *theories* from him. But his mind was not in the theoretical mode. He was filled with more practical questions, like how many such specimens were there in the area, and why were they still hiding while the boy was treating him to a near-orgy of self-display? And how was he going to keep up with this dynamo in his weakened condition? If Hendrijks and his men reappeared, what would they do, and most imperatively, what could "cowboy Lauder" do to defend himself and his find?

As Ken kept stepping closer, the boy looked up over his clear-skinned, almost hairless shoulder, which shone as if oiled. He clearly had very active sweat glands that were dependent on water. If Ken followed him, he was sure to end up near water.

The boy tightened his lips and squeezed his eyes together, in an expression of concentration, or warning. Ken reminded himself not to press closeness, and squatted a few yards away, all the while forming a new avalanche of questions in his mind. What exactly was the kid's age? His playful curiosity and wonder put him between six and eight. But he had the agility and mastery of his environment of a ten-year-old. If he was indeed alone, it was nothing short of magical that he'd survived in the bush. The boy had the age of the place itself; he was eternal and fresh-born every minute, like the savanna.

Ken studied the little body, particularly the long and outspread big toes. When he stood still, the boy's feet looked like narrow hands with comparatively short fingers and overdeveloped wristbones that had become heels but still looked somewhat like wrists.

Ken was amazed that such a primally shaped foot could walk and run so well. He wondered what the boy ate. There had to be plenty to scavenge here, he reflected, aware of the sun's heat on the crown of his head, and the soothing breeze on the back of his neck. Behind him, the grass spread out lushly into a garden-type savanna that was in striking contrast with the aridity on the other side of the black rocks. This side, nesting in a pocket of the Mau's spurs, was like a narrow strip of moist vegetation, far more luxuriant than the place where Ken had found the fossil. The crown of the Mau kept the humidity alive, through that continuous suspension of clouds. Even now, with the sun out, the escarpment soared into mist, and its higher forestation seemed more of the jungle than the savanna type. Weather- and flora-wise, the place was a haven, but practically that meant there was plenty to eat, both fresh and rotting.

Now the boy gathered his stones, stuck two in his left armpit, letting his arm hang over them. With his eyes, Ken measured the clean little bulge of muscle in the arm. The boy spun around and walked off, leaving more of the footprints Ken would have killed for just days ago.

He walked slowly, peering above the grass. Ahead, the boy was monitoring columns of birds that rose, broke, reformed. Large birds were a good sign of carcasses, and also of the resting spots of felines, who most often dozed off right by their kills. If the birds were smaller, that usually meant water, where they could pick at grass and soft-shelled snails.

In only a few minutes they had come to a much larger water hole, clearer in color, sandy-shored and irregular. The boy had dropped the stones. He ran, his dirty hair waving back, his eyes at the ground, and dived at something.

Ken, straining to muster a run too, came up behind the boy just as he was rising again, his hands seeming to flutter. He was gripping a large mole shrew that was over twenty inches from snout to tail. Its now useless snout was twisting impotently. The hominid whacked it over the throat with the edge of one palm, gripped it with both hands again, and drubbed it hard against the ground, annoyed that the sand's softness didn't instantly kill the shrew. He hit it against the sand again and again, then somehow had a sharp stone in one fist. The shrew squeaked thinly as it was being gored. The hunter fell to his knees, waited for the prey to twitch its final spasm, then searched around with his eyes.

He spotted Ken. He then lifted the prey and sank his teeth in it.

His skill had been witnessed, and he was eating. A complex action, doubly gratifying, had been fulfilled.

Ken sat by the water hole. The sun was hot, and he no longer had his bush hat. He dipped his hands in the water, scooped up a palmful, and poured it on his hair. Then he waited quietly, happy just to be watching.

He watched the kid eating, biting with hunger and showing

his teeth repeatedly. His teeth were flat, his canines rising barely at all above the level of the molars and incisors. A big ape's canines would be long, pointed, and interlocked. But there was nothing apish about the boy's teeth. In fact, the way he sat now, toes dipped in the sand, his only somewhat apish feature was that low forehead, indicating a smaller brain. But who was to say that a larger brain was preferable? Ken smiled at the child, at the water hole, at a little flock of sandpipers that waded in the water, probing it with their long slender bills. He spread his legs in relaxation, exhaled a breath of thoughtless contentment, but then he bolted up, all his senses cranked back to speed. With his fingers, the boy tore out a piece of soft shrew belly. The bright red gob, dripping blood, traveled in the long brown hand, not to the boy's mouth but toward Ken's face.

It was an offering.

He blinked at the shapeless, bright-red piece of meat, wondering what to do. If he took it, he would establish a more intimate link. So he took it. It was soft, bleeding, warm from the life that had just left it.

The boy watched him.

I'll fake it, Ken thought. He lifted it to his mouth, as the australopithecine gazed at him. He touched it against his upper lip and was seized by a desire to taste it. But there was also a churning revulsion agitating his stomach while his throat swallowed emptily. It was raw protein, and he hadn't had any lately, except for those few nuts. Here was food, and it meant food poisoning or survival.

He'd take just a small bite, he pacified himself. The shrew was an insectivore, not a meat-eater, certainly not a scavenger. In fact, it might be cleaner to eat, and certainly closer to what the human body was initially designed to consume, than the chickens sold in American supermarkets. He had drunk the water in that puddle, and so far had no signs of stomach disorder. He hesitated with the warm meat close to his face, then took a small bite.

The meat was almost tasteless, and slippery. An atom of it slid down his throat unchewed, and the thought almost made him throw it up. Then it found its way to his stomach and his hunger seemed stimulated by that first bite. He'd eaten only a little bite. He tried to make himself drop the meat, but he felt depleted, and here, within reach, was food.

He took another bite, chewed it, feeling its juices flow and fill his mouth. The tissue was soft, and did not feel very nutritious. A light meal for the Stone Age.

He felt a huge revulsion, jumped up, tried to reach a bush and vomit out of the boy's sight, but he fell on his knees and retched the small piece of meat, and all his gastric juices. They poured out of his mouth, while he gave himself a failing grade for survival adaptation. Others had survived in deserts and jungles by eating their belts and shoes, or uncooked mice and birds, or even dead comrades. He wasn't in their league.

He wiped his face with the sleeve of his shirt, then reeled back, famished and humbled, and terribly down on himself.

The boy was where he had left him, making a tiny crunching noise as he crushed the shrew's head with his teeth. He was part of an evolutionary stage where there was no respect for another creature once it was dead. Meat was meat.

Ken watched the boy. The child picked up Ken's discarded meat and stuffed it in his mouth. Then he sprawled lazily toward the water and drank. Ken scooped water out and drank too, as if modestly reapproaching the stage of healthy savagery. The child burped, contentedly passed a hand over his swollen belly, and reached to pick up his stones.

MOMENTS LATER, THEY WERE WALKING AGAIN, STONE AGE boy in front, older, modern human bringing up the rear.

The boy carried those stones with such natural ease he must have grown up handling them. Ken was now convinced that the stones came from that black jumble of lava rocks. There was no other bed of black rocks around. This meant that the stones he and Ngili had first seen twenty miles to the south must have been carried there. And that alone made them tools. The carrying and usage in hunting made the user a handy human, a virtual *Homo habilis,* who was not supposed to have arisen, said classical anthropology, before the human mind enlarged to at least seven hundred fifty cubic centimeters.

But the mind walking ahead of Ken, twisting right and left, throwing glances at the bush and back at Ken, could not be more than five hundred tops, and might be even less, depending on how thick the skull bones were. That brain mass would increase some, as the boy matured, but not much, not enough to make the threshold.

The child's delicate limbs were like those of a particular australopithecine, the *gracilis* (''slim'' or ''slender,'' in Latin), who was even smaller-boned than his cousin the *robustus* (''husky one''). Some scientists believed that *gracilis* was in evolutionary competition with *robustus*. Either way, neither *gracilis* nor *robustus* made the threshold of toolmaking and tool-using smarts.

Ken suppressed a laugh. There were no thresholds here. This child, which seemed like a *habilis* in the body of a *gracilis*, was clearly his own species. And God only knew how many evolutionary ape-man lines had once existed, competing or cooperating and interbreeding, until *sapiens* (Ken's and Ngili's line) pushed all the others into dead ends, and emerged supreme.

Ken felt a bizarre affection for the boy, who walked in front of him shining with sweat. He was losing minerals at a terribly high rate, no doubt about it, which meant that he needed to replenish often. So you're just an eating and drinking machine, Ken thought warmly. His heels rose and fell energetically, his buttocks sweated, and his head dangled right and left as if listening to his own playful rhythm.

They were approaching the black rocks and Ken saw the parachute's orange umbrella and white severed lines clearly against the rock face. This reminded him of Hendrijks, and he almost panicked.

Then the mungongo tree came into view. He saw his knife on the ground, which he took as a sign that his enemies had not penetrated the area. He felt giddy with relief. He signaled with his palm held up, and the boy stopped.

He threw the knife at the mungongo's branches and several nuts fell. He picked one, cut it open, sliced it in two, munched on one half as he offered the other half, exactly as the boy had offered the meat. The boy reached out. Fleetingly, Ken felt his fingertips. The boy thrust the nut into his mouth. He chewed, made a displeased face, spat it out, spraying saliva at his guest.

I guess you don't like my cooking any more than I like yours, grinned Ken. The child watched, then grinned back with blinding white teeth. He and Ken could enjoy a good laugh together, but he was no fan of mungongos, which happened to be the nut most prized by all the tribes in East Africa.

That said something about the boy's life in isolation, or about his stage of evolution. But the boy's expression, that blinding grin, that look of trust, chased the scientific speculations from Ken's mind. He felt so gratified that he fought himself not to reach out and stroke the child or catch him in an affectionate hold. Don't scare him, Lauder.

He enjoyed the child's expression, while vaguely debating a few issues that remained mysterious: Where were the boy's kin? Would the child lead him eventually to the adults of his breed, or to some kind of lair? And why had the boy moved his grounds, from miles to the south, by the fossil site, to here?

He hoped that those questions would be answered soon, though not too soon. There was a kind of magic to being alone with this creature. He decided to do what he could to prolong it, so he sat under the mungongo tree, and after a brief hesitation the boy sat down too, not very close yet not at a forbidding distance. The boy also seemed to enjoy that closeness, in the sense that he had his chance to observe his visitor, which he did as attentively and actively as Ken.

Ken was not aware of how relaxed he felt. He fell asleep practically sitting up.

He started keeling over to one side, and blinked awake, and saw that he was alone again.

Didn't trust me with his lair, he thought.

Never mind, there's always tomorrow—the short sleep had restored his strength and confidence. When I see you next, we'll search together for some "honey guides." These were small bush birds, brown and white or olive and white, who fed upon beeswax and bees' larvae. If you followed a honey guide, you almost always ended up at a honey-laden beehive hung in a tree. Nomadic tribes smoked out the bees and then stole the honey, usually leaving thankful pieces of hive for the guiding birds.

I'll teach you a few skills that are supposed to take you another ten thousand years, thought Ken, smiling at the deserted bush, momentarily happy.

The diarrhea hit him right after sunset.

KEN RAISED AN INVOCATION: O DANTE, POET OF WORLD renown, in your *Divine Comedy*, section "Inferno," you forgot to include among hell's most horrible tortures the one about African runs.

He was squatting for the sixth (seventh?) time in the last two hours, pouring foul-smelling fluid out of his rear. In between defecations, he had to lie down because he was so exhausted and defeated by belly pains. With no control over his anus muscles, he took off his pants and left them in the grass.

It was possible the mole shrew had poisoned his gut, but more probably, it was the water. There was a cruel irony in this because the diarrhea was going to dehydrate him so completely, he'd have to replace the lost water by drinking again if he wanted to live a few more hours. The only clothes he had were his pants, shirt, underpants, and the woolen socks he wore in his desert boots. So he wouldn't soil them, he took them off one by one, until he was down to his boots. He piled them on the grass, and thanked the night for drawing the curtain on his humiliation.

Even if Hendrijks had shown up at that moment, Ken couldn't have felt more miserable or closer to his end. In between bouts, he lay on his back, with his palms gently massaging his belly, trying to talk his gut into quieting down.

Come on, boy, he coaxed, you've punished me enough.

But his gut would not forgive him.

The pain felt as if a crowbar was piercing him through the small of his back.

The moon rose, and the bouts became more frequent. He started running a high temperature, and shivered so hard that his teeth chattered to the stars. He considered eating grass, or chewing tree bark, to hopefully distract his stomach, but he had no energy left to rip out clumps of grass, or hobble to a tree.

He knew there was a moment soon when he would no longer move but just ease his gut on himself. To make matters worse, his thirst returned, blazing his insides, and singeing his mouth. The fever made him feel that he was breathing fire.

Then he heard himself beginning to rave out loud. He gave a lecture about bipedalism, and took questions from the audience. When the questions were over, he found himself by the freshet's puddle, drinking. The puddle had shrunk, and the next time he crawled to it, there would probably be no water left.

He staggered away, wondrously feeling a little better. The bouts were coming less often, perhaps one every hour. Then every two, maybe three hours. At one point, he found his underpants and forced them back onto his body, but he couldn't find his pants and shirt. His limbs ached so deeply that the act of dressing made him moan. He tried to walk back to the mungongo tree, but instead found himself somewhere on an arid stretch, under a hallucinatory moon. He was so wasted that he expected his heart to stop spontaneously. In that state, he heard the sound of drums, but they were not drums. They were large, rare, slow-falling raindrops, crashing down on grass blades and leaves.

The escarpment's mist came down in a big lazy rain, the last of a delayed rainy season. Ken lay on the grass with his mouth open and eyes closed, drinking in the bland-tasting rainwater, which made him choke and cough.

Then the rain washed him into senselessness.

*   *   *

WHEN HE BECAME CONSCIOUS AGAIN, HE LAY IN A NARROW dark space, breathing air that smelled cool and pungent like that of bats' droppings in a cave. Maybe he had tumbled into some subterranean hole and fouled it with his own droppings the way he had fouled the grass. He could not tell. He was still extremely feeble, though luckily his fever was gone.

An indirect glow of light was coming from somewhere, but he couldn't guess its source. He lay on his back, his gut momentarily not aching, but he was so exhausted that he could not raise his arms, though he was aware that they were touching what felt like cool moist soil.

Feeling like a buried mummy, he followed the gradual change of the light through what seemed like many hours. Finally, he raised himself on his elbows, then sat up, only to be met by a crashing pain as he bumped his head into a low ceiling of rock.

On his back, he crawled clumsily away from the low ceiling to a bigger and taller space. He looked up and saw a round, grayish opening that turned out to be the lower mouth of a chimneylike passage. This tube of rock led to a surface hole covered in bushes. The sunlight made the bushes look airily transparent and pretty. He was probably only a few feet below the earth, but this tube of rock, once the blowhole of a volcanic gas emission, was long, and looked quite difficult to climb out of.

Still, it was a relief to realize that he was not buried alive and probably wasn't a prisoner. The tube was climbable. All he needed to do was wait until his strength was somewhat restored.

The daylight filtering through the hole kept getting stronger, and the brighter it got in the cave, the more Ken saw that this chimney had been in use for a while—though he wasn't exactly entitled to complain about smells, he told himself. A space on the dark-gray floor looked like somebody had been sleeping there, and right next to it were two objects.

Hesitantly, Ken reached with his hand, and came back with a white piece of bone, which he quickly put back, and reached for the other object. It was his cigarette lighter, which he had dropped on his last trip to Dogilani. The boy had picked it up, knowing it was his. Altogether, the boy was more familiar with Ken Lauder than Ken Lauder had imagined, which explained the relative ease of their first contact and the boy's trust.

His next thought was that he was now in the boy's lair, and there was no sign of anybody else. The boy was alone and had been without parents or kin for at least ten days, perhaps even longer.

The boy hunted in the open but spent his nights here, in this very protected sleeping place. The boy wasn't hiding, but he was very aware of predators—and maybe even of enemies.

Finally, Ken realized that the boy was reinforcing their initial trust by bringing him into his lair. Ken couldn't help but be touched by this.

He picked up the bone again. It looked like a human arm bone. Why did the boy have that bone? Was it a tool, or a play object, or a bond to a dead kinsman?

He opened his cigarette lighter, flicked it on. At the second rotation of the flint stone, the flame sparked and started burning, blue and low.

He turned it off, feeling that having fire, even in this modest quantity, catapulted him back to a sapiens' normal skill and power.

Suddenly, blinding light poured down the chimney as the screen of bush covering the surface hole was pulled aside. Then the light was shut off instantly, by a body beginning to crawl down, four-legged. Looking up, Ken saw an enormous face with a pair of close-set eyes. Whatever it was was making a *mhmff, mhmff* sound as it crawled into the cave.

Ken was too weak to feel much panic. This is the end, he told himself, a quick battle between a hungry animal and his debilitated self. A blind, brief, and unknown struggle under the earth. He tried to figure out what kind of animal it was by its sounds, but it sounded neither feline nor primate.

It was the boy. He was surprised to see Ken at the other end of the cave from where he'd left him, and yelled his surprise, dropping something out of his mouth.

It was a dead hedgehog, which the boy had skinned, except for a piece of hide above its tail.

They sat in the dark, sizing each other up. Then the hominid turned and rushed back up the chimney.

Instants later, he crawled down even more slowly and carefully, this time moving on three limbs only. His right hand was carrying a big palmated leaf that held a few ounces of water.

IT WAS ALMOST MORE EXTRAORDINARY TO HEAR THIS CREA-ture than to see him.

In these close quarters, Ken was even more aware of the youngster's restlessness. The boy put down the leaf and sat throbbing impatiently, his chest letting out a *haah-haah-haah* kind of sigh, which was nothing but his panting after carrying in the food and drink. He shook his head from side to side, sneezed and snorted his own mucus back in, then sniffed at the air, as if he were checking how well Ken's scent had mixed with the smells of his home. He stuck out his light-brown hand, which in the indirect rays of sunlight looked devilishly dark, and pointed at the hedgehog. Ken could smell the light odor of blood and torn guts and it made him want to vomit again. He clenched his teeth, managed to control himself, and felt a triumphant sense of being back to his familiar self. The boy must have picked up on this because he became momentarily still and carefully scanned Ken's face.

Then he fussed again—fussed being the only word for it. With a long finger, he pointed at the water, which glinted inside the big leaf. With the same finger, he poked at the little hedgehog, somewhat cruelly, it seemed to Ken, but with the cruelty of the bush: quick and unsadistic. There was no doubt about it. He wanted to know whether Ken was going to eat it; if not, he was still hungry. Ken started laughing quietly. Then he stopped, realizing that the boy's fussiness was also because they were at such close quarters, and for the first time the child probably saw him as a potential aggressor. Aboveground, he could scurry off quickly, but here, he was at the larger animal's mercy.

Ken laughed—a pure nervous discharge.

The australopithecine child laughed too, quite suddenly.

He let out a high, thin sound, from the larynx that wasn't deep enough to really utter vibrant speaking sounds. But it was a laugh—a tense, humorless, and utterly human laugh. The boy was responding like an uptight, stilted human caught in a narrow space, like a stalled elevator, with a stranger.

Keep him laughing, Ken thought.

Ken raised the palmated leaf quickly, trying to think up something humorous. Before he could come up with anything, he sneezed hard right into that cupful of water, splashing it all over his face and chest. The child raised his protruding lips and weakly formed chin and let out a high-pitched guffaw, almost a howl. Ken angrily lapped the leaf, lapped his wet hand, sucked in his sprayed lips, lapped his hand again for any drops he might have missed. The child, now laughing for real, broke his howl into a chopped-up sequence of giggles, like barks. Wet, disappointed, and weak, Ken laughed too.

Ken thought about how much he wanted a tape recorder, and chuckled to himself about the absurdity of this. He was in the Pliocene now, where there were no tape recorders.

What mattered was the laugh. He had seen many animals being playful or satisfied, but they didn't have humor per se. Chimps were known to play tricks on each other, often quite rough ones, and to become overjoyed when the tricks worked, but humor as a trust builder was uniquely human.

Still chuckling, Ken gestured toward the dead hedgehog, letting the boy know he could have it.

The boy reached out to grab it, in a gesture so instinctive and animallike that Ken pulled back. The boy stuffed the hedgehog's soft belly in his mouth, his eyes widening from the big mouthful in a way that made Ken catch his breath. Careful, he felt like warning. He felt an intense tremor. A large, barely chewed gob was traveling visibly down the boy's throat, and the little thing rapped at his own chest, to help himself swallow.

Ken breathed in relief.

The hedgehog was a blood-smeared little carcass, and its Stone Age consumer momentarily full, and burping satedly.

Ken started laughing again. The boy joined him and chuckled as well but with a slightly surprised expression. He wasn't sure why they were laughing now, but he'd certainly join in. The hominid seemed to be laughing so that his guest would not be laughing alone.

Impossible, Ken thought with brusque anxiety. This boy is much too resourceful and adaptive to be what I think he is.

He's got the apish facial angle, and the jaws, illustrated even more vividly when he eats. And he's got the funny feet too.

Ape and little man, man and little ape, he had to be what he was. He simply could not be a case of multiple atavism, packed with so many throwback features all at once. Modern humans sometimes had lower foreheads, longer faces, heavier browridges, longer hands and feet and toes, but never all at once.

Where is your kind, kid? he felt like asking. But there was no way to ask that.

He might never be able to pose what amounted to a question to a specimen like this one, who was now getting restless—as Ken had already observed, the child had spans of concentration that were deep but brief. Here he was, dropping the carcass on the dirt floor and starting to rise. He clucked his tongue against his teeth, put his palms inside the chimney's tube, and pulled himself upward.

Go where youth calls you. Ken was astounded that he'd had such an old man's thought. After all, he was only twenty-eight. But twenty-eight was a ripe old age for a protohuman.

*　　*　　*

KEN LOST TRACK OF TIME. HE DOZED, AWAKENED, SLEPT, feeling in between how his strength was slowly rebuilding.

It was another morning.

He heard that giggle, low like the cheerful yapping of a pup, and then the hominid scaled down the chimney, bringing a green, gross-looking tuber. He skipped the last few steps and jumped onto the cave floor, his big round knees flexed, his long feet thumping down with unhesitant nimbleness. He let out that brief laugh again, which had become their shared little ritual, as he had scurried in, out, in, between Ken's spells of unconsciousness. Ken quickly gave a chuckle of his own, their way of greeting, instead of a grunt, sniff, or touch.

The boy plopped down and bit into the tuber to show Ken that it was to be eaten. Ken noted that so far the boy had not scavenged, but had eaten meat he had hunted; he also seemed to recognize the value of at least one type of vegetable. Were these skills learned from his kin? Had he learned them himself? There was no telling. Under a coarse skin, the tuber tasted watery, bitter, and unfilling, but Ken needed nourishment. He ate it complete with skin, while the child restlessly turned to climb out again.

"Bring me some more," Ken uttered, softly but loudly. The boy just eyed him, then turned his back and hoisted himself up the tube. He didn't seem scared of Ken's voice, or surprised by it. I've talked in my sleep, Ken told himself. Or raved when I had that high fever.

Ken was annoyed with himself, having again expected the creature to react cowed, stunned, even scared into running off. He would have to fight off his expectations. Relax, Lauder, and enjoy not having to be a scientist. For one thing, this boy's forehead may be low, and his frontal lobes less developed than yours, but that's because his memory and abstract speculation don't need to be so developed at this stage. That's what those lobes are for, and just now he doesn't have any real use for them. After all, what's he got to remember other than survival? What's to speculate about? Besides, you always made fun of classical anthropology, which assumed protohumans to be clumsy apes. Be glad to be studying a long-toe who's so spontaneously adaptive.

He stopped himself again. He had never liked "studying." But wasn't this studying?

Every time he and the boy were face-to-face, he felt he was no longer Ken Lauder—much more than Ken Lauder, and much less. He became an unknown being, faced with another unknown being. He was aware that he was not analyzing all this but was *absorbing* it. With nose, ears, eyes, sense of temperature and touch, he absorbed the boy and the boy absorbed him back.

Through sickness and relief, Ken still lived with one terror. That of Hendrijks's reappearance by the lava rocks. What would he do then?

He prayed that the manhunt was over. "You might as well not see us sapiens at our worst from the start, Long Toes," he muttered at the darkness. "Might as well lose your illusions slowly, if you have any."

The lid of leaves above him came off again and something was flung down at him. It was his rumpled pants, cleaned by the rain.

The boy had found them. Who knew what he made of them, but he had flung them at his guest just when his guest no longer felt sick and powerless.

Ken stood up, feeling light and a little shaky. He was sure he'd lost weight. He picked up his pants, plunged one leg in, then the other—back to the modern feeling of being more powerful and protected if clothed. He stuck the cigarette lighter in his pocket. It was just an object the boy had picked up, but that was how the invasion of the wild always started, with objects.

He felt strong enough to climb out. A few steps up the chimney, he heard a plane. He stopped, straining to remember how long he had been there.

Ngili and the scouts had left Dogilani on a Sunday. Ken had trekked feverishly for two days, then met the boy, then spent another two, maybe three days fighting the fever. That still did not make it to the next Sunday, when Ngili would return to bring supplies and to pick up Ken's first field report.

He heard the plane closer, and recognized its engine.

It was Hendrijks's Beech Lightning.

He stopped, frozen, inside the lava chimney. Then he tried to climb faster, finding the chimney surprisingly slippery and hard to grip. Thoughts banged around in Ken's mind: Where was his shirt? Seen from the plane, it could be a dead give-away. Also where were his nightviewers, which he had lost sometime after finding the parachute? They were another giveaway; he cursed himself for not having searched for them already.

He also thought about the hominid boy. What would happen to him? He might have to watch Ken being injured or killed. Or worse, he might be captured. Hendrijks would hardly fly this unique specimen to the University of Nairobi, Department of Paleoanthropology. Ken pictured the boy being tied and dragged like a freak, among rough male laughter, to a smelly poachers' camp or a decrepit border post.

He made it up to the lip of the opening and clawed his way out. Stepping outside, he tripped, blinded by the light.

The boy was standing by a bush.

THE HOMINID HAD HEARD THE BUZZING OF THE PLANE AND was excited.

The alien had arrived without his tuber/bug, which was rather disappointing, but now the tuber/bug was following.

He lifted his face at the sky, glowing like a child expecting a big toy.

He was in a good mood already, because the last few days had been a feast of new events. The alien was more fascinating close up and more intriguing as he got to know him better.

He was very shocked to see the alien jump out of the chimney's top in his rumpled pants. The alien made ugly puffing/rattling sounds—Ken was panting and cursing—and was running around like crazy among the tract of grass, the jumble of lava, the mungongo tree, and the stream, looking for his shirt.

THE PLANE BUZZED CLOSER AND KEN MANAGED TO CONtrol himself and tried to use the reassuring power of his voice: "Nothing wrong, Long Toes." He wondered whether he should speak Swahili instead of English, and realized again that both were lost on the boy. "Just a little game we sapiens are playing. Intraspecies war."

He was struck by a cruel sense of guilt about the boy that made him think he should rush out into the open and turn himself in. But even that would not guarantee the safety of the hominid.

He needed a weapon. His knife might still be lying around the scrub by the cave, but that wasn't enough. *I need a weapon.*

The plane's buzzing varied in volume, as if it were flying low, circling around one stand of trees after another.

He could not find his shirt. The rain had swollen the little stream and leached the ground where the bushes did not hold it down. His shirt had probably been washed away, but he had no time to make sure of that—the plane's noise grew even closer. He had to get himself and the boy out of sight, somehow.

He searched his pocket. "Look, Long Toes," he muttered, holding up the cigarette lighter.

The hominid saw the shiny stone in the alien's hand. The alien's thumb rubbed its top.

The boy had seen fire before, bush fire, but never as a tiny breath of yellow glow. The alien brought it close to his own face, and blew it out. Then he made it appear again. He raised it to the boy's face, letting him enjoy the tiny live fire. Then Ken backed toward the cave's entrance, showing the boy that the flame looked even fuller and sharper against the dark.

*   *   *

KEN'S SHIRT HAD BEEN FLUSHED AWAY IN THE RAIN, THEN carried down several miles. Spread out by the water and then folded again by the whims of its flow, the shirt netted torn branches and lumps of dirt, finally clumping up and stopping the water like a little dam. By the middle of the next morning, with the rain gone, the shirt rose in its midst, bulged and muddied like a drowned animal.

A marabou stork flapped down and pulled at the shirt with a curious beak. It freed a sleeve and dragged at it, but feeling no tissue or blood in it, lost interest and let the sleeve drop and took off.

The bog dried up under the soaring sun. Hours passed.

IN THE CAVE, KEN MOVED HIS FINGER QUICKLY ACROSS THE tiny flame. He felt its bite and began moving his finger across in the other direction, running the whole experiment before the hominid's glittering eyes.

He tried to show the boy that this little game wasn't dangerous. But the little hominid would not check the flame's friendliness. This suited Ken fine. The longer this took, the better chance of the plane turning around and flying away.

He had to be careful though, because the lighter's fuel was not unlimited. And he didn't want to lose his only direct source of fire. He would have to find something else to kindle from that flame. But what?

Just then, the boy reached for the cigarette lighter, and Ken guided the dark thumb, which felt shockingly muscular for its size, to the flint's igniting device. He worked the thumb against it, his body mastering at the same time the shiver of his first direct body contact with the boy.

The boy's thumb rubbed, pressing too hard. It missed. The lighter was hot, and the hominid dropped it and pulled his hand away.

Ken patiently picked up the lighter and started working it again, while also listening to the plane's sound and straining to analyze his situation in the most practical terms. He had not found that survival cache. The other survival cache was at the very opposite end of his area of research. It would take him or them several days to trek back to it, practically in the open. And now he was sure he was being hunted.

The answer was somewhere other than that cache, and away from his meeting place with Ngili. What would happen if he missed his next appointment with Ngili—assuming that Ngili was not part of the conspiracy?

He realized that those forested little valleys dipping between the Mau's spurs were the answer. They were narrow and twisted, and almost impossible to search with a low-flying plane. His pursuers would have to come on foot. That offered him a far better chance.

I need a weapon. I can't let another leopard attack us. Or a lion.

I need a weapon. I'm going to make one.

The lighter's flame was very low now, and almost on its last drops of fuel. He had to find something else to kindle before the fuel gave out.

The child took the lighter from his hand while the flame was still burning. His throat rolled out a warning "rrrrr" sound. Ken tore out one of his pants pockets. It was crumpled but dry from the contact with his body. He touched the little flame to it, and grinned ever more widely as the fabric caught fire and the bluish flame grew back to a ripe yellow.

The boy became silent. Only his eyes, at maximum size, testified to the moment's specialness. Their globes had become brilliant, opaline white with a fine reddish iridescence surrounding their fully dilated pupils.

Then the boy caught Ken by surprise. He backed off two steps, then fell to the ground on all fours and remained there, face held high, signaling subservience and lack of self-protection.

Ken dropped the burning fabric and sat down. The boy tumbled over and sat almost shoulder to shoulder with Ken. Then he leaned against Ken, fearfully but at the same time with urgency, as if that contact gave him the strength to face the fire. They sat shoulder to shoulder, both training their eyes at the low flames, both knowing that the other was watching the same capricious being of light.

Ken was sweating and gritting his teeth.

Bingo, he thought. Total trust.

He felt that the trust was expressed not in words but in a deep quality of the moment, touching the foundation of their beings.

Perhaps it was the power of that moment, perhaps it was his imagination. But he thought that the plane was sounding more distant now.

Then, finally, he no longer heard it. The buzz of its engine had vanished completely.

IN MIDAFTERNOON, A CLAWLIKE HAND REACHED DOWN TO pick up Ken's crumpled shirt while several pairs of feet in scrub boots gathered around the dried-up bog. Modibo held up the shirt, turned it on all sides, felt it with his hardened fingertips.

"He's dead, dead!" was all Hendrijks could say. He performed a kind of grotesque dance, hopping about, reaching for the shirt. Modibo yanked it away. Hendrijks pushed his hat back, showing his crimson forehead slashed halfway by the hat's stricture.

"He's dead, isn't he? Isn't he?" he bellowed, no longer holding back the strain of the last five days of flying and landing, flying and landing, of scouring the bush with one eye ahead and one over his shoulder, and one hand always on his .45 Sig/Hammerli Swiss pistol. He'd slept in increments of fifteen minutes at a time, which he'd seen baboons and bush birds do. He had paid Modibo and the other Africans for five days of manhunt, but had neglected to take another *witte* (Cape Dutch for "white") with him. So he had spent the worst nights of his life, paranoid that the blacks would kill him and sell his plane.

"Speak, dammit!" Hendrijks yelled at Modibo.

The sergeant was stretching out the shirt, holding it close

to his beady eyes, turning it. He even smelled it. Then he let it fall.

"Maybe not dead," he advised thoughtfully. "Dere is no blood on it, I don tink."

"But it rained! The rain washed off the blood!"

"Maybe he tirsty, and drank de rain."

Hendrijks felt like he was going insane. He glanced at the heated flatlands, saw a jackal sitting in the open between him and the hazy escarpment, tongue hanging from the heat but eyes glinting with what looked like sarcasm.

"Maybe he troo us off wid da shirt, da way he troo us off wid da car." Modibo scratched the naked, dusty calf of his left leg with the wornout front of his right boot.

"Where is he, then?" foamed Hendrijks. He tore off his hat, but instead of whipping his clothes with it, he flung it at a bush. A sudden hiss rose from under the hat, and Hendrijks lunged to grab it. He leaped back grotesquely. A boomslang snake twisted out from under the hat and the bush and seeped away. Hendrijks was so furious that he leaped forward to crash down on the reptile but missed. The boomslang twirled on its tail; it rose up straight, mouth open, upper fangs held tall. The fangs caught the sun as they sprayed a cloud of fluid venom that settled on Hendrijks's lower chest, thick middle, and legs and feet.

Hendrijks heard the Africans laugh. He jumped out of the snake's reach, and turned with one hand on his hip holster.

They stopped laughing. Hendrijks stared down at the film of venom over the front of his shirt. He feared irrationally that it might penetrate the fabric and then his skin.

"You let it dry in da sun. It's okay," said Modibo with insight into his fear.

Cooled off just for an insant, Hendrijks was boiling again. "You think the kaffir got back here somehow, and joined Lauder?"

"Da kaffir?" asked Modibo with ever so slight derision.

Three African faces watched Hendrijks. He stuttered. "The . . . I mean, Ngiamena. The geologist."

"No," said Modibo. He spat through a gap in his white

lower teeth. "Da mzungu and da kaffir, very strong team." Modibo remembered how Ken had raced with the rifle in hand, dropped to his knees, and pointed the rifle at the Safari Cub. Ngili had raced one step behind him, yelling fiercely, "Shoot the tires! Shoot the tires!"

"Very strong team, dey might kill us," Modibo said, enjoying the look on the white pilot's face.

Hendrijks swallowed the mucus in his mouth, which tasted bitter, as if filled with bile. "If he's alive, what do you think he's up to?"

"He maybe go dere." Modibo pointed at the forest on the Mau.

"And then?"

"Maybe he die." Modibo acted truly amused. "Or come back, and we do."

He did not expect Hendrijks to answer that one and he didn't.

"Get back in the plane," he grunted instead. "I'm dropping you back at the camp."

"Where you go?"

"To Nairobi," said Hendrijks, with an intimation of vengeful plans. He tried to put his hat back on, but its bill flapped, ripped from getting caught in the bush.

The Africans knew when to laugh at the white pilot, and when not to stretch it. This time they didn't. One picked up a rifle he had let slide to the ground, and they trooped away, toward the Beech Lightning.

Hendrijks seemed lost in thought.

He stood facing the escarpment, scanning its higher reaches. For an instant, mist cleared at high altitude, bringing the green into sharp focus, making it feel as if it clung to Hendrijks's eyes. The white pilot started, then shook his head as if chasing off visions or memories. He remembered Ken's shirt and bent down to pick it up. He bundled it messily, stuck it under his arm, and started toward his plane.

T HE GAME OF MAKING FIRE IN THE CAVE LASTED SEV-
eral hours, and when it was over, they climbed outside
again. About a hundred yards from the cave's mouth, Ken
found his knife.

Soon he would have to eat meat, he told himself. Meat,
the great protein-storer that gave hominids their initial energy
for exploring open spaces, abandoning their nonstop grazing
of leaves and seeds in favor of just two or three meals per
day. Meat meat meat. Meat. He was craving it. Even uncooked meat. He found himself fantasizing about a steak tar-
tare, raw, gooey, its sanguine juices smearing the corners of
his mouth.

This is not me, thinking like this.

But it was.

HE CLIMBED ON THE JUMBLED ROCKS AND LOOKED FAR AND
wide for the plane, but did not see it or hear it.

He climbed down, gave the hominid boy a wide smile,
then led the way around the rocks, into the first of the fingerlike shaded valleys that wrapped around the escarpment's
spurs. They checked one, two, three valleys, and liked the
fourth. They stopped under a shelter of branches, where the
boy saw the alien start to act tense and pressured because

night was coming and he still had no weapon.

The boy wasn't particularly concerned about this because he was so captivated by the alien. In the beginning, the alien had moved slowly, seeming almost incapable of running. When the boy had found him lying on the grass under the rain, he had dragged him into the chimney and had felt the weight of that muscular mass which the alien did not seem to use. He had heard Ken rave and had marveled at the sounds he made. The boy had even gone out of the cave and tried to duplicate some of the alien's sounds, but had failed. Still, the alien was a real feast for the eye and ear, and more.

Now, as they sought that sheltered valley, the alien was acting far more in possession of his strength. He moved fast, and his posture and direction were obvious. He even appeared handsome in his own alien way, and reassuring.

The boy was enjoying an abstract pleasure: that of remembering that something new and exciting was happening to him. He had awakened the night before in the chimney and realized wordlessly he was not alone. The next day, he would again enjoy this incredible partnership.

In the darkness, Ken snored peacefully, which caused the hominid to be aware that certain actions and expressions of the alien's sounded or looked similar to . . . To his own kind. But that sensation was quickly contradicted when Ken had slurred a few words in his sleep.

The boy lay down again but could not sleep. The play, the show, the ever-renewed surprise of the alien's presence, made his mind race. Through the day, like a cub pulling at blades of grass or discovering the tip of an adult's tail, he had been in a constant state of wonder.

And now came the second act of the play—remembering it. He followed the alien until they came to a spot where elephants had uprooted an acacia and several wild chestnut trees weeks before. The boy sat trustingly in the grass, the firestone in his fist, watching Ken climb on a broken lower branch to cut off firewood. Ken knew that it would take him a while to cut the wood with his small, inefficient knife, but he had no choice. The night was starting to fill the valley, like a late tide.

KEN LIT THE FIRE USING HIS FAILING LIGHTER AND ANOTHER pocket ripped out of his pants.

He was bending to carry over another armful of dry broken branches when he heard the boy's high-pitched sound. Next to the rising fire, the boy stood openmouthed, screaming for no apparent reason. Ken's first reaction was that he had been bitten by a snake, and he rushed over.

But the boy was clearly not hurt because he broke into a flurry of motion, pushing and kicking more branches into the fire. Still screaming, he dropped to the ground and started plucking grass and throwing it into the flames, followed by a flowering bush, most of it too green to burn. The fire started smoking, almost threatening to go out. The child raced off. Screaming intermittently and stopping to breathe and screaming again, he ran around the bushes and trees, looking for things to heap on the flames—an old nest hanging from a branch, a dry vine that had fallen to the ground, another vine, live and green, a shriveled cluster of wild nuts trampled by an elephant's thumping foot, a mound of dirt full of live ants. He flung all these into the fire, then stood leaping in place and slapping the ants on his hands and arms without even looking at them, his eyes totally fixated on the flames.

Petrified, Ken saw the child break into a sweat, while his eyes flashed, wildly at first, then only playfully. He stopped screaming but kept leaping and twitching as he exuded a sense of relief that suddenly one of his old fears, the fear of bush fire, the lethal scourge of the African flatlands, was being exorcised. The boy had harbored that fear for a long time. It had lasted on in his flesh, in his bones, like a tragic memory.

It was being expelled now, in favor of a sense of power over the flames. Apparently happy with his outburst, the brown-skinned little devil raced about the place again, looking for other stuff to incinerate. His hands plunged into the grass and he came up with a large, twisting black-collar lizard, which he hurled into the core of the fire. It squirmed for an instant, then was asphyxiated. The smell of roasting meat shot a pang of hunger into Ken's stomach, a message of unhoped-for food into Ken's brain.

Ken squatted and tried to pull the lizard out of the flames with a branch, but it had clutched onto the fire in death and could not be moved. It popped loudly when its throat and stomach swelled and burst. The odor of burning protein haunted Ken's nostrils, mocking his feelings of fleeting compassion for the innocent animal. His own instincts had become basic: a hungry man, an excited child, a fire consuming life to protect other life—theirs in this case—the dark bush, and the chance of a meal tomorrow.

The boy, in a frenzy of triumph, was leaping over the fire. He yelped as he burned his feet. Eyes narrowing, he stepped back to leap over it again, and again, until the man dropped the knife and a dry branch, and lassoed the child by the waist, with both arms. They fell on the grass, the boy in a lunacy of kicks, punches, and laugh/cry, which Ken finally controlled by pressing the low forehead against his own chest, amazed with the strength of the little being.

He let go of the boy. Unfed, the flames had decreased. The boy staggered to them, and in a postscript of conquest, peed on them.

THEY HAD NOT HUNTED SO THEY DIDN'T HAVE ANYTHING for dinner.

They shared the fire, the man whittling a long straight chestnut branch, while the boy watched the flames, his face seeming ready to explode from the unverbal thought that the fire stirred in him. At one point, Ken saw the boy turn away from the fire to look at the dark wilderness. The eyes of an owl glittered in a tree. Zigzagging bats flickered into being and then back into nothingness, as they whirled above the dancing light; their sharp cries sounded absolutely identical to the way they had always sounded, but bats illuminated intermittently by fire were totally new. As was the irregular flight of a bug catching the fire's glow on its wings, and the rich rain of smaller insects falling into the flames, and the sight of the ground close to the fire—just regular ground made up of humble dirt, yet lit now radiantly, in a fantasy of colors and movements never witnessed before.

Whittling at his chestnut branch, Ken kept glancing at the boy and was pleased by his subdued behavior. Good going, Long Toes. You've got what it takes, in that little box in your head. Ken suddenly started—he had cut his finger.

He put it in his mouth, thinking as he sucked on the bleeding cut, Good-bye, Prometheus. Man never stole fire back from the gods, with or without his liver being chewed on by an eagle as punishment. There had never been a *quest* for fire because fire was always at hand, ignited in the bush by the sun. But man had no pressing need to use fire until the first major glaciation, when he rediscovered its gift of warmth, and also how to cook food, most probably out of the need to thaw frozen hulks of mammoth meat.

The yellow wood of the chestnut caught the flames' reflection. The branch was slowly turning into a spear.

He stopped whittling and slid the almost finished weapon across the grass, to the boy's feet. The boy explored the spear with his palms, then forgot about it, his eyes caught in the fire.

The spear had not been hard to make, but it would be much harder to use. Ken pictured himself running with it, missing, scoring, all that under the critical eye of a young australopithecine.

He was suddenly filled with disbelief at what he had become part of. This is not happening! He felt that if he closed his eyes and reopened them, this other creature would be gone. This is not happening, he repeated. But he was barely twenty miles north of the site where he had found that fossil, and there, too, he had at first uttered that line of denial: This is not happening.

It was happening.

He knew he would accept this unreal reality more easily

had he met not one such specimen, but several. A family, to whom he could leave this child, and then—then what?

Eventually, turn his back on all of them, he admitted to himself. Head back to where he had come from. But there was no such family present, and maybe there wasn't one at all—just he and the youngster, an odd breed of two, from which he could not split.

That thought brought on another, overpowering in its responsibility. If that was the case, what was he to do? What should Ken Lauder do as a human and scientist about having met a solitary prehuman?

I got myself in a fine mess, he thought, and not just because of Hendrijks.

But there was that too.

If only he could void his memory of anything that had happened before the last few days. He was here, he wasn't sick anymore, and he had an extraordinary companion. What a fantasy. All he had to do was forget why he had come here, and where he was from. And then, what liberation and fun—to join the object of his science, but without any obligations as a scientist, and prance about the Pliocene together, and just *be*!

The boy had curled up by the fire, still watching it with half-mast eyes. His eyelids descended, blinked feebly, descended again, and remained closed. Ken lay on his back, preparing for a night of fitful sleep. Float away on sleep's dark tide, then bolt up, hand on the unfinished spear. Scan the darkness, check the fire, sleep again, wake again. Two minutes of checkup to every ten or twenty of rest, that was the ratio. He would sleep like an early man.

He became scared. He felt the oppressiveness of silence. It had been far too long since he had talked, but he would not be understood and would only baffle his friend. But he had to communicate with him somehow. He could not think of a way, even though he had drawn him to this new site, and they were watching the fire together.

We'll hunt, he decided.
We'll hunt. Tomorrow.
It sounded magical. As accurate as language, or better.
We'll hunt.

I N Nairobi, there was a curfew that went into effect every evening at eight P.M. But the roaming army
patrols had reinforced it for only a few days. After that, an
industry of fake curfew exemptions had sprouted up, run by
the army itself, which set roadblocks at main intersections to
stop the motorists with fake exemptions and fine them. Very
quickly, the city's gridlocks and traffic jams returned. While
the downtown area occupied the patrols' attention, the suburbs pulsated again with nightlife.

"Fine me twice the amount, but just let me go," Cyril
Anderson begged, leaning out of his Toyota Land Cruiser,
toward the metropolitan police lieutenant. His permit was
real—it was issued by the Department of the Interior—but
he had been sitting in gridlock for half an hour and wanted
to get away from this boulevard filled with smoke from over-
heating cars and matatus.

The policeman told him to wait his turn, which meant that
if he came back in a minute and Anderson increased the
amount, he might let him go. Anderson cursed out loud in
his Shakespearean voice, reached for the cellular phone, and
dialed an overseas prefix, then a number he had come to
know well over the last two days.

When a receptionist answered at the Mayfair Hotel in London, Anderson asked whether Mrs. Corinne Anderson had

returned to her room; if not, she should be paged in the lobby, bar, restaurant, et cetera. He waited with mounting rage. Earlier that day and the day before, Corinne had not been located, no matter what hour he had called. He was therefore shocked when her calm and limpid voice answered. "Cyril? I knew it was you. You just caught me. I'm going out again, for drinks with the chairman of the conference."

"Living it up, huh?"

A brief pause. "Don't you think I should a little, after years of waiting for you to return from your conferences and symposia?"

He knew his answer should be: Of course, darling, and this is your first scientific event, so play, I don't mind. But it seemed to him that a faucet had been turned on inside his wife, a faucet of "now it's my turn." No matter what he said, she would switch it around and relate it to the imbalance of their relationship. For years, he had done this and that, and now it was her turn to open the door and go in and out as she pleased. He felt like roaring over the cellular connection that she'd lost her mind, that she'd be nothing without him. And besides, he'd married her for her looks! It would feel good to diminish her so completely, but he could not do that so much anymore because just recently she had turned on him like a snake and hissed that she married him to have a career in science, and it was time she took care of that career, since he had not delivered much else. The hurt she had inflicted back was much worse than the one he had hurled at her.

That little heart-to-heart changed their relationship. He tried to figure out when she had stopped responding to the Anderson aura. He had of course taken other students to bed and filled them with his warm emissions and watched them pant and moan their awe at him. Or so it had seemed. He thought now that had he married any other, she might also have awakened to independence and revolt, just like Corinne. Perhaps the professorial bed wasn't a real mirror of his prowess, but instead a stage where his students playacted orgasms with him, while in real life they enjoyed them with stiff-cocked bastards like Lauder and Ngiamena.

Through the six years of his marriage, he'd experienced great pangs of jealous anger over Corinne's affair with Ken. It had happened before he set his sights on her, but her "It was nothing at all, darling" told him it had meant something, and that he had been outclassed before he even got started. She had dropped him though, said his voice of pride. But was his pride correct, or mistaken? Corinne had preferred Lauder for her selfish joy, but she had only dropped him for her opportunity with Anderson.

Now she had flown to London for the conference on the enlarged brain, and he realized that he wanted her next to him. Even if there was no bed to really bring them back together, or exciting new discoveries, there was . . . there was . . . habit.

He wasn't even paying attention to her, now that he knew where she was, and that she was with a nonthreatening French evolutionist he had known for years.

"It's so fascinating," Corinne said. "The researchers here are presenting papers that sound directly inspired by what you say to me around the dinner table. Lebenson presented a genetic analysis of brain-weight increase as relating to changes of diet. Fidos and Oppelman presented the allometry of the brain's blood irrigation in relation to the cooling of the climate."

He cut her off. "Fidos and Oppelman are German. You'll see how the Third World scientists tear them apart for suggesting that the human brain grew to its largest size in Europe."

"That's not my point. All these directions, you think them up at breakfast."

He knew where she was headed. "These people are lab rats, Corinne. They're not worth a partnership with me."

"A few of them are quite brilliant. Lebenson is presenting not one paper but two. His second's about the neural component placement optimization in higher primates. He compares it to the microchip layout wiring minimization problem in a computer. . . .''

"Would you stop the mumbo-jumbo? I decided that I wouldn't join the computerfication of our science!" *Couldn't* join was more accurate than wouldn't, but he wasn't going to hand her that card. "Find me a foundation interested in me, Corinne, or an international program that I can run. Otherwise, you're wasting my time!"

"Pardon? I thought you called *me*. I'm making the chairman of the conference wait, so I can talk about your problems."

His problems! He felt like strangling her, if he could only do it through the phone.

"Any news about Ken's search?" she asked suddenly.

Through the smoke of the street, Anderson glimpsed a mob on the sidewalk—men, and one lonely female wearing a turban, a huddle of heads and shoulders moving in a rhythm, hitting someone caught in their midst. A pickpocket probably. Justice had passed into the hands of crowds. That kind of cruelty seemed fateful to Anderson. Recently he'd felt like that anonymous victim, suddenly getting blows from all sides, from age (he was rather nervously waiting on a prostate checkup), from the political crisis, from the disloyal wife.

"Why are we talking about Lauder, anyway?" He never called Ken by his first name.

"You kept talking about him, about how interesting the piece he brought back looked, even at the most superficial examination. And you asked Ngiamena whether Ken went back to Dogilani alone, and Ngiamena clammed up but didn't really deny it. . . ."

"So?" He reached into his wallet. He rolled all the cash he had into one wad, waiting for the police lieutenant to come closer.

"Ken is lucky, luckier than both of us. But maybe his luck can be yours too, Cyril. If he went back to Dogilani alone, he can't have it easy. Why don't you go out there after him?

Offer *real help*. He'll make you scientific coordinator, he'll have no choice.''

"Don't talk nonsense. He offered that to Phillips, I'm sure." He thought of himself and Ken together in the bush. He had sparse field experience compared to a young fire-eater's stamina and sense of improvisation. God. No way. "Lauder needs Phillips because he's a poor conceptualizer, that was always his weak point." He drew the cop over with the wad of money.

"So you're a great conceptualizer, greater than Phillips. Phillips is away, Ken needs help, and you need a find."

"Why Lauder's? He can't even . . ."

"Stop it, Cyril. Ken doesn't have to talk the talk, he walks the walk." Terribly scientific way of phrasing it, Anderson thought in scornful anger. "The easiest find you could be part of is his . . ."

He stuck his hand out the car window and the cop took the money. Somehow Anderson overcame his desire to yell into the cellular phone; instead he breathed, "It would be beneath me to be part of someone else's find, rather than they be part of mine."

"What would it take," she asked, still patiently, "for me to convince you?"

"What makes you think that find's so unique?"

"You think so yourself."

He squirmed under her logic. But a little door of opportunity to alter their rapport seemed to open, and he rushed toward it. "Very well, we have to talk more about this. When are you calling me tomorrow?"

"Now I'll say a time, and you'll tell me you're busy then, and give me another time, just to show me how important you are." Her tone was even, but irritated. "You're so manipulative, darling."

"I don't know what you're talking about," he said dryly. She was right and he did not care; the main thing was to have the last word. "Tomorrow noon is good for me, darling. I'm having lunch in the tutorial. All right, Corinne?" The cop put the money in his pocket. He motioned another car to reverse and make way for Anderson to get out of the traffic.

Her silence was full of contempt.

"All right?" he yelled, blowing all his composure. "Corinne?" Silence at the end of the line. Had she hung up? "Corinne?"

The dial tone.

He dropped the phone, floored the gas, bursting forward so hard that the cop staggered back against another car. He drove on the sidewalk, honking at African faces that had to leap away from the crazy car, cursing the driver.

He thought about calling Corinne again, and fought so hard not to do it that he sweated. He wiped his forehead with the sleeve of his white jacket. The stain of sweat would show. She had hung up on him. What did it mean? Would she still call the next day, or would he have to chase her?

He maneuvered around a torn open stretch of pavement and hit a roadwork sign. The car jumped, and it helped him regain some control. He took his foot off the pedal. He glanced in the rearview mirror, then sat up to see himself. He looked the same, his rich white hair well groomed, his face imposing. In the car's darkness, his hair looked luminous, his face carved, imperially middle-aged. He made contact with what he saw in himself—a master of the field, and of his life. *But she had hung up on him.*

ANDERSON GLANCED AT A NOTE WITH AN ADDRESS, AND drove out of downtown, into the chaos of low, unmaintained buildings surrounding the old railway station. The area smelled of urban despair, and he was aware of how conspicuous his Land Cruiser was.

He parked in the inner court of the Nyassa Motel, locked up the car, and stepped out. His ears instantly distinguished the sounds of human sexual moans above a few radios and a lawn mower that was absurdly cutting the grass at that hour.

A boy ran past him carrying a stack of steaming paper

boxes that said PIZZA BUCCI, BEST IN AFRICA! on the top. Anderson, note in hand, knocked on a door, while the boy
knocked one door up. A woman wearing a white bra opened
the door to the pizza boy, and the sexual moans were louder.

The door in front of Anderson creaked inward, and he was
confronted with a plump red-faced man in a V-necked T-
shirt. "Professor," said the man, smiling. "I thought you
were not coming."

"I almost didn't, Mr. Hendrijks."

He peered behind the pilot at a round table lit by a lamp
suspended from a chain. He made out the shape of another
pizza box. Hendrijks stepped back invitingly, but Anderson
did not come into the room.

"I reflected about our first meeting, Mr. Hendrijks. There
is no way that I could pay you the money you asked for."

Their first meeting had happened in the cluttered rooms of
Zhang Chen's Herb and Fossil Shop. It offered seeds and
roots at "Sensible Prices, Cures for All"—meaning all people, or all diseases. Hendrijks had suggested it.

"Come in just for a minute. I got something that might
change your mind, Professor."

"No, really. I came to say that I'm not interested, please
stop calling and sending me notes."

"Just one minute, verdomma!" Hendrijks became aware
of his tone, of the curse. "Sorry," he laughed. "I speak loud,
because . . ." The sexual moans were filling his room, louder
than outside. "Sex movie shooting next door. Comes through
the air-conditioning pipes. The sound equipment's so old that
they have to yell. . . . One minute? Please?"

"One minute." Anderson stepped in.

Hendrijks closed the door, went straight to the table, and
impatiently pushed aside the pizza box. It slid, revealing
something else lying there—a disassembled pistol, with a
magazine whose loading end showed the silver-and-brass
pattern of the top bullet. Anderson briefly feared that Hendrijks might grab the gun, but instead he raked the table with
his fingers, moved two photographs closer, then reached up
to adjust the length of the chain supporting the lamp. He

elongated it, showing Anderson the two photographs that contained the perfectly clear footprints of a hominid.

"Lauder took the pictures," said Hendrijks. "The boot in that picture is his boot."

"Did you see the footprints too?"

Hendrijks nodded.

Anderson cleared his voice again. "Did you see the live specimens?"

Once again, Hendrijks nodded. Anderson turned crimson. He cleared his voice. "How many specimens did you see?" The pilot was silent. "Where's that place?"

Hendrijks laughed and shook a finger like an adult at a child: Nah, nah, no more information until they agreed on a figure for payment. Even then he would not disclose the place. Anderson would find out where it was as they flew into it together.

"Why did you tell *me* all this, instead of someone else?" asked Anderson.

"Because they kept mentioning you. Lauder and Ngiamena. I heard them say how much you'd want to take over this find. I heard it in the plane, and in the bush."

"You're not very forthcoming," said Anderson. He kept clearing his throat. "How can I trust someone who obviously stole this information?"

Hendrijks laughed the same way: Nah, nah, he did not steal anything. He simply went to a certain bank and talked to the manager, inquiring about a safe-deposit box in the name of Lauder, a client who had not paid him for a week of flights. The manager agreed to let Hendrijks open Lauder's safe-deposit box.

"Agreed?" asked Anderson between clearing his voice.

"I know how to convince people." Hendrijks took the Sig/Hammerli gun, started clicking its pieces back together. "Didn't it surprise you, Professor, that I knew your phone number?" Anderson started; indeed, he had not questioned the way Hendrijks had found his unlisted number. A visit to the phone company, grinned Hendrijks. A talk with a supervisor. Phone company supervisors were paid a pittance.

"You see, Professor, someone like you doesn't have the street smarts to stalk someone like Lauder." Hendrijks completed the Sig/Hammerli's reassembling. "Bet you don't even know how to shoot a gun." He slipped in the magazine. "Or read tracks, or find water in the bush. I have someone after Lauder. Name of Modibo, an incredible tracker and a poacher for years; even though he's in the army, he's still a poacher." He turned to pull at a drawer which refused to open. He set down the gun, used both hands to open the drawer, took out a crumpled, discolored shirt, threw it on the table—it fell over the gun and the pizza box. "This is Lauder's shirt. Me and my tracker found it right by the Mau."

"Is he dead?"

"We don't think he's dead. In fact, we think he was found by the funny feet."

Anderson breathed. "All right, we'll make a deal. Where is he?"

He knew where Ken was. When Ngiamena had called him, anxious about his son's whereabouts, Anderson had guessed Dogilani. The next day, Ngiamena had confirmed that the game park plane had spotted the two young men at Dogilani, which was exactly where Anderson had assumed they were. So where else would Ken be now?

"The price of all the information depends on what kind of deal we make. Just to follow Lauder is one price. To get Lauder out of the way"—Anderson made a horrified face, and Hendrijks chuckled—"is more. But still affordable."

"I don't know what you're talking about."

"Take Lauder out," said Hendrijks. "Not expensive. Five thousand."

"I have to think," Anderson said. "I've never made such a decision before."

"You don't do stuff like that for science," chuckled Hendrijks. "But think of it as a war. He's the enemy, and he's in your territory."

"You're talking about murder, Mr. Hendrijks."

"You kill Lauder, you get what he found, on a platter.

You think five thousand's too much? Okay, will you pay four?''

Even cheaper than you, Corinne, Anderson thought. Live hominids, at four thousand.

He leaned against the table. "Aren't you afraid that you might get caught and tried, and I'd testify against you?"

Hendrijks made the same amused face, like an adult talking to a child. "No one's going to be tried in this country, not for a long time. What is coming is a completely new power, and I have the connections to it."

"Mr. Hendrijks, Lauder was my student."

Hendrijks laughed. "In life, there are times when thefts are not thefts, Professor, and murders are not murders. They're very rare, so you're lucky that you hit one."

Hendrijks picked up Ken's shirt. Anderson lunged at the Sig/Hammerli just as the crumpled fabric was lifted off the pistol's dull shine. He grabbed it, cocked it with his thumb, pushed it hard under Hendrijks's rib cage. The contact of the barrel to the body muffled the shot like a silencer.

Hendrijks weakened from the knees, and seemed to break toward the floor; he touched down, but one of his shoulders met a chair, which stopped him from sprawling and folded him in an almost sitting position. He died sometime during that movement. Anderson had heard of the surprise on the faces of murdered people, caused by their brains synapsing life's final disappointment. But Hendrijks did not show that surprise. He looked dull, as if he had accepted what was happening to him.

Anderson held the gun up for a few seconds, then let it fall next to the pilot's body. He was feeling a strange daze of amazement: This had been so easy.

He waited. He expected to be sick, but was not. Hendrijks's features were agitated by a brief tremor. His eyes rolled back, and air escaped from his lungs, making him utter a dead man's cough.

Anderson turned, reached for the air-conditioning unit, turned it on. Moans wafted in from the room where the sex movie was being shot.

It had been so easy, but now he had to find something to wipe this gun with.

He pulled at the bedsheets, but they were heavy, and filled with the smell of a sweaty old male. The smell made Anderson choke. He walked into the bathroom, found a filthy towel hanging by the sink, tried to get hold of it, but could not make himself do it. He gritted his teeth, looked at a mirror with green cracks in its reflecting surface that resembled algae. He saw himself beyond the algae. He still looked like the man he knew, and that man still looked good. Looking at himself, Anderson did not find it hard to accept what he had become. He found it harder to handle the dead man's filthy personal belongings.

He gritted his teeth, took the towel, walked back into the room, and wiped the gun, his mind beginning to hum a kind of crazy song. It was easy. Ea-zeeee.

The dead man wasn't Lauder, but that would be easy too.

He dropped the gun back, threw the towel on the floor, rattled through the closets and drawers, looking for more evidence of the hominids, in photographs or notes. There were none. But he found a map of Dogilani, with a particular location marked with a cross in red pen. He studied it, finding that it matched almost identically his own deduction of where the rocks stratigraphed by Ngili and Ken were—right by the southernmost spur of the Mau. He folded the map and slipped it into his inner jacket pocket.

That reminded him to take his jacket off and examine it. He found no blood on it. Or anywhere else on his clothes. He thought of how fast, how skillfully and efficiently he had killed, and also how he had limited the blood spilling to a minimum, by dipping the gun into the flabby adipose midriff of the aging pilot. He thought about it, and his mind hummed that new song. Ea-zeeeee.

All would be easy from now on.

He still had to be careful, he told himself. He toweled his fingerprints off the surfaces of closets and drawers which he had left hanging open on purpose; now, he pushed them shut one by one, with his shoulder. He wanted to drop the towel, but for some reason became paranoid and stuck it under his jacket, then turned off the light by brushing his shoulder against the switch. He opened the door, stared out into the crowded parking lot, and knew he would go to Dogilani, to kill Ken Lauder.

It would be easy.

He thought of the others who knew about the find. Ngili. Randall Phillips. Raj Haksar.

Haksar had called Anderson and surprised him with a story about having once visited Dogilani himself. He had refused to say when, but had said he'd seen a strange population that took to the forest when they realized that they were being watched. He had given no details, and Anderson had not paid close attention because he had assumed that Haksar had spotted some unknown tribesmen. Anderson was interested in fossils, and Haksar had not found fossils, but he had seen a tribe. Suddenly the notion of a tribe of protohumans inundated Anderson. He forgot about Hendrijks, and stood in the doorway of the open room, realizing he had, at last, gotten his own find.

Had Haksar published anything about that tribe he'd seen? Anderson felt like rushing to his car phone and calling the old man, but he controlled himself. Just because things would be easy from now on, he didn't have to behave carelessly or hastily.

Haksar had told Anderson that he wanted Anderson's cooperation. He had alluded to going back to the area with Anderson. What did Haksar really want? Money, like the pilot? A chance to eliminate potential rivals? He chuckled. Haksar was frail and gravely ill with diabetes. Anderson couldn't imagine him becoming dangerous.

One thing at a time, he told himself. Tomorrow he would visit Haksar. He would find out what Haksar was talking about. Then he would go to Dogilani, to get Lauder.

Get Lauder. That was imperative.

The thought of his find (it was already his), of its enormous and barely glimpsed value, inundated him again. It had come to him out of the blue, in a mysteriously fateful way that involved a killing, and would demand at least one more killing, that of his wife's erstwhile lover.

And that would be easy.

He realized what he was doing, and pulled the door shut behind him.

The door of the next room was closed. Pizza boxes were stacked up outside, and just then the moans stopped and a voice inside called out about another camera setup, and then they could all take showers.

Anderson made it to the car. It was not dented or scratched and had all its tires, which was good. He settled inside, turned on the headlights, and started the engine, noticing that his hand did not shake, his foot did not throb on the gas pedal, and he no longer bit his lower lip.

He rolled out of the motel's yard.

Five minutes later, torturing the Land Cruiser's quality tires over rusty railroad tracks, he threw the towel out the window. Then he turned back and headed for downtown, debating whether to call the Mayfair Hotel in London and leave Corinne the elliptic message that it had been easy.

No. That would be too early. He would do it after dealing with Haksar, and more important, after getting Lauder.

Part Four

SAVANNA SONG

E VERY DAY, THEY WOKE UP AT ABOUT THE SAME TIME, even though it was not measured by a clock. Besides, Ken was beginning to forget what it was like to wear his watch. Here, time wasn't made of regular increments, equal and abstract, like hours, minutes, and seconds. Instead, it was made of spells of safety and danger, of chasing or being chased, and of being alive and successful in their hunt.

Their wake-up time always felt the same. Daylight appeared, making the landscape turn from dark to shades of gray, and then to the spectrum of live, warm colors. The birds started to chirp and twitter, and a breath of coolness blew down from the Mau, creating a humid mist that made Ken cough.

When he coughed, the boy stirred or sometimes even bolted up. His eyelids fluttered, the mucous excretions of sleep cracked along the rims of his eyes, and the boy would look around with a quick, darting glance.

When he saw Ken, his lips would curl up, recognizing him. He would throw up his fists and rub his eyes roughly, while his legs twitched as if fighting off sleep, kicking Ken with the spontaneity of a teenager.

Then he would burp. Not from fullness after food, but the burp of morning air trapped in the stomach being forced out by a change in the body's position. It was also a burp of hunger; most often, the child would jump up and lunge for whatever was left of their last meal, which he had covered with dirt the evening before. That was the protohuman breakfast: shreds of meat with broken bones, severed veins and tendons, and dried-up clots of blood sticking out—all was homogenized by the swarming of savanna ants.

The boy would blow at the ants, or even pick them off with his fingers, before attacking the carcass. Ken sometimes crushed open a large bone to suck at its fresh and lukewarm marrow. And that was breakfast for two hominids, one ancient, one contemporary.

Ken was learning that almost no animal despised the kill of another. Even if the badger was fabled to eat just wild honey, the zorilla insects and eggs, and the mongoose lizards and snakes, none would turn down meat just because they had not fought for it or hunted it. Meat was top-of-the-list natural protein, no matter how fouled it was by earlier hunters, how scarce, how dried up, or how decomposed it was.

Ken was growing used to the smells of decomposed carcasses and found they carried a certain sweetness of rotting protein. The only other sweetness in the wild was that of blooming flowers and ripening fruit. They were the two lone streaks of candied, nectarous taste and scent, lost in the savanna's olfactory palette, which was crammed with raw, bitter, brutal odors: of antelope manure, of lion, hyena, and jackal urine marking territory, of trees burned by the last bush fire, of rotting meat, of mud boiling in the sun, of ancient dust, insignificantly cleaned by the rain twice a year.

Ken felt that his sense of smell had been transformed. His nose, which was so small compared to many animal snouts but so large compared to the boy's, had become as critical to him as his eyesight.

He even smelled his own bodily odors differently. He was in tune with what his smells meant, and hardly cared that he hadn't showered, cleaned his orifices, or brushed his teeth in . . . how many days now? He could not tell.

He had been alone in the savanna eleven or perhaps twelve days, but that number sounded so abstract. He scratched his grown-out beard, accepting the time that it indicated, yet not being able to relate it to a savanna day's unfolding. There were no hours here, at least not in modern, artificial time. The days and nights were divided into five main spans:

1) wake-up and preparation for hunting
2) hunting
3) eating the kill and then relaxing till right before dusk
4) dusk, which was the anxious time span of selecting a sleeping site, and
5) sleep.

And Ken's life was mainly directed at watching the protohuman boy, protecting him from dangers and sharing in the functions of his life. And he lived to *absorb him,* to grasp him and carry him inside his own modern self, or whatever was left of it—Kenneth T. Lauder was not too sure how much Kenneth T. Lauder there was left at this moment, and didn't have much time to care.

The two of them together had to sleep and eat.

But in order to eat, they first had to keep from being eaten.

Ken was learning to escape an endless variety of lion jaws, hyena fangs, warthog and antelope prongs, buffalo hooves, serpent's teeth, elephant and rhino tusks, insect needles and stings. At night when he closed his eyes, he saw a parade of the past day's dangers. They were innumerable. Some he had escaped too fast even to register them properly. Others, the felines, warthogs, charging buffaloes, and barking hyenas, were imprinted so strongly on his senses that he wondered how he had been so unaware of their challenge to the human race.

The boy fell asleep so fast. For the boy this existence was normal, but for Ken this was survival in the extreme. In that sense, he felt weaker than the boy.

But notwithstanding which of them was "better," they had to avoid danger, and yet face it all the time. They also had to hunt, which took time, energy, extraordinary physical exertion, and, on Ken's part, a kind of wordless prayer for luck.

So far, their hunting tools had primarily been stones. Ken had made another spear, but spear-hunting had still not replaced stone-hunting. Most of the time they carried the stones with them, but when they were caught empty-handed, they could pick up any of the stones scattered throughout their hunting grounds.

Keeping those stones in hunting order meant remembering where they were and leaving them purposely in certain spots. Thus, Ken trained his mind to know the territory. The stones were utterly dependable. The animals would not touch them unless they were left on the top of some burrow or lair, or in a busy cross avenue of paws and hooves. He had to leave his hunting caches outside the path of game, but close enough to it to guarantee a successful hunt. Of course, learning to distinguish good spots from bad ones brought even more knowledge of the territory.

And Ken's and the boy's activities were still not finished. They also had to look for foods other than meat. That meant mungongo nuts, shrubs, seeds, tubers, and roots, all of which they had to taste first, because some were edible and some were not. In fact, some were violently toxic so they had to be assessed through tasting and waiting.

The boy did not seem to know many of those edible vegetables, except for the tubers filled with fluid. This led Ken to believe that his kin were primarily meat-eaters.

Finally, they had to look for water, the life-giving drink that Ken pictured as clear streams and transparent lakes, but that was never limpid and clean out here, unless they found it gathered in rock crevices after a rain shower. Ordinarily, it came in puddles, bogs, water holes, mucked up by drowned bugs and alluvial dust. This water maintained its life-giving status only because if they didn't drink it, they would certainly die of dehydration.

Ken's stomach might never have adapted to this water if it hadn't been for the boy's help. During Ken's third major bout of diarrhea, just as he was again passing fecal fluid through his cruelly sore anus, the boy suddenly brought him a piece of wet dirt, which he stuffed into Ken's mouth. Ken chewed and swallowed it, then lay exhausted on the grass, until the cramps and diarrhea abated.

Something in that soil tablet had a peptic effect. He smiled gratefully at the boy, who seemed so content that he ran to the clay shore of a fading freshet, scraped up some more dirt with his fingers, and came back, chewing it. The chewing reminded Ken of a pharmacist's stirring a remedy with a spoon in a bowl. The boy's bowl was his own mouth, the stirring device his teeth and tongue. The boy spat it out and pushed a mouthful-sized gob between Ken's open lips, while with a clear stare he urged: Come on, swallow it!

Ken knew he couldn't have learned this on his own. Ken chewed the wet clay, experiencing both disgust and an interesting sense of bonding. The boy had to have learned it from his kin. Where were his kin?

THE BIZARRE MEDICATION MADE HIM FEEL BETTER, AND soon he was eating raw meat again during the day. In the evening, when he made the fire, he would roast pieces of their catch. The roasting was superficial, but it made the food taste much better. However, he simply did not have the strength to build a fire each time he needed to ingest protein, and at those times, he had to eat raw meat like an overtired sapiens munching on a cold slice of pizza, unless he could gather enough nuts. But with the help of a dirt pill now and then, his stomach seemed to start adjusting to that mixed sapiens/protohuman diet.

The episode with the dirt pills sealed a pact between Ken and the boy. They were taking care of each other. Another critical function.

And there were still many other important functions. Keeping oneself clean mainly consisted of wiping off the drippings of eating and defecating. If chimps knew how to turn leaves into sanitary towels (and even into menstrual tampons), two hominids could also figure out the many uses of leaves and grasses. They also had to watch where they squatted down. Ken learned to defecate without giving a snake or a bug a chance to bite his bare ankles or buttocks, or a predator to come close enough to lunge hungrily to eat his feces. Hyenas and wild dogs never despised feces, beginning with their own. They were the wild's ultimate recyclers, and as a result the wild stayed clean.

Life in the Pliocene was so demanding that at the midpoint of their day, Ken and the boy needed a quick but dedicated rest period, which they took by plopping down on the grass and sitting back to back, leaning on each other. This way they could look out at the bush, always alert for swaying grass that might indicate the advance of big carnivores.

Ken would feel the boy's firm and skinny back against his. Or the boy would drop his head, hard and surprisingly heavy for its size, onto Ken's shoulder. The boy was not soft or gentle with Ken. He had showed gentleness only once, and not much then either, when Ken had been lying sick in that chimney of lava.

To gain Ken's attention, the boy kicked him, or stopped him by gripping his arm roughly. He threw his body against Ken's in friendly excitement or to make him change direction. He would pull pieces of kill out of Ken's hands with a casualness that would have seemed petulant, except that Ken saw it as a mark of confidence and trust.

Ken was completely disarmed by that trust. He found himself yearning for the next little kick, poke with the elbow, or head thrust back hard onto his shoulder. There was no way that the child could really hurt him. He was still a hulking mass of tall modern man, refined into a muscle machine by an additional two million years of evolution. He had lost weight, but he was still in top form.

Ken had lost enough weight that he'd had to tighten his belt to its last buckle hole—his belt, like every other item of his clothing, was now cracked, discolored, and dirty. His pants were torn and bleached from harsh sunshine, and caked with dust and mud; they looked like an old layer of skin that for some reason would not peel off. His hiking boots were shredded, and their laces had snapped, forcing him to tie them back together with big ugly knots.

As for his filthy underwear and smelly socks—they lay abandoned somewhere within the adjoining territory, probably turned into nests by mice. He had also lost his hat, which meant that from morning until sundown, his eyes squinted painfully against the sky's glare. He also carried around the stinging pain of a sunburn that was especially acute on the bridge of his nose.

He mentally joked with himself that the reason early man had a flat nose was to escape sunburn. He laughed at the joke, and was sorry he couldn't share it with the boy. Scratches and cracks in his sunburned skin now scarred every exposed surface of his body. His tongue felt swollen. His dislocated ankle had healed, but not completely because he kept exerting it. At night, he tried to massage it, while the boy watched, and Ken reflected that this one simple gesture needed no translation, no explanation. Two million years ago and now, a dislocated ankle was a dislocated ankle.

And then one morning, the boy's waking kick caught him right on his sore ankle. He stopped himself from shouting out a curse, sat up, and smelled lions.

In a panic, Ken jumped up. They had slept on a shelf of rock, softened by the warm ashes of a few nights' fires. The boy stirred, turned on his stomach, and fell asleep again.

The boy probably smelled the lions, too; his olfactory warning system was certainly as accurate as Ken's. Had he decided that the danger was still remote? Or was he reassured by the hulking presence of his alien friend? If so, the boy would be taking a chance with his life.

Ken looked at the tiny face. He felt his fist hardening around the spear. Reflex action. No need for thinking. He would do his best to protect the child, and himself.

He smelled the lions again and heard a faint roar. The sounds were distant, or perhaps just blurred by the mist.

He felt a not unpleasant sense of solidarity with all the humans past and present who had fought felines. Hominid versus feline, man's longest and fiercest interspecies war. He was part of it now, taking his station in a war for the breed.

He felt that specific tightening of his scrotum and contraction of his anus. The stab of fear shooting up from his groin, shooting up into his stomach, ramming into his chest, and rising until its harsh, unpleasant tension hit his jaws.

His survival reflexes sought to establish where the enemy was, how far and how strong. He had to *see* the enemy, and for that, he needed to be up on his feet, erect. Up on the closest height available. He was already scaling the rocky outcrop, using the spear as a climbing stick.

He stepped on the top, inhaled the mist, coughed, then cursed himself for making a noise that could betray his presence. He smelled the distinct stench of male lions.

Damn. I wish I still had my binoculars, he thought.

But they were lost along with his other camp gear, where he'd fought with Modibo. He still had not quite figured out what Modibo had been doing in his camp, or the role of the other people and events (connected to Modibo? separated from him?) that had brought him here, standing spear in hand on this rock top.

Now his eyes had to become his binoculars.

He waited, his heart beating hard.

Slowly, shapes started moving in the mist. Two spots of yellow acquired shape, then direction. Two blurs of dark brown became the maned heads of two male lions stalking ahead, directly toward the rocky outcrop.

Damn. Two males. Big hungry ones.

He could see their empty distended bellies, hanging between the rotating movements of their shoulders and hips. He panned his eyes right and left, praying that an antelope would appear and distract the lions. One kill and they would lie sluggish and passive for days, enough time for the hominids to switch to new grounds.

Then Ken saw something else in the mist, and it was so unexpected and forceful that his heart sank.

Only fifty yards to the right of the males, a much vaster mass of yellow spread out in the fog, like a bank of rolling, creeping, living matter. At first, the mist made it look homogenous, but it wasn't.

Ken was straining his eyes so hard that the veins on his temples bulged, but he started to make out separate animals. He counted one, two, three. . . . There appeared to be silhouettes, sashaying above a low, golden mass. To the far right, the mist was beginning to thin and numbers four, five, six, seven, eight appeared, and as each one added itself to the number, Ken's heart sank lower.

He was staring at a large pride of lionesses, seven or eight adults, plus an untold number of cubs. Small and low to the ground, the cubs were becoming distinct too, like wet gold with streaks and specks of dark brown that were their little muzzles, ears, and eyes.

There were no large blurs of brown in the pride. No manes. No grown male lions.

The pride was heading straight toward the rocky outcrop and the Mau, and in its path lay a wide, irregularly L-shaped water hole, with grass dressing its shores but no bushes or reed-type vegetation. He and the boy had drunk there, and there the boy hunted small rodents. This was *their* waterhole.

We'll have to give it up and move camp *today,* he reflected. We'll have to be careful trekking out of here.

Even though each passing second added to the danger, for a few instants Ken let his eyes feast on the lionesses' movement. The smooth rolling of shoulders under their yellow coats, the necks lowered flexuously, the haunches rounding the thinning mist with almost human sex appeal.

He shook himself alert, turned, and bumped into the little brown hominid, whose vivid eyes and teeth smiled as he panted from climbing up fast. Three days before, Ken had made a second spear, hardened it in the fire, and given it to the boy. The new spear shone in the boy's dark fist. The boy opened his lips into a grin, and there they were again, two million years of evolutionary difference disappearing in a split second.

The boy turned to look at the lions; and briefly his cheeks swelled, and his eyes shone more brightly. Then he glanced at Ken, examining Ken's spear like a military man checking that his comrade was armed and combat-ready. His expression was so stupendously modern that Ken was aware that all it lacked was words. As usual, there were no words, but there was sound. There was that *rrrr,* the boy's basic rattle, which rose in his throat, and was followed by an *eeeee,* of surprise and excited challenge. *Eeeee,* those are lions. *Eeeee,* there are a lot of them. *Eeeee,* let's have some fun by getting close to them.

Ken had learned that the *eeee* often signaled action. It was the number 5 sound in what he had begun calling the boy's "Ape 36" language range. Ken based this system on a chimp's range, which comprised at least thirty-six different utterances, all standardized and intelligible to other chimps. Ken had noticed that the boy's signals for emergency and danger were defined and standardized, just like those of chimps, and they occurred without fail, while the sounds of satisfaction, joy, and relaxation were far more random and sloppy. Language was deeply societal and born of the primal need to warn others against dangers.

Sounds 1 to 4 in the boy's lingo were all warnings. The basic *rrrr* was itself a warning of presence. A much fiercer *grrrrr* was a clear declaration of hostility, which the boy used when he hunted. A loud, brutal *wraaa!!* topped the warnings. Ken had also heard the boy utter it in his sleep, and had seen him bolt up after it, as if fighting off a bad dream. A low, wasted *waah* indicated tiredness, and the boy would utter it if they trekked too long without resting or drinking. *Eeee* was excitement, and *maah* or *naah* signified hunger.

"Eeee!" Ken tried to duplicate the boy's sound, but the boy gave him a startled little look, then grinned. Mocking my accent again? he seemed to say. He hopped down the rock face. Where the hell was he going? Ken panicked. Wait, Long Toes! We gotta hurry away from those lions. We . . .

The boy continued down the rock face, the brown soles of his feet seeming to fly over the rock's natural steps until he vanished. Ken cursed, grabbed his spear, and let himself fall from rock top to rock top. In his mind he pictured the boy being caught by the lions and shredded before he could intervene with his big voice and ridiculously light spear.

He ran down, tripped and fell, jumped up and ran down again. I'll break my neck trying to protect this little hunting machine, who so far has done quite well without my protection. He leaped off the rock to a strip of gravel running the whole length of the rocky rampart. Beyond those pebbles from millions of years of erosion started the tall grass. Between rock and grass, the gravel strip stretched and twisted and stretched again like a corridor.

He saw no one.

He stamped his naked foot down inside his clammy boot. His ankle was sore, and he felt that he was ready to give up. No one could stand this emotional roller-coaster. And if he were to lose the hominid to a pair of lion's jaws . . . well, that would be just tough.

He whipped around.

The boy was right behind him, narrowing one eye almost into a wink. Ken dropped the spear and threw his arms forward, ready to pluck the boy back to some semblance of safety, but there was no safety other than in their continued teamwork against the surprises of the wild.

Off the boy went, down that gravel corridor, but he stopped briefly and flagged his arm down the almost straight rock wall, letting Ken know that they were to pass the lions that way. And off he ran again.

This was a smart switch of territory, and Ken knew that the boy's energy level meant he was ready for hunting.

All right, Long Toes, panted Ken. Let's go catch us some lunch. Or be lunch to beasts that deserve to pass on their genes more than we do.

THE TWO MALE LIONS HAD NEVER BEEN THIS CLOSE TO THE Mau escarpment before, and they had been advancing toward it every day for over a week. The older male was limping from an injury he'd received during the fight with that lioness defending her cubs. His limp cut down the male's speed, but the females they were stalking could not elude them because they were burdened by their cubs, some barely two weeks old.

This large pride was really two prides that had come together after these cub-killer males had attacked them repeatedly. The two depleted prides had fused into one in which the lionesses hadn't figured out a clear hierarchy and pattern of teamwork.

If the pride had taken a common stand against these two males, they would have stopped the stalkers short, but the lionesses were conflicted about accepting the males. The females who had already lost their cubs were the weak links; their hormones had already begun to urge them to be mothers again. Waves of sexual heat throbbed in their flanks and the insides of their vaginas as they swayed through the tall grass. Under the swatting protection of their tails, little corks of mucus had begun to form, scenting the air behind them with a call to copulate. The males took heart in that signal, and took their time.

The males had eaten little for the last two weeks, so they looked very mangy. Their coats were dull, their eyes narrowed and lusterless. Their usually shiny dark lips were now badly chapped. They were looking forward to eating as much as they were to mating. And they would gladly eat the lion's share of the kills of the fast-running, long-leaping, hardworking lionesses.

The lion's share was in fact the males' share. In lion society, there are no pampered females. And no hardworking males, unless those males live entirely on their own.

Thus, the two marauding males kept advancing, and the lionesses kept retreating.

That day, as soon as the dawn grayed the horizon, the two males started roaring, forcing the females to get up and herd their cubs away. Then the males stopped roaring and followed the pride into the mist, where they could hunt and kill the straggling cubs.

The lionesses darted their eyes at their cubs, losing them in the mist, stopping and prancing about nervously to find them. Surprised and scared, the cubs meowed, and sneezed, and inevitably began to fall behind and get lost.

The males stalked closer, on padded feet, with furry ears at full alert. When they heard the whines of the cubs, they charged in that direction, into the floating mist, their big carnassial teeth eager for babies, their smoldering yellow eyes on alert for the mothers.

This morning, the limping old-timer led the killer patrol, jumping with his whole mass of over four hundred pounds. He uttered low basso grunts to the younger male, who was doing a good job of pushing off the females with his scent and roar. The old male squinted up toward the sky, noticed that the sun was thinning the mist, which meant he had only a few minutes left for hunting.

He stopped and waited, totally still, until he heard two separate bleats, from two lost cubs.

He yawned, baring his carnassial fangs, which from root to tip were five inches long. He smacked his brownish tongue at his whiskers and lay down flat against the grass. He let a paw lie flat on the grass, then pushed it ahead while he crept forward. The paw mowed the blades of grass until it found a cub no larger than a puppy.

It was a female. She had a short neck, a dotted coat, and a tail that was sharp-tipped, knotty, and short.

The cub saw the big paw, but did not identify it as such. It was almost her size, and quite unthreatening. She put out a tentative little paw of her own, then she got up on all fours, her eyes turning into grains of quicksilver, and jumped on the paw, her little tail slashing the misty air in glee.

Quickly, the large male brought his head down like a huge hammer, knocking her down on the grass, breaking her spine. A last bleat came out, while the yellow carnassials went into her neck like cleavers into a steak and came back dripping red.

One cub less. One more step toward taking over the pride.

To his right, nearby, another cub was calling. A stronger, deeper voice indicated a male, or perhaps an older cub.

The killer again flattened himself in the grass and pushed his limp paw forward, like a bait.

Like his sister's, the little male's eyes became attracted by that furry decoy. He was about to scratch the paw with his own, when he looked up. A pair of jaws snapped at the mist, close but not close enough. The young cub reared on his fragile hind legs, more in amazement than in defense. The old male fleetingly felt a laceration on his muzzle from the cub's two-week-old claws. Again, the carnassials slashed like steak knives into tender meat.

The old-timer did not hold back on this one. With the cub in his fangs, he shook his formidable jaws, tearing off the little head from the dotted body, sucking it into his big throat. Just then, an older cub, confused and scared, ran at the old lion, saw him, and in a suicidal attack, flung himself right at the killer's face. Startled, the big lion tried to inhale, and swallowed the little head unchewed.

Momentarily without air, the big male jumped up and crashed back down, thudding his chest against the ground. That thud rammed the unchewed cub's head into his empty stomach. Air rushed back into his lungs. He roared, blowing away the third cub, killed him with one bite at the jugular, and sipped his blood to lubricate his throat and resettle his jolted stomach.

He got up.

The lionesses had heard his jumps, and they rushed back, too late. The young male came back with them, his face bleeding from a lioness's paw. The old-timer hobbled over to the tall grass and flattened himself down again.

The mother of two of the cubs ran into the clear, ears pulled back and voice at full tragic volume. She found her mangled daughter first, then her decapitated son. She took almost a minute, calling out in stunned, crying roars, before she fully realized that two of her cubs were dead. She had two others, somewhere ahead with the rest of the pride. Fear for their lives made her turn around and charge again toward the Mau, crying her loss into what remained of the mist.

As the sunlight poured over the lions' morning exercise,

Ken saw that the mother was gone, and he watched as the big male lumbered like a drunk man toward a cluster of bushes. He stopped at a bush, started biting off leaves and grass and ingesting them quickly. The younger male stared at him with the stupid look of inexperience. The old one knew what he was doing, because he froze in a pose of odd discomfort, opened his monumental jaws, and smokily vomited the undigested cub's head. Ken and the boy saw it pop out of the killer's throat and roll stickily on the grass.

The smell of the regurgitated head, wrapped in pungent gastric oozes, was caught by the savanna air as it curled back against the cold descending from the Mau. The stench from the lion's stomach wafted over to antelopes waking from their standing sleep. It was sniffed by the monkeys waking in their trees, and by a family of warthogs wallowing in a dip of mud. It was a vile warning to anything that had a nose, and a reason to fear lions.

Ken glanced at the boy, who was making a new sound. It was not a warning, and not the excited *eeeee* of curiosity of barely an hour before. It was a prolonged *uuuurrrggghhh* from the bottom of his gut, a growl so full of hate and bile that it made the little creature seem frightening. An unexpected thought touched Ken's mind: The environmentalists of his time might worry about the demise of the big feline, but here, in the Pliocene, all that was human would revolt against the wild's most murderous teeth and claws.

And the only protection he and the boy had against those teeth and claws was their bare wooden staffs and their minds.

He put his palm on the boy's naked shoulder. The boy looked up at Ken and his hate started to fade, replaced by another, more practical mood.

Let's go on with our own hunt, the bullet-black irises seemed to be saying.

And with a spin on his heels, the boy dashed back into the gravel path and tore off, leading as usual.

They left the lions behind, and sped on. There was another water hole a good run away. It was small, attracting a reduced array of herbivores, but it was safe from felines because its shores were muddy, and thus free of bushes and tall grass. Any large predator approaching it would be easily spotted by sight or smell. But with the felines at the other water hole, the drinkers here had become complacent. Ken had made a mental note that if they were to start hunting with spears, this was the spot they should try first.

And now his spear was in his hand, and the boy's was in his little brown fist. Today I'll give him his first spearthrowing lesson, he thought excitedly. Today. It made all the more sense to head for the "easy" water hole because Ken, the teacher, had yet to learn how to hunt with a spear.

He would be learning on the job.

Running, he started chuckling. I'd be a lot less nervous if the combined departments of paleontology and anthropology were watching me instead of this eight-year-old with a fist-sized brain. But I'll figure something out. I saw *him* hunt duikers with stones. What does he do? He creeps behind their rumps when they drink and throws his stones, not at one duiker in particular but at the big target of a whole damn herd. They get scared and stampede, and more often than not knock down a weaker female or a fawn. He gets the fallen one. It's not high-precision hunting, but it works.

I'll figure out something like that, and I'll get lucky. There's this thing about antelopes. Very often, they don't flee danger in a straight line. They start veering in a kind of loose circle, trying to get back to their herds or to the abandoned grazing site. There must be a way to predict that kind of movement. Otherwise, with our speed of running, we humans would've never had a chance.

And then there is precision throwing, pure and simple. Just don't miss. From throwing stones to shooting basketball hoops to launching spaceships, just don't miss.

Sounds simple enough.

Dammit, Long Toes, the kind of stuff you make me do, he thought, and grinned on, despite their hard, sweaty run. His nervousness was dissipating, and he felt just as confident as any hominid would, spear in hand, on a plain rich in game. I'll get lucky.

They reached the water hole, and he did get lucky, though not in the way he had expected.

They waited awhile before a big male kudu antelope approached the water, alone. It was fully antlered, majestic, and gray. The white stripes on its sides moved as it advanced, like a swaying robe. Ken had always felt that kudu males had a priestly air because of the way they held their spiral horns, like a solemn headdress. It stood as tall as Ken while it inspected the two hominids.

Don't miss the kudu, Ken told himself.

But he had never thrown a spear, and he knew that if he missed it would show the boy that he didn't really have a clue about what he was doing.

And then he figured it out: DON'T MISS. That was all there was to it.

He raised his hand with the spear, feeling the tension in his elbow and shoulder.

He quickly inhaled, exhaled, and inhaled again. Whoa! he thought, as he galloped forward, and launched the spear directly over the water. Pain exploded in his elbow joint but it didn't matter. His target was moving and the spear was chasing after it, slashing forward until it gored the kudu's left shoulder.

The big animal turned and ran off, dangling the spear from its body like an additional horn, odd and out of place. Ken looked at the boy, while his face, aching from sunburn, burst into the most delicious grin of pride. *I did it.* That joy flowed inside him, pure and primal as if it had waited in there for two million years.

Then the spear slipped off, and the animal ran on, its spiral horns rigidly high.

Ken raced around the shore to pick up the spear, the boy thudding behind him.

The spear's tip was crimson with blood. The boy grabbed it from Ken and held it right in front of his face. This tool had now become something else—an effective long-distance weapon.

The boy uttered his "Eeeee!!!" at high pitch, broke it off

with a yapping laugh, and began slapping the spear back and forth from one palm to the other. He touched the bloodied part and gave Ken a look of congratulation.

The boy's foot stepped on the other spear, which Ken had brought along and abandoned in the muddy grass. He kicked it toward Ken, holding on to the one that had already made a hit.

Ken circled around the water hole, away from the boy, trying to collect his thoughts, but the boy followed him like a puppy. He's too cute for words, thought Ken, wondering if another sapiens would merely see the boy as skinny, punily built, odd-shaped, downright ugly? Would he shock Ken's contemporaries? Ken remembered Fuegia, the Patagonian Indian woman discovered by Darwin. Darwin thought she was beautiful, but his contemporaries saw a flat-footed, chunky creature, whose breasts were rude pendulums, and whose womb was a bestially warm procreating oven. Torn from her habitat, Fuegia became the freak of the day.

Ken paced around the shore alone, thinking. He was scared that too much of his older self was tumbling down. What am I becoming? he wondered. What's left of the twenty-eight years I've already spent in a civilized life?

"Civilized" sounded so unnatural. He had started to see the earth's population as prisoners who are denied the right of primal living by a jail system made up of technological and cultural achievements. Now he had broken free. But it wasn't like him to see civilization as a jail. He had always been a healthy outdoorsman, but never an extremist. Civilization had a value that had to be protected as much as wilderness. The two were not self-exclusive.

But none of those lofty words sounded convincing.

The near-spearing of the kudu had increased Ken's excitement for their first true, full-tilt spear-hunting. With that in mind, they zoomed away until they emerged into a mosaic of trees and grass and spotted several herds of yellow-backed duikers.

*   *   *

THESE DUIKERS WERE FAT, AND THE YELLOWISH STRIPE ON their backs broadened like a loose triangle around their wide rumps. Ken raised his spear, mimicking the beginning of a throw, but the boy instantly lifted his own spear and raced forward.

Damn. Ken had meant to signal him that he would try the first strike. Now how was he going to stop this dynamo?

He ran behind the brown feet, feeling his own heels touch down, the soles land full length, the calf muscles pull up the feet again by their heels, while the balls of the feet gave the legs a strong upward boost. A big shot of physical energy was pumped up from feet to calves, continuing into the knees, thighs, buttocks, and spine.

That was how *Homo sapiens* ran.

The boy ran like that too, and yet differently. His heels touched down the same way, but dipped hard, leaving an imprint that seemed out of proportion with his small body. His long curved toes dug deeper and used more effort to free themselves. As the balls of the feet sprang the boy back up, his calf muscles bulged out like a soccer player's. No wonder the boy tired faster than Ken and consumed comparatively enormous amounts of food and drink.

The boy glanced back at Ken, then jerked his left arm at the pack, while swerving away to the right. Ken understood that he was to stir up the pack from the left, making them run to the right, where the boy would be waiting. Well-suited strategy, Long Toes.

Ahead, the herd sensed Ken. Several bucks, the herd's sentinels, lifted their heads from the grass, their jaws still chewing. Then one of the bucks bellowed like a truck's horn. Swiftly, the females turned and kicked back the torn grass, as Ken raised his spear and raced toward them with his lungs burning. For an instant, he expected to overtake the pack. One particular fat rump was falling behind and Ken prayed that the boy was in position. When the fat animal turned, presenting its flank and one scared herbivore eye, Ken felt a guilty hesitation and lowered the spear.

He raised the spear again, but he had fallen behind. The

duikers started giving the race all they had. Ken began to slow down, his lungs burning and his eyes smarting from stirred dust.

Ahead, the duikers jetted past a mass of bushes. Ken did not see the boy stand up; he saw only the spear, shining as it cut through the air and fell between two duikers. The others stampeded, turned. One buck fell and was trampled. The rest started fleeing right back at Ken. He could easily have speared one more.

But he glimpsed the boy standing up, and lost sight of him the next second, as if he had been knocked off his feet. He forgot about hunting and started running ahead, angry and fearful. What the hell had happened? The boy was tiny, so easy to knock down and trample. Why wasn't he getting up again?

He ran, jumping aside from charging duikers, finally getting close to a big flurry of kicked-up dust, which became the boy himself, being dragged on the ground by that fallen buck—the little devil couldn't pass on impaling it right in the neck. The dying buck dragged the spear and the boy in a big arc of whirling dust because the spear wouldn't break, and the boy wouldn't let go of the spear, and the buck wouldn't die without a big dramatic flurry.

Ken rushed, but before he could decide what to do, the flurry collided with him, and the buck's hoof blasted him right in that sore ankle. He plunged at random, found the animal's hard spine, gripped it, and slowed the buck. The boy staggered up and fell again, injured or perhaps just dizzy. Through the unspeakable dust, as Ken and the boy fought to untangle from the buck, they saw a head rise, looking huge from the dark halo of its mane, hanging open its jaw with the carnassials bared and white.

It was the younger marauding lion.

Earlier, the lionesses had camped by the water hole, so the two hungry males had decided to look for game or for the cubs they had killed but not eaten. And the younger lion had decided not to share what he might find, and had gotten away on his own.

He had been awaiting a herd of prancing duikers to bring some easy prey right under his nose. Now the lion saw the writhing motion of the dying duiker buck. He rose to full stature and loped forward with confidence. All he had to do was finish the prey. There were no knots of excitement in his stomach, just churning gastric juices eager to receive food.

A man rose up beside the writhing buck, and a similar shape, smaller, stood up next to him; together they looked like a little herd of two. That made the charge more fun, and even warranted a full roar from the lion.

In Ken's brain, one lonely thought took shape as he raised the spear: DON'T MISS.

From the boy's height of less than four feet above the ground, he saw the lion grow three times in size in less than two seconds. The carnassials dripped foamy saliva, the eyes dilated, and the nostrils snorted. The boy let out a hoarse little whimper. The loping lion was just too big, and was charging too fast. There was no time to flee.

Without any of his usual bravado, the boy threw his body against Ken, who was raising his spear.

The boy glanced up, horrified and mesmerized.

Ever so slowly Ken aimed the spear, until its wooden tip pointed straight at the lion's face. He lowered the tip of the spear, keeping it aligned with the lion's jaws, then dropped it just slightly lower. DON'T MISS.

He could not afford to miss the point of alignment between the tip of the spear and the charging lion's throat. As the beast charged closer, its silhouette grew exponentially, making it almost impossible for Ken to keep his hands still.

He fought the urge to drop the spear and flee. Sweat flowed out of his body so profusely that his pants, already stiff with the bodily salt of earlier days, turned dark in seconds.

DON'T MISS.

The boy lasted almost until the last instant; then he could not take the lion's charge any longer. Ken opened his mouth wider than the boy had ever seen it, making that wide alien mouth, studded with such small, flat teeth, look almost ridiculous. And out came a high and yet deep howl.

Ken had not planned to make this sound, but it had unaligned the spear. He had to jerk it back down to its target. DON'T MISS.

He continued to howl fiercely, raising the sound ahead of him like another spear. In its final leap, the feline seemed as large as the escarpment itself. It dwarfed Ken, who howled and aimed the spear straight up, and then thrust upward with it.

The spear gored the lion under the throat, piercing the mass of feline muscle. The lion's collapsing weight kept pushing it down around the spear while Ken's arms were throbbing so hard that he feared they might be dislocated. The spear held up the beast's weight for a miraculous moment, while foam from its gaping jaws splashed at the man's face.

Ken had to force his hands to let go of the vibrating staff, and the lion broke the unsupported spear like a matchstick. Then its hulk slammed on the ground, embedding the broken spear tip deeper into its chest. A mute quiver seized the hanging tongue, and the beast was still.

Ken staggered backward. The boy's arms laced frantically around his right knee. Ken looked at the broken spear.

He tried to laugh, and uttered a gross hiccup.

The boy pulled the other spear out of the duiker, groping, looking not at it but at Ken. He held it up, and with a jerk of his shoulder invited Ken to follow: Come on, we're out of trouble, and there's more game and the day is young.

But as the boy took a few awkward, lumbering steps, Ken guessed that the boy was too shocked even to know why he was moving. Ken tackled him from the back, toppled the little body on the grass. The boy was so sweaty that he slipped from Ken's hands like a fish. But with a wide throw of the arms, Ken grabbed him again, pinned him on the grass, and raved softly: "You're going nowhere, nowhere, you hear? Nowhere, nowhere," he repeated, putting in one frantic word all of his need to capture this little body and to keep it in relative safety.

The boy squeaked some protest, but as if a common language had been found, they cried at each other at the same time. Through the rain of sweat on both faces, tears or something like them filled the boy's eyes, while Ken, his face soiled with the lion's dying salivation, gritted his teeth to control his emotion.

"Nowhere," he exhaled finally.

And the boy, as if breaking up inside, lifted his apish lips toward the savanna sky. In a thin howl of his own, a howl of liberated joy, he told the surrounding landscape how frightened he had been, and how amazed he was to still be living. And then he cried, fists clenched, chest heaving against the chest of his strange protector.

S OME TIME PASSED AND THE FLAPPING WINGS OF EA-
gles, vultures, and marabou storks gathered over the
dead bodies of the lion and the duiker, ready to eat.

Ken and the boy lay on the grass, depleted but feeling that
somehow the lion's death had granted them a temporary im-
munity.

Ken thought of the moment when it had taken everything
in him not to turn away and run, but instead, to show a
degree of courage and fierceness he never knew existed in
him. Never had known it, never, never—he repeated, just as
he had done minutes before, muttering "nowhere, nowhere."
He had hugged the boy, feeling that nothing mattered other
than having him right next to him.

Unexpectedly Ken thought of his father, the pothead postman, who had vanished from Ken's life as if the sperm he
had injected into a woman's egg, and the resulting offspring,
had meant nothing to him.

Yinka came into his mind, too. But hadn't their mating
been simply a case of strong mutual arousal that an uninhibited man and woman had consummated spontaneously? That
was all it was. Or was it?

He found himself picturing Yinka's naked belly. The image was so powerful that he tensed up, but he was not re-
acting with lust for that clean flesh and those delicate pubes

that had tantalized him in his cluttered bedroom. Rather, he appreciated the wideness of her hips, the rich size of her pelvis, and the perfection of her motherly organs. Yinka was a healthy, perfectly proportioned female, an ideal repository for a male's genes.

His mother's face flashed up, in her home in Oakland. He berated her silently. She was supposed to be a sensitive female, but she had not noticed anything about him last Christmas, nothing indicating some hidden emotion ripening quietly in her son. She had babbled about herself, as usual. She had guessed nothing, had asked nothing. That dim-witted vegetarian, she was no more insightful than a savanna herbivore.

He imagined her sitting him squarely in a chair in the dining room and asking him: Ken, my boy, when are you going to marry? His heart would have started to pound. When are you going to make me a grandmother? Ken, son, to hell with macrobiotic food and New Age cuisine, I want to be a grandmother. Even though I did not want to be a mother. I need to know that there is a mother out there, for your own children. Is there one? Is there one, son?

Of course, she had not asked those questions, but what would he have answered? He had no answer, he thought innocently.

They got up and walked away, in their usual formation, the boy walking ahead. Scanning the tracts of grass, Ken glimpsed the older lion, the limper, sitting in the grass. Three young lionesses prowled around him, competing for his attention. One leaped past his nose and whipped his face with her tail. The others stalked, growled flirtatiously, then rubbed their labia on the rough vegetal texture seeking relief from their hormonal itch. They were consumed with getting pregnant.

The boy bumped him with his shoulder, then hurried ahead, glancing back to make sure Ken was following.

Ken wiped an itch on his face. The lion's saliva had dried on his cheeks and lips. He grinned as he broke that film of feline body fluid, and stepped along faster.

The boy swerved behind a column of petrified lava that lay among bushes, like a broken pillar in a lost temple. Ken plodded around it, briefly leaning his palm on it. The rock surface felt so familiar that he smiled, stepped into a narrow space between rocks, and landed hard on a human skeleton.

He tried to leap onto a clear spot, but bones were lying everywhere, in a narrow irregular rectangle between the rocks. He tripped and fell, and lifted himself onto his hands and knees.

Just a couple of feet away a skull sat on the ground. Its forehead sloped far back; its left cheek was missing, as if it had been shattered from a blow. Next to it lay a big boulder, and several flaked-off stones. Their shapes seemed Oldowan—primal cutting tools, which Mary Leakey had named after the Olduvai Gorge.

The boy stopped and faced Ken with an unreadable look, but Ken paid no attention. He was sprawled on his stomach, his nose almost brushing the bones of a foot. He reached for them with an urgency left from the night spent in Randall's garage, cleaning the fossil.

This foot was not a fossil. It was just picked clean and dry. Its toes were scattered on the ground, mixed with the tarsal bones, the cuboid, navicular, and cuneiforms, and the talus and calcaneum, the ankle and heel bones. Apparently the whole foot was there.

He picked up the heel and weighed it in his hand. Whoever had trodden on those bones had a large fleshy foot. He picked up the big toe and could tell that it pointed outward, just as in the pictures he had taken. It had been thick and muscular, to grip and to climb. This foot was nature's early-model walker, before humans had completely abandoned tree climbing. It was from the age before evolution produced the streamlined, svelte feet of the sapiens line.

Ken had found the missing link of bipedalism.

HE SCANNED THE ROCKY ENCLOSURE. THERE HAD TO BE A dozen skeletons here, whole or partial. He reached out to gather the foot bones, ignoring the boy who was standing silently on those little feet that would grow into the full-size feet lying now on the ground. He thought about how he would collect this find.

For an instant, he was Ken Lauder, scientist. He was even annoyed that the boy was there. Then he became self-conscious. The child was watching him. *What's he going to think? I can collect that foot later.*

He got up and paced around carefully. The bones were protohuman. The skulls' facial angles were low and the jaws elongated. The pelvises had broad, un-apish ilia. Those bones should have been fossils, but they were recent. They were firm, but had not mineralized. The earth under them was humid and compact, suggesting that the skeletons had been lying there through just a couple of rainy seasons, rather than a few million years of rock decay.

He looked up at the boy, down at the bones. Then he gazed at his crusty boots. All were real, though they belonged to different times.

The sensation of time contracting and expanding made him dizzy.

A rib cage lay just a few feet away, its sternum crushed in, the lower ribs almost pulverized, as if an elephant had thumped down on that chest. A sizable rocky boulder lay nearby. The little quarry was a graveyard for the boy's breed, perhaps even for his close kin. Here was proof that the boy was not a wild child with freak anatomy. Ken remembered the human arm bone he had found among the boy's possessions.

An image flashed into his mind so fast that he staggered. Seeing the rock enclosure with the little hominid standing in it, he also saw an adult protohuman, a male, muscular but short, barely over five feet tall. The male held a stone in his hand. His arm rose, flexed, extended, and the stone whizzed past Ken—in his imagination, but he still shrank back.

Ken could almost hear a high little laugh that the boy would make. Ken imagined the boy running giddily after the stone. *He brings it back and tries to hand it to the grown male protohuman, who doesn't take it but instead closes the boy's little fist around the stone, and then faces the boy away, toward the open savanna.*

The protohuman guides the little arm, pulling it back, flexing the little biceps, teaching it how to release the stone.

His father lies here. One of these dead protohumans was his father.

That arm bone he was carrying around, that was from his father's arm.

The vision faded.

Ken realized something almost as astounding as the vision—the boy had communicated with him.

THERE WERE ELEVEN SKELETONS IN THE STRANGE GRAVE-yard and all of their pelvises looked narrow, unfit for pregnancies, which meant they had belonged to male australopithecines. All of them were badly broken. It looked as if an elephant had broken into the little enclosure and trampled the corpses. But elephants would not stray into these rocks, where there was no grass, leaved trees, or water. Who or what had killed the protohumans?

There had not been many floods in the area, even when the rains turned the trickles from the Mau into gushing streams. The eleven males had not drowned.

The bones did not look charred, so a bush fire was out of the question.

The dead bodies might have been carried into that corral of rock, but why and by whom?

Ken moved about the place, feeling that he had to relate to the boy in some way. The boy had brought him here and expected a reaction.

He paced awkwardly, now and then with a timid grin at the boy. The child did not respond, but walked about the boneyard with an easy step. He was familiar with the place.

Ken gripped his spear so frantically that the veins on the back of his hand stood out and his fingertips pressed so hard they turned white.

This is a story he is telling me. He brought me here to tell me why he is now alone.

The boy was communicating. His father must have been one of those dead. His father, who had once taught him how to hunt.

A NUMBER OF LARGE BOULDERS SEEMED TO HAVE FALLEN from the heights of the escarpment looming above. Was it possible that they had rained down on that little cluster of hominids while they had been hiding here—perhaps during a skirmish in an interspecies war?

The hunting stones, hand axes, and choppers certainly showed that the males had retreated in here armed. If that was so, was the boy the only survivor of his breed?

With all these thoughts overloading his brain, Ken hit on another: Maybe the boy will answer that question, and soon.

He took the boy's clenched little fist and pried open his clutched fingers. He took the stone out of his little brown palm and replaced it with the spear, which the boy took.

Ken dropped on one knee to the ground. With cupped palms, he gathered the foot bones, then pushed them under a hanging ledge and sealed them with a primitive rampart of rocks. He knew he was leaving behind something that was incredibly valuable, but he simply could not handle the bones and the child all at once.

He stood up and looked into the child's eyes. As an anthropologist, Ken had heard about cultural chasms being quickly erased by the intelligence of primitive tribespeople, of "savages." But with this hominid, the sense of being understood was more overpowering than anything he had lived as an anthropologist. It was downright absurd. This child couldn't possibly understand him, and yet . . .

Whatever Ken did, he felt the child understood it in such a basic way that of the two of them, Ken was the less informed. He was the slow one, the student.

Ken took the boy's other hand and gently pulled him out of the graveyard.

* * *

"THIS IS A PLANE." IN THE DIRT KEN DREW AN AIRPLANE'S shape with his finger, reducing it to its minimal details. "See? A *ppha-lane*." He broke the word into its basic sounds, uttering them patiently, though he knew they conveyed nothing to the five hundred cubic centimeters of brain behind those expressionless little eyes.

He drew a propeller, sat up, and made his own two arms—holding one arm up, one down—into a set of propeller blades, and rotated them. He made a buzzing sound. He stopped and pointed his finger to the plane drawn on the ground.

The boy's shiny eyes took all of this in, but didn't respond.

Ken drew himself: a hulking modern man, with a spear in his hand. Still this did not get a reaction.

I'm an idiot. It's not that he doesn't understand—but drawings are two-dimensional, while his reality is three-dimensional. I've got to use another method.

He placed the knife on the ground and then drew its image with his finger. Two-dimensional reproduction next to its three-dimensional model.

He didn't expect a reaction to this either, but the boy lifted the knife and looked at Ken. He swept his forearm over the drawing, then placed the knife in its stead.

Of course. What a clever little ape-man. Who needs the inanimate, unusable image of a knife, when you can have the real thing?

He sat back, tired. No more ethnocentric experiments. If he wanted to get a message across, he had to devise one that belonged to the boy's world, not to his own.

Something moved in the boy's little eyes. He knuckle-walked to Ken and threw himself on the ground. His smooth naked skin rubbed against Ken's brutally sunburned chest and his wet and filthy pants. Settling down, the child let out a little snort that almost sounded like: We're here together so what the hell was the point?

He was communicating again. With the simplest means, but it was entirely effective.

Ken lay down on his back next to the boy and watched the savanna birds sail above them.

Sometime later, they walked back to the dead lion and duiker. Hyenas were pulling at both carcasses, which were so shredded now that it was hard to tell the feline from the herbivore. The boy charged the hyenas, scattering them, then plunged at the filthy bloodied mess. He tore a hind leg from the duiker's carcass, hauled it up on his shoulders, and led the way back to the rampart.

There he dropped the meat on the ground and covered it.

DUSK.

Ken was gathering firewood so they could take on another wilderness night.

What am I going to do? he thought with near panic. What have I done to myself?

But who was that "myself"? Recently that self had killed a lion with a self-made weapon.

He carried the branches back to the rampart. They had found a nice spot for sleeping, on a smooth, even rock face, some eight feet above the ground. Ken carried the branches up the rock face, made the fire, and they lay down.

The boy reached for his hand, and started touching his fingertips to Ken's fingertips. He got up on one elbow and with the flames dancing in his eyes, he started touching Ken's face. His hard little palms tapped him lightly on the cheeks. A finger followed the curve of his chin, then the crest of his nose. Then the boy played with his hair, and even pulled at it.

He knows that I'm going to leave, Ken realized suddenly. He wants to remember me.

Ken blushed violently. Thank God for the dark. But the child brought his eyes so close that Ken started swallowing dryly, and wondered whether these australopithecine eyes could see in the dark. Maybe extreme dilation of the eye's lens, the iris, made them act like natural nightviewers.

He could not endure the child's eyes and closed his own, then reopened them and studied the play of the flames on the boy's chest and shoulders.

I cannot leave him here.

But what's the alternative? To take him to Nairobi? To London? To Berkeley's Institute of Human Origins?

It was easier to close his eyes again. He did and saw his mother, young, her womb swollen by pregnancy. He saw his father, a tall and gangly youngster with glasses and a ponytail, helping his mother out of a battered VW and toward the entrance of a medical building in Oakland. But he could not possibly remember his mother pregnant because he had not been born yet!

He felt the child's fingers again. They were back exploring Ken's face.

HE REMAINED AWAKE AFTER THE BOY FELL ASLEEP, STARing at the fire, obsessing silently. Would he leave or stay? Would he take those foot bones back to the civilized world, make a splash in the scientific community, and have every name in the field rush back to Dogilani? No one would judge him harshly for putting the spotlight on this paleohabitat and its one-of-a-kind creature.

No one but the creature itself.

He pictured Dogilani turned into a hot scientific attraction, with planes and helicopters buzzing back and forth, the air crackling with radio messages, the rocks dug up, the plant varieties counted, the animal species tagged. With park rangers keeping vigil, journalists would ingratiate themselves with researchers, the country's board of antiquities would issue permits, and he and Ngili and Randall would preside over man's zero hour of evolution.

He wondered what a true scientist would do. One who was never concerned with success and notoriety, but with science itself?

Stay on, he answered. Stay on, and observe the child. Try

to find the location of his breed, and observe the breed.

What would a father do? he asked himself.

He tried to stop his tossing, so he wouldn't wake up the boy. He was *not* a father. He *could* not play father to this son of the wilderness.

He had to go back to Nairobi and share this with his fellow scientists, who now felt like total strangers to him. He wondered how they would have reacted to the boy. Raj Haksar might have known how to handle the situation; he was an expert in primitive tribes. Anderson would have gone for the publicity, called a scientific convention, and put himself on world tour with the protochild. About Randall Phillips, Ken wasn't so sure. He had seemed so stressed and bitter. His wife was a basket case, his marriage a mess. Beware of a man who loses his support system. And then there was Ngili, with his moodiness and dependency on his African ties. Ngili would have behaved the most scientifically, and the most humanly too.

He missed Ngili.

He thought of him and of Yinka.

The child turned faceup, and snored lightly, his breath vibrating under his long low palate. Ken groped for one of the hunting stones, then rose and scaled down to the grass level.

He walked across the grass vaguely illuminated by the fire's dying radiance. He wondered about what Yinka had told him in Nairobi, about Anderson and Haksar visiting Jakub Ngiamena on the night before Ken and Ngili's return. Haksar claimed that there was a tribe living at Dogilani, and that he was trying to organize an expedition. That could mean that Haksar had traveled to Dogilani. Maybe he had seen one or several protohumans. But why would he have kept it a secret?

Ken retraced his steps, wondering whether anyone else had seen the protohumans. The Masai had an interesting legend about a breed of original humans called the *mangati*. According to that legend, the Masai had defeated the mangati and chased them into Kenya's forested mountains, from which they had never reemerged. Was there some truth to that legend? Were the mangati truly the original humans, not just in a folkloric, but also in an anthropological, sense?

A pack of wild dogs had broken into a fight over what was left of the lion. Listening to their barks and snarls, Ken thought of the other lion, the limping cub killer, and wished he could kill that one too. Maybe one of these days. He shivered from the night air. How much longer would he be here?

He had missed his first rendezvous with Ngili, but if his sense of time's passage had not been completely affected, then Ngili was due to fly over the plain again in two days, maybe three. He's going to be blown away when he sees me, and when he sees the boy. . . . But what will happen when the boy sees Ngili? He wondered, abrubtly anxious. How will the boy react?

The answer to that, and to many other questions, lay back by the fire, snoring lightly and innocently.

"**R**AJ?" CYRIL ANDERSON SPOKE INTO HIS CAR PHONE. "I stopped at your door and rang your bell, but you didn't answer. Didn't you hear the bell?"

Raj Haksar responded in a faltering voice. "When was that? . . . I didn't hear anything, Cyril. . . ."

"Really?" Cyril was driving through a pissy rain on the streets surrounding Haksar's house in Little Benares, the oldest part of Nairobi's East Indian section. "Twenty minutes ago. I heard the bell myself, and I rang it at least a dozen times. Where exactly were you?"

Haksar's front door was made of burnished teak inlaid with ornamental Hindustani inscriptions. Cyril knew the house well. The entrance led to a round atrium that rose through all three stories, into a roof domed like the *stupa* of a Sri Lankan temple. That made the house into a giant resonance box. It was impossible that Haksar had not heard the bell.

"Twenty minutes . . . Oh, yes. Sorry, Cyril, I was . . . out."

"Where did you go?"

You old tandoori liar. Anderson had seen Haksar's car, a venerable late fifties British Humber in the driveway, its tires flat from lack of use.

"Nowhere. I have these spells of fainting. . . . I suppose I was in the middle of one. . . ."

That was possible. His diabetes had gotten worse and lately he'd developed an intolerance to insulin, the very drug that controlled his disease. Anderson knew that ongoing low insulin levels eventually fried the brain. Diabetics who lived alone—as Haksar did—often became so irrational that they stopped eating, or discontinued their medication, which could bring on diabetic coma.

"I feel a little better now . . . and my doctor promised to change my medicine. What's going on?"

"Open your door. I'll come back and tell you."

"Tell me on the phone."

"Didn't you say that we should meet?"

"I'm so very tired . . . I'm saving my strength for my doctor; he said maybe he'll come by today. . . . He's so busy. . . . Why can't you tell me on the phone?"

"Raj!" Anderson braked quickly at the last second to avoid hitting an Indian woman hurrying two children across the road. The rain liquefied the yellow of their naked feet and the red of the woman's sari. "Raj, what kind of partners are we in this? How am I to find financing for your expedition if we talk only on the phone, in between these whimsical appearances of your doctor?"

He wasn't sure what to believe about Haksar's health. When the two of them had visited Jakub Ngiamena on the morning before Lauder and Ngili's return, Haksar had appeared to be in almost decent shape. He had used a handkerchief to mop his forehead and had excused himself to the bathroom three times, but he was a diabetic. Anderson wished he had made it clear to Haksar that day—not a minute of my time, not a penny of raised money, unless you tell me the *whole bloody secret*!

But of course he had not known that there was a secret—not until Hendrijks showed him the footprints in Lauder's pictures.

The memory of killing Hendrijks wriggled through Cyril's body. So ea-zeeee! But the buzz of killing had overtaken his reason. Only after dropping Hendrijks on that filthy motel floor had Cyril realized that a live fossil was more precious than any skeleton, and yet Cyril, the apprentice killer, had just fixed it so that the pilot couldn't tell him where to look for it.

Had anyone other than Ken and Ngili seen that creature? Had Haksar?

In Jakub's presence, Haksar had talked about seeing a tribe once, at Dogilani. "An anomalous tribe" was the phrase he'd used—a phrase that kept wheeling around in Cyril's mind.

Did that mean a tribe of live fossils? Only Haksar could answer that.

Two days after killing Hendrijks, Anderson had visited Haksar and told him that he'd seen the pictures of the footprints, but not who had shown them to him. Haksar had suddenly complained that he had a headache and was feeling faint—signs of sugar depletion. He had asked Cyril to hand him a vial of insulin from the medical closet in his office and to come back later. He didn't like anyone around while giving himself a shot. Several hours later, Anderson had driven back to Little Benares. Haksar had shuffled to the door, told him through the peephole that he wasn't feeling well, then dropped the peephole's lid shut, and shuffled off. For a week after that, Haksar either did not answer Cyril's phone calls, or claimed his disease and cut the call short.

This, Anderson concluded, meant he knew about the creature and didn't want Cyril to know. It also probably meant that Haksar was selling to someone else.

That drove Cyril crazy. The *secret* might be sailing away from him just now, to the glory of another scientist, Lauder even. Maybe Lauder and Ngili were in cahoots with Haksar, and Haksar's request for help from Cyril was just a ploy. That made Cyril want to call Nairobi's new chief of police, the powerful and feared Arnold Kalangi. They had grown quite friendly at the cabinet meetings and routinely did favors for each other. But that meant exposing the secret to an outsider. . . .

These thoughts whirred obsessively inside Cyril's brain. They made people fall into two neat categories—the ones who would help him reach his deserved glory and the ones he would have to crush to clear his way.

"Ra-aj," he now modulated persuasively, "what you know about that place is bigger than you . . . and bigger than all of us. You need a partner." *Maybe he's already got one,* his paranoia inserted. "Meanwhile, you cannot ask me to go after scientific financing on hints alone. Especially since money is very scarce, and so far I haven't located any backers."

That was true; he hadn't even started looking for them.

"If you haven't located backers, what's there to talk about?"

"Raj! For fuck's sake!"

The Indian woman with her children had joined a modest Indian crowd that withstood the rain in front of a popular curry diner, some under black umbrellas, most of them unsheltered. They waited for actors to come out dressed and painted as the gods Brahma, Vishnu, Shiva, and his godly wife, Parvati. Then the procession would trundle off in rain and mud to the Nairobi River, where the traditionalists held a festival at the end of every rain season.

The Nairobi River was hardly the Ganges—a disgusting little stream with wallowing pigs and yelping stray dogs— but the hard-core believers had to have their sacred flowing water. They had thus earned the name of Little Benares for that part of Indian town, and even constituted a modest tourist attraction to anglicized Indians straying from Hinduism.

"I can't even come to the door, Cyril," Haksar repeated. "I'm saving my strength to edit some notes about what I observed in the savanna. . . . Why is the money situation so bad?" The mention of money was hard, practical.

"I shouldn't tell you one word, the way you are behaving to a colleague above suspicion."

Notes, Haksar had said. What kind of notes?

"Then let me hang up. . . ."

"Raj! Wait!" Cyril almost overturned his Toyota Land

Cruiser. "Raj, I swear, you are the most cunning, untrusting . . ." He heard a sound at the end of the line and yelled: "If you hang up on me, I'll call Chief Kalangi! Antique treasures are national property these days, and you're withholding information leading to one. I'll obtain a warrant, I'll break into your tatty temple and have you carted away, and then I can rifle freely through all your drawers and files. You cannot do this to . . ."—he was about to say "to me," but like an actor sensing the need to improve a line, he quickly changed it—"to science!"

"I'm sorry, Cyril . . ."

The dial tone.

Anderson wished he had that Indian woman and her brood in front of his car again so he could bump her with his bull bars, just to see her sari fly through the rain-filled air. Maybe Haksar would die from a heart attack. Or be locked up in jail without his insulin shots.

Haksar had hung up on him. Just like Corinne. Corinne had not returned to Nairobi. She had stayed on in London, and never called back.

In that way, Cyril and Haksar were similar. They were both without their women. Cyril remembered Ranee Haksar, Raj's wife, a brown little dwarf of a woman, who always had the red cherry of her caste painted on her forehead, and was always serving and obeying Raj to near-idolatry. Before she had died of cancer, Ranee used to throw elaborate dinners, feeding practically the whole faculty. She cooked everything personally and by hand and also waited on every guest. But she ate alone in the kitchen after the dinner party was over, all because her godly husband wished it so.

You've gotten better mileage out of her than I out of mine, Anderson thought with added irritation.

He noted the movements of the neighborhood to determine how risky it was to break into Haksar's house. He had to find out what Haksar was hiding. Probably it was a record of what he had found. The notes.

He concentrated on the house. It stood morosely alone between *dukkas*—shops—now closed because of the festival.

Newspapers piled up in the driveway, not far from the un-used car. The windows had harvested muck and cobwebs. On the sidewalk outside, a street artist had drawn a giant chalk painting of Hanuman, the Hindu monkey god. More important, Cyril had spotted zero patrolling police, a good sign that this neighborhood was on the wane.

He parked the Land Cruiser by a long flower stand shel-tered by a tarp on poles, and locked the car door. He walked in the rain, aware of how different he looked from the other pedestrians. A street shrine to Rama and other mythical fig-ures was being guarded by a man who seemed to be dis-playing proudly the monstrously amputated stumps of his arms. Unglazed pots were sold next, and a group of kids were kicking brass rings, trying to keep them vertical as they rolled in the mud.

All of them see me, thought Cyril. So? He passed the dead stare of the sidewalk artist. None of these people exist, thought Cyril. They are alive and real but so low in power and influence that it doesn't matter if they see me or not.

He stepped over the uneven cobbles of the driveway. A broken fountain figure, in the shape of Vishnu with four arms, trod the waters of creation while a tiny Brahma sprang from his navel. This Vishnu had lost most of his twenty fingers, and someone had tried to rip the Brahma out of the godly navel, managing only to bend it. Anderson pictured Haksar lying lifeless and thought fiercely: You won't die with your secret, you old chutney. I'll rip your nails if I have to, to make you talk. Ea-zeee. He pummeled the doorbell.

"Hel-lo-oh," Haksar gurgled out of a speaker set by the bell.

"Dr. Sharwati here," said Cyril, using the name of the Indian laundry that did his shirts.

"Pardon? Who are you looking for?"

"Professor Haksar."

"There must be some mistake. I am Haksar. My doctor is Dr. Gupta."

"I know, Professor. Dr. Gupta is busy today, so he assigned you to me. Diabetes mellitus, correct? He gave me a sample set of new pills to give you.''

"I take shots, not pills. . . . Too many shots . . . six a day . . .''

"I know,'' Cyril replied cheerfully. "That's why Dr. Gupta thought he would try these new pills on you.''

"What is the name of the pills?''

That he had not thought about. "They're insulin-based . . . with a new . . . liquefier added.''

"I want to know the name of . . . the medicine . . .''

"There's an army truck up the street, easing the pedestrians of what's in their pockets,'' said Anderson promptly. "If you wish me to leave, it's your choice, but they'll probably open my bag—and these pills come from Switzerland. They'll probably think they're ingestible hallucinogenics. So long, Professor . . .''

"Wait . . .''

Cyril glued himself to the door so that Haksar wouldn't be able to see him from a window. He could hear footsteps coming to the door.

"Cyril!'' In the crack of the door, Haksar looked like death warmed over, but his stare was alert, a surprise. "What kind of trick are you pl . . . ?''

Cyril threw his weight against the door and burst into a hallway. Haksar crashed back into a stack of newspapers near an umbrella stand, releasing a cloud of dust. Cyril banged the entrance door shut. "What kind of trick are *you* playing, Raj? What's all this secrecy?''

Haksar, in a Nehru-style jacket with a round collar, looked sleepless and dirty. He was starting to sweat big pearls that rolled down his caved-in cheeks, and whined something about needing money.

"What the hell d'you need it for?'' snickered Cyril. "You can hardly jerk off by yourself!''

Cyril was completely unprepared when Haksar grabbed a walking cane and hit him with it, the steel tip skiving Cyril from above the end of his eyebrow into the gut of his cheek.

As blood splattered onto the unread newspapers, Haksar scurried farther into the house.

Cyril stormed after him, noting the house's pitiless marks of neglect. Doors hung open, rooms gaped empty, a kitchen stove showed the lava of overflowed meals. The house smelled of spilled spices and stopped-up toilets.

At the foot of a wide stairway, Haksar tripped and fell but threw the cane into Cyril's legs, causing him to bang to the dusty floor, while Haksar rose moaning, his right hand limp. "My wrist, you broke my wrist. . . ." He still found the strength to pad up the stairs before Cyril could stop him. The thought that Haksar might reach his hiding place and destroy some information boosted Cyril off the floor.

BOOM! Huge drums started outside, too loud to be muffled by the rain. The actor who played Lord Shiva, face painted blue, torso nude, stepped out of the diner and parted the crowd, followed by his "divine aspects": a huge drum worn over the head of another actor, a huge trident carried by yet another, a huge papier-mâché lingam, or phallic column, draped like a humongous condom over the head and shoulders of a fourth. All four strode ahead to meet a similar column of performers symbolizing Shiva's wife, Parvati, with her own avatars. There were raps of drums, screeches of flutes, and more clamors. At the same moment Shiva raised his hand to appease the crowd, Cyril finally grabbed Haksar.

The crash of Cyril's fists onto the frail Indian was muffled by the festive noise from outside. Anderson beat the defenseless old man until the blood dripping from the gash on his face made him stop and zoom to a bathroom, where he found nothing to stop the blood but toilet paper. He blobbed some together, pressed it on the cut, then stormed back to find Haksar . . . on the phone! He ripped the receiver from his frail fingers and pulled the phone cord out of the socket. "Who were you going to call? Who?"

Then he stopped. Haksar hung limp, like a dead man.

"Drop the sham!" Anderson ordered. He pushed Haksar into an aluminum chair beside a clean, functional desk with a computer, fax machine, and the phone. Haksar's study was minimalist and modern. Anderson whipped out Lauder's photo of the footprints, but as he stuck it under Haksar's nose, ready to start his questioning, he heard someone ringing the doorbell.

"Who's out there?" asked Cyril.

Haksar barely blinked. Cyril slapped him softly. Haksar opened his eyes.

"It must be young Ngiamena. . . ." breathed Haksar, barely alive but with a sneaky grin. For an instant only the unrelenting doorbell stopped Cyril from wringing Haksar's neck.

The loathing in the old man's eyes made Cyril wince, but he had no time to punish him yet. Ngili was here, Ken Lauder's friend and partner.

"Why is he here?"

The sneaky grin widened. "For the same reason as you, Cyril."

"What do you mean, the same reason? What the bloody fucking hell do you mean?" He shook Haksar, noticing how light the sick man was, skin and bone.

"He wants to know . . . about Dogilani . . . and the forest . . ."

"The forest?" asked Cyril, perplexed.

The bell rang again.

"Where did you park your car?" Haksar grinned.

Anderson's Land Cruiser was known among students like a personal badge, like a blazon. He had wanted it that way. Now anyone who saw it and knew Cyril would know that he was here in the area. And anyone could figure that he was visiting Haksar, not shopping for curry sauce.

"Don't pipe a word, or I'll kill you," Cyril warned. He would go down and get rid of Ngili. Still, he didn't trust Haksar. He grabbed a pair of scissors off the desk, cut the phone cord into pieces, and used one length to tie Haksar's hands behind the chair's back, and another to tie his ankles. Then he passed a hurried hand over his ruffled clothes and ran down the stairs.

Halfway down, he realized that he didn't have his Sig/Hammerli gun. If he had to take on Ngili, he would have to do it with his bare hands. That injected some rationality into him. Fight Ngili? Ridiculous. Cyril would simply tell him to get lost.

He tore open the door.

"Anything wrong?" asked Ngili in surprise. He stood in the doorway, in dark slacks and a sweater, graciously slender and tall. He epitomized an African Cyril hated. An African sure of himself and undefiant because he was neither scared of nor impressed by whites.

Ngili pointed at Anderson's face. Cyril had forgotten that he was bleeding. "You all right, Professor Anderson?"

"Uh . . . yeah . . . yes . . ."

"What are you doing here?" asked Ngili. "What's going on?"

Cyril mopped the cut with the back of his hand. He felt so lowered in the African's eyes that he could have killed Ngili just to erase the insult.

"Professor Haksar is very sick . . . he asked me to help him to the bathroom . . . and fell . . . and I fell with him," he blurted.

Ngili's clever eyes went over his clothes. Cyril prayed that they didn't look like he'd been fighting, but he knew they did.

"Shall I call an ambulance?" asked Ngili.

"It's not necessary. He's fine now. What do you want here?" He stepped heavily toward the Masai. Ngili reached out a hand and stopped Cyril by touching his arm, not brutally but firmly.

"Professor Haksar called me and asked me to come over." He withdrew his hand, somewhat like a sober man after steadying a drunk.

"He called *you*?" asked Cyril. "Well, he cannot talk to you now." A memory flickered up in his brain. He grabbed at it thankfully. "It's your brother's wedding this week, right? Gwee's wedding." Ngili's brother's name felt like the hardest word Cyril had ever uttered. "You must be busy with all sorts of arrangements. . . ."

"We are, the wedding is tonight. But Professor Haksar told me it was rather urgent that we speak." Ngili moved to step inside.

"He didn't . . . didn't know what . . . what he was talking about. . . ." Cyril blocked his way, hoping to sound embarrassed by an old colleague's deterioration. He twirled his index finger against his temple. "Insulin depletion . . . makes him cuckoo. . . ."

"But he insisted."

"It's unnecessary. He's already forgotten. Everything's taken care of."

Anderson felt he couldn't take the clever eyes of the young Masai staring at him much longer. They had dilated like a wide lens, taking in his whole body. It was the same way that Masais, standing on one foot in the plain, checked on a whole herd; they didn't roll their eyes right and left but simply dilated them for a wider view.

Ngili stepped away toward the street, but he turned quickly. "Let's not beat around the bush. When you and Professor Haksar came to my father together, he said that he had once explored Dogilani and seemed irritated that we were there too. You said nothing like that; but now you are telling me that I shouldn't talk to Professor Haksar. Now that's pretty strange, because Professor Haksar asked me to come here and even said something about a legacy he wanted to entrust to the right person. . . ."

"And that might be you?" Cyril laughed genuinely. "You couldn't even protect your friend Ken!"

He hit a nerve. Ngili looked at him so hard that Cyril cursed himself for not carrying that Sig/Hammerli. He prayed that Ngili wouldn't do anything more than maintain his stare, which had taken on the smoky dullness of tempered iron.

But Ngili restrained himself; Gwee's wedding was in a few hours. Ngili had agreed to visit Haksar at such short notice because he had had to pick up a load of wooden staffs of tribal office and Masai shields covered in cowhide which had been refurbished by an East Indian craftsman.

"Tell Professor Haksar that I'll be back," Ngili said warningly. "You've got some wire coming out of your pocket—I think it's phone wire."

Then he turned, and walked toward the street.

As Ngili faded into the drizzle, Cyril felt his pockets and found a piece of phone cord he'd stuffed into his right pocket.

He stepped back inside and slammed the door, but he almost didn't hear the noise. A sour smell of fire hit his nostrils. He raced up the stairs to the door of the study, where he saw a plume of smoke.

He dived inside. The back of the aluminum chair lay on the floor; it was detachable, and Haksar had disconnected it from the seat simply by standing up. Then he had untied his hands; his ankles still tied up, Haksar was now sprawled on the floor, feeding pages covered in dense and regular handwriting to a fire he'd made on a brass tray.

"Just in time," Haksar squeaked sarcastically, as the fire blackened a last wad of pages. Big dark agates of sweat dripped from his chin, caused by the fire's heat and by the racing insulin depletion.

Anderson plunged and ripped free a few pages. They were covered in drawings—of monkeys, as far as he could check quickly. "What did you destroy, Raj?"

"What everyone's after . . ."

"And what was that?"

Haksar shrugged; he wasn't going to talk.

Anderson took a step. "You didn't want to tell me . . . but you called Ngili. . . . Why did you ask me to help you in the first place?"

"To find out whether you knew anything," said the sick man sanely. "You're always sniffing, Cyril, always sticking your fingers into what isn't yours. So I had to find out. . . ."

"You teased me," growled Cyril.

"Didn't t-tease you . . ." The insulin depletion made the sick man stutter. "Just wanted t-to s-see who would b-be the best c-custodian . . . of what I f-found. . . . It's not you, Cyril . . .''

Anderson stepped back and started opening the study's cupboards and closets. Despite his depleted state, Haksar's heartbeat went up like an engine from idle to high speed. Cyril was getting closer to that particular closet where . . .

Anderson opened the closet; row on row, insulin vials reflected the light, each packed with its disposable needle.

With one sideways sweep of his hand, Cyril reaped one whole row. Then another. The vials cascaded down, most of them breaking. Then he trampled the surviving ones.

The life-giving fluid flowed onto the dirty carpet, gathering into a little pool. Haksar pulled his tied-up ankles under him and sat cross-legged like one of the sages in the street, looking at the insulin puddle.

Breathing hard, Anderson pulled on the chair without a back, and sat heavily on it. He too stared at the little pool and the broken vials.

''You see, Raj? Your life is in shards on the floor. And it will dry up there unless you tell me the whole story.''

NGILI CURSED ANDERSON: BLOODY BWANA BASTARD, *nyoka,* snake, *mbaya ugonjwa,* ugly pest. Deeply angry, he drove the Ngiamenas' big Mercedes at pedestrians, stamping in their minds an image he didn't deserve—the spoiled young black upstart. But Anderson had spoken one truthful thing, and as an African proverb had it, "The liar's tongue speaks the bitterest truth." Ngili had not protected his friend.

Ngili had let Ken get lost in the savanna by himself. Ken's disappearance was an accident, but the Masai ethos was a warriors' one. Ngili felt that he had abandoned his partner and comrade. For warriors to abandon their comrades was only a little less dishonorable than losing the war.

And this day was deeply immersed in tribal imagery. The Masai shields and wooden staffs were clattering behind him in the backseat, their sound somehow live and accusatory.

Ngili told himself that he had carried out his father's request. But anytime he gave himself that excuse, he remembered flying over those plains covered with herds, looking for Ken—he had done it twice already, scanning the grasslands with his binoculars stuck to his sockets, to keep out the sunlight glaring at the park rangers' plane. As usual, the animal's movements were exciting and colorful, but Ngili's eyes sought obsessively for the movement of a human.

But he hadn't seen any humans down there.

Ken seemed to have vanished.

I did it for my father.

The thought brought no relief. Ngili missed Ken, and was worried about him. More deeply, he missed a special sense of himself, formed during his friendship with the white American. Like many educated Africans, Ngili swung back and forth between his roots and his own Western ways. With Ken, Ngili could express those Western ways honestly. In fact, Ken had helped him become aware of another Ngili, one who had grown quietly inside him, unseen to his ever-observant father.

At moments like this, Ngili almost hated his father. An astounding new feeling that scared him.

He did not dare tell his father how much he had liked being that mzungu's friend. And that he felt like dropping his family duties (which were made incredibly more complicated by the wedding event) and rushing onto a plane again, to zoom out there and scan some more.

But Ken could be a bagful of bones by now, scattered over a few square miles.

And there was something else. Hendrijks's death.

Ngili and Yinka had been called to the downtown metropolitan police morgue to identify Hendrijks's body. It had seemed strange that Chief Arnold Kalangi had asked Yinka too, but she had met Hendrijks, and she agreed to go. And she had walked into the morgue, breathing with her mouth wide open: air-hunger, a typical sign of fright.

The police morgue was a cube of cement that looked like a giant cinder block. Inside its basement crypt, Chief Kalangi had personally pulled out of the vault a tray with a bagged body that looked compact, swollen. The superintendent had unzipped it. Pale as green wax, Hendrijks had stared out, bloated like coarse ceramic.

Yinka had run to a gross spittoon of brass, and heaved dryly, without managing to vomit. Ngili had raced to hold her up.

The chief pushed the tray back into the morgue freezer.

Yinka mopped her face with Kleenex, looked at her brother, and saw a greenish sheen of fear spread under his cheeks. Was he afraid because, after Ken's disappearance and Hendrijks's death, he was the only one left from that trip to Dogilani?

Ngili was tempted to involve the police in a search for Ken, but knew better. Too many cops were involved in drugs and poached stuff, even though Kalangi, a recent appointment, had promised to clean up his department's act.

Kalangi asked if the Ngiamenas had personal enemies. Ngili shrugged, staring back at the tall, white-haired, and repellently skinny chief. He felt that volunteering any information could turn against him. And suddenly he was stunned to hear the chief recommend an outfit of ex-lawmen, for personal protection. They could take care of anybody anywhere, even overseas.

Yinka had recoiled in shock, while Ngili asked icily, "You're sure that those men are ex-lawmen, and not active ones?"

The chief grinned and put a hand over his mouth to cover a cough. " 'S all ri', if you don need you don buy.'' He had a thick Kikuyu accent, which sounded fake to Ngili, and teeth blackened from chewing sweet m'koko wood or betel nuts.

"What a dangerous old sleazeball," said Yinka, once in the car. She looked at her brother. "You don't think this is reaching somewhere far and ugly, do you?"

"No," he said, thinking exactly that. "Hendrijks got offed because he ran something. Maybe drugs."

She hadn't asked him whether he thought that Ken was still alive.

That had been three days ago, and now, ahead of the Mercedes loomed the Naivasha Hotel, where the wedding would take place in just a few hours. This was where Ngili and Ken had served drinks and shared dreams.

* * *

YINKA STOOD ON THE FLOOR OF THE NAIVASHA'S BALL-room, wearing a grand kikoi that was as red as a flame. She had a storeful of chains on her forehead. She was supervising the dress rehearsal for the up-and-down, the unabashedly sexual Masai courting dance.

Twenty girls, all related to the Ngiamenas, were to hop the up-and-down in front of twenty boys who had been hand-picked from the best Nairobi Masai families. President Noi's own son—not a Masai, but who would raise that point?—had been invited to be the lead male dancer. It wasn't known whether he would attend. The boys wore hunting dress, but also Vacheron and Rolex watches. Both the boys and girls hopped on long bare feet to the accompaniment of Digo drums, of chains jingling on foreheads, and of silver and brass hoops clanking on ankles and wrists.

The meaning of the dance was implicit, and done with all the stamina available—some males soared four feet from the ground and some females three. It was spelled out clearly in the shaking of shoulders, breasts, hips, and rumps. For the males, the hopping and shaking symbolized youth, power, separation from dull daily experience, eagerness to hunt and to impregnate. For the females, it symbolized youth, fun, cheerfulness, wish to attract a male and make his seed into offspring. Under their straight, narrow kikois, the girls jig-gled their breasts, and the boys dangled their genitals. The boys thrust at the air with hips and crotches, the girls rotated their pelvises forward, then pulled them back teasingly, pre-tending to shy away from the boys' thrusts. All done not just to music but to giggles on both sides. The girls, practically blinded by the adornments hanging over their faces, had to sneak glances to keep their places in formation, and to tease the male dancers without bumping into them, which was quite a feat of skill.

In the years that Yinka had spent in her grandparents' village, she had witnessed that dance performed by true tribal youngsters, some as young as ten. No Rolex watches there. No shiny hotel floors under their long feet, just village dirt. The dance was even wilder there, and spicier. It was truly a courting/mating rite. After the dance, the physically most developed dancers headed in pairs for the scrub, without parental supervision or restriction. Physiology itself was the mark of adulthood, the coveted right to love, drink, and behave as an adult. The tits that were barely blooming held themselves back. The penises that rose hesitantly inside the hunter robes did not press their advantage. Kids knew when they were still kids, and also when they should become men and women.

Yinka remembered all that, and it made her a good dance instructor. She had arranged the girls by size and age, the smallest in front, to dance before the shortest boys. They were also the shyest. They would warm up the crowd by hopping innocently and without true emphasis. As they hopped, they were to draw sideways, and allow the older ones, who had far more definite plans about their counterparts in the group of the opposite sex, to come face-to-face. Then the dance would quicken, the Digo drums would turn their still linear pounding into a frenzied *burrrrr,* and the feet, bodies, and faces would fly, while the eyes burned like fire under the tribal adornments. Sweat would glow on the young skin like extra glass beads. The audience would feel the drumming churn their blood, no matter what their age. A connecting sense of youth would flow in everyone, and a shared pride would make relatives smile at each other, forgetting rifts and petty jealousies.

This was probably one of the most graphic dances in the world, yet it was very pure. Many of the dancers were virgins, and none of the older boys and girls were married. The boys and girls put such heart into their thrusts, boosts, and swirls that through its very sincerity the dance lost its prurience. It was a celebration of the future.

Being a city affair, the Ngiamena wedding's up-and-down had been modified to include the older relatives and the prominent guests. After the first three rounds, executed exclusively by youngsters, the dance would be open for all who cared to join. In jest, Yinka had told Ken she expected him to dance the up-and-down with her. That would've looked funny, and they would've done it to the family's confused grins. Now she realized how much she had anticipated it. How she had pictured herself and the settler hopping together, he clumsy but smiling, she giving a virtuoso performance. She had planned to soar like a bird in front of him, to fly her breasts at him, to come close until her knees knocked against his, and to keep urging and encouraging him with quick hot glances. He would have tried his best, good sport that he was, and bobbed around clumsily, with his wide American smile. Or who knows? He might have found in his savanna-trained body a rhythm all his own. Who knows? Yinka had a true African's belief in dance as communication. She was curious about that part of Ken. And that would've become their dance. She would've been proud to be an expert, way above him and totally in her element, yet she would've welcomed his inventiveness, or at least his courage to play along.

If he had been here, but he wasn't.

The memory of the visit to the morgue clutched her stomach again.

Hendrijks's face. And then, instead of Hendrijks's face, Ken's.

Again, she breathed with her mouth wide open. Airhunger, the sign of fear.

Where was Ken? Why had he gone out there alone, the *idiot*? But it had been her own smart idea to help him go there alone.

It was impossible not to think about him constantly, because, after the visit to the morgue, her fear for his life ran alongside her fear for her brother's life.

Now, Ngili carried a gun, and he would carry it tonight, under his tribal dress. Yinka had refused to carry a gun, and she refused to openly admit her worry. When she saw Ngili step into the ballroom, she ordered the dancers into a break and ambled to Ngili with a big smile.

"Everything all right, my brother?"

"More or less." He walked to a makeshift fitting stall so he could change into his tribal dress.

She walked after him. "What did Haksar want?"

"I don't know, I didn't get to see him."

He stepped into the stall, pulled a curtain along a wire, and told her what had happened. She was silent. "You disappointed?" he asked angrily. "You thought he'd tell me something that would help us find Ken?"

"Yes," she confessed, wondering why he sounded so angry.

"I'm afraid we have other stuff to worry about. Downstairs, Um'tu was talking to Jack Dimathi. He called me over." Yinka listened, neutral. Jack Dimathi owned East Africa's only private passenger airline. Ngili opened the curtain. He looked so handsome that even his sarcastic sister momentarily lost her breath. Ngili scanned the dance floor and saw that no one was nearby, but he still lowered his voice. "Jack thinks that there's going to be a coup. And that we Masais will be targeted."

The knot that grew in Yinka's throat almost choked her. "Why us? We're such a small tribe . . ."

"Precisely. They wouldn't dare target a numerous one. The Kikuyu, their own people. Or the Embu."

"Who's they? The army?"

Ngili nodded. The army. Africa's one institution that everyone feared. Expected to ensure stability, but always fostering strife. As an airline owner, Jack Dimathi was one of the country's best-informed civilians. Ngili explained to Yinka that Jack had noticed a pattern. Troops were moved out of their usual barracks into the areas of tribes they didn't belong to. Troops were maneuvering, and pitching their tent camps, near Masai grazing areas. Meanwhile, a number of Masai chiefs had started to talk of "tribal representation."

"Someone's putting those words in their mouths," finished Ngili. "Someone's organizing a Masai provocation, to give the army an excuse." He waited a beat, staring at his flabbergasted sister. "At least that's what Jack thinks."

"And Um'tu's taking him seriously?"

"Yes. The tribal chiefs are having drinks in the main

lobby, and Um'tu's going around pumping them about army moves in their areas.''

The wedding was not to start for another hour, but the greeting line was already in place, because the tribal chiefs had driven in with their families well ahead of time in their not-too-reliable cars and trucks, leaving time for breakdowns. A good crowd had gathered outside the hotel's entrance, under wet umbrellas, waiting to come into the lobby at the rate of one family every five minutes—that was how long it would take each family to cross twenty yards of space, greeting Jakub and Itina, Gwee, the bridegroom, who wore a garb of lion skin studded with lion fangs, and Wambui, the nanny who had raised all the Ngiamena babies.

Wambui was a mess, crying her eyes out, and not just out of love for custom.

The guests walked in with ear-to-ear grins that were oddly devoid of laughter, being formal expressions of courtesy, not outbursts of feeling, and started down the line: *Hujambo! Habari?*—Hello. How are you?—to which the Ngiamenas responded simultaneously, *Hujambo! Habari?* Then both sides at once: *Mzoori, ahsante*—very well, thank you—and threw arms around each other, with the same fixed grins, not an iota less formal than at a colonial garden party. Then the guests asked the same identical questions—about everyone's health, about the bride's price (the Ngiamenas had paid no bride's price; the bride was from an urban family and had a law degree—but the custom of asking had to be upheld), and about why Ngili had not been the first to marry, to which Jakub was to answer with feigned embarrassment, but hint that Ngili might have been gifting his seed to someone already, and a potential spouse might be among the guests, not revealed because of some lovers' fickleness. Ngili meanwhile would hunt ever harder, to compensate for not giving his aging parents the gift of nimble obeisant grandchildren.

The male guests wore caps of leopard skin and tunics of leopard and zebra, the women elaborate kikois and tiaras of multicolored feathers of green-tufted turaco, brown-necked parrot, red-headed lovebird, blue-breasted bee eater, yellow-mantled widow bird or black-bellied seed cracker, not to mention the many varieties of sunbirds. One could tell, by the way the guests carried themselves, which ones wore these adornments often, and which ones were more familiar with suits and ties and high heels. In one respect, the old and the new mingled freely. The women wore together their tribal copperware and their mounted gems from Cartier and Bulgari.

The noise of the party reminded Ngili that he and his sister had to be down there with the guests.

"By the way," Ngili whispered to Yinka. "The president's son is not coming. I called palace protocol, and they gave me an excuse."

Wonderful, she felt like saying. The man had pawed her after the last up-and-down, and she'd had to pinch him hard. But she didn't say anything because if the president had allowed his son to attend, it would have been a positive signal, while this was something of a quiet shunning.

Ngili looked at his sister and noticed how beautiful she looked. Yinka whispered to him, "I'm sure Jack is paranoid. Targeting the Masais is ludicrous; only a few of them have any power. And there's not going to be a coup from the army against the president; the army's having it too sweet."

"What about the president and the army purging all potential opposition, with us as a pretext?"

"Um'tu should have the sense to enjoy the wedding," answered Yinka angrily, hurrying off down the stairs leading into the lobby. "What about Ken?" she asked, when she heard his footsteps catching up with her. "Aren't we going to set up a rescue party?"

"What if we can't do it?"

"You mean we're going to abandon him?"

He muttered obscurely, "Ken's a survivor, and might be safer than we are. . . ."

She stopped dead, halfway down the stairs, and threw her head back to stare at him from under her tribal apparel. "How can you talk so callously about your best friend?"

"I meant what I said, Yinka." He caught her naked arm,

making her bracelets jingle. "Yinka, Ken loves one thing only: science. . . ."

She smirked. "Really? He's not a robot."

"Yinka! He is . . ."

"White?" she snapped.

"American!" he blurted, and she laughed. Wasn't every other Kenyan dreaming of marrying an American? Or did it make a difference because those Americans were usually black?

"What if I just decided to live not as a dutiful native daughter," she asked defiantly, "but as a female opportunist? Isn't that what you call females in your debates on genetic strategy? What if I decided that there's nothing wrong with Ken as far as I'm concerned? He's young, dedicated, genetically valid, as you would say. He may become a star in science, if he gets back alive. . . ."

"*If*," he mouthed portentously. He looked at her darkly. "Yinka. Did you . . . ?"

"None of your bloody business!" And she really felt that the reason she was worrying about the settler had nothing to do with having gone to bed with him. They had been intimate for just hours, and maybe he'd already been dead for weeks.

"Listen." Ngili's features had narrowed, his posture had become rigid and blank. But she knew that his posture meant the opposite of what it signaled: He cared. "What if Ken comes back, and nothing happens between you?"

"You're right," she said flatly. "Maybe nothing will."

She hurried down, he followed, and a round of applause started below in the lobby. As Ngili and Yinka came down the stairs in tribal apparel, they made such a striking couple that the crowd reacted to an ideal image of itself. With a jingle of chains, she went toward an arriving group, to throw her arms around a high school friend.

Yinka's kikoi had been worn by Itina at her own wedding, and in its collar was sewn the big seed of a forest tree. A love fetish, a juju. It was guaranteed to make a man think about the woman who fancied him, while at the same time she thought about him. Come on, juju, show your power,

Yinka thought fiercely. Make him think of me, if he's alive! Make him think of me!

She felt that the dried-up seed had gotten heavier, and it pressed against her collarbone. She hugged her school friend's family, then stepped into the greeting line and stood a little sideways, facing toward the unseen Indian town. She touched the seed in her collar, and wished that whatever Haksar knew about Dogilani, it would help Ken.

"THE NEXT GLACIATION . . . IS IN . . . TWO THOU-sand . . . years. . . . That means . . . a hundred human genera-tions. . . . That's enough time to fixate . . . a new human type. . . ."

Haksar lay on a couch now, no longer tied up. His insulin depletion was so advanced that Cyril wondered why it was taking so long for the old Hindu to die.

The house was now dark except for a desk lamp. Anderson sat there, wrapped in the dust of the old books and papers he had rummaged through, mixed with the septic scent of spilled medicine and stopped-up toilets.

"But long before that . . . the planet would sink . . . under the weight of its overpopulation. . . ." Haksar went on, like a tape programmed spastically to cut off and restart every few seconds. "In two thousand years . . . there would be over two thousand . . . billion . . . people . . . on earth. . . . Project-ing at current . . . birthrates . . . the weight of the Filipinos alone would . . . surpass the weight of the earth. . . ." He cackled at the notion of the Filipinos' weight.

Anderson stood and stretched, letting out a good crack from his back. A new human type would be nice, but how could one get rid of the old one? And what about the deple-tion of the resources? Suddenly he jumped from the desk and posted himself menacingly in front of Haksar. "Why are you ranting about a new human type, Raj? D'you mean you met those creatures, and copulated with them?"

Haksar still hadn't told him anything. Nothing had helped, not even inflicting pain—Cyril had squeezed hard on Haksar's injured wrist, feeling the jagged, perhaps broken bone underneath. The tortured man had screamed, but he hadn't sputtered one bit of information.

"No . . . that wouldn't have been . . . science. . . ."

"I'm glad," laughed Cyril. He waved the few pages he had saved from the fire. They were diagrams of male genitals, hairy and realistic—they showed the testicles and members in various species of primates. They were anatomically correct and life-size. Anderson laughed again: "Did you draw these, old boy? I guess you were hot as a pistol in those days. Is this what you got off on?"

"I drew those . . . yes . . . back in '53. . . ."

1953. Anderson was at Oxford. There was nothing else special about that year except, oh, yes, of course: In Kenya, the blacks were getting themselves zapped by the RAF, during the independence war against the British.

"Yes . . . I was studying zoology then. . . . Leave those . . . alone. . . ."

"Relax." Anderson scanned the few pages, marveling at how accurate the small drawings were, marveling that a male gorilla's erect prick was under 1.5 inches long (the figures were noted next to each drawing), while an orangutan's was 2 inches, a chimp's 2.5 inches, and a sapiens human's a whopping 5 inches at least. "Should've thought that the bigger the apes, the bigger their dongos. . . ." he muttered.

"On the . . . co-hontrary . . ." stammered Haksar. "The big apes . . . are strong enough to . . . scare off . . . co-hompeti-tors . . . so they don't need big penes to . . . keep their females faithful. . . . You're foggy on . . . biosociology, Cyril."

"Shut up."

"Too much faculty politics . . . God . . . what I saw out there . . ."

"In the savanna?"

"In the savanna . . . and in the forest . . ." Haksar rose, his features looking almost monkeyish. From his eyes seeped an evil glint. "Stay away from that place, Cyril. . . . It kills . . .

it doesn't bring glory . . . but death. . . . You get to see . . . humanness rising . . . and then you die. . . .''

"D'you think Lauder's dead?"

"Maybe . . . not . . ."

Cyril resisted belting him one. "Why . . . not?" he mimicked the moribund.

"Very strong . . . genes . . ."

Haksar's head flopped onto his chest, but Cyril was wary. What if the old sneak was faking? In that position, with his breath down to a thin inaudible draft, Haksar could reduce his expenditure of energy to twenty calories per hundred pounds per hour. In fact, since Haksar weighed less than a hundred pounds, he could get it down to even less. Maybe he could even sham his death; Hindus knew all sorts of weird techniques. . . .

Cyril watched the old man as he examined the back of another page. Blood rose to his cheeks as he saw a spread of frontal views of vaginas, minutely but realistically drawn, from lemur to ape to human. They were all endowed with distinct and sizable clitorises.

"Is this what you did at Dogilani, Raj, chase monkey pussy?" He could not believe the effect those drawings had on him. "I'll buy you a subscription to *Penthouse*, Raj. Raj?"

Haksar looked now like a corroded deity. From his eerie immobility came a thread of sound. But it was clear and without stutter:

"D'you know how big a gorilla's balls are, Cyril? Twice as big as a human's . . . Yet he climaxes in under ten seconds. . . . How large are your balls, Cyril?"

"What? None of your bloody business!"

"Field studies show that the larger an ape's balls, the less faithful his mate is. The reason he needs such large balls is so he can occupy many females because he can't keep any particular one. . . ." He stared at Anderson full of innuendo. "Someone told me that Corinne's staying on in London. . . ."

Cyril jumped, grabbed Haksar and shook him. "Stop pretending, Raj! You're still here! I'll drive you to a hospital, they'll give you a shot of insulin, then you tell me what you know, and we'll make some money together!''

"How much money? For a new human type? No one has enough money to pay for that!''

"I waited too long for something this big to come my way!'' Cyril yelled. "I'm not going to stop for an old man who's already half dead! What?''

"I want a lot of money,'' said Haksar. "And what I am going to tell you takes time. Get me some''—his voice was slowing again, that unexpected cache of energy was getting exhausted—"insulin . . . now!''

"How? Shall I suck it off the floor?''

There was still some fluid in that narrowing puddle on the carpet.

"Get some in a spoon . . . and aspire it with a syringe. . . .''

Anderson had missed the plastic syringes, which were packed in a separate box.

Cyril pushed his face so close to Haksar's that the sick man's breath filled his nostrils: sweet/bitter/stale, a horrible smell. He didn't care. He blasted him back with his own breath. "This better be worth it. . . .''

"Hurry . . . a spoon . . . in the kitchen . . . let's see who's faster . . . you . . . or my death. . . .''

Damn you, thought Cyril, rushing out to the stairs. Too bad I can't really kill you!

Alone, Haksar planted his feet on the floor, straightened his back, and rose shaking like a leaf. He staggered to the window. He bit his skinny lips to muffle a moan of pain and managed to open it.

Humid evening air hit his face. The street was deserted in front of his house, but by that curry diner, people with candles, bells, and drums watched the bare-chested Hindu hermits, who walked chanting toward the little river, their nude torsos coated in ashes. The hermits kept their eyes to the ground. Their beards and tangled locks of hair, as well as their ash-covered bodies, shone, drenched where the rain had washed off the ashes. The din was reaching its paroxysm. Tonight these people were Hindus, nothing but Hindus, connected deeply with their faith and ancestry.

Haksar stared at them and frantically wished to connect too. To forget science, and the strange events that had brought him here. He wanted, in the face of death, the power to transfer into the eternal what this chanting crowd believed in.

What he knew about the world and the human race weighed on him like a sacrificial stone. And he felt an enormous regret that he had not found a trusted heir to whom he could leave what he knew.

The forest, he thought. *Don't go into that forest, Cyril.*

He was still alone.

On his desk, he saw a book that looked pregnant from repeated readings. He dragged himself to it and opened it. It was annotated on practically every page. It had been lying next to the only connection with the outside that had escaped Cyril's vandalism: the fax machine.

He leafed to a particular spot, tore off a few pages. He glanced at a sticker with phone numbers pasted to the desk, fitted the pages into the fax, and dialed an overseas number. He pressed the "send" button. With a light hum, the pages started to sink into the machine, to reappear as copies in another fax machine, eight thousand miles away.

WHEN CYRIL RUSHED BACK IN WITH A SPOON, HE SAW THAT the window was open. Haksar was standing by the window in a kind of vertical wallow, his face oiled with sweat. Haksar collapsed. Cyril jumped forward but failed to stop his fall. Haksar seemed dead except for his fluttering eyelids.

Cyril scooped fluid off the floor with the spoon, dipped a syringe needle in it, worked the plunger. Cyril had never administered a shot before. He looked for a spot of healthy tissue and settled on plunging the little needle into Haksar's palm. Haksar suddenly gave a big throb. Cyril grunted joyfully. Haksar had decided not to be a traitor after all!

"Wait! Raj, wait just a minute!" shrieked Cyril, not hearing the morbid humor in his call. He fumbled, scooping up more fluid, tried to dip the needle in it, and pricked himself in the hand. Shit, shit. Dripping blood onto Haksar's cadaverous hand, he plunged the syringe back into the dying Indian's palm.

The old man spasmed, then stared at Cyril.

Outside, the hermits reached that muddy stream and fell into it crying, "Shiva! Shiva!"—the god of destruction but also of regeneration.

Haksar was dead. And the god was not telling in what form he would regenerate.

CYRIL DID THE ONLY PRACTICAL THING THAT FITTED THE moment. He closed the window. Then he stepped into Haksar's library and rifled again, fast and at random, tearing off pages, crushing tomes under his feet, desperate that he hadn't more information from Haksar than he'd gotten from Hendrijks. Finally he found a box with black-and-white photographs that had been pushed neglectfully under a desk. He scattered them on the floor. One of them showed the dark, hairy crest of the Mau escarpment.

Three men stood before the Mau. Cyril recognized, younger by some forty years, a thin, jowly Hendrijks. Next to him stood Haksar, also young and wiry and big-eyed, looking like a grenade of nervous energy about to go off.

The photo seemed to have been taken in the early fifties while Anderson was at Oxford. Haksar wore a military-style tunic, with discolored patches on its shoulders and collar. Cyril wondered if those patches were the places where rank stripes had been ripped off. Next to Haksar was an African, a very young, skinny, crab-legged fellow, with a square tattoo on one cheek. He also wore military-type clothes with rankings torn off. An Enfield rifle was slung on his shoulder, its leather strap replaced by a cord that looked braided from animal hair. The Enfield's butt had been broken below the lock. It reminded Cyril of the comical yet deadly homemade weapons the Mau Mau guerrillas had used during their independence war against the British.

The Mau Mau. . . .

He looked at the escarpment, then looked at the African. Hendrijks and Haksar smiled with adventurous youth, but the African laughed from a great sense of cruelty. His expression said, I'll kill you.

The African might have been a bush tracker, and Hendrijks the pilot. But what was Haksar doing there?

Cyril tried to remember what he knew about the Mau Mau guerrillas, but he'd been out of Africa then, and the independence war had not imprinted itself on his memory the way it had on other Europeans'.

Darkened by its forest, the Mau loomed above the three men in the picture like a Pliocene battleship and for the first time Cyril realized how dangerous it would be to follow Lauder there and steal his find.

He stuck the picture in a pocket. Haksar was dead, and Ngili had seen Cyril here, only hours before.

Ngili had seen Cyril bleeding.

And he had threatened to come back.

Cyril looked around. Based on the astounding mess, it could appear that Haksar had been robbed. But the insulin vials smashed on the floor suggested that he had been murdered.

The inexperienced killer lost his nerve.

Minutes later, Cyril emerged from the house and ran in the rain to where he had parked his Land Cruiser. He noticed in passing that the street artist, perhaps chased off by the rain, no longer guarded his sidewalk painting.

He drove the car around a corner and surfaced in a back alley. A rain-rotted door in a wooden fence led to the back of the house. He parked the Land Cruiser in the alley, reentered the house, and found the body where he had left it.

With warped logic, he decided that the incriminating element was the body, and that it had to be disposed of.

Instants later, he exited the house carrying Haksar. He carried him upright, easily managing his weightless body. From a distance it seemed as if two men were hurrying off together, almost cheek to cheek, in a walk of Siamese twins. Thus, they arrived at the car, where Cyril slipped the body into the backseat.

Cyril felt that he was driving by instinct, along the north bank of the disgusting little river. Out the open window, he saw people bending to sift through the garbage. A dead body would be less conspicuous here than Cyril's well-kept and expensive vehicle. He turned off the engine, grabbed the body, and pulled it and himself out of the car.

Luckily, Haksar wasn't heavy and it was easy to drag him along. Cyril couldn't tell where the river was, but he heard it. He stepped toward it, finally saw it—a red, muddy puddle—and dropped the body in it, thinking that of all homages to Haksar, he was giving him the most symbolic, by committing him, Indian style, to the sacred flow of a river.

He stepped toward his car, and . . . he stopped as if shot. Arnold Kalangi, the chief of police, stood ramrod straight by Anderson's car. For a millisecond, Cyril believed this was a hallucination.

"Good evening, Professor," said Kalangi, in his Kikuyu-accented voice.

One exchange of words was not enough to make the hallucination disappear. "How did you get here?" breathed Cyril.

"I followed you," said the chief. "I left my car up there." He pointed with his chin.

Cyril saw a dark, unmarked car at the terminal crest of a range of garbage hills. It was parked on the maneuvering space of the city garbage trucks.

"Why?" asked Cyril.

"Because circumstances dictated that we should meet and talk a few matters over," said Kalangi. "Are you free now, Professor?"

"Huh? I . . . Yeah, I was just . . . going home."

"Would you mind accompanying me? I'm due at a place behind the bazaar at Muindi Mbingu Road. You might know it. Zhang Chen's herb shop. Could you come there with me?''

Cyril wondered how much Kalangi knew of what had occurred in Haksar's house. Was the sidewalk artist an undercover agent? Had Kalangi tapped Cyril's phone, or Haksar's?

The cop glanced at the place where Cyril had dumped Haksar's body: "Professor Haksar was really very sick. He wouldn't have made it much longer.''

Cyril didn't comment.

"I don't think he kept many notes in his house," said the chief. "I'm sure there are notes from his earlier expeditions somewhere . . . but I don't think they're there.''

Cyril lit up: "Where are they?''

"We can discuss that," said the chief. "Come on.''

And, to Cyril's astonishment, Kalangi held out an arm to help him over the mounds of garbage and toward the unmarked car.

ABOUT THE SAME TIME, AT THE NAIVASHA, ALL THE WEDding guests were assembled and the party was in full swing. Jakub Ngiamena unexpectedly took Ngili aside. "Ngili, our friend Jack Dimathi is feeling tired. He says that big parties are no longer for his age. Mind running him home?''

Dimathi stood behind Jakub. He was a short, carefully groomed fiftyish African, in a tuxedo that stood out among the kikois. He was notorious as one of the elite's few overt gays—his much younger partner, an Arab from Zanzibar, played Digo drums in the band hired for the wedding.

"I also forgot my wedding gift at the office," smiled Jack, who did not look tired. "If we stop on the way, Ngili, we can pick it up.''

Ngili remembered that Jack didn't drive but was surprised that his father had suggested him for the errand.

He looked at his father and figured out that this was an order.

"Sure," muttered Ngili, "let me change my clothes.''

Minutes later, wearing slacks and a windbreaker, Ngili

drove Dimathi off across the city's serial roadblocks to Jack Dimathi's downtown office. Jack unlocked the entrance of his office, spent five minutes inside, then returned with an unsealed manila envelope and a three-ounce bottle of Annick Goutal perfume. He apologized that the gift wasn't wrapped. Puzzled, Ngili took the perfume—it looked like a duty-free item Jack had picked up on one of his trips. Ngili opened the envelope. It contained seven one-way plane tickets to Johannesburg, on Jack's airline.

"You can fly on from there to anywhere else—London, New York," explained Jack. "The tickets are open and valid for three months."

Perplexed, Ngili asked if he had to pay him for the tickets.

"Wire me the money later. If you use the tickets, of course. Let's hope it's not going to be necessary."

There were enough tickets for Ngili's parents, Ngili, Yinka, Gwee and his bride, and Wambui, who was considered part of the family. Ngili's cheeks blazed as he looked back at the elegant little man. Jakub had made sure that he could take his family out of the country.

"No one saw us, no one knows anything. Now you can take me home and then go back to your party."

"Jack . . ." Ngili knew the man well; for years the Ngiamenas had flown in Jack's planes, for years, they had attended Jack's events and all of them had attended other elite events together. Even Jack's homosexuality, a thing terribly frowned on in Africa, had been accepted as a quirky feature of a family friend. Yet Ngili had never spoken to Jack this directly before. "Jack, are you worried about anything?"

"I'm never worried." Jack smiled thinly. "I'm just aware of some developments. The army just bought four new Embraer planes from Brazil, after their transporters proved insufficient during that refugee airlift. . . . Of course"—his thin smile widened—"the Embraer is not really a transporter, it's an attack plane, with cannons mounted on the wings; but the officers who made that mistake and signed the purchase order were too embarrassed not to go on with the deal. . . . The usual mess, you know. . . ."

It wasn't the usual mess. Not if Ngili related the planes to the concentrations of army around Masai enclaves. And they might be around other tribes' enclaves as well.

"Don't worry about these trivia; you're a scientist," Jack concluded, bending to get back into the Ngiamenas' big Mercedes.

Ngili fired the engine, tore down the street, and braked hard at a roadblock clogged up by a half mile of cars. He reversed, tried Kaunda Street, found another roadblock, bypassed it by taking a back lane, dropped to Uhuru Highway, found it clean, and gunned over to Jack's bungalow on University Way.

He dropped Jack at his place and tried to return to the highway, but saw a roaming army truck stopping broadside against the traffic. He returned to Muindi Mbingu Road and kept hopping off to little lanes of poor Arab dukkas and African stalls, until he just followed those lanes, hoping they wouldn't be throttled by roadblocks. He kept seeing roadblocks down cross streets, and armed patrols jumping out of trucks to shake down the motorists. Along its main arteries, the city, one of Africa's biggest, seemed to be caught in a strange game of apprehending itself. But back here, poverty guaranteed a sense of freedom.

Ngili saw with his peripheral view the envelope with the plane tickets in the passenger seat.

He had to stop behind a puckered matatu taxi that had stalled while it was unloading a passenger. Off to one side was a converted warehouse, with the sign ZHANG CHEN'S HERB AND FOSSIL SHOP clearly readable under a naked bulb. A police notice was pasted on the sign.

A burly Chinese gentleman in his sixties, Zhang was an enduring fixture. Although often closed down by the cops because he dealt in poached items, he always reopened for business after greasing them. If he lost the lease on his building, he always managed to come back in a new location, sometimes next door to the old one. This was where Ken and Ngili had found the top of that *Australopithecus* skull that Randall had ruled unfit for dating with potassium-argon. Tonight, the shop was in one of those lulls between being closed and reopening.

Peering from behind the Mercedes's wheel, Ngili suddenly sat up.

He saw Cyril Anderson and another man, an African, walking toward the shop.

The African was Nairobi's police chief, Arnold Kalangi.

Anderson looked rather haggard. Ngili noticed that he was wearing the same clothes he'd had on that morning.

Ngili flipped the rearview mirror to an angle framing the two men, then sank down in his seat. In the mirror, Kalangi seemed to explain something, acting forceful, while Anderson's body language was reserved and cautious. Kalangi walked to the shop's door, unlocked it, let Anderson in and then himself. A light came on. Through a window, in silhouette, Kalangi sat down, while Anderson paced back and forth.

The noise of the matatu's engine coming back alive made Ngili start. He pressed the gas and drove after the taxi, away from the store. A couple of doors down, a body shop was staying open late. Ngili pushed his car into its open gate, jumped out, struck a deal to park his car in the body shop. Then, with all his senses sharpened, Ngili ran back to the herb store.

Kalangi and Anderson were still inside, but now Anderson was seated too, as if having agreed to be patient.

Pure instinct told Ngili that he had hit on a vital clue. He looked around for a hiding place. A row of pushcarts was stacked for the night against a wall that stank of urine. But Ngili was too concentrated on the store to care about the odors.

He slid quietly into the niche between the wall and the pushcarts.

Only minutes later, a dusty truck showed in the lane and pulled up to the store. On its flatbed, horns and hardened animal hulks thudded noisily. Two men in extremely tattered army fatigues jumped down from the flatbed. And out of the front came a crab-legged, tattooed bush character, whom Ngili recognized as the scary man who had joined Ken's camp right before Ken's disappearance—Sergeant Modibo.

T HE RAIN CLOUDS HOVERING OVER NAIROBI WERE PRE-
vented from drifting westward by the crests of the Ab-
erdare Mountains. Only a few clouds, too thin to produce
rain, made it over to Dogilani. By the time they arrived over
the savanna, the night was descending, cool and dry.

The hour of reckoning for the savanna's hunters and
hunted struck again.

The hulk of the dead lion was revisited for the second
night in a row by two competing gangs of scavengers—a
family of hyenas and a pack of wild dogs. The night before
they fought each other, leaving the hulk almost intact.
Through the following day, the hulk, its lion smells still active, had scared off a number of carrion seekers—dead lions
lying about were not common. Finally, the birds figured that
the lion was harmless and descended carefully to take out
the eyes, the soft pieces of muzzle and face, the hanging
tongue, the testicles, and morsels of the tail where it joined
the buttocks.

On the second night, the hyenas and wild dogs decided to
give the hulk another chance. But again the slope-backed
hyenas, with hind legs that seemed chopped off compared to
their much longer forelegs, had to reckon with the wild dogs,
whose big funneled ears were shaped like the horns of old-
fashioned gramophones, while their coats were spotted dis-

gustingly in black and yellow, as if some bigger beast had puked all over them. They were both hungrier than last night and spoiling for a fight. The ratio was two hyenas to three dogs. The dogs had no big advantage other than being infinitely bolder. The hyenas relied on their weight and superior strength, the dogs on the ferocity of their jaws. The hyenas jumped and rolled in the dirt, crushing the dogs who bit like land piranhas. The howls of these two breeds rose above the valley, pulsating under the shrinking moon.

Throughout the racket, the australopithecine boy snored peacefully on a wide flat rock face. Next to him, Ken spent his second sleepless night after killing the lion.

He sat on the rock face and noticed that over the last few weeks his eyes had gotten better at picking out movements and objects in the dark. He saw several dogs throw themselves on one large hyena, the family's dominant female, and tear at her neck to render her family leaderless. Though other hyenas jumped in, their help was hesitant and confused. Yelping in panic, the dominant female raised her muzzle toward the moon, and when the biggest dog cut her jugular, she trembled and then collapsed. The dogs howled victory, and performed stupendous leaps and lunges, like four-legged acrobats. The hyenas switched their barks to whines and broke off. The wild dogs jumped up on the lion.

Ken slid down the rock face until he stood at the edge of the grass again. He stopped by that subtle border, where the night's perils multiplied a hundredfold. He knew that he had caused the hyenas and dogs to fight because he had left that lion's carcass on the plain. He had killed that big ferocious thing that everyone in the bush fears. He was now a hunter. He had been a nerd in high school, and not even a Boy Scout, and yet he'd killed a lion.

He felt he was looking into his own soul, wondering if he could live so naturally, so directly, without the eternal self-questioning of modern humans. Could he just *live*? Like Long Toes?

But that was just a romantic notion. Long Toes did not

live unconflicted. He had confessed in that rocky graveyard that the past haunted him.

Ken flexed his knees, slid his back against the rock face, and sat.

He found beauty in all he saw and heard—what he would once have called a cruel beauty, but there was no cruelty here, any more than there was goodness. There was instead a kind of global and sloppy perfection lurking in all things. The wild dogs, small, bad, and happy, appeared like perfect creations, justified in everything they did. The dead lion had taken on an odd postmortem charm; it was a naïve beast that had given Ken an unexpected trip back into a hunter's soul. He was thankful to the lion. He was grateful to all those creatures, alive and dead, and even to the grass they blood-ied, trampled, or ate. Ken was like a tribal hunter, who thanked his prey after killing it, then kept the horns and hooves as amulets.

All the anthropology he had read, all the tribal culture he had studied, now made sense. Fetishes, charms, hunting songs, tribal beliefs and superstitions, all made sense and had become a part of him.

All because of killing one lion?

Or was it really because of the boy, Ken's continuous source of revelations?

It was all of it: the boy, the lion, the kudu, all the other game they had hunted. And the fire, kindled with his city-boy lighter. It was everything that had happened over the last incredibly magical weeks.

But again, first and foremost, it was the child.

Killing the lion had even reduced Ken's fear of Modibo. The man seemed predictable now, just another hominid, with wicked tools, firearms. If he found Modibo in his path again, they would sort this out. Man to man, hominid to hominid.

He remembered the boy, and he decided against venturing into the grass. He turned and started to climb the rock face.

*   *   *

HE LAY ASLEEP, WISHING HE WOULD REMEMBER HIS thoughts in the morning, to jot them down. Then he remembered he had no pen and paper. He would have to keep repeating them to remember them. He turned to one side, and his hand found the boy's body. Reassured by its warm presence, Ken rolled on his back, the cold night on his face. He should perhaps sit up and relight the fire. But he was too tired. He tossed to get all the warmth out of the ashes. He dreamed about their warmth, softness, and delicacy.

The spread of ashes was suddenly covered by a shadow that extended over the sleeping man and child, reducing their grayish luminosity and making the sleeping bodies appear darker. A foot, large and with a widely spread big toe, patted the ashes. Another foot stepped next to the first, and the fingerlike toes of both played in the ashes, while the being towering above them fought a brief shiver of pleasure. The being squatted, dropping a knee in the ashes, and put its fist in front of that knee. A hand with very long fingers but a short stumpy thumb touched the white, quietly shining spear, the only one Ken had left.

The hand picked up the spear by clamping four fingers around it, while the stubby thumb tried to match that movement, but only curved inefficiently. Then both hands clamped on the spear. Vibrating from the hairy muscles twining around the arms, they brought the spear down, held flat, over Ken's throat.

Ken felt the choking weight of the spear on his throat, and his eyes fluttered open.

He looked up.

Immediately in his face was a hirsute head.

Two eyes caught a pale reflection of moonlight and glittered at him. A warm breath hit Ken's face, so close that he inhaled it into his lungs. As the spear weighed on his throat, he felt his skin being cut. Ken's breath passage was obstructed, and he wasn't getting any oxygen. He gripped the spear and pushed it up, rolling the air back out of his lungs. He yelled in shock, folded his knees back to his chest, and kicked at a fiercely hairy creature.

Like a brown streak of flesh, the boy bolted up beside him. Ken jumped up, bumping into another unclear shape. The attackers were hairy and strong. The face Ken had seen was flat, without a baboon's doglike muzzle.

Another creature gripped Ken at the ankles, and he fell facedown. Jumping up again, he turned toward the new attacker, gripped its arms and chest, feeling its packed hairy muscles, and they plunged together off the rock face.

They touched down hard, though the crash was lighter than the zap of surprise—he was losing the invincibility he had felt after killing the lion. The creature he'd fallen with gave a whine of pain, while he threw himself in the other direction and tried to call the boy. But the boy had no name and they shared no language!

Ken opened his mouth and yelled: "Eeee!"

From above he heard the puffing grunts of the aggressors, and a blunt moan, as if through closed lips; Ken pictured the aggressor's hands pressing down on the boy's lips, silencing him, and killing him. With the sweat of fear erupting on his shoulders, he threw himself on the rock ledge, heard a thud of flesh hitting flesh, saw one aggressor creature staggering back, hairy hands at its crotch. Ken guessed that the little australopithecine boy had hit his attacker in the *balls*! The attacker looked rather like a mangabey monkey, with the hairs on the top of its skull forming a stiff crest, but it was too large to be a monkey. Trying to grab the boy again, the crested male turned full profile, and Ken immediately noticed the angle of his face. He was an australopithecine, but not of the boy's gracile, light-boned kind. He was the heavy, crested, robust kind. These hairy hulks were protohumans, like the boy, but they were from a different variety.

The jolts to Ken's mind continued, in rapid succession. The boy was desperately fighting the robusts, and the robusts were lunging for the boy as if he were a delicious morsel. As a last jolt, Ken realized that he had been included in this nightly raid only by accident.

He had no more time to think. The boy grabbed Ken's arm and tripped him back into the void. They both fell. . . .

Ken landed on the ankle he kept injuring, and moaned. The boy was instantly at his side, propping him up. Several of the creatures emerged in the high grass. Ken shouted at the child, "Run, run!" in useless English, but the boy sprinted off. The closest crested creature lunged out to seize Ken. Ken ducked, broke into a hobbling run, while ahead of him the boy kept turning back; then suddenly he streaked away, directly toward the Mau. Panting, Ken gurgled a half-hearted call. The boy vanished into a stand of trees.

Cursing out of confusion and fear, Ken burst into an uneven grove of Cape chestnuts. He looked up through the branches and saw the Mau's forested slopes hanging almost above him.

He ran to the middle of the grove and stopped. A breath of cool undergrowth wafted at him, and he smelled the dusty rottenness of forest floor, and a scent of tree mushrooms.

Behind him, but almost on top of him, he heard the rough sound of breaking foliage. One of his pursuers was up in a tree, and it was *brachiating,* arm-swinging after him. It was moving so fast that he could see its dancing shadow. Dazed, Ken charged out of the trees and uphill, across a stretch of tussocky grass which his pursuer couldn't brachiate across. He was lashed on his bare chest by a ropelike liana, swinging at him from a wild flame tree absurdly reminiscent of the ones shading the avenues of Nairobi. The tree rose on a slightly higher promontory and he saw the boy up in the flame tree. He wanted to yell in relief and bit his lower lip to stay silent. Looking almost like an ape, the boy waved his arm at Ken.

It started as a round gesture, like a wave for attention, but became a straight one, with the hand held up, like when they hunted. He was pointing toward the escarpment, as if he were urging Ken to keep climbing straight up.

Then the boy sank into the foliage, while the liana he had used to signal dangled limply, meaningless.

Behind Ken, husky apish shapes were jumping down from the branches. Ken turned and counted five of them. They were slowed down now that they were out of the trees and in the grass. Ken was less worried about them than about losing Long Toes. Where was Long Toes headed? Had he fled into the trees out of sheer fright, or with a plan?

Then he saw him again, far ahead, in the branches. The boy was ahead, and his pursuers were behind him, and the forested Mau had essentially only two directions: uphill or back down the incline.

If he ran straight up, as Long Toes was doing, maybe he wouldn't get lost.

With his lungs burning, he passed under tangled branches, once seeing a big shadow and panicking that his pursuers had caught up—but it was only a grotesquely large bird's nest of mud.

The forest floor was dry and rustling; it made a deafening noise, a jangle that let any creature nearby know that he was there. Then he realized the floor wasn't uttering that noise. It was coming from the foliage on the trees behind him. His pursuers were still after him.

Part Five

THE OTHER HUMANS

K EN RAN UPHILL.

He ran, wondering if the boy truly wanted him to keep climbing up the steep slope of the Mau. As the vines and branches lashed at his arms, he shot them forward and macheted through the tangles, dreading the venomous creatures that might sting him at any moment. He also wondered if Long Toes was still somewhere in the lower canopy and what perils he was encountering. That was the habitat of leopards lurking between savanna and forest. Maybe the boy had stopped, and was looking for a hiding place. *I'll stop too.*

But when he slowed down, he could hear the robusts chasing right above him. He plowed on through. Ken expected that soon there would be a change in the terrain from the thicket of the lower ranges to a wide band of big trees, with canopies so dense that no nourishing sunlight or water could filter down. In those areas, he wouldn't have to deal with the wild growths on the ground. Come on, big trees, come on! he prayed.

Finally, he burst into an area free of thicket and raced under the irregularly broken archways of lower branches. A dark huddle stirred and he made out a herd of pygmy forest antelopes, *mbolokos,* that started bleating and scattering. Ken stepped with his boots onto their slippery turds and the wild figs they had been eating.

He slowed down, no longer able to sustain the chase, and his pursuers blasted on right above him.

The roar sounded continuous; no matter where he went, he couldn't escape it. Ken stepped back, hearing the crawling-creaking-snapping noises that became a kind of global hum from above. Finally, he realized that the night breeze was ruffling the canopy tops as it descended the escarpment.

He wasn't being chased, at least not right now.

But maybe he was being stalked?

A fear came over him that was so potent and inventive that every noise he heard sounded like a roar, and even the darkness itself seemed to move, as if it were breaking into a billion hungry creatures. He tried to decide whether to move or wait. If he waited, he might be found; if he moved, some deadly ground creature could find him. And whether he moved or not, some other night hunter—a reptile, a bat— could plunge at him from above. He made out a thin sapling, put out his hand to tear off a branch, and a sticky liquid suddenly plopped onto the back of his hand, a warm excretion that same animal had innocently dropped in its sleep. He wiped his hand on his tattered pants, then tore off the branch and aimed it ahead of himself. He stepped forward, down a natural passage toward a spot where a pale rain of moonlight was coming down through the frayed canopy, and in that moonlight, the boy passed quickly upward.

Ken froze.

The boy did not stop, though he did scan the bushes and trees right and left. Looking for me, Long Toes? Ken thought. But before he could utter a sound, the boy had hurried off, still upward, and vanished. Forgetting caution again, Ken strained his body, ready to bulldoze through the thicket after him, but . . .

Just behind the boy, and moving as soundlessly as in a bad dream, were three of those hulking robust creatures. Ken saw them clearly, moving in profile, their long jaws hanging, their low mouths open from the effort of climbing without making any sounds.

They walked with their knees bent, as if from holding up their bulging torsos. They passed Ken's terrified eyes, in which Ken's scientific attention was immediately on alert but then instantly overpowered and killed by the pure dread that something so unknown and lethal was on the prowl for the boy, and for him.

He drew back in an instinctive movement to blend in the foliage. The boy's pursuers vanished.

Several moments passed. He reckoned that he had to stay still until he stood a better chance of finding his way, devising some better weapon than the stick he was holding. He was not giving up on finding the boy, but roaming the forest at night was a sure way of getting killed. He'd almost gotten killed when he was fighting the robust attackers on that rock ledge. There he'd fought from pure survival instinct, without knowing what he was fighting. But now, the dread of what he'd seen almost loosened his bowels.

He knew that these creatures were not the boy's kin.

A number of minutes passed, during which he tried to regain his self-control.

I'm Ken Lauder, he thought, as if making his name into a tool to sort out the situation. I came here as a scientist. I may leave tomorrow. I may leave because ... because ... because I am not this child's guardian. Endangering myself like this is senseless. I may never see him again. That glimpse of his passage between trees, minutes ago, might be the last time that I see him.

In the womb of foliage, Ken lay down, thinking he was back to his old self. He could think about his own survival, and if he survived, he would snuggle back in the bosom of science, where surprises were not permitted unless they were scientific.

His eyes began to close. He drifted into sleep.

*   *   *

"WHAT ARE YOU GOING TO DO WITH HIM?" ASKED YINKA. She tossed against Ken's body, as both of them lay on the forest floor. Her naked body was as dark as the darkness, and yet somehow distinct.

Ken wanted to plead with her to get up because a nude body on the forest floor was exposed to a multitude of risks. But Yinka folded her bare arms under her head, and let her breasts be freely stroked by the cool night air, while her eyes glittered with the intensity of her question. "What are you going to do with him?"

He mumbled something about the scientific value of discovering Long Toes.

She shook her head with contained anger. "He's a child, Ken, first and foremost a child. What do you think you're doing? You've intruded into his childhood. You're now intruding into his breed, and you'll draw the whole world after you."

He inhaled the delicious smell of her body, so different from the forest's. He was madly aroused and felt he would do anything or say anything, just to take her in his arms. "What would you do in my place?" he mumbled, bending over to muffle her answer with a kiss.

She pulled her arms from under her head and sat up, clearly not welcoming a sexual advance. "Leave!" she said authoritatively.

"I can't do that. . . ."

"Haksar left."

"How do you know he was here?"

"How do you know he wasn't? Why did he come to see my father on that day, mentioning that he once visited Dogilani?"

He pondered. She was right. Why else would Haksar be so interested in this wilderness, unless he had visited it himself earlier?

"You've got to stop being so selfish," she said.

"*What?*" Selfish? Ken wondered if he had heard her right, as she continued, "You've got to stop thinking of yourself, and start thinking of him."

"But that's all I'm thinking about. . . ."

She stood up and walked off. He watched her flesh and skin disappear into the forest, and urged himself to get up and rush after her; he could not leave her alone, unprotected. What answers did *she* seek, as she crazily dived into that wilderness all naked?

This has to be a dream, he told himself with that strange lucidity that some dreams have. He thought of Yinka and her wonderful body in his disorderly bed in Nairobi. A tickle of male pride. What had she been doing since he left Nairobi? She would have danced at Gwee's wedding, with some beautiful Masai males, valid would-be husbands. That must've made Ngili happy. He wondered if his years of friendship with Ngili, or his instants of intimacy with Yinka, were just trespasses in a hostile and forever divided world.

The main thought, the one that really mattered, rose from among all the others and drifted into focus: Long Toes.

Ken closed his eyes, but Long Toes promptly jumped behind his closed eyelids. Long Toes grinned with those brilliant white teeth. He scratched with his little fingernails. His belly was swollen up from having just eaten; his navel, like a little brown button, stuck out of his body. He jumped up, walked, ran, sat down, dozed off, snored—all inside Ken's memory, in a million poses of an incredible childhood.

Ken had never paid much attention to children before. He had always craved to be an adult, autonomous, and rational, and invulnerable. Fatherhood had never really interested him; he rated men too overtly fond of their kids as soft and sappy. Long Toes had erased all those attitudes. That unpinchable little thing (nothing to pinch, no plump parts, no cute folds), that unhuggable minikin (he had never let Ken catch him in an affectionate hold), that tiny weirdo, with his outpointing toes and all, fretting and touching and burping and giggling and vocalizing in Ape 36, had done this. Long Toes had a gift for causing in Ken a basic feeling he could not put in words. It did not belong in words. It came from far deeper than mind and language.

While in the grip of that feeling which no words could

describe, Ken pictured himself making love to Yinka. He was copulating with her not for the wild thrusts but patiently probing at her uterus door, and climaxing to guide his seed to her egg.

It took fatherhood. Fatherhood makes humans human.

And he too could become a father, if he survived.

That thought helped him control his other fears. He lay back and chose, as a survival strategy, to try to sleep.

IN THE EAST, THE SUN SOARED OUT OF THE INDIAN OCEAN, and minutes later, its light had traversed the whole width of East Africa.

The Mau's treetops caught fire. Below them, the darkness beneath the trees diluted into dirty, salt-and-pepper tones of gray.

Still asleep, Ken was stung under his left nipple.

He reached for the spot and caught a little insect, which he pressed between his thumb and index finger, crushing it all except for a piece that remained hard and intact like a pinhead. It was a safari ant's head, with its pincerlike jaws still moving.

He felt two, three, four, a dozen bites on his stomach that made him bolt up, sweeping his palms across his skin. Next to him, he saw a little brook flowing over the forest floor. He rose, dipping his knees in that brook, but was amazed that he didn't feel any sensation of wetness. A cloud of insects, moths, sleepy butterflies and grasshoppers, flew up, all running away from that brook which had already stretched out in all directions, as if in defiance of gravity.

What Ken thought was a brook was actually a flood of safari ants, leaving their nest in search of food and a new nesting place.

Ken stood up, his knees swollen into grotesque spheres of crawling ants. All around him, creatures were running for their lives—often too slowly. A snake zigzagging along was so loaded with ants it would be dead in instants, carved off so efficiently that only its skeleton would remain. One of those pygmy antelopes galloped across the tide, its graceful lopes keeping it above the carnage. A huge forest moth wheeled crazily, loaded with clinging ants, then crashed in the swarm. Ken looked right and left but couldn't see any flat place that was free of ants. Ken knew the ants migrated in all directions, their only strategy being to flow everywhere until they found a satisfying new habitat. They could be as many as five or twenty million, and a column of safari ants could stretch for a hundred yards, and roam for several days, moving at forty yards an hour.

He took a breath, and charged off across ground that was already glittering with that swarm. The ants kept pouring out. Had rivers gotten in their path, they would have built bridges woven from their own bodies. The only thing that could stop them would be fire, in which several million of them might be killed, only to be replaced within days with eggs from one of their twelve new queens. She would mate with one of the half-dozen winged males.

Hollering in triumph, Ken reached a stretch of uninvaded forest floor ahead, threw himself to the ground, and frantically peeled off his pants. He slapped ants off his ankles and knees and thighs, then rubbed his wrists and forearms, smearing the ants as they pinched his skin. He kicked off his boots, cleaned them inside with leaves, pulled them and his pants back on. He returned to picking pinlike ant heads from his palms and arms and looked over and thought he saw the boy, leaning against the trunk of a tree.

He dived toward him, and fell. When he looked up again, all he saw was a big brown knot of tree bark, shaped like a human head.

He felt the need to walk up to that tree, and touch it. Then he retraced his steps until he saw the swarm of ants and knew that they too were real.

Come on, Lauder. Come on.

He staggered upward.

*　　*　　*

SLOWLY, THE DAY WENT THROUGH ITS PHASES OF VARYING sunlight. Rainwater collected in the foliage, and Ken stopped to drink it.

Then he climbed on, until he was finally deep inside the empire of the big trees.

For thousands of years, these camphors, yellowwoods and cedarlike conifers had taken all the sun and moisture, letting nothing grow below other than the skimpiest scrub. Underneath the putrid leaves on the forest floor were tiny rodents, worms, grubs, spiders, centipedes and millipedes, while on the floor itself lived the bongos, sweet-eyed forest cows, the okapis, and the mbolokos. Higher up, the forest's real estate was crowded with monkeys, eagles, and other winged raptors. And in between there were pottos and small reptiles and minor carnivores that spent their whole lives in the trees.

Man himself was so different from the forest, Ken thought, even though he had been created there.

Noon came and passed. Ken was so numbed by fatigue that he was almost sleepwalking.

The Mau's slopes rose unevenly now, leveling into plateaus. The tree canopy above was becoming uneven, allowing some daylight to flow through, which created tracts of grass on the forest floor.

When Ken finally stopped to rest, he glanced upward and saw, lost in the green tangle, clear shards of sky.

T HE CLAN OF GRACILE HOMINIDS WAS LOUNGING IN THE grass of a high clearing, surrounded by several giant lobelia trees and a bank of wild bushes. Over the tufted spears of the lobelias, one could see the edge of the Mau, and the sky beyond it.

A crowned eagle was circling stubbornly. Underneath, a woman who stood just over four feet tall turned up her face and glanced at the crowned eagle. Her eyes were light brown. She decided that the eagle's flight did not signal any close peril so she started looking about, checking the hominid band scattered around her.

Things seemed peaceful. Enjoying the warm air on her hairless breasts and stomach, she stood up, throwing back the thick brown strands of hair that brushed her cheeks. These strands were long and straight and grew tightly, and when she bent forward they shaded her face like a natural hood. Her forehead, cheeks, and mouth were all hairless and smooth, giving her a look that separated her and her kind from all the other forest animals.

The woman put one of her long hands up and combed her fingers through her hair, a self-grooming movement she made often. In her other hand, she held an infant whose plump legs were clutching on to her skinny waist. The baby's little mouth sputtered as one of her nipples fell out of its lips, and they smacked around searching for the other nipple.

The infant didn't look like the woman. It had large features and long jaws and thinner lips. But its lips felt the same way on her nipple as her own children's lips had felt. With her free hand, she pressed down on the top of her breast, helping the milk flow—many generations farther on, the flow of the milk would go much more easily, making it more pleasurable for the mothers of the future.

The woman had endured the pain of the little mouth on her nipple for over a year, nursing this baby who was not her own. This had been an effective way of not becoming pregnant again. She had avoided becoming a mother again because she was the leader of the clan, but that could be terminated by violent death at practically any moment. The clan was going through an unpredictable and violent time.

She did not need words to know how things had come to be like this. She remembered the reasons for the present situation in the way of her evolutionary level, which was by storing pictures and other sensorial cues of past events in the incipient memory lobes in the front of her brain. Those recollections—combinations of images, smells, and sounds—were as many as a sapiens had words, and she could recall them, discard them, shrink them, or enlarge them in milliseconds, for even a brain of a few hundred cubic centimeters contained several billion neurons, each sending electrical currents to thousands of others.

Holding another female's baby, she looked apish, but also like a modern woman. Her forehead sloped back at forty-five degrees, her eyes sat underneath strong eyebrows, and her nostrils were well carved, though she had only a minimal nose. Her lips were hairless and full, and the hint of a chin gave her a resolved look. Her navel was elevated and large because her mother had chewed it off when she was born.

She too had chewed off the umbilical cords of all her babies, after she gave birth to them while standing with her legs wide apart, her long hands gripped around a low branch. Her belly was well shaped, but without one ripple from motherhood or from her age, which was over twenty, almost mid-life in her breed. A good pubic tuft forested her crotch. Her waist was svelte, her legs hale and muscular, and her feet with their splayed-out toes had palmlike soles.

When she was seated, she used her feet often, to touch and stroke, to kick gently to get an unruly child's attention or roughly, to warn and punish. Altogether, except for her sloped forehead and unusual feet, her body was very much like a modern woman's.

And yet *she* was different. Her naked body was a call to other hominids that she was there, still a young, warm, genetic mechanism. It was the outward translation of that anxiety in her brain, about what was happening to her species.

She was the clan's alpha woman and she had not been pregnant in two rainy seasons. With three exceptions, including the baby she was breast-feeding, she was related by blood to everyone else.

Of the seven adult females, three of whom were pregnant, two were her sisters, two more her half sisters, and the others cousins of some degree. Of the fifteen or so children, running, playing tug-of-war with fallen vines, three were her own daughters and one was her son. She also had a nephew she had not seen in a while, the child of a sister who died about the same time her youngest infant had died.

Now that nephew was sitting on the low branch of a tree, his face swollen, his cheeks and chest scratched and bruised as if he'd been beaten.

Long Toes sat just high enough to kick away any of his cousins who might try to pull him down to the ground and start spanking him as they'd already done twice that day.

But he would pay them back in kind over the next few days. That is, if he stayed on with the clan.

Right now he wasn't sure he wanted to do that, after the punishment he'd received for going away for months, and after eating nothing all day but grass and leaves that rasped up his tongue and made his breath go sour. That woman who looked and even smelled like mother was still not mother, and her heavy stare meant absolute authority. He had forgotten the feel of authority, but he was reacquainting himself with it, and he did not like it.

Another female was lingering close to the alpha female. She was shorter, but she had longer jaws. Her hair was rougher and thicker, and she had broader feet. Her shoulders and buttocks were shadowed with short dark hairs that also showed on her face. But her eyes were equally brown and filled with a kind of vulnerable warmth that swept over Long Toes and made him uncomfortable.

She had a deep scar on her thigh, which had healed coarsely. She stayed near the alpha woman as if some bond tied them together. That crippling scar had been healed by the alpha woman, who had cleaned it with her tongue and then covered it with clay mixed with saliva. The baby that the alpha woman was breast-feeding was this shorter, robuster woman's baby.

Long Toes had never seen his long-limbed kin tolerate a robust australopithecine. This robust woman and her infant girl puzzled him greatly, because he was too young to connect the realities of breast-feeding, weaning, and ovulating again.

The robust woman did not protest the clan leader's proprietorial behavior, but accepted it as part of that deal and bond. The gracile alpha woman had saved her life and then claimed her baby to breast-feed, because her own baby had just died. Now and then, the robust woman's eyes swept darkly over the alpha woman, when her handling of the infant girl seemed brusque or careless. But she restrained herself and continued in her role of lady-in-waiting.

This robust woman also had another child, a male not much older than Long Toes, who was prancing now with the clan's other children. The clan's leader had saved the robust female's life, and then welcomed her with both her children into the clan. But Long Toes was definitely puzzled by the three robusts.

He wasn't surprised that there were no adult males around. That simply made him remember past events in the clan's life, including how and why he'd run off into the savanna.

Those were painful memories, which he'd blocked off in the savanna. But here, there was no keeping them at bay. Everything reminded him: the children's fatigue, the lack of meat, the tense alertness of his aunt, the forest's tangled and obstructed vistas. All of this combined into an oppressive sadness he'd felt since this morning when he'd picked up their trail and finally encountered the clan again.

He couldn't make himself be interested in anything, even in jumping down to find decent food. It was as if the forest were weighing on him, loading him with an unseen hopelessness unlike anything he'd felt in the savanna. The savanna was too active. There, he'd known fear as well as joy, but never this depressed powerlessness.

And for some reason, he felt that the alpha woman, who reminded him of his mother, was responsible for making him feel this way.

There were, however, a few things he liked about being back with the clan. There was the music of busy mouths trading sounds, and the smelly, warm closeness of the bodies. A few things were new and baffling. Long Toes had been away long enough that some of his young cousins had grown up dramatically, becoming almost unrecognizable. Small domes of breasts now adorned the subadult females, including two of the alpha woman's three daughters. The way they looked at him, with their rounded eyes and raised brows, gave him a peculiar feeling that almost made him forget the spanking and the vegetal diet.

The alpha woman's daughters walked about in a giggling threesome, holding up their forty-five-degree profiles and pretending to see no one but themselves. They picked flowers and fruit and threw them at Long Toes and at the other male youngsters. When Long Toes had rejoined the clan that morning, those three girls had scratched and punched him viciously. Yet they did it with a kind of strange intent, as if they were trying to gain information about him.

All of this had left Long Toes with a pleasant/unpleasant feeling that was complicated enough to make him plan to steal away later, after they fell asleep, and return to the flat savanna. No giggling, budding cousins there. No confusions.

On his way down, he would search the lower forest for his friend the alien, who had gotten lost. This hadn't exactly shocked Long Toes, who had noticed that his friend had a peculiar way of getting distracted by things which he, Long Toes, didn't find at all fascinating. That must've happened in the forest. Long Toes was not worried about his friend. He had seen his friend spear a lion while uttering a roar like nothing heard in nature. He must still be roaming down there unharmed or else the boy would have heard him utter again that incredible roar.

Long Toes would find his friend and then they would head down together and make it back to the grassland.

From his perch in the tree he saw one of the subadults, the robust woman's son, ambling slowly toward the tree. He was about three feet tall but sturdier and hairier than the other male youngsters, and he had a sagittal crest across the top of his skull. His matted hair built up around his crest, like a crew cut. His arms were longer and thicker, and he had broader feet than the others.

As he walked toward the tree, several yongsters tried to tease him into chasing them. He knew he was slower, so he snarled. But the others wouldn't lay off, and suddenly he caught one, and growled, showing his clenched and interlocking canines.

The others promptly answered with fake cries, meant to alarm their mothers. The alpha female stood up in the grass; next to her, the robust female looked up and uttered a whistle of warning. The alpha female's three daughters zoomed over to play arbiter, as did their one brother, a gangling, nervous youngster, whose lips constantly pulled back showing his glaring teeth. All together, they overran the robust boy, who began to moan. Finally, his mother strode over, shaking her heavy buttocks, which, Long Toes noticed, displayed the inflated lips of her vagina. Deprived of breast-feeding, she was in estrus again.

The young princesses released her robust boy, who got up on one knee, red-faced and almost crying. The robust mother looked ready to spank her son too. The two of them exchanged stares that said how much they disapproved of each other's behavior. The boy turned his shoulders aside, stepped past the tree, and suddenly grabbed Long Toes, clamping his snarling teeth down on the runaway's leg.

Gashed in the calf, Long Toes punched at the robust boy's head and howled. He freed his leg and kicked at the robust boy's chest, but lost his grip on the branch, and fell on top of his aggressor. Anger erupted in both of them, and in a millisecond, they were rolling on the ground, snarling, punching, kicking, and biting. The robust boy had an advantage with his interlocking teeth, but Long Toes had converted all his stored-up savanna fears into desperate fierceness.

The other boys and girls gathered around them, whooping and yelling, but Long Toes emerged on top of the other fighter so quickly that it scared them. They caught a dark glimpse of the deathly encounters he'd survived while away from them. The robust mother was also scared. She plunged at the fighters and easily pulled them apart because the robust boy was happy to leave the fight. Then she punished him with a crisp blow to the jaw, while Long Toes grabbed the low branch, swung up into the tree, then sprang upward toward the higher branches.

The alpha mother handed the robust baby to another female and closed in, ready to punish everyone involved. The bratty cousins scratched up palmfuls of dirt to throw at Long Toes, who was now twenty feet above the ground.

He wished for his hunting stones so he could have revenge on his cousins and his aunt. Below, she crossed her arms under nipples smeared with seeping milk and remained quiet and still. And into this disarray stepped her ever-smiling son, who swiftly kicked the robust youngster.

Long Toes had seen enough, and was disgusted. He licked the gash in his leg, while looking across green foliage. Down the incline, two hulks were climbing toward the clan's ground.

He broke into the "Grrr" of maximum danger.

* * *

SINCE THE MORNING, WHEN HER NEPHEW RETURNED, THE alpha woman had relaxed her vigilance. She was less scared of intruders up here, on the higher plateaus, where the foliage wasn't uniform and was easier to see through.

The forest floor was drier and rustled more loudly on these sunlit slopes, and for the last few years, there had been less rain during the rainy seasons. Those things together made her aware that the Mau was slowly drying up.

Over the last ten generations, her own breed had been increasing its life span. She had already lived longer than her mother. A longer life span gave the breed more opportunity to notice repetition in life, which in turn had created a primitive sense of what was normal and what was not. They had also experienced physical and mental gains that had helped increase the population and had steadily prepared them for an evolutionary upsurge.

But three generations ago, there had been a cruel disruption.

Today, the clan was still struggling with its consequences. The leader had not witnessed that disruption herself—she was born one generation later, during the retreat from it, but she had lived a life of strife and loss, violence and improvisation. She had lost several mates. She had narrowly escaped being injured and killed.

With the increase in brainpower of the last ten generations, she met the challenge of the future restlessly, sifting through her experience and through the experience remembered from her ancestors, and planning.

Even though her brain was only five hundred cubic centimeters in size, it was already large enough to be complex, and it functioned with such coordination that her basic instincts were present at once in all her brain areas, benefiting from all their various functions. Her instincts of territory, aggression, fight for survival and for power, continuation of her genes, telling her own genes from other genes in her clan and her own genetic species from other species, were not terribly different from the same instincts in simpler mammals, or even in reptiles or birds. Yet they were essential to her humanness, because they were so uncommonly strong. Much stronger than in all other animal breeds.

The little woman with straight brown hair harbored in her brain the beginnings of a conscious anxiety about the future of her race. In that sense, though similar to the brains of other breeds, and almost identical to the brains of many apes, her hominid brain was already utterly different.

Otherwise, the various parts of her brain were not original, though the way they worked together was quite novel. It was their phenomenal cooperation and integration that made this brain an utter success, even without language. For instance, there were certain pieces in her brain, some round, some curved, which science would later call the limbic system. That system concerned itself with primal emotion and motivation. It dealt in unseen processes, which had an unusual translation into obvious physical reactions; accordingly, feeling certain emotions, or becoming aware of certain purposes, this female's eyes would shine brighter, or her pulse would quicken, or her temperature would rise, or she would sweat without having expended any physical energy. Emotion and purpose changed the tone of her voice, or brought rushes of blood to her cheeks and breasts.

Why were such changes deemed valuable, when in most other species expressions were few or even absent? Why should hominids advertise so overtly what they felt, when at the other end of the scale of animal composure, a crocodile would remain still and jagged-faced through all stages of its life?

Because hominids lived to communicate and communicated to live. Even when a hominid was alone, the physical expression of its own emotions went on unabated, for the hominids, out of all species, continuously communicated with themselves about what they felt.

The very primal thinking and planning that usually saved her also absorbed and distracted her. This morning, she had not posted lookouts to warn the clan about intruders. And now, by the time she became aware of the danger, one of the marauding robust males rose right above the nearby scrub.

She instantly let out a sharp rattle from her throat, whipping everyone into action. The babies were yanked off plots of grass, and the young were herded into the thicket at the clearing's other end. Young males of fighting size tore off branches to wave as sticks, but the females chased them into the thicket after the other children. Long Toes looked back to the lower end of the clearing, where the clan's leader and her robust henchwoman were on the ground, wrestling two males with hairy faces and sagittal crests. They did it barehanded; the clan had weapons of flaked stone and bone, but they'd had no time to arm themselves.

The robust female with swollen genitals had instinctively turned to gather her infant and grown son, but the leader in her path had swung her hard toward the intruders. The robust female found herself face-to-face with a male of her own breed. On his chest and belly, long hair radiated sideways, as if from a vertical central axis. His testicles, each apple-sized, were heavily brown, yet his penis seemed deeply retracted, almost absent. His arms dangled almost to his knees, and the hairs on his head pricked up around his sagittal crest. He was twice the size of the woman.

The robust female's sexual emotions churned, but she knew how to hide them. She could have turned and fled, but the gracile woman's sisters and half sisters had her children. Primal deception was thus set in motion. She bared her teeth in a welcoming grin, and rocked from side to side, to swing her pendulous breasts. Turning, she faked running back, stumbled quite artfully, and landed on her palms, exposing her estrus-swollen parts. The male behind her should respond appropriately. Then, aware of no panting charge behind her, she staggered up.

The male had moved aside, as if deferring to the other male, a giant, the crest on his skull fringed with white hairs, his grin revealing missing teeth. This time the robust female tripped genuinely, while both males lunged forward.

The larger male caught the alpha woman and threw her to the ground. On her back, her forward-rotated vagina was dangerously exposed, so she fought fiercely, nails plucking into the attacker's face. The fear of being impregnated by the robust male's short penis made her remember her last baby lying dead in a wooded gully, two rainy seasons back. She had lingered next to the tiny corpse for hours, blowing her breath into its lips, chasing the bugs off the tiny face and limbs that hardened slowly, finally raking dirt with her hands and putting it on top of the tiny thing, gently, as if afraid to wake it up. And that death had made her resolve to avoid other pregnancies.

Not long after that, she had led the clan into the forest's lower range, where they found the robust female, injured and pregnant. This was where their strange bond was formed, and a few weeks later, the robust woman gave birth while being taken care of by the gracile.

Now the robust female didn't want to be pregnant either. The mate she had lost had been a gracile, and she hoped that he was still alive and hiding in the forest.

Almost penetrated, she pursed out her long lips and hooted for help so loudly that the other females across the clearing cringed.

The clan's subadult males just could not resist it. Two, three, four, including the robust woman's son, sprinted out of the thicket looking for branches and sticks. They saw Long Toes ahead, plopping down from his tree, landing on all fours, and clawing hard at the ground.

All he could find was a lump of sandstone, which was brittle but heavy. There were no better stones in view. It would have to do.

His own memories were rushing back. The bones of the eleven males in the quarry seemed to come alive in front of his eyes, and he saw them fight their robust attackers. He lifted the sandstone and raced.

The robust woman had thrown off her attacker with knee kicks at his furry stomach. The alpha woman, struggling to keep herself closed up, bit her attacker until she could get out from under him, but was grabbed again, from behind. Fortunately, the folds of her labia were dry and taut. Teased by her resistance, his penis was erect, and seed that was designed to be quickly and randomly spread came surging out. It was then that a large lump of stone slammed at his head, making him slip down to his death.

Sticks and dirt were pitched at the other robust male, who jumped upward, caught a branch, and lifted himself into a tree. He brachiated away.

The cheering little males would have chased after him, but the alpha woman sprang up, her face so pained that it looked as if her eyes had disappeared. She gave her savior, Long Toes, a terrible swat for having rushed to help, and let out the high sound of checking the clan's numbers and packing up and leaving. Then she tore off a big leaf, clumped it into a vegetal mop, and wiped that wasted seed off the back of her thighs.

Now, trekking through the trees with his kin, Long Toes remembered everything. He remembered other treks like this when the young were escorted away from a location that had become unsafe by the tense and unusually harsh mothers, while the fathers went away, on mysterious forays of their own.

The fathers came back from those forays thinned in numbers and limping from injuries, their arms painfully sprained or broken and held close to their bruised bodies. And some of them did not return at all.

When they returned, the fathers had a strangely savage look in their eyes, which made them seem repellent and yet heroic. All those shades of feeling had grown up inside Long Toes into a powerful yearning to follow the males, to find out what they were doing, and to become one of them.

Finally, he had sneaked away from the clan, four rainy seasons back, almost two years ago. He followed the males, scared that he might be discovered and be forced to face his father's wrath, yet also hoping for the right moment to show himself and be accepted in the warriors' party.

For several days, he followed them out of the forest and across the flats, biding his time.

As he was mustering his courage to let his presence be known, the gracile males were hit by a strange invasion from the flats that chased them back. They ran bleeding from cracking lightnings and strange roars until they ran into an ambush set by a band of hulking robust males, who were waiting up in the safety of the rocky spurs. The robusts pushed an avalanche of boulders down onto the graciles, crushing all eleven of them.

This was how Long Toes' father had died, never knowing that his little son, the boy he had taught to hunt, had been stalking him.

The son had witnessed the carnage, blocking it out of his tiny memory. And yet he had stayed on the savanna, free also of the memories of his clan duties.

But now he was back with the clan, and with his memories of them.

THESE MEMORIES WRAPPED THEMSELVES AROUND HIM, AND held him shivering in the grip of a cool, remembered fear.

But it wasn't in Long Toes' nature to remain in the sad land of the past. He became aware of his feet pounding the forest floor, of his cousins' bodies moving nearby across the brush. He looked ahead into the forest and into the present.

Far off, he saw a tall shadow, and his heart quickened. It was his friend the alien carrying himself with that weird gait, so rigidly straight.

He couldn't help chuckling. The alien looked so funny.

Then, pictures of what he should do to keep the clan from hurting his friend flashed up in his mind. He should race down and turn him around, and force both of them back down toward the open spaces but there was no time to do it. The clan spotted the stranger. He looked utterly different from anything they had ever seen. The stranger looked up, and the surprise on his face seemed to light up the undergrowth. He raised both arms, with a greeting that was almost a prayer.

The victory over the two robusts had filled the clan's little males with confidence. Now they charged down, their strong heels flashing, and fell on the stranger, slamming him against the dry forest floor.

T HE ADRENALINE ELECTRIFYING KEN'S BODY WAS UN-
like any he had felt before. It was as if a drug had been
injected into all his organs at once. His heartbeat deafened
him. His eyesight gained such clarity it became an almost
surreal daze. His empty stomach knotted up, distended, contracted again, while his bile shot quick bitter squirts into his
throat. He tasted blood, and wondered if he had ruptured a
vein. He hadn't, but he had clenched his teeth so hard that
he'd lacerated his gums.

He could not afford to acknowledge this fear if he wanted
to survive. There were easily thirty hominids, and a dozen
of them rolled in his direction to capture or kill him. They
were all young, all between three and four feet high.

He saw Long Toes too, who was cutting back and forth
through the rolling tide, making sounds. Ken recognized him,
but wasn't sure Long Toes still knew him.

Another boy, barrel-chested, with longer jaws and a distinct sagittal crest, ran ahead of the others. His hair was
pricked up stiffly on both sides of his crest. Long Toes tried
to deflect him by bumping into him, but the one with the
crest was able to clutch at one of Ken's shoulders, while one
of the subadult females pushed Ken. At the same time, a
young male whose lips were pulled back over his uptight

little smile kneed Ken in the stomach, making him fall to the ground.

They all had slants to their foreheads, but otherwise were so varied that Ken's eyes jumped feverishly among them, noting details that his mind could not organize. The youngsters landed on Ken, and a fire of panting breaths swept his face.

As he took their repeated blows, he understood why they had seemed so varied. His mind had sealed Long Toes' image onto his fantasies of Long Toes' breed. He had expected them all to be mass-produced replicas of the boy, who was clearly one of them. Except for their remarkably similar sloping foreheads and protruding jaws, they all looked different—in the shapes of their faces, in their varying amounts of muscle, in the way they reacted to him. But what had he expected? These were *a living breed*! No two chests were alike, and no two stomachs were swollen in the same way. Some of their lips were thin, apish, while others showed the beginnings of an almost modern fleshiness. The same was true of their nostrils and ears. Their only identical feature was the breathless astonishment with which they stared at Ken.

Ken felt the same astonishment. He couldn't make his eyes wide enough, or his brain roomy enough, to take all of this in.

He heard them rasp and screech over him, and could make out Long Toes' voice like a distinct motif of his own. He liked the way that pile of bodies weighed on him because it reduced his trembling. He smelled their spiced sweat. Dark fingernails pulled at the hair on his chest—he groaned, and they pulled at it harder. He squirmed, and the young protohands, frighteningly strong when added together, held back his arms and legs so that other protohands could pat his ribs and feel his belly and crotch under his pants.

The button above his zipper popped, and the zipper itself tore open. The hard fabric of his bush pants gave way as the hominids began tearing his pants and boots to pieces. Some rough grabbing and pulling made him cry out and fight, but suddenly he was captive and naked.

Ken instinctively pouched his hands over his crotch to protect it, but his feet seemed to draw the most curiosity. He had never been ticklish, but the fingers scurrying over his soles, toes, and ankles were unbearable. With a giggling moan, he managed to kick his feet free.

They drew back just a few inches, and he gawked back at them, feeling like he was dreaming.

Long Toes pulled his cousins back by their elbows and shoulders—Ken saw his anxious expression, checking whether Ken was still alive. He got the impression that the boy wanted him to do something, but he didn't know what. And then he guessed it—Long Toes wanted him to utter that dreadful howl that could frighten a lion.

Out of the corner of his eye, Long Toes saw his aunt, the alpha woman, hurry down, followed by the adult females, including the robust mother. The group around Ken parted, and she saw him staring up with terrified and astounded eyes.

She silently bent over him.

A knot in Ken's throat stopped his breathing. All he could see was the alpha woman's eyes. They shone like the eyes of a live sphinx.

He noticed the enlarged areolas of her milk-filled breasts, which added a touch of softness to her otherwise aggressive stance. Her long-fingered hands and lightly downy arms gave off a wiry strength. She put out her hand and touched him briefly, as if to make sure he was real. Her touch felt hard as wood.

As she stared at him, Ken got up face-to-face with her, breathed deeply, and started howling so loudly that he blasted the female back with the sheer strength of his voice. Then he stood in front of all of them, defiant though terribly vulnerable without his clothes. While the spell of his howl still lasted, he headed for the closest climbable tree. The males of the clan could show up any minute, and they might not be as intimidated by howls.

Quickly, he was hugging the tree, naked like the protohumans, equal to them. *Muscles, limbs, don't fail me now.*

But a rumble behind him stopped him from climbing, and he turned.

The alpha woman was hustling the clan away from him and into the trees, in a chaotic little column. Long Toes and some of the others glanced back at him. Their over-the-shoulder glances seemed like the strangest way to close that scene, leaving him behind, one solitary naked visitor.

Instantly, Ken hurried after them, trampling dead branches, grass, forest floor debris. He briefly thought about the clothes they'd destroyed, but quickly forgot about them and what they represented. His own future was the next few minutes; his world was the next few yards with that naked breed hurrying off ahead of him.

He was not used to walking barefoot but kept up fairly easily because his feet were more streamlined for walking than theirs.

Ken remembered that female's sphinxlike gaze and her obvious confusion. She had spared him for now. She wasn't clear about what he was, or how to deal with him. Long Toes had helped too. Ken's life hung now on the will of an alpha woman and on the influence of an eight-year-old.

And yet he was rushing insanely after them instead of thinking about saving his own life. He ran faster. He tore through a giant spider web. He had wanted to be caught up in this web, he had striven, worked hard, hoped and prayed to be where he was now. His bare feet were stepping into prints left by true primal feet, and his naked body was fighting its way through a naked and unprotected forest whose every beat of life was naked, undisguised, unprotected by culture.

He had wanted this, and now he had it.

He pictured Ngili on one side, and Haksar on the other, all three of them naked, trampling the forest floor. Haksar's knowledge about uncontacted tribes would have been invaluable now.

He followed the clan's movement up ahead. From the back, they could be any aboriginal tribe, except for their slightly sidling gait. They wore absolutely no ornaments, shells, necklaces, or plugs in their ears. It was as if their sense of personal beauty had not surfaced yet.

His mind suddenly focused on the enigma of their presence. He forgot his hunger, fear, and exhaustion. How could this be? How was it scientifically possible that they had survived and remained undetected?

His only answer was this habitat. He told himself that this was a unique tract of wilderness—a slice of live Pliocene.

It sounded like a joke.

And where were the males? Away hunting? And when they returned, how would they react to him? Were the furry creatures from last night this breed's males? If so, it made no sense for them to raid the forest's lower limits while this matriarchy hid on the higher slopes. But why had the boy wandered into the savanna by himself?

There was so much Ken did not understand. What good were his fifteen hundred cubic centimeters of brain, if he did not understand what he saw?

He tried to tell himself that he wasn't alone, that he had him, the boy. It didn't work. That sense of oneness was simply not there.

The boy and he were no longer a species of their own.

Ahead, the clan moved into a clearing made up of midsize, densely packed lobelias, and of giant alpine heathers draped with a moss known as old-man's beard. The heathers made Ken wonder if they had reached seven thousand feet of altitude or over, though the air wasn't particularly cold and his breathing was not strained. Heathers were usually found on high crests, where the winds inhibited the growth of tall trees. There were also bushes loaded with an unknown type of nut that grew in clusters like grapes. They were shaded by two wild banana trees, whose fruits were wrapped in an unusual reddish rind.

In the banana trees, Ken saw creatures he had never seen before: big tarsioid animals with giant eyes that moved slowly on their handlike paws, peeled the red bananas, and munched on their pulpy flesh. Tarsioids were the breed from which monkeys had developed. Ken studied the lobelias and heathers, and was struck by how tightly they ringed the clearing, shutting off the rest of the forest. This habitat was even more ancient than these protohumans, Ken reflected. *I'm trapped in a Pliocene black hole.*

The alpha woman stepped toward Ken and stood just a few feet away, scanning him until he realized that her stare was a message of some sort. He backed away until he hit a tree; then he slid down to the grass and covered his face, praying that his gesture would convey submissiveness.

He waited behind his closed palms, his face in the dark, his mind so cranked up that it felt strangely dry. Dry like a tinderbox waiting for a spark to turn it into a blazing flame.

After a few minutes, when he hadn't heard anyone rushing toward him, he sneaked a look.

The children had started playing their tugs-of-war with the lianas hanging from the trees. The alpha woman was headed for the banana trees, with the infant girl tottering after her. The robust female tore off a strand of old-man's beard and entertained the infant with it, while the alpha female dug between the banana trees and pulled up a large dried branch with cashewlike nuts hanging from it. And then she yanked up a side of mboloko antelope shiny with worms.

So they ate meat, and this clearing was where they kept it.

Ken wondered why they would eat forest carcasses when there was so much fresh game in the savanna. The antelope was old and its forelegs knocked against each other like sticks. Yet, he hadn't eaten in twenty-four hours, so the mboloko carcass looked only mildly repellent to him.

The clan gathered around the alpha woman, elbowing each other into a certain pecking order. She stepped away carrying the meat, indicating that some of the hominids should follow her. When she sat down again, she had arranged her family in a different pecking order. Her designated nanny, the chunky short woman, sat on her right. The young male with the perpetual grin sat between her legs, like a true firstborn. The others sat farther away, giving each other a stroke or a scratch before the food started coming toward them. The mothers held their children between their legs and shared the food with them. On the whole there was little fighting, as the bits of rotten meat were passed down. Old meat for appetizer, dry nuts for entrée, guessed Ken, and indeed the nuts followed. Then the ones with better teeth tore the branch into bits and chewed the dry wood.

Long Toes kept staring at Ken. The alpha woman glanced at him, and Long Toes instantly looked down at the meat in his hands and chewed on it, acting completely integrated.

The chunky short woman got a few good pieces for herself and her infant girl. She chewed them into a paste and fed them mouth to mouth to her baby, who was momentarily back in her arms. Other adults fed their children mouth to mouth, making the meal look like a show of sloppy kissing.

This might be it, Ken thought. *The birth of the human kiss!*

A silent and rough affectionateness overtook the scene. Chewing on a piece of wood, Long Toes made eye contact with Ken. Maybe he had wanted Ken to see this scene. Maybe he had sent Ken that message, after the robusts' nocturnal attack: Follow me, and I will show you my clan. Follow me, and I will lead you to the other humans.

Ken tried to laugh, but his laugh was close to tears. Some lion killer he was.

The alpha woman stared at Ken with a kind of defiant immodesty. She rubbed her feet together in the short grass, as if in a nervous tic.

What would she do if I got up and walked closer? he wondered.

He knew that she would not tolerate anything that would endanger her little tribe.

Long Toes was now sitting on the grass, mobbed by a bunch of children who were uttering short but insistent sounds. Were they asking about the savanna? Perhaps about Ken too? Their little faces kept turning around to stare at Ken, then they would turn back toward Long Toes. And every time Long Toes met Ken's eyes, he would turn his stare quickly to the darkening canopy, perhaps signaling that they had to wait until dark.

Ken replied with the slightest nod.

The adults started roaming about the clearing, preparing places to sleep. They moved back and forth right past Ken with curious glances, yet never ganged up on him. Ken wondered if the alpha woman had somehow declared him off limits.

It was clear that they had a good sense of time, because their shelters were ready just before the sun slipped beyond the horizon. Then it was night.

KEN WAITED UNTIL THE CLAN'S SLEEPY SOUNDS DIED DOWN before he crawled closer to where Long Toes had lain down to sleep.

The big fireflies kept kindling up and pursuing each other, and he turned on his back to watch their flickering night missions crisscrossing the darkness. Then he started to hear sounds. He sat up, and saw two bodies lying down in an embrace. One was Long Toes; he was uttering a whine that sounded more or less like "niawoo, niawoo." The alpha woman was squeezing him in her arms, her mouth to his body. She was soothing his bruises with her lips and tongue.

Ken held his breath, sharing their unique intimacy.

The boy made that sound again. She responded with soft grunts, which seemed to make the boy cuddle tighter against her. Again, with her tongue and lips, she appeased the pain of his scratches and cuts or maybe just expressed a love she had withheld before. Long Toes responded to her squeeze with his own and called out to her, "niawoo, niawoo," while she worked on his shoulder. She caught something, a splinter perhaps, with her protruding teeth, and then pulled. Her lips made a spitting noise—if it was a splinter, it was out now. Then she made her own "oowai, oowai" sound, almost like the wailing of a baby, while he responded with "niawoo." Both sounded more meaningful and complex than any of the sounds the boy had made in the savanna. They sounded almost syllabic.

Niawoo . . . A similar sound, *niawo,* meant "mother" in Swahili.

Was this the sound of human offspring whining for the motherly tit? Would it come to really mean "mother"? Who was to say that the most basic words had not been created that way? Ken listened, breathless. Were they really "talking"?

He shifted his position, ruffling the grass. The female raised her face, her tenseness showing instantly in the stance of her shoulders, and her larynx started that warning rattle that sounded rudimentary and apish.

Ken pulled back and waited. The alpha woman lay on the grass again, and the primal dialogue resumed.

There wasn't anything he could do but fall asleep listening to the music of protohuman larynxes.

He became aware that it was cold, and that the gray forest floor was wrapped in amorphous mist.

He blinked and saw that it was dawn.

He looked up and saw the alpha woman hunkering down beside him. With the hardened edge of her palm, she split open a tuber, bit from it, and chewed. She put her palms on his shoulders and drew him to her; she wanted to feed him mouth to mouth!

He hiccuped in shock and fought her. Chewed tuber paste fell from her mouth and she scooped it up with her fingers and pushed it into his mouth. Tasting the lukewarm, sour and watery paste, Ken started spitting and coughing.

There was a round of throaty titters. He did a double-take. The three young girls who resembled the alpha woman had squatted right behind him. He felt the warmth of their breaths, welcome on his frozen back.

He angrily wiped his lips and chin, then combed his fingers through his hanging hair, which made the females guffaw because his fingers had smeared the goo on his hair. He jumped up and was instantly aware of his dangling naked-ness. The alpha woman got up too, and he was afraid that she would next become fascinated by his genitals. His stomach was churning mercilessly. I should've taken that tuber, he scolded himself. Prissy idiot. I've passed on food and on a friendly gesture that might have admitted me into the clan.

One of the daughters eagerly bit from the tuber. He felt so starved that he dropped disappointedly into the grass, while the girls rose and pranced off, amused with how they had started their day. Ken dipped his face in the grass. Tiny droplets of dew sprayed his face, and he fished a few with a parched tongue. He was deathly thirsty.

He looked for Long Toes, who was just stirring up, next to two other boys, the one who always smiled and the one with the crew cut. All three had hugged in sleep, letting their rivalries go.

The alpha woman came over to Ken again and handed him a palmful of leaves.

He took them and stuffed them into his mouth. They tasted awful—bitter, dusty. He spat them out and uttered a whine, clutching his hands over his stomach, aiming to show her the most pleadingly starved look a paleoanthropologist ever gave an ape-woman.

She pulled her lips back in a smile. The mother in her needed no more explanations. She rose and walked off, and he jumped up and stepped right after her, resolved not to screw up again.

Long Toes stared after them with a frown, then eased himself from the clasp of the other boys and stood up.

Ken braced himself for another dusty carcass. If there was any meat on it, he'd bite off the outer layer and chew again until he found some edible protein. His stomach's rumbles seconded the plan.

She was treading on at a healthy clip, quickly getting away from the clearing, so he enjoyed being able to watch her amazing body in its bipedal motion. She paused to dip her lips in a puddle, and he drank from it too. She printed her bare feet on a plot of wet earth, and he stepped right on her footprints. She turned and gave him a fully toothed smile, and walked on ahead. As he caught up, she brushed a shoulder against a moss-covered trunk, watched him with raised brows, then lowered her eyes, down and away. He whined again and made that slashing gesture against his stomach. She raised her hand to touch him. He jumped back and broke into a panicked giggle—had she brought him to this quiet spot with that need for seclusion that even apes had when feeling sexual?

She thrust her warm knee at him, and tripped him. He crashed down.

She was down next to him instantly, sticking her hands in the ground and pulling out a long white worm. She bit off its head and presented it to Ken's twitching lips.

As hungry as he was, the sight of that decapitated worm made him shiver. He closed his eyes and took it. The worm was cool and tasteless; its real taste was the twisting movements it made against his tongue and palate. He struggled hard, closed his eyes, and swallowed. When he opened his eyes, he saw the woman put the last of the worm in her own mouth and close her eyes too, as if she were trying to learn a new trick.

He started to laugh. Her eyes opened instantly, but he couldn't stop laughing, so he covered his face with his palms. When he dropped them, she had also covered her sloping face. Then she dropped her hands, rose on her knees, and, with a strong roll of her shoulders, let him know she wanted him to dig in the soil for his own food. The thudding of their knees on the ground had made a whole crop of worms sprout out of the dirt, and she threw herself on her stomach, yelping, to catch as many as possible. A dew of perspiration covered her amazingly thin waist. She sat up, munching with hunger, and it struck him irrevocably: She was a savanna creature. She and all her kin were misplaced in the forest.

He struggled with the same feeling the boy had forced on him in the savanna, that he could not ask questions or expect answers. It was a magically frightening feeling.

The alpha woman got up and laid a dozen of the worms

on the ground. Then she stepped toward him. He hopped back to maintain his distance, but she lunged to stroke his belly. A storm of panicked thoughts filled his head—could she be meaning . . . ? Then he realized that she was worried about his gut, which was already gurgling and rumbling. She stroked him up-down, up-down, as if trying to soothe a child. Then she paced away, yanked a purple potato-shaped fruit from a bush, and brought it to him. As if to prove its edibility, she bit on the fruit. She held a piece in her mouth without chewing it, her lean cheeks swelled out, perhaps to show him that he had to hold it that way to absorb its juices.

He did as instructed, letting the fatty juice seep out of the fruit, oiling his throat.

She put out both hands to feel his upper body and palpated his chest, shoulders, and arms until he grew nervous again. Then she walked to the lowest point of the gully, hunkered down, buttocks in the air, and dipped her hands in the ground again. She dug slowly, until the hole foamed with muddy forest water. She looked up. Again that roll of the shoulders, telling him to try it.

He dropped to his knees and dug in, vaguely aware that her gesture might have some additional meaning. Soon muddy water wet his fingers and her meaning became clear. He jumped up.

She was gone. She had finished teaching her survival course, and abandoned him. She had zigzagged too many times for him to be able to follow their trail in reverse.

She must have done this intentionally. She didn't want him around because he was a disruption and he might bring danger to her clan.

At least her Stone Age pharmacopoeia had calmed his churning stomach. He felt full, and comfortable.

He started hearing sounds ahead, not unlike the clan's. Wondering whether he'd been wrong about her, he walked up across thick brush. He moved forward for a few instants, then stepped on a slippery pile, and when he looked down, he dived away from it, muffling a scream.

What he had stepped on was a hominid's torso that had

been halfway eaten. He could see into its chest cavity, where severed blood vessels hung where the heart and lungs had been. The head, the arms, the lower parts of the body had been torn off; ligaments, tendons, shreds of muscle purple with dried blood showed instead of the missing limbs. Bloodied vertebrae, detached, lay on the forest floor, like shattered beads lost from a macabre bracelet.

He jumped ahead, cleaving through foliage, and saw four robust australopithecine males tearing the corpse of another hominid. They were eating it.

Sweat drenched his skin. The closest eating male was hairy and red-eyed, and had a tall sagittal crest. His jaws were so huge that they resembled that ''black skull'' that made students wince when they visited the university's fossil vault. One of the robusts bit from the other dead hominid, to a soundtrack of grunting and sloshing syncopated by the snaps of breaking bones. The dead one's face was ripped up except for a cheek and ear and one side of the neck. That was all that was left from the gracile hominid, whose features were like those of the woman who had just abandoned Ken in the forest.

Two of the feeders leaned back in opposite directions, to tear apart a crotch whose scrotum rolled flaccidly from that tug. A loud crack announced the parting of the pelvis. Across the grass, other robust males rushed to claim pieces of that delicacy.

Somehow Ken managed to hold on to his sanity. He pulled back. The leaves in front of him merged again, blocking his view of the feast.

ALL AT ONCE, HIS SCIENTIFIC BRAIN, AN AMAZING MACHINE of abstraction, drew everything together: The Mau and the plain right below it, where he had met the boy, formed an *ecotone*, an overlapping zone of several eco-geological habitats. The savanna and the forest, the wooded slopes and the grassy clearings, allowed a multitude of life-forms to survive together. But this particular ecotone's uniqueness was that it overlapped not just in life-forms but also in time. Ancient tracts and pockets, like that Pliocene clearing, became the meeting place of older and younger species. Among them, not one but two breeds of human ancestors had found the needed conditions to follow their own evolutionary clock, slower than the rest of the planet by two million years.

But . . . What clawed at Ken's heart was the evidence that while other breeds had successfully accepted each other, these two hominid breeds were fighting to the death. Which meant that they had been recently forced together into an area far too narrow, a slice of the ecotone that was this particular southern end of the Mau.

The ecotone's magical coexistence was shattered right here, by the war of its two most evolved species, the forest hominids and the displaced savanna hominids.

I don't want to see this, thought Ken fiercely.

But there was no way that he could step back and leave, forgetting what he had seen. He curled a finger around a stem, and moved it aside, letting himself back into the cannibal feast.

He watched. Ahead of Ken's flimsy cover, a female moved in, on all fours. Her hanging genital cleft showed between her buttocks as she knuckle-walked past him. She had no breasts, just fully grown nipples. A baby was clutched around the back of her neck. Another female with a baby stepped erect out of the thicket, followed by a gang of females, walking either upright or on their knuckles, all of them carrying infants, all of them nippled but breastless.

Ken's eyes were goggling out of his head. The robust female he'd seen in the clan was limber and had fully formed breasts. She must be a second, perhaps third, generation crossbreed. These archaic robusts had repeatedly mixed their genes with the graciles, by raiding the graciles' unprotected females.

Ken remained crouched behind his cover, noting that the males showed some crossbreeding too: The sizes of their jaws and sagittal crests varied. Not all displayed the same interlocking canines. These hominid pockets had been mixing their genes for some time.

The meat made the females laugh excitedly. One, large, young, her waist still unthickened by childbearing, shook her head, signaling sexually with her hair. The females squatted behind the males until every male had a harem of several mothers, each balancing her baby while pushing for a spot, with obvious subservience toward the males.

Ken listened, wondering if he was losing his mind. These hairy hulks walked and they "talked." Their calls went beyond being just signals for danger, hunger, or sex. They had to be carrying personal messages; indeed, the women's sounds took on the ring of *chatting*.

Ken clenched his fists. He remembered fighting the hairy robusts that had attacked him and the boy. They had been raiding the savanna's edge that night for gracile meat. He flashed on the exposed grave of those gracile males in that rocky corral.

They had fallen in an intraspecies war, but what had started it?

As the males finished feasting, the females made room to eat what was left. They bit the dead flesh differently from the males, less gluttonously. A young mother kept glancing at the large robust male that had first caught Ken's attention. She was hoping they would get together sexually after they had both finished eating.

Ken could not believe how much his eyes had adapted to this horrible scene. His stomach was knotted and his nails were stabbing into his palms, but essentially he wasn't repelled by it. Now he watched as the large robust male got up on slightly flexed legs. Seeing him full stature, Ken realized that despite his size, he was quite young. His muscles had the strapping roundness of a teenager turning into an adult. A very large scrotal pouch adorned his crotch, and its pubic hair was just setting in. It was the least scary part of him. The penis itself seemed absent; eventually, Ken glimpsed a tiny mushroom-shaped glans, with a dot of an opening, squashed up against the pubic bone by the unusually large testicles. The male looked around, and another female, the one that had thrown her hair about, came toward him, swirling her mane again to interest him.

The young male could not make up his mind between the two willing females. Ken couldn't resist seeing this and stepped out from behind his bush, then raced in the clear and plunged behind another bush. The females, sensing the male's indecision, started sending more flirtatious signals. All three approached a bush with the purple potatoes the alpha woman had given Ken. The younger female zoomed over and bent down to pick a few of the fruit, which exposed her swollen cleft. The one with the child figured out what the other female was doing and bumped into the male, rubbing her hand between his legs. Instantly, his penis pointed outward, still shockingly small for his size, but the more experienced female guided her lover into her posterior lips, without letting go of her baby. She shoved herself at his loins, once, twice, three times, then peeled off and knuckle-walked away.

The young female rival did not seem discouraged. She bit off one of the fruits, then enticed the male after her by holding up the rest of it. He playfully hurried off, his little glans already beginning to stiffen again.

Run, stud, into the jungle of fatherhood, Ken thought with a chuckle.

He got the sense that the horde was slowing down, ready perhaps for a deserved siesta. He heard a faint rustling of foliage above him. Looking up, he saw a thin-limbed hominid arm-swinging in the tree. Strong but clumsy, he dropped from a higher branch to a lower one, utterly silent, for all the while he carried a hunting stone in his teeth. He looked like a larger version of Long Toes, except that his face had a scraggly beard. He was a gracile male, and he crawled along the lower branch, stopped, and took the stone out of his mouth.

Quickly, Ken scanned the trees but didn't see any other hominids, so he looked at the scrub and saw a thin file of gracile males approaching, ducking, then inching their faces over bush tops, then ducking again. Each time their faces rose above the bushes, they stared at the robusts lying lazily in the clearing.

Ken opened his mouth to shout, then bit his lower lip.

The gracile male in the tree raised his stone in a precision grip and waited for the branch to stop swaying. The advancing gracile warriors looked thin and stylized, and there were shockingly few of them. As they passed him, one glimpsed Ken through the grating of a bush.

The stone thrower in the tree launched his hit, and the other graciles charged forth, howling high and hard. As they fell on the unsuspecting robusts, the two breeds looked like two clashing mirrors of humanity, one just slightly more refined than the other. Ken yelled out before he could check himself. The gracile that brought up the rear guard launched his stone at Ken but missed. Ken remained standing and yelling until another stone struck him in the head. He sank in the bush as if he had never been there. Ahead, the band of graciles launched their stones at the robusts, who would have been sitting ducks if they hadn't been warned by Ken's yell. Still, three of them were pelted, and the others ran away. The robust females seemed better organized; the young females swung up into trees, then reached down from low branches, and the mothers lifted their babies to them. They were lighter than the males so they could swiftly brachiate away.

Several of the robust males dived to claw dirt and pick up downed branches. The graciles retrieved their hunting stones from the bodies of the dead, but as they prepared to throw them again, a naked alien creature rushed into the scene, and howled and yowled, bouncing up and down like a crazy baboon. The graciles re-aimed their stones at Ken and pelted him on the forehead, in the chest, and against his hairless belly. But he kept bouncing and yelling, until both breeds pulled back. When he finally collapsed, they stopped stoning him. The robusts drew back without retaliating, and the graciles vanished toward unseen heights, without claiming victory.

* * *

KEN SHIVERED AND CAME TO HIS SENSES. THE BATTLE WAS over.

He sat up and staggered to his feet, terrified of what he would find.

He saw the fallen bodies of one gracile and three robusts. One of the robusts' handlike feet twitched. It belonged to the young male who had been frolicking just instants before. Pink foam sputtered out of his nostrils and lips. His throat rattled. His chest heaved spasmodically.

Ken rushed to lift him. He passed his arms under the robust's armpits, latched his fingers over the massive chest, and then, supporting the head with his own head, Ken started dragging him toward a tree, to prop him up in a sitting position. Under the ape-man's left pectoral, he detected a heartbeat. Ken felt like urging him not to die. The ape-man was so heavy that he had to stop several times until he reached the tree and sat the hominid against it.

Instantly, the ape-man's big head fell to one side. Ken gently lifted it, feeling that the head itself must weigh almost thirty pounds. Blades of grass were stuck on his hairy, long-jawed face. The big creature blinked its eyes open, dying but still curious. It saw Ken. Its big teeth tried to lock in an aggressive snarl, but didn't make it.

Hang in there, Ken prayed, and he thumped gently at the big chest. One minute ago you were prancing about, alive and giving life. Hang in there.

Ken took the thick wrist and felt for the pulse; there wasn't one.

The head was sinking to one side, but the eyes kept up that glassy inquisitive expression. Then the huge shoulders dropped, as if losing their inner support. The big creature had died.

From somewhere behind him, Ken heard Haksar's voice, as clear in Ken's head as if he were really there.

"He was dead already. Not worth dragging over," said the old professor. "Besides, the robusts are evolutionary dead ends. They didn't make it past the middle Pleistocene."

Haksar is not here, Ken thought. I'm imagining that polite, learned voice.

He replied, to the empty forest, to the old teacher who wasn't there, "The robusts are not dead ends, at least not here. And you came here once. Yes?"

"Let's say that I did."

"Why didn't you publish a report? Why did you keep it a secret?"

"Let's say that this was my joke. The joke of an old tandoori on everyone else. Now, you amaze me, Lauder. Risk your life for that of a near-ape. You're made of the stuff of saints, and of delusional psychotics."

"Thanks."

"What do you want to change, Lauder? What can you improve, by making this place known? Evolution has spoken, natural selection has spoken, man's history has spoken. These hairy australopithecines, big or small, robust or gracile, were ruled inferior. End of the story, and beginning of science."

"Your kind of science. What did you do here, Raj? How did you find this place? How did you leave it?"

"Why should I tell you?"

"The graciles are clearly savanna creatures. They would never have returned to the forest of their own choice. This is the other breed's habitat; no wonder they're fighting for it. So, something happened. The fact that you didn't tell anyone proves that something happened."

"There's a clue in this forest. If you find it, you'll know the story."

"I'll find it."

"Be sure to live to tell. Good luck, Lauder."

"Raj!" It was all a fantasy, and yet Ken called aloud at the man he had not seen for years. "Stop! You can help me with this. And not just me, you can help . . ."

"What? Humanity?" Haksar's voice, with its discreetly Hindu-tinged Oxford accent, acquired a viciously satirical edge. "What for? I wanted a better humanity too, Lauder. I sought it in the past and found my lesson. Besides, humanity is entirely relative. You're freaked out that the gracile woman might fancy your lily-white dick; well, doesn't she seem entirely acceptable now, compared with these protocannibals? Doesn't she look human, comely, fuckable?'' His voice in Ken's head thickened with a kind of stayed vengefulness. "I always hated you, Lauder. You and Ngiamena. A black Masai and a fair and freckled Scot. Your genes are so extreme. Mine are in the bloody middle, neither Aryan nor black. . . .''

"You hate yourself, Raj. And you're dishonest.''

"Possibly. I'm weak. Weakness begets dishonesty. Good luck, Lauder.''

The voice started echoing, taking on a strange chopped-up resonance, as if falling through layers of time. "Good lucklucklucklluck, Lauderlauderlauder . . .''

Ken was awake. The corpse next to him was real, and so were the corpses a few feet farther away.

THUNK! A hunting stone zapped the tree trunk next to his head and rolled down between him and the dead robust. Another stone thwacked next to his chest and hit the corpse. Another stone lugged hard at the dead chest, and Ken saw that another line of brown faces was hurrying across the brush, coming for him. Thank God they did not brachiate as fast as the robusts. He hurled himself down, feeling a pang of guilt that he was leaving that body unburied. The graciles could easily be cannibals too. Those gracile males were stalking sadly in an uneven forest war, and they hated the forest's green hell, its tangled pressure cooker, its incestuousness. They yearned for the open, just like Ken and Long Toes did. They yearned to return to the magical savanna. But something held them back.

Those graciles were gaining on him. THUNK! A stone hit a sapling next to him, and decapitated it.

He started to run and glanced over his shoulder. They were running too, closer now, but a little disadvantaged because they had to plunge down to pick up the stones they kept throwing at him. But they kept throwing and chasing, and he wondered, if they caught him, whether he'd be able to kill one or two of them before they ripped him apart.

They were getting closer.

He took a terrible hit under his left shoulder blade that felt as if it had jolted his heart out of its place. Cheering voices behind him made him imagine the joy of the hunters. Good hit! One more like that, boys! He knew that the next shot might throw him to the ground, and they'd overcome him before he could jump up again. He began to hear thudding feet. A few seconds, and their breaths would be on his back. He felt a great sense of waste. He'd seen man's ancestors, but would never live to tell. . . .

Fear so disrupted his logic that he hoped for any wild thing that could save him. Long Toes, where are you? Talk to these madmen! But Long Toes had run off to the savanna to be away from these madmen, or from what had made them so mad. Passing a big tree, Ken thought how relieving it would be to dive into it headfirst, smashing his brains. That would be it. Lights out. End of the show. Finis.

Feeling that his heart was giving out, he stopped and turned, expecting the charging warriors to reach him and kill him.

He was so shocked that he gasped. The charging warriors were slowing down.

He whipped his head right and left, frantically looking for an explanation. Through the trees, he saw a kind of indistinct low tower. He found his last strength and raced instinctively toward it.

He passed a line of trees and stopped, so shocked that he lost awareness of everything else, including his pursuers.

He stood in front of what looked like a macabre work of art.

A tree that had been split in half by lightning rose before Ken. Its branches had shriveled, and its bark had curled up and fallen off. As if on a pedestal, two skeletons had been propped up erect and fastened to its dried-up trunk with vegetal twines. The skeletons had been yellowed by time, overgrown with moss, and had lost many segments of bone, but

Ken could tell immediately that one was a sapiens and the other was a protohuman.

The sapiens skeleton wore a colonial helmet and an old camouflage jacket, which the bugs had eaten into a green doily. The protohuman skeleton was covered with old-man's beard moss to lend it its apish look. The one in the helmet had thrown a rusted wire snare around the protohuman's neck, and the protohuman's hands were tied to the snare, giving the rude but clear impression that the creature was fighting that choking device. The legs of the sapiens skeleton had been bent out at the knees, giving it a crab-legged air. Its skull's gaping cheeks had been filled up with packed dirt, which had hardened into a face; on one of the cheeks, a gummy stain, dark and square, looked like . . .

Like Sergeant Modibo's tattoo.

Ken's mind jetted back to the present.

He quickly turned around to see if the graciles had followed him to the gruesome exhibit.

They had not, but he could hear their noises and knew they had not departed.

He stepped toward the morbid ensemble, and other bones cracked under his bare feet. Like vanquished fighters, more hominid skeletons lay around the tree trunk. They looked like they were from light-boned graciles. Time had stripped off their flesh, except for a few fragments of tissue too dry and hard for the bugs to care about.

Climbing lilies had found their way onto this structure; their color varied from lively red to a purple that looked a lot like stagnating blood. That vegetal blood had not been planned by whoever the gruesome artist was; the flowers had simply invaded the old bones, giving them a look of fresh massacre.

By the look of the bones and their state of disarray, Ken concluded that the creation was twenty to thirty years old. Of course, it could be even older. Forty to fifty years.

He kept looking back at the two fighting skeletons. Modibo and that anonymous australopithecine. Their stance depicted a kind of cruel smugness on the part of the sergeant and a stunned desperation in the protohuman.

I should've killed that crab-legged gnome when I had the chance, thought Ken. Next time I meet him, he's a dead man, he promised himself.

Finally he escaped the spell of the fighting skeletons and moved away to inspect the clearing, until he stepped on something round and hard. He stooped and picked up a tin can, its lid still in place. It was an old packet of Zebra insect repellent, advising: "Caution. Avoid contact with plastic spectacle frames, and fabrics such as Acetate, or Rayon." Ken was familiar with this bush supply, but had never seen it in that kind of package. He figured it was really old, from the fifties. Maybe that monument was built in the fifties? He dropped the can, took a few more steps. Something shone faintly on the ground, so he bent down and pulled up a round, corroded object hanging from a rotted leather strap.

It was a wristwatch.

Ken wiped it with his fingers, stared at its greened-up face. On the back, he read the name of a Swiss watchmaker, and three engraved initials: I. V. H.

He stared at it a moment before he realized what they spelled: Induprakash Vasant Haksar. Ken looked back at the helmeted skeleton, at that cheek that had been stained to evoke a tattoo. Modibo and Haksar?

That thought baffled him completely. It could not be. What did they have to do with each other? How could they have ended up here together? And why had they fought the protohumans, and erected that grisly memento?

"Raj, what did you do here?" he asked loudly. "You are a scientist. How could you become mixed up in this . . . in this . . ."

He could not name it. It was a crime, but of a kind and purpose he could not fathom.

Ken lingered a few more beats, wondering whether the tattoo might not personify Modibo, or whether the initials spelled someone else's name than Haksar's. But that could not be. Before Ken and Ngili brought back their fossil, Haksar had never disclosed any interest in Dogilani. And Modibo had shown up at Ken's camp right after he'd returned to the savanna.

This watch is an important piece of evidence, Ken thought. He strapped it onto his naked wrist.

Then he picked up a branch to defend himself in case of a gracile ambush. But no one was waiting when he walked out of the circle of trees.

That gave him a clue about the monument's purpose. Maybe it was a kind of no trespassing sign, reminding the graciles not to return to the forest's lower ranges and eventually to the savanna. At any rate, it had something to do with the graciles and the robusts being forced into one habitat.

Still fearful, Ken stepped away, trying to get his bearings, and was rammed hard in the loins. He jumped and turned and locked his hands on the horns of a charging mboloko buck.

Nearby, two does were watching the buck, their eyelids low as if they were urging silently, Come on, hotshot, do your stuff. The buck, a stupid male, charged again, catching Ken in the lower abdomen. Ken lifted it by the horns and thrashed it hard against a tree, falling with it. He got up on one knee and watched the vein in the buck's neck pump its last seconds of life.

The does cantered away, little yellowish tails raised like flags. Ken stepped down the slope a few paces, but returned and hauled the buck onto his shoulder.

Then he started down again, man bent under his prey. His body ached and his feet hurt. He became aware that his toes and soles were bleeding. He was leaving a blood trail on the grass.

Then he saw a male hominid standing in his path, leaning against a tree. A lookout.

He misjudged the lone male's size. He's so small, Ken thought. If he's alone, I can take him. He eased the dead antelope off his shoulders. Just moving the dead body seemed to make his own thinking flexible. I'm not going to fight him. We'll share the buck, there's enough for both of us. And then I'll go on my way back to the savanna.

The hominid was one of the clan's youngsters. He was the boy with his lips pulled back in a nervous grin. He allowed Ken to approach him to almost an arm's length, then turned and sidled off at a run. Ken put the antelope back on his shoulder and followed the streak of the running boy. An uneven clamor rose somewhere ahead. Childlike gracile bodies fought through the thicket toward him. In front, his eyes as big as half of his face, ran Long Toes.

As the tide of youngsters got closer, Ken sensed a change in how they approached him. They sounded noisy and hyper and friendly. Following them, in contrast, was the cool, almost glacial presence of the alpha and her henchwomen. She saw the stranger and stepped toward him slowly, her eyes tightened to slits, her lips thinned by contained anger.

Ken saw her, and smiled broadly, with a glint of inspiration in his eyes. He threw himself to the ground. His face against the rotted leaves, he crept toward the leader in a pose of submissive offering, pushing ahead the dead antelope.

H E WAS STILL PUSHING THE BUCK IN FRONT OF HIM
when the alpha mother sat down on the ground. The
other females gathered beside or behind her, while the children dropped down behind Ken, breathing hotly on his heels.
And he, not dumb for a sapiens, sensed that with every inch
of crawling closer he was gaining a degree of acceptance, so
he pushed the dead antelope ahead till it touched the female.

She clutched it by the horns and pulled it onto her naked
lap, while the youngsters behind him breathed loud and
whooped, ready to tear at the fresh meat without any of the
prescribed pecking order. Ken sat up, grinning. The clan had
lost its Stone Age table manners, and almost its whole sense
of discipline.

Some of the females held back, trying to read the alpha
woman's expression, and some dropped to the ground to gain
seats close to the meat. The leader stubbornly lowered her
sloping brow. But it was hard to resist the children's shining
eyes and panting breaths. The robust female leaned over,
holding a flaked stone knife. The leader took it from her hand
and started butchering the meat while holding it at her chest.
As the hungry youngsters pushed, almost knocking her over,
she pulled herself back, and bumped into the sweaty stranger.
He stayed where he was, firm as an anchor. She tried to shift

away from him, but the hungry clan pushed her back against him.

The buck's body had been opened.

Ken dipped his hand into it as if into a tray of food.

Inside the warm buck, he touched hands with the bolder youngsters. He also felt the alpha woman's hand, which was hard and nervous and fast, like an unpredictable little animal.

He tried to court her gaze by glancing sideways at her, and then by dipping his eyes at the meat, showing both shared interest and respectful patience.

She stubbornly looked down at the feeding children.

The buck's innards, still steaming warm, were highly prized for their softness and lack of bones. The eager fingers were fighting for the heart and liver. Ken dipped in, found the slippery liver and tore it out. He lifted it up, above a bevy of hands, and tore off a piece for Long Toes, who lunged to grab it.

The alpha woman shot Ken a brief glance, so narrow and dark that the corner of her eye seemed filled with ink. He leaned toward her, and she chewed noisily, as if to keep him at bay. He sensed that she was nervous almost beyond her brain capacity, and totally at a loss about what was in the best interest of the clan. Should she be suspicious and chase away the stranger? Should she be friendly to a possible ally?

He offered her the rest of the liver. She took a hearty bite, and let it drop into a clutch of begging children's hands. Ken caught a glance from Long Toes to the alpha woman, a glance that was shockingly mature and reassuring, in which he told her that the alien was all right. How long had the boy been staring at her like that? He had seen her take the meat from Ken, and grinned his approval.

Humanity is relative. . . .

The alpha woman leaned briefly against Ken to boost herself up. She stepped to a low branch, tore a clump of old-man's beard, and mopped herself clean from the blood of the slaughtered buck. He watched her. When she stood up, she looked tall from the natural uplift of her skinny, athletic body.

He enjoyed being at rest and out of danger, his stomach processing food, his body warm from the tight ring of youngsters' bodies pressing on him from all sides, his nose taking in the raw and unwashed scents of sweat and dust dried up on skin. The whole translated into a familiar feeling of being at home.

But he feared something in this peaceful scene, and he finally identified it. He'd lost his own sense of being different. *They* were already so human.

He looked around at faces that were already familiar and felt he needed to give them names. Long Toes had been Long Toes for a while. The little boy with a sagittal crest became Crew Cut. The robust female he baptized Busta. And the alpha woman, *the* mother of the whole clan, whether by blood or just by position, became Niawo, mother in tribal idiom. And her ever-grinning son he nicknamed Smiley.

The champing and gnawing youngsters weighed so hard on him that he finally moved to push them away. He freed his legs. Long Toes uttered a whoop of surprise and pointed at his feet, which were swollen to double their normal size and were leaking blood onto the grass. Instantly, a huddle of children gathered over his feet again, touching, pinching, tickling. Acting reassured. The alien bled, like any normal creature.

With her usual nervous impatience, Niawo stepped to see what the fuss was about. She tore leaves, kneaded them into a mop, spat on them, and dropped on all fours to clean his bleeding feet, not gently but fast and efficiently. She took one foot in her thin and hard hand, felt it for broken joints, moved Ken's silly stubby toes, and did the same with the other foot. Then she flung his feet back in the grass, like a spoiled child's. And he tried to hold back an emotional meltdown like the ones he'd felt in the savanna, with the boy.

Back in the savanna, he'd fallen in love with that boy. He couldn't afford to fall in love with all of them. He started laughing. Niawo stared at him, and nervously raked her long fingers through her tangled hair.

Then she rose, and her entourage, including Busta, followed. They trailed away, trading sounds he could not understand. Busta pointed in one direction, then in another, perhaps "discussing" the system of lookouts for the night. Niawo seemed very irritated. She nodded her agreement to Busta, but then made some high-pitched sounds and slashed the air with her hand, making a gesture which, from chimp to sapiens, always sent the same message: She'd had enough.

Ken sat up, watched by the children. The females were momentarily away. This was as good a moment as any.

He grabbed a stone knife that lay bloodied on the grass and swept aside dry leaves, leveling a stretch of dirt with his palm. He started drawing a turaco bird—beak, claws, feathers. Even a primal mind would recognize such features.

Long Toes hunkered down and peered curiously; other youngsters gathered, while Ken cleared away more ground so he could draw an acacia tree with zebras trotting underneath.

Warm breaths wafted over Ken's neck and shoulders, but the ongoing chorus of whoops and whimpers was one of surprise, not recognition. After all, most of these children had never seen the flats, he told himself, while drawing a giraffe. He drew it picking at the acacia's top with its long prehensile tongue. He drew, erased, drew again, trying to capture the animal's realistic details. The sky, the openness of space, the distant horizon, the sun, could be rendered only with agreed-upon visual symbols. No matter how much he wanted to, he could not really draw the savanna.

The children buzzed hotly among themselves. Long Toes made noises, perhaps explaining. Ken pointed his finger at Long Toes and made all the others laugh, which made Long Toes squint at him, confused. Then the other children pointed their own fingers at Long Toes, and there was more laughter. Ken took the boy's arm, held up his little hand, and closed it into a fist. Next he squatted and drew the boy's fist clutched around a hunting stone. He glanced up over his shoulder. Their eyes were narrowing, bladelike with concentration. He drew the rest of Long Toes, throwing his stone at a savanna hare.

Ken had sweated, and his tongue hung out—why did humans stick out their tongues during work requiring attention? What part of the brain's older wiring was being reactivated? Ken assumed that those were archaic reflexes, left from the prehominid apes, who still used their mouths to catch and hold, just as man's fear of falling was another leftover from when all future humans still swung around in trees.

He felt an unexpected coolness on his shoulders and looked up. The ring of attention had recentered; the faces were no longer aimed at him but at Long Toes.

Long Toes appeared to be telling a story. Ken stepped forward and dropped down behind a crowd of tiny naked backs.

Long Toes "talked," but his talk was as much for the eyes as it was for the ears. He turned in semi-profile, and made a sound that was not his usual "rrrrr." Holding his head to one side, with both his arms lateral, he flapped his hands quickly, then slowly, like a . . . like what? Like a plane's propeller coming to a stop? Ken choked, realizing that Long Toes was miming Hendrijks's plane landing.

He was more than stunned; he was awed. And yet he wasn't truly surprised. Miming predated language. These creatures didn't understand drawings, and they didn't need them. They had learned to mime out in the open spaces, where voices don't carry far and where visual signals are essential for hunting and stalking.

Ken felt stupid about the drawings he had sweated over, and yet he was excited that they had prompted Long Toes to tell his story. Long Toes was already showing them that the alien had appeared out of that thing from the sky. His finger pointed at Ken; the children's faces turned toward him, then back to the little narrator. Long Toes "talked" using the short sounds he had used in the savanna, but his gestures and changes of expression were much richer. He grinned, frowned, smiled again, glared, sulked, blinked in dismay, all the while standing up straight, then relaxing, then bracing again; he was describing scenes of suspense and high drama. He raised a palm, raised both hands, clenched his fists. He shrugged, swelled his chest, and pointed at Ken with his hand or his eyes. But Ken noticed that the audience was turning toward him only briefly or not at all, because as a notion he'd been accepted and was part of the story.

Long Toes playacted hunting scenes. He evoked an enormously challenging character, the lion, by simply yawning with his lips wide open; and then he roared uninhibitedly, and jumped back looking terrified, playing himself now, scared by that lion's charge. Using a mboloko bone, he demonstrated how the spear was used to kill the lion, apparently done by Long Toes himself because no faces turned toward the alien! He playacted the heavy feline's fall, and the pulling of the spear out of the body. Then he held the bone up above his little face, and let it drop, and Crew Cut instantly grabbed it.

Long Toes had fun, that was obvious, and he knew how to grip his audience. The children's faces had become little mirrors of his stormy expressions, and their fists balled up involuntarily. They squawked in surprise, then sighed in relief, as if they were watching a movie.

Long Toes' richness of gestures would be superseded in his later offspring by complex, fully developed language, but gesturing would remain in the wiring of the human brain, making the modern sapiens move their eyes, lips, eyebrows, hands, arms, shoulders continuously. That gesturing would be automatic, as a remnant of a much less verbal, much more visual ancestral language that Long Toes was speaking now to his enraptured cousins.

Ken lowered himself to the grass, watching Long Toes tell them how they had met and hunted. Brilliant, Long Toes, he thought. First step toward getting all of us out of here and back into the savanna. He smiled, with hope, and confidence, and, truth be told, with no small amount of ego. It might never get in the papers, nor be discussed in scientific forums, but in the scientific forums of his fantasy, Ken saw himself being recognized for guiding an ancient breed back to its habitat. He was helping to establish the natural course of evolution in the planet's other humans.

He felt in his arms and chest the memory of dragging away that dying robust male. He glimpsed Haksar's watch on his wrist and remembered the morbid monument of skeletons.

He did not want to think of death. He looked around. The adult females were watching Long Toes, but their reaction was more subdued. Were they worried that their children might be lured to the open hunting grounds? Ken noticed that Busta was breathing hard, and the others stared fixedly and shook their shoulders from side to side—like irritated chimps before a full-tilt tantrum of charging and throwing.

He got up on all fours to move away and to find someplace to be alone and think. Apishly lumbering on all fours, he found Niawo in his way. She had cleaned herself of the buck's blood, and primped herself, it seemed, for she had stuck a number of green lanceolate leaves in her hair. She put one of the leaves in her teeth and munched on it, making it give out a pepperminty scent.

He looked at her. She looked back.

She looked almost vulnerable now, nothing but a core of life weighing less than a hundred pounds. But he reminded himself that she had unhesitatingly dumped him in the wilderness. What would her little mind be up to now?

Long Toes finished his story, and the excited gaggle scattered in the grass around him. The other females mingled with the children, giving Ken guarded stares. He felt he knew what they were thinking and he thought they were right to be worried. He was a big problem.

Ken lay down next to Long Toes, who leaned close and threw a possessive arm over him. Ken closed his eyes. Visual memories of the savanna paraded across his mind. He saw his first encounter with the boy—the two of them drinking from that mucked-up water puddle. Then he felt that something was wrong with the way he was remembering those scenes. Reality had descended very close to the ground. The colors were not as bright. The perspective seemed flat. But he could make out the animals' movements with incredible accuracy. The charging lion appeared in his head and terri-

fied Ken more now than when he had stood alone in the
lion's path.

And then he saw a light-colored being, whose top organ
seemed familiar and yet utterly stunning; as did its other
limbs; as did its movements. That unknown creature raised
an object that seemed to shine, though it was not luminous
or transparent; it had a special shape, straight and thin, that
gave it uniqueness and made it glow. The lion rushed into
that object, was gored, and fell, shaking the savanna. The
odd being let out the glitter of its eyes, and the jarring sound
of its throat, a loud, discordant bray. The odd being was . . .

It was himself, and he understood the meaning of the
strange visuals, the odd angle at which they framed reality.
He was seeing the savanna, and himself, as Long Toes did.
He was receiving the boy's view of their encounter, a view
in which Ken, the sapiens, was the other human.

Ken opened his eyes. He felt the need to sit up and utter
some skeptical expression like "Come on," or "This is too
much."

But his sapiens language seemed to have vanished from
his brain. Instead, he found himself in *their* space of cognition.

He became very scared.

He looked around the clearing. Everything in it, every leaf,
every blade of grass, was closer and looked flatter, and yet
stood in sharp contrast to all other shapes and objects. Probably because australopithecine eyes were not as good at far
sight, not as familiar with open spaces. The womblike closeness of the forest needed much less awareness of space. But
anything that moved and existed within that close range felt
more powerful and real, as if its influence on an individual's
life was dramatically stressed.

His senses other than sight and motion had also sharpened.
His skin became a kind of vibrational field for the body tem-
peratures that surrounded him. Dirt on his own body felt very
irritating, and yet he wasn't repelled by it. He reached and
scratched himself, on his chest, shoulders, and belly, on his
legs, between his toes. His body was layered with leaf and

dust and forest decay. He freed his pores with his fingernails, and let them breathe. Somehow, he noted that early man's bath was a scratch and pick and groom affair. It did not use water, which was for drinking. Later, when water was encountered in abundance, in the savanna, it would be through swimming that early humans would learn to clean themselves with water.

He saw himself as the protohumans saw him: top-loaded, uttering brays and performing a collection of strange, jagged actions. Yet he was acceptable, relatable. A gushing happiness came over him, and it was warm and blind like a climax. We're not so different!

He *knew* that the graciles wanted to make contact with him, even though they were scared and puzzled about his role in their future. He saw Niawo, who seemed very close to him, probably because of that flattening of the perspective. She breathed on him and he felt he was smelling not a hominid female body but a *desperation of the genes*, which included a burning curiosity about a certain part of his body.

That part was his loins.

There was nothing unusual about his loins per se, but Niawo sensed that he had no offspring and was even more mystified because she also sensed that he was not here to find his female.

That desperation of her genes awed him. He looked into the protowoman's eyes and felt that it was something so basic that it encompassed all her other faculties, physical or mental. It became part of her intelligence, resilience, courage, sense of purpose, and quickness of choice. It was so strong, and appeared so legitimate, that anything in its service, even killing other humans, seemed justified.

Ken looked at the protowoman's gift with envy, and then reached within himself, to see if he, as a sapiens, still had that gift.

Unexpectedly, he touched deep inside himself and found such a parching yearning for a female, such a thirst to unite with a woman, that every atom of his body and every pore of his unwashed skin shivered. He felt he was lying not on his naked back but on the unexplored mysteries of his lineage, on an ancestry that stretched back into the Pliocene.

He tumbled into Niawo's eyes, as if into a bottomless well of instinct. His heart quickened, and he prayed wordlessly, though he wasn't sure for what. He prayed until, mercifully, she got up and walked off, away from him.

Then he slipped out of the protohuman's cognition. The desperation of the genes had not left him, but its throb subsided. And his sapiens language skills kicked back in.

HIS FIRST CONSCIOUS THOUGHT WAS: I'LL KILL YOU, RAJ Haksar. And you, Modibo. I'll kill you all if, willfully or not, you did anything to steer this breed toward their extinction.

Then he called out in his mind: Ngili, old friend, you gotta come here and try this. It's stronger than Uganda Blue. Uganda Blue was a variety of grass the two of them had smoked when they tended bar at the Naivasha Hotel. It was a wretched, lethal weed that was said to kill if one indulged long enough.

The desperation of the genes was not fuzzy. It was the most limpid hallucinogen, because it was not a drug. It was just the reason to be, itself.

NIAWO LED THE FEMALES INTO BUILDING THAT NIGHT'S shelters while Ken watched her, feeling her tenseness.

She picked out young stems, bent them, and tied them at the top with an awkwardness he had never witnessed in her. He started sweating. Was she building a shelter for her . . . and for himself?

No, no. Enough madness.

How could he know what was in her mind? She had deceived him that morning, so he knew she was capable of deception like all humans, even if she did not have an abstract mind. Her mental abstraction was survival-oriented; it was deception, the skill of not communicating directly, of withholding. Physical reality was concrete and honest, but survival required scheming and seducing the others into a made-up reality, which could be done very well without language or abstract thinking.

Ken lifted his face to the alpha woman as she trod back toward him. He was ready to tell the proto-temptress that he was aware of her abstraction/deception skills, and that he would stick around, tempting her back with the benefits of an alliance until he figured out why he was really here. And maybe . . .

No, no.

I'm not the Ulysses of these islands of ape-nymphs. I'm a modern man. I am . . . Kenneth T. Lauder.

His name, which he'd never been at odds with, now sounded ridiculous. She gestured for him to crawl over and tumble inside that green home she had built. He stared at the little hut of leaves, trying to figure out whether it was for one, for two. When he passed the woman, he was sweating again, and he shivered that she might read that as some form of sexual interest.

He was halfway inside when he felt the push of a warm body, hitting at his buttocks, making him fall inside. He turned on his back, desperate to fold up his knees and defend his genitals.

It was Long Toes, pushing to make room for himself like a pup in an already occupied doghouse. Outside, Niawo caught Ken's eyes and snorted. She spat out the wild peppermint she was chewing. Then she got up and tied the roof above both of them. Ken grabbed Long Toes as if he were a shield. The boy snuggled contentedly against Ken's sweaty skin and burped one of his end-of-the-day, I'm-happy-and-tired kind of burps.

The alpha woman grunted away the other children who'd gathered around. Her ever-smiling son tried to loiter, and she pushed him, then busied herself breaking more stems and tying them up, adding on to the shelter. When she lay down, she did it almost spoon-style against Ken and Long Toes, and he felt her warmth combining with his own and the child's.

He had become so appreciative of any bodily comfort. Though he was nervous about her closeness, her warmth eased him into a deep sleep.

HE WOKE UP TO A FINGER TOUCHING HIM ON THE BACK OF his calf.

He sat up numbly, blinked at the dark, and found out that he was being touched not by a hand but by a foot. Niawo was rubbing her long, fingerlike big toe on the back of his calf.

She was leaning into the hut's opening, staring at him. Then, brushing against him, she reached inside. He held his breath. But she only shook the boy by the shoulder. Long Toes bounced up, hitting his head against the roof of leaves.

With her outstretched arm, she motioned over the sleeping clan toward the forest beyond the sleeping site. She was telling them they were free. They could go now if they liked, back to their beloved savanna. Now, while the clan was asleep.

What the hell should I do? Ken wondered.

The little primal female seemed very tiny and vulnerable.

Ken felt a paralyzing lack of decision, mingled with a kind of cowardice. He had been asleep in the warmth of other hominid bodies. He did not feel like confronting the night.

A sound in the distance made all three of them start. It was a kind of heavy yowl.

Long Toes sat up instantly, shoulder to shoulder with Ken. He was tense though not panicked. The yowl came again, followed by a wild racket of voices clashing with other voices, some of them jagged with aggression, others foggy and hoarse as if from sleep. One sleepy voice soared into a bloodcurdling scream, and the vast unseen territory came awake with cries of pain, as if a lot of creatures were screaming and dying all at once. The two breeds were fighting again, and one of them was gaining the upper hand.

Easy, Ken told himself. You were lucky you didn't walk away into that ambush. It will be over in a second. Better hold on to this little creature. The boy was now shaking with his whole body. Ken pulled him close, thinking again: *Enough,* how many of you savage males are there, killing each other blindly, in the night? There's no sense in this killing, there's plenty of space, there's no need . . . More bloodcurdling screams. Thuds. Yells of encouragement, loud urges, signaling a second attack. It was an almost musical fracas of . . . what? Of death, in the dark, in the Pliocene forest. Ken clenched his teeth. Enough. Enough. ENOUGH.

All the females had bolted out of sleep. One, close by, yowled in such loud panic that two others finally jumped on top of her, muffling her with their own bodies. It was Busta, the robust female. The other females exchanged brief sounds, like commands on a ship in a storm. Their offspring began to cry, and the mothers slapped their hands over their crying mouths. Niawo rose and stepped hurriedly into the trees. Two other females followed her, and all three disappeared, while the remaining ones squatted nervously, ready to clutch and silence anyone else who panicked. But no one else did. Everyone, even if they couldn't guess the outcome of that distant battle, knew what it meant. Even the children's silence suggested that they were horrified, although not amazed.

Finally, the battle began to subside, and the screams and hoots of pursuit moved farther away, making the night feel endless. Then there was silence.

Ken kept cradling Long Toes at his chest. He felt the boy's heartbeat like the flutter of a bird's wing.

Then Ken saw Niawo walking back through the trees. The others followed, with slow steps, as if they knew the outcome of the battle. The females that had been holding Busta prisoner freed her, and the little robust woman rushed in her swaying manner to the alpha woman, beginning to sob. The leader received her at her breast, and the two females staggered back together, in an embrace that spelled loss for the robust woman, and relief for the gracile.

Ken lay down, trembling, trying to fight his own selfish relief. In the forest, the graciles were the winners again.

"Y OUR APE-MEN, CYRIL, ARE GETTING EVERYONE EX-
cited, but no one's opening their checkbooks," said
Ramsay Beale, a top London investment banker, who had
been at Oxford with Cyril back in the fifties. "Harry Ends
at Royal Dutch Shell passed on investing this morning, after
asking me with wild eyes, What do those chaps look like,
Rams? How big are they? How do they boink? Everyone
asks about how your creatures boink, Cyril. Harry'll be at
my dinner tonight. I thought I'd give him a chance to change
his mind. He'll pump you breathless, you'll see, but I doubt
that he'll commit a shilling."

Ramsay and Cyril were driving toward East London in
Ramsay's Bentley. They were taking an unusual route, south
of the Thames, down Jamaica Road and other streets that
had once been London's historic heart. Now they were the
main arteries of colorful ethnic sections. Anderson had suggested this route.

"What about Her Gracious Majesty's government?"
asked Cyril, using mock formality to ward off another potential rejection.

" 'Fraid it's a blank. The prime minister said, 'This project's a billionaire's toy.' I hope your friend doesn't expect
us to chip in."

427

"Not anymore. Is the prime minister coming to your dinner too?"

"I don't know. I did ask him."

London was wrapped in a methodical, microscopic, nasty drizzle. It made the traffic look like a primal universe ejecting four-wheeled nebulae. A truck nebula formed dead ahead. Cyril yelled, "Watch out, Rams! For god's sake!"

Ramsay avoided the truck. Anderson caught his breath and mumbled, "This city's always the same—wet, busy, and hard to impress. I have a mind-boggling discovery. I can't believe that no one's jumping at it."

"Maybe it's too mind-boggling." Ramsay glanced at his old friend; Cyril was acting frighteningly strained. "If you're asking for millions of pounds, maybe you've got to show us one of those creatures. Why didn't you bring one with you?"

"How would I have done that, Rams? They're not lizards that you can catch and slip into a jar."

"Well, sorry. Our executive crowd is pretty unimaginative."

Anderson had every reason to act strained. A week before, the London *Times* had run a notice on its science page about palynologist Corinne Anderson accepting a researcher's position at the London Museum of Natural Sciences. Her first job at the museum lab was to date an ancient skeleton dug up in Africa by Professor Randall Phillips. Randall was claiming that he had found the skeleton "with assistance from former student Kenneth Lauder." Ngili was not mentioned. In a brief joint statement, Corinne and Randall speculated about the possibility of live protohumans surviving in the unchanged habitat of the Mau.

Anderson had received that issue of *The Times* in Nairobi, in the same mail that contained a brief letter from Corinne. She had decided that their marriage was over and had hired a divorce attorney. Cyril correlated her decision with her name and Randall's printed side by side in *The Times*. He called a few British scientists and learned that instead of going on to his sabbatical at Davis, Randall had stopped in London and was taking the scientific community by storm with samples of bones and shots of footprints. He and Corinne went everywhere together. Corinne had rented a flat in South Kensington, and Phillips was receiving his mail and faxes at her flat.

And they had hired a certain Luke Merrick to help them sell "their find." Luke charged three hundred pounds an hour and was one of the top ten promoters in the British Isles.

The renegades were riding on *his success,* and they had to be stopped. Anderson had called Ramsay Beale, a friend outside the scientific community but infinitely better connected and more powerful, and announced that he would be coming to London and he needed his help.

At Oxford, Anderson had studied paleontology and Ramsay business, but they had become friends thanks to intra-college "pub crawls." The crawls had continued over the years, during Cyril's visits to England, in fancier drinking places, some with ladies' quarters attached. The two men's relationship was in essence empty except for the drinking memories and the extraordinary esprit de corps of old Brit boys who should've ruled the world and hadn't. Men like the two of them had become, in Ramsay's words, "deluxe servicers in the Yank era."

There had always been an unspoken pledge that they could one day call on the friendship born during the old pub crawls. From practically the moment Anderson emerged from customs at Heathrow, he had called in his pledge, by asking Ramsay's help to sell "real protohumans, Rams, which I just saw in the bush. Not just their bone crumbs, not the *possibility* of their survival, but their certified existence. Must find the people to cough up ten mil to study them, and fast, before these three ganefs"—Cyril had used Hollywood Yiddish to sound à la mode to Ramsay, who stemmed from a very Briticized and knighted Jewish family—"steal this from us." The three ganefs were his estranged wife, Phillips, and Lauder. Anderson had explained that Corinne had had an affair with Lauder. Now that her marriage was on the rocks, she was warming up the sheets with Randall, but she still wouldn't let go of Lauder. "Adultery is, alas, not immoral, Rams, not in terms of genes strategy. Corinne wants Phillips for professional security, and Lauder for genetic replenishment. Those are perfectly normal female options."

"And what are the males' options? The girls we keep on the side?" Ramsay had chuckled.

But deep inside, Ramsay had not felt like laughing. The Beales had two sons, one predictably dark-haired, the other inexplicably redheaded. Rams had long wondered why his sons looked so unalike. "I'll help you, Cyril. I'll help you blow Corinne and Phillips out of the water."

"Thanks, old chap. By the way, I'll need you to manage this venture if we get it going. And for now, I need some money."

Ramsay had written Cyril a check for ten thousand pounds and then taken him to Claridge's Hotel. "With a find like this, it's not political to stay anywhere else. But, Cyril, I'm going to talk about this to the world's top investors. So you better have the goods."

"Don't worry." That was called winging it, and in that department Cyril had no rival. Cyril's voice had risen. "I've seen our past, Rams, and it's stupendous, but what's even more stupendous, it's got the future wrapped in it. There's as much to gain from one brain crease, from one tooth of my creatures"—how right it felt, to describe them as his— "as from a space discovery."

"Did you really see those beings, Cyril?"

"As I see you now," lied Cyril unblinkingly.

Ramsay had worked the investors' circuit, at breakfast, lunch, drinks, and dinner. There were stunned reactions but no bites. Money was tight. Cyril had pressed Ramsay to throw an informal dinner for friends, including some of the top people who had said no. He was convinced that in person he could turn them around. "Wait till I describe those café-au-lait little buggers, Rams; they're astounding. With a little breeding, we could perhaps get a new human type going."

"In how long?" asked Ramsay practically.

"Ten years maybe. Pity you couldn't get Royal Dutch

Shell involved; I need someone like them. Good for years of funding and uninhibited by the press and other riffraff.''

This was the morning of the dinner. The Tower of London had fallen away behind them, and the Bentley was racing down Jamaica Road. Rams kept squinting at the rearview mirror, because Cyril had told Ramsay that they might be followed.

"Why would anyone follow you, Cyril? So far, you've had no bites."

"Because, Rams, let's assume that my little chocolate paranthrops can be tamed and observed, et cetera. D'you realize that I'd be letting loose on the human race, on *us,* another kind of human? That would create some dreadful problems." Anderson's tone made Rams stiffen involuntarily. "Like, guarding such a find alone would be a huge logistic headache. And then, if they exist, that sends a certain signal: We sapiens are no longer the chosen, so to speak. They might be. I'd be introducing an unknown that would tear up the world as we know it. Do you understand?"

Pure Anderson. With his voice, with his stance, he opened in Ramsay a cache of visceral fear. The banker felt he had to serve a warning. "We must leave some room to get out of this, Cyril. To backpedal, so to speak . . ."

"Of course," agreed Cyril. "We won't say no to some hush-up money, if it's decent." The banker looked proud to be involved, and rather scared.

"Who are you meeting in Greenwich, Cyril? Another scientist?"

"Yes. One who is puzzling, just like us, the implications."

They entered Greenwich, peacefully wet under the rain. Greenwich Park appeared, staid but still royal under its multicentenary oaks and chestnuts. The Maritime Museum appeared, gray with age, facing the dirty river.

"Can you stay nearby for fifteen minutes, Rams? My date's waiting in the park."

"Sure, there's a little pub in that lane, the Lord Nelson. I'll park by it."

"Thanks." Cyril threw himself out of the Bentley and ambled into the park.

WHEN ANDERSON WAS CONCEALED UNDER THE OLD OAKS, he eased a light portable phone from his jacket and dialed a number in South Kensington. A man answered with a brief, flat "Yes." Cyril identified himself. The man told him that Corinne and Randall and Luke Merrick were across the road, in Corinne's apartment. Cyril asked if the rain had interfered with the taping of their voices. The man replied that the reception had been blurred earlier because the raindrops confused the laser beam, but now the rain had stopped and the reception was clear. Did he want to hear a snippet?

Anderson answered yes. There was the crack of a connection being made, then a voice came through. Cyril recognized Luke Merrick. "I know that other humans than us are an incredible concept, but that's concept only. We need followup. Can we assume that your monkeys out there have in their bodies, in their DNA, some kind of fluid that might treat impotence? or cure baldness? or make us capable of living two hundred years? or . . ."

"Cure AIDS?" asked Corinne's voice, clearly and cuttingly.

"Why not?" countered Merrick innocently.

"What the fuck are you talking about, Luke?" That was Randall. Rumbling in the background, burly, uncouth, especially against the Brit's pedigreed tone. "What are you babbling about? We gave you a sensational find, and we want it sold on its merits. . . ."

"Randall, Randall," Corinne prayed.

Anderson felt himself shake. Corinne addressed Phillips so intimately. There was no doubt about it.

"He's trying to turn protohumans into some kind of E.T.," groaned Phillips.

"Well, yes," countered the promoter. "Why should anyone sink millions into this thing unless it flies through the air or does something else miraculous?"

"It's the wrong approach, Luke," said Corinne, calmly but firmly. "And that's exactly what I had to put up with for years. Cyril is the most insufferable sizzle-seller. I thought I might finally live with a little integrity. . . ."

"Let's not quarrel," said the promoter. "In ten minutes, nine of London's hottest trendsetters will come in through that door." Involuntarily, Cyril gritted his teeth. Over the talk, the recordist's flat voice cut in. "Like the reception?"

Cyril made himself speak. "Yes. I hope they can't hear us."

"Course not. This is sophisticated equipment. Relax."

Halfway up a deserted pathway leading to the Royal Observatory, a man in a hat and a raincoat appeared. Cyril braced himself, whispered hurriedly to the recordist, "Keep taping them. I'll be back there in an hour."

He folded the delicate phone set, thinking that Corinne had been pretty nervy to mention integrity.

He started up, noticing that the other man was sixtyish, with cold gray-blue eyes and a gray little mustache showing between the hat's brim and the coat's upturned collar. He looked like the caricature of a fifties detective.

"BACK IN THE FIFTIES, HAKSAR WAS AN AGENT IN THE Kenya CPS, the Colonial Police Service," said Anderson's interlocutor, as they cruised the park's empty footpaths. "He was fluent in African dialects, and really had no choice but to work for us because he needed the money to continue his studies." The money, always the money, thought Anderson. "Now, when the movement for independence started in Kenya, we easily put it down. There were all those horrible stories about the Mau Mau guerrillas. About their secret oath and how they tortured villagers who wouldn't take the oath, and gouged out the eyes of those who betrayed the oath, and strung them on sticks to dry. It did happen. But we easily put a stop to it because we had the firepower and the planes."

The drizzle fell over Cyril's pumped-up hair and bristled

the other man's mustache, which was small and correctly trimmed, a typical colonial male emblem.

"Do you remember a pilot named Hendrijks?" asked Cyril.

"A Dutchman from the Cape? Yes, we had all sorts of wogs working for us. And more spies and traitors helping than we could handle."

He continued, talking of the waste of war in a voice too passionless to cause sadness or reflection in his listener. "And then we found ourselves in a pickle, because we needed that war to go on, to justify arms and supplies. And to win our stripes, you know. So we came up with this story—*I* came up with it actually." The mustachioed man chuckled with pale pride. "The story was that the Mau Maus had retreated under the Mau escarpment. I looked at the map, saw the name of that mountain ridge, which was the same name as their movement, sort of. So bang, I reported to London that they had retreated there. . . ."

"But didn't they?" interrupted Anderson. "I wasn't in Kenya then, but I heard about it."

"My foot they did," said the man scornfully. "We had put Jomo Kenyatta in prison and scattered the others to the four winds—maybe a handful were still freezing in the snows up on Mount Kenya. Anyway, this started a whole other thing. A head-count frenzy of how many Mau Maus we were catching, and how many we shot. There were never enough to shoot, you know. So I assigned Haksar to the Mau because he was a good spy and I wanted to stress the area's importance, and I doubled him up with a local constable, Kalangi, a real bastard. He must be the one who told you to look me up."

"No," lied Anderson, although Chief Kalangi was indeed the one who had told him how to find the man with the little gray mustache. "I went through the Nairobi press of the time and saw your name mentioned. Then I called a friend here who was in the last cabinet and asked him to track you down."

"I suppose one does that now, even in our privacy-loving

England," muttered the ex-colonial cop philosophically. "Anyway, I got Haksar and Kalangi some poachers, trotted them out of jail, you know—they were in jail at the time. And I sent them all to the savanna under the Mau, with orders to find someone to kill. The poachers had been near that area before. Haksar hadn't. At any rate . . ."

He stopped and looked away toward the river. Even in the rain, the view over the former Royal Hospital and onto the river was nostalgically majestic. "Can you believe," he asked, "that this beauty is for sale?"

"What's for sale? The Maritime Museum?"

"Yes. Upkeep's too steep. And they can't even find a buyer."

Anderson nodded sympathetically. What was England coming to?

"That creaky old empire wasn't so bad," said the ex-cop rancorously. "After all the wars and revolutions, one finds out how much less happy one is with the new deal. By the way, do you have my money?"

"Did you bring Haksar's notes?"

The ex-cop nodded. Cyril looked out across the rain, beyond the park's tall wrought-iron fence, at that pub said to have opened in Nelson's days. He could see the shiny hump of Ramsay's Bentley against it. Anderson pulled out an envelope and handed it to the ex-cop, who took it and put it inside his coat without attempting to count the money. He produced a short and stubby notebook, discolored, with leather covers closed by a rusty clasp. Its stark, ugly design looked military. Anderson took it; it felt heavy and compact, like a shallow rectangular stone.

"There's nothing else of Haksar's you kept?"

"No." Anderson studied him incredulously. "Come by my place to check, if you like. My wife wanted to see who would pay a thousand quid for this."

"Never mind. So what happened after you gave that order?"

"The poachers spotted some kind of oddball bunch under the Mau. Naked, you know. Nomadic, I suppose. The poachers killed some of them and chased the others into the forest. . . .''

"What did Haksar do?"

"Went round the bend a bit. He and Kalangi followed those oddballs into the forest. They lost them, but according to Kalangi, Haksar broke down or something and wouldn't leave the forest. Kalangi came out alone, and turned in this notebook. Then Haksar came out too, but that was a good two weeks later.''

"Did Haksar file a report?"

"He didn't have to. I filed the reports. I made them up."

"Did you see any of those natives' bodies?"

"No. The poachers stripped them of flesh—which I had not ordered. While Haksar and Kalangi were in the forest, the poachers deserted and made it back to Nairobi, where they sold the skeletons to shops that ground them and resold them, as cock-stiffening stuff, you know? So I threw them back in jail. The trouble was, now we had human bones, supposedly of guerrillas, being sold in the market. The press got hold of it. London freaked. Meanwhile, the real Mau Maus regrouped and started recruiting new soldiers. I withdrew the force and redeployed it, but it didn't matter. We lost the war."

"And you never had any interest in reading this book?"

"No. I only took it out of Kenya because I used books as buffers to secure my collection of antelope horns—still, most of them got smashed. Why should I remind myself of that sad mess?"

"At the time, didn't you have the curiosity to question Haksar?"

"Why? He was a raving basket case. The whole story was best forgotten, and we were all expected not to talk anyway. We were under the limitations of war acts. When you're in a war, it's best that you know less, not more."

"But you keep up with Kalangi, don't you?"

The ex-cop's empty voice was enlivened by a shot of anger. "I certainly do not. I don't give a damn if the murdering bastard became chief of police in my place. I'll tell you, if you want to hurt someone, he's the one to ask for help. Best murder cartels are in the Third World; they're of first-world quality, if you know what I mean. If Kalangi asks about me, don't tell him you found me.''

"I won't tell him. Thanks for the help. Haksar's notes might be scientifically relevant, even posthumously.''

"Glad I still had them. I read Haksar's obituary. Never thought he'd make it at selling curry, let alone at teaching.'' The ex-colonial cop lifted his hat; his thin glued-down hair was as gray as his mustache. "I'll be off. Pity about this park, isn't it?''

They turned away from each other in the rain.

Noon struck at the Greenwich Observatory. Cyril calculated quickly. It was a half hour to drive back to Ramsay's office in the city, where Ramsay would stay on to work the phone again; then it was twenty minutes by cab to Brompton Road, in South Kensington.

As Cyril had promised, he could be back within the hour to an apartment across the road from Corinne's apartment. There, in a room without furniture except for a desk, a chair, and the laser equipment used during the Cold War to "cook" the windows of foreign embassies, sat that recordist, a young man with a short and strikingly vertical hairstyle. He targeted Corinne's windows with a laser beam that caught the air vibrations caused by the voices inside and bounced them back across the road to a receiver that reconverted the vibrations into the voices of Corinne and Randall and their promoter. The recordist listened to the voices and recorded them on tape. Cyril had hired his services at a reasonable five thousand pounds; this kind of equipment had become affordable after corporations started using it in their merger wars.

Cyril hurried toward the Bentley, leafing through the notes, reading here and there and frowning as if confused.

Suddenly, he stood still.

He read with growing attention.

A smile rounded his lips, but he wasn't even aware of it. He read avidly, until a raindrop splashed into the open book.

Then he looked up, hid the book under his coat, and hurried the rest of the distance.

AT THE SOUND OF THE DOORBELL, THE YOUNG MAN WITH A vertical hairstyle took off his earphones and pulled out an automatic. He marched to the door and stuck his eye to the peephole; behind the door, distorted by the lens like a fat carnival dummy, stood Anderson.

The young man let him in, frisked him with one hand while keeping the automatic aimed at him, then stuck the gun in his belt and nodded Cyril into the room with the equipment.

"They blew it," he said, touching his beautiful vertical hair. "They had a posh brunch catered in, with caviar and eggs Benedict and champagne, and only two out of nine guests showed up."

"Really? Why?" Through the window, across the road, Corinne's apartment seemed so close that Cyril instinctively stepped back.

"Relax, they're busy," said the young man. He touched his hair again. "The promoter said they didn't come because that fossil's not really a fossil. Short by a thousand years or so. Sounds like people think fossil, not fossil species." Cyril gave him a look that said, you catch on fast. The young man started affixing a silencer to his automatic. "We do it now? You want to come and watch?"

He held the gun so close to Cyril that he noted a tiny speck of black, an atom of carbon, encrusted in the smooth gray side of the steel. "Not yet. Let that promoter leave first."

"I don't care. Two funerals, instead of three. She's a pretty tough tart, by the way, and comely too. How long were you married?" He touched his hair again.

"None of your bloody business. Your hair's amazing. Where do you have it styled?"

"None of *your* bloody business. I asked 'cause I thought, if you decided to go so far, you can talk about it too."

"Ever heard of a Mr. Kalangi?" Cyril asked instead.

Kalangi had told Cyril of the recordist's services, during an astoundingly brief conversation. "You want something done in London?" the chief had asked. "Five thousand dollars, and I'll give you a telephone number."

Cyril had paid the five thousand. "Memorize this number," the chief had said. London phone numbers had seven digits, but the one the chief gave Cyril had only five.

The man with the pretty hairstyle shook his head. Never heard of Mr. Kalangi. Anderson asked him the name of his boss and the man responded that he had no boss, he was an outside contractor and didn't know the name of the company who referred him for jobs. He did know that the company was an international network providing services that governments, police organizations, private security outfits, and Mafia families could not afford to undertake directly. Cyril remarked that the company must make sizable money. The man replied that the company was said to have offshoots that were public and legal, and issued stock. Cyril asked if such a company would be headquartered in England. The man suspected that the headquarters were in Africa, which, of all continents, was the one least open to international scrutiny.

The man put his earphones back on. He smiled, took them off, and held them up for Cyril. "They're having a pretty hot fight in there, about who botched what. Want to listen?"

IN CORINNE'S APARTMENT, THE LAVISH BRUNCH OF CAVIAR and eggs Benedict lay on the dining-room table, practically untouched.

The only two guests who showed up had stayed a very short time. Over champagne that tasted too cold and acidic for the weather and the hour, they had examined the bone fragments cleaned up in Randall's Nairobi garage. They were exhibited on the dining-room table, on a big piece of burlap. Next to the lavish brunch, the fragments looked small and insignificant, even sad. Randall had fought to make his voice cheerful as he explained why these little shards were so unique: They were *not* a fossil, though they belonged to a fossil species. They had clocked only seven thousand years in Corinne's potassium-argon machine, which meant that a creature of a breed officially extinct two million years ago had lived in modern times! That and the footprint pictures (enlarged copies of Ken's photos were displayed by the bone shards) suggested that protohumans were still alive *today*!

The two guests sipped champagne, whispered politely that the shards were "gorgeous," and didn't get it. Was that a fossil or wasn't it? And what did it have to do with live protohumans? They had looked at Randall and Corinne in puzzlement. Luke hadn't helped, because he kept calling it a fossil, and Randall had to correct him and explain why it wasn't one. Under ten thousand years of ancientness, mineralization was incomplete, which meant this was a subfossil. That confused things even more.

The guests left Corinne, Randall, and Luke alone to ponder this inauspicious start.

Corinne was furious, and outspoken. "You screwed up, Luke. You brought us a couple of simpleminded morons. They don't get the difference between some very clear concepts."

Rarely talked to like this, Luke filled a glass with champagne, heaped some caviar and eggs Benedict onto a plate, and managed to keep his cool. "I'm afraid your concept is a bit confused, my dear." She raised her eyebrows over her steel-blue eyes; she hated his patronizing British tone. "You show bones, but you talk of live beings. You should've brought over one of those beings if that's what you're trying to sell."

"Our associate Ken Lauder is out in the savanna," she said quickly, "observing the australopithecines even as we speak."

"Then maybe we should wait for your associate." Luke wondered if that Ken Lauder had more to do with the find than these two. "You're lucky that Cyril has not presented a live australopithecine either. I've been tracking him and

Ramsay, and they've got the same problem: Where's the thing they're trying to sell?"

"I don't want to hear about Cyril. Help us sell what we have!" snapped Corinne, deeply angry. After repeating the tests three times to ensure against errors, she had gotten so excited that she had pulled Randall into the lab and kissed him dead on the lips. "We'll be famous," she had whispered, blowing Randall's mind with the "we," with how fast she was moving, and with how promptly he himself was responding.

Randall found Corinne only moderately attractive. She wasn't exactly his fantasy of the woman he'd choose to finally cheat on Marcia. But Corinne was the one who had advised hiring Luke, and going after major funding. "They'll fall to pieces, Randall. They'll beg you to take their money," she had crooned as she straddled him in her apartment, half an hour after testing the bones for the third time. She copulated greedily, and mostly on top.

Luke refilled his glass of champagne. "We have to reconceptualize based on your apes, and I think what a buyer would want in them is either some extraordinary mental powers, or sex. Do they have clitorises?"

Randall nodded astonishedly. Yes, they did.

"Brilliant," triumphed Luke. "Why did they develop the clitoris; what in the clitoris is critical for human evolution? Or maybe they can do math without numbers. Einsteins with fist-sized brains. I'm terribly sorry, but with our current globalization of crises, we want a global benefit to sink our money into. We don't want just ancestors. We want ancestors who have the answers, to everything."

"I guess we have to figure out those answers ourselves," said Corinne with sarcasm.

Luke felt tired and unrewarded. He checked his watch. "I'll have to pop off now." He thought that he perhaps should join Anderson's team. But they too had difficulties. He moved toward the coatrack by the entrance door.

"Wait." Randall marched over, heavy and red in the face, a male intent on mending his ego; Luke stepped faster to his coat. "We're going to go back to Africa, Corinne and I. We're hopping on a plane tonight, and we'll be in the bush tomorrow afternoon. We'll get new evidence, boxes of it, and then we'll sell it, not here but in New York, or Berlin. Call Oppelmann and Fidos," he barked at Corinne. "Those are the top German experts. They work with the Max Planck Institute, with the Von Stein Foundation, which are not just science beacons but major funding chests. We tried with you, Luke. We'll do the rest without you."

"Swell, see how far you get . . ." murmured Luke, "and I'll send you a bill." He opened the door.

"The Germans have a sense of culture," Corinne raised her voice at the departing promoter. "They'll go nuts hearing that australopithecines were around when Luther wrote his sermons and Dürer did his drawings of Adam and Eve."

She was angrier than she sounded. She had let herself be carried away by her enthusiasm. The find was not ready to be sold. And Randall was a mess.

"I've got to pee some of that champagne," muttered Randall. He slipped into the narrow bathroom.

With his foot, he lifted the toilet seat, noticing that it wobbled on its brand-new gilded hinges. Expensive apartment, show-offish, and rife with shoddy work. He bubbled his stream out with pain from the carnal excesses with the insatiable Corinne. "Call British Air and book seats to Nairobi," he yelled through the closed door, wondering how long his credit cards would support all this extravagance.

He had impulsively walked off the plane in London, leaving his family on it, feeling that without Marcia, and with the bones in his pocket, the world would open to him in a way that it hadn't when he was twenty, thirty, or forty. But the London scientists were as difficult as the ones in Berkeley or New York. They wanted documentation, proof that the bones were not contaminated, a lengthy paper to be reviewed by peers. They too were puzzled about what exactly this find pointed to. They resisted the notion of the unchanged Pliocene habitat. Instead of becoming an overnight star, Randall had found himself auditioning.

Meanwhile, Marcia had flown on to California with the kids, and now she sent him faxes in care of the De Vere Hotel, which Randall had checked out of when he moved in with Corinne. The hotel forwarded the faxes to Corinne's fax.

Those unpleasant thoughts made him drip on the bowl's rim. He tore toilet paper, wiped the rim, flushed, and washed his hands. He walked out of the bathroom, and found Corinne bending over the fax machine. He stiffened—another whiny message from Marcia?

"Same three pages you got before, from Haksar," she commented, puzzled.

She held them up while her other hand started undoing a button on her dress. He took the pages. "Marcia must've refaxed these by mistake." Drunk, Marcia might do worse; she might leave the coffeepot on, causing a fire.

The pages made no sense. They described the unusual communicating powers of a tribe of Amazonian Indians, the Mayoruna, who had been observed by a *National Geographic* photographer who had been captured by that tribe. Throughout weeks of being with them, the man could not talk to his captors. They, having never seen white people, spoke no Spanish or Portuguese, and he, an American from Seattle, spoke no Mayoruna dialect. And yet the Indians had talked to their guest by telepathy.

She perused the pages over Randall's arm. "This might be the selling angle we're looking for!" She undid another button on her dress. "If earlier brains were wired differently, if they used nonverbal means of communication, that's a tremendous angle for the communications business."

"But why would Haksar send this to me, a couple of days before he died?"

"Don't you get it? To fuck Cyril over!" Corinne crumpled Haksar's pages and launched them at the wastebasket, missing. "We should try the communications angle. It's cold here in these London apartments. Let's stimulate our blood circulation." She stepped out of the dress, rubbed her breasts' areolas, pale and very large, against the front of his shirt. He pinched his lips. "What's wrong?"

"I wonder what Cyril is doing. I wouldn't like him showing up at your door."

"That would be embarrassing, but not dangerous. Cyril's a braggart and a flake, not a killer." She pulled him into the bedroom, kissed him, captured his reluctant tongue. Then she broke free, panting. "I'm getting great ideas about the sex angle too. Like, why did the vagina rotate forward, from being back under a monkey's tail?"

"Because of that damn bipedalism." Her bush was blond, sandy-blond, like her hair. The worst for Randall. His penis hurt around the rim as he pushed in; he'd asked her to buy some Vaseline, but she'd forgotten, while preparing for that brunch. "If you receive a male's sperm, then get up and walk around, I suppose it falls out less easily if your tube's not pointing straight down. . . ."

"Tube. You're so coarse. *Oh.*" She was good at achieving quick orgasms. She exhaled, blowing the hair off her dank forehead. "You're a good lover."

"Thanks. How was Ken?"

"Fine. Uptight and obsessed with science." She pushed him onto his back, with herself on top.

"Aren't you sorry you didn't stick it out with him?"

"The only thing I'm sorry about is wasting my time with Cyril. But that's okay, I'm still young. As soon as I'm a name in the field, I'll go to the best sperm bank around, and I'll have a child all by myself." She was pumping toward another orgasm. "No husband, no co-parent; who needs you insecure male lumps? Maybe you were more secure as protohumans." Coming, she squeezed his penis to wincing pain, then peeled off and fell next to him, while he shrank, too sore to climax himself.

"CAREFUL CROSSING THIS ROAD, IT'S A TERROR," SAID THE man with the vertical hair. He stuck out his arm, grabbing Cyril to a stop. "Particularly for foreign tourists—last month, a car with four Italians took the wrong turn here, into the front of a bus. All four died.''

He looked at the rushing traffic, at the changing lights, and signaled to Cyril, who crossed, weak in the knees. He saw the opposite sidewalk coming at him. Shadows of pedestrians, falling away on both sides. A news man hawking an evening edition announcing a soccer team's win.

The man with the vertical hair carried two gym bags. Amazingly, he had bunched all of his monitoring equipment inside them. He touched his hair once more, before leading Cyril into the lobby of the building across the street. A Jamaican doorman was busy talking on the phone. He gave them an indifferent look.

They stepped into the elevator, and Cyril caught the other man's eyes. The other man returned a reassuring smile. Everything was under control. Failsafe.

I SHOULD GET A DIAPHRAGM, THOUGHT CORINNE. SHE HAD been doing it on top, peeling out at the last second, but still ... Next to her, Randall was silent and still, as if lifeless. Then he whispered, ''There's someone here ... someone came into the apartment. ...''

''Nonsense. The bed was creaking.''

''There's someone ...''

She was so angry she could have punched him. She jumped out of the bed, grabbed a robe, and burst into the living room as she was pulling on the robe. But she felt utterly naked when she saw an unknown man with strangely vertical hair. He was raising a gun with a silencer. Next to him stood her own husband.

Cyril had fantasized about this moment, but when the man raised the gun, something in him tore. This was his wife. He ran to the entrance door, which the gunman had opened with a burglar's picklock, opened it, ran out into the lobby. Behind him, the gunman fired.

Corinne did not realize that she had been shot because the gun made a muffled noise, *skukk,* like a suction cup coming off. She was hit in the chest, as if with a stick. Losing her balance, she reached blindly, grabbing her killer by his vertical hair.

Outside, Cyril heard the muffled shot and a roar. The roar of pain came from a male and so fierce was it that Cyril jetted back inside, not to miss Randall's death. He had no qualms about Randall. Cyril thought he was going crazy; the gunman was rolling on the carpet, pressing both hands over his bleeding head, which had lost all its hair. Corinne lay dying, one hand clutching the hair, which was made of implants that she had ripped off the killer's skull.

Randall was just walking in from the bedroom.

Cyril did not know when he had dived to the ground, clutched the gun, and raised it. The shot aimed at Randall made the same insignificant noise, which Cyril was too busy to savor. Randall fell. Cyril turned the gun on the killer and fired again, *skukk, skukk,* bringing to the face that was contorted in pain an instant relief.

Corinne had fallen faceup. Cyril rushed to the windows and drew the curtains shut. He turned, found his way to the bathroom, where he grabbed a bathrobe and a towel, and rushed back to throw them over his dead wife. Then he spun around. The apartment's front door was still open. He kicked it shut. It had a dead bolt. He turned it, sealing himself inside with three corpses: his wife, his rival, and the hired killer. This had not been so ea-zeeee.

A light noise made him start.

The fax was buzzing again. Cyril stepped over to it and looked. The fax was retransmitting the pages that had puzzled Corinne. Cyril lifted them out of the machine, skimmed them, failed to connect them with Haksar. But he recognized how intriguing they were. He folded them and stuck them in his pocket, then jumped over Randall's body to get to the phone.

Cyril dialled Ramsay's office.

*   *   *

"WHERE'VE YOU BEEN?" RAMSAY CRIED OUT, WHICH Cyril instantly knew that it meant bingo, his friend had good news. "When I got here, I found three messages from Harry Ends. Harry's leaving Royal Dutch Shell to run a capital venture of fifty million pounds, and he needs a really fantastic start-up. So I did something you'd never do, Cyril, I hope you'll forgive me, but I had to. He wanted an answer right then and there, and I couldn't find you, so I wanked off, I winged it. I told him that your paranthrops had a non-baldness gene, which indicated that they might have others like it, maybe a non-impotence gene too, or non-cholesterol, or whatever. Should've called it a youth gene, period. Didn't you tell me that those creatures never made it past thirty? So they lived young all the way. Anyway, I got Harry to fund your project. He flipped."

"Really, Rams?" Cyril's eyes hazed up with a blessed feeling of fate. He stammered lightly. "My creatures g-got even mm-more ff-fantastic stuff...w-wait t-till I tell y-you. . . ."

"Can anything be as good as non-baldness? Anyway, you can make your creatures as fantastic as you like, the more fantastic the better. You'll tell us all about it on the plane."

"On the plane?"

"We're flying to Africa together, day after tomorrow, on Harry's jet."

"What?" squawked Cyril, his stutter canceled. Damn. This was going too well.

"Let me see if I can patch Harry over to you, I have him on the other line. He'd love to say hello. I know you're not at the hotel. Where are you?"

Cyril saw Corinne's apartment number on a sticker glued to the phone set. A London number like a million others. Ramsay would forget it in a second. What the hell.

Ramsay told him to stay by the phone, and hung up. In the few seconds that passed, Cyril realized that Harry Ends would probably ask to see an australopithecine; why else would he want to go to Africa? The time pressure hit him like a giant hammer. He hadn't yet seen the australopithecines himself!

The phone rang.

"Cyril? Hold on, here's Harry."

"Awf'ly glad to talk to you, Cyril," said Harry Ends. His voice was very low, almost like a ventriloquist's.

Cyril braced himself. "So am I," he rushed to respond. "I've seen those creatures, and they're simply absolutely . . ."

"I know," said the deep voice. "I'm awf'ly excited about our new project." Cyril frowned: Proprietorial already, are we? Harry continued unsuspectingly. "And since I was due in South Africa, I decided to stop over for two days in . . . Nairobi, is it? You and Rams fly with me, yes? Free, of course." He laughed; so did Cyril, as if Harry had said something humorous. "Now, we'll see one of your little bugbears down there, yes?" He laughed again. "Can't sink such dough into something I haven't seen." Cyril started to say something, and Harry rode over it with the ease of a man used to ending dialogues when he wanted, and on his own terms. "You've got tomorrow to make the necessary arrangements. If you have to make a lot of phone calls to set things up, don't hesitate, I'll pay for them." He laughed so candidly that Cyril wondered if Harry wasn't reading Cyril's mind, which had at once flashed: telephone. Telephone to Nairobi.

"Great talking to you, Cyril. See you at the airport, yes?"

"Yes. Absolutely. Airport." Cyril no longer stuttered. He just spewed out basic blocks of meaning.

Cyril hung up but his mind clicked on, spewing the same basic blocks. Nairobi. Bugbear. Telephone.

He took a breath, pulled out his appointment book, and flipped through its telephone directory. Harry Ends had been quite clear: Can't sink such dough into something I haven't seen. Gotta get him a bugbear. But wait a second . . .

He had read through Haksar's notes enough to know that Haksar had described that place in his diary. Haksar had described and documented everything. Cyril remembered the photographs he had found in the old man's house, the grossly realistic drawings of the primate anatomy. . . . And Haksar was dead, safely dead.

Instead of rising from the grave to point his finger at Cyril, Haksar was leading Cyril through a journey Cyril had never taken. And Cyril still had time: tonight, tomorrow, and the following night. The day after tomorrow, which would be spent flying, and the night after. Three nights and two days. There was still time.

How lucky he was to have been cuckolded. Without Corinne's adultery, he would never have come to London, he would never have laid his hands on these notes. . . . Fondly, he patted the ugly notebook. Almost affectionately, his eyes stroked his latest victims.

He started; the phone was ringing again.

He hesitated. Letting Ramsay call him here had been a risk. He shouldn't answer the phone. But what if it was Ramsay again?

He connected with his real curiosity. This was Corinne's place. Even though she lay dead on the floor, who was calling her?

I'll pick up, but I won't talk. . . . He lifted the receiver again and felt that it was slippery; his palm was sweating.

"Cyril?" It was Rams again.

Cyril let out a big sigh of relief. "Yes, Rams. Thanks for the good work, old boy, that was fab. . . ."

"Just where the hell are you?" Cyril did not have time to panic. Ramsay's tone indicated that he had no time to listen to an answer—things had become supersonic. "Must absolutely, *absolutely* produce one of those things for Harry to see! A couple of big companies called Harry and told him that they might get involved. They want to sponsor, in their own words, 'a healthy, glorious African project'! The stakes are finally as high as you wanted them, Cyril. They are immense! So make your calls to Nairobi and line up at least one hairy crit. And the last point: Harry already faxed me an intelligence report about that country. It seems that there's a civil war of some type ready to break out over there. . . ."

"Huh?"

"Some ethnic thing? Units of the army concentrating around Masai villages, or something like that?"

Silently, Cyril cursed his friend Kalangi, who had assured him just before he left that nothing would explode while he was gone. But give Africans the glimmer of a chance to mess up, and by Jove they'll do it. As for what was brewing, or why, Cyril truly hadn't the faintest. His best defense was to laugh it off. "The army's on maneuvers, Rams, they're always on maneuvers. Anyway, how would Harry know about that? He sounded fuzzy about where he's flying to."

"Believe me, the database he's using isn't fuzzy. They've got the latest satellite shots at their fingertips. The point is, you know that government, Cyril. Tell them to hold things off for a few days. Or if they're not involved, tell the other side, whoever they are, to hold off. All right, Cyril? Everything in hand? Ciao, old boy."

The line clicked off.

Cyril sat quietly for another instant, pondering whether to make another phone call from Corinne's apartment. He decided against it. What he had to say to Chief Kalangi was truly a little too charged. He would leave this place, stop at a bank, get a bag of change, and use a pay phone.

"You lied to me, Arnold," Cyril admonished a stunned Chief Kalangi. "You said you could get me some interesting bones through that filthy polecat Modibo. You didn't tell me that you and Modibo and Haksar and Hendrijks saw the australopithecines back in the fifties."

Cyril spoke from a pay phone on the first floor of London's famed department store, Harrods. Twenty-two thousand miles above London, a geosynchronous satellite picked up the call's radio impulses and redirected them back down at the earth, into a phone set inside the cinder-block building of the Nairobi metropolitan police.

"Nor did you tell me," Cyril continued, as he kept clinking coins into the pay phone, "how all of you attacked the australopithecines, and slaughtered the males who tried to fight back, and chased the others into the forest."

Kalangi started to protest that he himself had never . . . But Cyril cut him off.

"How unwise of you to put me onto someone who kept a document of that event. That old British cop. You didn't know he had taken Haksar's diary, did you?" The thin, gray-haired, ramrod-stiff Kalangi said nothing. "How many australopithecines did you kill since, Arnold? You take a cut of selling their bones in Hong Kong? How much is your cut, Arnold?"

Kalangi found his voice. "I don't know what you're talking about. No one lives back there. There's a legend of some odd tribe, the mangati, whom the Masai once defeated and pushed back into the forest—but of course that was just an old tale. . . ."

"Spare me the folklore. Your mangatis are alive and well, and if you keep denying it, Arnold, I'll make two copies of this very interesting notebook and take one to the Forum for Restoration of Democracy. They have an office right here in London. And I'll give the other one to Richard Leakey." Both threats were bluffs. The Forum, Kenya's most powerful opposition party, would've jumped on Cyril's own back. And Cyril would've never shared anything with the brilliant younger Leakey.

But the bluffs worked. There was a pause; then the chief spoke again. "So, Cyril . . ." In using Anderson's first name, Kalangi conceded defeat and openness to negotiation. "Are you going to ask for my help again? Help for the white man to rob my land of yet another treasure?"

"That treasure doesn't belong to one land alone, and maybe I should ask the help of Jakub Ngiamena. I wouldn't have to pay him, and Jakub's park rangers would be the best at searching that wilderness."

"My men are as good as Jakub's," snapped Kalangi. "As for paying, that's an ugly word among friends. Haven't I proved my friendship? Haven't I dismissed the testimonies of those beggars who saw you drop a body in that garbage dump?''

Cyril laughed out loud. ''You've got to be kidding, Arnold. The word of some beggars against that of a world-class scientist? I think I'm the better friend, in holding back this disclosure. You did England's dirty work, Arnold.'' Anderson stared out at the cheerful animation of Harrods; it matched his own excitement. ''You betrayed your black brothers and almost destroyed a breed valuable to the whole world.''

Kalangi didn't make a sound. He had been totaled.

''This notebook, by the way, is not coming back to Africa with me, Arnold. It's staying here, in a friend's safe, to ensure my security while I'm back in Nairobi.'' He was experiencing great pleasure in torturing the other man by slowly twisting the knife of power. It wasn't as much fun as killing, but killing was so quick. ''Now one other thing. The protohumans you killed, were they gracile or robust?''

''They were . . . the skinny kind.'' The chief offered his own capsulation of the two varieties' difference.

''Figures,'' snickered Cyril. ''The others would've snuffed you out.'' A pause. Cyril's pile of coins was decreasing. ''I'm thinking of forgiving you, Arnold, in spite of what you did to science. I'm thinking of giving you another chance.''

Kalangi was silent, but it was no longer the silence of fierceness. It was soft, punctured, vanquished. Then he said, ''Very well. What do I have to do for the white man?''

''I'll tell you. That trouble that the army is gearing up to stop . . . or start . . . Reschedule it, Arnold.''

The chief of police protested, perhaps sincerely. ''But I'm not behind any . . .''

''Find out who's behind it, and put it off.''

A pause. ''Very well. What else do I have to do for the white man?''

''I'll tell you exactly what you have to do.''

TUCKED IN A CREASE OF THE SAVANNA, THE POACHERS' camp could not be seen from the air because it was hidden by the flat tops of six acacia trees. Under their sparse umbrellas the narrow corrals for the live catch were camouflaged by fences of unwhittled thorny branches, whose tips had been bent inward and tied with other tips into spiny roofs.

From a plane, especially to an inexperienced searcher's eye, the whole looked like an acacia grove suffused from below with a fierce growth of bushes. If animals were moving in there, they must have broken into those bushes to seek relief from the heat. Even park rangers and police officials could be deceived by that camouflage, if they hadn't been on the job long enough. On the other hand, those more experienced were also the likelier to close an eye and take a bribe—a ranger's or cop's salary was a misery for supporting a wife and children.

One thing that could not be detected from several hundred feet of altitude was the disgusting buzzing of the flies that always occupy a place where animals are being butchered and skinned. Fifty to seventy percent of the poachers' catch were zebras, because their skins were in such worldwide demand that the camp had to constantly produce them. When the generator was working, the camp played a tape of gunshots to scare the birds. When the power was out, gourds filled with dry seed were tied to the tips of the acacias' highest branches and provided rattling noises meant to have the same effect. But neither noise helped much because the wild's predators quickly guessed that the men in the camp were just another kind of predator, and their prey was thus disputable. Marshal eagles and marabou storks and vultures and hawks raided the grove constantly, while the four-legged thieves trafficked incessantly around it, and at night constellated the bush with their glittering eyes. It was as if the savanna claimed back a little of what the poachers had stolen and killed from it.

Eventually, when the camp became too gross with bones, discarded meat, and blood drippings, and with the adjoining piles of excrement of the men living in it, it would be abandoned. The precious generator would be hauled onto the poachers' truck, followed by the crude wooden tables where the animals were skinned, the big tubs where water was boiled to clean the skins, and the chain saws used to cut through the thick elephant feet and the tough knees of zebras. These were followed by the mallets that pounded the inferior horns into powder, the rifles, the spears and knives used to finish snared animals, thus saving bullets, as well as the radiotelephone. Finally the pots and pans the poachers used to cook their meals were packed up too. The camp would be off to another tract of wildlife, like a rapist off to his next virgin victim.

Early on a day reserved for such a move, the cold dawn swept slowly over the camp, and the five men sleeping in it, directly on the ground; they were all young except for a crab-legged little man in a faded army greatcoat, who snored, turning toward the brightening sky a square tribal tattoo on one cheek. The eye of dawn moved on to a stack of hunting snares, which were nothing but plain round coils of steel wire. They were wide enough to catch a water buffalo's neck, even a midsize rhino's, and their steel wire was so sharp that it could cut through those necks almost like a razor, decapitating large beasts in under thirty seconds, if they chose to fight being captured. The large ones invariably did, saving the poachers most of the work of cutting off the heads with the chain saw. The water buffalo and rhino heads were great for wall display, and were priced accordingly: ten and twenty thousand dollars respectively per head of buffalo or rhino, on the Asian markets. From Singapore to Taipei and Seoul to Tokyo, the Pacific Rim was going nuts over the trappings of power and rugged luxury once reserved for the white man. Their executives went to work in stark, high-tech interiors but relaxed in decors of big-game hunting clutter that made them feel like latter-day Teddy Roosevelts.

The Asian elites, who did not forget that they were Asian, believed in curing sicknesses or boosting sex appetites with ground, dried, roasted, and pickled animal products. Those were of all kinds, and came from all over the world. Bones and horns. Gallbladders and livers. Bear paws. Monkey eyes. Crushed shells of pygmy tortoises. Amazonian fire-fishes. The Asian elites, traditional consumers of poached stuff, had boosted world poaching to twenty times the levels of the 1960s because they paid well and with cash: two thousand U.S. dollars for a package of bear-paw soup for four; five thousand per fish for certain varieties of tropical fishes; a hundred thousand for a midsize set of elephant tusks; between a half million and a million for a whole elephant.

Modibo did not know about those astounding prices but was perfectly aware that the Asian market was bouncing. Only about 10 percent of the money paid in Taipei or Tokyo trickled down to his level, but that 10 percent had recently doubled in amount, and then tripled, despite some new competition—Russia had entered the poaching market with a vengeance. Lately, animal medicines had been on the rise, and not just for Asian customers. The world was getting turned off to antibiotics. Almost anything caught in the wild was considered to be curative because it had the aura of something natural, and of surviving by its own genetic powers. "Savanna food" was also in high demand. In Modibo's youth, the elephants hit by trains on the Mombasa-Nairobi railroad were merely pulled off the tracks and left to rot.

Today, any dead elephant, if cut up fast enough, could be sold as a treasure of protein bred on pristine savanna grasses. In certain exclusive clubs of Tokyo, one ate *life* in the guise of ostrich-egg omelet, antelope cutlet, and elephant steak.

The rising prices made the business more ruthless. Where there was more money, there were also more palms to grease. The park rangers harassed Modibo's men constantly; that year, they had burned three out of their six camps. Also, poaching was changing. The younger poachers were poorer trackers than those of the previous generation. They wanted their drinking water purified; they balked at eating snake or monkey and wore down their radio batteries listening to rap music. Like everywhere else, the young were a disappointment.

Modibo was asleep on the bare ground, snoring after a late meal of tough wildebeest steak seasoned with long drags from a joint of Uganda Blue. He and his crew had been busy last night trying to snare a family of civets, twenty-five-pound wild cats that were so agile they could stalk grass sparrows and knock down several before a flock flew off. The females had little glands in their vaginas that secreted musky oils the pharaohs had first used to make perfumes. Now these civet-oil perfumes were back as part of that craze for all-natural stuff. If one didn't harvest the civets fast enough, the hyenas ate them in the snares, occasionally getting trapped too. Running from snare to snare in the beams of flashlights, Modibo had had a workout, and was in no mood for the camp's radiotelephone to start buzzing first thing at dawn.

But it did.

Tired, dazed by too much Uganda Blue, the old poacher crawled half-asleep toward the radiophone, waking fully when he hit a cooled pile of shit, plopped on the camp floor by a panicked animal or by one of his stoned men. Swearing, Modibo swatted around with his hands to find something to clean the military greatcoat he was so proud of. He encountered nothing but hard ground, cold dust, and spiny branches. Scratched, stinking, he opened his eyes and picked up the receiver. "*Ndio?* Yes?" He blinked, amazed to hear who it was at that hour. "Chifi?" he asked, adapting the word "chief" Swahili-style.

In one of the corrals, a baby rhino, not yet three months and only two hundred pounds, raised its head at the increasing light. Its nose, still hornless at this age, made it look like an armored piglet. A deep jagged cut around its neck showed that it had been caught in a snare. A bandage of mud had been crudely applied to its wound, and the hardy little animal, very playful and funny in the wild, seemed to be on the mend, though it had lost a lot of blood. Modibo planned to sell it alive, to a dealer connected to zoos. It was worthless dead and would have been chopped up for steaks for the poachers. But just now, it found the strength to get up from its bed of bloodied mud and looked back at the dawn with the untamable spirit of youth.

Talking on the phone, Modibo stood at attention as much as his crab-leggedness permitted his body to rise straight. "Yes, Chifi. Sorry you call last night . . ." He was trying to keep his voice down, but the caller barked at him to speak up, dammit, so Modibo spoke up, resigned to wake up his men and be seen in a posture of fright—Chief Kalangi seemed to be in a particularly foul mood. "Sorry you call last night, Chifi, I was out afta da civets. . . ."

One of the poachers opened his eyes, lifted up a messy head of Rastafarian dreadlocks. He was Bilal, the youngest of the team. Between Bilal's locks shone long white objects that looked like hair rollers.

"You dry hyena turd," said Kalangi. He always swore colorfully, a legacy from the colonial army. "Can you guess why I'm calling?"

"No, Chifi, I don guessed. . . ." The cold bite in Kalangi's voice gave him no inkling.

"You've seen mangati come out of the forest again, Modibo, and didn't tell me?"

The question was so unexpected that Modibo hiccuped. When his glottis reopened, the redirected air vacuumed out of his lungs, carrying chopped-up blabber. "Wha . . . ? Deyz no mo' mangati, Chifi . . . I told you, all gone. . . ."

"Don't lie, monkey cunt. That mzungu you couldn't catch, he saw their fresh footprints. Didn't you just kill some and sell the bones all by yourself?"

When the Asian market had started bouncing, Modibo had decided on a bold move. Chief Kalangi deserved no cut of certain species. He had lied and told him that the mangati were utterly depleted, and had started selling them directly, through Zhang Chen's store. Knowing the penalty for skimming the chief, Modibo almost creamed his greatcoat. "No, Chifi, who sez? Da Chinaman's a liar, Chifi. No one knows about da mangati, and deys none left. . . ."

"You're the liar, mole shit. There's plenty left, and rumors about them, all the way to bloody London!"

The dawn, ever brighter and wider, focused on the awakening men. Bilal's hair rollers could be seen clearly now, but they were not rollers; they were reefers of Uganda Blue, which he had deemed safest to store in his hair.

Besides being the youngest on the team, Bilal was also the softest-hearted. He had bandaged the baby rhino with mud and had nursed him with water over the last two days. By Modibo's terms, he was a bad poacher—he smoked too much, ran sloppily after fallen prey, giving predators a chance, and talked back. He, of course, was happy that Modibo was getting such a dressing-down.

"I only got five men, including me, Chifi. . . ." Modibo was listening now, with a dull, unalive kind of fear in his features that made them hang heavy. "To do dat, Chifi, I need good radios, also ammo and nightviewers. When? All ri'. All ri'. We do it, Chifi. We ready as soon as da plane drop da stuff." Modibo hung up.

He reached down for a tattered straw mat, tore off a corner, and cleaned his greatcoat. Then he paced around, kicking one man who had slept through the phone call. The man grumbled and raised his hands from his genitals, to rub his eyes. Modibo reached under his greatcoat, brought out a Browning P 35, whose barrel looked freckled and mucked up as if it had been lying in a swamp. He walked to the corral with the baby rhino, aimed the Browning, and fired a loud shot. Then he fired another shot at another animal. And another. All four poachers had jumped up, fully awake, and watched Modibo shoot animal after animal—some of which had required hours of stalking.

He reloaded and moved over to the little wire cage with the civets; inside, the cats, sensing death, meowed and clawed the wire until the sergeant hit each with a bullet, and the noises stopped. There was no trapped animal left alive in the camp.

Bilal stood by the corral with the baby rhino that had died instantly, one eye gouged out by a single bullet whose path had continued into the brain. Bilal frowned. "Why you kill da kifaru, Sarge? He was gettin bedda."

"To cut out its teeth, and make jujus for me and fo' ev'one," said Modibo with a nasty grin. The shooting settled Modibo's nerves. He barked at his men to get ready, a plane would be here within the hour bringing ammo, a new radio, and instructions for a job that would pay each man five hundred dollars. He heard someone utter a stunned gasp. None of them had ever made that much in one whole season.

"We going afta dat mzungu again?" Bilal asked.

Modibo laughed at the idiot. "No. Da mzungu is dead for sure. He coond make it in da forest." He stepped up to a stack of snares; their steel coils had rusted where animal blood had repeatedly dripped on them. He took another step, faced a drum of gasoline, tapped it with his finger to gauge how much fluid was left in it.

"If da mzungu is dead, why we go in da forest?" asked Bilal.

Modibo turned to face him fully. "Who sez we do?" Noting at the same time that the youngest poacher was too clever for his own good.

"Oddawise you don shoot all da catch," said Bilal, glancing aside toward the other men. "If we stay in da plain, dere'z no need to shoot da catch, and burn it." The smart bastard had guessed why Modibo had tapped on the gasoline drum.

"Go cut up da rhino for steaks, and den get da truck ready," Modibo said lightly. "We eat an' we leave." He stared past an acacia's trunk at the Mau escarpment, rising some twenty miles away. At that hour, it looked cool and black, but by midday it would simmer in the heat, green like a viper's skin. He saw a man lingering unoccupied, and ordered him to wash the snares. And there was no need to be shy with the water, because that plane was bringing plenty more water.

The chief had given him two days to bring a live mangati back to Nairobi.

"I DON'T UNDERSTAND WHY WE HAD TO WASTE A BUSINESS day," grumbled Harry Ends, "leaving London before lunch so we can arrive in Nairobi at night."

In his shirtsleeves and socks, a glass of Chivas Regal in his hand, he sat in the lounge section of his jet, opposite Cyril and Ramsay. The way Harry threw back half of his drink, Cyril could tell he was afraid of flying and was bracing himself for the takeoff.

Cyril smiled and told him larger planes like this one always landed in Nairobi either at night or before dawn because during the day's heat the city's high-altitude air became too rarefied to support big planes. "If we arrived in daylight, we would plummet into Nairobi instead of landing into it."

Harry Ends tensed up and his eyes narrowed. He hated not knowing something, and especially hated being educated about it publicly. "I wouldn't've thought that we had so much payload. . . ." he muttered.

"We can make it a workday while cruising over the Mediterranean, and Egypt, and the rest," said Cyril casually. "Want to hear the program I've put together for us?" Harry grunted and sipped more whiskey. He was very short and unmuscular and tanned, with longish hair and an excessively deep voice that came out of the body of a choirboy. And he was "terribly, terribly competitive," Rams had warned Cyril.

So Cyril couldn't pass up the chance to teach him a thing or two.

"We will spend the first morning at my office at the anthropology department. See the fossil vault and watch some film of my previous expeditions." The expeditions were those of his students, but Cyril had made sure to be featured in all of them. "In the afternoon, coffee with the government." Harry started to object—he hated meeting officials— but Cyril cut through. They would have to win over the government. "Evening, I'll show you the town: artifacts, girls. Terrific girls, by the way, and very accommodating," he reinforced, unsure of Harry's persuasions. In Cyril's time, a male could smell another, but who knew with this executive breed, even their balls were high-tech.

"Next day, we fly to Dogilani by small plane—those can stay airborne at every hour," he smiled amiably. "We dig for fossils for a day. The next day, we truck over to the Mau. Trek, stop, observe. Same the following day. And that concludes it."

"That's it?" asked Ramsay.

"Isn't it marvelous?" countered Cyril rhetorically. "In four days, Harry, you'll know more paleoanthropology than all the world of business put together."

"Wait a second." Ends fidgeted nervously with his belt, making sure it closed properly. Cyril was still unbuckled though the plane was rising steeply. "I thought I was clear that I wanted to see one of those things."

"With luck, we'll see footprints left by those things." Cyril purposely rose. A stewardess who had stepped in to check on the passengers frowned, but Cyril intentionally ignored her. "We may find a freshly used occupation floor."

Ends fidgeted, fingered his belt, glanced at the no smoking sign. "You still have a day, Cyril. Can't you send some bush scouts or whatever, to flush some out?"

"You mean, rouse them out of the bush, like quail in Yorkshire?" Cyril loved Harry's expression; the man looked trapped. What was he going to do now, order the plane back to Heathrow airport? Cyril noticed that the frowning stewardess was no longer frowning and was listening. "They are human, Harry, as human as you and me, except for having cities, cars, and credit cards or the extra brain mass that results in cars and credit cards." The woman was listening with increased attention. "That is exactly the value of this find, the *humanness*. And I'm lucky, of course, that someone like you doesn't expect to immediately quantify it in stock market points. . . ."

Ends made an annoyed gesture. "Of course, of course. I know they're like us. I was thinking all day yesterday about finding our common paradigm, our unified field theory, so to speak. . . ."

You're making up words, boy, thought Cyril. He glanced at the stewardess. Did she understand that Cyril had a great mind and that Harry was just a parrot? Whether she got it or not, she wet her lips, met his eyes, then looked away. Not gorgeous, but she'd be all right for the next twelve hours.

"Let's not get lost in words. If we become operational, I promise you, Harry, that we'll soon watch that breed come out of the forest. It will be, Harry, like watching the emergence of man, out of the trees and into the savanna. . . . You might even think of inviting our backers to the show, or our stockholders."

Rams was enthusiastic. "Cyril. What a hot idea."

"I know. Now I have to go call Nairobi and see how things are shaping up." Turning, Cyril faced Ramsay and tilted his head, signaling for his friend to follow him out.

He waited several seconds behind a set of curtains until Ramsay stepped out of the lounge. Cyril grabbed him by the elbow and whispered, "What did you think?"

"The emergence of man? What a show. Can you really do it for the stockholders?"

"I can do it for the stockholders. Give me six months out there, and I can do it for anyone." At that instant, climbing from twenty to thirty thousand feet in less than a minute, he felt lightheaded and certain that anything was in his power. Even field anthropology, even *hard work*. "Even for other investors than Harry. Who incidentally hasn't yet given us any papers, not even a memo of agreement.''

"Relax, for Christ's sake. Harry's for real. Cyril, what drives you so hard?''

"Science,'' said Cyril. He let a long smile float behind him, as he strode off to the private jet's telephones, by the galley.

The stewardess asked him if he wished to have a drink. He ordered a Courvoisier cognac, stopped her hand in his while he took the vaulted glass, then put his nose to it, sniffed, sneezed. The stewardess tittered and handed him a napkin; Cyril wiped his nose and winked at her, and proceeded to the phones.

"HOW IS MY MAN IN NAIROBI?'' CYRIL INQUIRED JOVIALLY. Kalangi responded in an echoing voice that he was busy, and Cyril asked why he was using the speakerphone. Kalangi denied that he was—that echo was from the satellite connection. Everything was proceeding according to plan. Anderson's camp was being built at the foot of the escarpment, and Modibo's team was climbing the lower slopes. But there was no way they could bring out a creature in such a short time.

"They have to. I don't care how they do it. Are you tailing Ngili and Yinka Ngiamena?''

"Yes. The girl withdrew all her cash from her bank account yesterday, I don't know why. Ngili, according to a servant we're bribing, quarreled badly with his father and is moving out of the house.''

"What did they quarrel about?''

"Ngili wants to fly out there and look for Lauder, but his father's trying to stop him.''

"Boring. What's new with the rumored army coup?''

"You've been talking so much about that, you made me ask some friends of mine in the military. They laughed at me. There's no coup, Cyril, nothing's going on. Where are you?''

"Thirty thousand feet up in the air, above France. So long."

"So long," Kalangi mimicked him.

Anderson asked the stewardess to tell the other two passengers that he needed to quietly do some work; then he sat by a window in the aft section, and with almost childlike eagerness opened Haksar's notebook.

IN HIS NAIROBI OFFICE, KALANGI TURNED OFF THE SPEAKerphone and looked up at four military men seated on the other side of the chief's very large desk, which was empty except for a half dozen phones.

The men ranged in rank from captain to general. They sipped from cups of kahawa. The general, who was also the oldest, had tattooed cheeks. Three vertical streaks carved his skin under each eye, which made his face look as if it were peering across hanging lianas. He slurped his kahawa through the stick of aromatic m'koma wood he held in his teeth.

"So, when are you planning to start?" Kalangi asked, speaking now without his pretend thick Kikuyu accent.

They all looked at the general. He finished a slurp. "Sometime during your friend's visit."

"He was never my friend. I have to know, if I am to do my part."

"It will be between Monday and Thursday." The general slurped again, laughed. "Monday or Thursday, but not excluding Tuesday or Wednesday." Kalangi shrugged, impatient with the general's games, but the subordinates shook their heads and sucked their lips noisily; the general was so clever, and his answer so subtle.

"Where are you going to be, Arnold?" asked a lieutenant general. "In the savanna, with Anderson?" He was small, tense, with a parting line that looked laser-traced. Kalangi knew that he was the brain of the operation.

"Probably, but I'll leave things here well in hand. You

know, Cyril's bringing over an incredibly influential character . . .''

"Good," said the lieutenant general. "He'll see us in action and realize how determined we are." A cold stiff laugh went around the room.

A line lit up on Kalangi's phone. He picked up. "Chief Kalangi." He listened. "Don't lose sight of them," he instructed the caller and hung up. "Ngili and Yinka Ngiamena are at Wilson airport, trying to rent a private plane."

"Jakub has figured out that he's on our list," said the general. "This quarrel with his son is a cover. He's sent the kids to rent a plane so they can all sneak over the border."

"They're not going to find a plane. I already put the word out among the private pilots," Kalangi reassured him. "Anyone rents to them, they get a bangalore torpedo from us as a present. Anything else?"

"Bring one of those things alive to Nairobi, so we can decide on its value," said the general, taking the m'koma stick out of his mouth and rising. "We must rebuild this country's portfolio, you know." His subordinates laughed again, and Kalangi joined them.

"THANKS FOR LENDING ME THE MONEY, YINKA, BUT YOU don't seem fated to part with it," said Ngili, dropping tiredly in the big Mercedes's passenger seat. "I found no plane to rent, except for an old crop duster. I turned it down."

"So what are we going to do?"

"Keep looking for a decent plane. It won't help Ken if we get one that comes apart in the air."

Nothing will help him if we wait much longer, thought Yinka, looking away at the tarmac. It simmered in the heat of the dry season like a giant mirage. "What about your friend Mtapani," she asked, turning on the engine and pulling away from the airport. Mtapani, an air-safari operator, was a high school mate, and a Masai.

"I went to him and asked his price, and he told me he'd do it free, if I help him with this." Ngili pulled a computer-printed sheet of paper out of his pocket. "Listen to what he's into." He read aloud with a mixture of amusement and concern: "This is an oath to Engai, and the one who betrays it will be struck dead by Engai's lightnings." Yinka frowned at that portentous beginning; in Masai myth, Engai meant the sky and also the supreme deity. Ngili read on, "In the beginning, Engai gave the Masai people all that exists in the way of cattle, and promised the Masai to watch over their destiny. In exchange, he asked for an oath of obedience, and a pledge of blood. Blood dries up, but never loses its color. Loyal warriors suffer the throes of capture and death, but never betray Engai. Today, Engai's warriors are rising to fight for their freedom again. Whoever serves the Mzungu, or the Mzungu's black servants, shall perish by Engai's lightnings. It is a thousandfold worse to be a black servant to a Mzungu than to be a Mzungu. This is the pledge that we are renewing today, that the Mzungu's servants shall be killed, whether they're strangers to us, or whether they're of our own blood. . . . If we break it in any way, let Engai's lightnings turn against us." Ngili folded the paper. "Not too different from the Mau Mau oath, eh?"

She shrugged, steering the car, but he could tell that she was affected.

Ngili added in a light tone, "Mtapani asked my opinion about slaughtering a calf at the initiation of new members and asking them to wear armbands of its hide. He came down on me very heavily to sign this, telling me that they needed a name like mine to attract members. How many guys do you think signed this already?"

She shrugged, steering the car, her legs stretched to work the pedals, her kikoi taut over her flat stomach. She had lost weight.

"About sixty," he informed her. "Mtapani said that a lot are from our old high school."

"Sixty is hardly enough to make a difference in current politics. Especially if they come from a tribe as small as ours. Who's their leader?"

"I hope not someone we know," said Ngili. "Mtapani

wouldn't tell me unless I signed, but he made it sound like it was someone really high.''

"So I suppose you didn't sign?"

"Are you joking? D'you think 'Mzungu's servants' means the black maids in white families? It means the government, anyone dealing with the International Monetary Fund, with OPEC, with the World Bank. . . ." He paused; when he continued, she heard the alarm in his voice. "This oath is a license to kill just about anyone. But Mtapani is not an impoverished Kikuyu or Kalenjin, Yinka. And I told him that. I asked him, are we back in '53? He said, 'We Masai were chickens in '53. We had signed preferential agreements with the English. Most of us stayed out of the Mau Mau war. We have to redeem ourselves, and show our Africanness.' I told him that we couldn't become a secret society against other Africans and he said, 'D'you think other tribes don't have secret societies against us? I fired all my Kikuyu mechanics.' I then asked, 'Did you fire the mzungu English dealer who gets you the parts for your planes?' "

"The mzungu," she commented angrily. "After twenty-three years of independence, we're still obsessed with the mzungu."

Growing up free and affluent, she and Ngili had rarely used that word before. Now they did, and it felt heavy with bitter legacy. Strictly, the word meant European, or white man, but its emotional gamut was astounding. The Waganda king Mtesa had hailed explorer John Hanning Speke with it, meaning that the discoverer of the Nile's source was a wondrous stranger, an almost destiny-sent guest. But for the blacks who hauled the litters of white colonials on their shoulders, and were bullwhipped for not moving fast enough, the word *mzungu* had a quite different meaning. It had yet another meaning for the fearful black mother who brought her sick child to a European doctor, who was sometimes helpful but often uninterested and cynical. A few mzungus— a missionary who built a school in the jungle, a bush pilot who flew a tribesman stung by a boomslang to a hospital— deserved deference and gratitude. But the word never lost an initial foundation of fear, an occult load of pain and hate. For Yinka, the word signaled the African's most vulnerable condition. That of a scared native, assailed in his own land by a race that, unfairly, was more resourceful.

Affluence had also protected Yinka and Ngili from the land's lingering tribal jealousies. Seventy tribes in Kenya and over two hundred in East Africa had stepped into independence limping from the colonial system's heaviest chain, its ramified prejudice. The elitist Masai, who were warriors and cattle growers, had always despised the majority tribe, the Kikuyu "blockheads," who were poor and cattleless. The Kikuyu said the Masai were bush savages. But both of them agreed to hate the sloppy, lazy Kalenjin. Most tribes thought the pygmies were ugly, and that the Bahaya had mated with monkeys because most of East Africa's prostitutes were Bahaya. The situation had been further complicated by the wars for independence, after which many groups had been re-evaluated, based on how hard they had fought the English. Again, as an honored fighter for independence, Jakub Ngiamena had raised himself and his children above the lingering grudges and suspicions. And things had seemed fine, as long as the country possessed enough money.

"How long has it been since Ken left?" Yinka turned the car into the freeway.

"Six weeks," Ngili said, after an instant of reckoning silently. He gasped and muttered, "I mean, almost four weeks. . . . What's the matter with me?" The Masai week had five days, like the fingers of a hand. Ngili had figured in five-day weeks.

"Very promising mistake," grinned Yinka. "Your friend Mtapani would be proud."

"You're such a bitch. I think you're getting better."

"A month is the longest anyone is expected to survive alone in the bush, isn't it?"

"Yes. According to some experts."

"So. If that one mzungu is to die, maybe it's happening right now."

"Stop it."

"Seriously, brother. We could tell Mtapani that we killed our own mzungu. By letting him go there alone, and then by not going back there in time. We could join his secret society as honorary members."

"Shut up. I made a mistake at a time when the family, the country, seemed the only important things. I'm sorry, I am. So shut up."

"I'm sorry too." She drove against a high wind that whipped tall palls of dust and slapped them onto the moving cars. "Because, despite all my bravado, I was a big coward. You and Ken were about to fight, you and Um'tu were about to fight, so I chickened out, I didn't want to see you fight each other. I suggested that deal to Ken, and he jumped at it. I knew he would, and I knew you would too."

He nodded, his profile outlined against the shantytowns strangling the city. His handsome looks seemed empty now, unjustified. He whispered, "I'll find a plane."

"Physically, it's not possible for him to last much longer, is it? How could he find enough food, enough water? How could he defend himself?"

"That's one of the things he set out to discover."

"And he probably did, and didn't come back to tell us."

"Stop it, you're hurting yourself." Ngili stroked her shoulder, then whispered softly, "Is it possible that you liked him so much, and didn't know it?"

She laughed. "Yes, brother, it's possible. I, the intuitive one, the arch-female. Always in touch, and mocking Ken for not being in touch. Great trick Engai played on me, isn't it?"

She headed off the lethal freeway and into the infested downtown streets, where Ngili wanted to stop at a safari shop to buy bush supplies. As she waited for Ngili, she let Ken fill her mind. Now it seemed all right to think about him. Before, it had always been difficult. Now, all the barriers, spoken and unspoken, had fallen. By vanishing, Ken had given her total freedom to remember him.

If the African saying was true—that after a man's seed touches a woman, she can never get rid of him and he becomes like her second shadow—then she'd thought about him more after he disappeared than she had since they'd met. She had fantasized about their brief time together, vowing in one corner of her mind that if he returned, she would reward herself by taking him to bed again, to enact those fantasies. Even if nothing else happened, and he didn't fall in love with her, she would deserve that, and it would be enough. A woman's sexiest part was her mind, she thought, not what was between her legs, as so many think.

She smiled, recognizing that other Yinka, the one who shocked and challenged. She would become that one again. She would be sad for a while, but then she would be all right.

I love my brother, she thought, as he opened the car's door again, arms filled with packages. He sat in the car looking very thoughtful. "Can you help me talk Um'tu into leaving Nairobi?" he asked her. "When this strife comes, I'm afraid it will be a stupid murderous tribal bloodbath like everywhere else, and everyone will take advantage of it to try to fix their own enemies. And Um'tu has enemies. I want him out of Nairobi, and you and mother too. I want you all out of the country until things cool off."

"Where are you going to be?"

"In the savanna," he answered unhesitatingly. "I don't want our find to become a pawn in anyone's political games."

"Ambitious talk, brother. I'll try to help you with Um'tu."

The big car entered their street. Karen still looked shockingly affluent. In one of the front yards, a black family was loading suitcases into a Volvo station wagon.

"What the hell is this?" muttered Yinka, as the Mercedes rolled through the gate.

Parked by the guesthouse where Ngili and Gwee had lived as bachelors was a dusty bus with a rural number plate. About a dozen sticks were planted in the ground next to it. The guesthouse was empty: Gwee was on his honeymoon, and Ngili, after quarreling with his father, had spent the last four nights at a YMCA. But as Yinka stopped the Mercedes, a cloud of smoke wafted out of the guesthouse's doorway.

The two of them stepped out of the car, and Yinka began coughing from a raw odor of rural tobacco. Ngili reached out and touched one of the sticks. It was a warrior's spear; all the sticks were spears, and some, judging by the rustiness of their blades, were quite old. They had been stuck savagely into the well-kept grass.

"Mother!" Yinka called in surprise, seeing Itina step out of the front entrance. Blank-faced, Itina walked down the steps of the main house with a tray of sandwiches, followed by Patrick with an identical tray. Seeing Ngili, Itina heaped her tray onto Patrick's and ran to throw her arms around him, bursting out, "I'm so glad you're here!" She passed an arm around Ngili, the other around Yinka. "A bunch of chiefs from Nakuru are here, and also some friends, talking to Um'tu." She was a small woman, the only one in the Ngiamena family who was small. She had smart eyes and a filigree of tattoos on her forehead, and had always been the little dynamo powering two big machines at once—her husband and the house.

"What's Um'tu doing at home instead of being at the office?" Ngili asked.

"He won't be going to the office anymore. He resigned as commissioner of the parks."

"What? When?"

"This morning. The president called him on the phone and they spoke for half an hour; then Um'tu went into his study and wrote a letter of resignation. He was made to resign." Ngili felt his mother's panic. "The men in there are trying to talk him into some kind of uprising, to set up a separatist government. Don't let him agree to it, Ngili. If he says yes in there, it will be enough for it to be known, and he'll be branded as a traitor and killed."

"But, Mother . . ." Ngili gently freed himself. "Um'tu's not even a member of an opposition party. . . . What kind of separatist government could they be talking about?"

"Something tribal. Come with me, you'll see." She took her tray. Patrick, following with the other tray, looked relieved that reinforcements had arrived. "*Karibu chakula!*

Come and eat!'' Itina called in Swahili, as she stepped into the guesthouse; she rarely used Swahili at home.

Stepping in behind her, Ngili saw the familiar interior, still filled with his books and samples of rock. The visitors, all men, middle-aged or older, sat directly on the floor. Pipes and self-rolled cigarettes had turned the room into a smoke chamber. Jakub emerged out of the smoke, standing alone before that seated crowd, his forehead glittering with sweat.

The guests wore rural clothes: cotton pants, shirts, and leather sandals, some worn with woolen socks. A few wore suits that were worn out and old-fashioned. Over their clothes, they sported brass necklaces and glass beads and signs of tribal rank and office: the *okiuka* clubs, the whips and fly swatters marking the status of *olaiguenanis, olobolosis, olotunos,* and *laibons.* As councillors, seers, leaders of elders, selectors of the bulls that were wrestled by young boys before they were circumcised, and guardians of the warriors' weapons in time of peace, these men had exerted authority most of their lives. Ngili understood instantly why his father was sweating. In their rather comical appearance of today (some wore glasses; one spat out his chewing gum, preparing to try Itina's sandwiches) there was an enormous amount of tradition.

"Stop talking now, and eat!'' his mother called shrilly. Ngili wondered if she had made the food without being asked, merely as a way of interrupting a debate that was too uncomfortable for his father.

"Honorable chiefs, here are my son and daughter,'' Jakub announced.

With stiff nods, several men saluted Ngili (but not Yinka), then reached for Itina's sandwiches. Yinka crossed her arms and planted herself right in the middle of the room. Munching on the floor, an old chief seemed ready to spit at her thighs. Jakub looked at Ngili. Expecting a tough beam from those regal eyes, Ngili was stunned to see them fluid with mute pleading, as if to say, I'm glad you're here, son, because I need your help. Damn, Ngili thought in response to that gaze, how warm and open you are, Um'tu. Might it be because you just lost the power of your office? But he hurried across, hitting folded knees of laibons, to stand next to his father.

Once there, he took the onslaught of tribal eyes coming at both of them out of the tobacco fog. One chief yelled through a sandwich, "You shared in the government's perks for years, Jakub! But we never did! Is that why you don't want us to form a government of our own, because you left the government?"

"I didn't leave, I was made to leave," Jakub retorted.

Ngili recognized the yelling chief. He was Desmond Ndbala, elder of a cluster of Masai clans allowed to graze their cattle on the Magadi Reserve. "We want a government of our own, right, laibons?" Ndbala trembled from searing and long-contained anger. "A republic, a flag, a nation of our own, right, laibons?"

"Yes, yes!" yelled the laibons. A few of them even chanted "Tribal power!" and made a fisted salute that brought jingling from their tribal bracelets.

"You want a republic for every last tribe in the land?" Jakub trembled, also from anger. "You think the president and the army will allow that? You want the perks, Desmond, the power! You realize what it would take for such a republic to be created? Plunging the whole country into tribal war!"

"So what's wrong with that? We're asking you to be commander of our tribal forces. With a chance to become our first president!" Ndbala stepped over sets of folded knees, and Ngili felt his father brace himself so rigidly that he feared he might have a heart attack. Ndbala, cheeks swollen smugly, leaned into Jakub's face. "Your government put you in a sick sheep's hide," meaning that the government was biding its time before killing Jakub. "Now we have the warriors ready to attack the government house and the presidency. Put yourself at their fore, Jakub."

"You'll be killed one way or the other, so you might as well die a martyr," reinforced another chief. He had only two teeth in his upper jaw, and they were black like chips of obsidian.

Yinka suddenly had to clutch her mother, who was springing forth, shouting at Ndbala and the other man to get out. She told them that they were crazy and murderers to boot. Jakub shot forth his vast hand. But he did not strike Ndbala; he simply anchored his hand on Ndbala's shoulder and pushed down until the other man's aging knees cracked and folded. Ngili rushed to separate the two, but Ngiamena gave way, and Ndbala fell to the floor.

"I fought the British right next to Mzee Kenyatta," growled Jakub. "We who fought then were not Kikuyus, Merus, Embus, or Masai. We were just patriots. What you are suggesting will split up the country."

"It doesn't work, the country doesn't work!" the old men clamored, through gums emptied of teeth. Ndbala was getting off the floor. He was ranting: Jakub was a traitor. A black mzungu. As the Masais' ancestors said, surrender your bow, but not your eye. Jakub had surrendered bow and eye to President Noi's government.

"Get out, out!" screamed Itina, escaping Yinka's hands. She caught Ndbala off balance as he was getting up and pushed him, sending him into two other men. Patrick looked at Jakub to see if he should chase out the other guests. But somehow Jakub had overcome his anger and began pleading with the visitors. "Kiihuri, Djikane, how long have we known each other? Listen to me!" But they started trooping out over furniture that had fallen over and sandwiches that were squashed. Behind them, Jakub pleaded hoarsely. Shards might shine, but only a whole pitcher could fetch water. And one should know one's arm's power, before clenching one's fist.

Remembering the spears planted outside, Ngili rushed out. He started yanking the spears up from the ground and suddenly had a vision, superimposed over the dusty bus and the scramble of angry men. He saw himself and Ken at that bazaar on Muindi Mbingu Road, before they took the bones to Randall Phillips. Something had been said between them that afternoon. Ngili kept snatching the spears out of the ground. What was it? He gathered the spears into an awkward bundle and threw them into the bus, hearing them fall inside with a big sloppy clatter. The old men were jumping angrily into the bus; in passing, Ndbala gave Ngili a punch, an old man's punch but still nasty. Ngili pushed him inside, slammed the door after him, and then ran after the vehicle, getting smelly exhaust in his face, just to see it gone.

He slowed down as the bus hurtled into the street. He turned and walked back up the driveway with a frightening feeling that everything around him looked new and unknown: the luxuriating garden, the house he grew up in, and even Patrick, the familiar servant he'd always taken for granted. Itina rushed to her son again, tied her strong thin arms around him. "Are you going to stay, and obey your father?"

Again he freed himself. "I'm not going to go to that School for Diplomats. I'm not going to go to New York, even if Um'tu never speaks to me again. What we have to do is get out of Nairobi. Now."

She stood on tiptoe to swiftly kiss his cheek. "I know," she whispered. "Go inside and tell him that."

He saw Yinka come out of the guesthouse. Again, he experienced that feeling connected somehow with himself and Ken on that afternoon at the bazaar. But now Yinka was connected with it too.

Yinka stood aside to let him in, then walked away toward her mother. The times might be scary, thought Ngili, but the women are still excluded from the heart-to-hearts of men. I'll tell him that. This time, I'll tell him a lot of things.

He stepped inside and forgot what he wanted to tell his father. Jakub had pulled aside the carpet, revealing the floorboards. Next to the wall, there was a kind of trapdoor. Ngili had never noticed it because he hardly ever looked at the floor. He usually left the guesthouse before Patrick led the servants inside to clean.

Jakub lifted a floor plank like a lid and pulled up a cardboard box from under the floor. He opened it, and then turned to Ngili, his hands holding a most unusual weapon.

It was a piece of common pipe, narrow, rusty, its open

end topped with a nail secured with a wire, to form a crude set of sights. Impossible as that seemed, the pipe was the barrel of a homemade pistol. Its trigger guard was made of a bent strip of brass, and the trigger from yet another nail. The grips were made of wood that was neither polished nor painted, just dulled and smoothed by handling. Out of the grips' bottom hung a narrow tin box that looked like an old anchovy can. That was the gun's magazine. The whole weapon looked monstrous and ridiculous, a crude toy but with the power to kill.

Jakub saw the surprise in Ngili's eyes, and lowered the weapon.

"A Mau Mau gun?" Ngili asked.

"It is, but I made it myself." He allowed his son to step over and take the weapon.

"Did you ever fire it?" Ngili asked.

Jakub nodded. "And I killed with it."

Ngili was silent. He handled the gun with a mixture of respect and repulsion.

"The barrel is from a water pipe," said Jakub. "The hammer is a piece of World War Two shrapnel and it's released by a barbed-wire spring. The grips are from wood—hard wood, thirikwa tree. It never cracks from heat or bloats in water. With this gun, I fired regular Browning nine-millimeter bullets, which we stole from the British; I looked for a pipe that size and checked it against a nine-millimeter bullet. For other homemade weapons, we had to file down the bullets. But I had a real knack for finding pipes that fitted existing calibers, and I was experienced—I picked up that kind of gunsmithing as a kid, from an uncle who hunted all his life with a homemade rifle. He did blow off three fingers from his right hand," laughed Jakub, raising the pistol and taking aim toward one of the walls.

He pressed the trigger, which let out a screechy empty click. Jakub saw that Ngili had braced himself for the shot, and laughed. "D'you think I'd leave this under your floor loaded? I didn't even want to show it to you."

Ngili breathed. "Then why did you put it under my floor?"

"Superstition. It saved my life, so I felt that if I put it down there, it would protect you too."

"Who made this niche in the floor?" asked Ngili.

"The whites who owned the house before us. During the Mau Mau war, the whites riddled their homes with holes for guns—of course, their guns were not homemade. They thought they'd be protected if they were attacked inside, by their own servants. But the servants figured out where the holes were and got to the guns before the masters." Ngiamena hesitated, as if looking for words. "You thought your father was a leader, a strategist in the independence war? I was a gunsmith first. That's how this smart Masai boy became popular with the Kikuyu guerrillas. They kept passing our village and saw me and my uncle gunsmithing together, and finally they took me to meet Mzee Kenyatta. They had other people trying to build weapons, but they were not as good as me."

The erstwhile pride showed in Jakub's voice. "I ran a real factory; we manufactured up to four rifles a week, plus one pistol. Most of them blew up the first time we fired them. So we tested them by pulling their triggers with a cord, while we ducked in a ditch. Those that survived saw combat against the English. That's how we won that war." He paused, bent down to put the gun back in its box. "That's how we won that war, so that kids like you and your sister could go to fancy schools and play with the whites on your terms."

Ngili had heard those words before. He stuck his fingers in his belt, and swelled his chest, determined not to be weakened by guilt. But when he looked at Jakub, he realized that his father was not trying to make him feel guilty. Jakub spoke with awkward sincerity. "I saw combat six months after I joined. Then I was arrested with the Mzee. I became a leader in jail, not in the field." Ngili reached to the box, took the gun out again. He raised it, aimed at the wall, and pulled the trigger.

The barbed-wire spring responded. The gun clicked. Ngili handed back the gun. "I want you to leave Nairobi, Um'tu. I want the family to leave Nairobi."

"Wait. Those old clowns, someone put this tribal-power idea in their heads. I wouldn't be surprised if it came from the army, because it would give the army a great excuse for action. The army would hit at us, we'd hit back, and we'd become a black Yugoslavia. . . ."

Ngili cut in: "Is that why you were forced to quit? In the hope that you'd get caught in such a scheme?" Jakub nodded. "But you fought the English, Um'tu! You fought them, right along with the Mzee!"

"That's precisely the point. We fought the white man, we kicked him out, and after that we felt that we could look him in the eye, and even allow him back as a guest. But now there's a new breed of African leaders. They did not meet the white man in the field, weapon in hand. They're too young. They met him at the United Nations, at the International Monetary Fund, at the World Bank. Where the deals are made. Where the white man is so powerful that he can buy whole governments."

"And they were bought?" asked Ngili, guessing the answer.

"They were bought. But on condition that one day they'd pay back. Now that day has come, and our new leaders are defaulting—to the foreign banks, and to their own nation. This is what all this is about, defaulting. And let's throw some of the blame at the white man too. Why not?"

Ngili was silent, remembering the manifesto that Mtapani had given him. Then he cleared his throat. "Who will gain from the trouble, Um'tu?"

"The army and the police. The police, especially. That chief, Kalangi. If things start, and you find him in your path, shoot first. Shoot for the gut or the balls," advised Jakub cruelly, yet his cruelty sounded strangely unobjectionable. "so even if you don't kill him, you know that he won't get up to kill you. He betrayed comrades to the English, Ngili. There is no evidence, but I know it. He's involved in drugs.

probably in poaching too. . . ." Ngili remembered seeing Kalangi lead Cyril Anderson into Zhang Chen's store, and then seeing Modibo arrive at the store with a truckful of poached stuff.

His father took his hand, squeezing it in his vast palm. "Ngili, what exactly does Yinka have in mind, concerning Ken? I need to know."

Ngili suddenly figured out what his memory meant. Ngili and Ken, never before divided by anything, had faced each other like two enemies that afternoon at the bazaar because Ngili was aware that Yinka liked his friend.

"I have no idea." Ngili swallowed a lump. Jakub frowned incredulously. Ngili cleared his voice, but it came out jagged with anger. "How can she have anything in mind, when he's not here, and probably not even alive?"

"Did she like him a lot?" asked Jakub.

"Yes . . . And he liked her too, I'm sure." Just now, Ngili felt that he and Ken had been friends in a sadly superficial way. Male comradeship, with the luxury of flaunting interracial equality, and sharing the romanticism of the digs. Yinka might know him better than he did, better than he ever would now that a month had passed since Ken's disappearance. To fight the certainty of Ken's death, Ngili asked with hostility, "Why are you so concerned about Ken, Um'tu?"

"I'm not really. But I want you to understand why I'm not telling you to go to the savanna and find out what happened to him. I know you want to go, both out of friendship and in order not to be less than Ken. But you can't go"— he squeezed Ngili's hand, as if anticipating his resistance— "because I need you to take Yinka and your mother to Johannesburg. Gwee's still honeymooning there. I want all of you out of the country until the trouble is over. I've left the parks department, but the word won't be out immediately. In the next twenty-four hours, I can get you a private plane. You have to help me, son. You'll help me, won't you?"

Ngili stared at him with his black-bullet eyes. Then, with one try, he freed his small but powerful hand from his father's ample palm. "What if he's not dead, Um'tu?"

"He had a radio, and he never made contact. You flew back there twice and he didn't show up. What are the odds?" asked Jakub with the same uncruel cruelty. "But your family needs you, and *I* need you. We are alive. I need your help, son."

"You want me to accompany the women. Where are you going to be?"

"I have a hiding place, here in Nairobi."

"Where?"

"Best that you don't know. I've got comrades, and we have weapons. There's a few of us who didn't give up the fight for this country. I'm only telling you now because I didn't want you to feel that you had to choose between me and your friend."

Ngili glanced over at a set of rock hammers of different sizes. His scientific equipment looked unreal. Next to the hammers was a duplicate of the photo Ken had in his apartment, of Ken and Ngili on a dig. They were younger by a few years, unshaven and dusty and happy.

He gave his father a look that staggered the old man with the sacrifice in it. A sacrifice tied to that American dead in the bush, and to a sense of identity Jakub could not understand. "Very well. Line up that plane. And after it's over, I'm free to go back to the savanna, or anywhere I choose."

Jakub wanted to speak, but was afraid of endangering their new alliance. Breathing loudly, he bent and lowered the strange weapon into its hiding place.

"Come to my study," he said on a tone he wanted light. "I have real guns, for you and Yinka."

"All right. Give me a minute."

Ngili listened to his father tread heavily out, then sat down and glanced over the samples of rock and the pictures from digs. The feeling that his father was still fit for the fight amazed him. Not with a son's love just now, but simply with a sense of what mattered, he prayed: God, let the old man emerge the winner.

Then he thought of his friend. His friend the mzungu. Ngili said it to himself, several times: the mzungu, the mzungu. The prejudice had exited the word because his friend was dead. That limpid, cold-headed hallucination helped Ngili see Ken, lying lifeless on the forest floor, surrounded by a clan of protohumans.

T HE CLAMOR OF THE BATTLE HAD ENDED, BUT KEN never went back to sleep.

With the boy cradled in his arms, he listened to his breathing and felt the rhythmic rise and fall of that fragile, naked chest. Haksar's old watch was no use in counting the minutes, but it seemed that every fifteen minutes or so the boy was dreaming; his body tightened, his breathing quickened, and he gritted his teeth.

The dreams seemed to have a beginning, middle, and end. They started with the tightening and gritting, went into an action-packed middle during which the little body twitched and kicked, then eased into a gradual relaxation.

Modern scientists believed that protohumans were incapable of abstractions, but could one call a dream an unabstract experience?

We know so damn little, Ken thought, and found in that thought a reason for hope. Nothing could end if knowledge hadn't ended. And there was still a chance that Ken Lauder—bearded, filthy, exhausted, with nails grown so long they looked like claws, with rashes itching in the creases of his skin, with canker sores on his gums and one even on the tip of his tongue, and with all he knew of the world tumbling in chaos inside him—could bring this adventure to a productive end. To make this unwitting derring-do into . . .

what? A meeting between these other breeds and his?

What could follow from such a meeting? They, the ancestors, had their own fate and future, which could not, should not, be twisted so that sapiens could have access to more knowledge.

A few hours before, when he'd heard the screams of fighting and dying, he had fought an urge to jump up and shout, "Stop it, you fools. You have a duty toward us. You can teach us things that no one else can!"

But had he managed to make the hominids understand that, and had they been able to glimpse their distant future children in him, they'd have answered with equal passion, "You stop it! Stop what you're doing with our inheritance!"

Ken pictured Long Toes' breed having a dialogue with the modern world, and he had to fight a rueful chuckle. God, how that face-to-face would pull the rug from under scientists and philosophers, historians and moralists, priests and rabbis and mullahs, and from under the politicians, both the elected ones and the self-enthroned fascists of the right and the left. And he could just imagine the scuffle among scientists, to be the official interpreters at such a summit of the human race.

Unexpectedly, the prospect of being one of those interpreters, perhaps *the one*, quickened his pulse. What dizzying glory and power! For the first time, he felt he could understand someone like Cyril Anderson.

I'm not fated for that, he thought. Anyway, I'm probably going to die soon, from exhaustion, from a breakdown in my immune system, or from being caught in one of these battles. Quiet, cool death—Ken had witnessed its presence since he was first alone in the savanna. It struck everything and everyone, and it might soon strike him. He was surprised that he wasn't more frightened. Death would be fast, instant. But would it come with a millisecond of illumination and understanding, before his brain stopped synapsing? Maybe, or maybe not. All his functions might stop in less than a millisecond, without his ever getting any kind of revelation about death. There had been poems about death, speculations, religions, but no reports. There would be no report from him, either.

But it wasn't time yet. Quietly grateful, Ken wondered if the miracle of the boy and the hominid tribes he had found here in the wilderness meant that perhaps other unthinkable wonders might also occur to him. That he might die, but not disappear completely, and hover in spirit over the world he had loved.

Who would miss me most? My mother?

Ngili?

Ngili appeared in his mind, full of life, rich in seed though not yet a father. Ngili would be all right. And he would miss Ken, for a while.

Yinka?

He squirmed on the forest floor that had taken the shape of his body. He felt he needed to be with a woman again before he died. He felt this need racing in his blood, stirring in his genitals, so intensely that he was glad she was not there. He pictured her face after they made love, her skin shining as if it were haloed, and he felt love not as an infatuation, but as a grateful bond with the female who would accept his seed.

I'll never really know what it's like, he thought. I understand it now, but I'll never really know what it's like.

He thought of the note she had written him that afternoon. Please don't get killed out there. Come back, and maybe you'll show me what else they did to each other back then. Hey, you remember it word for word? Scary, Lauder! This is too bad. We would've had such fun, had I gone back and told her what I found up here.

Just a few feet away, Busta squirmed and grunted in her sleep.

As Ken listened to the sounds she was making, he understood exactly why she was among the graciles. She had left her robust breed and, like a homely girl seduced by a handsome high roller, she had fallen under the spell of one of those gracile hunters. They had made love. She had endured the pain of his penis that was so much wider and longer than the penises of robust males, and was also so much slower in climaxing. But in making love face-to-face, his pelvic bone had rubbed her clitoris in a way she had hardly ever experienced with the robust males who mounted her from the back, usually after a chase. The stretching of her labia by the wide penis had been another dizzyingly new sensation. But nothing had matched the bond itself—swelling up with her pregnancy, she had remained in the plains, and her mate had brought her meat that he had hunted and had shared it only with her. As her belly filled up with Crew Cut, she still had to make love to her insatiable partner almost every day, way beyond a robust female's appetite, but eating meat almost every day made up for the exertion. The unborn Crew Cut had rounded up in her belly, nearly killing her when he came out, but she recovered and found her breasts full like tubers, their skin almost snapping from the stored milk. During the unusually long recovery she still had the attention of her male. He kept bringing the meat, and also pestered her, making it clear that if she didn't receive him again soon, he would take the food elsewhere. An instinct she'd never felt before told her to receive him as soon as she wasn't in dire pain and to rely on his help instead of the help of the other females, who were also locked in one man/one woman bonds of pain and pleasure. The gracile females were not cooperators, like the apes or the robust females. They competed for the forageable tracts of ground, and only helped each other when a large predator showed up nearby.

Busta did miss some of her old ways. The playful sexual free-for-alls. The rush of the estrus days and the repeated mountings. But there had been no prize of food, nor any scary/strange throb of waiting every evening for one mate to come back with a hunting day's catch. There had been no exhausting but somehow reassuring chore of fulfilling a permanent male's demands.

She had taken to the ways of the graciles, and really thought of herself as a consort, a spouse, as they raised Crew Cut together, the blend of her egg and the gracile father's seed. Then she had lost her spouse. And she had joined the retreat of the gracile widows, into the forest.

Now when she heard the clamor of the battle, she knew that not far off in the darkness, the fate of two breeds, the one she had left against the one she had joined, was being played out. She had fallen asleep with a heavy heart and dreamed with more confusion and violence than the other females.

The clan around her sailed into the night, united in their anxieties, preparing for one breed's victory over another, or for the total depletion of both. These notions were totally uncomplicated for the hominids, while Ken, the alien in their midst, sleeplessly bubbled with thought, and felt, with the worried excitement of a scientist, that he *understood*.

And he was so grateful for this understanding that he hugged the child sleeping in his arms. Without Long Toes' eager little footsteps, leaving prints on the savanna's face, he would not have had any of that understanding.

Again he became scared about death, which would not only separate him from his sapiens world but also from this world. From Ngili and Yinka, but above all others from the little being in his arms.

Several thousand feet below, the poachers' truck hurtled up, until the Mau's lower spurs rose right in front of it.

MODIBO WAS DRIVING WITH HIS BRAND-NEW NIGHTVIEWERS on; they were expensive Night Hawks that Kalangi had sent in on the supply plane that morning.

A cluster of fetishes and amulets clinked in front of Modibo's nose, hanging from the rearview mirror. There was a five-inch-long Virgin Mary made of plastic, a hyena's penis bone, a dried-up whole sunbird, a shotgun slug, and various fangs and teeth, including a chip from a grossly large hippopotamus molar. Tied to a coarse frame of brass, they made up the *imani* or faith tree of the poacher gang. In the camp, the imani tree was hung from a pole, but when the poachers moved, they usually stored it with the cooking utensils. But this time, Modibo had said he wanted it hanging in the truck's cabin.

Modibo forced the truck uphill until its engine started to grind; then he stopped the truck and turned off the engine.

"Come on," he ordered the two other men in the cabin, and jumped out. The others descended after him, cradling in their arms more of the brand-new equipment dropped off by the plane: two E. F. Johnson radios and a Bushmaster scanner. The Bushmaster was just a bit larger than a portable telephone, but its ten-inch antenna could scan anything within nine thousand square miles, from approaching park patrol planes and vehicles to the radio stations in the regional townships of Narok and Magadi.

That morning the pilot who brought the supplies had told Modibo, "In Nairobi, we plug with this scanner into what's said inside police cars and banks' armored trucks." Modibo had let out a whistle at how sophisticated the equipment was, and concluded that these mangati were getting more valuable by the hour.

Up on the truck's platform, the red dot of a reefer flared, then subsided. Bilal and one other man jumped down, slinging their rifles over their shoulders. Bilal glanced up at the Mau's forested incline, which seemed to hang over the truck and the men. Suddenly he felt the touch of fingers against his throat and he jumped; Modibo was trying to clip a wire hung with a baby rhino's tooth on it around Bilal's neck. Modibo wore one himself, and with his nightviewers on, he looked like a horned monster.

"*La.* No," grunted Bilal.

Modibo clicked the other jujus in his hand and grunted back that they were good for imani. Bilal shook his head, and started walking toward a tulip tree with unusually low branches. The greenish brightness of Modibo's nightviewers made the tree's fiery red lobed flowers look now like gruesome funeral decorations. Bilal suddenly retched, from the Uganda Blue he'd smoked earlier on an empty stomach in the hurtling truck.

"Get yoself togedda, or I leave yo' here," threatened Modibo.

Bilal made a pained face, straightened up, wiping his mouth with his tattered sleeve, and trailed back. But when they arrived at the truck, Bilal saw the other men unloading the snares—two stacks, full size and baby size. The snares had been washed that morning and they gave off a lingering shine in the moonlight. Bilal muttered something about it being bad imani if they snared any more baby animals. And he was sure that this whole chase after mangati was real bad imani.

Modibo unslung his Enfield. "Yuh know who give da orders here? I do. We snare what I say we snare. Yuh shut up, or I snare yuh ri' here fo' bait, yuh undastand?" He cracked back the Enfield's lock.

Bilal looked at the barrel's cold round mouth, and muttered, "I undastand. Yuh give da orders, Sarge."

"Good. Bilal, yuh walk ahead and aim dis at da ground, so I can read da trail." Modibo handed Bilal the big flashlight. Maybe the idiot will blind a boomslang snake, he thought, and get a deadly bite. "Yuh turn da flashlight at mah nightviewers, I kill yuh," Modibo warned, aware that if a light beam shone into those glasses, the person wearing them would be blinded.

"All ri', men?" There was a muffled rumble of confirmation. "Up we go!"

Modibo touched his juju and stepped into the trees. As they started the trek up, all the men touched their jujus, except for Bilal, who didn't have one.

WHEN KEN WOKE UP HE FELT THAT HE WAS HAVING AN out-of-body experience. He saw that the vegetation surrounding their sleeping site was bright green with morning light.

He heard a loud *Wrraaa!* come from several chests. Before Ken could rub the blurriness from his eyes, the gracile males, their bodies like rough naked statues, rushed through the edge of the brush. They must have been watching the clan because when they jumped on the sleeping females, their penises already had firm erections.

For an instant, Ken marveled at how perfect their penises looked, so purposely pointed. He wondered if he was having a graphic wet dream, but he felt Long Toes kick in his arms and jump up.

Two males were already toppling Niawo. Four or five other males started grabbing several of the shrieking females, who threw themselves on their backs on the forest floor—to avoid being hurt? to welcome seed they had been expecting? Niawo seemed to disappear under her aggressors, but then there was a dull thud of a knee or foot, followed by a high cry of pain from a male, and Niawo emerged undefiled and threw herself at the male, who rose and fled. All the females thrown to the ground were fighting off their attackers with their knees, their fists, and their clawing fingers. They were also making harsh guttural calls as they threw the males off their bodies, while Ken, eyes bulging, noted that this frontal position was far from being an invitation, and was really a female's best defensive stance. If this was a primal rape, it seemed to have its own rules of the game. The males gritted their teeth and tried to withstand the battery, but soon they started to get up, massaging their groins. The women who had gotten rid of their males started shrieking them away, but with a similar glint of interest in their eyes.

The youngsters were up in a flash, aiding their mothers. Ken saw Crew Cut grabbing a male that had attacked Busta; he was strong enough to pull the male off his mother by his hair. Busta got up from underneath, leaves clinging to her breasts, her grin rather ambiguous, and Crew Cut instantly turned from her, and he and several boys hooted, chasing the male into the forest. Niawo also chased her attacker and managed to trip him. Then she crashed onto him like a feline onto prey, but he was strong enough to roll on top of her again. For several seconds, Ken saw the male's hairy back beginning to pump, but again the alpha woman slipped out from under him, and he was left hugging the forest floor. On her haunches, she waited an instant until he rose, well scratched in the face, and reached for her again; then she gave him a thudding kick in the chest and waved over two other females, who piled up on the male and scratched him like lionesses pretending not to be ready to pair up.

The children were now zigzagging all over the place, heading for a wrestling pair of male on female as soon as they saw one and turning it into a pile of bodies. The clan's sounds became so loud that they made the foliage rustle, and Ken became aware that the raid was not really a raid, but rather a kind of pairing play.

I better hide, he thought. With the females, it's foreplay. But if these males see me, it might get nasty. He was stunned to feel so much relief: These males were graciles of the same species as Long Toes' clan.

For now, the graciles had won.

He remembered that dying robust male. More like him were dead now. He closed his eyes, held them tight over that image of the dying prehuman, and wished it would go away. The stronger breed was winning. Let's be prejudiced in their favor, he thought. Might as well. They've got to be the ones that are more developed and more highly evolved. Don't judge, Lauder. And don't interfere. Don't be God.

He opened his eyes.

He was feeling very separate from the breed and decided to hide in a sprawling shrub that had red orchidlike flowers. It looked like a variety of bauhinia and he could see that it was prized by ants because its outer branches had been eaten into lacelike ghosts. He breathed and wondered how long it would be until the ants found him and he would have to dash out, hollering.

The males were escaping toward the clearing's edges. One of them was dragging a sprained leg. Bruised, his manhood flopping, he was still being harassed by the clan's young girls. Those giggling pests were more than he could take. He gathered his stamina, jumped into the shrub of wild bauhinia and landed nose to nose with Ken, who no longer looked as shockingly alien as he had weeks before. A thick brown beard had invaded the lower half of Ken's face, hiding much of his lightly designed jaws. His wildly tousled hair was full of debris from the forest floor that had clung to it in his sleep. His skin was tanned, unwashed, crisscrossed with scratches, and dotted with pimples. His chapped lips were still pinker and fleshier than the hominids' and his eyes were a lighter brown, his nose strikingly more prominent, and his forehead fuller and higher. And he was over six feet. Seeing how big Ken was, the gracile yelled in shock.

Quickly the ape-man's thin but muscled arms flexed and extended, and his fists shot at Ken's face with lightning speed. Everything was moving so quickly that Ken didn't really feel the blow. He collapsed and was viciously whipped by shattered branches. The gracile arched up into the air as he leaped away, streaked across the clearing, and joined his comrades. Ken could hear the high, staccato grunts as the males started spreading the news about the women's unexplained guest.

He rose, tasting blood in his mouth. He wiped his nose on his forearm, spreading the bloodied mucus on his skin. With his tongue he could feel that one of his front teeth had been shaken in its socket. Even so, he palpitated with hope. I'll survive, If I can make them see that I'm not after their females.

THE RADIOS AND BUSHMASTER SCANNER TURNED OUT TO be a big headache for Modibo. At the first rest stop, the men turned on the scanner and started tapping the frequency keyboard, looking for rap stations to tune the radios to.

Modibo had anxiously walked ahead to get a sense of where they were and where they were going. When he returned, all the men except Bilal were clanking snares like cymbals and thumping about in the murky light of the morning to the tune of Snoop Doggy Dogg. Modibo rushed at them snarling, ready to crush the scanner and radios. He kicked them with his rifle butt and ordered them back on the trail.

On they went. When the morning light filtered down, Modibo told Bilal to turn off the flashlight. Only minutes back into the climb, someone turned the scanner back on, hoping to find the morning news. Modibo hit the culprit in the face, thinking that they needed an example.

Kalangi had sent him as detailed a map of the area as could be found. Using the map as well as readings from his compass and his bush tracker's memory, Modibo hoped to reconstruct the trail opened back in '53 by the anti–Mau Mau commando Modibo had been a part of. But in those thirty years, the forest had changed tremendously. New vegetation had overgrown and enriched some of the inclines, and leaching of the soil had made others bald and frittered. The trees had taken over some of the cliffs and abandoned others. Modibo remembered that the old trail meandered up until it finally ran into an open terrace. Beyond that terrace there was an abrupt drop that faced straight east. That terrace would be critical in defining all other geographic coordinates such as elevation, distance, and isolation of the mangati area. He was finding that his memory was more reliable than any of the latitudes and longitudes noted on the map. He had an innate sense of distances, even though he realized soon that the distances he remembered no longer seemed to match the terrain he was in now. Falls of trees, growth of brush, mud slides and other movements had seesawed the incline, adding or subtracting distance. And so much of the growth had become so thick that certain areas had to be bypassed.

It seemed that they were sinking upward, deeper, deeper, and deeper into a higher and wider unknown space. Two hours before, by Modibo's reckoning, they should have passed a landmark left by the '53 unit. A particularly noticeable one. Truly impossible to miss. It had been left there to scare the mangati and to discourage them forever from reexiting the forest.

Where the hell was it?

Behind him, the young generation kept banging the scanner's keyboard, looking for the sounds of Snoop Doggy Dogg or LL Cool J.

Bilal, who had trained for three months in forestry at a

regional vocational school before he stole the teacher's pay-
check and ran off into the bush to avoid arrest, was now
coming out of his reefer daze and discovering how marvelous
the alpine forest was. It was unlike anything he'd seen during
his brief training. Species he knew were mixed in with trees
and bushes and flowers he'd never seen. He felt like he was
still tripping. To regulate his thoughts, he concentrated on
his footsteps—the footsteps of poachers in the forest, the
footsteps of old army boots from a ragtag little army that
preyed on the wild and never thought twice about it.

The trees and plants brought back memories of his childhood. His first eight years were spent in a highland village,
before his family moved to a Nairobi slum and disintegrated.
He passed a m'deeree shrub, which tribal people used to
make a concoction that cured fevers. A broken, uprooted
m'cherenge tree smelled sweetly, reminding him that its
wood was used for milk pots. The large yellow flowers of a
m'talawanda reminded him of the village drums he had
banged on as a kid. Most of those names were prefaced by
an *m'*, like tribal names—which made a kind of sense. Bilal
remembered that in his childhood stories trees had been people.

Feeling momentarily better, he turned toward the sergeant.
"Look, Sarge, dis is a m'toondoo tree. Good for boats,
drums, troughs—and da leaves you can make ropes." Modibo looked up and saw a majestically somber tree, with its
vast foliage. "Can camp a whole regiment under it, huh,
Sarge?"

"Shut up," Modibo muttered.

Bilal looked behind at the other poachers. Their sweat had
cut shiny little paths in the dirt on their foreheads, cheeks,
and necks. He still felt funny from the lingering reefer, making him want to impart to those men a feeling of . . . what?
Beauty? Yeah, a kind of beauty, which he had almost forgotten. Bilal stepped closer to Modibo, his eyes so shiny that
the sergeant veered off to keep his distance.

" 'S all ri', Sarge. Dat"—Bilal pointed at another tree—
"is a m'oosimbatee. Fruit good for cough." He looked at

the other men with warmth; they looked back blankly. He asked the sergeant how exactly they were going to locate those mangati. Modibo did not know, but faked it. They were not far from the outer edges of the mangati territory; they would make a leaf cabin, as they did when ambushing rhinos, and sit inside it and let the mangati come close.

"After we kill dem, do we pull out deir teeth and put dem on da imani tree for luck?" asked Bilal, looking at that baby rhino tooth dangling on Modibo's chest.

"We don kill dem, we bring dem back alive. Dey valuable," said Modibo.

Bilal felt the eyes of that baby rhino, peering from beyond death into his reefer-moistened soul. He could not take the snaring of one more creature, but he didn't know how to say that to the other poachers, or to Modibo.

"What if da mangati fight us, Sarge?" Bilal asked.

"Don worry 'bou' dat, worry 'bou' make a good leaf cabin," countered Modibo. "Remember, five hundred dollar each, if we do a good job." He raised his voice at the other men. "Five each. Lot o' money."

"I don want to go," said Bilal. He dropped on the ground and started to take off his boots.

"Insa-bordi-nay-shun?" snickered Modibo. He raised his left arm and poked at his watch and compass, their only orientation devices, which were strapped next to each other on his wrist. "I go alone," Modibo warned. "I leave all yuh here, and go alone."

A throb seized the poachers. One of them poked Bilal in the ribs with his boot. "Get up, and stop make da trouble."

Bilal got up but started mumbling, "Da mangati, dey people, not apes, I see deir teeth in Zhang Chen's shop, dey look li' people teeth. Fo' catching people, we should get mo' money."

Modibo walked on, his eyes alternately on the trail and on the compass. Then he stopped. "Hold this," he told Bilal. The young man obediently took the scanner. Modibo unslung the Enfield, stuck it in Bilal's chest, and pulled the trigger

The shot was muffled by the body. Erupting out, the slug blew a hole in Bilal's back.

Bilal fell, twitching. Modibo deftly caught the scanner and stuck it under one arm; then, holding the smoking rifle, he jumped into a bank of bright red climbing lilies.

One poacher squeaked, "Ss-sarge?" There was no answer. Another muttered that the sarge had gone off with their money. Unslinging their rifles, all three poachers plowed forward across the shrub. They saw Modibo crossing away quickly, then stopping, then standing dead still. They rushed toward him and froze in front of a strange monument.

A tree that had been split by lightning stood in the middle of a clearing, supporting a gruesome sculpture of human skeletons held together with brownish withered twine. The poachers saw the morbid likeness of Modibo. In his ant-eaten camouflage jacket and helmet, he was snaring a helpless mangati. More hominid skeletons lay around the tree trunk, like vanquished fighters. Old-man's beard moss had been wrapped around their bodies, to make them look apishly hairy.

"Who build dis?" a poacher dared to ask.

"I did," Modibo rasped hoarsely. "To scare da mangati, and keep dem in da forest. Now, anyone got da cold feet, yuh free to go. But if yuh stay, yuh take my orders. We catch da mangati, take dem back live to Nairobi, and we sell dem ou'sevves. We sell widdou' da chief, dah-reck to the customers." He waited a beat. "All ri', men?"

He waited. They were too scared to answer.

"All ri'," he answered for them. He kicked a skeleton, as if to affirm his power in the clearing. "We ready, men?" Someone whined an acquiescence. "Den up we go."

Off they went, stepping over the hominid bones.

Modibo was suggesting an arrangement identical to the slave-trading operations of yore. The Waganda chiefs of the interior had also sidestepped the Swahili kings of the coast and the Arab princes of Zanzibar and sold slaves directly to the Muslim rulers of Oman, and to the nabobs of India, and then to the Europeans. Since the pharaohs' times, East Africa had been poached, by strangers and by its own people. It had been poached of slaves, of beasts, and now of its ancestors.

NOW THAT THE RAID WAS OVER, THE FEMALES SHOWED their excitement by prattling and hooting.

Niawo, who had a bruise under one breast and leaves in her hair and sticking to her thighs, prowled about with a catlike look.

The children were chasing each other with an excess of energy which, Ken guessed, was a result of the ambiguous emotions they felt while watching their mothers engaged in that rough pairing game. Crew Cut seemed to be angry at Busta. She reached out to touch his cheek, but he rejected her and grabbed a gob of dirt and leaves and flung it at her. Then he ran off with Smiley and Long Toes.

None of the females were foraging for food that morning. The motherly instinct had been replaced by the urge to produce more children in the near future.

Ken saw the females start walking off, in pairs, for some reason choosing to fight their way through the dense brush instead of taking a clear path. After he'd lost sight of them, Ken heard them explode into high cries and shrill laughter; they had run into the stalking males again, and were returning quickly, glancing back over their shoulders. The children felt that they had permission to investigate. They zoomed into the thicket, then galloped back, then plunged into the thicket again. The females dropped into the grass, and some of them went through the motions of foraging, but they were really too stirred up to have patience for anything. Some jumped up again and paced, this time with a kind of strut.

The guys are close by, Ken concluded. They're watching.

But Ken couldn't tell exactly where they were. He started to step into the thicket, and Niawo hurried over and followed right behind him. He saw her eyes and was surprised by the concern in them. Am I in danger? he wondered. Will I be stoned to death in front of her?

The hair on the back of his neck pricked up. Out of the

thickness stepped three males. They approached fast, with their slanted profiles hung forward and their arms dangling unarmed. Ken could see that they didn't have any sticks or hunting stones.

All three barely reached up to Ken's chest. He felt so silly being so tall and big-headed. Their eyes were focused on his midriff, like radars scanning another male's gonads. His were at rest. He felt the anxiety of being seen naked by other males who were overtly appraising his sexual mechanism. He was scared, but he wished Niawo would go away—what the hell was she doing here?

Nothing, apparently. She watched the males step closer, and then she crossed her thinly muscled arms under her breasts and bit her thin lower lip, almost in a challenging pose. Ken looked at her, and she looked straight back at him. The gracile males were now so close that he smelled their hot sweaty bodies. One came so close that his forehead was right under Ken's chin. And then he reached . . .

For Ken's arm. The ape-man's nimble muscled fingers, chimpish but much less hairy, felt Ken's biceps muscle. Ken flexed it slightly. The *Australopithecus* blew warmly at Ken's neck, while his fingers quickly palpated one of Ken's shoulders, then his pectoral muscles, then retreated.

Yes, I'm made of flesh and bone just like you, Ken thought, and I yearn for a mate just like you, but I'm not here to claim your territory, or your females.

Of course, they could never understand that.

The hair on Ken's body still stood up, but he withstood their inspection. Two million years of difference on both sides were separated by a few feet of air. Then one of the males almost pinched one of Ken's nipples, which were smaller, with thinner areolas, than theirs. Ken understood, and started truly laughing. This was one of his features that wasn't larger, stronger, and coarser-looking than theirs. They stared at his navel, and at his crotch, but dared not touch them.

They turned and hurried off.

Ken turned. Dead into Niawo's eyes.

He grinned, I think they were impressed that you showed them your pet—me.

She turned. A few leaves were still stuck to her back. He started to put out one hand . . . no. No, he would not pick the leaves off her naked back.

She did something very clever, he thought. She somehow let those males know that I was no trouble. Then he changed his mind; maybe she'd signaled something completely different. Maybe she'd told them that Ken wouldn't stand in their way of wooing her clan because . . . Ken was her mate!

All right, all right, Lauder. You can't be raped by a female if you don't feel like it; that's one advantage of being a male. So cool it.

In a disorderly formation—females in the middle, escorted loosely by children racing back and forth—the clan started to migrate eastward. The sun's warmth dripped like honey through thinning foliage. Ahead of them a sparsely forested gully lay between wooded cliffs.

Niawo led the group right into it, which was like courting an ambush, but she had done it on purpose. On the left side of the cliff, they could see the hairy heads of males showing in tangled branches up in the trees, like ripe fruit ready to drop.

Niawo even slowed down the pace.

The females passed by the attentive eyes of the males, who clustered among trees like boys lingering on a sidewalk, watching the girls go by.

The males started walking down, singly or in pairs, some faster, some slower. Finally, more than a dozen of them stood along the gully, touching the women's territory but not entering it yet. Their chests, arms, and legs were interlaced with vines and bushes. They were still so much a part of nature, thought Ken, entranced with that mix of skin and leaf and stem.

The males didn't even try to block the women's path. Their dark glances seemed to figure out how difficult this courtship would be.

Niawo came to a bank of shrub loaded with wild peanuts,

and behaved like a teenager, fussing loudly over them. The other females allowed her to pick the peanuts and distribute them. They dropped down or sprawled, and ate slowly, making a lot of gestures and sounds. Were they sending the men a message by being so enthusiastic over food? Were they letting them know that the way to their hearts was through their stomachs?

It was possible.

Niawo was emphasizing food sharing by giving out those puny nuts so importantly. There was a very strong connection between food and sex.

Ken fought a recurring worrying thought. Ngili would eventually put together a rescue party to come looking for him, and when they found him, they'd find *them*. Park rangers and scientists power sawing through the brush or dropping from helicopters would face this "savage" humanness with their own modern humanness and then . . . what would happen?

But there might not be any search parties back in Nairobi because they might think that I'm already dead.

So what will happen to me? Will I stay on here? Will I *live* here?

No. Impossible. I'm too different.

He wondered whether the males might still try to eject him from the scene. He knew they would, eventually, and decided he should probably slip away. He looked around for Long Toes. Unconsciously he assumed that they would leave together. He and the boy. The way it had been in the savanna.

He shook his head.

He saw Long Toes appear and disappear among the crowd as he ran around with Crew Cut and Smiley. They made a rather handsome threesome. The peanuts had turned into a regular picnic, with most everyone sprawling in the warm grass. Ken noticed Busta go off with a party of other women and come back carrying branches of climbing lilies, with crisp and rippled petals that curved upward. Was this dessert after the nuts? No. Their naturally curved ends were perfect to clamp in the girls' and women's hair. Busta did it first;

she took a handful of petals, threw them up in the air, and stood under the petals' rain like a playful chimp, letting them snag in her hair. Then she got up and paced about, her eyes at half-mast, as if she was trying to decide if she was pretty wearing that flower apparel.

And she was.

Beauty was such a deeply rooted human instinct. Here it was, already at work. Making oneself pretty was such an ingredient of womanhood.

Suddenly something about Busta seemed to correct her heavy features and make the angle of her face less steeply slanted. Her gait seemed lighter, and her breathing, through her wistfully open lips, evoked an innocent freshness. She twirled around, arms high. One of the other females uttered a snickering sound, but Busta opened her eyes and planted herself in front of the critic, her much more robust arms dangling menacingly. She had a right to adorn herself before mating, just like everyone else. The offender sat up hurriedly and looked down at her own prettier breasts and conceded her error. Busta strutted away close to Niawo and dropped in the grass. Knowing the sisterly ways of those two, Ken didn't read that much in Niawo's fingers rising to Busta's face. Niawo gave her a little tug. And one more. Busta's shoulders were twitching. Ken found himself ambling over, hurrying, scared that he would miss this. Out of breath, he dropped right next to them, eager to photograph that moment with the lens of his mind.

Niawo was not tickling, not squeezing. She was plucking those long hairs off Busta's lips. She was making Busta's lips more like a gracile woman's. Freeing them of that robust fur.

Busta tilted her head back, blinking in pain, but her lips, where they had been plucked, were clean and pink. Ken was struck by a realization of how simply and effectively women signaled their sexuality with their *faces*. The pink of their vaginal lips had sunk out of sight in the australopithecine stage of evolution, hidden between legs that were held tightly together. But this pink had been transferred onto their faces.

And even though this breed would diversify enormously over the next few million years, the pink of these hairless lips would remain the essential feature of femininity.

The sun filtered through the trees and the air became warm. Ken felt drunk from all the knowledge, unlearned, undeduced, he was being taught in the raw by this species.

He and the species were so busy now that none of them saw the forehead, topped by frizzled black hair, that rose above a fairly distant bush. The eyes under that forehead were used to looking at things from a distance. They watched, dilated with excitement, while the mouth on that face twisted nervously, repressing its gnomish grin.

Modibo ducked back behind the bush again and retreated sideways like a crab, computing how many australopithecines he'd just seen. He figured it would take his men at least until the afternoon to set snares all around that terrace, turning the mating grounds into one giant trap.

WARMED BY THE SUN, THE FLOWERS BEGAN TO WITHER AND fall out of the females' hair. Niawo, losing one cluster of petals, put it up again, then losing it again, suddenly tore them all down, and rubbed them hard between her fingers. The crushed petals showed between her palms, which she slapped on her cheeks.

She's playing, Ken told himself.

No, she's not. She's signaling for you, Lauder.

He felt himself blush, under his tan and his crusty dirt. Freaky stuff. What was he going to do?

Niawo massaged her cheeks and stroked her closed eyelids. Then she got up and again led the clan down into the widening gully.

Ken felt an unexpected desire to walk closer to her. He followed behind her, his wide steps easily overcoming her much shorter ones. He swallowed nervously. Step before her, stop, turn around, that's it, easy, boy. Turn and look at her, as if completely by accident. He felt awkward, and scolded himself. How could he feel that way? No one watched him. No one? Well, no one at his evolutionary stage.

He stepped in front of the little woman, and turned to her with the best faked indifference any man could muster.

He throbbed from top to toe. Her irises looked dilated, perhaps from the juice of that flower.

He gaped. This could not be.

She was letting him know about her own interest by dilating her pupils like opening lenses. In all species, that dilation signaled interest. She sought his eyes, and when she caught them, she stared at him so intently that he shrank back from the edge of her stare as if from a dizzying drop.

They were still stepping down that gully. Unexpectedly, the trees receded, and they entered a terrace that was wooded on both sides but open in the middle. The opening pointed over the escarpment's edge at the savanna.

For the first time in days, Ken stood in the full sunlight. He let it flood his nakedness and kindle his face. When he turned back, blinking, he found the little female right next to him. He tore himself away abruptly, almost tripping.

I PROBABLY MISSED MY CHANCE WITH HER, HE THOUGHT. That's good. No sense in thinking more about it.

He faced out onto the far savanna and saw the moving specks, dots, stripes, of grazing animals. There was plenty to do here, at the edge. The children had clustered there, staring and babbling and pointing. Long Toes was back explaining and telling tales. He raised an arm, flexed it like a long neck, made his palm hang limp from the wrist, and with fingertips brought together he imitated the head and neck of an ostrich. Scanning the savanna, Ken saw that ostrich, stepping around a cluster of eggs. There didn't appear to be any baboons around to steal them, or any hawks to puncture them. The ostrich lowered itself on its eggs, but raised its neck like a periscope. Long Toes raised his own arm to imitate that neck.

Ken wondered how visible they were for someone standing in the savanna below. He stepped so close to the precipice that the grass and dirt frittered into scree under his bare feet, and began to roll down. He saw a wide bald spur half-way below, with a pattern of feet stepping in a circle.

This was the spur he had seen from Hendrijks's plane.

Part Six

THE CHOICE

HERE IT IS, NGILI, KEN THOUGHT. THAT FAMOUS PATtern of footprints we saw from the plane. We racked our brains over its meaning and almost began to think it had been a mirage. But here it is. The proof that they existed here long ago, when only *they* were the humans. The proof of their magical continuity.

He felt an amazing wealth of memories connected to those footprints. They had been the first clue to the existence of this unique breed.

The wind on the lower cliffs whipped up a cloud of dust that covered the foosteps briefly and then swept it away again. A whirlpool of wind picked up some of that dust and carried it up the slopes of the Mau until it sprayed Ken's face.

He stepped back and turned toward the terrace, where again he saw the males of the breed.

They trooped in, a compact column of about two dozen, but they quickly broke off into twos and threes. They started pacing around, as if taking the measure of this or that female reclining in the grass, now and then pausing to allow the children to streak in front of them. Most of the younger children were loitering around, trying to guess which of the males would be chosen by their mothers. The older boys had gathered at the mountain's edge, looking out at the open spaces. It was clear that they coveted those open spaces that were so full of color and movement, and game they could hunt.

The males walked around like neighborhood boys checking out the girls at a dance, trying to figure out which one to ask. These graciles had been kept away from females by the wars between the breeds, and now that the war was almost over, and they were its momentary victors, they had come to court. Here and there a male hopped on one foot, then on the other, dangling his crotch in front of a certain female. Then he would walk off, strutting and prancing. Some of them returned several times to the same females, whereas others strutted and hopped in front of any female in their path.

Ken guessed that the males who were returning to one particular female probably knew her, and might have mated with her already, and might even have had children with her. He noticed that some of the children approached their mothers' suitors and sized them up with intense curiosity. Still, everyone's behavior was careful and inhibited.

Ken was sure that the war had been the reason the spouses had separated. The war had made both males and females weigh the advantages of freedom against the comforts of a bond with a mate. But clearly, the bond, or the need for it, was turning out to be stronger because, in contrast to that morning, the males were here, trying to negotiate with the females. The females sat up straight and rocked side to side, chimp fashion, and stared less at the males' faces and more at their hips, upper thighs, and genitals.

He watched them long enough for the sun to sail overhead westward and for the shade of the Mau's crest to fall over the terrace, bringing with it a gust of cold that made Ken shiver. He looked up and saw that the crest appeared to be on fire with the radiance of the sun slipping behind it.

The women started getting up from the grass, and several of them gathered in the middle of the terrace and walked around, first in a loose irregular circle, then in a tighter one. The males that had pursued them joined the circle, enlarging it. The women pulled closer inward, tightening the circle, leaving the men out. Again, the men broke into the circle, walking with them.

Ken felt a small hand push on his back. He turned, expecting Long Toes, but instead saw Niawo, whose hand was not much larger than the boy's. She pushed him toward the walking circle.

After Ken broke in between two females, several more males broke in simultaneously, enlarging the circle to almost the size of the one Ken had seen on the spur. Most of the males had managed to maneuver themselves next to a female, separating them from Ken in the process.

Ken thought of Ngili. He and Ngili had wondered so much about that circle, and now Ken knew what the hominids were doing in it. They were choosing their mates.

Ken started slowing down but was pushed forward by a knee knocking into the back of his knees. He glanced over his shoulder at one of the males, a short, young, muscular australopithecine who was panting, not from exertion but from excitement. He had very large nostril holes, and a hint of a future nasal bridge. His look said to Ken: Move, dummy, this is no time to think. Ken jumped ahead and bumped into another warm hominid. Walk, Lauder, dammit.

His feet stepped in the footprints left by the feet ahead of him. He tried to match the pace of the group and to land his foot right in those prints. But the circle was still shrinking and enlarging, and the males kept juggling their positions, slipping out and back in, trying to get a spot next to the female of their choice. The females were aware of this and watched the jockeying with that half-mast gaze Ken had seen earlier in Busta. Every now and then, one of the females missed a step, fell behind, or rushed forward a few steps. They were also trying to be near certain males.

After Ken had been walking between these other bodies for some time, he saw a female still standing outside the circle, and realized that it was Niawo. She was holding back a shiver, making him aware of how much colder it must be now. But he did not feel the cold inside the warm circle, which now included almost every adult male and female on the terrace and was easily as large as the ancient circle.

Far off above the savanna, Ken saw that the moon was almost full again. It seemed strikingly round, strikingly like the circle they were carving in the cliffside. Darkness would follow, and then the circle would break, like a huge live necklace fragmented into paired pearls. The pairs would step toward the brush and lie down with each other. And the moon would rise enigmatically overhead, evoking one notion only: godliness.

He was walking almost diametrically across from Busta, who was enjoying this so fully that she started hopping wildly.

The circle was breaking up, and the other females and males began hopping too—like the Masai in their up-and-down dances. Yes, Ken reflected, that hopping and this hopping were both exhibitions of sexual power, flauntings of organs that were ready to unite. Maybe the custom had started here. The up-and-down. The dance that had shocked missionaries with its unabashed sexuality. The dance Livingstone tried in vain to defend as a beautifully innocent rite of fertility. Here it was. Here was its ancient source.

As the pairs broke off, the circle was depleted. Ken realized that he had to slip away now. He could not join this all the way; he could not break its magic by his intrusion. He finally stole away from the pairing graciles. There wasn't a trail down to the savanna, so he would have to cut one, fighting the scrub downward.

He spotted Long Toes on a large stone anchored at the edge of the terrace; he was watching the darkness thicken below. The boy looked at Ken, who was naked and unpaired.

Ken read the boy's eyes and knew that they were saying good-bye. If the alien didn't pair up, there was no chance that he would stay. Why would he? What would he be to the clan? So the stranger was not staying and there was nothing to do but say good-bye.

What are you going to do, Long Toes?

Long Toes tilted his head to one side, showing his indecision. But he clearly thought he might give the old crew a chance, for now. This home gang of his had possibilities.

Ken smiled, trying to signal back that he thought Long Toes was making the right choice. The boy had playmates here, and uncles and aunts, and with his precocious skills, he might someday emerge as a leader.

But what about the savanna?

Perhaps Long Toes was thinking the same because he looked out at the ocean of open space where the hungry felines were roaring and the herbivores were bellowing until their sounds filled the night. This was the savanna they had known together.

Ken looked out at the savanna again, and then at the boy's feet. Maybe he would be back sometime. Stop it, Lauder, he told himself. This was a onetime experience that would never happen again. This is it. So long, prehistory.

Long Toes uttered a call, and from nearby, Smiley scurried over, trailed by Crew Cut and the other youngsters.

The alien was leaving. Their big live toy was saying his farewell. Ken gripped a groundsel sapling and used all his strength to uproot it. He would need a hardy stick to hack his way down the sloping Mau for another hour or so; then he would find a place to sleep and continue at dawn. Ken was bending the sapling and letting it go and bending it again until the youngsters started cackling and laughing and joined in to help him. It was better that he do something like this, instead of allowing his feelings to overflow. He tried not to look at Long Toes while he worked at the sapling. Finally, he felt it snap and held it up and the children helped him tear off the leaves.

In seconds, he was ready to go.

He stepped out to the edge of the terrace and felt it roll down with him as the dirt gave way under his feet. He changed tack with the stick, like a skier, and began sliding down the incline on the backs of his swollen, aching heels. He skied like that for a time, and the children followed him for a long way. They didn't seem at all scared of the dark, perhaps because they had Long Toes, vanquisher of both the jungle and the savanna, with them.

* * *

NOT FAR BELOW WAS WOODED BRUSH, WHERE HE WAS CERtain the children would no longer follow him. Ken looked down and tried to concentrate on the trail so that he wouldn't look back at the little faces behind him.

He heard their little grunts and giggles and longed to see their expressions. But he didn't want to see Long Toes. He didn't want to meet the darkness in his eyes, though he hoped it meant nothing but the growing darkness of the cliffs. Still, he glanced back when one of the kids tripped. Clumsy Crew Cut was quickly picking himself up. And of course he also saw Long Toes. The boy immediately looked down as if checking the bushes, boulders, and shrubs. His lips were open, and his whole face seemed sad. He was walking down without the giggles and liveliness of the others.

Ken swiftly looked ahead again—hearing the other children but also hearing Long Toes' silence.

He looked out at the open flats and pressed one hand against his chest and squeezed the other around his stick to keep his body from feeling the days of hunting and the nights of sleeping curled up next to that primal child. To get away, he could not let himself face that.

Stop it, Long Toes. Goddammit, stop it; don't do whatever you're doing to that pump in my chest.

Ken was suddenly struck by an ugly, selfish longing to be back in the city, among casual, self-possessed modern people. It tried to drown out the giggles of the children, but it failed. He looked back, and Long Toes gave him a little grin of encouragement. The alien might have once killed a lion, but now he seemed frail and lost. Ken winced at almost every step and was bruised all over. He was no longer the same man.

As they continued down, they crossed the band of shrub, and just yards ahead there was another that was taller and more tangled. Now I'm going to stop and shoo them away, Ken told himself. This is far enough. They should go back home.

But before he could do it, he stepped on a vine that closed around one of his ankles. It felt hard, as if it were made of metal. Two steps behind him, a child cried out, and as Ken jerked his head back to see who it was, his other ankle was snagged.

All at once, the sky and earth tumbled at each other, as another of these vines caught his neck. Grabbing it, Ken's hands recognized the noose of a wire poaching snare. It tightened, pulling him ahead. He fought the strangling sensation by pushing his stick against the wire, watching it slice the green wood like a soft-boiled egg. He heard a radio, followed by a voice nearby. "*Upesi! Upesi!* Quick! Quick!"

Ken tried to twist his neck, to see the children, to warn them—me, but not them, not Long Toes!—but he could not turn his neck. The wire had stiffened it into blocks of panicked muscles and was beginning to slice into them. The other snares tore the ground from under him, and he slammed into the dirt.

A man stood in front of him. He wore faded army fatigues and had on nightviewers that made him look like a huge strange bug. He was carrying a rifle in one hand, and in the other he had a toggle that twisted and tightened the snare. Ken knocked the man down and could smell his pungent sweat. He saw the man's snarling grin, as evil as ever.

"*Upesi, mangati!* Quick, the mangati," Modibo kept yelling.

Modibo jumped up but seemed unwilling to shoot his Enfield. He grabbed the heavy brass flashlight in his belt and hit Ken over the head with it, not realizing who he was. Modibo thought Ken was the largest mangati he'd ever seen. There was a clang of metal on bone, and Ken almost blanked out. He lost the stick, but put both hands inside the wire noose and loosened it enough to take a raspy breath. As he tried to stagger up, Modibo hit him again with the flashlight, toppling him and dropping the flashlight.

Just yards beyond, the baby mangatis had been snagged either by their ankles or their necks. Modibo heard them cry out in shock and pain. He wondered where his men were, and why they had left him alone to reel in the catch. This made the sergeant so mad that he gave the big mangati another blow with the Enfield's butt, then hopped off toward the little ones. He'd try one rifle butt in the head to knock out each of them but still catch them live.

Ken came to, groped around, found the flashlight. He heard a whack, followed by a child's feeble scream. Not the children, he moaned. Then there was another whack and a high cry of pain. He struggled up. The snare around his neck was loose because Modibo had been in such a hurry to knock out the baby mangatis he'd dropped the toggle he'd been using to garrotte Ken. Ken slipped the snare off his neck and moved to free his ankles. The children cried in the snares, and Modibo jumped about crab-legged, rifle in hand, hitting their vulnerable skulls.

''*Upesi, haraka, upesi!* Quick, get over here, quick!'' he kept yelling.

Another poacher finally showed up, also wearing night goggles and carrying a shotgun. He rushed to help the sergeant by bringing the shotgun's stock down on a child's head.

Ken gripped the heavy flashlight. He thought: Don't miss. As he dashed upward, he bumped the second poacher just as he was about to hit the head of one of the children for a third time. Was it Long Toes? There was no time to find out. The poacher turned, and Ken's brain moaned, DON'T MISS! His thumb flicked on the flashlight and shot a beam of light into the poacher's face. The nightviewers multiplied that glare seventy thousand times, and the poacher was blinded instantly. His shotgun fired into the air and fell to the ground. The man grabbed Ken around the neck, but Ken was able to hurl him into the clear, turning him into a groping, screaming ghost. Other poachers smashed through the shrub, their rifles pointed. They saw the ghost and fired at it without thinking.

Modibo had instantly ripped off his own nightviewers and hit the ground one second before the shooting started. He had lost the Enfield and crawled away without it.

Ken lunged out with the flashlight and hit one of the

poachers, knocking him down just as Modibo had done with him a moment ago. He grabbed the man, picking him up and using the twisting, yelling man as a battering ram against the other poachers, making them scream of death and doomsday. He chased the other poachers toward their radio, which he couldn't see but could hear. Chief Kalangi's voice boomed out into the forest: "Modibo, where the hell are you? Modibo, this is Chief Kalangi, report your position. The expedition's plane will land at the foot of the spurs tomorrow morning. . . ."

One of the surviving poachers got away from Ken and raced off, kicking the radio and knocking it over. Ken threw himself at the bodies of the others, looking for Modibo. He searched the bushes but found no one. He turned and raced back to the snared children.

He hadn't had enough strength to break the snare that had trapped him, but somehow he found a way to break these. There was an extra beat in his heart that made him ignore the pain of his bleeding fingers. He ripped up the wires, freeing the little ankles and necks. The children started moving feebly, almost unconsciously. Long Toes opened his eyes at Ken and puffed softly through his mouth.

Far above, on the terrace, the breed had heard the screams of their young and the aggressors' gunshots. The mothers, joined by half of the males, raced down frantically.

But the brief battle was already over. One child lay totally still, lifting his little crossbreed profile at the moon. Ken held his wrist. But there was no pulse.

Crew Cut was dead, strangled by the snare and battered with the shotgun. For him, there would be no more evolution.

"KEEP CALLING MODIBO," KALANGI ORDERED HIS AIDE, Lieutenant Sampa. The chief rose from the dining table they were using as a listening station in the second-floor suite of the Naivasha Hotel. "And keep scanning the air. If the bastard stopped transmitting because he caught something, then I'm sure he changed his frequency to call his buyers."

"We put men at all his contact points in town," said Sampa, "and none reported that he made contact. Maybe something happened to them." Sampa wore an undercover outfit that was the tattered robe of a kamba witch doctor, with amulets for sale hanging from tiny hooks sewn across its front.

"How could anything happen to five able men, all armed and carrying the best equipment?" asked Kalangi. Sampa shrugged, making his amulets jingle.

Kalangi had turned the hotel suite into a field operations center. It was packed with bodyguards and orderlies, and reeked of cigarette smoke. Kalangi paced to the bedroom. The bed hadn't been slept in, but it was covered with Xeroxed pages from Haksar's notebook. Just hours after Harry Ends's party had checked into the hotel's penthouse suite, Kalangi's agents had slipped in, taken the original, run off a copy, and then returned the original.

Kalangi took out a list of foreign guests staying at the Naivasha and reviewed the ones he'd already met with. They included an envoy of the U.S. Agency for International Development, the boss of a Swiss hotel chain interested in branching out to Africa, the secretary of the World Council of Anglican Churches, and a German builder of safari vehicles. In three days, if Clean Sweep went well, all those people would identify Kalangi as one of the new team.

In five minutes, Kalangi was scheduled to meet with two envoys of an African-American organization called Giving Back to Africa.

"Where are Harry Ends and the two others?" he asked Sampa, stuffing the list back in his pocket.

"After a tour of the fossils vault, Anderson and Ends left Ramsay at the university and went to meet with the president. The meeting went well and lasted eight minutes. They've reconnected, and now Anderson is taking them shopping at Muindi Mbingu Road."

"Cyril didn't call me in the meantime?"

"No, Chief."

"They'll probably be back any minute. Be ready for

them.'' Harry Ends's penthouse was bugged with voice-activated mikes that were connected to listening devices in Kalangi's suite. A special operator stood by. Bored, he was looking through a new porno magazine published in censorship-free South Africa.

"All right. I'll be back in half an hour."

"Yes, Chief."

Kalangi stepped out of the suite and headed for the elevator.

TWO MINUTES LATER, HE WAS WITH THE TWO ENVOYS FROM Giving Back to Africa.

"I am sorry that you were carjacked," he said. "Unfortunately, your mishap is not unique; we had four carjackings against foreign guests last week alone, two roadside robberies of tourist buses in game parks, and that's not all. . . .''

The two African Americans, both barely over thirty and both bruised from scuffling with the carjackers, were in a belligerent mood. Lucius Conroy was the son of a California high school principal and himself a teacher. He was six four and barrel-chested; his bubbling energy made him resemble a young black Orson Welles. He blasted out a list of mishaps that had occurred since they'd arrived: Thieves had drilled a tunnel in the wall of the American cultural attaché's residence, and made away with native art and electronic equipment. The economic mission of Malawi caught fire on the day they were scheduled to visit it. The dwellers in the poor suburbs started their days with fistfights with transients, over access to the local water pumps. Fighting seemed to occur all over town, almost as a prelude to any social transaction. Mob justice hung in the air. Conroy had been here five years ago; he could not recognize the place.

The other African American was a petite and bespectacled young woman. Cynthia Palmer was an attorney for trade unions and had been raised by a single mother. She declared that she had rarely seen women being treated so primitively. Paid way lower than the men, they still had to bribe and/or give sexual favors to get their jobs, and they bore the brunt of domestic violence. . . . Kalangi finally stopped her, telling her that everything she'd heard was a rumor, spread by the government's critics. This was a democracy.

Conroy jumped in. "Is the disappearance of six hundred million dollars from your treasury also a rumor? That was reported by your own press. Hell, that's an amount equal to three years of foreign aid."

Kalangi decided to tread carefully. Giving Back to Africa was a dynamic institution, both tougher and more knowledgeable than the U.S. Peace Corps. And being black, it could not be accused of bias. Conroy and Palmer had been received in South Africa by President Mandela.

Kalangi broke into a wide smile. "I come as a friend," he said, lowering his tone as if the room were bugged (as it was), "to advise your foundation to hold back on investing here at this time. There will soon be vast political changes."

"Will they affect the incredible sense of casualness, the better-do-nothing mode of your officials?" Conroy spoke like a disillusioned idealist.

"Absolutely." Another telling look at the walls. "I myself can't do anything because of those older bureaucrats, but I came here to inform you that a new team is coming in. . . ."

"It better," said Palmer. She had sat down on a chair, her dress pulled up over her pretty knees. "Our foundation is entirely community-funded, and we're not the richest American minority by a long shot. You're saying in effect that we should give our money to the next regime here. Very well, but we'd still have to see them perform. When are they coming in?"

Kalangi thought fast. Clean Sweep was about to restart. He didn't want them around to witness it. He needed a momentary diversion. "May I use your phone?"

They nodded. He called his own suite and asked in cryptic phrases what was going on. There was no news of Modibo, and Anderson had still not called, which upset Kalangi as much as not hearing from Modibo. Earlier that day, he'd let greed advise him and had told Anderson that without an additional five thousand dollars he would not get that army plane to fly them to Dogilani the next morning. Anderson had told him to go to hell. Now Kalangi was nervous about his standing with Anderson, especially after having read Haksar's notes.

He hung up.

"Would you like to take a trip up north, to a truly uncommercialized game reserve? One of my aides will drive you"—he managed another smile—"as protection against more mishaps. And believe me, this country's more lawful than many others—in Nigeria, nine environmental activists have just been hanged for criticizing the rape of the Niger delta by Royal Dutch Shell." He didn't tell them that Harry Ends, former VP of Shell, was in the same hotel. "Change cannot be brought about here by Western means. But there will soon be change. Good night. God bless."

"Good night," the guests murmured in reply. Kalangi exited.

Behind him, Lucius Conroy commented on the appropriateness of "God Bless" in a place of such turmoil.

RAJ HAKSAR'S NOTEBOOK LAY IN ITS RUDDY MILITARY covers on Harry Ends's desk in the penthouse. Cyril had given it to Harry that afternoon, and Harry had started reading it between meetings and rides about town, captivated by it like a schoolboy with a new comic book. He read it with his elbows anchored firmly on the desk and his forehead in his palms.

The writing was small but very regular and clear, produced by a steady hand and controlled by a patient and observant brain. The opening page was marked March 24, 1954.

"My name is I.V.H."—Cyril had explained to Harry what those initials stood for: Induprakash Vasant Haksar—"I am, I should think, the only civilized man who has ever visited this area—excluding my companions, who include some officers of the colonial police and some poachers turned soldiers of fortune in this already lost war."

Harry Ends read, feeling that he was becoming hooked on something enormously significant. As a VP at Shell, he'd seen a lot of the Third World, and had found that its squalor, poverty, and illness held no interest for him. Riding from Nairobi's airport to the hotel, he'd already determined that this place was on the brink of major trouble. Yet he'd also felt an amazing sense of human continuity here, which had first come into focus while he was staring at the empty skulls in Cyril's vault. When he looked away from them, at one of Cyril's assistants, a long-headed, bright, and quite pretty Kikuyu girl, Harry was struck with the thought that these Kenyans were ancient—perhaps in a direct line with the ancestors in the vault. That girl looked like the fossils' exquisitely stylized granddaughter. Harry had started to stare at the driver of their minibus, at the kids who rushed to wash its windows at intersections, at traffic agents, at hotel receptionsts. *All could be stemming from back then.*

Curiously, this time he was not impressed with tycoons, magnates, or crowned heads, but with the simple people he had glimpsed from the car or from the windows of his penthouse. He felt a sense of archaic kinship with them that he had never known before; he was an elitist, and did not like, or know, minorities. And this contact with scientists was equally flattering; he felt he was becoming one of them.

Noting Harry's exhilaration, Cyril had whispered to Ramsay, "Harry's a textbook case. Ancientness has smitten him. Next thing we know, he'll be learning Swahili."

Cyril had counted on this, and even Ramsay had not escaped the excitement. Earlier, Cyril and Harry had hurried to the president's residence in Uhuru Park. Ramsay, who had been described to the president's protocol department as a simple "adviser," had not been included in the meeting, so he stayed on at the university and browsed through the anthropology department's library. On a list of recommended reading, he found the account of the *National Geographic* photographer's encounter with telepathic Amazonian tribesmen. Ramsay leafed through it and found it annotated in hand by Raj Haksar. Later, when he reconnected with the other two, Ramsay raved about Haksar's comments on telepathic nonverbal communication. Could protohumans have had similar powers, and had Haksar communicated telepathically with them? Or at least thought he had?

Harry had quipped, "This is getting more interesting by the minute. By the way, Rams, Cyril, I knew that your non-baldness gene was just sizzle. Lucky for you, now we have something much better to sell."

Cyril swallowed. "What's that, Harry?"

"*Us*," said Harry.

They had returned to the hotel, where Harry ordered dinner in and steeped himself back into Haksar's notes.

Haksar engaged his reader with words of candid immensity: "In view of my discovery, the history of humanity as we read it in high school becomes only half of itself. There were protohumans all along, in good numbers. They were here during the Ming dynasty and during the Mogul conquest of India, when Shakespeare wrote his plays, through the Renaissance, during the American Civil War, and later. In pockets of tropical forest, in Africa but perhaps on other continents too. Evolving more slowly than the rest of the planet, on a clock of their own.

"Their discovery will have vast consequences for the future, especially because I'm turning these creatures into a new humanity."

Harry Ends frowned. What exactly did Haksar mean by "a new humanity"?

The notes were an unpredictable mix of field observation, evolutionary speculation, and autobiographical references. Raj Haksar was born in India, when it still was the brightest jewel of the English crown. The schoolboy Raj was sometimes hired to beat drums in an Indian forest, to rouse birds that were being hunted by visiting Englishmen. Having dived in a pond once to bring back a downed bird, the boy heard an Englishman snicker to a local Indian official, "How do you like my brown retriever?" That Indian official happened to be Raj's father, who indignantly jumped out of the Englishmen's coach, picked up his drenched son, and headed home on foot.

The Haksars were not of a high caste. They hoped that by emigrating to Africa they would get closer to the top. But Africa turned out to be an even more layered cake than India. Raj's father did poorly in business, and they had little money. Good with languages, young Raj learned Swahili and served as an interpreter with the colonial administration. He saved all his money to study anthropology, planning to get his Ph.D. and teach. But then came Africa's wars for independence. The Mau Mau guerrilla movement kindled Kenya, and the English drafted young Raj into the colonial police. "How big of them," Raj noted sardonically, "that after being the brown retriever, they're making me a good little Englishman, ready to die in 'defense of the realm.' "

"So here I am," he wrote, "discovering the world's most astounding secret, as a British intelligence officer, or crudely put—truth suits this place better—as a spy. O Hanuman"— his tone swung to lyricism—"help me forget how I got here, and inspire me with your symbolism. As in Hindu myths, the creation of a new humanity will include a horrible secret. Hanuman, if you were here with me, you'd be enchanted by these two young graciles rolling on the savanna grass, obviously having sex for the first time. The male exhibits the massive penis that has replaced the short, inconsequential one of the *robusti* males. It's almost as if they have given up bulk in the body in exchange for bulk in the prick."

Then Haksar's notes went on for several pages about the distinguishing emotional qualities of sex in humans—"the intimacy, the specialness of the act itself"—that separates humans from chimps and apes.

"I conclude that a lot of these physiological developments have to do with the results: a connection between the mates that is highly personal. A bond."

Haksar interrupted his speculation to note: "According to this vile poacher M, the hominids that live in the forest are quite different. They are much bigger, he says, but with smaller genitals, and given to the apes' free-for-alls. He says that they move about on their feet a lot. I must see them. My breath cuts off, as I fantasize that the forest ones might be of the *robustus* type. God, what a layered secret lies here, in this derelict piece of wilderness!''

Then again, Haksar theorized about how sexual anatomy determined behavior, until he finally returned to more anecdotal material about the gracile couple he'd observed on the savanna.

"Those two consummated, stopped, consummated again, and finally became aware of my presence. She closed her legs, jumped up, and sidled into the brush, while he tore a branch of whistling thorn, with no regard for the injury to his hands, and stood in an aggressive posture covering her retreat. His eyes were falling out of his head with amazement (never having seen a sapiens before—and I am brown-skinned; what deeper shock he would've lived facing that pink-snouted pig Hendrijks!), but he knew what he had to do—stand guard, block my way to that live vessel now holding his genes, even at the price of his life.

"The enlargement of the human penis over any other ape species truly created man's culture. Most of our mythologies start with penis cults and fertility tales. Even you, Hanuman, are an extension of such myths. I'm sure that the ancient Hindus encountered surviving pockets of protohumans, of the *Ramapithecus* species. Culture does not arise from nothing. We'll talk more about it soon, Hanuman.''

Harry turned to Cyril. "Who the blazes is Hanuman?"

"Some Hindu hero. It shouldn't be too hard to check out. I'll call Asian Studies and ask them to messenger over a book of Indian mythology.''

"Do it.'' Ends plunged back into his reading.

THE BOOK ARRIVED AS THE THREE MEN ATE DINNER. HANuman was a deified monkey mongrel, of great valor and virility, who had been conceived in the forest by a god and a monkey queen. He was a servant of prince Rama, one of Vishnu's avatars. Thus he was connected with the Hindu cult of Ekamukhalinga (penis with a human face), which split the penis in three, making each section represent one of the three top gods, Brahma, Vishnu, and Siva. Turning a page, Cyril found a photo of a statue of Hanuman. He had a man's body and an almost protohuman face—the long jaws, the bridgeless nose, the eyes sheltered under prominent brows and the slanting forehead.

"Half man, half ape, Haksar's mongrel," he laughed.

Harry Ends turned sharply, "Are you saying that Haksar sired some crossbreed out there? Is that what he means by a 'new humanity'?"

"Oh, no. All that business about Hanuman is pure hyperbole. Haksar was a Hindu proud of his legacy."

"Then what does he really mean?"

Cyril grinned. "You'll see. Read on."

Harry returned to the pages. Ramsay planted himself by Harry's desk and started to scan the lines over Harry's shoulder. They lingered over a brief entry. "Up on the Mau. Yes, I saw the forest dwellers. They are indisputably of the robust variety. And they are as majestically primitive as the graciles are touchingly human. The new world could be of one kind. What a dream."

Then there was a speculation about when the next Ice Age would arrive, the conclusion being sometime in the next one to three thousand years. Then, scribbled obliquely, over a whole page: "I cannot play God. Or can I?" The writing was shaky; the point of Haksar's pen had punctured the paper.

Then, in a shaky but condensed hand, "A. K. brought our new orders. They are as horrible as before. We'll kill more graciles, and the rest of them will flee into the forest. Thus achieving, brutally and on a wide scale, what I would have liked to achieve experimentally, and with a limited number of subjects.

"Is fate forcing my hand? What shall I do? Shall I kill M. and A. K.?"

Harry asked, "D'you know what those initials stand for, Cyril?"

"No, I'm afraid I haven't a clue."

Harry continued reading. The next note stated tersely: "In the forest with the other two. I missed. I could've killed them, but I was chicken.

"I have not slept since Wednesday, but tried to convince myself that a new breed would gain the fabulous muscularity and fierceness of the forest variety, and this new mix would be admirably equipped to face the next Ice Age." The writing was again jagged and feverish. On the next page, in a more settled hand, it read, "The man who follows me here, if accepted by these creatures, will watch the beginning of a new mankind. To that man, I say . . ." Hurriedly, Harry turned the page.

It was the manuscript's last page; Harry stared at the ugly, discolored inner side of the back cover.

He looked up. Ramsay was both awed and confused. Cyril had crossed his arms over his chest and hummed smugly.

Harry lost his patience. "Well?"

"It's all in there. Don't you get it?"

"Stop playing games, Cyril."

"He's talking of the breed I just found, which I named *Homo andersoni*—Anderson's human," Cyril explained, certain of Harry's limited lore in Latin. "A new human type, created by crossing graciles with robusts. Haksar's unit had orders to kill someone, anyone, right there at the foot of the escarpment, and then claim that they were guerrillas. They killed some graciles and chased the others back into the forest. By forcing the two breeds into one habitat, they inadvertently forced them to interbreed. That's what Haksar wanted to experiment with. The military action started it for him, time completed it, and I . . . I discovered it," he finished.

"You mean"—Harry Ends jumped up, knocking the notes off the desk—"that a new type already exists?"

"I saw it," lied Cyril.

He could not believe Harry Ends's reaction. His face turned crimson, and he rushed around the penthouse, shaking the floor, rattling dinner plates filled with uneaten food. Then he galloped over to Cyril and grabbed him by the arm.

"How advanced is that interbreeding process? Is there enough left of the two original breeds?"

Cyril almost choked. "Of course there's enough. As long as there's a pair of individuals left of each, there's enough!"

"Then start making calls now," Harry blurted, "to the best zoologists and veterinarians. I'll fly them over, to stop the interbreeding! What other scientific help do you need? How much would this government ask for, to put the air force and army at our disposal?"

Ramsay spoke up. "What do we need the army for?"

"To stop the interbreeding!" yelled Ends. "To surround that . . . what the hell's that place called, the Mau? To surround the Mau, enter the forest, and separate those two breeds by force if necessary!"

Cyril blurted back. "Are you crazy? You want to bring crowds trampling like elephants into something that has to be carefully observed and assessed? What about the secrecy we agreed to?"

"To fuck with secrecy! We can afford full coverage now; in fact we want it. Shell will be saving two breeds of our ancestors, not one but two. . . ."

"Shell?" asked Cyril, stunned.

Ends shook his head furiously, as if denying a slipup. "And why not Shell? You wanted a giant trust, Cyril! Otherwise you would've taken this to one of your piddling scientific symposiums!"

"I don't want a giant trust to completely take over my find! And why should we undo my *Homo andersoni,* if it's as brain-evolved as a gracile but stronger and fiercer?"

"Because it's wrong to mix them, dead wrong!" Ends paced, blasting like a large-caliber cannon. "How could Haksar allow such a thing to happen? And if he couldn't stop it, how could he remain silent about it for all those years? What was going on in his damn noodle?"

Cyril was surprised by Ends's passion. "I guess, having known discrimination firsthand, he probably saw in the creation of a new breed a kind of salvation for mankind." He turned toward Ramsay. "There's value in mixing, no? You Jews should know that because you were always kept apart. . . ."

Ramsay snapped, "We Jews were never fond of mixing, thank you, whether we were forced to it or banned from it, and I'm really getting fed up with your goddam quips, Cyril! Now"—he turned to Harry—"what would be so wrong with a new human type?"

"Everything! It would be terribly wrong to make one artificially! That would be against nature, against evolution, against everything . . ."

Harry Ends seemed to regain control. He opened his mouth to speak again, but Ramsay stopped him. "We should perhaps go down to the bar to continue this. . . . These matters are too sensitive to be discussed in a hotel room. . . ." He circled the room with his eyes.

Harry Ends understood. He closed his mouth, stepped out onto the penthouse's wide balcony, stepped back in, and called the two other men with his finger. They followed him out and found themselves right under the grating buzz of a huge orange neon sign with missing letters.

Ramsay grinned and spoke up against the buzzing. "This is more like it. A hotel room might be peppered over with bugs, but no one could bug a neon sign."

"I don't give a monkey's ass," yelled Cyril to cover that maddening buzz. "What does Shell want to do with my *Homo andersoni,* Harry?"

Harry made the same beckoning gesture, signaling that he was not going to yell back. He drew the faces of the other two so close to him that they could hear him whisper.

Then, suffering the maddening noise and the orange glare of the neon on his face, Harry explained that this was a chance for big business to prove that it wasn't a killer of the environment, a destroyer of nature's balance, but just the opposite. Big business could be a savior, the savior of our race, the guardian of our ancestors. This was a chance Shell should jump at. They'd had their worst luck in Africa last November, with those nine environmental activists being executed in Nigeria, where Shell was pumping oil out of the Niger delta and money into the pockets of the ruling clique. Those activists, headed by a certain Saro-Wiwa, a playwright and poet of repute, had demanded a share of that money for their people, the Ogonis, one of twenty ethnic groups living in that petrol-rich delta. That would have started an avalanche of nineteen other movements asking for payments and environmental protection. So it just couldn't be done, and Shell had glanced the other way while the nine men were hanged. But now Shell looked horrible, so they needed a big "positive" African project to restore their image. Big and expensive. This was it.

Harry stopped to breathe, and looked away from the neon. Cooled by the evening, Nairobi's air smelled of car exhaust and burning garbage. Beyond the traffic, the darkness flickered with low-voltage ghettos and squatter camps lit by garbage fires. Their lights were jarringly different, the ghettos' bulbs stable and cold, the camps' fires pulsating and weak but warm. Nothing about them indicated Africa specifically. The view from the roof could have been any corner of the Third World that was isolated, dangerous, and angry with its fate.

Harry Ends turned and concluded definitively, "Shell cannot possibly be involved in an interbreeding. That would look like we were genetically reengineering our own ancestors."

"But that interbreeding is far from complete!" Cyril hated how quickly Ends made decisions, as if he owned not only the find but Cyril as well. "A process like that takes many generations. . . . Rushing there with an army would completely traumatize . . ."

"We need to secure this country," said Harry to Ramsay. "We need the cooperation of the highest authority."

"The chief of police is pretty high," said Cyril, cursing himself for not having paid Kalangi the extra money.

"Shell can't work with a chief of police," said Harry, "not after what happened in Nigeria. It sends the wrong signal."

"Just a second, Harry. Is Shell in this already?" asked Ramsay.

"You bet," snapped Cyril. "You must think I'm stupid, Harry. Your leaving Shell was a ploy, wasn't it? A ploy for Shell to acquire me and my find at a lower price. . . ."

"This is not your find. From what I've read, it was Haksar's," countered Harry head-on.

"All right, I'm out," Cyril blustered in Harry's face—the man was so short and unmuscular, Cyril felt that he could bounce him off the roof with one punch. "This was never meant to work. Sorry, Rams. I and my find are out of any deal. . . ."

"You want to play chicken with me?" snarled Harry. "You know, there are some strange facts that you wouldn't want to see connected, Cyril. Like Haksar dying right before you claimed the find, and then your wife dying, and that guy Phillips." Cyril stepped back, and Harry instantly stepped toward him. "I'll tell you what. If you promise to follow my cues, I'll let you work under me. If you don't, I'll make sure that those connections are established, and believe me, a thousand other scientists will flock to work with me and tell the world that those two breeds are being allowed to live exactly as they did two million years ago. You get my meaning, Cyril?" He looked up into Anderson's chin. "You dig?"

Cyril made a choked noise against the buzzing neon. Ramsay, petrified by Harry's insinuation, couldn't help reflecting that the murders would explain Cyril's frantic behavior in London.

"Do we understand each other?" Harry asked again, with a sideways glance that included Ramsay.

Cyril nodded. They understood each other.

"Cool," said Harry. He started for the door of the penthouse. Ramsay started to mutter that he had not weighed all the consequences of this, and perhaps should not be involved. . . . "You're already involved," Harry Ends cut him off dryly. "And I'm running this. All right?" He led the way back, short, unexceptional, but endowed with the power of one of the world's top businesses.

Inside, Cyril walked to a side table with drinks, grabbed the scotch, poured a dark stiff drink, and killed it. A mirror reflected his face above the colorful tops of whiskey and brandy bottles. Suddenly, instead of his face, Cyril saw Hendrijks over the tops of the bottles. The pilot had crumpled on the floor of that seedy motel. Haksar had followed, gaunt as a mummy, deprived of his precious insulin. Then Corinne, lying in her flat next to Randall, both warm from each other (the bitch). And that hired killer, scalped and pierced by bullets from his own gun.

Five deaths. Had they all been useless?

Ramsay stepped next to him to make himself a drink. He dropped the ice cubes and muttered, "Cyril? All that isn't true, is it?"

Cyril peered into the mirror. Harry Ends had sat down at the dinner table. He was eating the cold food on his plate, with big mouthfuls that he obviously did not enjoy or even feel.

"Don't be an idiot, old boy," Cyril said lightly.

The phone rang. In the mirror, Cyril saw Harry pick up, listen, then wave with the receiver at Cyril. Cyril walked over and took the receiver. Harry sat down again and ate absent-mindedly, vaguely hearing Cyril answer someone with yes and no, and then hang up. Then Cyril sat down at the table and pleaded that the three of them go to the savanna alone first, to check on the state of the breed. Cyril would also ask Kalangi along. The chief could help them more than anyone else. Harry finally consented.

Busta was crying. She uttered an ugly yowl and tried to lift Crew Cut. But her little son was too heavy, and her strength failed her. She hunkered down and stared at him, letting her tears roll down on the cheeks that Niawo had plucked free of hair.

She touched her fingers to the snare's burn on Crew Cut's neck, and stroked his skin, as if she were trying to mend the tissue and bring him back to life. She fell by her son's body and scooped the boy's head into her long-fingered palms, and held it delicately against her cheek.

A small circle of the females, including Niawo, stood by silently.

After a moment, Ken heard the angry grunts of the males, who had fallen on the poachers' hideout. They were tossing it upside down, throwing things in the air. Ken saw a plastic water canister, followed by a rifle. Ken gritted his teeth, raced into the hideout, and grabbed the rifle by the barrel, jerking it free. He could tell by its weight that it was loaded. He threw the strap over his shoulder and dived for one of the radios.

The males howled and jumped on Ken from all sides. He had to surrender something to them, and it had to be the rifle. He worked the breech, spilled the slugs out of the magazine, and hurled the rifle to the ground. He then dived toward another one of the snares that was peering up from the grass. He showed it to the males and started searching the grass for more of them. The males followed him, as if they understood—without words, without language.

Modibo had set up a ring of snares that fanned out from the hideout and hugged all around the incline. By thrashing with the branches through the grass, Ken taught the males how to find them. With the simplest gestures, he indicated when they should walk single file behind him and when to fan out. They went from an undisciplined gang to a clean, well-structured formation.

Ken found a short lobelia tree and hung the snares around its fluffy straight stem. As long as they were in the tree, the snares were harmless. As they searched for the snares, the males walked deeper into the brush and came to a pool of blood spilled by a bushpig that had been caught in one of the traps. The male walking right behind Ken helped him untangle it, but it was already dead. Another male lifted the bushpig onto his shoulders. This was edible meat. Good thinking.

Ken glanced back and saw another hominid pick up two more snares, stick them on a branch, and grin widely at his accomplishment.

By the end of their mission, they'd picked up twenty-four snares in all. They circled the cliffside until they came upon a polished basaltic rock that shone like a giant forehead in the moonlight. The rock shut off the trail.

Twenty-four snares. Ken found it strange to think in numbers again. They also had several radios, a scanner that was easily worth three hundred dollars, and nightviewers that were twisted and broken but still recognizable. They were Night Hawks, a top-of-the-line brand that cost about eight hundred dollars. Ken knew that ordinary poachers couldn't afford such fancy gear, and they definitely didn't get radio calls from Chief Kalangi. He remembered Kalangi's message to Modibo. What was that soon-to-arrive expedition? And whose expedition was it?

Ken and his troop retraced their steps, eventually hooking

up with the clan. As they stepped again past the destroyed hideout, Ken saw Long Toes, sitting up unaided, his stance somewhat frail, but his eyes wide open and alert. Then he saw several females pulling at the dead body of one of the poachers. The body had been stripped of its clothing. Ken heard a mocking voice inside him: Rush, boy, rush, and stop them before they tear it up and eat that flesh. He was ready to lunge toward them but restrained himself. That bastard would've stripped those females' flesh and sold their pounded bones. One of the males following Ken dropped the bushpig down on the grass, and the females left the human for it.

Ken was wrenched from his thoughts by a sudden cacophony of white-nosed monkeys right above him in an ironwood tree. Their furry, brown coats blended into the dark, but their white noses were perfectly visible. Their sleep had been disturbed by some other animal that was now making them screech and jump about crazily. Whatever it was, it was sliding down the ironwood's trunk; it hit the ground and flashed its teeth.

It was Modibo, who jumped to his feet, looked around, and spotted Ken. He looked very small without his greatcoat, clad only in khaki shorts, a shirt, and oversized boots. If it hadn't been for those monkeys, he could've gotten away. His hand raised a poacher's skinning knife, and like a wound-up devil, he raced past the females, who were busy with the bushpig. He threw his arm around Long Toes and picked him up.

He raced right past Ken. As Long Toes fought him, the skinning knife rose in Modibo's clawed hand, but the little gnome tripped, stabbing his knife into the ground.

Modibo pulled it out, grabbed the boy again, and tumbled like a human ball down the incline with his catch. Ken dived down, stumbling, himself a rolling human ball. Modibo raced down the hill with the boy bundled over his shoulder. Ken ran down behind him. There were prayers he wished he could remember. There were orders his brain was shouting at his limbs. There was a cold breath from a terrace lower down.

Racing after Modibo, Ken ran into a low branch and staggered. When he stepped into the clear, Modibo was on the ground, and Long Toes was up, pummeling him. The boy was fighting back.

Ken was still dazed from his fall, but the next thing he knew he was at Modibo's side. Using nothing but his bare fists, Ken put all his strength behind one lethal blow aimed at Modibo's face—and missed. The movement swung him against a tree. He turned, just as Modibo came at him with the knife. Ken jumped aside, and Modibo turned. Long Toes was scratching at the ground, and suddenly he had a stone in his hand. It ripped the air and flew into the poacher's forehead, knocking him to the ground. Modibo's jaw twitched and his limbs fluttered, a no-longer-scary windup toy.

Rushing over, Ken stepped painfully on the stone, which wasn't a stone at all. It was a gob of mud from an ant's nest that had hardened like iron. Long Toes had found it by pure chance.

Ken saw Long Toes' little mouth split open in a snicker of delicious cruelty. Bruised, scratched, and exhausted, Long Toes stepped up to the comatose poacher and kicked at his ribs. Then he stopped to look, enchanted by that twitching of arms and legs, which became more rapid, until it stopped abruptly. With a spasm that made his old boots screech against the forest debris, Modibo was still.

The moonlight seemed to shrink him in size even more.

Ken bent over the grotesque little man who had filled his nightmares for the past few weeks. His chest, which still carried the juju that had not protected him, looked so narrow and his limbs were so wiry and thin that nothing about him suggested wickedness.

Ken heard the clan, tearing through the trees, rushing after them. He realized then that he wouldn't be able to lead them to safety. The clan would see Modibo on the ground, defeated by Long Toes, and decide that they should wage a battle for their territory.

Overwhelmed, he crossed to where the trees thinned, expecting to look out over an oceanscape of savanna under the moon. He peered over the edge of the terrace at moonlight bleaching the flats beyond the lower spurs. He saw grass, dotted with bushes of whistling thorns. And he also saw a narrow band of cleared ground that was probably an unfinished airstrip.

The clearing had been done by hand. He watched it, overwhelmed by a feeling that the encounter of hominid and human would now take place. The battle was set.

He took a breath, and cut through the warm clan, heading upward. He breathed the dark air and climbed until he could smell the jarringly different odor of the poachers' hideout. He stepped into it, fell on all fours, and groped around until he found the radio.

It had been damaged; when he lifted it, he heard something clink feebly inside. He set it back on the ground, crouched down by it, and turned the on button. Its little red light came on in the darkness, making it into a strange one-eyed beast.

IN NAIROBI, THE NGIAMENA HOUSE WAS QUIET AND SHOWED barely a few lights. Itina and Jakub were out. They had gone to a dinner party because Jakub insisted that they behave as if escape was the furthest thing from their minds. Itina, Ngili, and Yinka were leaving for Johannesburg the next day.

Ngili was in the guesthouse, sifting through old records of his geological research, while Yinka stood alone in the garden, staring at the coffee bushes and trying to get used to the feeling of leaving Nairobi. When she heard the phone ring in the house, she ignored it, trying to understand why leaving was so hard. It was complicated by many other feelings. Not only would they be leaving their native place but also losing their status. Her father was going underground, a decision full of peril. Yinka pictured how they would be living through the next weeks or months, not just among strangers but also dangling on a rope of hope and expectation that would break if Jakub was betrayed and captured, or killed.

She heard the phone again.

Remembering her father's orders to make everything seem normal, she hurried inside and picked up the phone. "Hello?"

She heard the hum of static and a kind of echo, as if she were on a radio. Then a man's singsong voice said, "Hello, this is the Magadi game reserve, calling Mr. Ngili Ngiamena. . . ."

"Wait just a second, I'll get him." When game reserves called, they usually asked for her father, not for Ngili. "Are you sure you don't want Mr. Jakub Ngiamena?"

"Yes, we are sure. We have a radio caller who asked us to patch him to your number, to talk to Ngili Ngiamena." The reserve operator made brief pauses before the names, as if reading them from a freshly jotted-down note. "A Mister . . . Lau-dah?"

An absurd explanation thundered through Yinka's brain. Perhaps a relative of Ken's was calling from America, but why would such a call be routed through the Magadi reserve? Then, suddenly, she guessed: Ken was calling. He was out in the bush, and he had a working radio. He'd radioed Magadi because he knew its radio frequency. Magadi was close to several fossil digs, and Ngili and Ken had used its office in the past to get messages and collect supplies. And the head of the Magadi reserve knew the Ngiamenas' private number.

"I'll send someone to get Ngili, but you can put Mr. Lauder through," she said, and felt a strange easing in her head, as if a lengthy migraine had suddenly ended. A weight of anxiety dissolved, and she felt stupidly light, as if she were filled with air.

The storm of static increased, and the operator's voice echoed far away. "Go ahead." Yinka's nails scratched the phone. No, no! She couldn't bear the thought that the connection might be cut off. And then there was a strange voice, flat and hoarse, from somewhere in another world. "Ngili? Hey, Ngili?" A pause. "Are you there? It's me, Ken."

He didn't sound like himself.

"Ken, it's Yinka!"

Ken was quiet. Then he started laughing, and said, hoarsely, "I'm sorry . . ."

"This is Yinka, Ken, Yinka! What are you sorry about?"

"I mean . . ."

He seemed to be making a silent, unseen effort. She wondered if he was sick. Or was he so depleted that he couldn't think straight?

"I need Ngili," he said. "I'm using a radio that's been damaged. I don't know how long it will keep working. . . . Yinka . . . something terrible is happening. . . ."

"Are you all right?"

"No . . . Yes . . . We are . . . we are being hunted, Yinka. . . ."

"We?"

He was silent again. She prayed that he was not insane and hadn't suffered some absurd transformation, but that he was simply at the end of his energies.

"That's why I wanted to talk to Ngili. . . . Yinka . . ." Even in these circumstances, she enjoyed hearing her name from his mouth. "You remember . . . what I told you last time I was at your house?" She nodded, silently. "When I gave you . . . those fossil flowers?" She started to chuckle nervously, while her mind urged: Yes, yes, you're making sense, keep talking. He heard her chuckle, chuckled too, and sounded one more fraction closer to the normal Ken Lauder. "Yinka . . . I don't want to scare you. . . ." She shook her head, but had no courage to speak. "That breed . . . it exists. . . ."

She breathed and felt she understood.

She was a little less scared for his life.

"So? What are you doing out there? Are you watching them?"

"I'm with them . . . I'm surrounded by them. . . . Please get Ngili. . . ."

"Ken!"

"Yes?"

"I'll go get him, but I want to talk to you."

"You can stay on the line. . . ."

"I want to talk to you!"

"I want to talk to you too. . . ." he said, almost reluctantly. "But we're being hunted, Yinka. . . . We just repelled an attack. . . ."

"Get out of there," she cried. "What are you going to do? Defend them by yourself? Why? Why are they so important?"

The light hit her at an angle and reflected in a little tear on the side of her nose. Yinka touched it, and it rolled down her cheek. She stamped her foot angrily; that for some reason reminded her of Gwee's wedding and the up-and-down she had not danced with Ken.

She started to cry in earnest.

"Yinka!" he said with astonishment.

"Stay right there . . . I'll get Ngili. . . ."

She put the receiver down, wiped her cheeks with the back of her hand, and headed for the guesthouse.

Somehow, in the next few instants, nothing happened that would tell her that all this was a dream. She told Ngili that Ken was on the line, and he looked up, breathless as if he'd been punched in the stomach. He noticed his sister's shiny cheeks, put his arm around her shoulders and squeezed her briefly but firmly, then hurried into the house.

She went to her bedroom and picked up the extension. Over the hovering static, she heard the two men exchange a grunted greeting—Ngili's voice breathless from shock, and Ken's raw from exhaustion. She realized that he was probably more depleted than the radio he was using.

She had wanted so much to know that he was alive. Now she knew that.

Ken was telling Ngili where he was, and that *they* existed. They were right there, surrounding him, and he and Ngili had to save their lives.

"Ken, I can call Don Johanson, at Berkeley's Institute of Human Origins," said Ngili. "And Sherwood Washburn, and Phil Tobias at Witwatersrand, in South Africa. But even if I get through to them, and they talk to me and they believe me, what will it take for any of them to get over here? A week at the least? And to make some international body take some kind of action would take much longer. Several weeks, or more."

"I know . . . it can't be done that way. . . ."

"Ken, listen . . . What are they like?"

Yinka watched her brother through the open bedroom door—the same door through which Ken had once watched her naked. She got a knot in her stomach as she waited for Ken's answer.

"They're incredible . . . unique. . . . But we need help tomorrow, Ngili . . . tomorrow . . . one kid already died. . . ."

We again!

She saw Ngili's fingers curl up the phone's cord, his face still shining from picturing what the breed was like—his find too—and then gradually losing its shine. "Ken, nothing can be done that fast. Something very bad is happening here. . . . We are . . . we are leaving Nairobi. . . ."

"What?" Ken broke into a cold, lugubrious laugh.

"You don't understand. We are on a kind of blacklist. Still . . ." Ngili seemed to debate in his mind, and Yinka felt like shouting through the open door: Now that you know he's alive, are you going to leave him alone out there until he gets killed? But she bit her lips. What was she doing? Urging her brother to plunge into mortal danger after avoiding it here in Nairobi?

How important was Ken? How important was he really?

Ken spoke. "They're going to come back, I know it . . . with guns and snares. . . . But if they don't, maybe I can get us out of here. . . . It's four hundred miles west to Uganda. . . . There are tracts of forest there that have never been inhabited. . . ."

Madness. And Ngili answered it as if it weren't madness. "No, Ken. Uganda's got poachers and drug traders . . . it's got the 'blue highway,' with all those weed runners. You can't take them west. . . ."

"North, then?" asked Ken. "Eight hundred miles north . . . then we reach the Sudan or Ethiopia. . . . Miles and miles

of empty brush . . . no airfields . . . no roads, and no
tribes . . .''

"Ken, that's crazy."

"All survivals are crazy. . . .''

Up on the Mau, Ken was lying in the grass, watching the
red eye of the radio as it flickered like a drowning candle.

Long Toes sat hunched right by the radio, the little red
light making his features glow.

Ken was fighting to keep his wits together. Ngili's words
had made him frightened. And he was also trying not to think
of Yinka.

He tried to think about heroic things. The cause of science.
If the world lost Ken Lauder, it would be losing less than if
it lost that kid sitting up in the grass. And if Ngili couldn't
come to the rescue, he might still lead the breed to salvation
somehow. He felt he was willing to die, if doing so might
help them.

"The radio's dying. . . .'' he mumbled.

"I'll come tomorrow," said Ngili suddenly.

"How are you going to manage that?"

"I'll manage it somehow. Ken, listen. I'll come, but . . .
are they really there with you?"

Ken started laughing; he felt clearly how much he had
missed laughing with another sapiens. "You think I'm that
gone? You want me to pinch this kid here, so you can hear
a yell from a larynx as shallow as a spoon?''

"No, no. It's okay. I'll get there.''

"Ngili . . .'' But he couldn't think of the right thing to say
about friendship, about Ngili's courage and dedication. He
breathed awkwardly. "Is Yinka still there?''

She gestured to Ngili that she didn't want to speak.

"No, she's not here now."

"I'm glad. She's so beautiful, your sister.''

"I know. I think you should save whatever's left in that
radio.''

"I think I should too. Good-bye, Ngili . . .''

"Tomorrow!'' Ngili reminded him with anxiety. "Ken!
Hold on somehow! Help them survive! I'll find a way!''

"All right . . ."

Yinka dropped the receiver on her bed and stepped into the den. She saw Ngili hold the receiver with such tension that the muscles of his arms bulged as if he were lifting a heavy weight. She looked at his eyes, which were dry. He was putting all of his feelings into that fierce flexing of muscles.

"We'll do it, Ken, we'll save them somehow," Ngili said quickly. "Take care of yourself. Take care of yourself!"

There was the scratchy sound of a bush radio being turned off. Ngili and Yinka looked at each other, then Yinka walked over to throw her arms around Ngili, who still held the receiver to his ear.

Ngili heard the operator at Magadi, asking if the call was over. Ngili said yes, and thank you, and he hung up. Then he hugged his sister.

LEAVING HARRY ENDS'S SUITE, CYRIL ANDERSON searched his pockets for the keys to his empty house.

What if I let it all go? he wondered. What if I let them fly out there tomorrow, all by themselves? Ramsay, and this bastard Ends. What if I don't even show up?

He knew what would happen. Harry Ends wouldn't even bother to try to find out what had happened to Cyril. As Harry had said, a thousand other scientists would line up to work with him ("under him") and tell the world that the two breeds were the same today as they were two million years ago.

Waiting for the elevator, Cyril tried to remember the images of his victims in that mirror, to reawaken his newly discovered killer instinct. But it didn't seem to be in him now. When the elevator opened onto the lobby, Cyril saw Chief Arnold Kalangi sitting in one of the armchairs. He got up and walked toward Cyril, who greeted him with a gruff: "So, what is it?"

"Cyril, I want you to listen to something. It's a tape of your former student, Lauder. My men recorded it half an hour ago, as they were scanning the air to make radio contact with Modibo. Lauder is up on the Mau, apparently leading"—Kalangi took a breath—"a band of protohumans."

A band of protohumans? Leading them?

Cyril felt as if a silent, but lethal, thunderbolt had struck him. He was almost surprised it hadn't cracked open the lobby floor.

"What happened to Modibo?" Cyril asked.

"I don't know," said Kalangi, "and it's not important. Professor Anderson . . . Cyril . . . I'm afraid Lauder's presence out there gives me a very interesting option. To consider him as a potential partner."

Cyril paused a moment, then spoke. "Lauder would never go partners with you. . . ."

"You'd be surprised what men would do," said Kalangi, "to save their dreams. And I could help him. I could help him save those creatures." He waited a beat. "On the other hand, if you want our partnership to continue, you have to be able to afford it. I wasn't joking about the price of that plane. It's a military transporter, and its operational cost is high. In fact, it went up since we last spoke."

"All right. What's the new price?"

"Come into my suite," suggested Kalangi almost affably. "I have the tape of Lauder speaking from the Mau. It's very garbled, and not long, but you should hear it. He was speaking to another ex-student of yours, Ngiamena. Ngiamena wants to fly out there tomorrow, to rescue Ken and the creatures. But I suppose we can take care of that. If we reach a new understanding."

He led the way to the elevators and punched the call button. Cyril stepped next to the chief and waited for the elevator that would take them upstairs.

CYRIL ANDERSON WAS IN KALANGI'S SUITE FOR LESS THAN twenty minutes.

When Cyril left, Kalangi sat motionless for a few minutes, then reached for the phone. He called the general he had received in his office the day before and asked him if they could meet in front of the Naivasha Hotel.

A half hour later, a black Oldsmobile without license plates pulled along the sidewalk opposite the hotel. Almost immediately, a little army of streetwalkers started approaching the three men inside. One of the men bent out of the car window and barked a few words at the girls that made them scatter immediately in a clatter of high heels.

Seconds later, Kalangi crossed the road, entered the car, and seated himself in the backseat next to the general. He told the general that Operation Clean Sweep should be restarted the next morning, but only after a certain plane had taken off, carrying himself and the Shell Oil man and his party to the savanna. Kalangi had information that Shell was prepared to pay millions to exploit that piece of the wild where the mangatis lived. He told the general and his aides that he would tell them more only if they agreed to give him a prime position after the new government was installed. He was getting too old for police work, and suggested that he be named finance minister in the new government.

That caused some shock in the car. One of the men pointed out that finance minister was an important job, and such an appointment would have to be discussed with the new regime's revolutionary council. Kalangi laughed and replied that the council could discuss the matter right now because the entire council was sitting in that car. Depending on their decision, the police would decide whether to support tomorrow's operation.

There were a few minutes of silent glances exchanged between the military men. Then the general announced that the revolutionary council thought Kalangi was a valuable choice as finance minister. And now he wanted to personally examine Kalangi's information about the Shell man's plans. Kalangi invited them all into his suite.

Meanwhile the streetwalkers had moved back toward the hotel's entrance. As the four men got out of the car and walked inside, they heard the general quip that by the time the Shell man's party flew back, the situation in Nairobi would be resolved and under control.

T HE TWIN-ENGINED EMBRAER MILITARY PLANE HAD been tugged out of its hangar and was being readied for its flight to the savanna. Even though it was primarily a troop carrier, it held a considerable amount of armament. Two cannons peered out of the housings in its wings, there were two smaller and nastier machine guns, and the bomb chutes on its belly looked like two sets of gills. The plane's Brazilian manufacturer had designed it for escorting, attacking, bombing, and moving troops, making it easily adaptable to the messy and unpredictable nature of Third World wars.

Its hatch for dropping paratroopers was open, and a ladder leaned against it.

The crew washing its insides was surprised when a silhouette appeared in the early-morning light, coming in through the parachute hatch. It was Cyril Anderson, wearing dust boots, safari pants, and a bush jacket with layers of pockets. A bush pack was strapped to his back, and on top of his head was a dramatic wide hat with a floppy brim. He saluted the plane's washers with the customary *"Jambo."*

The crew's overseer hurried over to tell him that this area was restricted. Cyril smiled. "Chief Kalangi chartered this plane, and I am one of the chief's guests." Then he looked around the plane, breathing through his mouth because of a very foul odor; some live animals must have been transported

544

in the troop carrier. Even though the metal floor was foaming with detergent suds, it still stank of manure and blood like a poachers' pen.

A sinister-looking Kikuyu steward in a white jacket came up the steps behind Cyril and gruffly asked for permission to step inside. Cyril moved out of his way, then leaned back in and breathed the air. It still stank. That would give Harry boy a taste of the real Africa. The Kikuyu steward asked if Cyril wanted his bush pack hung up. Cyril handed it to him, then turned around and faced out of the parachute hatch.

He checked his watch. It was just barely eight A.M., and they were scheduled to fly out at nine.

He faced the airport, shining brightly in the morning sun. Beyond it, there was a shantytown nicknamed Kanisa Kusini. In the far background, Nairobi threw its vertical towers into the high-altitude air.

THE CHILDREN OF KANISA KUSINI WERE NOT UNHAPPY WITH their life in the shantytown. *Kanisa* meant "church" and *kusini* south, but the once active Mission of the South, a Belgian Catholic operation, had been closed down in the sixties by the new independent government, and the shantytown had engulfed its destroyed vegetable gardens. The church was covered with graffiti and didn't have a roof; inside it was divided up into a number of shops that sold oil, flour, butane for cooking stoves, and herbal remedies.

The water pump once built by the mission was the center of the shantytown's social life. In Africa, the god of water was more important than the god of the heavens; water ruled the people's lives and excited their imaginations. When the shanty children got older, some of them would travel and see water in abundance, in the shape of a big lake, a ten-story waterfall, or the blue infinity of the Indian Ocean. But even after that, they would keep in their souls a devotion to water that few people carry as ardently as the Africans. For the shanty kids, water was miraculous—even the drippings from the old corroded spout of the mission's water pump. It quenched thirst, it turned dust into kneadable dough, and even helped keep a hungry stomach quiet.

Lucius Conroy and Cynthia Palmer had taken on quite an aura in the shantytown when they announced their plan to bring a modern supply of water to Kanisa Kusini. The kids had appropriately baptized them Mmerikani Maji, the Water Americans.

The events of that strange day started as the Water Americans drove their rented Toyota van into the area. The children—skinny but dazzling, with lusciously black skins, lips of unreal pink, and teeth so purely white—rushed to mob the Toyota, shouting, "*Polisi hapa, polisi hapa!* The police are here," as if reporting exciting news. Lucius and Cynthia stepped out of the Toyota and saw several police cars, two trucks, and a bulldozer, all converged upon the pump square, which was packed with two hundred women lining up with their pails. The two dozen in front were already shoving back and forth with a platoon of armed police, while some city workers were taking apart the pump.

Then things happened very fast.

Lucius hurried forward, ahead of Cynthia, into a storm of shouts. A city official was yelling that the pump was being dismantled because of poisoning of the water. Angry women's voices responded that once the pump was dismantled it would never be returned, and what were they going to drink meanwhile, or cook with? Conroy rushed to the official, to plead the obvious: Taking away the pump without replacing it with any other supply would start an uprising. The women, most of them mothers with infants strapped to their backs, were rushing the city workers. A photographer was calmly snapping pictures. A police lieutenant was leaning into a walkie-talkie, calling for an army backup. Conroy grabbed the lieutenant by the arm and asked why the army was needed. This was not a riot. Lieutenant Sampa asked to see Conroy's papers, and Conroy pulled out a big, folded wallet with his U.S. passport. Sampa grabbed the whole wallet, put it in his pocket, and said clearly, "Go to hell, Mmerikani."

There was a shot, and Conroy fell, his eyes stunned. A

volley of fire came from the lopsided tower of the church and took down several of the mothers.

Cynthia rushed toward Lucius, but she saw the dust exploding in front of her as bullets hit the dirt road. She could also hear the *tukka-tukka-tukk* of Soviet-made Kalashnikov automatics. She had learned their sound in Africa. She realized that she would probably not save Lucius and might lose her own life, so she turned and ran toward their rented Toyota.

"Elikopta! Elikopta!" voices cried around her from the doorsteps of tin-and-cardboard houses. As she looked up, the shadow of an assault helicopter covered her face and the narrow dirt lane. She was certain it was targeting her, and so she was stunned when explosions started going off a whole block away as the flimsy houses of the shantytown were blown up.

Cynthia jumped behind the wheel of her van and started the engine; the radio came on. She gaped, hearing a commentator say that an incident around a water pump in Kanisa Kusini had turned violent when tribal instigators had attacked the civilian population that was asking for the protection of the police. The police had tried to intervene, but had come under heavy fire and had asked the military for help. The military had swung into action. The government warned other agitators not to take advantage of the violence. . . .

Cynthia had just witnessed that incident, and now it was on the news almost before it happened. Cynthia hadn't seen any tribal instigators. But she knew about Africa's civil wars from her earlier trips to Mozambique and Rwanda.

The bullets hit the dirt closer to her van, and Cynthia threw open the doors on one side of the Toyota, letting a bunch of kids dive in. All were practically naked and were in a car for the first time. Cynthia hurtled the van down the dirt lane and found an unexpected passage with access to the freeway. Behind her van, that helicopter circled and came in low again, to fire another rocket at the tin-and-cardboard homes.

* * *

SEVERAL MILES TO THE SOUTH, NEAR THE AIRPORT, AN-
other helicopter rattled through the sky, bore down, and hit
an auto junkyard not far from the terminals. The bang wasn't
very loud, but a volcano of smoke and burning car hulks
erupted and was visible from the terminals. Then the helicopter scored again, right by a clogged-up traffic ramp. It
dug an ugly burning hole in a bank of jacaranda trees. A
tower of fire blew upward, knocking out the outer windows
of the Simba restaurant and the Barclays Bank office.

Jakub Ngiamena was in the bank, arguing with a teller
who had refused to let him withdraw ten thousand U.S. dollars. Since that morning, transactions in foreign currency
above one thousand dollars had to be approved by the finance
minister. Jakub asked to talk to the manager, and started to
tell him his name, when the man interrupted him. He knew
who Jakub was and asked him to wait. Soon he came back
with a tall wad of shillings in his hand; he said that the local
currency was not covered by the new limitation. Jakub could
see the pale green of U.S. dollars under the shilling notes on
top. He asked the man's name and thanked him, then hurried
out.

In a busy lounge, Itina stood waiting next to Ngili and
Yinka.

Itina's eyes were red because the four Ngiamenas had
stayed up all night arguing about what they should do. Finally, they decided that Itina and Yinka would leave for Johannesburg alone the next morning. Ngili was adamant that
he was staying, and claimed that he would be safer in the
bush than in Nairobi. Jakub kept getting up to answer phone
calls from regional chiefs who were preparing to return to
Nairobi. Finally, Jakub agreed with Ngili's wish, and Ngili
drove off to speak to his friend Mtapani the pilot. When Ngili
returned, they ate a silent breakfast after their sleepless night.
Jakub put on a suit he rarely wore, and they drove to the
airport.

Now an announcement came over the P.A. system: All
flights were canceled, and the passengers should vacate the
terminal. This brought shouts from the passengers, who

started milling about in confusion. Itina spotted Jakub fighting the crowd toward them. The P.A. voice was mute for a few instants, then another announcer said that a rogue helicopter, probably flown by foreign agitators, was attacking the airport. The air force was scrambling to intercept it. For safety reasons, airport security recommended that they lie on the floor facedown. Near Itina, two elderly African nuns in full habit crossed themselves, then lowered themselves to the floor, but other travelers were less compliant and began yelling for explanations. Ngili noticed an airport security man on the upper concourse as he flung his arm out above the crowd. Then a deafening blast rocked the lounge, and a wall of dark fog rose. There was a gaping moment of silence, followed immediately by yells of *"Hatari, hatari, moto! Danger, danger, fire!"* and *"Msaada, daktari! Help, doctor!"*

The security man had thrown a smoke bomb to panic the crowd. A swell of screaming people pushed Ngili toward a door marked NO ADMITTANCE. Jakub grabbed the two women and followed Ngili through the door out of the smoky lounge. The cries of fleeing people echoed in a kind of underground passage, which opened soon into the blinding sunlight of a parking lot.

The crowd was streaming in all directions, but the Ngiamenas stopped so they could figure out what to do. Ngili was scheduled to take off in Mtapani's plane, bound to Dogilani. Jakub had spoken to the Magadi reserve camp and asked a cousin of his who worked there to send his rangers to the savanna to meet Ngili there. Mtapani's plane was waiting over at the light aircraft terminal. Jakub made a rapid decision.

"Ngili, run ahead to Mtapani and convince him to take Itina and Yinka and fly them over the border to Tanzania. After that he can fly you to the Mau."

Itina started protesting. "I don't like this. How are we going to get from Tanzania to Johannesburg? And I don't want to leave you here alone, so you can play underground hero again."

"Shut up. Everything's organized. Go, Ngili."

All four of them were raising their voices. The parking lot they were standing in had turned into mass chaos, and people were honking and bumping into each other's cars to get out of the airport.

"Run to the plane, Ngili; we'll follow you," Jakub ordered. He gave Ngili half of the wad of bills.

Ngili stuck the money in one of his pockets, jumped over a hedge of boxwood, and ran fast and hard among cars and frightened people. He reached a runway and headed toward the sun and the old-fashioned hangars of the light aircraft section. He had packed a .45 Colt Commander with a seven-shot magazine into one pocket of his windbreaker and had two boxes of bullets in his other pocket. The two weights beat against his ribs, but he didn't feel them. The money knocked against his thigh, but he didn't feel that either. Straight ahead, he saw the plane, a Cessna for four passengers, parked within the arched open entrance to a hangar, and ran toward it like a true Masai, holding his torso high and rigid and making big, jumping strides.

Mtapani and a hangar mechanic were standing by the plane, talking. A Land Rover marked AIRPORT SERVICES pulled slowly along the hangars. Ngili could see two men in it. One of them threw out something that looked like a rolled-up newspaper, which fell on the tarmac, clanking and rolling toward Mtapani and his plane. It blew up at the front of the Cessna, disintegrating its nose, dislodging the propeller, and blowing a hole in the hangar's wall. Through the smoke, Ngili could not see Mtapani or the mechanic; they couldn't have disintegrated, but he simply did not see them anymore. The AIRPORT SERVICES vehicle turned and came toward Ngili. The man who'd thrown the explosive leaned out again. He was young, wearing nondescript civilian clothes.

"Ngili Ngiamena?" he asked, his tone almost friendly. He held out another rolled-up newspaper that had a clearly visible, lighted stick of dynamite in it. Ngili remembered that they were called "bangalore torpedoes." They were excel-

lent for disabling a small target at close range. The man was
about to hurl it at him.

Ngili wrenched the Colt out of his pocket and released the
thumb safety catch, but forgot to deal with its other safety
catch, the one in the grip. The bangalore torpedo hit the
tarmac and was rolling toward Ngili as he aimed the gun and
uselessly pressed the trigger. His body acted before he could
give it an order. He jumped forward and slammed one foot
down on the fuse, while his brain remembered the gun's
other safety catch.

His finger loosened it. DON'T MISS. As the Land Rover
was almost on him, he took several shots at it point-blank,
cracking the windshield and killing both men. The vehicle
was careening out of control, without a driver, until it ran
into another jeep parked at the edge of the tarmac and came
to a dead stop. The jolt made the driver fall out onto the
tarmac. Ngili ran over and jumped into the bloodied driver's
seat of the Land Rover. He kicked out the other body and
looked behind him.

A Toyota jeep was racing at him, and three men in plain-
clothes were shooting Kalashnikovs. Ngili saw the shots exiting the barrels and turned the Land Rover around on two
wheels, gunning it away west. He floored the gas pedal and
ducked under the broken windshield as a chain-link fence
rose to stop him. He burst through it, raining bits of chain
all around him.

He stood up in the Land Rover and looked back to see if
he was being followed, but all he saw were two personnel
carriers rolling onto the tarmac and disgorging armed men.
He looked around, spotted army trucks moving on the road
from the city to the airport. Suddenly he remembered his
parents and Yinka and was frightened for them. They might
already have been captured. A helicopter rattled west above
him toward the savanna. His guilt over abandoning his family was matched by the guilt of having abandoned Ken. He
sat down in the driver's seat, floored the pedal, and kept
going. He could hear faint sounds of explosion, and when
he looked back at the city, he saw tall columns of smoke

rising between the glass and cement buildings.

The gasoline tank was full. He drove on, trying to understand what was happening. He turned on the radio. One station blamed "tribal instigators of violence" and another mentioned "foreign provocateurs," a vintage government line. He switched off the radio. He was roaring toward the Magadi game reserve, and prayed that the army wouldn't invade it in the next few hours. If it wasn't invaded, he could use its radio to find out what had happened to his family.

He drove out of town and roared down a country road that descended the eastern wall of the Rift Valley, toward an alkaline lake he and Ken had nicknamed "the cauldron of prehistory." When the silence started to weigh on him, he turned the radio back on and heard a communiqué explaining that the army had restarted Clean Sweep, but now it was targeting "corruption at the highest level, and tribal conspiracy." Dumbfounded, Ngili listened as Mtapani's manifesto was quoted as proof of a tribal conspiracy. A permanent curfew was in effect. A national commission had been set up to assess the culpability in the crisis of all politicians and elected officials. The president, withdrawn in his palace, had not made any statements.

ABOVE THE SAVANNA, THE FLAPPING OF BIRDS' WINGS WAS overtaken by the rattling noise of a helicopter that appeared from the east and moved straight toward the Mau. It flew higher as it approached the Mau and took a hovering, sideways path around the richly wooded incline. As it moved sideways, it dropped a number of large glass flagons with lit fuses of rope coming out of their necks. They fell into the forest a few hundred yards from each other, breaking on impact and catching fire.

The helicopter turned, rattled back east, and vanished.

Minutes passed before the airplane appeared. It was the Embraer that Kalangi had chartered, cruising on a northwest-southeast course right along the ridge of the Mau, as if surveying its entire length.

The plane's steward had gone around several times with a tray of plain tumblers of whiskey. The plane's interior still smelled of trapped animals so Harry Ends had taken a tumbler and was burying his nose in it, drinking it with little sips. Ramsay had done the same, while Cyril had thrown back two whiskeys, one right after the other. All three were pretty lightheaded as they looked down to the green Mau, dizzy with the thought, repeated aloud by Cyril, that this particular forest had not changed since the Pliocene Era.

Kalangi was in the cockpit, talking on the radio to Nairobi. Things were not going quite as planned. The airport had been easy, but the presidential palace guard had repulsed an army attack, inflicting casualties. More alarming, Kalangi couldn't make contact with his command post at the Naivasha Hotel, which made him wonder if the Naivasha had been overrun by troops loyal to the government.

Outside the window, Kalangi noticed a bald spur with a circular formation on it. He stared at it through binoculars, then told the pilot to fly over it again.

Harry was trying to call London on a Mitsubishi ST 151 satellite phone (complete with a fax option) when the steward stepped over with a message from Kalangi that made all three men pile over to look out the window. They couldn't really see the spur very well so Cyril led them back to the parachute hatch. The plane had descended considerably and was flying slowly. Cyril moved the massive lever and opened the hatch. Harry and Ramsay were so excited that they stuck their heads out and peered through narrowed, tearing eyes at the footsteps on the spur.

Cyril stood right behind them. Under his jacket, in a holster at his belt, he wore Hendrijks's Sig/Hammerli pistol.

He looked at the men in front of him, peering out of the plane, trying to find the ring of footsteps. Then Kalangi walked into the cabin.

"Close that hatch and get back to your seats!" he snapped angrily. "We're going to land."

* * *

IN THE FOREST, THE BROKEN FLAGONS BEGAN TO BURN slowly. Known as "bush cocktails," they contained a mixture of two-thirds gasoline and one-third vegetable oil. Poachers used them to start wildfires that would flush out a lot of animals. In the open, their effect was instant, but up here, under thick canopy shade and with no wind, the flames would build slowly, consuming the forest-floor debris, crawling over to bushes, and eventually finding a large dry tree killed by lightning. Only then would the fire start blowing flaming dry acorns and bits of dead branches onto neighboring trees to raise a wall of fire. But that would take a number of hours.

YINKA, JAKUB, AND ITINA HAD MADE IT TO THE EDGE OF the tarmac in time to see the Cessna blow up and to watch Ngili's shootout with the Land Rover. They saw him take it over and run away with it.

Yinka was trying to figure out what to do next when she heard a familiar voice call her name. It was the Ngiamena's friend Jack Dimathi, the airline manager. She ran toward him. His hair was covered with what looked like peeled plaster, and the shoulders of his spiffy summer suit were white. Dimathi pointed up to the roof of the terminal.

"I've got a helicopter waiting up on the roof. Jakub should take it and fly out of here. The army's looking for him everywhere. . . ." He stopped to take a strangely painful breath.

"Who's going to fly the helicopter?" Yinka asked.

"My own pilot. He's up there." Jack pointed to a metal staircase leading up to the roof. He collapsed forward unexpectedly, and Yinka couldn't find enough air in her lungs to scream. In the back of his well-cut suit, there was a great bleeding hole.

Yinka felt a surge of anger and bitter disillusionment that almost cut off her breath. She jumped over Jack's body and raced to her parents. When she finally drew breath, her hands were struggling with her father; they tore inside his coat and pulled out his gun.

She darted up the steps, and saw a light helicopter on the terminal's roof. Three soldiers were amusing themselves by jumping up, catching the rotor blades, and hanging from them. Another soldier was unsuccessfully trying to get them to leave the helicopter alone.

Yinka saw a dead man lying on the terrace, seeping a stream of blood. She was sure that this was Jack's pilot.

"What are you doing?" whispered Jakub. Stunned, he and Itina were right behind her on the stairs.

"I'm going to ask if any of them can fly that thing," Yinka whispered. She raised the pistol and looked at it with the attention of someone gone crazy. Then she looked at the front of her dress. "If I undo my dress, d'you think they'll be distracted long enough for you to shoot them, Um'tu? You're a man, Um'tu, what do you think?" She handed him the weapon, which felt heavier to Jakub than anything he'd ever handled.

Itina spoke up. "Don't be crazy, Yinka . . . Let's . . ."

"Jack said they're looking for Um'tu," she countered fiercely. "And probably for you and for me too!"

Jakub had never pictured such a scene. Or had he? Had he subconsciously dreaded death in his children's presence?

He prayed that if the three of them had to die on the top of an airport terminal, at least Ngili, his firstborn, would survive. Then he saw his daughter move forward with her long giraffelike strides; he had never realized how graceful she was. He watched as one of the soldiers glimpsed her out of the corner of his eye. This soldier let go of his rotor blade and dropped onto the roof. The others turned too. Jakub heard Yinka talk to them and heard her say something about her father being Jakub Ngiamena. Abruptly, as the soldiers turned sharply, ready to grab Jakub, he lifted the gun—DON'T MISS—but didn't aim. He yelled at his daughter to jump back.

Jakub swept with his gun from left to right, across the soldiers' silhouettes, while pulling the trigger repeatedly, sweeping and firing and never stopping. His weapon was an eight-shot Mauser HSC. The three men who had been playing with the helicopter blades fell dead, and Jakub smelled an eruption of feces; fear had made one of them empty his bowel. With two bullets left in his weapon, Jakub turned to the other soldier, who claimed in a frightened stammer to be a pilot.

"Maybe he can't fly this thing," Yinka said.

Jakub turned the gun on the man.

"I swea' I can fly da 'elicopter. . . ." He gasped that he did not have his license yet, but had picked up flying while working for a mining company. His eyes were those of a desperate little creature clawing at the edge of life.

"If you aren't lying about flying, and you get us out of here, nothing will happen to you," Jakub promised.

The soldier whimpered that he did not know why the airport had been attacked; he had been drafted only two weeks before, and his unit had been ordered out of the barracks that morning because "the government had been infiltrated by foreign agents."

"What's your name?" Jakub asked.

"Uledi Kinanda. I'm from Mombasa."

"I am a member of the government, Uledi," said Jakub. "This is a criminal plot against the government and the constitution. When you were drafted, you swore to defend the constitution."

The soldier nodded and begged Jakub to turn his weapon away. Jakub stuck the gun in the wide belt that girthed his waist, grabbed the soldier, and pulled him up. He looked at his daughter and wife. "I need to get to a radio station. We expected this but not so soon."

"Who's we? You and your other tin soldiers?" asked Itina. She suddenly straightened her shoulders and scowled at Jakub like a true African wife.

The pilot expected anything except for a family quarrel to start in his cockpit as he lifted the helicopter into the air. Jakub blasted Yinka for her boldness, which had turned out all right but might have ended in disaster. Itina called Jakub a fool for sending Ngili ahead to the hangars, and his friends double fools for not having foiled the coup. Jakub snapped that their forces were in place and ready to fight back. Itina asked the pilot how much he would ask to fly all of them over the Tanzanian border, but Jakub told Itina and Yinka that they could go. He had to stay. Yinka gaped at the panic and disarray below in the downtown streets.

"Look, the army is looting!" she cried.

"That'll make them botch the coup. We're lucky," exulted Jakub.

On the ground, army trucks and personnel carriers blocked streets and key intersections, and soldiers rushed out of shattered stores carrying TV sets, CDs, computers, clothes, and cases of liquor. They stacked them onto their trucks, which started to look like bizarrely festive floats. There was smoke everywhere, and bodies lying in the streets, and yet the looting gave it all a farcical air.

The helicopter flew over a hospital, and Yinka saw a Toyota pull up in front of the emergency admittance and a young black woman herd a dozen kids out of the car, some stark naked. The pounding of mortars ripped through the air, shaking the helicopter, and shells zipped past the cockpit. They could see that the Naivasha Hotel's windows were blackened and that there was a big, gaping hole in its side. The sunshades and chaise longues were burning on its lawns, and the body of a large dog floated in the swimming pool. A bedsheet turned into a white flag was hanging from the marquee. A seemingly well-disciplined army of irregulars—their uniforms were jeans, unbuttoned camouflage jackets, even T-shirts—advanced on the looting carnival a few blocks from the hotel.

They felt a powerful bang under the cockpit and saw a piece of floor crumple, then fall out, letting air whistle in. Jakub yelled at the pilot to soar away while Itina cried at him to land. Then there was another bang, which shattered the fuselage. Yinka turned and saw that its midsection was bursting into flames.

"Put her down! Put her down!" Jakub yelled, his face squeezed against the glass.

Though the rotor did not stop, the helicopter dropped some

fifty feet before restabilizing. A hail of gunfire burst around the glass bubble. The helicopter hurtled low, then clanged loudly as it touched down in front of the hotel.

On the top of a barricade made of burned cars stood a man in a faded, unbuttoned military jacket. He also wore a shiny Masai necklace made out of hammered copper, and he had on extra-large Masai copper earrings. His hair was white, and he was commanding the operations with a walkie-talkie in one hand and a panga, the machetelike Masai knife, in the other. His face showed the joy of a child fulfilled in old age.

Soldiers surrounded the helicopter's bubble, fogging it with their breaths. This is it, thought Yinka, this is where we get raped and shot in the head and left for the flies. She was aware that the bubble was being opened, and two soldiers pulled her out to the ground. She felt the whole history of Africa in their hot, frantic fingers on her bare arm. She heard her father yell something and saw the white-haired commandant climb down from the barricade and rush over. He was followed by two young aides, who wore Masai copper earrings hanging low from under modern military helmets painted in camouflage patterns.

She recognized the commandant. Under his unbuttoned jacket, he wore a T-shirt printed with TRIBAL POWER. A feeling of relief invaded her, mixed with a need to vomit. The commandant was Desmond Ndbala, the separatist Masai chief who had raged at her father just days before, in Ngili's guesthouse.

The soldiers let go of her. Jakub opened his arms and hugged Ndbala, who returned the hug, smugly but not nastily; victory made him generous. Ndbala announced to his soldiers that Jakub Ngiamena, hero of the independence war and a comrade of the Mzee, supported Tribal Power. A clamor burst out of the soldiers' chests, and Ndbala hugged Jakub again. The soldiers, half of them wearing Tribal Power T-shirts, fired festively in the air.

*   *   *

ON THE SECOND FLOOR OF THE HOTEL, NDBALA AND JAKUB found Kalangi's command-post suite. His chief aides had deserted, except for one who had slept through the fighting on the floor of the suite's spacious dressing room. A young prostitute snored next to him, and both of them were zombied out on Uganda Blue.

Ndbala and Jakub woke them and began interrogating them. The woman had nothing to confess except perhaps how much she had been paid. But the aide, who was shirtless and pudgy and scared of the naked panga blade in Ndbala's hand, confessed who the mutiny's leaders were, and that they planned, once in power, to establish a drug hinterland in the savanna adjacent to Uganda.

Ndbala turned to Jakub. "Those bastards! Isn't our Tribal Power better?"

The aide went on in his confession with a wild story about Kalangi and foreign oil tycoons, and the precious mangati, and Cyril Anderson. Yinka and Itina had followed Jakub upstairs. Yinka watched her father blink incredulously at the mention of Anderson's name.

"Are you sure that was Professor Anderson?"

Kalangi's aide nodded. "He came in here las' night, and da chief played 'im an intah-cepted radio message. . . . And den Mr. Anderson wrote a check for da plane. . . ."

"What plane?"

"Da troop carrier what flew all of dem out to Dogilani dis morning . . ."

"Who were they?" asked Ndbala.

"Da chief, Professor Anderson, and some big oil guy . . ."

Ndbala turned the panga in his hands. The naked blade's shine made the man volunteer more. "And da chief sent a 'elicopter to da Mau to drop bush cocktails, start a big fire . . . on da crest. . . ."

"Why?" asked Yinka.

The man shrugged; he didn't know.

Jakub didn't know what to believe. And Ndbala wasn't interested in the mangati story; the army coup had lost its momentum and the mutineers had been thrown back by loyal units at the TV station and at the presidential palace. Ndba-la's men had gathered around the dining table that was loaded with scanners and radios. Jakub asked them to radio the weather station on the top of the Aberdares, which had a view of the Mau. He wanted to know if the Mau crest was on fire. The weather station was reached, but it reported that no fires could be seen on the Mau.

"What do you make of this, Yinka?" Jakub asked his daughter.

"I wouldn't be surprised if Anderson flew out there. Ngili and Ken always said he was a scientific raider. And Ken was still alive yesterday. I spoke with him."

"I know that," said Jakub.

Ndbala stepped up to him just then and slapped his shoulder. "Jakub, let's radio the police districts and army bases and urge the commandants to surrender in exchange for no prosecution. Then we'll talk to the president. He's holed up in his palace. Now's the time to pressure him about 'tribal power.'"

"Yinka, get Magadi on the radio and see if Ngili's there," Jakub instructed. "He probably went there; it's the closest safe place."

ALMOST TWO HOURS LATER, YINKA WAS FINALLY ABLE TO make contact with Magadi. When she heard Ngili's voice, she waved wildly. Jakub ran over from another radio set, and Itina bolted from a chair.

They both spoke to Ngili, who told them that he was fine. Itina threw her arms around Jakub and leaned her head on his sweat-darkened shirt, and they stepped aside to let Yinka talk to Ngili too.

"I can see the edge of Lake Magadi, and a bunch of pink-backed pelicans," Ngili told Yinka over the radio, "and twenty rangers oiling their weapons. They want to drive over to Nairobi and rescue Um'tu."

Yinka laughed, although she felt close to tears. "Guess what. Um'tu's already rescued, and the president called the

Naivasha and asked Jakub to form a caretaker government. Even one that's based on tribal representation. His only condition was that he stay on top."

"It figures," Ngili replied. "Have you gotten any more messages from Ken?"

She said she hadn't but told him about the stunning confession made by Kalangi's aide. Ngili became incredibly excited. If Anderson had dragged a money man into the bush, that was definitive proof that the breed was not a product of Ken's raving imagination.

"Put Um'tu on, Yinka. I'm taking these rangers and driving to Dogilani." He was almost shouting. "And we'll find Ken alive for sure."

"You think so, Ngili?"

"Yes. He's a maniac. Guys like that survive."

"Here's Um'tu." She gestured wildly for her father to hurry. Despite his bulk, Jakub flew to the phone, while Itina crossed over behind him.

Yinka heard Jakub ask Ngili what kind of weapons the rangers carried. Then Jakub asked Ngili about the rangers' truck and snapped gruffly, "If the truck's got a problem, how are you going to drive out there?"

"The reserve has a competent mechanic," Ngili said, "and their truck is a German-made all-terrain Magirus in pretty good shape, except for a little carburetor problem that the mechanic promised will be fixed in a few hours."

"Can you trust that man? You know you have to drive straight across the brush." It occurred to Jakub that if the truck broke down outside the reserve, but before it reached the Mau, Ngili's life would be safer there than if he faced Kalangi and his men by the Mau.

Ngili was adamant about going. "Wish me luck, Um'tu."

"Think about it, son. Think about it while that truck's being fixed."

"I've already thought about it. You don't want me to go?"

"I want this to be your decision, Ngili."

Ngili took a breath like a swimmer before diving. "Yes, it's my decision."

"It's over a hundred miles before you can even start see-ing the crest of the Mau," Jakub warned.

"I know," said Ngili determinedly.

"How are we going to know what happened?"

"I'll radio from there, Um'tu."

IN THE FOREST, THE FIRES HAD BEEN BUILDING.

Each separate fire had been meandering, munching at this and that tract of forest floor. So far the fires hadn't killed any large creatures, only ants, leeches, and worms. But this was the dry season, so the fires went on. And then one of the fires encountered the dead body of Bilal the poacher, lying where Modibo had shot him.

The fire started to roast him in his clothes. Like a funeral pyre, his dirty army fatigues started smoking, then burning with full, live flames. The tired fabric charred, and the dried deposits of body salts crackled at the armpits and the crotch. Heated in the clothes, the skin and flesh caught fire. Human protein and fat started broiling and sizzling. An odor of cooked meat filled the undercanopy.

That one corpse suddenly gave the fire the strength to leap, reaching the lower branches of nearby trees. Sticky, honeyed sap had dripped onto them from higher branches and was juicy and alive. Together, the wood and the sap combined to feed the beast of flames. It was a strange beast that was never sated. And feeding it made it even more insatiable.

The flames found another unexpected bonanza when they reached the gruesome monument of protohuman skeletons. The dry old-man's beard went up in flames with loud, quick crackles. The flames built up twenty feet high and attacked a dry mahogany tree nearby, causing it to catch fire in one burst. The flames began a self-sustaining cycle. They heated the air so dramatically that the space under the trees' stifling canopy began to feel like an oven. Leaves, shrubs, thorns, hanging snares of lianas dried up and caught fire. Now every-thing that was combustible, whether dry, fatty, oily, or res-inous, caught fire twice as easily as before. Certain leaves were thin enough to dry up in instants, becoming as combustible as paper. Younger aerial roots and thinner buttresses began to blacken and twist and curl up, as they fed flickering flames of their own. In turn, the warm air became lighter, rose and pressed at the canopy above, though it wasn't strong enough to burst through the foliage. Pushed back down, the warm air breathed fire back at the forest floor. Heat penetrated several inches of litter. Centipedes and millipedes surfaced and writhed on the ground. Rats, moles, skinks, ground frogs, and uncounted bugs exited their world of never-seen tunnels, holes, and dens and started running in panic. Winged insects rose, only to disintegrate in the heat from above and fall down as a powder. Into that parched tinder burning branches began to fall.

By this time, the larger animals had started to panic. Alpine forest fires were quite uncommon in these latitudes, and the monkeys began a frenzy of jumping and screeching. Their sense of smell and their eyesight were among the best of the wooded species, and they saw and smelled the fire through gratings of branches, and started twitching and shaking and defecating in fear. The carnivores were growling and clawing at tree bark; those with children began bumping them toward the still unkindled brush. As usual, the ungulates, from pygmy antelopes to the large, cowlike bongos, were the most scared. They snared their horns in the thickets and brayed in panic.

The smoke was now percolating upward and steaming out above the canopy, but it was still hard to distinguish with the naked eye because it mixed into the roaming mists of the Mau's crests. Still, as dusk approached, the flames grew into the clearings, kindling the dry grass. The flames in the clearings reminded the birds of prey of the savanna fires, which were virtual orgies of food for eagles, vultures, hawks, and owls. All they had to do was flap down, pace among the burning ranges, picking up cooked creatures.

A whole column of sharp-beakers had formed in the sky and started circling close, monitoring, getting ready for a forest fire feast.

*   *   *

AT ABOUT SIX IN THE EVENING, IN THE THREE-TENT CAMP by the airstrip hacked out in the savanna, dinner was being prepared. They were having goat steaks and cassava mush, and flatbread, which would be washed down with Cokes and water smelling like plastic from the plane's containers.

Harry and Ramsay and Cyril were out for a hike in the savanna, with Cyril in the lead, lecturing about how ancient the place was and picking up bits of bone and throwing them away. Harry and Ramsay were falling all over themselves about the *feeling* of the place. In a grove sprawled on the horizon, elephants were using their trunk tips to finger the foliage atop acacia trees. On a hill, a pregnant leopardess gave a sultry call.

"Tell me, Cyril," Harry asked, "if simple mammals are such geniuses at adaptation, why can't business, which is run by humans, adapt faster to changed economic environments?"

"Precisely because you want it faster," laughed Cyril. "Faster is your main concept and goal. Adaptation needs time. It never sets itself any deadlines."

Harry fell silent. They walked until the shadows reached their maximum stretch.

Cyril stopped and pulled out his gun. Harry thought he had done this because it was getting dark and they were so far from the camp.

"You're afraid of thieves, Cyril? I thought this was an untouched wilderness," Harry asked.

"This is because you don't believe in *Homo andersoni*," grinned Cyril. Then he grew serious. "Hands up, Harry, and stay where you are. Rams, hands up, and stand right next to Harry." Cyril cracked back the gun's safety catch. "I'm sorry, but there's no use pretending. This is not working. And what we're dealing with here is far too important."

Harry looked at the gun in disbelief, but Ramsay understood, and his chest began to heave.

Ramsay spoke, wheezing and stuttering. "Cyril, d-don't

d-do it. Are you willing to c-compromise your discovery, a lot of money, everything, for . . . for what? You can't do it alone, no one can!"

"I can do whatever I think is necessary for the future of our breed," said Cyril, as if answering an intellectual argument.

"Cyril," exclaimed Harry. "Have you gone crazy?"

"Perfectly sane, old boy. I killed Haksar, who had more vision for our future than twenty of you put together. Haksar realized that our breed needs *Homo andersoni,* not only to survive the coming Ice Age but to survive its own self-destruction." Cyril laughed in self-awe; those were great words to use on the lecture circuit.

Harry was following him carefully. "You're talking about that stupid mongrelization? You want to replace our species with that sham?" Harry was so stunned by Cyril's madness that his brain canceled fear. He was cool and practical. "How much do you want for us to forget this insane little incident? I can have a money order for any sum faxed over from London in five minutes."

"You should turn and face away," Cyril advised Harry. "It will make dying easier."

Harry looked at Ramsay, whose eyes did not leave Cyril's hand. Harry said in a voice too normal for its meaning, "You're such a horrible bastard, Cyril."

"There's no point for such words here," said Cyril. "This is two million years ago, remember?"

None of them heard the footsteps as Kalangi caught up with them. He saw the three white men standing among round thorny heads of brush, one with a gun pointed at the two others. Kalangi threw his hand to his waist, but he'd left his gun in the camp. He twitched at the sound of the first shot, and watched a long jet of blood erupt from Harry Ends's throat, almost spraying Cyril.

Harry fell, and Cyril turned the gun on his friend Ramsay, who spun around and started running at random into the bushes. Cyril fired twice. Ramsay stumbled, then knelt down, then spread out on the ground and stopped moving.

Kalangi started shaking so hard his teeth chattered. The noise was clearly audible, but he could not stop it. He saw Cyril walk to the bodies and probe them with his foot. Then Cyril turned and saw Kalangi.

Cyril stepped heavily toward the police chief until they were standing face-to-face. "You're crazy!" Kalangi blurted.

"No, I'm not." Cyril motioned toward Ends's body. "He was crazy. I am what Haksar tried to create. That mix of fierce power and brilliant mind." Kalangi was blinking uncomprehendingly, but Cyril finished his thought and enjoyed its beauty. "I am the beginning of our new breed. I am *Homo andersoni.*"

THEY RETURNED TO THE CAMP—KALANGI IN FRONT OF Cyril, who had his weapon trained on the chief of police.

They immediately noticed that the pilot, the steward, and all the camp crew—about eight men in all—were standing motionless, facing the Mau. Under its hairy top, about a third of the way down, there was a yellow dance of fire. The fire made the rest of the incline look black and gave the savanna a feeling of immensity.

Cyril stopped, petrified. His hand still held the gun aimed at Kalangi, but his eyes were focused on the fire. He felt as if the flames were kindling his mind, curling crazily among its combusting neurons.

Then Cyril turned and hit Kalangi with the pistol's butt. When the chief fell to the ground, Cyril kicked him, yelling hoarsely, "You scumbag, you did it, didn't you? You set the fire, didn't you? Why did you do that? Why did you do it?"

He then spun around and fired a shot above the head of one of the men who had moved.

Everyone froze.

"Throw your weapons on the ground," ordered Cyril. The men did, dropping one handgun and several knives.

Their rifles and automatics were all in the crew's tent. Cyril raced over to it and returned with a Kalashnikov automatic in one hand and two others strapped over his shoulders. He also carried an extra magazine in his other hand. Kalangi was sure he would kill them all right then, but instead Cyril rushed to the plane and fired a forty-slug magazine into one of its landing wheels. The bullets hit, and bits of rubber sprang out of the wheel until the plane leaned to one side, unable to take off.

During that spell of crazy shooting, some of the men might have tried to run away into the savanna, but they didn't. They waited in terrified fascination to see what the crazy mzungu would do next. Cyril detached the empty magazine, slammed in a full one, then backtracked to Kalangi and asked him again why he had done it.

Kalangi moaned through his teeth that he had planned to flush out some mangati, and also blackmail that corporate man into paying more money. He moaned that the fire could be put out by dousing it with water from a fire-extinguishing aircraft.

Cyril ordered him to radio Nairobi for such an aircraft. Kalangi moaned that he could not do that, at least not now. He'd had Nairobi on the radio, before following Cyril and his friends into the bush. The fighting was over, and the coup had failed. He whimpered that the fire would put itself out during the night, when the humidity would descend over the ridge in heavy drapes of fog.

The camp crew watched. Most of them were no longer young and had seen plenty of death and destruction. But madness terrified them, as it always scares simple people, who think it's a disease they can catch.

Cyril aimed the automatic at them and ordered them to take down their tents. He told them they'd all have to sleep in the bush, unarmed, under the stars.

"Now bring me a chair," he ordered.

They brought him a collapsible bush chair made of canvas. He turned it toward the fire on the crest and sat down.

The men stumbled away into the darkness, turning now and then to stare back at Cyril, who sat enthroned on his bush chair, watching the fire on the crest.

* * *

THE MAGADI RANGERS' TRUCK WAS NOT FIXED IN TWO hours, or three, or four. Ngili paced by the vehicle like a caged lion while the mechanic plunged repeatedly inside the engine.

Finally, night fell. Ngili stepped inside, sat on a bench in the office, and remembered that he hadn't slept the previous night. He lay down, confident that the hard wood of the bench would keep him awake, and sank into a deep sleep.

Several hours later, he was awakened by the mechanic, who muttered that the truck had been ready for a while, but the rangers had not dared wake him. But now his father was calling again by radio from Nairobi.

"I have good news, Ngili," his father announced. "The armed fighting is totally over. Now the political fighting begins. I'm calling you from the presidential palace."

"What the hell are you doing there?" asked Ngili, remembering that the president had just forced his father out of the cabinet.

"It appears that I'm going to play grand mediator. The president invited all the fighting parties to send envoys. But that's not the main reason I'm calling: Remember what I told you that scumbag said, about the fire on the Mau? He wasn't lying. The weather station on the top of the Aberdares has reported a fire, right below the crest. A big, racing one."

Ngili was quiet. He saw the fire in his mind. And he knew what it could do to that slice of the wilderness.

"The truck was just fixed," he answered indirectly.

"Good. We caught Kalangi's top aide, Lieutenant Sampa. He told us that Kalangi has only eight or nine men with him, and most of them are poachers, not soldiers. Are you still going there?"

"Yes," said Ngili.

"Kalangi's pretty trigger-happy, son."

"The rangers are armed with hunting rifles. They also have some sticks of dynamite."

"I don't know about this, Ngili. . . ."

"I do, Um'tu. Didn't you say that I shouldn't be less than my friend?"

"You're right, son . . ." Jakub sighed deeply. "I'll assemble another force here and put it on a plane and send it over as soon as I can see our way through this mess. . . . Good luck."

"I'll radio from there, Um'tu."

Half an hour later, the German truck, with Ngili at the wheel, two rangers in the cabin, and ten more wrapped in blankets on the truck's platform, groaned out of the swinging iron gates of the reserve's office.

THE TIDE OF SCREECHING AND SQUEALING RODENTS HIT the hominid clan's sleeping site at just about the time their attempt to get away from the fire was turning into a mass frenzy. There were giant forest squirrels, bushy-tailed dormice, crested rats with white side stripes, moles. They galloped over the clan's naked bodies in three or four squealing waves, waking everyone.

Ken bolted up, one hand in Long Toes' hair. He had fallen asleep stroking the top of the boy's slanted forehead, ensnaring his fingers in the coarse strands of his hair.

The tide passed as quickly as it had come, and just as soon as its cries faded away, others took their place. There were screams uttered by monkeys, oinks from forest pigs, and the broken basso of an old leopard. And in between, there were others, which Ken could not identify. But the one thing that seemed clear was that all the noises came from up the Mau's slope.

Ken jumped up, rubbing skin with other bodies, and felt their muscles twitching. The panic, whatever it was, was coming from up the hill.

Long Toes bumped into Ken's thigh, and Ken grabbed him by the shoulders and forced him down. The night air was warmer than usual, and there was a glow among the trees, a hint of luminescence, that was vague but also distinct. Ken smelled what was happening before he could think the word: fire. Whenever fire occurred in nature, it was always a disaster.

What the hell, he thought. There was a fire, but it seemed to be *above* them! He took a deep breath and the smokiness in the air made him cough so badly that he gritted his teeth.

Something big was happening.

He took a few strides and let his urine out. He couldn't stop it, nor did it stop him from moving. He pressed his teeth together, folded up his fear and tucked it away inside him. No fear allowed, Lauder.

He heard the hominids behind him and turned impatiently. Several of the males were following him. They seemed to trust him instinctively and they sensed his fear. But he was active and not confused, so they wanted him on their side.

The color of the air was turning from black to gray to golden, and it was getting warmer.

Ken tried to remember the geography of the incline. He knew there were several terraces above him, most of them wooded but a few that were just bushes and grass, no trees. And somewhere above them hung that basaltic cliff, which was naked, like a polished forehead. Not much to burn there. For the fire to expand, it had to move down.

Son of a bitch! He'd left the radio back where they were sleeping.

He decided to finish his search before going back. The fire was getting brighter. He jerked back his head and saw four gracile males behind him, fanned out, their big knees flexing regularly, their arms swaying along. Their eyes locked on to Ken's with a serious look of comradeship. He wondered if they thought he could save them from the fire.

There had to be some explanation for a fire in the middle of the night at this altitude. He had to get his head out of the Pliocene and back into the present. He kept walking, searching, and then he saw one of those bush cocktails. One flagon of gasoline and oil had malfunctioned at landing; its fuse had extinguished and its incendiary fluid had leaked into the forest floor. Ken knew what that meant, and he was stunned by the diabolical cruelty of this attack.

And there was no way he could explain this to the other males.

The air had become yellow, and animals began to roll down from above. They were too scared to try to hide from the humans. The fire was getting brighter, and he was able to distinguish the animal shapes in the darkness. He could also clearly see the shininess of the graciles' eyes. They were very scared, but they stayed with Ken as he moved forward into the flaming forest.

Ken threw his arms out to the side and grabbed the elbow of one of the males. He pulled the male over, grunted an encouragement, and then groped the other way and caught another arm. With staggering steps, all five males laced arms and, shoulder to shoulder, tore through the bush, looking for bigger passages, closer and closer to the fire. Now they could hear it crackling.

The little team shared a shiver when they saw a big leopard ahead of them. It was injured and wouldn't attack them: The leopard's right shoulder had been badly mauled in some drama probably caused by the fire. It averted its sulfur eyes as if ashamed, and limped downward quickly, grateful that the hominids gave it no trouble.

Ken and the hominids had their own trouble to deal with.

Moving farther upward, they broke through the last screen of green and stood facing the fire, five hearts hammering as one. A whole upper terrace was twisting in the flames. There, with horns caught in thorny saplings narrowly growing together, stood a cow-sized bongo with shiny eyes, heavy horns slowly spiraled upward, strangely immobile in the flames. Already asphyxiated, it was held up by its horns and by the stiffness of death.

One of the males tried to detach himself from the group. Ken gripped his arm harder, forcing him to stay in place. Ken felt the pulse that went through the hominids' arms and struggled hard to hold them together. Then he let go of them, and all five broke apart, sweating from the heat of the fire.

That's what it's going to come down to, he thought. The

strength of our arms and legs along with the brains behind our sweaty foreheads—against this fire.

Ken shook his head, grinning bitterly. The odds were not good for the graciles. Their numbers were low, and their weapons were not equal to those of the forces they would face. Whoever was after them would do what they'd set out to do.

And then—what?

He stepped away, across heated air until he reached the end of the incline. The foliage and branches thinned against the escarpment's end, and on that side, there was a sheer drop toward the savanna.

He retraced his steps, followed by the other males, who acted confused but patient. There was a sheer drop on the other side as well.

On both sides, Ken had looked up through gratings of branches, and glimpsed the starry sky; there was no chance of a rainstorm.

That meant the fire had nowhere to expand but down.

Very well, he thought. We'll simply have to leave this place.

AFTER TWO HOURS OF DRIVING, THE GERMAN TRUCK'S EN-gine began to overheat. Ngili jumped out and threw up the hood. He opened the coolant tank and refilled it with drinking water taken from the rangers.

He decided to wait a half hour. The truck was not about to break down; it was simply showing the strain of having driven across open country.

After fighting to control the wheel for two hours, Ngili's neck, shoulders, and arms hurt as if he had been hauling rocks. His mind felt empty. He remembered the countless glittering eyes of animals he'd caught in the beams of his headlights. He felt as if he had been driving into an enormous, yellow/green eye, the eye of the wild at night.

He stepped away from the truck, shivering from the cold, the fatigue. He'd eaten at the reserve, fried eggs and a salad of unripe tomatoes prepared by a ranger, but he was still hungry. He'd shared his food with the other men, aware of how unprepared they were for what they were going to do.

Beyond the dark mass of the truck, an outburst of whooping and yowling suddenly started. Ngili rushed to look, expecting to see some curious hyena that the men were trying to shout away, but instead it was a man the rangers were bringing over between their lowered rifles and crossed beams of flashlights.

Ngili froze. The man was barefoot. Below his knees, his legs were bleeding from scores of cuts and scratches. There were scratches all over his face and every inch of his exposed skin. His stare was haggard, as if he'd seen ghosts. One of the rangers gave him a drink of water, which he gulped, splashing it over his destroyed shirt.

He was the one survivor from Modibo's team of poachers.

Minutes later, the truck was razing its path across the brush again.

The poacher sat in the cabin next to Ngili. He was so listless and frail that Ngili had tied him with a rope to the seat; the Magirus truck, though fairly new, had already lost its seat belts. The poacher had told his story about that one extra-large mangati (Ngili figured that this must have been Ken) who had decimated the poacher's team.

Ngili began to drive faster, putting the Magirus to an incredible test of its sturdiness. He raced ahead, trying to imagine what Ken would look like after those weeks in the wild, comparing the features he knew with what the poacher had described and coming up with a kind of monster. But that monster had used his resources well enough to survive and to be accepted and trusted by the strange breed, and even to defeat the breed's attackers.

How did you do it, Ken? Ngili wondered, with friendly concern, and also with a completely new feeling. He didn't know that Ken; he had never really known him. Science had always hung between them like a transparent screen. But the true Ken and Ngili were now discovering themselves in adversity. And they could be friends, truly, only now.

The German truck leaped over large rocks, and the rangers on the platform pounded angrily on the cabin's roof. Had Ngili gone crazy?

No, he hadn't gone crazy. Friendship, he thought. Real friendship.

He looked around, at that cosmos of wilderness, filling himself with its starlit beauty. Things were not so desperate. Things could be made better, by people like him. Even here, in Africa.

THIRTY MILES AHEAD, THE FLAMES ON THE MAU HAD EX-panded so far downward that Cyril's face began to shine in its glowing light as he slumped on his canvas chair.

The camp crew, the steward, and the pilot slept fitfully in the bush on beds of dirt they had dug with their hands.

It took Kalangi over an hour to crawl to the plane, stop-ing every few minutes and flattening himself to the ground because he imagined that Cyril was about to jump up and nail him with the Kalashnikov.

Finally he made it to the plane's ladder and up through the hatch, into that smell of poachers' pen. He tiptoed to the radio, which worked on auxiliary batteries, and got it work-ing. There weren't many army bases he could count on to be still in the hands of friends, but one of them had to have an operational fighter plane.

AT THE SLEEPING SITE, LONG TOES WAS BUSY SCRAPING AT something with his hands, helped by other youngsters and some adults. They were breaking up an ants' nest and shap-ing its hardened pieces into hurling stones. As Ken and the other males walked down from the fires above, Long Toes straightened up and showed Ken one of those hardened gobs of mud mortared with ants' saliva.

They were getting prepared.

Ken was shoved in the side by Niawo, who passed him, heading toward a bunch of little arbors covered with small, scaly berries. She was starting to tear down the berries, first one by one. Then, impatiently, she jumped up and hung from a higher branch, causing a big cloud of berries to rain onto the ground. She looked at him, and he felt a strange impulse to rush to help her. She was jumping up again, with a boost from the strong muscles in her calves. Tearing another branch, she fell with it against him. Warm-bodied. She tumbled on all fours, and using her teeth, she made a vegetal pouch out of the leaves. She nodded to him to gather the edible berries and put them inside. He swept together a little heap and collided forehead to forehead with her. He felt that enormous pounding of his heart, and knew what it meant.

There it was, the beginning of their first real adventure together.

Maybe she felt the same thing because she put her palm on his chest, then signaled to him with her eyes that a certain branch was too tall and too thick for her to get down by herself. They pulled at it together until it broke, and they fell into the leaves, and with a rain of berries over them.

She rolled on top of him, weighing on him with a body load that surprised him, and her lower belly and pelvis thrust out at him. Just once, hard and briefly, like a call from those organs that had rotated forward when the females began walking erect. Her movement was so strangely effective that he lived an erection and a climax, not in his body but in his mind, and when he pushed her off him, she fell back between the leaves, legs spread and grinning. Then she got up and hopped onto her palms and knees again, to bite off other wide leaves.

He got up, afraid to know what he felt. He leaned on a tree, breathing explosively, aroused, stunned, and fearful.

"Here it is, Lauder," said Haksar's ghost from somewhere nearby. "Womanhood in its formative stage. Is it any worse than today's? Is it any better? You could be the only sapiens to find out, Lauder."

Ken breathed. He tried not to think.

"Try it, Lauder. You have the sapiens' curiosity."

He managed to respond, "Am I still a sapiens?"

"Of course, Lauder. No one regresses out of their species. You'll always be a sapiens, but you could try this other species, Lauder. Try it and find out."

Ken became so afraid that he stared away, down and past his own aroused body. "Find out what? They need help. They need to be led out of here...."

The ghost laughed. "You want to be their leader? Same old sapiens ego. They don't need leaders. They have their own leaders. But they'll take you as a genetic partner. You have good genes, and that's what they want. You've proven the strength of your genes."

No, he thought. No.

He saw Niawo again, dragging two bags of that edible fruit. She had a bounce in her step that he thought was related to him, and it made him shiver.

He bashed his head against the tree trunk, hard. It helped. He staggered away from it, somewhat calmed.

He felt he had found his control, but she crossed his path, hands free now, and faced him. He happened to be standing down the incline from her, which put her almost at eye level with him. She gave him a look that had no inherent message. It was just a statement of interest, a quest for a mate issued from so deep within that he feared she could completely distort his thinking. She was making her being seem the most desirable, her smell the most enticing, and their union the most appropriate. It was a savage determination to mate.

Ken staggered back. Then he turned and did what he had not been able to do for so many days. He ran.

ONLY A FEW HUNDRED YARDS DOWN, THE BRUSH FELT CONsiderably cooler.

He stopped, feeling that his cowardice was among his life's bravest acts. He touched his head with both his hands, and felt he was touching his mind. What a magnificent organ it was—honed by two million years of additional evolution. He could not give it up.

He heard rustling in the foliage above him, tilted his head

back, and saw large shadows brachiating limb by limb in the trees. A big furry belly passed over him, then another, and then several others. And then a smaller, more delicate female shape, carrying an infant on her back.

They were a column of robust hominids, brachiating like apes down the incline, away from the fire.

Ken felt that the disaster was bringing on a truce; for now at least, he didn't have to fear them. One of the larger robust bent a tree trunk, which made an opening in the canopy, and he saw that it was daylight now.

Off in the savanna there was an explosion that was clearly man-made. Then he heard more explosions, and he started racing farther down.

I N THE DISTANCE, A PLANE CAME LOW OVER A DOT THAT moved in the savanna, kicking back a tornado of dust. The plane zoomed down near the dot and fired several shots—the man-made explosions were heard for miles around. The blasts raised curtains of dust on the ground, but the moving dot kept advancing.

The explosions rocked Cyril in his chair. He jumped up, into a world all crimson with emerging sunlight. Even the nose of the lopsided troop carrier on the ground looked crimson, as if someone had daubed it with bright red paint. And in the bush, the other men jumped up too. Gripping the Kalashnikov, Cyril remembered the fire on the crest. He spun around to take a look; but just as Kalangi had predicted, the mist had wrapped itself around the crest. But this mist looked very dark, as if it were mixed with smoke. Then a gust of morning breeze pulled at the mist's lower hem, and the fire showed through strongly. It was much lower on the incline than it had been the night before.

Cyril heard the unknown plane zooming past its mysterious target again.

Panicked, the camp crew rolled toward Cyril. "Where are the guns? Give us the guns!" they screamed. Cyril let loose a volley from his automatic, and most of the men threw themselves to the ground. The steward rushed to the plane, with the pilot chasing behind, shouting to him not to try to start the engine. The plane could not take off on that shattered wheel. Already up the stairs, the steward kicked the pilot, who gripped the steward's foot and pulled him down in a heap. Cyril started laughing and fired off another volley of bullets at the side of the plane. The shots cut off one of the hooks that attached the ladder to the plane, and as the ladder wallowed in the air, its other hook came undone and the whole thing fell.

The pilot turned and charged toward Cyril with his bare fists. Cyril waited for him to come close, and then stopped him short by planting a few bullets right at his feet.

"I'm *Homo andersoni*!" he raised his voice in one of his grand thunderings. "Where's that scumbag Kalangi?"

"I have no idea!" shouted the pilot.

"He's in the plane!" guessed Cyril. "Kalangi, get out of there, or I'll torch the plane with you inside it!" Cyril fired two volleys, puncturing the shiny aluminum, and Kalangi stuck out his scruffy face through the open and ladderless hatch.

"I was trying to radio Nairobi for a fire-douser!" he cried pitifully.

"What's that other plane?" asked Cyril, pointing.

"How the hell should I know?"

But Kalangi knew only too well. Last night, reaching an air base still occupied by the rebels, and remembering Ngili's promise to come to Ken's rescue, he had told the pilot to be on the lookout for any ranger planes or trucks in the area. If that plane was firing at a ranger truck, the truck had to be Ngili's.

"Come down and get over here right now," Cyril shouted and fired another shot. Kalangi almost fainted. He had instructed the pilot to spare the Embraer, but to nail anything that might be skulking around it. Therefore Kalangi didn't want to get off the plane and become an unprotected target, but how could he argue with a loaded Kalashnikov? Cyril fired another shot, and Kalangi jumped onto a bed of dirt, staggered up, and dragged himself over.

The other plane was now soaring away, leaving a trail of smoke from its starboard wing tip.

"It got hit, it got hit!" cried someone.

The plane banked, turned, and almost disappeared, hidden by its own reflection of the sunlight.

When the people on the ground saw the plane again, it was almost above them. Kalangi tried to sprint away from the little group, but Cyril knocked him to the ground with the Kalashnikov's butt. Still, Kalangi jumped up and shouted at the air, "Don't shoot, don't shoot!"

The plane zoomed by, and shots fired from its wings hit the steward, whose body waltzed upward and seemed to separate in midair. It came back in several pieces. The other men cried out in panic and scattered into the bush. Kalangi tried to get up but was knocked back to the ground again by Cyril. Cyril had recovered his voice and was roaring at the sky, the bush, and at the traitor Kalangi, who had called the plane to kill Cyril. Kalangi screamed that he had called no one and had no idea why this plane was strafing them, or that truck.

"Who's in that truck?" Cyril yelled.

"It's got to be Ngili Ngiamena," moaned Kalangi miserably.

Cyril knocked Kalangi to the ground a third time. Ngili was in the savanna, just a few miles away. Cyril was so enraged that he felt no fear as the plane zoomed by again. He actually stared at Kalangi, enjoying the fact that the chief was shitting. He became really aware of the plane's strike only when he saw a slash in the side of the Embraer's fuselage, as the slugs ripped through the aluminum. Then an explosion blinded him. When the smoke blew away, he saw that a whole wing of the Embraer was gone, and one of its engines lay in the dust about thirty yards from Cyril.

A FEW MILES SOUTH, NGILI'S TRUCK HAD SURVIVED THE first strike because Ngili had cleverly driven it into an acacia grove. The plane had come in low and fired at the grove, uprooting a tree next to Ngili, but that was all the damage.

Several rangers on the truck's platform had aimed their rifles at the plane's cockpit but hit the wing instead. Then came the shatter of the slugs against the distant Embraer, and the engine being blown off the wing.

Now the fighter plane was coming back. It trailed a slightly thicker plume, but the pilot did not appear concerned.

There were two things that Ngili could do: He could order his men down and abandon the truck and let the plane destroy it, or he could drive in a zigzag pattern, forcing the plane to bank and turn, during which time the rangers could try to shoot the pilot. The latter plan was risky, but that way they'd save the truck.

Ngili gave the plane time to set its course, then roared out of the grove. The plane fired a missile this time, which incinerated the grove. Ngili gunned hard and turned a sharp right. He saw the plane soar, which meant that the pilot was confused and was climbing higher to take a wider look. Ngili was so preoccupied with the plane that it wasn't until the last minute that he saw the spot where he and Ken had unearthed the fossil. He reversed so hard that he almost knocked over the truck, then he turned and saw the plane charging straight at him.

He roared the Magirus forward, counting on its speed to make the plane's fire land behind its target. At the same time, he yelled at his men not to miss.

DON'T MISS!

The plane scored, but far behind the truck. Ngili rose, holding the wheel and weighing on the gas, and saw the puffs of the rangers' shots against the plane's nose—and then he heard a shattering of glass as the cockpit was hit.

The rangers cheered from the depths of their beings.

The plane soared steeply but joltingly. Ngili drove with one hand and bashed his other fist into the cabin's ceiling. The rangers, equally excited, drummed their fists back at Ngili, and they drove off almost on a tribal drumbeat, while their eyes looked out to see what would happen to the plane.

It was lowering itself, either because it was disabled or because it was still eager to kill.

Cyril saw the plane coming down, becoming larger and more detailed by the second. He noticed the plane's underload of armament, a tiny but greedy-looking barrel opening (it was a 30mm high-speed cannon), doubled by two clusters of missiles, and he saw the slits where the machine guns were. He had a flashing sense that if he'd entered the military, he would have been as brilliant at warfare as he was in science. The plane seemed suddenly to trip in the air; it somersaulted, and then one of its wings pointed almost straight down. Anderson started firing the automatic, probably at random, and felt he had inflicted a deadly strike.

The plane roared over his head toward the Mau, where it hit with a thud that shook the mountainside and the savanna under Cyril's feet.

KEN WAS RUNNING DOWN TOWARD THE THUDS AND BANGS of the savanna war when the shock of the plane's crash sent him to the ground. He fell on one side and felt the heat of the plane's engines on his skin. The wings detached from the fuselage; they flew into the ironwood trees and stayed entangled while the fuselage slid ahead like a giant aluminum pod. Then the pod split open, sending out objects, perhaps even bodies, all around Ken.

Ken was still scrambling up when an engine burst into flames, and he was thrown to the ground again. He looked over at a soldier who had been ejected from the crashed plane. The man was in combat dress, with extra belts of bullets strapped across his shoulders.

A splinter of fuselage had impaled him through the chest, and an automatic submachine gun lay by his body. Ken picked up the gun. It was an AKM, the newest version of the Kalashnikov, with a foldable stock.

Marveling at how heavy it felt, Ken stood up in an almost trancelike state. His index finger curled naturally around the trigger. His mind seemed to puncture, letting the Pliocene flow out of it, like air out of a leaking pressurized cabin. He was hurled back to the present. Reversing from the ancient being he had discovered inside himself, he became an out-of-place naked man who feared for his own survival. He had been terrified facing the fire, but it had been a different kind of fear.

Now, with the wreck of a fighter plane charring in front of him, and long *tukk-tukk-tukks* of automatics weaving into each other in the savanna, he had something modern to fear. But he could meet that fear with this weapon in his hand and with a mind identical to his aggressors'.

There was a second explosion—the plane's other engine—that catapulted him backward into a flowering bush. He rose, numb, bewildered, and pulling with a reflex action the trigger of the AKM. A short burst of slugs whipped hotly at the foliage, splintering branches and pulverizing leaves. Technology, technology! He stared at the cartridge shells that had been ejected onto the forest litter. He strained his ears, to try to count the rifle reports below, trying to figure out how many people were exchanging fire.

He also heard the roar of the forest. The crash of the fighter plane had finally maddened all the wildlife. The forest was yelling out its fear.

Ken heard a loud tearing of leaves above him and threw his head back. Many robusts, several dozen, were brachiating down now, panting and calling to each other with frantic grunts. Frightened, they instinctively responded by arm-swinging downward, chased by the unrelenting forest fire.

Ken's senses short-circuited, and yet his eyes were able to focus on the parade of hairy bodies. Males, youngsters, passed above him, arm-swinging, making their lives depend on their biceps, wrists, and fingers to hold them onto the branches of the trees. The females' swollen genitals sailed above him, buttocks like round cups of naked flesh that evolution would double up in the next stage with cups of flesh on the females' chests. Increased arousal, more hope for the breed. The feet that were more like hands grabbed hold of the branches and swung the hairy bodies along. Like a last hurrah of their tree life, they fled downward. . . .

And then they were faced unexpectedly with a new wall of flames caused by the blazing aircraft.

The wind, or perhaps it was sprayed gasoline, made this fire spread faster than the other one, and its heat easily climbed to the branch level. Between trees, there were still passages that the fires hadn't reached, but the robusts were not jumping down and taking advantage of them.

Get down and escape, you idiots, Ken felt like shouting.

He thought about firing his weapon, but he knew that wouldn't bring them down. It would only make them cling even harder to those branches.

Desperately, Ken considered one impossible plan after another until he realized that he alone could not do anything. He would have to go down there and interact with those killers, whoever they were, and convince them to act humanely. Or he'd force them to, at gunpoint!

He rushed to the dead airborne soldier, whose body was about to catch fire. Ken snatched several bullet magazines. But he was naked and had no pockets, so he hoarded the magazines in his arms and threw the AKM's strap over one shoulder. Loaded and clumsy, with the AKM beating painfully against his body, he ran toward the thinning edge of the trees.

"GIVE US THE GUNS!" THE PILOT AND CAMP CREW RAGED at Cyril as he kept waving the naked muzzle of his automatic at their chests.

Behind them, Ngili's truck charged the camp, with the rangers firing their well-aimed shots from their scoped hunting rifles. One of Kalangi's men cried out, then vomited blood through his mouth and fell.

Cyril realized that it was a matter of seconds before Kalangi's men grabbed him. Even if he could pump out all of his bullets, one of those bastards would be left to strangle him with his bare hands.

He tripped on the little pile of weapons he had amassed by his canvas throne the night before. He bent, grabbed two automatics, slung them on his left shoulder, and grabbed a handgun. Then he lunged to grab Kalangi, who was too exhausted to fight back and just twitched in Cyril's hands like a chicken about to be slaughtered.

Cyril pressed the handgun right into the chief's throat, propping up his fear-slacked jaw. One traitorous move from the others, and the chief would be gone. He stepped aside from the weapons.

"Get your guns," he growled. The crew dived to pick them off the ground. "Now go there"—he pointed toward the edge of the trees—"and build a line of defense."

Then Cyril stuck the gun in his belt and shook Kalangi. "Into the forest!" he ordered.

Kalangi seemed catatonic, so Cyril kicked him behind the knees to set him in motion. Even loaded with several automatics, and with his hands full with the chief, Cyril still moved astonishingly fast and thought and made decisions with deadly efficiency. Just like the real *Homo andersoni*, his nature fierce and undiluted by civilization.

"Are you crazy? What about the fire?" Kalangi asked.

"Into the forest," Cyril repeated, undaunted.

"I can't make it," rasped Kalangi. "Kill me here, you fucking mzungu."

"You can make it if I can."

And he pushed the chief with a strength that belied his years. The other men were running past them to the edge of the forest, but as they reached the edge, another *tukk-tukk-tukk* started. The camp cook, a poacher, could see gunfire being spewed from up between the trees, and a strange vision of a naked, apelike gunman. Then a bullet hit the cook in the chest, stabbing into his heart. He died staring at the Mau.

From up on the hill, Ken had recognized Cyril and Kalangi, and was now firing at them and screaming in a frenzy. When Kalangi recognized Ken, though the young mzungu was stark naked, he found his energy and pulled Cyril to the ground.

The Magirus truck was so close now that Ken could hear its engine. The heartening thought that Ngili could be driving it made him hold his fire and save his bullets. From below, Kalangi's men started firing back, some of them upward at the forest and others at the truck. But by this point, the truck was entering the abandoned camp. Ngili jumped out and waved his hands crosswise in front of his face, urging a cease-fire. When Ken saw him, he started screaming. "Get down, Ngili, get down!" Unsure if his voice carried that far, he leaned out of his cover and a poacher behind a bush below fired a bullet that hit him in the right shoulder.

Ken stared in amazement as his flesh ripped up and he saw the red tissue inside. The little hole filled slowly, as if reluctantly, with dark blood. Another bullet wheezed past him, forcing him back, between the trees.

He could lift and move his arm, but it felt heavy. He threw the AKM's strap over his shoulder and clapped his left hand over the wound, which was not bleeding heavily. He could stop the blood flow with the pressure of his palm.

It seemed a minor wound, though he knew that few bullet wounds were minor in the bush. As he stepped back, the blazing heat of the fire enveloped him, and he started to feel dizzy.

Long Toes . . . he thought, unexpectedly and groggily.

Then he thought about this friend who'd arrived in the truck. Ngili, Long Toes is still alive. *They* are still alive. Get here, Ngili, now that you've decided to come.

The passages between the trees were still open. Providing exit from the fire into . . .

Into the bloody mess below.

Bloody sapiens mess. Truly so.

This was not how evolution intended man to exit the forest.

He stopped dead.

He saw Long Toes.

"INTO THE FOREST, BASTARD," ANDERSON KEPT MUTTERING as he hit Kalangi in the back with the muzzle of the automatic.

Kalangi turned and sputtered, "You're crazy. We'll die in the fire. We should go back and make a deal with Ngiamena."

"Into the forest," Cyril repeated, knowing that Ngili would not make a deal with them.

*   *   *

THE ROBUSTS SLID DOWN FROM THEIR BRANCHES AND GATH-
ered in one of the passages between the trees. Their mass of
bodies looked like a wall of hairy muscles. The graciles were
also filing down from on high, in a stunning formation. In
front was Long Toes, both of his fists loaded with the projectiles they'd broken up from the rock-hard anthill. The
adult males followed immediately behind him; they were also
armed with gobs of mud and torn branches. The young boys
were sprinkled among the adult males, and behind them
stormed a fanned-out escort of males herding the females,
who were loaded with their infants.

Long Toes' upper teeth tensely gripped his thin lower lip,
and he looked as decisive as Ken had ever seen him. He was
so hardened that Ken caught himself smiling, sending the
boy a message he himself had learned as the cardinal command of the wild: Don't miss.

DON'T MISS, LONG TOES.

Filled with a protective pride, Ken wondered why Long
Toes was leading the graciles' march. Was he the leader?
Were they valuing his experience with aliens like Ken? But
didn't the clan realize, as Ken did, that Long Toes was still
just a boy on his way to becoming a man. Maybe the clan
could hear the murderous racket of the aliens down below,
and they had crowned him leader because he had survived
the snare and fought that final battle with Modibo and won
it. Long Toes was already unafraid of the wide spaces; he
was already a hunter. But just then, something happened that
gave Ken the clue as to how Long Toes had gotten in front.
One of the adult males tried to overtake Long Toes, who
jumped to keep his advanced position and elbowed back the
male. Long Toes raised the fists filled with the anthill stones
toward the battlement of the waiting robusts. He had rushed
to the clan's fore all by himself. He had emerged as a leader
spontaneously, and now his clan trooped behind him, parad-
ing its armed technology of gobs and sticks.

The robusts had needed both hands to brachiate, so they

were unarmed. The evident resolve of the graciles, plus their weapons, made the unarmed robusts hesitate and finally decide not to attack. This gave the graciles a momentary advantage and allowed them to tear through the narrow passage and out of the flaming forest, right under the dark stares of the robusts.

The two breeds, the graciles and the robusts, were separate but were now being forced to step out of the flames almost at the same time, even though the graciles were escaping first. As the fire roared behind them, they all lived a long instant of incredible suspense.

Long Toes stepped past the robust clan and on past them.

Good going, Long Toes! Ken broke into a grin: The two breeds' final battle would not take place. At least not now.

A burst of automatic fire from just below and just outside the trees awakened Ken from his awe.

He slipped between two trees, rushed down, and emerged on a treeless incline sparsely dotted with bushes. Blinking in the sunlight, he spotted Kalangi just a few yards down, a smoking automatic in his hand. Kalangi ducked behind a bush. Cyril Anderson, bristling with an automatic and a handgun, stepped toward the bush, his face a mixture of stupefaction and colossal wrath. With one arm, he pointed the automatic and fired several shots, none of which hit Kalangi.

Ken started shouting, "Stop shooting! They are coming out! You can have the find, Cyril, just stop shooting!"

From behind the bush, Kalangi yelled, "Kill him, he's crazy!"

Then Cyril commanded, "Help me get him, Ken!"

Cyril pointed the automatic at the bush and pulled the trigger again, but only a click followed. Kalangi bolted up above the bush and fired, causing a squib of blood to pop out on Cyril's chest. Ken pointed his automatic at Kalangi, but his arm was so numb that it pulled his weapon down as if it were made of lead. By the time he was able to hold it up again, Kalangi had scrambled up the incline and into the smoky trees.

Ken staggered, found himself a few feet from Cyril.

Cyril touched his chest, then lifted his fingers to his eyes. They were smeared with blood. "Hurry, Ken . . . I've been hit, but lightly . . . take me down. . . ."

Ken felt like laughing. Even now, Cyril's immediate thought was of himself.

Cyril stepped closer but fell on one knee. "Help me!" he snapped, making an impatient gesture that caused him to smear blood on his rich white hair. "Ngili's down there! My blood type is O!" He clung to Ken, pulling him downward, his speech beginning to slur. "We can work together. . . ." Then, as if annoyed at Ken's lack of response, Cyril pointed the handgun at him. It looked small in his big hand.

Ken cracked back the trigger of his own gun and fired. Cyril fell backward. Now his chest was a mess of bloody bullet holes.

Above them, charging into the trees, Kalangi heard something whiz past his head. It was a hurled stone. With a dry whack, another hurled stone caught him in his forehead. As Kalangi stumbled, he saw a rush of graciles above him and tried aiming his weapon, against a salvo of stones. The stones hit him, and his weapon fell from his hands. He was engulfed by the graciles, who trampled over him, turning him in seconds into a grotesque hulk.

Stepping over Kalangi, the clan marched down the stony incline, their eyes taking in the openness of the wide savanna before them. Ken and Anderson waited petrified, one standing, the other collapsed. Ghostly, Anderson raised himself on his elbows.

A few robust males appeared behind the graciles and rolled down toward the savanna too, on their knuckles like chimps. They stopped, then growled loudly, signaling their mates and offspring to start moving out of the trees. Some were upright and some were knuckle-walking.

Ken bent down and tried to lift Anderson, aware that his own right shoulder and arm were barely obeying him. Anderson gestured to be left where he had fallen. He was raving softly, and Ken had to strain to understand what he was saying.

"We could've worked together.... This place ... supports ... several breeds.... *Homo andersoni* ... and we could have named the other after you...." Cyril smiled, generous, and then coughed blood. His eyes sought Ken's.

Ken watched the egotistical smile on Anderson's dying face. Even in death, his ego was apportioning glory.

Cyril turned to stare at the protohumans, and Ken stared in the same direction. They were heading down the fractured cliffsides toward the majestic grassland. It had never occurred to Ken to count them. Now as they hurried past him, he fought two conflicting feelings. They seemed to be under a hundred, less than any living modern tribe. On the other hand, almost a hundred of them seemed like an enormous treasure.

Ken couldn't see if Long Toes was still leading them.

As he followed their movement, he saw that it changed direction; they were bypassing a little crowd standing to the side. Ken recognized the park rangers' khaki outfits; then he saw Ngili.

Ngili and the rangers were watching man's emergence.

Ken felt that Cyril had died at his feet, and he was afraid to look down, as if such a sight could jinx his own survival. He staggered on from where he was, stepping on the short grass that had been trampled by protohuman feet.

That was when Ngili woke from the spell of watching the protohumans and saw his friend. Ngili started running uphill, his windbreaker swelling like a balloon.

As he got closer, his face became a kaleidoscope of emotions: elation, curiosity, shock, concern, joy. And again concern. Ken was bleeding. Ngili started to shout at him to lie down and not move.

Ngili felt his mind exploding. The closer he came, the more real Ken's battered, bleeding, emaciated body became. Ken staggered down until Ngili was close enough to touch him. Then he collapsed in Ngili's arms.

"Y OU'LL HAVE TO HOLD HIM DOWN," SAID A VOICE with a strong East Indian inflection, "because we have no anesthetic. He's lucky he has only one bullet in him and that it's so close to the surface. . . ."

Ken heard the voice through a dreamy fog. He blinked and stared, trying to see, but his eyes were full of a cool viscous solution. Through it, he made out the blurred outline of three faces hovering over him.

Then he heard Ngili's voice. "All right, we'll hold him down. But how could you have forgotten to bring anesthetic with you?"

A doctor, Ken thought. And this is Ngili, and he's alive. And the clan is alive. I saw them come out of the forest. But when was that? A black gap seemed to stretch between that time and now.

And what are they doing to me?

"My hospital was shelled during the coup," said the doctor, "and the supply rooms were looted. He's lucky I could bring antibiotics. Now, this is not going to be for the faint hearted," the doctor continued. "Are you going to be able to help us, miss? He will bleed."

"I'll be all right," said a woman.

She had Yinka's voice.

Ken started squirming, feeling that his wrists and ankles

had been restrained. With rough ligatures, it seemed, probably rope. He tried to smell the air to understand where he was. He did not smell the city or a hospital. He heard a turaco bird and the buzzing of an airplane. He was still somewhere in the bush.

"Yinka?" he asked tentatively, afraid that naming her might wake him from a dream.

There was a pause that frightened him. Then she spoke, very close to his face. "Yes?"

"Hey, Ken," said Ngili. "You slept a couple of days."

Ken pictured himself, filthy and naked, and he could feel the air touch his naked body. He was afraid that he might pee on himself and maybe already had. He blinked fearfully at one of those blurred faces and whispered, "What's in my eyes? What the hell did you put in my eyes?"

"A disinfectant," said the doctor. "I'll clean it out as soon as I'm done with your arm, Mr. Lauder. How are you feeling?"

"I'm . . . fine. . . . Yinka . . ." He paused, not knowing what to say to her. "What are you doing here? You writing . . . a story?"

"Yep." She sounded calm, but spoke with a half beat of delay, as if from a distance. "A story about: Fellow Sapiens. Let's behave ourselves; our ancestors are watching." She took his hand.

He gasped, feeling for some reason that all his nakedness had gathered in his palm and fingers, and they were ashamed of touching her cool narrow hand. "I'm going to cut his hair," Yinka announced to the others present. "It's so filthy and tangled."

"Good. He has no injuries to his cranium. All right, Mr. Lauder?"

"Yes?"

"Ready? This will hurt a little."

"I'm ready." He squeezed those cool fingers, and Yinka squeezed back, almost painfully. And above that pain, another pain, a searing agony, seemed to plunge into his upper right arm, like the beak of a vulture. He thought, That's what they feel, the savanna animals, when they're pecked at while still alive. The pain increased until it felt like a knife slashing directly through his brain. He brought his jaws together, and yelled through them, spraying an atomized spit. Then he was still.

"He fainted," said the doctor. "That's good." Something metallic clanged into a bowl of tin. "Take his pulse," he said to Yinka.

She let go of Ken's hand, pressed her fingers inside his wrist, and ordered herself to feel the beating of his blood.

She felt it. It was there.

She took a long breath, and looked at the still face. Ken's hair had been bleached unevenly by the savanna sun, and his face was so battered that she almost didn't recognize it. A laceration ran on its left side, from the end of his eyebrow to the corner of his mouth. It was healing and looked almost like a tattoo. His skin, which had tanned unevenly, had been parched by the fire. The bruises and cuts gave him a feline look, like a leopard's.

Yinka looked at Ken's body; his chest, abdomen, hips, thighs, looked emaciated to the bone. His shins, ankles, and feet, thinned like all the other parts of his body, were checkered with pink bandages, applied by the rangers before the doctor's arrival. He even had bandages on the soles of his feet.

She looked back at the shoulder. Ngili was mopping blood, while the doctor was stitching the wound. "Must work quickly; this faint is like an anesthetic, but it won't last," he muttered.

Ken coughed. Then he moaned softly from the pain.

"Thank you, Miss Ngiamena," said the doctor, "you'd make a good nurse. Now I'm going to bandage this shoulder and arm really tightly, and then he has to lie down, very still, and let's hope that he doesn't start running a temperature."

"How long does he have to be still?" asked Ngili.

The doctor was short, with thick glasses and bulbous big eyes, perhaps from a thyroid condition. He bulged his eyes at Yinka. "Today and tomorrow at least. You're the more patient one, aren't you? You sit by his cot, with a book.''

She nodded.

She felt that her courage was like a kind of drug. It cleared her mind. And it also made the time pass. She would sit by Ken's cot but would not have to read. There was too much to think about.

Ngili was staring at her. ''The camp boys will take turns watching him, Yinka.''

''I'll watch him first, for a couple of hours.''

''Good. In a couple of hours, I'm going to drive around, and see what's happening. You want to come with me, Yinka?''

''Sure.''

THE CAMP BOYS CARRIED KEN FROM THE MAIN TENT, WHICH had been used as a field operating room, to one of the sleeping tents. They laid him down on a cot. And he slept, exhausted from the pain, and from everything else.

He woke up sometime later and saw Yinka on a canvas chair close by his cot. She was leaning her knee against his leg, and he felt her knee's roundness, motionless and firm. Her head was lolling down on her chest—she was dozing. He smelled the air, trying to distinguish a scent that was specifically hers among the smells of the tent. For the last few days, he had been enjoying the smells of the sapiens world. Man's most haunting memories were based on his sense of smell. How primal, he thought. Ken had verified that truth, in the savanna, in the forest. And now here, too.

He lived powerful emotional jolts when he recognized the simplest smells of civilization, like the cool scent of clean bedsheets.

But he couldn't smell Yinka. Maybe she sat too far away.

He fell asleep again, trying to remember something, to remember several words he'd been repeating through the last days, words that had a very specific meaning. But as meaningful as they were, he'd lost them.

He slept, aware of movement and noises. There were small

planes landing and taking off. And there was time here, the time of civilization, divided into hours and days. And it was passing.

LATE THAT AFTERNOON IT RAINED, WHICH HELPED TO EX-tinguish the fire on the Mau. Since the day before, a douser plane from Nairobi had been fighting valiantly with the tall black columns of smoke. The problem was the lack of a steady supply of water. The plane's pump had been sucking the muddy fluid out of water holes, disturbing the drinking of animals. Resupplied, the plane took off toward the escarpment again and again, lowering itself dangerously to see if it was hitting the flame cores or just pissing away the water into the smoke. The pilot, a Kenyan, was doing a hero's job.

During the rain, Yinka and Ngili were driving in the truck at around ten miles an hour, literally creeping across the bush.

The rain quickly washed the savanna dust out of the air, and every color, shape, and hue, every grille of branches and lacework of leaves, became almost painfully defined. Through the windshield, swept clear by the whining wipers, Ngili saw a huddle of brownish bodies far away in the tall grass.

He turned off the engine but did not brake. Mute from tension, he showed them to Yinka, while the truck still rolled forward. The creatures stared back at the truck in silence. Ngili could not tell whether they were robust or gracile. They had huddled under the shelter of an acacia, their eyes shiny like berries.

This was Yinka's first time seeing them. She had flown in one day after Ngili, but by that time, the breed had scattered into the tall grasses. This morning, however, a ranger had found an eaten kudu, with its leg bones crushed open and the marrow sucked out.

"They don't seem to be afraid," said Yinka.

"Yes," said Ngili. "They're readapting to savanna conditions pretty nicely."

She breathed, staring at what Ken had seen for the past few weeks. "So, what are you going to do? What are you and Ken going to do?"

"It's very simple," said Ngili. "I don't think we should reveal the find."

"How can such a secret be kept?"

"It probably won't be for too long. So we might as well keep it for as long as possible." He turned the engine back on, reversed as gently as possible, and they drove back to the camp.

IN HIS TENT, KEN WOKE UP REMEMBERING THE WORDS. *THE desperation of genes.*

They seemed meaningless at first, until Yinka stepped back into his tent and smiled at him.

"I saw them." She sat down on that canvas chair and took his hand, simply and naturally. "Ngili and I drove around a little, and we saw a bunch of them, under a tree, waiting for the rain to pass."

He sat up with a shudder, and she rushed over to push him down again. Maybe this was because she had mentioned the australopithecines, or maybe for some other reason, but suddenly it seemed that there was another female's face, under Yinka's. He glimpsed it, as if Yinka's features had become transparent. He didn't see Niawo in Yinka, but instead he saw a kind of ancestral woman who had begotten both of them. And it was there in those ancestral features that he saw the desperation of genes. He remembered having felt it in Niawo's features and body because it was present there, and it was present in all women. It was in the graceful, relaxed way Yinka sat, and the way she let go of his hand and reached over and touched his face. All of it was part of desperation, such a very inappropriate word because it wasn't a desperation, really, it was the awareness of woman's destiny and purpose.

"Thank God you're not feverish." She grinned. "The stuff you put us through, settler. The rangers told me that they went into the forest to assess the fire damage, and saw your footsteps. . . .''

"Footsteps," he smiled. "Always, footsteps."

She stared at him, then grabbed his hand again. His fingers felt emaciated too, like a primal claw. He felt suffocated by emotion. She looked at him with her fantastic dark-brown irises, and he panicked, the way he had while tumbling into Niawo's irises. She breathed right in his face, and he finally recognized and connected with her smell. A cool clean smell, of good healthy flesh, of intact teeth. The warmth of genes, the same as in the forest but stored inside the cool wrapping of smart modern living.

He suddenly burst into tears. He thought of Long Toes, almost strutting as he'd led his clan into the open and started cutting that virgin path into the savanna grass.

She became frightened and stroked his hand. She didn't understand why he was crying. He tried to explain to her that he was worried about Long Toes' survival the way they, the sapiens, had been worried about him.

She frowned, perhaps not happy with the comparison. "That boy must be some creature."

He nodded, and told her about Long Toes. About their first meeting by the water hole. There was that amazing, flat-headed little being . . . who was now guiding his breed into relearning the basics of savanna life. Ken stuttered the key events of their friendship: Being saved by Long Toes when he was feverish and unconscious. How the little *Australopithecus* dragged him into his lair under the ground. Then the cigarette lighter. Building their first fire. Whittling their first spear. The spearing of the kudu. The graveyard with the bones of Long Toes' father. And the lion.

That flat-headed little being. He . . . he . . .

Ken wanted to tell her that the boy had turned him into a different Ken Lauder, but he didn't make it.

Yinka was staring at him with an overpowering concern, and he feared again that he would fall into a female's eyes. He said in a voice that sounded flat and stupid, "That boy was a magician, in his own prehuman way." He despised himself; what he had said was untrue, a betrayal of their days together, of their hunts. But did it matter? She could never understand.

She looked as if she had made a kind of decision. "Tomorrow, if you're strong enough, we'll drive to that water hole." She put her arms around his shoulders and bent to kiss him, awkwardly, first on a corner of his mouth, then on his closed lips, with her closed lips. He felt her trembling subtly against his chest. "I thought you were dead. I pictured you eaten by hyenas."

"There are no hyenas in the forest."

"Eaten by whatever . . ."

"Someone's going to walk in. . . ."

"I don't bloody fucking care." But she didn't kiss him again, just kneaded his arm with her fingers, with an emotion that was not sexual and seemed scary for her too.

There were shuffling feet in front of the tent's entrance, and Ngili asked softly, "Ken? Can I come in?"

What the hell's Ngili doing, Ken wondered, announcing himself so formally? Is he acknowledging Yinka's right to be alone with me? Yinka got up. Ngili came in, smiled at his sister.

"Hominid physiology is amazing," he said. "Isn't he already looking better?" Then he sat down. "Ken, you need to make a decision about reporting the find, because I just learned of a new development. Someone from Shell Oil just contacted my father and told him that they still want what they call 'the project.' They're claiming a kind of authorship right."

"What?" Ken started chuckling tiredly. Again? After Anderson, Shell Oil?

"Believe it or not, they tried to convince Um'tu that their late VP Harry Ends was a pioneer in the saving of hominids. And they've got Haksar's notes."

"Are they threatening to make this public on their own?"

"Not exactly threatening, more like pressuring." He waited. "So, what's your decision?"

Ken spoke in a low voice. "We're not going to make this public, Ngili."

"Great," said Ngili. Yinka could tell that he was entirely in agreement with Ken. "Um'tu will never be in a stronger position with the president; just now Um'tu practically is the government. So we can map out here an area of a few thousand square miles and have the government declare it off limits. And Shell can't do anything, even if they publish Haksar's notes. Everyone else who knew or witnessed something is dead, thanks to Cyril." He laughed. "Dammit, Ken, isn't it amazing? Cyril, the one man we feared most, became an unwilling protector of the breed? Ken?"

"What?"

Ngili beamed with excitement and energy. "You and I will be the custodians of this place. We'll find a way with our bureaucracy. And I'm never giving up geology." Ken nodded, he'd figured that. "The douser plane is leaving tomorrow morning, Yinka. You want a ride to Nairobi?"

"Can I wait a day?" she asked. "If Ken's okay tomorrow morning, he'll show me the water hole where he met the boy."

Ngili lowered his eyes. He patted his friend on the arm, turned, and left the tent.

DRIVING TO THE WATER HOLE THE NEXT MORNING, YINKA asked Ken about the other hominids. She'd heard plenty about the boy; but what was it like to trundle around with all those naked adults? What was that like? Ken answered carefully that it was pretty . . . stirring, so to speak.

She stopped the Land Rover by the little puddle where he had first watched Long Toes drinking. He stepped down in a pair of boots he'd borrowed from Ngili, grimacing from the pain in his bandaged feet. He had a strange sensation that something was changed in the surrounding emptiness, though he couldn't tell what.

He saw a thin black object on the muddy shore of the water hole, and called Yinka to follow him over, as if her presence might protect him. He hurried toward it, feeling an invasion of déjà vu, which made him shiver. Could the spell restart, and perhaps—he shot a glance at the pretty young woman behind him—overpower both of them together?

The object was a branch, straight and without knots, like a short spear.

It was black because it had been charred in the forest fire.

He picked it up, while the feeling of déjà vu increased frighteningly. It was so physical now that he felt it like a contagion, infecting him through his fingertips.

Long Toes, don't do this to me.

He knew for sure, without any chance of error, that Long Toes had left it there for him. Now, after his clan had left the forest. The boy had picked it off the forest floor, hurriedly, still warm from the fire. Once in the savanna, he had noticed that it was very short, hardly a hunting tool. But now he could use it for a message to his friend.

Ken told Yinka that he had taught Long Toes the use of a spear, and that the stick in his hand was a reassurance from Long Toes that he wouldn't forget that lesson.

She stared at him as if he were crazy. "You think you'll ever get over this?" She answered herself, with healthy anger. "I guess not; no one will from now on."

"What do you mean?"

"We won't be the only humans anymore, and God knows what that will do to us all. Great!" she cried out mockingly. "Give me that!" She tore the stick from his hands, but as she spread her feet apart, positioning herself to fling it away, she uttered a short cry. He jumped toward her, fearing that she had been stung or bitten.

Long Toes stood in a clump of reedy grass, looking straight at them.

Yinka tried to utter another cry but couldn't. She groped back with her hand and found Ken's arm. Ken looked at the boy, finding him utterly strange-looking and at the same time enormously familiar.

Long Toes was staring with his shiny eyes. He had just eaten something that had dirtied his face. That was enough to bring back for Ken all the memories of their encounters, their face-to-face stances as they sized each other up, the stunned stares they had exchanged, the first time they had touched their fingertips, their games, their hunts. . . .

He was imagining. There couldn't be so much regret, so much reproach, in the boy's eyes.

But yes, there could be.

Here's where we meet again, Long Toes, and here's where I fail you.

The boy stepped back and made his lips into a whistle of flesh. One sharp sound. A few feet back rose Niawo, astoundingly short and primal-looking, and wide-eyed. Niawo stared quickly at the woman next to Ken, and then at Ken. Then she gave Ken one gaze of secrecy and illicitness, as brief as it was fantastic.

It said: We've been together, but in another time.

And Long Toes' eyes said: I want to be with him. My alien, my strange big clumsy pet. Ken started to step toward the two protohumans. But . . . next to them, a male stood up. A male who had no chin, just jaws, and a brutally slanted forehead. He was much larger than Niawo, and looked somewhat younger. He spotted the modern human pair, and his face carved itself into a mask of fierce, almost suicidal devotion to his own female and to her youngster.

The male called them back toward him, with a strong, brief grunt. They stepped back behind him, though Long Toes did it slowly, like an undisciplined child. Still, they stepped back behind him, and the male waited, dead still, challenging the aliens, until his woman and her child sidled off.

Then he moved too, turning, following the pair.

It took a few minutes before the three silhouettes disappeared, into the savanna with the buffaloes and the lions and the mysteries of evolving humanness.

"Maybe you want this," Yinka said, holding up the spear. Ken took it, trying to find on it the warmth of the child's hands. He didn't find it.